Nicholas Christopher is the author of two previous novels, *The Soloist* and *Veronica*, seven books of poetry, and a non-fiction book, *Somewhere in the Night: Film Noir & the American City*. He lives in New York City.

www.**books**at**transworld**.co.uk

Critical acclaim for *Veronica* by Nicholas Christopher

'I was so impressed with the poetic imagery of this beautiful work,
I wanted to press it into everyone's hands . . . [a] unique and
highly recommended mystery'
Daily Express

'Beautifully written, this is the thinking person's Batman, a
Gotham City of brilliant insights, as visual and necromantic as
a Fellini film, just this side of lunacy, but at a high poetic pitch'
Mail on Sunday

'*Veronica* is written in beautifully simple poetic prose . . . A joy
from first page to last: the plot is compelling, but the sensuous
language draws one on. Its recurring images – triangular mirrors,
a blind fish, an island that exists only on a map – linger in
the mind'
New Statesman & Society

'Lingering, sensuous and provocative, Christopher's unusual
fantasy is a masterful exercise in the necromancy of poetry
ripened into prose'
Scotland on Sunday

'An original fantasy of phantasmagoria, passion and conjuring
. . . This is a richly visual book, in which both Manhattan and
other magic cities are constantly present and are almost
characters themselves'
Good Book Guide

'An exceptional novel, the beauty, magic and readability of which
penetrate your soul . . . Dip into the first few pages, get hooked,
and recommend it to all kinds of readers'
Sarah Broadhurst, *The Bookseller*

'As oddly familiar as déjà vu and as intriguing as moments
of synchronicity, [*Veronica* is] a fresh and innovative
novel for our times. It feeds our imagination, shuffles reality,
and questions daily occurrences, life patterns, concepts of time,
spiritual awareness, and love. This is an alchemist's fiction
and Christopher becomes both scientist and magician,
creating a novel of great force, a nonstop, exciting page-turner,
and more'
Booklist

'The sort of novel which cults are made of'
Bookseller

Books by Nicholas Christopher

Fiction
A TRIP TO THE STARS (2000)
VERONICA (1996)
THE SOLOIST (1986)

Poetry
ATOMIC FIELD: TWO POEMS (2000)
THE CREATION OF THE NIGHT SKY (1998)
5° (1995)
IN THE YEAR OF THE COMET (1992)
DESPERATE CHARACTERS: A NOVELLA IN VERSE (1988)
A SHORT HISTORY OF THE ISLAND OF BUTTERFLIES
(1986)
ON TOUR WITH RITA (1982)

Non-Fiction
SOMEWHERE IN THE NIGHT: FILM NOIR & THE
AMERICAN CITY (1997)

Editor
WALK ON THE WILD SIDE: URBAN AMERICAN POETRY
SINCE 1975 (1994)
UNDER 35: THE NEW GENERATION OF AMERICAN
POETS (1989)

A Trip to the Stars

Nicholas Christopher

BLACK SWAN

A TRIP TO THE STARS
A BLACK SWAN BOOK : 0 552 99888 5

Published in the US by The Dial Press, Random House, Inc., 2000

First publication in Great Britain

PRINTING HISTORY
Black Swan edition published 2001

1 3 5 7 9 10 8 6 4 2

Set in 11/12pt Melior by
Phoenix Typesetting, Ilkley, West Yorkshire.

Black Swan Books are published by Transworld Publishers,
61–63 Uxbridge Road, London W5 5SA,
a division of The Random House Group Ltd,
in Australia by Random House Australia (Pty) Ltd,
20 Alfred Street, Milsons Point, Sydney, NSW 2061, Australia,
in New Zealand by Random House New Zealand Ltd,
18 Poland Road, Glenfield, Auckland 10, New Zealand
and in South Africa by Random House (Pty) Ltd,
Endulini, 5a Jubilee Road, Parktown 2193, South Africa.

Printed and bound in Great Britain by
Clays Ltd, St Ives plc.

for Constance

Contents

1.	The Planetarium	13
2.	New Orleans	18
3.	Brooklyn	28
4.	Spiders	33
5.	The Abandoned Factory	44
6.	The Hospital Ship	52
7.	The Hotel Canopus	68
8.	The Hôtel Alnilam	95
9.	The Education of Enzo	124
10.	Islands	189
11.	The Sky-City	208
12.	Kauai	267
13.	The Stardust	339
14.	Naxos	407
15.	The Hotel Rigel	433
16.	Dead Letter	477
17.	Honolulu	522
18.	Ice	535
19.	Houston	554
20.	Fire	565
21.	A Trip to the Stars	594

I saw a child carrying a light
I asked him where he had brought it from.
He put it out, and said:
'Now you tell me where it is gone.'

— HASAN OF BASRA

1

The Planetarium

We had voyaged far into space and now we were returning. Before leaving the solar system, we orbited the moon and several planets – skating along Saturn's rings, probing Jupiter's red spot, and skimming the icy mountain ranges of Uranus. We trailed a comet and threaded a swarm of meteors. And after Pluto, we were out among the stars: glittering clusters, bracelets, and crescents that swirled around us. We followed the long curve of the Milky Way, past Alpha Centauri, the first star beyond the sun, and witnessed the explosion of a supernova and the collapse of a neutron star into a black hole. Traveling two hundred light-years to the red star Antares, we took a long look at the next nearest galaxy, Andromeda, and then reversed course.

In the darkness, to the jagged strains of electronic synthesizers and the roll of timpanis, the crowd was hushed, padded seats tilted back, necks craning, as we made our return journey at the speed of light. I clutched the armrests of my seat and blew away the motes of dust tumbling around my head. Against the spectral glow from the overhead projectors, my aunt's silhouette shone black. Her hair smelled fresh, even in the stale metallic air of that windowless place. It was cold there too. I had my coat buttoned up to my throat and inside my boots was curling my toes to keep them warm.

Finally the blue and white sphere of the earth re-appeared before us, suspended in the void, and the godlike voice of the announcer thanked us for taking 'A Trip to the Stars', which was what they had called this show, running from Thanksgiving to Christmas. There was a burst of applause and a clatter of seats snapping into place as everyone stood and the houselights came up and the great domed ceiling went black. The electronic music faded away, replaced by a slow ragtime waltz as the ushers opened the doors in the back.

Pulling on my cap, I preceded my aunt to the nearest aisle and felt her hand lightly on my shoulder, guiding me. We had come to this old planetarium at the northern tip of Manhattan to celebrate my tenth birthday. The show had been sold out and the large crowd, closely packed, buzzing with conversation, poured up the narrow aisles of the circular room. We slid into the stream of bodies and were carried along with it. I could see nothing but people's backs and hands. Scents of perfume and sweat filled my nostrils and then the smoke of cigarettes as people began lighting up.

When we reached the back, my aunt took my hand and picked up her pace. Her grip was gentle, but firm, her suede glove soft against my palm. It was only when we had stepped out into the pale winter light – the wind on the sidewalk swirling dry snow, ticket stubs, and programs alike – that the crowd dispersed enough for me to look up at her in order to speak.

And then I could not say a word.

The woman, who was pulling me hard now to a blue sedan idling at the curb, was not my aunt. Until she opened the rear door and pushed me in, I thought she must have mistaken me for another child. Then, before stepping in after me, she looked me full in the face and betrayed no surprise.

A man was behind the wheel wearing a brown coat and a brown homburg tilted low. Even before the woman had pulled the door shut, he threw the car into gear and sped away.

'Hey!' I cried. But as I coiled up to dive for the left-hand door, the woman flipped open her handbag, fished out a black atomizer, and hurriedly squirted a cloud of perfume into my face. My eyes stung and I started coughing. A scent like Easter lilies caught sharply in my throat. I felt woozy, and my heart slowed to the point that I could hear its beats in my ears, broadly spaced, like a distant drum. Everything blurred, as if a gauzy filter, woven of shifting colors, had been placed over my eyes.

'Stop crying!' the woman snapped, not at me, but at the man behind the wheel, as she removed her gloves. They were black suede, like my aunt's.

My hands and feet tingled, then felt heavy, as if my bones had turned to iron. My tongue was thick. When my eyes cleared a short time later, I stared out the window trying to read the street signs. Even if I could have, it wouldn't have mattered: our route, filled with twists and turns, was impossible to follow. We had entered a factory district of narrow streets, rusted loading ports, and broken sidewalks. Pigeons lined the eaves of the warehouses. In the vacant lots bums rubbed their hands over the jagged flames in oil drums. I still felt light-headed, but my vision was less blurred. And already my heart was speeding up and the heaviness was draining from my limbs.

The woman beside me was a complete stranger. She was young – older than my aunt, but still in her twenties. And she was pretty like my aunt, tall and slim with long, light brown hair; but my aunt's eyes were bright blue, and this woman had brown, nearly black, eyes that were darkly made up. I thought again of diving for the far door at a red light or when we slowed for traffic, but we ran every light and there was no traffic on those streets.

We pulled up abruptly at a white brick building beside a vacant lot. The building occupied half the block. Caged windows sealed and dirty, it looked like another factory that had closed down a long time ago.

The large doors at its loading zone were chained and padlocked. Its paint was peeling, but the whiteness of the building's facade stood out among the dark gray buildings that lined the rest of the street. The sign over its entrance had been corroded by the elements: only the letters CHINE – a fragment of a word – remained legible. A man wearing a white coat and oversized gloves was crisscrossing the vacant lot with a metal detector, stepping gingerly over the shattered glass and strewn twisted rubble. He peered back at us over his upturned collar, then turned his eyes back to the ground.

Our driver, frozen behind the wheel, lit a cigarette. His smoke filled the car. He had never turned his head, and I had failed to glimpse his reflection in the rearview mirror.

The woman opened the door and gripped my hand again. 'Don't be afraid,' she said, her first and only words to me. But her face, rigid and severe, did nothing to allay my fears. My heart was racing now, and the moment I was on my feet, stiff and weak-kneed, I had trouble catching my breath. I wanted to bolt, but managed only token resistance, yanking my arm briefly from the woman's grip and feeling utterly helpless as she led me into the building through an unlocked metal door that slammed shut behind us.

My first sensation was the smell of burning tar. The air was just as chilly as it had been outside. I felt the small clouds of my breath condense on my cheeks. But I could see nothing. As the woman led me by the hand, I stumbled every so often and she pulled me that much harder. We made successive ninety-degree turns along a dank, narrow corridor, with fine cold dust swirling by us. I heard wind howling faintly in a distant shaftway.

Suddenly we stopped and a door slid shut behind us. We were still in pitch-darkness, standing in a large room that was descending through space. Its floor hummed beneath my feet, cables whined overhead, a distant generator whirred. I started shivering. Where was this woman taking me? And where was my aunt now, I asked myself as the elevator carried me deep beneath the abandoned factory, little knowing that it would be fifteen years before I saw her again.

2

New Orleans

I had a gift for dead languages. Latin, Greek, a smattering of Phoenician. Every night the first year he was gone, I dreamed of Loren. And in the dreams with a piece of charcoal he was writing letters to me in Latin on a long white wall. *Cara Alma*, he began each one, in his rounded script, trying to tell me where he was. But I could never translate fast enough to make sense of the contents, and what I did remember when I woke up made no sense at all.

Though I am not the kind of person who ever cried herself to sleep – not when my closest relatives died, not when people hurt or left me – on some of those nights, when I woke suddenly, I drenched my pillow thinking of Loren, whom I had hardly known.

The police were of little help. From the start, they told me that a determined kidnapper, professional or otherwise, was among the most difficult criminals to thwart. And that I was a victim too – a ripe target since I was young and unaccustomed to having children in my care. The wariest adult, they said, when properly distracted – I had merely been tapped on the shoulder, only to find no one behind me and Loren gone when I looked down again – could have a child plucked away from under her nose. None of this assuaged me. On my own I kept looking for him. I dropped out of school, though I was in my last year. I had some money – about four thousand dollars – that I had inherited from my mother. It was she who had raised Loren after my sister Luna and her husband Milo Haris were killed nearly three years earlier. Luna and Milo had been itinerants, living in over a dozen different cities in the seven years after they adopted Loren in Reno, Nevada. The next city would have been Pittsburgh, but they died on its outskirts. As a baby, Loren had known only the road. They had adopted him, and now, somehow, I was his only surviving relative.

I used most of my inheritance to hire a private investigator after Loren disappeared. In two months he came up with only one thing: a woman fitting my description exactly had been seen getting into a car with a boy fitting Loren's description – navy pea coat, black watch cap, plaid scarf. After that, nothing. It had been very cold that day, and he and the woman had vanished like the vapor of my breath. The fact that the woman so closely fit my description did not make things easier with the police. Especially when no ransom note, phone call, or message of any sort arrived from this look-alike kidnapper. The police had begun to look at me askance, with a mistrust bordering on suspicion – of, at the very least, my sanity.

Beginning to doubt the latter myself, I walked around the city carrying Loren's photograph for weeks. It was the only photograph of him I possessed, taken one summer at Coney Island: wearing a sailor cap aslant, hands on hips, he was squinting into the sunlight. My mother didn't believe in photographs. She said they didn't preserve memories, they diluted them. She had other such odd, but firmly held, beliefs. Like her proud claim that she never dreamed. And that a dreamless sleep was the sign of a clear conscience.

Radiating outward in circles from the planetarium, I showed the dog-eared photograph to everyone I could think of – taxi drivers, storekeepers, workmen, doormen, dog walkers – and then, in desperation, to people who couldn't possibly help me, like random pedestrians and obvious transients. No one had seen anything.

19

Before my circles reached the city limits, the photograph had crumbled, days, then months, had blurred away, the seasons had run their cycle, and finally, exhausted, I gave up my search. The police gave up, too. 'It's an open case that is never going to be closed,' they told me. '"Inactive", we call it.'

During that year, all of 1966, I stayed in my mother's house in Brooklyn. I slept not in mine but in Loren's bedroom, which had been my sister Luna's room before she ran off with Milo. At night I lay on his small bed, under the blue quilt, with his things around me, and for hours in the dark I went over and over the last day I had spent with Loren. From the little I had seen of him, I had drawn a strong impression. In his pea coat and cap he walked with something of a rolling gait, like a sailor. He was a wiry, athletic kid with the straight posture and the intense, direct gaze of someone who, on his own too soon, had grown up too fast. As, strangely enough, often happens in these cases, he had ended up looking a good deal like my sister, his adoptive mother: symmetrical features built around wide cheekbones and a straight nose, and the same dark wavy hair and gray eyes. But while Luna had nervous hands, quick gestures, and a staccato way of talking, Loren was steady and unhurried. Perhaps with such peripatetic parents, this had been his only recourse – a positive development.

That last afternoon, before going to the planetarium, we had stopped at a diner nearby. I drank coffee and Loren picked at a western omelette. This was only our second time out since my mother's death. The night before, we had gone to the movies. Though I was nominally his aunt, not only did Loren and I hardly know each other, but we shared almost no history together. Before my mother's death, I hadn't seen him in nearly a year. And suddenly I was the only person between him and an orphanage. Two months short of my twenty-first birthday, with a cramped studio apartment in Boston, three hundred dollars in my checking account, and my secondhand Impala, I now had a ward to care for – by default.

My mother, robust all her life, had died suddenly of a cerebral hemorrhage while getting ready for bed. Loren had discovered her the next morning. After calling for an ambulance, he had sat on the floor with her head in his lap. Though the police operator had instructed him not to move her, Loren told me he had known right away that she was dead, and, after holding the mirror in her compact under her nose to make sure, he couldn't stand the idea of just leaving her there like that, on the cold wooden floor. After they took her body away, and telephoned me in Boston, the police wanted Loren to go stay with one of the neighbors, but he refused to leave the house. The woman next door came over and cooked him dinner and then sat up in the living room after he went to bed. When I arrived in the evening, I found Loren in my mother's bedroom. He was lying on his back in her bed, still dressed and on top of the covers, with the lights off, gazing into the darkness. I switched on the lamp and sat down at the foot of the bed. His eyes were bloodshot and his face grief-stricken. But whatever crying he had done was behind him and his voice was composed.

'What will I do now?' were his first words to me.

'You'll be okay,' I said, keeping my voice steady and pressing my hand to his cheek. Though I had been asking myself the same question – on his behalf and my own – all during the drive from Boston, I did not yet have a real answer for him.

When I went to the bathroom to get him a glass of water, I closed the door behind me, buried my face in a towel, and cried – not for my mother, but for Loren. As much as I felt I had gotten a raw deal when it came to family matters, it didn't compare to what he had been through: twice orphaned and now orphaned again because of an untimely death – all before the age of ten.

My mother and I had been estranged for three years – since I had left for college, just months before Loren arrived at her house. Our estrangement was the culmination of the eight years since her own mother's death in which we had lived alone together, in an atmosphere that alternated between suspiciousness and outright hostility. I never knew my father. He enlisted in the Marine Corps at the height of the Second World War and was sent to the South Pacific in June, 1944. At the time, Luna was eight years old, and my mother didn't know that she herself was barely a month pregnant. I was born the following February, seven months after my father was killed in the battle to liberate Guam from the Japanese. Posthumously my father had been awarded a Silver Star for valor, which my mother kept framed in the living room. My mother never remarried, and the three of us lived frugally on her salary as a salesclerk at Macy's and the veteran's benefits she received for my father. For the first ten years of my life, until her death, my mother's mother moved in with us, to help out. Not surprisingly, my mother never spoke of it (an aunt from Staten Island filled me in on the story) but my grandmother had been a drunk. My mother always told Luna and me that our grandmother, the long-suffering widow of a fireman, had died of 'a broken heart'; but according to this aunt, the toxic agent at work in my grandmother's bloodstream when her heart gave out one night had been, not love, but Seven Roses rye, which she drank from a teacup. So I was raised by widows, in a house of women seldom visited by men.

When I was eighteen I had an abortion – illegal in those days – and because of complications afterward my mother got wind of it. At the same time, I was busted for selling marijuana, in order to pay the doctor, and what little communication existed between my mother and me broke down completely. One year I only came home from college on Christmas Day, and another year it was on Thanksgiving – for half a day – but that was it. And because of the way Luna moved around, I hardly ever saw her – or Loren – for more than a day at a time, also, inevitably, in chaotic circumstances. In her will my mother had made no provision for Loren. Not surprisingly, since the will had been drawn up twelve years earlier, before his birth or adoption, when my mother had bequeathed her small savings and her sole asset, the house, to Luna and me.

So Loren and I had sat in that diner and tried to plot our next move, each of us squirming. An orphanage was out of the question. In my mind, there were three possibilities: a foster home for him, with a new family; a continuation of his life in my mother's house – the same school, neighborhood, and all the rest – with me assuming her role and getting some sort of job in the city; or if I sold her house, he could move up to Boston with me, into a bigger apartment, while I finished school. From our previous conversations I knew that the foster home was anathema to him. Living in my mother's house, working in a dead-end job, was equally repellent to me. Which left option number three. I was six months away from my degree in classics, and after plowing through Strabo, Lucretius, Tacitus, and Procopius – the natural scientists and historians – I had planned an extensive trip around the Mediterranean basin the following year before entering graduate school. If Loren moved in with me, that would all go out the window. And even if I managed to obtain more financial aid, and we lived on a shoestring, yoking our lives until he was old enough to go away to school himself, what kind of existence would it be for either of us? I who had no desire for children of my own, and he who desperately needed a parent and not someone, however well-intentioned, with the age difference of a sister rather than a mother – someone who surely exuded the same sort of ambivalence as had Luna and Milo, his late father.

Some of this was spoken between us, some we kept to ourselves, but, in the end, the hour we spent huddled in that red vinyl booth, our breath clouding the window as we stared at the stream of traffic on the West Side Highway, felt interminable. We ended up talking mostly about Luna and Milo. I told him about how they had met, waiting in line outside a movie house when Milo was playing hooky from his job at a music store and Luna was on Easter break from the fashion design school to which she never returned. And about Luna's peculiar desire as a girl to live on a houseboat, which she never realized. From my mother Loren had acquired a skewed – highly sanitized and fanciful – version of their lives. For someone who insisted others hew a taut line with regard to the truth, my mother took many liberties.

For example, she insisted to Loren – who knew better – that Milo was a construction engineer, though in fact when he worked at all after his marriage it was as a carpenter with minimal training who did pickup jobs or short-term stints on construction sites. Between jobs he drank, smoked reefers, and pursued his fantasy of becoming a disc jockey by practicing incessantly with a tape recorder and taking his demo tape by every radio station in every city they passed through. The rare times he was summoned to audition, he never got the job. Luna all the while provided a small but steady income as, variously, a cashier, a waitress, and a manicurist. My mother had also informed Loren that Luna had become a psychic at the end of her life – a strange admission (or fiction) for someone who boasted that she didn't dream. My mother claimed to me that in the last month of her life Luna dreamt the circumstances of her death and sent them to her in a letter. I never saw the letter, and when I spoke to Luna at that time, late one night, long-distance from Kansas City, she didn't prophesy her death or anything else. Her voice thin, exhausted, she told me that Milo was drinking more heavily than ever and that the following week they were setting out for Pittsburgh, where he claimed to have lined up a job on an evangelical radio station.

Instead, on a highway entering the city, he swerved across the double line and slammed into an oncoming milk truck.

And this was very much on Loren's mind that afternoon at the diner. Until then, he had never once mentioned the accident to me.

'See, I wasn't killed,' he told me matter-of-factly, 'because of the way I used to sleep in the back of the car. They always traveled at night. They would build me a little tent with a suitcase jammed in front of the seat, where I was stretched out on a blanket, with another blanket suspended over me so that headlights and the highway lights wouldn't wake me. Sound was muffled, too. I remember how low, how far away, their voices sounded in the front seat when I heard them at all. When we crashed, I was asleep, snug in there, with no place to get thrown. The sound that woke me was awful: a roar, then screeching metal and breaking glass. My ears rang so hard I couldn't hear anything else. It was pitch-dark and things were pressing down on top of me. I opened my mouth to scream, and then I felt two pairs of hands groping for me. I thought: they're okay and they're going to pull me out. But it was the state troopers. Lights were flashing everywhere. Police cars and ambulances. A big milk truck with its engine on fire. Our car was crushed, but I had no cuts, just a bump on my head and a broken finger which – see – never healed right. It's still bent. When one of the ambulances drove away, I knew they were inside it. And I knew from what was left of the front of the car that they must be dead. It was horrible,' he said, and here his voice broke. 'All over the highway milk was streaming from the truck, which had been ripped open. It was ankle-deep in places, and bright white. Except in front of the car, where their bodies had been thrown, the milk had turned red.'

Twelve months after Loren's disappearance, on New Year's Eve 1966, I left the city in the dead of night after scraping the ice from the windshield of my Impala. In November I had sold the house in Brooklyn to a couple who promised me that they would always keep a lookout for Loren, should he show up on the doorstep. That brick house, on the shady street in Bensonhurst with a dozen other brick houses, had been the only home he had ever known for longer than six months. The proceeds from the sale would enable me to pay off my student loan and go without a job for a few months.

At that time, I changed my name. My first name, too. Moving the letters around, I changed it to Mala. Of course I knew that Mala meant *bad* in Latin. In Spanish and Italian as well.

On the road, I felt cut loose, isolated – an island unto myself. It seemed for a while I was following my sister's example, though not her path. I drove south, stopping only for gas and, once, to eat, and spent the next night in Charleston. Then I veered west, never sleeping in the same bed for two nights running for a month. To Birmingham. Nashville. New Orleans. San Antonio. Amarillo. I zigzagged to California, then eastward to North Dakota, and south along the Mississippi, keeping as close to the river as I could, back to New Orleans, which I had liked the first time around more than anyplace else.

I stayed in New Orleans for four months, in a furnished room on Perdido Street. Though my money was holding out, I got a job, to be busy. It was a temporary position in a remote branch of the public library in the Saint-Eustace parish, filing books that were being taken out of circulation. Slotting them away on dust-caked shelves where they would never be opened again. Quite amazing books, some of them, like *A Catalogue of Imperfections in Venetian Glass in the 17th Century*; *The Journal of Timothy Marlin, Physician to Prince Henry the Navigator*; *The Funereal Jewelry of the Chaldeans*; and *A Geological Survey of the Island of Remóra*.

I worked in the basement, which was called the morgue, and it was there I met a man named Zaren Eboli. He was an arachnologist, writing a book about the arboreal, cannibal spiders of the Caribbean, which I felt sure would one day be shelved beside these other curiosities by one of my successors. Within a week, I went to work for Eboli, in his old, three-story, faded blue clapboard house on the river. It was my knowledge of Latin, primarily, that had led him to hire me on the spot. Every afternoon I catalogued the dead spiders preserved in their jars and fed the live ones in their terrariums.

On my first night in New Orleans I lay awake under the rough sheet on a narrow iron bed. The bed was pushed up against the wall, and through the window I looked across the street at the old asylum that was now a dance hall. Now, even when I slept at night, I didn't dream. In fact, the moment I left New York I stopped having those dreams about Loren writing to me in Latin. When he filled my thoughts, as he often did, I heard only the language of guilt and remorse, spoken dully in my own voice.

It was nearly dawn, and through the parted venetian blinds I could see the first pale blue light reflecting off the tall windows of the dance hall. All night a fine drizzle had been falling, and as the light slowly shifted, now orange, now yellow, across the trees, glistening in the wet leaves, I turned against the wall in my cramped bed and began to cry, clutching and digging my nails into the blanket and biting the sheet to stifle my sobs. Crying as I had never heard Loren cry, not when my mother died, or even when he had finished telling me in the diner how it was he hadn't been killed along with Luna and Milo. Instead, he had turned to the window beside our booth and with his index finger in the thick vapor drew a face like his own with hands clapped over the ears, no mouth, and closed eyes below which he dotted tears, all down the cheeks.

3

Brooklyn

As the elevator lurched to a stop, I was suddenly sure I would never again return to my grandmother's house.

The previous night I had found Alma hunched over the dining-room table at two a.m. in the dim rays of the overhead lamp. I was on my way to the kitchen for a glass of milk to help me sleep when I stopped short in the foyer, and gazing across the living room, saw her in the small alcove that was our dining room.

Wearing an old green bathrobe, her long hair tucked over one shoulder, she was lost in concentration, scratching away at a legal pad with a well-chewed pencil. She was massaging her forehead with the fingers of her free hand and tapping her feet nervously. Beside her, in an ashtray filled with stubs, a cigarette was burning. In the living room she had left the television on, the blank screen flickering with snow. A glass of wine, untouched, was on the table beside the easy chair where she had been sitting. She must have gotten up impulsively, I thought, to do whatever it was she was doing on that pad.

I watched her for a long time. After she had smoked another cigarette and crumpled and tossed away a few more pages from the pad, I called out her name as I entered the living room. She was startled, and turning to me, covered the legal pad with her arm. In the morning I would find one of the crumpled pages under the table: a tortured page of computations, figures every-where, many of them crossed out, at the center of which was a list of expenditures – *rent, utilities, car insurance, food, clothing, medical* – below my name and hers. She had been trying to draw up a bare-bones budget for the life she thought we might be sharing. It pained me at that moment to think of her plight: twenty-one years old, with barely any money and her whole life ahead of her, suddenly burdened with what must have felt like a bag of bricks around her neck. After I had smoothed out that page, it was hard standing there in the dining room, watching the sun, the color of ice, rise through the frozen trees, and trying to understand how Alma must feel. At the bottom of the page there was a small anno-tation, obviously an afterthought to all the arithmetic: *Find a job & learn to cook.*

I hardly knew Alma, but I had always liked her in the way kids like relatives they seldom see. She was beautiful, smooth and elegant in her movements, with piercing blue eyes, long chestnut hair, and lips that made the back of my neck tingle whenever she planted a kiss on my cheek. To me she had always been a mys-terious, even exotic figure. Wearing sunglasses and a suede coat and a beret when she came home, and always some flashy earrings. She smoked and played blues records on the old phonograph in her room, and after one or two nights she'd be gone. Probably I liked her for the very reasons my grandmother so disapproved of her. Alma certainly didn't like to cook: this was one of my grandmother's pet grievances about her. As well as the fact that Alma didn't relish housekeeping in general, or socializing with my grandmother's friends, or family holidays, or attending church. My grandmother's all-purpose modifier for Alma was 'no-good'. When she was feeling more generous, she limited herself to 'wild'.

I, on the other hand, could do no wrong in my grand-mother's eyes. I enjoyed keeping my room in order (how could I not when having a room at all was such a novelty) and raking leaves and drying dishes and even going to church, where I loved listening to the choir sing hymns. I was at that time, in my Brooklyn life, a quiet and orderly boy who had already had a bellyful of being tossed around on rough seas during my years with Luna and Milo.

All the more reason that I should so admire Alma's attitude. And her independence, which was so much more solid and real to me than Luna's scattershot rebelliousness that never took her anywhere. Luna was constantly returning home and then taking off again in a huff. Alma just stayed away. And when she did show up, say for Christmas, she never took the bait when my grandmother tried to provoke her. About her studies: *You can't become a priest, yet all you study is Latin*; her private life: *Your sister had bad taste in men, too, but at least one of them married her* (I was still trying to figure that one out); and her appearance: *If that skirt gets any shorter, and you grow your hair any longer, you won't need a skirt at all.* I realized soon enough that Alma hadn't always been so composed in the face of such attacks, that she had come by her detachment the hard way – after years of heated arguments and recriminations – and I respected her all the more for it. Despite my dependence on, and loyalty to, my grandmother, I resented her meanness toward Alma. I had developed bonds with my grandmother, I loved her, but I also felt most uncomfortable with her when Alma was around. So I kept my mouth shut and, to make it easier on myself, stayed out of the way – even out of the house – during Alma's infrequent visits. This was another reason we felt like such strangers when we were thrown together for that brief period after my grandmother's death.

My room in that house had been Luna's room before she ran off with Milo. It still had the same pale blue walls and blue drapes, the narrow bed and low chest of drawers of matching cherry wood, and the full-length mirror screwed to the back of the door where Luna had primped herself and combed her hair. That afternoon, before Alma and I left for the planetarium, I dressed before that mirror. There were many things my grand-mother had done for me in my two and a half years with her which were brand-new to me and for which I hope she knew I was grateful: laying out a hot supper, however bland, every night; buying me new shoes and sneakers in the fall; and, unlike Luna, making sure that the shirts I wore to school were not only laundered, but also the right size. I pulled on the last of these from my top drawer, a blue turtleneck, creased neatly where she had folded down the sleeves and tucked them under.

I heard Alma start up her car in front of the house, so I hurried, throwing on my pea coat and pulling on my woolen cap. As I locked the front door, she was gunning the engine, trying to get the heater warm, her breath misting up the windshield and the car's exhaust fumes sputtering into the snowbank along the curb. She had the radio turned on, and the announcer went from the escalation of troops in Vietnam – fifty thousand to be shipped out right after Christmas – to the launching that morning of the Pioneer 6 satellite from Cape Kennedy. I had seen the satellite on television the night before, atop a tall white rocket on the brightly lit launchpad, and now I closed my eyes and imagined it streaking out of the earth's atmosphere.

After lunch, during the drive to the planetarium, we hardly talked. There were snow flurries, and then it snowed harder, but the snow wasn't sticking on the highway. Alma seemed far away, rarely looking away from the road. I was sure she was still preoccupied with those figures I had seen on the scratch sheet, still trying to make it all add up in her head so that the two of us wouldn't end up in the poorhouse.

Just before she parked the Impala in a lot near the planetarium, I felt I had to speak. 'Alma,' I said, 'I wanted you to know that Grandma loved you, even if she didn't say so anymore.'

Her eyebrows went up. 'It's okay if she didn't love me,' she replied. Then she softened her voice, and added, 'But you may be right. Maybe she did in her own way.'

I nodded.

'The fact is, Loren, she was a different person after you came into her life.'

I wasn't sure this was true, but I said nothing.

'You know,' Alma went on, 'Mom and I got off to such a bad start. She never saw my father again before I was born. She must have been angry about that – frustrated, at the very least – but she never talked about it, ever. She just held all that in, and then she and I went at it over the years.'

I thought about this. 'I don't know my father, either. You know, my real father. Maybe he's dead, too, and that's why I was put up for adoption.'

She switched off the ignition and dangled the keys thoughtfully. 'Maybe so. But, you know, sometimes I feel like I know my father just as if I'd met him.'

'What do you mean?'

'I mean, it's like I actually remember him.' She was gazing out the window. 'I spent so much time trying to imagine what he was like.' She patted my shoulder. 'But that's because I had nobody else. That won't happen to you. You'll have other people to love.'

Again I nodded my assent, though I was thinking: And who will they be, these people I'm going to love? It felt like, in ten years, I had already used them all up.

4

Spiders

Zaren Eboli was holding up a large glass jar in both hands and speaking to me loudly over the rain that lashed the windows and drummed on the roof. He had been born with only eight fingers – no pinkies – and as I looked at him through the refraction of the jar, his long fingers looked even longer. Around five three, he was at least four inches shorter than me and must have hovered near my own weight of one hundred twenty. He was pigeon-toed, with stooped shoulders and a salt-and-pepper goatee. Invariably he wore soft Turkish slippers with silver stitching, a black velvet smoking jacket, and a string tie with a clasp in the form of crossed swords. His wire-rimmed spectacles were thick: without them he could barely make his way through a cluttered room.

And all the rooms in his house – fifteen of them not counting the enormous basement – were cluttered. With books, magazines, looseleaf folders, specimen jars, slide racks, and filing cabinets packed to capacity. His furniture was of a dark, heavy, rococo design, imported from France by a spendthrift ancestor just after the Civil War: big-legged tables and chairs, overstuffed sofas, deep-drawered cabinets. Musty wall hangings alternated with thickly lacquered oil paintings of Louisiana swamplands, the myriad birds and insects that populated them rendered so realistically – a swooping kingfisher or electric dragonfly – that they often startled me when I passed them.

'The trap-door spider,' Eboli was saying in his up-and-down-the-scale singsong voice, 'a close relative of the tarantula, ambushes his prey from a silk-lined burrow covered by a hinged door. His life span is one year, in which time he never strays more than a few inches from the entrance to the burrow.'

Wearing the leather gloves with which I handled live specimens, I paused with my back to a tall window where the light from the storm powdered the air like phosphorus. After working in silence for four hours at opposite ends of the second-floor library, I had just stood up to take my one break, for coffee and a sandwich, on the screened-in verandah downstairs.

Without so much as a glance at me, Eboli knew he had my attention, for he seldom addressed me directly when he was working. Afterward, before I'd drive back downtown, he would sometimes sit on the verandah with me to chat for a few minutes, but in the twin sanctuaries of his study and his basement laboratory the silence was palpable, subliminally fed by the hum of countless heat and sun lamps, infrared bulbs, air filters, miniature humidifiers (for the jungle spiders) and dehumidifiers (for their desert cousins), and of course the constant complex spinning of hundreds of webs.

'Among all spiders, the trap-door is the most accomplished burrower and the most gifted artisan. Up to three and a half inches in length, he lives alone in a tube-like burrow five to twelve inches deep, which he digs with a comblike rake of spines on his chelicerae. Then he waterproofs it with saliva and lines it with silk. His burrows vary in complexity, from a simple tube secured with a beveled door to a cylinder capped with a trapdoor that has an oblique side tunnel with a second door. Some of these doors are even fitted with a set of bolts. And all the burrows are designed against a single predator: the spider wasp, which is capable of prying open the trapdoor and cornering the spider. With superior

34

sensory equipment and agility, the wasp quickly over-powers the spider and paralyzes him with venom. Then the wasp deposits an egg on the spider's abdomen and a larva hatches which feeds off the spider before and after he dies.' He lowered the jar onto the table and adjusted his string tie. 'His death mirrors the fatal sequence spiders inflict on their prey: ambush, entrapment, paral-ysis, and slow death.' Preparing to open the jar, he slipped on his own gloves, custom-made without the pinky slots. 'Still, the trap-door spider must be counted, among all creatures, as one of the finest natural architects.'

That afternoon I ate half my pepper-cheese sandwich and drank two cups of black coffee on the verandah. It was a relief to be out there, even in the heat and humidity, which were not nearly so oppressive as the overheatedness of the house; on the job I wore only the lightest cotton dresses and rope sandals, and still the sweat ran down my back. The river through the man-grove trees in the driving rain was wide and turbulent, overhung with green mist, rushing toward the gulf. In the canopy of the foliage I saw a pair of red birds huddled with folded wings. And, higher up, one of the striped green owls that hunted by day. The arboreal spiders, I knew now, wove exquisite, complex nets im-pervious to water. I had learned, too, that all spiders are carnivorous. That they never take in solid food through their mouths, but after predigesting their prey with a secretion of fluids, suck the liquid remains into their stomachs by means of powerful muscles. That though their average life span is one year or less, the female tarantula can live to be thirty years old. That most spiders have eight eyes and eight legs. And that there are spiders who live underwater, inside silken diving bells that store air, spinning their webs, laying eggs, and preying on other aquatic insects. In the high grass below the mangrove trees they could be found in the mesh of slow-moving streams that fed into the river, but not in the river itself.

Eboli, who had been born in that house forty-five years before, told me that he traced his interest in arachnology to his discovery of those underwater spiders during a boyhood swim. Working in his house, I saw other antecedents of his obsession at work; for example, the photographs of his mother that covered the lid of the baby grand piano in the living room. An imposing, dark-skinned Creole woman with pursed lips and thick eyebrows that met over her nose, in all the photographs Eboli's mother wore a black lace shawl, intricately woven, and a matching veil that had been lifted – apparently for the photographer's benefit – back onto her tightly bunned jet hair. The shawl and veil fanned out around her smooth round head as if they were one with her – as if she had spun them out.

'Her name was Cela,' Eboli remarked quietly when he found me examining the photographs. 'She lived here as a recluse for some years after my father's death.'

That was all he ever told me about his family, of whom he was the only survivor, himself a recluse in that same house. But despite his soft-spokenness and generally furtive air, I never thought of him as secretive: he spoke freely of himself, without affectation or any of the high seriousness that entered his voice when the subject was spiders. To my surprise, for instance, he told me he had served in the army in Europe as a young enlistee in the Second World War.

'Disqualified from combat, of course,' he drawled, holding up his hands with their missing digits. 'Believe it or not, I ended up in the clerical corps as a typist. I tested out, in those days of two-ton manual machines, at ninety-two words a minute. And I got as close to the front lines as I could, working in a mobile command post. I had harbored only one strong ambition before the war, when I was studying the piano: to meet the late, great Ferdinand La Menthe. He lived in New Orleans, but in his last years he avoided public appearances, and try as I might, I never met him before he died on December 16, 1941. Three months later, I enlisted. After my discharge, I lived in Paris for a year, playing in small clubs, and when I came home I resumed my piano studies. Then in 1949 when my mother died, I gave it up and began my work with spiders in earnest. I'll play you something,' he said, beckoning me into the living room.

With an amazing touch, he set his eight fingers flying on the baby grand's keyboard, first drawing forth a highly embroidered baroque waltz, then shifting into ragtime, improvising variations on a theme from the waltz. For several minutes he played with fierce concentration, finally isolating and returning to the waltz theme, which he played slowly and emphatically before spinning around on the piano stool. 'Ferdinand La Menthe, you see, knew his Bach,' he smiled. 'That was his very own *Goldberg Variations*.'

As often happened after lunch, Eboli asked me to drive down to the library to take out some books. I did so, then went to the newspaper files, and picking through the 1949 obituary columns of the *Delta Mirror* soon came on the notice for Cela Marie Eboli, who had died on March 7. To my surprise, in the same issue, there was a news article about her death, accompanied by one of those photographs atop the piano, from which a single sentence leapt out at me. *According to the police, Mrs Eboli, wearing a black dress and with a long rope noosed around her neck and tied to the leg of her brass bed, jumped from a top-floor window of her house to her death.* And hung there, on the long rope, for several hours before her son Zaren, *a piano player at the Black & White Club, came home and found her.*

Suspended like a spider, I thought with a shiver, closing the drawer before sidling down the dusty aisle, farther back into the past. I stopped before another green cabinet under a shaded 40-watt bulb encrusted with mosquitoes. Flipping through the yellowed clippings directly to December 16, 1941, scanning the most prominent obituary on the page, I discovered that Ferdinand La Menthe was the legal name of none other than Jelly Roll Morton.

Back at Eboli's house, as I parked my car, I cast my eye along the heavily curtained top-floor windows. I didn't see him again until the end of the day, when he asked me to come into his study. He was smoking a cigarillo in a long amber holder, ashes dusting his velvet lapels, and pacing impatiently. I stood nervously while he sat down behind his desk.

'Well, I hope my piano playing did not unsettle you,' he said, capping and uncapping his fountain pen, as he often did when he was preoccupied.

'I enjoyed it.'

'Please, sit.' He cleared his throat. 'I noted on my calendar that the period we agreed on for your employment concludes as of today.'

I had not noted this, and wondered how four months could have passed as if they were a single long day and night – with troubled sleep, no sex, little companionship, and sporadic eating habits. When I first arrived in New Orleans, I bought a bottle of bourbon, drank two glasses neat, and then, seeing the shade of my grandmother rise up filling her teacup with Seven Roses, I poured the rest down the sink. That was one road I wasn't going down, I told myself. In some ways, I might as well have. Since arriving in town, I had lost ten pounds, and the smudges under my eyes from my life on the road had darkened to rings. Sometimes when I was alone in my room, my stomach in knots and a stale astringency closing up my throat, I felt as if I were walking on a white airless road with the same flat scenery – bare trees, an empty house, an endless fence, a recurring windmill – sliding by me, like the scenery backdrop in a silent movie. And all the while I hoped to catch up with someone whom I was sure was just ahead of me, but out of sight. And who could it be but Loren, whom I knew I would never overtake.

'You have helped me enormously,' Eboli went on, the orange lamplight shimmering on his spectacles as he stroked his goatee, 'with the cataloguing especially. So

I wanted to ask you to stay on – same hours but with an increase in pay – for as long as you like.'

I hadn't expected this. 'No, I can't,' I replied. 'Thank you for asking, but it's time I moved on.'

And it was time, not only to leave Eboli's employ, but New Orleans altogether. Still, I wondered if I would have refused his offer out-of-hand like that just a few hours earlier, before I had been spooked by the description of his mother's death in the newspaper files. For I hadn't the slightest idea where I would go next or, as my cash reserves dwindled, how I would support myself when I got there.

'Of course,' Eboli sighed, standing up and pocketing the pen. He looked vaguely disappointed, but I was certain I also detected relief in his sigh. He had had other short-term assistants before, women as well as men, including doctoral candidates at the university, but I doubted that any other young woman had ever put in such a concentrated stint under his roof. 'Well, you have helped me enormously,' he repeated, stepping over to the nearest worktable. 'Would you just take one of these specimens down to the basement before you go?'

He had been working that afternoon with two spiders in separate terrariums. One, I knew, was a common wolf spider, *Lycosa carolinensis*, whose foraging habits he was observing. The other was a large spider, three inches long including his legs, that I had never seen before.

'Yes, he is a fellow I acquired only yesterday in the mail,' he said, following my gaze. 'All the way from Nevada.'

I peered into the terrarium. 'A trap-door?'

Eboli nodded. 'One with the most arresting markings, barely observable from this angle, which rival the red hourglass on the ventral side of the black widow's abdomen. This spider, a nocturnal member of the genus *Ummidia*, is known as *Stellarum*.'

'Of the stars,' I said.

'Yes. His black abdomen is speckled silver, like a night sky filled with stars. He is a desert spider and constructs his burrow near brush. He can withstand enormous amounts of heat, up to 130°. His favorite prey is a long-legged silver ant of the *Cataglyphis* species, who only emerges from his tunnels at night and possesses one of the most peculiar and sophisticated navigational systems in the animal kingdom. The upper half of the ant's cornea has evolved into a grid of the night sky above his territory – a kind of celestial map that shifts with the seasons. To travel, he aligns the grid of star points in his eyes with the stars in the sky. *Ummidia Stellarum*, in order to ambush the ant, is privy to his routes, though this is quite a mystery, for we know that even nocturnal spiders are too shortsighted to see the stars. So the silver ant, who lives by the stars, often ends his short life liquefied in *Stellarum*'s starry abdomen. Even more unusual is that *Stellarum* itself is one of those rare creatures who has no known predators. The average spider lays from 300 to 3,000 eggs, but the female *Stellarum* lays only one egg in a cycle. That's what checks his population. Without predators, *Stellarum* always dies a natural death in his burrow, which then becomes his crypt, sealed up by the desert sands. He is like a god among spiders – or at least a pharaoh. Some believe that his venom has a uniquely potent effect on human beings.'

'And what is that?'

Eboli was cleaning his spectacles with a striped handkerchief. 'Both the Hopi and Zuni Indians, who have used the venom in purification rituals, assert that it effectively reduces the human soul to its rarest elements, stripping away all that is false, illusory or fearful. Not for a few hours or days, but over the course of many months, sometimes up to three years, depending on the amount of venom ingested. It is a kind of long-term spiritual truth serum. In fact, the Zunis believed it would make their strongest shamans and

40

warriors almost godlike – or, if they were flawed, would just as surely tear them apart over time.'

I put my eye right up to the glass and saw the *Ummidia Stellarum* immobile on a flat rock behind the thick glass.

'But in the desert,' he went on, '*Stellarum* seldom has contact with people, and like other spiders, he bites only when cornered.' He reached into his jacket pocket. 'At any rate, here is your final pay-check, with a small bonus.'

'So you knew I wouldn't be staying.'

He shrugged. 'Perhaps our paths will cross again. I'll say goodbye now, Mala. And good luck.' He shook my hand, then turned away abruptly and left the room. I picked up the terrarium carefully.

The rain had finally stopped and the house was even more still than usual as I descended first the broad stairway with the faded Persian carpeting to the front hall, and then the cast-iron spiral steps, through a low door that led to the basement. All the way down, with the scent of drenched wisteria and honeysuckle filling my head, I couldn't take my eyes off the *Ummidia Stellarum*.

In the basement the whirring of filters and fans greeted me, and the hum of the lights that threw jagged shadows up the walls. I walked down the far aisle between long walnut tables and laid the terrarium beside those of the other desert spiders and plugged in its sun lamp.

The *Ummidia Stellarum* had not stirred, but his eyes revolved upward at the sudden blaze of light. Sweat was beading on my forehead. Even as Eboli was telling me about this spider, I had known what I was going to do. Slowly I lifted open the terrarium's metal lid and slid my left hand in toward the spider. He didn't move. My hand was steady as I walked my fingers onto the rock and nudged him. Still no movement. After all, he had been handled before. But, then, for months I had been handling spiders too, and I knew something about it

41

now. Quickly I slid the rock out from under him, and he jumped, scurrying for a hole in the sand. I blocked his way, then forced him into a corner, trapping him with my palm. Still my hand was steady as I closed it over him. And it remained steady when I felt him panic, fluttering and scrambling, and finally, desperately, biting me – a minute jab as from the corner of a razor blade, at the center of my palm. I knew this was the fang at the tip of his jaw that was a conduit from the poison gland. After a moment, I raised my hand, opening my fingers, and the *Ummidia Stellarum* darted through them, across the sand, and disappeared down the hole.

Suddenly there was a hot pulsing in my palm that moved through my wrist into my arm and shot rapidly upward. When it reached my chest, the jolt I experienced was far more powerful than what I had expected, but I felt no fear. Seconds later I stopped sweating and my head grew cold. My tongue was dry and my lips numb. My fingers and toes felt numb too, as if they had been injected with Novocain. I put my index finger to the vapor that had condensed on the outside of the terrarium and drew a face with hands clapped over the ears, no mouth, and closed eyes. Before I could dot in the tears, I spun around, certain I heard a rustle on the stairs. Had Eboli, in his silent slippers, been watching me? I rushed over, but there was no one. Later, I wasn't sure that I had closed the lid on the spider's terrarium. I wasn't clear, either, on how I managed to drive back downtown, my hands so numb they felt ice-coated and my head swimming.

But one thing I never forgot. As I climbed the steps from the basement in Zaren Eboli's blue house, the darkness deepened and I saw stars, thousands of them coming clear before me in the high stairwell, until they glittered sharply.

Two days later, and two years to the day after I had taken Loren to the planetarium – it would have been his twelfth birthday – I walked along the river to the recruiting office on St Clair Street and enlisted in the Navy

Nursing Corps and was assigned first to Savannah and then to Honolulu, for intensive training. Nine months later, in September, 1968, I was placed on-line aboard the USS *Repose*, a hospital ship, off Quang Tri, South Vietnam, in the South China Sea.

5

The Abandoned Factory

The woman led me down several dim dusty corridors, into a small, fluorescently lit room. The room had two doors: the one we had entered, which she left open; and another in the wall directly across from it, which remained closed.

This was the moment I had been waiting to seize. The effects of the perfume had worn off completely: my legs were steady and my vision sharp again. When I felt the woman relax her grip on me, I snapped my head around and sank my teeth into her hand. She let out a muffled scream, whipped her hand free, and whacked me a glancing blow behind the ear. By then I was already halfway out the door. I nearly succeeded in shutting it on her, but she was too quick, and before I knew it she had grabbed me by the scruff of my neck and dragged me back into the room. I was flailing my arms when she spun me around hard and shoved me against the wall. I trembled, thinking she was going to whack me again. Instead, she glared at me, containing her fury. Her arms folded across her chest, she squeezed the elbows repeatedly – a signal of her wrath that I would come to know well. Then she grabbed my hand and nearly yanked my arm from its socket, pulling me across the room to the other door. Without a word she opened it and pushed me through. I wanted to bite her again, but I didn't dare as I looked around at a room so cavernous

I felt for an instant as if I were falling through space.

The room was at least the size of a football field. Its walls were pocked brick and peeling plaster, and powerful lights hung from the ceiling rafters four stories up. There were craters in the floor where huge rusted pipes had been exposed. A half dozen workmen in blue jumpsuits were soldering electrical connections on the far wall. About thirty yards from me, two other men, one young, one old, were standing beside a pair of chairs upholstered in burgundy velvet. The younger man had dark, rust-colored skin, an angular face, and a black crew cut. His muscular arms bulged beneath the rolled-up sleeves of his checkered shirt, and he wore a blue and white tie. A pencil behind his ear, his face tight with concentration behind a pair of black horn-rim glasses, he was clutching a thin roll of blue paper and obviously explaining something to the older man.

Impeccably tailored in a black suit and gray silk shirt, the latter was listening with two fingers pressed to his temple, his chin resting on his chest. About sixty-five, short and stocky, he had white hair combed back flat and a thick white moustache, neatly trimmed. His expression was calm and relaxed. And it did not change when he raised his head a moment later. The woman released my hand and roughly – but more subtly so, with a surreptitious jab to the ribs – urged me forward, and we walked toward him.

The younger man stopped talking, and as I approached them, the old man studied me keenly with his pale blue eyes. He had a flower in his lapel unlike any I had ever seen: alternating yellow and red petals – jagged-edged like licks of flame – around a fiery orange center. I felt frightened, yet I wondered what kind of kidnapping this could be. Knocking around with my adoptive parents, spending more time in diners and bars than schoolrooms, I had seen a few things, and it struck me as more than odd that all these obviously well-heeled and otherwise occupied people had gone to such trouble to kidnap someone like me. I was an orphan, after all, a nobody, with no money, no connections, and no family aside from my young aunt. And the notion of her coming up with ransom money was laughable.

So what on earth could this old man want with me, I asked myself as he reached out and gently squeezed my shoulder. And it struck me suddenly, terribly, that their motivations might have nothing to do with money.

'Welcome, Enzo,' he greeted me. One side of his mouth went up in a smile and I saw a dazzling set of white teeth. 'You know, your real name is Enzo,' he went on.

I winced, rubbing my arm where the woman had yanked me around. When I looked up at her, she was staring at me coldly.

They really are crazy, I thought. 'I want to go back to my aunt,' I said, my voice breaking.

The woman peeled off her gloves and stuffed them into her handbag. 'I am your aunt,' she said acidly, to my further astonishment.

'That's enough,' the old man snapped.

'He bit me,' she said, holding out her hand, where there was a cherry-sized welt below the knuckle of the index finger.

'That's because you mismanaged things,' he retorted.

'It's because he's a—'

'I said, that's enough,' the old man cut her off in a low voice, and swallowing her words, she stepped back from us.

Turning to me again, the old man nodded toward the burgundy chairs. 'Please, have a seat,' he said softly.

'My name is Loren,' I said, shrinking from him.

'Listen to what I have to say,' he said, sitting down himself and crossing his legs, 'and afterward I promise that you will have a clear choice: you may return to your aunt, or I will send her a letter, which I'll show you, telling her that you are all right and choose to remain with me.'

'Why would I want to do that?'

'Just listen and maybe you'll see why.'

46

'Kidnapping is against the law, you know,' I shot back, surprising myself, but not him.

'There are other laws, Enzo,' he replied.

'That's not my name,' I said. Then something occurred to me. 'Hey, maybe you've got the wrong kid. Did you ever think of that?'

He shook his head. 'And they are important laws,' he went on in a kindly voice, 'never to be underestimated. By their lights, yours seems to me to be a very special case. What if I told you that I am your uncle – I mean your real uncle – and that we have the same blood flowing in our veins? To some, that is a more powerful sort of law.'

'What?'

'It's a fact,' he said gravely. 'But if I had told it to the woman you call your aunt, revealing my identity, and she rebuffed me, I might never have had another chance to bring you into my life. Certainly not without her permission, for I have no legal claim on you. Once I found you, I wasn't about to lose you – unless you wanted it so. I've learned that when something's been lost and you manage to recover it, you do everything in your power not to lose it again. I have learned too – the hard way – that if you do lose it again, you'll never recover it. I did not want to coerce your aunt, but, still, I undertook extraordinary measures to get you here. I have to live with that. From now on, though, what I want can only occur with your consent. You see, after investigating your aunt's circumstances, and yours, and learning just how tenuous your relationship with her is, I took this chance. I thought it my best chance.' He smiled. 'Understand, I used to be a gambler.'

I shook my head. 'No, I don't understand anything you're saying.'

'Just hear me out, please. Please,' he repeated softly.

I sat down, my mind racing. 'I can still go back to Alma if I want to?' I was still frightened, but, whether he was crazy or not, I did not think this man would harm me physically.

He nodded. 'Absolutely. You will hear many things about me, but never, ever, that I break my word. My name is Junius Samax. Your real mother was my niece. That lady's sister. The two are my brother Nilus's daughters, whom I raised – not very successfully, I'm afraid – after his death. Your mother died at nineteen, and unknown to me, she had given birth to you three months earlier and immediately put you up for adoption.' He took a piece of paper, folded into quarters, from inside his jacket. 'But first she gave you a name. This is a copy of your birth certificate. Two months ago I happened to learn of your existence. With a great deal of effort, and now satisfaction, I traced you to your current life.' He handed me the piece of paper.

The letters danced before my eyes, and as I read, my hands began to shake. COUNTY OF LAS VEGAS, THE STATE OF NEVADA was printed floridly across the top. Embossed on one side was a notary's seal over which I ran my thumb. The birth certificate was for one ENZO SAMAX; 7 POUNDS 14 OUNCES; blood type: DOUBLE-O-NEGATIVE; time of birth: 2:20 a.m.; place: LAS VEGAS, NEVADA; mother: BEL SAMAX; father: UNKNOWN. The birth date, DECEMBER 16, 1955, leapt out at me, for it was my own. And I knew that was my blood type because Milo – who, in all ways disorganized, was oddly and ironically obsessed with what he called 'accident preparation' – had made me memorize it along with the fact that I was allergic to penicillin. I also knew that I had been adopted in Reno, Nevada.

The old man snapped his fingers, and the young man with the crew cut materialized with a glass of water for me. I saw that his roll of blue papers was an architectural blueprint. The white in his tie was clouds. I wished that like a cloud I could float away at that moment, far away from that place, and touch down somewhere where these people could never find me again. I sipped a little water and told myself: if they don't really let you go, they still won't be able to hold you forever. When they let down their guard, you'll bolt, and this time

48

you'll pick your spot better, and once you're out, it won't be so easy for them to snatch you up again. Rather than convince me of anything, that piece of paper made me step back and take a deep breath and reconnoiter, as Milo used to put it. Then the young man patted my arm, and his black eyes were friendly.

'I'm sorry,' the old man said, and he sounded sorry. 'I know this is a shock, but when the subject is difficult I like to be as direct as possible. Double-O-negative is one of the rarest blood types: I have it, my brother had it, and you have it. That's significant. But this is about more than blood types. I have put myself in a position to live my life exactly as I please. I have only a handful of living relatives,' he said, glancing at the woman, who was pacing up and down out of earshot, her arms crossed on her chest. 'It's no secret to them that your mother was my favorite. I would like to share with you what I would have shared with her.' He paused. 'I'm being as frank with you as I can. There is much I would like to give you – a life filled with things I can't give to anyone else. Things you can't even imagine now. But I know full well that it will also be rewarding for me. It will fill a great void in my life, for there is much I know you will give to me, should things proceed as I am hoping. And should you decide you want what I am offering you.' He patted my shoulder. 'Now, take a moment, and then I'll tell you more of the story. Your story. Afterward, you can tell me your decision.'

He told me a good deal – at least it seemed so at the time. In fact, it was just a sliver off a far greater story than I could ever have imagined. Thirty minutes later, however, I was ready to see the letter the old man had written to Alma. The young man put a small table before me and laid down a sheet of yellow paper and a yellow fountain pen. Typed on the paper was the letter.

'As you can see,' the old man said, 'I have not signed the letter or used any of the names you have heard, but I have not once lied to her and I have told as much of the truth as I could without jeopardizing my position.

Primarily I want to reassure her as best I can.'

The letter was short and direct, and I read it carefully.

'If you would like to add anything,' he said, 'you may.'

'I can write whatever I want?'

'Except my name, of course,' he replied.

In the center of that silent enormous room with the craters, beneath the ceiling that stretched away in all directions like a sky, I thought about it for a long time and then wrote a single line to Alma at the bottom of the page, and then slowly added my signature.

The old man handed me a yellow envelope, already stamped and with Alma's name and address printed neatly in red ink. 'Fold the letter and seal the envelope,' he said.

'Don't you want to read what I put in?'

He shook his head. 'I trust you.'

He took the sealed envelope from me and beckoned to the woman. 'Ivy, please see to it that this is hand-delivered,' he said as she approached us. 'Use a Western Union courier at the airport. Then meet us at the plane.' He stood up.

Turning on her heel, she left without a word.

'Plane? Where are we going?' I said. Despite all I had heard, and the letter I had signed, and the fact my fear had momentarily been supplanted by the enormous curiosity the old man's story had aroused, I still had it in my head that I would have the option – however slim – of slipping away if I wanted to. That I had an out. Thinking ahead, I had imagined another car ride; it had not occurred to me we might travel a great distance that very day.

'We're going to Las Vegas,' he replied, the *s*'s soft off his tongue. 'And from now on you must call me Uncle Junius. And you must try to trust me. I apologize to you for the way you were brought here: while under my roof, you will never again be held against your will. You will be free to come and go as you please. I would ask only that you not attempt to contact your aunt again. It will

50

serve no useful purpose – for her, or us – as I hope you understand now. Can you promise me that?'

I nodded slowly.

'Good.' He reached into the same pocket that had held the birth certificate. 'This is your mother,' he said quietly.

He handed me a color snapshot of a pale, thin woman, very pretty, with long blond hair parted cleanly and grazing her shoulders. Wearing a red sleeveless dress, she was smiling in sunlight against an expanse of yellow sand, one of her eyes squinted half shut. The shadow of the photographer – a tall, broad-shouldered man with long legs – extended into the upper right-hand corner of the frame. And at her side the young woman was clutching a black hat, a man's hat, which he must have handed to her just before he snapped her picture.

'I never learned his identity,' he went on, 'but I do know that the man who took this photograph must have been your father.'

'My father?' I had wondered so often about my real parents over the years that it seemed incredible I might actually be holding tangible evidence of their existence. An image of my mother and the shadow of my father. It wasn't exactly like one of those memories Alma had told me about, that she had of her father. But it was close enough: if that shadow really belonged to my father, then this image would constitute a memory of his. One to which I was suddenly privy, and I felt a certain intimacy in that.

The image of my mother, that shadow, and the black hat combined to fill a place in my imagination where, until then, there had only been a vacuum. For a long time, they would be all I had of my father.

6

The Hospital Ship

The band of blood across the waist of my white uniform, where I leaned against the X-ray table, had dried and darkened by the time I got off duty and went on deck. The nurses had their own sundeck, which was off limits to all other personnel. By day, we could stretch out in the blistering sun or play cards at a fold-up table. At night, we stood at the railing smoking ganja and drinking White Angels – iced gin with a dash of bitters – from a stainless steel thermos with a red cross on its cap and US NAVY down the side.

I had scrubbed down quickly and still had blood under my nails. Sharline had bitten her nails all the way down and so didn't have this problem, I observed as she expertly rolled a joint. She stood close beside me, droning a song under her breath and never taking her eyes off the distant jungle that was lighting up, as it did every night, with flares and rockets – blue, green, and gold – like dragonflies whirring insanely in all directions.

Sharline shared a ten-by-ten cabin with double bunks with me and two other nurses. From Tulsa, Oklahoma, she was an operating room nurse, with five years of training, on her second tour of duty. I was an X-ray technician, the lowest rung of military nurse, trained in six months, with a three-month residency on an aircraft carrier in the Solomon Islands. Skilled surgical and postoperative nurses in the war were too essential to use on X-ray work, so the Navy relied on volunteers like me. And throughout South Vietnam, in military hospitals and on hospital ships, X-ray technicians were in demand; because shrapnel wounds were often undetectable by the naked eye, or were obscured by blood and dirt, every wounded soldier brought in for treatment was routinely x-rayed. Sometimes they were cleaned up before being wheeled into the X-ray room; sometimes I had to help strip them down. That night had been one of the worst since I had come onboard three months before: more than a hundred men had come in within a six-hour span, and working with a single orderly, I was covered with as much blood at the end of my shift as any O.R. nurse.

Sharline had her blond hair drawn back with a torn ribbon. She was about my height, with a very full figure – heavier, she said, ever since she had come to Vietnam. She smelled of iodine and disinfectant soap. Her eyes were bloodshot and her smile blank, as if she had already taken a hit off the packed buds of that pollen-dusty, jade Thai stick she kept in a thin plastic tube taped along her bra strap. After she did take her hit, drawing it in sharply to her lungs, she gazed back at those lights, thirty miles across the choppy sea, as if they were fireworks on the Fourth of July. Like everyone else onboard, at that moment Sharline heard no explosions, no artillery fire – nothing but the wind flapping the pennants on the mast and the slap of the waves against the ship's hull. But I could hear all the sounds behind those lights: mortar blasts, antiaircraft guns, even the crackle of small arms. No amount of ganja, gin, black beauties, or morphine lifted from the pharmaceutical stores either enhanced or erased them. I had more powerful chemicals at work in my bloodstream, which it seemed nothing could override.

Outwardly they had only manifested themselves at a single point, on my left palm, which was burning more intensely than usual that night. From the red dot that had formed there after the *Ummidia Stellarum* bit me, concentric lines had appeared, tightly packed in an area smaller than a postage stamp. Every month a new red circle rose up from below my skin, twelve of them now radiating from the dot, like the orbits of planets around a red star. I had long given up scrubbing my palm, or soaking it, or applying compresses, or ice. I was careful to keep it concealed, but whenever one of the doctors or another nurse saw it, I told them it was a tattoo. Which did not explain why it kept growing larger. After a while, I no more wanted to eradicate it than I would have wanted to reverse the strange effects of the spider's bite.

The new doctor specializing in tropical diseases, which were often transmitted by insect bites, had just come on-line, and I had borrowed several of his reference books one night, but under *spider bites* found no symptoms remotely resembling my own. I took my own pulse and temperature, and both were normal, but the temperature of my palm, which I measured with a flat thermometer, was always 105°. In addition to insomnia, my other symptoms were frequent loss of appetite: sometimes I went a whole day without food and didn't realize it until the next morning. At the same time, my weight remained exactly the same. Sometimes I drank two liters of water at a sitting, and like a spider craved the heat, but I never sweated, even on the hottest days. After leaving New Orleans, I began having very irregular periods, months apart, and then I stopped getting them altogether. In Savannah, when no rings had yet appeared in my palm, I underwent a complete blood workup after my induction, but it had been all clear.

I soon discovered that the powers of my memory were greatly heightened: I seemed able to scan its contents, no matter how remote or obscure the incident, to the minutest detail, as if I had at my disposal for review in my mind's eye vaults of unedited film footage encompassing my entire life. With the utmost clarity, I reviewed a visit to the Statue of Liberty with my third-grade class; a trek to the grocery store with my mother during the famous blizzard of 1948; and Luna's eleventh birthday party. I also suffered (or enjoyed) occasional bursts of visual hyperacuity, when I could perceive remote objects in great detail: the flags on ships crossing the horizon, the plumage of birds winging near shore, the auras around individual stars.

With battles, this meant I not only heard, but saw, far more than I wanted to – often more than I could bear. As I did at the end of that boiling night, when the last mortars streaked into vapor, and the choppers ferried us the wounded and the dead, and it became grimly clear, as always, that the fireworks display had been a ferocious pitched battle – one small corner of bedlam brought to us at dawn in the persons of soldiers, most of them my own age or younger, broken and blood-drenched, piled six deep in triage.

The USS *Repose* housed a crew of three hundred twenty men and thirty women – all nurses – and at any one time as many as two hundred male patients. Some of these – the lucky few – had come in with tropical diseases or 'natural' emergencies like appendicitis. The others had limbs blown off by land mines, eyes scorched by phosphorus bombs, feet and hands shredded in booby traps, torsos gaping open or riddled by gunfire and grenades, skin charred by incendiaries like meat in an oven.

'Wanna play name that tune?' Sharline said, moistening her lips.

Even if I had known it, I could not have identified the song she was droning.

'It's "Star Jam", by Jelly Roll Morton.'

Zaren Eboli's generous notion of a small bonus when I gave him notice had been five hundred dollars, which I had spent in one shot in Savannah on the night before my induction into the Navy. With a year of motels and furnished rooms behind me, I had taken a room for the weekend at the only four-star hotel in the city, paid for with the two hundred fifty dollars I received for my Impala. Then I spent my bonus from Eboli on a pendant.

Just around the corner from my hotel I had wandered into a shop so small it could only accommodate two customers at a time. Not that people were waiting in line to get in. It was just before midnight and the place was about to close. The walls were hung with posters of movie stars and faded tapestries from Indonesia. Behind the counter, the proprietor had long platinum hair and half-lidded eyes. He wore a tie-dyed shirt, an Indian vest, and a scarlet bandanna around his head. In the single cracked glass case before him, among a scattering of gaudy trinkets, cigarette lighters, and cheap earrings, my pendant stood out. Literally, a gem.

It was a piece of highly-polished volcanic stone – blacker than onyx and flecked with silver. According to the proprietor, it was created during a massive eruption in the South Pacific in 1701. Never cut, the stone was shaped by natural forces – lava hitting the raw tropical air and then cooling in the sea – into a seven-pronged star. The pendant hung from a black chain with a silver clasp, and had been brought to England in 1779, by one of Captain Cook's men after the captain was killed in Hawaii. Fifty years later, the proprietor assured me, it found its way to America in the possession of a woman who died at the age of one hundred and five in Savannah. Longevity was one of the qualities it might confer, he added. He wanted to fill me in on more of its history – he said he'd brew some tea – but I was in a hurry, and after paying him, followed the directions he gave me and joined an antiwar candlelight vigil in a public park across town. It was about that time the war had truly begun raging out of control, so there was a large crowd. Several speakers took the podium: a just-returned vet, a priest, and an activist lawyer who was aiding draft resisters. A pair of guitarists played. A Buddhist monk led a chant. In my last year at college in Boston, I had regularly participated in sit-ins and demonstrations. During the last of these, I narrowly escaped arrest after being gassed by the police outside Government Center.

Since that night in Savannah I had taken off the pendant only once, after riding a taxi out to the naval base at Point Vincent and stripping down for my physical examination. I had already cropped my long hair to fit the regulation length for the nursing corps, and after being vaccinated, photographed and measured, I was issued two uniforms, identification papers, training manuals, and a regulation watch, ultrashockproof, with radium numerals and hands.

Which were glowing now on my wrist at two-thirty in the morning as Sharline and I sat down side by side on two beach chairs. Prolonging our stay on deck as long as possible before submitting to the claustrophobia of our cabin, we turned our attention to the sky and I began picking out constellations – Cetus, Taurus, and Perseus – for her. The sky was velvety black and the stars were blazing so brightly they seemed to be falling toward us at great speed. But Sharline had already absorbed all the stimulation she could that day, and after finishing her joint and taking a last sip from the thermos, she fell asleep, her head cocked sharply to one side, her mouth open.

Aside from my pendant, I only had one other prized possession which I had brought into the Navy, the only object that I kept when I sold my mother's house: the Silver Star my father was awarded after he was killed on Guam. Living on the eastern seaboard all my life, that island had always seemed utterly remote to me – outside of time and space – but now I was due north of it, in the same ocean. I remember Luna showing it to me in an atlas when I was five years old, a tiny green dot far from any other dot, in an endless blue expanse. When I sailed back to Honolulu from the Solomons after completing my residency, we passed near it, but not near enough to see. Having polished the Silver Star, badly tarnished after all those years on the living-room wall in Brooklyn,

I kept it in my locker in the velvet-lined box in which my pendant had come.

Among our personal effects on board, we were allowed only three books apiece. The library in our cabin contained two Bibles, a dog-eared *Arabian Nights*, Sharline's copy of *The Dhammapada*, given her by a dying marine lieutenant, and some detective novels. I had brought along books on astronomy by Pliny and Manilius and a selection of Cicero, all in Latin, which were not of any use to the others and had previously been of no interest to me back in Boston, in my other life. In Pliny I read that Hipparchus had been the first ancient astronomer to question the notion that the stars were embedded in a solid sphere – like a giant Fabergé egg – which surrounded the earth. After witnessing a stellar nova, he realized the stars had not all been created simultaneously, and he began cataloguing them by position and brightness so that future astronomers could trace their evolution. And it was Cicero, drawing on Anaximander, who believed that the innumerable stars in the heavens were, each of them, gods. That night, a week before Christmas, I thought they must be so, certain that on occasion some of them fell to earth and mingled among us, shimmering with light or burnt out like cinders.

Later in the same book, trying to pin down a definition of the human soul, Cicero sets forth Democritus's theory that the soul, like any material object, results from an accidental collision of atoms, and Empedocles's that the soul is the blood permeating our hearts. Though many others, Cicero adds, hold that the soul is an unknowable substance in the brain, he concluded that the soul is simply breath; after a man's death, his soul – freed, immortal suddenly – rises into the upper atmosphere, where it is vivified by the same forces that stoke the eternal fires of the stars.

At the X-ray machine I looked into men's bodies for twelve hours a day. Sometimes longer. In studying X-rays day after day of these wounded men, who were often dying men, and always men in peril, I personally subscribed to the theories of those who called the soul an unknowable substance. Unknowable but not invisible. After a while, in that small room dark as a cave, I was sure at times that I could see a man's soul rising up at me from the photographic plates, floating there, piecemeal or condensed, among the bones and muscles and nerves and the dark shadows of the organs which I came to know so intimately. I scanned the smears and blurs, the fogs and mists, within each body, and the even darker shadows hovering behind the organs, for the white slashes of shrapnel or the duller streaks of bullets. Iron that had torn into, and settled deep within, the flesh.

At six a.m. every day except Sunday those of us who were asleep were awakened by 'The Star-Spangled Banner' on the PA system. I was usually up already, sitting on deck, waiting to assume my duties and watching the sun rise pink and hot across the sea. I no longer drank coffee − no longer needed it. I had quit smoking cigarettes just as abruptly. And no matter how exhausting my stint in the X-ray room, I never slept more than two hours at a stretch during the twelve months I served on that ship. In fact, I had required very little sleep since New Orleans: three hours a day at most. And Christmas Eve that year was no exception.

I got off duty at six p.m., skipped dinner, and slept restlessly for an hour. Then I went to the Christmas party in the mess hall. It had been a quiet day: only three wounded men brought in, around noon, and only one of them serious. Doctors and nurses were gathered around a long table with two bowls of wine punch, cans of beer in a bucket of ice, and a chocolate cake with red frosting. A small aluminum Christmas tree from Sears, Roebuck was set up in the corner. Someone had trimmed it with balls of cotton dyed green and cutouts of angels, from a coloring book. A tinfoil star adorned the tip of the tree. On the phonograph Elvis Presley was singing 'Silver Bells.'

I scooped a cup of punch, which I didn't drink, and someone cut me a piece of cake, which I didn't eat. In our tiny quarters I got along well enough with my three cabinmates, but otherwise I wasn't much of a mixer. In fact, this was the first social event, such as they were, that I had attended since coming aboard.

The next number, 'White Christmas,' came on, the lights were dimmed, and people began slow-dancing. First a surgeon, then a petty officer asked me to dance, but I told them both I wanted to finish my cake first. Instead, I slipped out and went up to the nurse's deck, where Sharline had dozed off with a joint stuck between her index and forefinger. I removed it and draped my jacket over her. She was skipping the Christmas party altogether. She and I, one of the orderlies had informed me, were considered 'the most desirable' nurses aboard by both the crewmen and those patients whose wounds still allowed them such considerations. At any rate, it was not a distinction that meant much to me one way or the other. Not so with Sharline. She had been getting it on with a sailor who had completed his tour of duty that month and then flown back to Honolulu. Several times a week we gave up the cabin to them for an hour. One of the other nurses had the same arrangement, with an anesthesiologist, but not so frequently. For fraternization of the carnal sort they could all have been discharged and sent home – which wasn't much of a threat to them, though it would have been to me, had I the slightest interest in fraternizing. There was some irony in this since I was the only one of them who had entered the Navy decidedly opposed to the war. An opposition I confided to no one, though most of my medical shipmates hated the war soon enough more than anyone stateside could imagine. This was not the case, however, with my one dour cabinmate, Evelyn, a starchy, taut-faced Alabaman from a fundamentalist military family who had intuited enough about my feelings on this subject to tell me, unsolicited, that it didn't matter what had brought me to Vietnam so long as I kept doing my job so well. She was most put off that I read Latin, which she considered a heathen tongue, without a dictionary. As for Sharline, she had been keeping even more to herself, and smoking even more Thai stick, since her paramour's departure.

'His tan was a shade lighter at the base of his ring finger,' she told me one day. 'By now he's back in Portland and he's put his wedding band on again.'

The nurses called such sailors 'territorial bachelors'. Most nurses avoided them, but they were the only kind of sailor Sharline liked.

'Definitely no emotional strings attached that way,' she observed, flicking her lighter.

The weather could change in seconds in those waters, and suddenly it began to rain, a dark squall that swept the deck with a staccato burst for several minutes. Sharline and I, once again sprawled out on beach chairs, were immediately soaked through, though she never stirred. Just that morning I had read in Pliny of a time during one of Rome's bloodiest civil wars, before a massive battle, when it was reliably recorded that milk and blood rained down from the sky, then flesh – snatched in midair by the birds – and finally iron. This was a rain which would not have been foreign to Vietnam, I thought, watching the squall, like a black top, whirl across the sea toward the jungle.

When the stars reappeared, I scanned them. In the constellation Perseus the Medusa's head has a winking eye, which my star books listed as Algol, a self-eclipsing double star, one star large and dim revolving around the other, which is small and bright. Every three days the larger star briefly eclipses the smaller one, and Medusa winks. As she was doing at the stroke of midnight when the PA system blared to life with a scratchy Christmas greeting from the captain and an announcement that a sleigh and eight reindeer would soon be touching down on the landing deck. Sharline woke up and without a word to me went down to our cabin.

Moments later, as I got up to leave, I heard a distant roar in the sky, farther out at sea. Straining my eyes, I finally saw a triangle of stars to the north streaking toward shore: a squadron of high-flying bombers. They were too big and too high to have come off any of the aircraft carriers, so I knew they were B-52s out of Guam. Vulnerable to sabotage, they could not operate out of Saigon, so they flew for eight hours to reach their targets and, after dropping their payloads, returned to the huge air base on Guam. Usually they made their runs much farther north of us. To someone in a faraway command center, I thought, it must have been a very important mission that required men to be sent up on Christmas Eve. Unless that someone had forgotten, or just didn't care, what night it was.

By dawn a number of the men in those jets were being wheeled into my X-ray room. Dressed in an elf cap, with a cotton beard, I had joined several nurses in serving Christmas breakfast to our patients when the call came in that the choppers were bringing out some casualties: nine airmen – pilots, bombardiers, and a single navigator – who had been shot down while taking out a series of bridges in the wake of a battalion of marines retreating under hostile fire. Their planes were hit with surface-to-air missiles and then strafed with antiaircraft guns as they crash-landed. The survivors suffered multiple shrapnel wounds, broken bones, and burns. Two dozen airmen had died in action, and their bodies, in black bags, were lined up on the deck awaiting transfer to Quang Tri.

So we had nine new patients: Santa and his eight reindeer, Sharline dubbed them.

The last one I X-rayed was the navigator, whose dog tag read GEZA CASSIEL.

They wheeled him in facedown because he had shrapnel wounds across his left shoulder in the back. He was lucky – that is, he was going to make it – because the shrapnel, six pieces running in an absolutely straight line, had missed both his heart and lungs, and his neck, by no more than an inch on either side.

I X-rayed him from head to foot, then the orderlies turned him over slowly and one of them supported his shoulder while I X-rayed him up and down in the front. None of the shrapnel had come out his chest. And the X-rays turned up one more piece lodged, inexplicably, in his right ankle. It, too, was extracted in surgery, but no entry wound was discovered.

Cassiel was an Air Force captain. Thirty-one years old. A tall, striking man, solidly built, with strong arms and shoulders and sleek black hair cropped short. He had been heavily sedated and his eyes were closed. His body had only been partially cleaned and there was still blood caked on his right hand – not from his wounds, it turned out, but from those of a fellow airman whom he had dragged free of their plane before it was engulfed in flames. Then he had crawled a hundred yards into the jungle, and with the shrapnel embedded in his other shoulder must have been in agony pulling a deadweight like that.

But it was something else – nowhere near his wounds – which the X-rays had picked up that most stuck in my mind. It was a small key, with a round head, clearly visible in the bottom of his stomach cavity. Its teeth were complex. At first glance, I thought it had two holes at the top. Then I realized that what looked like a second hole was really a circular mineral or gem set into the key that was the same size as the key-ring hole. During my training in Honolulu we had memorized lists of substances, including minerals, that X-rays could penetrate, and I guessed that this was one of them. At any rate, in other men's X-rays I had seen coins, marbles, even a soda bottle cap in their stomachs. But never a key. For that reason, and also because I wanted to see what his eyes looked like, I resolved to drop in on him the day after his surgery.

Sitting up in bed with his arm and shoulder

suspended and an I.V. in his other forearm, he calmly watched me cross the postoperative room from the moment I entered it, wending my way through the myriad beds, as if he knew I was coming to see him and him alone.

His eyes were gray, with silver highlights, deeply set beneath a flat, imposing brow. His hair had been combed, and bathed completely now, fully conscious, he looked even more striking: not just handsome, with finely shaped, symmetrical features, but intense. His eyes especially so. 'You must be Mala,' he said in a low, pleasant voice. 'You were asking after me yesterday when I was still out.'

I was surprised.

'The other nurse told me,' he said. 'She said Mala from X-ray had never been in asking about anyone before.' He extended the fingers of his right hand. 'Thank you for finding all that shrapnel. Including the piece in my ankle, which I've been walking around with for who knows how long.'

I touched his fingers, and they were cool. He had large hands and his fingers were long and powerful.

'I asked them to keep it for me,' he went on, indicating a plastic cup on the bedside table that held seven pieces of black iron, each about the size of a nickel.

'You're feeling all right, then, Captain?' When I spoke finally, my own voice sounded remote, hoarse in my throat. And my palm was burning more than ever.

'They gave me so much morphine that my shoulder and arm are numb right through. But I'll be all right.' He curled his fingers into a fist and compressed his lips. 'All the rest of my crew was killed, blown to bits. And they tell me there was nothing left of our plane.'

'I'm sorry.'

He shook his head. 'And I found out that the airman I pulled out was already dead.'

'I know. The crew that brought you in said it was a miracle you survived, Captain.'

'I used up a few of my nine lives, I know that. Won't

you sit down? And please don't call me Captain.'

I hesitated. 'I have to get back in a few minutes.'

'Then sit for a few minutes.'

There was a metal chair, which I drew closer to the bed.

'Not enough time to tell me your life story?' he said lightly.

I smiled, as I hadn't smiled in months. The tendons of my jaw and the web of muscles around my eyes seemed to relax all at once.

'Another time, then,' he smiled back, his eyes softening, answering his own question, as he would often do. 'Tell me, where did you get that?' He indicated my pendant.

'Savannah.'

'Can you tell me about it?' he said, studying the pendant.

I told him about the volcano, Captain Cook's crewman, and the woman who had lived to be 105, and I described the little store in Savannah.

He listened carefully, then said, 'It's probably iron-based, from the earth's mantle, which shares its composition with the stars. You know, the only pure iron on earth was brought by meteorites. Cook was one of those explorers who navigated by the stars, and when he needed food, he bartered the South Sea islanders iron – in the form of nails and fishhooks – that traced its origins to those same stars.'

'I didn't know that,' I said, fascinated by his words.

'Would you please get me the X-ray you took of my back before surgery? I'd like to show you something.'

All his X-rays were hanging at the foot of the bed beside his chart. While I sifted through them, he lifted a book from the bedside table and opened it to a page marked with a strip of gauze.

'I borrowed this from the map room,' he said.

My heart quickened when I saw that it was a star atlas with a Navy insignia – twin anchors composed of stars – on the indigo cover.

'This is a photograph of the outer rim of the Andromeda galaxy taken with an X-ray telescope,' he went on. 'Time-delayed to capture the movements of the stars. Now, hold my X-ray next to it.'

The shrapnel and stars looked the same: clusters of short white streaks against the blackness.

'Iron,' he said softly, 'here, inside my body, and there, in another galaxy, as far away from us as we can imagine.'

'Why are you telling me all this?' I said, leaning closer to him.

'I think you know why,' he said, tilting his head and turning his eyes back on mine. 'I knew I would be telling you from the moment you walked in here.'

I felt the blood rushing in my head, but he was right: I wasn't surprised. And we were both aware that whatever forces and impulses had drawn me to him in the first place were just as surely at work in him.

He reached out and took my pendant gently between his thumb and index finger. 'This stone,' he said, examining it closely, 'with all its stars – I've never seen one like it anywhere.'

'May I ask you something?' I held up the frontal X-ray of his torso and pointed to the shadow of his stomach cavity. 'Down here – surely this has nothing to do with the war.'

He smiled, and for an instant I was sure this was what he had really been waiting to talk about. 'The key? No, I put that there myself. Swallowed it a long time ago, for safekeeping, and never told anyone. It never came out and it's never bothered me,' he added.

'For safekeeping?'

He lowered his voice. 'It opens something very important.' He touched his stomach. 'I'll keep it down here until I need it.'

'You know when that will be?'

He shook his head. 'I'll know when the time comes.'

Hearing myself paged on the PA, I stood up and put the X-ray back with the others.

'I'll come back tomorrow,' I said.

'I was counting on it.' His eyes brightened. 'Merry Christmas, Mala.'

For the first time I focused beyond him, about a dozen feet, on the wreath of blinking lights that had been hung on the wall on Christmas Eve.

'Yes. Merry Christmas,' I said.

7

The Hotel Canopus

My first glimpse of the desert came from seven miles up, in an airplane. It was like a white mirror that, according to the plane's movements, tilted every so often in the blazing sunlight and blinded me. Sheer columns of rock, boulders piled upon boulders vertically, cast their shadows straight as compass needles for thousands of feet – shadows that led nowhere. Behind vast thermal currents, rippling faintly, mountains loomed in the distance. Eventually the great expanses of sand were replaced by rocky flats and choppy ridges of sandstone that ran to the horizon, where long red clouds, rough as stone, mirrored them in the sky. And there were ravines, deep blues at their lowest depths, dotted with brush, and canyons of graduated spirals, in the shape of tops. Of all the places I had ever gone with Milo and Luna, the desert was one we seemed to have bypassed, always taking the northern route out west and back. Furtive in their habits, they would have avoided those glaringly open spaces.

I had never been on a private plane before. In fact, until that day I had never flown. Buses, cars, and vans were the only vehicles I knew before I rode on the New York subways. My only interstate train trip had been from Pittsburgh to New York when my grandmother came to get me, and to make funeral arrangements for Milo and Luna, after the car crash.

But I knew something about planes, and Samax's was a twin-engine Learjet that seated eighteen. The fuselage and wings were painted yellow, with red markings. The seats were red leather and the carpeting was yellow, adorned with clusters of darker yellow pomegranates. Pillows and blankets followed the same design. There was a small galley in the front and a bar over which hung an antique mirror, its perimeter etched with balloonists in flight. The bar was stocked with liquor, but also with a vast assortment of fresh fruit juice. Samax was a fruit enthusiast, and he himself squeezed me a mixture of black grape and plum juice and stuck a wedge of kiwi onto the rim of the glass. From the galley I was served a piece of just-baked loganberry pie topped with thin slices of quince.

I was very impressed with all of this. Only later did I learn how much Samax disliked flying. He especially disliked commercial air travel because it involved putting his life completely in someone else's hands, which was anathema to him. So, because flying was a necessity in his business, he had conceded himself the luxury of the private plane – to keep control. But strictly in his own fashion. He hired a first-rate maintenance crew who worked solely on his plane, and the pilots were top-flight Air Force veterans, also on exclusive contract, whom he paid double what they would have received elsewhere. And, of course, as with all his possessions and habitations, he had had the plane modified to his own specifications.

I would come to see that though he was abundantly wealthy, and by any standard lived luxuriously, Samax in fact chose his personal indulgences with care and then always followed the same pattern: going all the way – and sometimes over the top – with them. One of the many paradoxes about him was that while he demanded utter control over his physical surroundings and treated his material reality as first and foremost a malleable thing, in his most private affairs and daily habits he maintained a rigidly spartan regime, which he kept to his entire life. At the center of the endless flux he himself initiated, he could remain – or retain the illusion of remaining – essentially unchanged. The inherent tension thus created, he would tell me one day, served him in twofold fashion: it kept those around him whom he had reason to distrust off-balance; and it ensured that he was stimulated at times when he might easily – constitutionally – have lapsed into intellectual or emotional torpor.

The takeoff had knocked the breath out of me, literally. Unlike a 707 or other big plane, the Learjet had taxied fast and then climbed even faster, nearly straight up – or what felt like straight up to me, buckled in tight by Samax, palms glued to the armrests – in a steep arc. As we rose, watching the Manhattan skyline recede in the winter smog, I thought of Alma somewhere in that enormous maze: I worried about her and hoped that when she got that letter she would understand and not be too worried herself. Then we passed over Brooklyn and I tried to figure out which of the sprawling cemeteries below was the one my grandmother was newly buried in, but seconds later the plane leveled off and there we were above the clouds.

Samax and I sat alone in the front, one seat apart. There were three other passengers, each in a different row far behind us. His niece Ivy sat with her seat turned to one side, her back to everyone. Then there was a beautiful young woman introduced to me as Desirée who had very long black hair and wore a leather jacket with silver studs and matching boots. She sat in the last row, wearing earphones, erect behind a silent portable typewriter at a small oval conference table. And at a window seat on the other aisle there was a man who boarded at the last minute and to whom I was not introduced. After a moment, I recognized him: the man in the white coat and oversized gloves who had been crisscrossing the vacant lot beside the abandoned factory with the metal detector. Now wearing a gray parka, he was a larger man than I'd thought, broad at the shoulders and flat-footed. His face was flat, too, with piercing shiny eyes, deep within corkscrew sockets that were fixed in a permanent squint. He spent most of the flight bent over a pocket calculator, making annotations in a notebook. Occasionally he muttered to himself, but I never heard him exchange a single word with Ivy and Desirée, nor did the two of them speak to each other. To my dismay – for I had felt comfortable with him even in the short time he had been with us – the muscular young man with the crew cut and the blueprint was not onboard. On the way to the airport he told me his name was Calzas and assured me that I would like Las Vegas. And after seeing us off at the terminal, he had sauntered off with a single well-traveled suitcase and a fedora pulled low over his eye.

I think Samax put a seat between us hoping that this space would take the edge off the fear he had seen grip me anew as we left the abandoned factory. He was close to me, but not too close. And he seemed at ease with himself, which helped put me at ease.

Soon after we took off, he gave me a deck of cards and suggested I try my hand at solitaire.

'You know the game?' he said.

'Yes, I've played before.' Milo had taught me when I was five, and said it was nearly impossible to win unless you cheated.

'Play with this deck.'

On the backs of the cards, red palm trees were outlined against a yellow sky.

While keeping one eye out the window at the rapidly changing landscapes below – green mountains and industrial belts easing into farmland and then open prairie – I also stole glances at Samax, who, having slipped on a white cashmere cardigan and a pair of glove-leather slippers, was absorbed in studying a map and making notes on a pad in red ink. Every so often he would look up and smile at me. I felt as if he and I were in our own little world in the front of the plane. Under the circumstances, I was surprised how comfortable

71

this began to feel and – as would often be the case in years to come – how little I cared that the people around us seemed so remote. At first I couldn't help staring back at them with curiosity, Desirée typing, Ivy rigid with her back to us, but by the time we were halfway across the country my mind was elsewhere. On the playing cards, for one thing, which I was examining much more closely after playing six games of solitaire in a row and winning every one of them. Samax had observed me doing so.

'Have any luck?' he said, his pen never slowing on the paper.

'Luck?'

We were over the desert now, and pointing his free hand toward the window, he said, 'Did you know that all of this was once the floor of an ocean?'

I nodded, and at the same time craned my neck to see the map before him.

'It's a map of the desert,' he said. 'Not this – another desert. Come, sit next to me.'

I unbuckled my seat belt. Sitting that much closer to him, I studied his profile and inhaled the scent of his cologne, which was dry and pleasantly citric. Above the neat white moustache he had a large, straight nose, broad across the bridge. Closely shaven, his cheeks were remarkably clear and unblemished for a man his age. His brow was deeply but cleanly lined, as if he had spent much time alone, in contemplation. But considering that he lived in the desert, he had few wrinkles around his eyes. Two simple reasons for this, I would learn, were that he seldom squinted – his eyesight was sharp and he regularly wore dark glasses – and that regardless of his changes of expression, from a smile to a grimace, his pale eyes remained open, level, and slightly inquisitive.

He turned them on me fully now. 'Do you like the plane?'

I nodded.

'Like to know the speed at which we're traveling?'

'About five hundred miles an hour.'

'Oh, so you're an old hand at this.'

I shook my head. 'I never flew on a plane before.'

He looked surprised.

'But I've read about them,' I went on.

'What have you read?'

'Oh, a book about the U-2 spy planes. They don't fly so fast, but they can cruise fourteen miles up. And they weigh much less than other planes. Without the pilot, they're not even one ton.'

He nodded appreciatively, stroking his chin. 'I didn't know that.'

'And I always liked to read *Aviation* magazine in the school library. Until they stopped getting it.'

'I think we can arrange to get it for you now.'

I shrugged.

'Well,' he said, and I could see he was measuring his words, 'I'm glad to be with you the first time you're flying. How about if we go up to the cockpit in a while and the pilot can show you some things firsthand?'

'Okay.'

'First, though, look out my window.' He tilted his head back so I could gaze past him. 'That's the Painted Desert. Also known as the Colorado Plateau. There's a point in its northeast corner, which we just passed, called Four Corners, where four states meet: you can walk in a little circle around that point and in about thirty seconds visit Utah, Arizona, New Mexico, and Colorado. I did it once. Most of the Painted Desert is in Arizona. Calzas's people, the Zuni Indian tribe, have their roots in the New Mexican part. It's called "painted" because of all the reds and oranges you see. Those ridges are sandstone, formed from massive sand dunes and clay hills that just baked in place 180 million years ago.' He pulled down the tray in front of my seat and laid the map on it. 'Now,' he went on, warming to the subject, 'this desert on the map is surprisingly similar to what you see below. It's a small section of the Sahara that straddles the border between Algeria and Tunisia, called "The Hammada of Fiery Stone".'

I studied it. 'The Sahara must be much bigger than this desert.'

'The Sahara is the largest desert in the world. Over three million square miles. But did you know that one-fifth of the earth's surface is desert?'

I shook my head.

'You see, a desert is simply anyplace that receives less than ten inches of rain a year. Of all the continents, only Europe has no deserts. Most of the Sahara is an "erg", which is a desert of flat sand and sandy dunes. Much rarer is a "hammada",' Samax continued, 'which in Arabic means a series of plateaus and ridges of bare stone – like the Painted Desert.' He circled a point on the map with his index finger. 'Here on the western edge of the hammada, fifty miles from the nearest village, in a small ruined temple dating to the time of Alexander the Great, there is an underground chamber containing a statuette of Meno, son of the god Ammon. The statuette is a foot high. It is carved from black marble and has inlaid eyes of gold with silver pupils. Except for one broken finger on the right hand, it is in perfect condition.' He paused for a long moment, until I looked up at him. He was smiling, but his eyes were gazing out the window, into the bright sunlight. 'In two days,' he said, 'I shall be holding it in my hand in Las Vegas. Calzas is on his way to obtain it as we speak.'

I had listened to this speech with astonishment, though soon enough such speeches would not seem so out of the ordinary to me. Out of all the questions that popped into my head, I even asked one – one which Samax seemed to approve of.

'How exactly will he get there?'

He further opened the map so that several more panels appeared. 'First he'll land in Madrid,' he said, then ran his finger across the pale green of Spain, over the rich turquoise of the Mediterranean, into the yellow of North Africa, 'and make a connecting flight to Algiers. From there he flies south to El Oued, an oil town with a small airport. Then he'll set out overland by Land Rover with a guide and two bodyguards, first to Bir Beressof, a village, and then here, to a former oasis east of Bir Lahrache. That is where the erg ends and the hammada begins. Over the hammada he will have to travel on foot for several hours until he reaches the temple. Here.' Samax lifted his finger and placed my own on the spot. In doing so, he ran his thumb over my index finger, the one I had broken that never healed properly. And, peering closely at me, he said aloud what had already crossed my mind. 'Yes, it is this same finger that is broken on the statuette of Meno.' Then, slowly, he folded up the map.

By the time we were descending over the Mojave Desert into Las Vegas, dusk was falling. It seemed to me that I had traveled across, not just time zones, but whole worlds since Alma and I walked out of the house in Brooklyn and set out for the planetarium. My head was heavy, and had we remained in the air much longer I would surely have rested it against my seat and fallen into a deep sleep.

Two blue sedans – identical to the one in which I had ridden earlier – awaited us on the apron at the private air terminal. My first gulps of desert air, taken on the tarmac with the wind whipping my hair, surprised me: for all its dryness, it felt as if I were swallowing, not air, but a cool dark liquid, and I was suddenly wide awake again. Samax and I got into the back of the first sedan, Desirée sat in the front with the driver, and we sped off. My first close impression of Desirée was the smell of her leather jacket mingled with a subtle jasmine scent emanating from her long hair, which was so lush and glossy, silver highlights twinkling in the black, that I wanted to lean over the seat and touch it. Instead, she turned around to me.

'Enjoy the flight?' she said pleasantly. She had a low, musical voice.

She smiled at me, and though her eyes, large and brown, were on my face, they seemed to be looking far away – so much so that she could have been smiling, too, at whatever she was seeing there.

Through the car windows, the lights of the airport had no sooner faded behind us than the glow of the city proper, a great golden cloud of light beneath the royal blue sky, appeared through the windshield. From a distance the garish flashing neon of the Strip was like an electric rainbow that had shattered and was sputtering on the ground. But we left the interstate highway for a narrower, less traveled road and gradually veered left, away from the city, into a network of dark, quiet streets. We passed ranch houses with sleek lawns and ironwood trees, Spanish villas with terracotta roofs, Tudor mansions with serpentine driveways, and even a mock-Roman temple flanked by a pair of brightly lit horseshoe swimming pools. Then we entered a long road paved with silvery asphalt on which there were no houses. Eventually it tapered into a single broad driveway through an iron gate that ended in a cul-de-sac. There, at the very edge of the desert, a startlingly large, white building with many lighted windows loomed before us. In a courtyard in front of the building, there was a marble fountain, adorned with a statue, from which a plume of water rose high in the air, glittering under spotlights.

'Welcome,' Samax said, smiling, holding the car door open for me.

Carrying her typewriter in its black case, swinging her hips, Desirée again wore an abstracted look as she smiled at me and walked up the marble steps to the building's entrance. A doorman in a white jacket opened one of the darkly tinted glass doors for her, and then I heard her heels clicking rapidly away.

'This is my home,' Samax said simply. 'The Hotel Canopus. Now it is your home, as well.'

My first look at that building, which was to figure so prominently in my life, has always remained sharply etched. Though I had traveled through many American cities, and lived in New York, where there were hundreds of far larger buildings, the Hotel Canopus, framed by a vast desert expanse, backdropped by the forbidding silhouette of the Spring Mountains, seemed enormous, looming there under the starlit sky. In fact, it was ten stories high, and about one hundred feet across. (Eventually I would come to learn all its specifications intimately, including the 290 windows, 110 doors, thirty bathrooms, three basement levels, and the tunnel that ran from one subbasement to a large greenhouse.) Purely rectangular, the building was constructed of limestone and white brick and had a slightly sloping, tiled gray roof. The design was straightforward but elegant, with baroque touches. It was detailed, for example, with fine masonry work, such as the figures of wild (and extinct) animals below window ledges and elaborate Islamic decorations – labyrinths, mandalas, and geometrical designs on brightly colored tiles set into the eaves and cornices. The entranceway was flanked by imposing, plainly fluted marble columns and there was a small arcade to the left, leading to a large circular terrace ringed with shade trees. The building's foundation was rimmed by yucca shrubs like thick fans and concentric circles of mesquite trees flowing away from the courtyard, beyond which were some outbuildings. I could also faintly make out the maze of a large garden, heavily shadowed, the equally large greenhouse, and a swimming pool. But, even as I took all this in, what most caught my eye was that fountain at the center of the cul-de-sac, which was more complicated than it had appeared as we came up the driveway.

I stood not ten feet from it now and saw that the plume of water was actually six jets of water from the mouths of six bronze dolphins that conjoined in mid-air. The dolphins were arrayed below a marble statue so supplely carved it appeared to be alive, in motion, beneath the umbrella of spray. The statue was of a woman wearing a necklace of stars who was sitting on a starfish throne. That is, it had five arms like a starfish, four of which were the legs of the throne while the fifth served as its back. She was young, with wavy hair cascading over her shoulders. A light robe clung to her body and her slender feet were sandaled. I thought I saw a smile glimmer through the veils of water, on an open, beautifully balanced face which was fixed on the heavens. In her hand she held a small bowl, from which water, rainbow-tinged, was overflowing in a steady stream.

As we ascended the steps, Samax saw me staring at the fountain. 'It's beautiful, isn't it,' he murmured.

I nodded, mesmerized by the complicated play of water amid all that marble and bronze – like a ballet in which everything was in motion except the dancer herself.

'It was commissioned by the original owner of the hotel,' Samax said, 'a Frenchman named Canopus from whom I bought this place. The design was by a Swede named Spica, who was also the hotel's architect. He oversaw the actual sculptors, and returned to the hotel to install the fountain when I became owner. I approved what he'd done, and after a couple of months Spica finished and left without a word. Just a note saying his design was based on a fable, though no one has been able to find its source. I hired both an art historian and a historian of religion to trace its origins, and they came up empty-handed. And I was never able to find Spica again.'

The doorman wore a white jacket with yellow epaulets and a black fez. The fez made me think of Egypt, and indeed he was Egyptian. Rectangularly shaped as the building of which he was the guardian, he had an impassive face, a thick nose, and unflickering brown eyes. Had he wanted to block the doorway, I thought, he needed only to step into it and he would have filled the frame as neatly as the twin doors themselves.

'Good evening, Azu,' Samax greeted him, and he responded with a respectful nod, politely looking me over as he held the door open.

Entering the lobby, I stopped in my tracks and whistled softly. It, too, was enormous, a long black desk along the right-hand wall, a pair of black leather couches on the left, and at the far end a bank of elevators. Samax merely smiled and stood aside as I stepped farther into the room, gaping.

The walls were great slabs of black marble, veined red, that ran unbroken to the ceiling about fifty feet above. The marble was inlaid with bronze and silver astronomical objects – comets, planets, and clusters of stars – and figures from the zodiac like Cancer, Pisces, and Scorpio. Polished stones, like lapis and onyx, highlighted their eyes, teeth, and scales. The white ceiling was unadorned, but the floor, a chessboard of white and black marble tiles, was centered by an enormous zodiacal wheel of polished brass set into the marble. I stopped in the segment representing Sagittarius, the Archer, who was poised intently with drawn bow.

'Of course, that's your sign, isn't it,' Samax observed, for, as I would learn, he was not someone who missed very much. ' Canopus was obsessed with the zodiac,' he continued. 'He put zodiacs all over the place. The basin of that fountain outside is an enormous zodiacal wheel. And there was another huge wheel in the garden, which I had removed. He consulted astrologers whenever he made a decision, but I'm afraid it didn't do him much good.' Samax caught and held my eye. 'No one can tell you how to make good decisions,' he said, 'they can only suggest where your decisions may lead you. Canopus was a bad businessman, and a worse hotelier, and no amount of astrology could save him from that. He ran this place into the ground. When he went bankrupt, I bought it for a song – for less money than a house would have cost me – and then I spent a fortune fixing it up, but it was worth it. I kept the name because I like it. Good evening, Della,' he called out to a woman who had appeared through a leather-padded door behind the desk.

She was slight and straight-backed, with slate-colored hair, a woman whose age, from a distance, was difficult to determine. She was wearing a red jacket, red hair band, and bright coral lipstick. 'This is Enzo,' Samax said loudly. 'He'll be with us now. Would you make sure that his room is ready.'

'Welcome, Enzo,' she said in a smooth, easy drawl as she crossed the lobby to the elevator bank. 'It's good to have you with us.'

'Thanks,' I said hoarsely.

'Come, let me show you something,' Samax said, and I followed him over to the desk. As soon as Della stepped into an elevator, and he and I were alone again, Samax took out a key which he turned in a keyhole beneath the desk; immediately a small hinged panel on the marble wall swung open, just beside the padded door, revealing an even smaller steel door with a combination lock.

It was a very public place to keep a safe, I thought, as Samax began spinning the wheel of the lock. The tumblers clicked into place, and when he opened the door I saw not the interior of a safe, but a pair of simple switches, one of which he flicked upward. Overhead there was a pneumatic hiss and a rumble and the next thing I knew the white ceiling was sliding into the wall, from right to left, revealing a dark hollow space. When the rumbling stopped and the ceiling was gone, Samax flicked the other switch and lights around its perimeter brilliantly illuminated a second ceiling, which could not have been more different.

It was a vaulted ceiling, entirely covered by a richly detailed mural depicting a celestial landscape. Around a moon rimmed with white fire hundreds of angels were gathered in concentric circles. They were youthful, with golden skin. Stars glittered around them as they played flutes and bells, scooped up water in crystal goblets, combed one another's hair, and preened their wings. The twelve animals and symbols of the zodiac adorned the circle farthest from the moon. At that point in my life I had only once visited a museum, and the church to which my grandmother took me possessed only standard-issue ecclesiastical artwork, so I was amazed at all these luminous faces gazing downward. For a moment they began to spin on me, circle upon circle, until I was so dizzy I had to close my eyes.

Samax came up beside me on silent feet. 'This mural was executed in the sixteenth century,' he said, 'by a painter named Francesco Gozzoli, who was commissioned by the Doge of Venice. It took Gozzoli and his apprentices four years to complete it, on the ceiling of the Church of St Antony on the Greek island of Naxos, at that time a Venetian duchy. The church was bombed in the war when the Nazis attacked the island, and so badly damaged that later the authorities erected a new church on the site, keeping only the foundation and a single wall. I salvaged the ceiling from the rubble before they carted it off. I paid them for it – the local arch-diocese and the government – with more than the usual quota of bribes thrown in.' He chuckled. 'The Greeks thought I was crazy – even the guys I hired to do the work. I like to look at it alone, usually, and I'm the only one who has the key to uncover it. Do you like it, Enzo?'

He could already see that I did. 'It's beautiful,' I said.

'Some say it's impossible to determine exactly how many angels there are in the mural.'

I was reminded of a game Milo used to play with me in the car, in which we would guess the number of people in a passing bus or the population of a town which we were about to reach. And so I said to Samax, 'Do you want me to guess now?'

'No, not at all,' he said. 'You see, they claim it's impossible because the mural is so lifelike that the number must always be changing. As if the angels can come and go.'

'Do you believe that?' I said, staring open-mouthed at the mural.

'I've never been able to count them,' he smiled. 'Soon you'll be able to try. But you've had a long journey, let's go upstairs.'

He flicked the two switches and spun the lock on the steel door, and in about twenty seconds the vaulted ceiling was covered over again.

There were three elevators. The first two had green doors, and the numerals above them ran to the second through ninth floors. It was the third elevator, with a red door, into which Samax led me.

'This is my private elevator,' he said. 'It goes to my living quarters on the tenth floor and the penthouse, as well as to the ninth floor, where you can connect with the other elevators. This is the elevator you will use. The green elevators go to the quarters of other family members and guests.'

The elevator was paneled in walnut and softly lit by a grid of ceiling lights. Beneath my feet there was a carpet with an Indian design – a red sun ringed with golden eagles.

'You'll meet most of the extended family tomorrow,' Samax went on as we hurtled upward. 'My guests you'll discover in your own time. Some are always out and around, others keep to themselves, often for long periods. They are not hotel guests, of course, in the conventional sense. Except for people who are here to do business with me, or people whom I employ, every-one is my houseguest. They may visit for a few days, or linger for months, and there are a number of long-term residents. Some guests are old friends of mine, others are interesting people I've met in my travels.' He paused. 'I can't imagine now living in a static environment, without new people coming and going.' He smiled. 'That's why when I truly settled down, I bought a hotel.'

I *had* taken a long journey, and as we rode up to the tenth floor, I was trying not only to absorb what Samax was saying, but also to grasp the incredible notion that I was about to start living in this place among a bunch of people of whose existence I had known nothing just that afternoon. I closed my eyes tightly, thinking for a moment that when I blinked them open again I might find myself back in bed in my grandmother's house, with Alma leaning over me, telling me that all of it – the planetarium, the abandoned factory, my first airplane ride, the mural of angels – had been no more than an elaborate, at times terrifying, dream.

If so, it was continuing, for when I did open my eyes, the elevator door slid open and Samax said softly, 'My rooms are in the penthouse. You are free to come up there at any time. Your room is E, at the end of this corridor.'

Standing by the open door to Room E, her hands folded at her waist, Della ushered me in with a small smile. She had brown eyes with the longest lashes I had ever seen, eyebrows plucked to a pair of thin lines, and a deep tan. Up close, she appeared to be in her fifties.

Room E was a large corner room that had obviously been prepared for me while I was still nominally a resident of Brooklyn. It had been freshly painted, the walls eggshell blue, the moldings and doors yellow to match the curtains and carpet. The room was shaped like a capital E – for Enzo? – without the middle bar, a rectangle which at either end, at right angles, gave on to another rectangle. The top rectangle was a sleeping alcove with a single bed and a night table opposite a tall window facing south, toward that aura of light over the city proper. The bottom rectangle was a bathroom.

In the main part of the room, another window overlooked the desert to the west. Against the same wall there was a rolltop desk, a swivel chair, and a set of oak bookshelves. Sketch pads, notebooks, and pencils were arranged on a stool beside the desk. And dozens of books lined the shelves, picture books of great art and famous buildings, adventure stories and desert tales, and an extensive set of travel books bound in green morocco, including *The Travels* of Marco Polo, the *Voyage of Magellan* by Antonio Pigafetta, Sir John Mandeville's *Travels*, and *The Journals* of Captain James Cook, as well as a complete set of the *Arabian Nights*. On the near wall there was a long closet and a chest of drawers, and in the center of the room an easy chair upholstered in red beside a reading lamp with an amber shade. Before the western window, on a tripod, there was a white tele-scope, which I saw at once was not a toy, but a professional instrument.

I looked at Samax in disbelief. All of this was daunt-ing, if not intimidating, not just because of its opulence, but because there did not seem to be a single frivolous item – such as a toy – in sight. This was a room, I would realize later, that had been set up with the person whom I might become – and not who I was – in mind. Which is to say it presented the seeds of how I would be molded by Samax.

'I tried to anticipate your needs,' he said matter-of-factly, 'but of course you'll let us know what else you need – and what you don't need.'

It was then that I noticed a copy of the current issue of *Aviation* magazine on the footstool before the easy chair. Even with all I had seen, this truly astonished me.

'How did you do that?' I said to Samax.

'It wasn't so difficult,' he smiled, then nodded to Della, who opened three of the closet's four louvred doors, one by one.

The closet was full: jackets and pants on hangers, shoes and sneakers on a rack below, shirts neatly folded on built-in shelves, and even some hats on hooks, in-cluding a baseball cap for my favorite team, the Houston Astros.

I turned quickly to Samax. ' And how did you know that?'

'I told you in New York that I investigated your cir-cumstances,' he replied. 'My people are very thorough, Those clothes should all be the correct size.' He sig-nalled Della to open the last louvred door.

'And I think you'll find the things in here to your liking.'

He had saved this for last: the left-hand quarter of the closet was devoted to toys. Much of it was stuff I would have put on a wish list myself. An archery set, a tennis racket, a fishing rod – strange for the desert, I thought – a pile of model plane kits, a chemistry set, a mineralogy kit, a stack of board games, and an electric train set, still in boxes.

'They're American Flyers,' Samax said, looking to see if I was pleased. 'With two locomotives, and all the accessories.'

In Brooklyn, my principal diversion had been constructing model planes, but I had never owned electric trains, and had always wanted them.

'Tomorrow I'll show you a room where you can set up the track,' he went on. 'I thought you'd want to do it yourself. If you're hungry, the kitchen is right around the corner. You can always get whatever you need. Are you hungry now?'

I shook my head.

His pale eyes were fixed on mine. 'What is it? Tell me what you're thinking.'

'It's a very nice room,' I said.

'It's a start,' he said. 'But it's your room now, and so it will change.'

I averted my eyes. 'I miss my things.' What I had in mind was my planes, mostly Second World War bombers which I had assembled, painted, and decaled, my stamp collection, which had been Luna's father's, a green pocketknife Milo had bought me in St Louis, and a black silk pouch embroidered with a full moon that Luna had picked up in Chinatown. The pouch contained a packet of snapshots and the few items of jewelry she owned – her wedding ring, a gold bracelet engraved *L. & M. Forever* that Milo had given her, and some pearl earrings. I also missed some of my clothes, like the sky-blue sweater my grandmother had knitted me. But it was Luna's silk pouch I missed most of all.

'I understand,' Samax said, moving closer to me, 'better than you know. And they are the very things I cannot bring you, or replace. I'm sorry.'

Of course as a collector, a man who took enormous pleasure in his things, he did understand – and for other, more intimate, reasons, too, as I would find out.

Still, there was a long silence between us.

'Are you afraid of sleeping here alone?' he said.

'No,' I replied honestly. 'That doesn't bother me.' I had gotten used to sleeping in unfamiliar places years before, when Luna and Milo had left me in motel rooms or furnished apartments while they went off to work.

'Just plain afraid, then?'

I sat down on the edge of the easy chair. When I didn't reply, a pained expression crossed Samax's face, which surprised me.

'I am very happy that you are here, Loren, and I hope it will not be too difficult for you. Try to get a good night's sleep, and perhaps if you think of it this way, it will help: you will go to sleep "Loren" and wake up "Enzo."'

This was the one and only time he addressed me as 'Loren.'

'I'll remember that,' I said.

'If you need anything at all,' Della smiled, 'I will be across the hall in Room D this week.'

'I'll see you for breakfast,' Samax said, squeezing my shoulder, as he had at the factory. 'Good night.'

On his way out, he took the red and yellow flower from his lapel and placed its stem in a slender vase on top of the chest. Then he closed the door after him, and suddenly I was alone.

I sat down on the bed and surveyed the rays of light from the city spraying up into the dark sky. Then I walked over to the chest and opened the top drawer, where I found socks of every color, carefully folded. I took down Marco Polo's *Travels* and opened it: . . . *at the point where the traveller enters the Great Desert is a great and splendid city. The people are idolators, use paper money, and burn their dead. They have silk in plenty, and ornaments of gold finely wrought* . . .

I returned the book to its place and slid open the rolltop desk. It contained numerous small drawers, shelves, and paper slots. I opened one of the drawers and found a box of tiny nautilus shells beside a magnifying glass. In another drawer there was a ruler and a pair of scissors beside a jar of white powder labeled DRIFT-WOOD DUST.

I looked through the telescope, without changing its position. It was already focused, on a red star twinkling at the center of a constellation which I couldn't identify. At that time, aside from the Big and Little Dippers, I knew nothing about the constellations.

I went into the bathroom, in which the white tiles, sink, and tub were gleaming, and took a pee. The toilet flush was silent. I had never had a bathroom that was not shared. I rinsed my hands and face. I filled the drinking glass with water and sipped, staring at myself in the oval mirror. I looked tired and pale, my eyes wide, my lips chapped. Seeing my reflection for the first time in such alien surroundings was not reassuring: so far away from everything I knew, and from all traces of my former life, I really did begin to feel that I was no longer Loren. Maybe if I had followed Samax's suggestion, and undressed and gone to bed at that moment, I would indeed have awakened the next day, rather painlessly, as Enzo.

But I chose to take the more painful route. There were two things I had to know before I could lie down in that bed and close my eyes with any degree of peace. First, I had to establish once and for all that, as Samax had assured me, I was not a prisoner.

I sat back in the red chair and waited, trying not to doze off, though at one point I jerked my chin up off my chest and saw on the desk clock that two hours had passed. I waited another hour, until five a.m., and walked out of Room E down the corridor to the elevator. I had not taken a single item from my new wardrobe; until I found out what I needed to, I would hold on to Loren's clothes, if nothing else.

My heavy winter boots squeaked on the marble tiles of the lobby as, heart thumping, I slung my navy pea coat over my shoulder and headed for the door. A man in a rumpled white suit and dark glasses had just entered the hotel. His face was buried in a book which he held in his left hand; with his right, he twirled a black walking stick with an ivory handle. The book's title was *Atlantis: The Seventh Continent.* When we passed each other, he did not so much as glance at me. That was not the case with a woman behind the front desk, whose eyes remained riveted on me from the moment I stepped from the elevator.

I did a double take, for though this woman wore the same red jacket as Della, and had similar – though more aquiline – features, she clearly was not Della. Heavily powdered, with bleached blond hair, she was as pale as Della was tanned. And she wasn't smiling. Nor did she seem particularly concerned to see me leave the hotel. The same was true of Azu, the doorman: with another polite nod, he looked me over once again, slowly, as he opened the door on to the cool velvety desert air and then closed it behind me.

A half hour later I was walking past the mock-Roman temple we had driven by earlier. Though it was still dark out, a pale red band lined the eastern horizon. Crickets were whirring in the brush beyond the houses, whose windows were uniformly black. I had passed no one, and had finally stopped looking over my shoulder to see if I were being followed. At first I had hurried away from the hotel, stepping into my own shadow which the moonlight cast directly before me, but as my eyes adjusted to the darkness and my nerves steadied, I settled into a slower pace.

When I reached the narrow road that led to the highway, I felt I had completed half of my small mission: I could tell myself now that I was not a prisoner at the Hotel Canopus. With four dollars in my pocket, I couldn't have gotten very far, but I could easily have walked into a police station or picked up a phone and called Alma. In fact, I had no desire to contact the police, and after the letter we had sent her, calling Alma was out of the question. It was the one thing I had promised Samax I would not do; beyond that, I did not want to call her. If Samax was telling me the truth on all counts, I had already decided I would be better off staying with him, and Alma would be far better off living her life without me. That was the gist of what Samax had stressed to her in the letter, couched in the most considerate terms; after my hopeless discussions with her on the subject of our future, not to mention the heartbreaking sight of her trying desperately to patch together a budget in the dead of night, it had made sense to me. *If* he was telling me the truth about who I was. What I had not promised Samax was that I would refrain from running away. Certainly Azu and that blond version of Della had informed him that I had left the hotel; and I wasn't so sure that the news would catch him by surprise.

I walked another quarter of a mile, some cars and plenty of trucks whizzing by me now, until I reached Route 15. A Shell station stood at the intersection, its yellow sign rotating atop a gigantic pole, across from a motel called the Twin Stars. In a phone booth beside the air pump there was a Las Vegas directory on a chain. I found and memorized the address I wanted in the blue pages listing government offices. Then I asked the kid in the office behind a Green lantern comic book – he was a few years older than me – where I could catch a bus into the city. He indicated the curb.

'It passes every half hour,' he mumbled, 'beginning at six. Just flag it.'

Soon that first bus rumbled in, carrying only a handful of passengers. Except for a pair of sailors, all the men wore cowboy hats and all of them smoked. I told the driver my destination, then sat in the first seat. Across the aisle were an old woman in a maid's uniform and a young woman in a vinyl jacket asleep with her mouth open.

In the twilight, before the sun rose, I had my first look at Las Vegas. As if the bus were stationary and the world outside in motion, long desolate streets dusted with sand slid toward me through the convex windshield. The contents of these streets never wavered: boxy apartment houses set back on treeless lots; miniature lawns without grass; parking lots patrolled by Doberman pinschers; drive-in wedding chapels with wedding cakes for roofs. And then a crazy quilt of neon signs advertising motels, topless bars, guns & ammo, palm readings, and charbroiled steaks.

And this was before we turned on Tropicana Avenue and entered the Strip. There the gaudier, more fantastical neon signs and larger-than-life marquees broadcasted the names of crooners and comedians, ventriloquists and dancing dogs. The signs were flickering off now at the tail end of the night and the last patrons were trickling from nightclubs the size of supermarkets. The famous casinos and hotels – Dunes, Aladdin, Stardust, Sahara, Riviera, and Tropicana – twenty-story towers and their long pavilions, with colonnades and arches, elaborate turrets, minarets, and ziggurats, were themselves like something out of the *Arabian Nights*, garishly updated and transported to the American desert.

The Strip itself was six lanes divided by a median strip along which double streetlights – like the wings of a gull gliding – ran as far as the eye could see. Alongside the curb there was less often sidewalk than a rough shoulder of burnt weeds, and beyond that, abruptly, the desert began, stretching away for miles, to the looming dark mountains. When we were still airborne, Samax told me that this city had materialized, in virgin desert, in seemingly no time at all – as if it had dropped from the sky – and that just sixty years before, it had consisted of some miners' shacks on dirt roads. The surrounding desert remained unchanged, and as the bus turned onto Sahara Avenue I watched the mountain winds whirl up a tower of sand far to the north.

By the time we turned again, onto Paradise Road, I had closed my eyes, which were burning from lack of sleep. The bus lurched to a halt more frequently now, at traffic lights and bus stops, and when I opened my eyes again, we were in a labyrinth of stark, narrow streets lined with low office buildings and dusty residence hotels.

At the next bus stop, beside a desiccated public park, the driver turned to me and pointed out the door. 'That's the building you want,' he said. 'Forty-seven twenty-two.'

The men in cowboy hats were all gone, as was the maid. Only the young woman in the vinyl jacket, still asleep with her mouth open, and one of the sailors remained onboard.

I walked up to Number 4722, a square white building with barred windows on the first floor and a set of limestone steps ascending to its glass doors. COUNTY OF LAS VEGAS was chiseled over the entrance, two flags hung limp on jutting poles, and in one of the doors a sign was posted with the building's hours. It wouldn't open until eight o'clock, so for the next hour I sat in the little park.

The park was more like a concrete bunker turned inside out: a circle within a square, with six benches facing inward. There were two leafless trees, and some gray weeds, stiff as sandpaper, that pushed up through cracks in the ground. An empty pint bottle lay on one bench and a ratty coat folded up into a pillow on another, where a bum had slept. Meanwhile, the sun was rising, eating away at the red brick of the surrounding buildings. Workers began filing into those buildings, including Number 4722.

Suddenly I was thirsty. I thought of my room – and its oval bathtub – at the Hotel Canopus. And the ceiling behind the ceiling in the lobby. And, playing that game with Milo as we approached Pollux, Kansas, the one and only time I had guessed a town's population correctly – 1,250 – after which he took a picture of me beside the sign reporting the number at the town line. Then, as I had at the factory when Samax told me I was really someone named Enzo Samax, I recalled again that bit of advice Milo offered for moments of crisis: to step back and take a deep breath and reconnoiter. That's what I'm doing in this concrete park, I thought; what I hadn't stopped doing, deep down, since that moment at the factory.

One way or the other, I would be moving on now, I told myself as I crossed the street after a security guard opened the doors at Number 4722 to the public.

The County Clerk's office was on the second floor. The air was overly air-conditioned and fluorescent lights buzzed overhead. I was directed to the Records Office, a pale blue room down a long corridor hung with faded photographs of the desert. There, at a barred window, I made my request of an elderly clerk, a razor-sharp woman with white hair in a bun who was smoking a cigarette in an amber holder. The planes of her cheeks were like paper and the bones in her hands were all clearly visible, as if I were looking at them through an X-ray machine.

'You want a copy of the birth certificate?' she inquired in a raspy voice.

'No, thank you. I'd just like to see the original.'

'And whose is it?' she demanded.

'It's mine.'

'You have identification?'

I shook my head. 'That's why I want to see it. I mean, I just want to see it. It's important.'

She pointed behind her at a sign over the wall of filing cabinets that read BIRTHS AND DEATHS. 'Everything here is important.' She picked the cigarette out of her amber holder and stubbed it out in an ashtray. But she kept the holder clamped between her teeth. 'You may have to wait a bit,' she said finally. 'Give me the birth date, and spell the name for me.'

I was still thirsty, and I took a long drink from the fountain across the room, the icy jet numbing my lips. No sooner had I settled into a plastic green chair than the clerk reappeared in the window. Beckoning me, she slid a piece of paper across the marble counter, and at the sight of it my heart started pounding.

'You must remain in this room with it,' she said, inserting a new cigarette into her holder. 'The fee for a notarized copy is five dollars, but for that you absolutely need identification or proof of kinship.'

The very fact she had returned with a document meant that there *was* an Enzo Samax born in Las Vegas County on my birthday. At that moment, which really did mark the end of my previous life, I was surprised at the extent of my relief, and at the first twinges of happiness that began to stir in me. The only lingering question was if the document would in all ways be identical to the one Samax had shown me at the factory. And it was. It confirmed to the highest probability that I was Enzo Samax. The son of Bel Samax and the nephew of Junius Samax.

Behind her spectacles and swirls of cigarette smoke, the clerk's eyes had narrowed. 'Your folks know you're down here?' she said.

'I'm going home now,' I replied with a sigh, sliding the birth certificate back to her. 'Thanks.'

Two blocks from the building, there was a taxi queue. The first cabbie had never heard of the Hotel Canopus, and I didn't know how to direct him there. The second cabbie knew where it was, but told me the fare would be more than $3.75, which was all I had left after the bus ride. The third cabbie agreed to take me there for that amount. He puffed cherry tobacco from a curved pipe and passed me a stick of hot-pepper gum as we sped along the Strip.

When I arrived back at the hotel, it was nine o'clock and a new doorman was on duty. As large and rectangular as Azu was, this daytime doorman, whose name was Yal, was thin and stringy, with a thatch of flyaway hair, small sad eyes, and sallow skin. From the side, he looked to be no more than six inches across. He let me in without a word. Behind the desk now, in the same red jacket and hair band, was Della, her coral lipstick gleaming as she squinted at me across the lobby above her reading glasses.

'You're up bright and early, Master Enzo,' she said cheerily. 'Ready for breakfast?'

I shook my head and hurried to the red elevator.

When I stepped out on the tenth floor, Samax was

waiting for me. He was wearing a burgundy robe and black slippers. Hands in his pockets, he was studying me closely, but with concern, not anger.

I stopped short. 'I—'

'Just get some sleep now,' he said quietly. 'We can have lunch together, rather than breakfast.'

When we reached my room and he opened the door, I turned to him.

'Good night, Uncle Junius,' I said.

I had surprised him: his face softened, his white moustache twitched, and closing his eyes, compressing his lips, he put his arms around me and drew me close. I returned the hug, and he said, 'Sleep well, Enzo.'

And he and I did have lunch – but not until late the following day. For I slept an entire day and a night and then nearly another whole day, and when I did wake up, lifting my head heavily from the pillow and studying my new surroundings, the first thing I discovered was that Calzas had returned from North Africa.

At the foot of my bed, on a wooden stand, was Samax's very first gift to me, the black marble statuette of Meno, son of the god Ammon, who was gazing at me with his gold eyes – the silver pupils glittering like stars – through the twilight of the curtained room.

8

The Hôtel Alnilam

Across the room a green ribbon fluttered on the cage of
the table fan. A pair of caged macaws squawked, back
and forth, in the courtyard below. Through the eucalyptus and colvillea trees, barking dogs ran in and out of
puddles, clouds of flies buzzing around their heads. All
afternoon the rain had thundered down, drumming the
rooftops, spattering in the muddy street. Red rain, like
dirt from the sky. On a phonograph in the next room
a jazz pianist was improvising around a theme. And
down the corridor, one of them tapping his foot, two
men were deep in conversation about a woman who had
died.

All these sounds flowed to me at once, as one but
distinguishable, while I kept my eyes glued to the fan
and its ribbon. Spinning ever so slowly, the fan blades
sliced the bands of light streaming through the venetian
blinds into even longer, golden ribbons which floated
up to the ceiling. And hovered there, rippling like
seaweed, in the deepening shadows.

A half dozen fans could not have displaced the heat
in that room. I soaked it up. And as usual did not sweat.
The sheet beneath me was rumpled and damp, but
my arms and breasts were as dry as they were hot. My
tongue stuck to my palate. My lips were humming,
my nipples ached, and the red dot and circles on my
palm glowed with heat. Cassiel, breathing softly beside

95

me, emerging from sleep, forked his fingers into my hair and gently tightened his grip.

'Mala,' he whispered into my ear.

He was the first lover to call me by that name, and despite how I had acquired it, it seemed to belong to me now, during my time with him, in a different way.

'Mala,' he murmured again, 'come closer.'

I could not have been closer to him, I wanted to say as he wrapped his arms around me again. I tilted my head back when he put his mouth over mine and slipped his tongue through my lips and slid his leg between my own. His broad shoulders and chest, beaded with sweat, cooled my skin even as my insides felt on fire.

We were in a hotel on the outskirts of Manila. It was the fourth and final day of our leave, January 14, 1969, and we had spent the better part of those days in that bed under the lime-colored sheet making love. Our uniforms hung side by side in the closet behind a curtain of beads. Because Cassiel was an officer, he had been able to requisition a jeep at the naval base at Subic Bay. We had used it to get around Manila and, once, to take a drive up the peninsula to swim at a secluded beach. After being shipboard for four months straight, I had been overwhelmed at first driving out in the open on a fast winding road, awash with scents and colors, flanked by the jungle and the sea. Cassiel had been discharged from medical care after being checked over at the base hospital the day the *Repose* put in at Subic Bay for refurbishing. From the dock, our patients were either transferred to the base hospital or to the airport, where transport planes would ferry them to Honolulu. Then the crew of the *Repose*, nurses, doctors, sailors, all went on R&R. Altogether Cassiel had been with us for just over two weeks – from Christmas Day until the tenth of January – recovering from his wounds. In that time, helter-skelter, he and I had shared what time we could. Some days I didn't see him at all. The first week he had a rough stretch, fighting off a secondary infection and fever. His shoulder swelled up and the pain became intolerable. In addition to antibiotics, the doctors administered morphine, which promptly knocked him out, sometimes for twelve hours straight. In the meantime, I wasn't exactly idle. The battle in which Cassiel had been shot down was just the beginning of a longer operation. Night after night during Christmas week the number of body bags on deck doubled, then tripled, triage overflowed, and our surgeons worked round the clock. We had badly wounded men jammed up and down the corridors on fold-up cots and, at one point, filling a section of the mess hall that was partitioned off. That was the worst time of all. Hearing the men moaning on their side of the partition while you picked over your breakfast or dinner and tried to get down enough food to make sure you could keep going. Even I, who needed so little sleep, was dragging myself around. X-raying five or six dozen men daily, I found that after a while not just their faces but their horrific wounds – jagged, burned, blood-caked – began to blur.

His second week on the *Repose*, Cassiel rebounded. Many of the most seriously wounded men, along with those who had healed swiftly, were ferried to Saigon. Cassiel fell into the middle group who remained aboard until we reached the Philippines. As we left the battle zone on January 6, my own duties let up a bit, and he and I were able to spend time together, first at his bedside, then in the cubbyhole office off the X-ray room where I'd bring him in his wheelchair, and finally on deck when he was well enough to walk on his own. There was little privacy on that ship even when it wasn't filled to capacity with patients, and it was amazing we were ever able to be alone for very long. It was on deck one evening just after sunset as we watched the flat green coast of Palawan Island slide by that he kissed me for the first time, pulling me close with one arm – his other still in a sling.

The jeep Cassiel requisitioned had no top, and we discovered the Hôtel Alnilam during a cloudburst when we pulled off the road to take shelter under the colvillea trees. Tucked away in a quiet, dusty, residential district, far from the flash and clatter of downtown Manila, the hotel was owned by an elderly Frenchman. A slight, balding man, he wore a white suit cut in another era and a pair of oversized eye-glasses. We were the only Americans at the hotel and when we checked in he made a point of telling us that he was strongly pro-American. In the fifties he had left the United States with plans to open a hotel in Saigon. But Dien Bien Phu changed everything and he fled to Manila.

'Whereabout in the States did you live?' Cassiel asked him.

'Las Vegas,' he replied. 'But I'll never go back there.'

Cassiel seemed surprised. 'I'm from Reno originally,' he said. I had learned this during one of our bedside conversations on the *Repose*, but Cassiel wouldn't say much more except to insist, like the Frenchman, that he would never return to Nevada.

'Why won't you go back?' I asked the Frenchman, glancing at Cassiel out of the corner of my eye.

'It's bad luck for me,' he replied.

'You lost at the tables?' Cassiel said.

'I never gambled in my life,' the Frenchman said, handing him the key to Room 9. 'Fourth floor.'

In the lift, when we were alone, I turned to Cassiel. 'Did *you* lose at the tables?' I asked.

'I lost worse than that, Mala,' he said without flinching. Then he took my hand. 'But we agreed, no questions for now. There'll be time enough later.'

I nodded, squeezing his hand.

We had agreed that in our four days alone together we would try to remain in the moment, each moment. Not look back, and try not to look too far ahead. On the other side of the world in what had been my previous life, I would never have made such a pact, never have thought to condition a relationship on these terms. (On the *Repose*, when I told him that I had no family, he replied that he hadn't seen his few remaining relatives in thirteen years, and we left it at that.) But in a war, with all I had already seen, it was not so difficult to lock myself into the immediate present. In fact, in Vietnam some self-preserving mechanism compelled you to do so. When you knew that everyone was living from hour to hour, acknowledgment of the moment could mean everything. The alternative to survival – vaster than Asia but containable by a body bag – was nothing less than the place where you gave up all your moments.

Our second day on leave, while driving up to a village called Orion near Pampanga Bay, we passed roadside stands with flowers so bright they hurt my eyes. We ate fried shrimp and mashed peppers at a small table under a faded awning. Then we hiked over sand fine and white as snow to an empty cove where the jungle, ending in a line of salt-singed palms, ran nearly to the water. Before leaving the city, Cassiel had stopped at the bazaar and bought a Japanese transistor radio and two pairs of pearldiver's goggles. Then on our towels in the shadow of the palms we listened to a Filipino rock station that, to celebrate the new year, was playing its top ten hits of 1968 over and over again. We swam underwater through reefs of pink and green coral alongside countless fish, some of which Cassiel identified for me when we returned to shore. Unicornfish, parrotfish, scorpionfish, hawkfish – each of them, it seemed, the incarnation of some other animal. There was even a spiderfish that clung to the underside of the coral.

While swimming, I discovered two things: like the circles on my palm during lovemaking, my pendant grew hot the moment it touched the seawater. In Honolulu during my training I had swum in a pool, but this was the first time the pendant had been immersed in the Pacific, where after all it had come into being in the form of volcanic lava. Suspended beneath my breasts as I swam, it trailed a stream of bubbles, but cooled again the moment I surfaced. The other thing was that I seemed able to hold my breath underwater for an inordinate amount of time. Much longer than I could while on land.

Cassiel had first asked me about the red dot and the circles when we were on the *Repose*. He had spotted them when he was feverish and I was cooling his throat and temples with alcohol. But I was able to put him off and he forgot about them. Only when he was on his feet again, his arm around me at the deck railing the night before we reached Subic Bay, did he see the dot and circles again, with a start of recognition.

'I thought I had dreamed them,' he murmured.

It was after midnight, and we were breaking the fraternization regulations – though not carnally as yet – kissing there under the black sky and the stars, he in his patient's robe and I in my white uniform unbuttoned to my breasts, barely able to keep our hands off one another in anticipation of our stay in Manila. Despite his being a hero, we both could have been severely disciplined. I surely would have been busted out of the Navy. Still, I preferred taking that chance to borrowing the cabin for an hour from Sharline and Evelyn. Previously, because of his wounds, Cassiel couldn't have done much in the cabin, and now that we knew we would be sharing leave, we were excited at the mere thought of a hotel room of our own.

Cassiel had been kissing my wrist when suddenly he held my palm up close to his eyes. 'Is this a tattoo?' he whispered.

I pulled my hand away gently.

'If so, I want one too,' he smiled.

'You don't want one of these,' I said, only half-jokingly.

I told him about working for Zaren Eboli, and about the *Ummidia Stellarum*. But I did not tell him that I had purposely stuck my hand into its terrarium. Nor did I get into the side effects of the bite.

'And it's been growing all this time?' he said with some alarm. 'Have any of the doctors looked at it?'

'Of course. It's nothing, and it'll be gone soon.' This was the only time I lied to him in our time together. Then I kissed him again.

'You know,' he said, 'you told me the other day that you were opposed to the war, but you never told me why you enlisted.'

For an instant I wondered if he could possibly have intuited the role the spider bite had played in my decision.

'It seems a strange jump from classical languages,' he went on.

'I wanted to start stripping away all that is false, illusory, and fearful in me,' I said slowly. 'Those are not my words, but they'll do.'

He wasn't expecting this, and I decided that, no, he hadn't intuited anything about the spider bite. 'Whose words are they?' he asked.

'A man in New Orleans passed them on to me.'

'Well, you picked a hell of a place to do it: everything over here is false or illusory, and everyone is fearful.'

'That's exactly why it was the right place,' I said calmly. 'Anyway, everything here isn't like that. I met you here.'

'Yeah, courtesy of a SAM missile,' he said, pulling me close.

As we sunned ourselves on the snow-white sand near Orion, blacktailed terns circling the palms, I pushed myself up onto one elbow. 'You know the name of our hotel?' I said to him. 'It occurred to me that Alnilam is an anagram for Manila, with an extra L.'

'I hadn't caught that,' he grinned, squinting up at me. 'Are anagrams another of your hidden skills – like speaking Latin?'

'So you think it is an anagram?'

'I don't know.' He sat up and took a swig from our thermos of iced tea. 'But I do know that Alnilam is also a star, named after the Arab astronomer who discovered it. It's the twenty-ninth brightest star in the sky, an epsilon, 900 light-years from earth, and it forms the center of Orion's belt.'

'Did you know about the stars before you became a navigator?'

He shook his head. 'But in navigation you learn about them right away. With just a few stars, you can navigate anywhere.'

'If you had to, you could use this star Alnilam to navigate?'

'So long as I had a sextant and a watch. On a navigational chart for this time of year you'd find Alnilam in the east at exactly zero degrees.'

'That's really all you need – a sextant and a watch?'

'The Polynesians didn't even have that,' he said, slipping on his sunglasses as he warmed to the subject, 'and they roamed the entire Pacific, between the tiniest islands. Magellan, maybe the greatest navigator of all, worked with little more than a compass. In his official portrait, he's pictured against the sea, seven stars above his head, with a compass in one hand and a map in the other. He named this ocean the Pacific because it happened to be calm through his entire voyage. Then he was killed here in the Philippines, in a senseless incident, hacked up by a swarm of islanders on Mactan soon after discovering his famous strait at Tierra del Fuego, and soon after discovering Guam. There's a statue of him near my base.' Cassiel took my pendant between his thumb and forefinger. 'If there was a greater navigator, it was your friend Cook here. Both of them circumnavigated the globe, but Cook sailed two hundred fifty years after Magellan, so he had two great advantages: a precision sextant and one of the first chronometers, to determine longitude. Oddly, Cook died the same way as Magellan, in a mix-up, speared and then dismembered in Hawaii, which he was the first European to visit. But that was on his third voyage. See, the purpose of his first voyage was not geographical, but astronomical. The Royal Society sent him to the South Pacific two hundred years ago, in 1768, to observe an eclipse of the sun by Venus. There have only been five transits of Venus in history, never in the twentieth century. By timing the passage of Venus across the solar disk, astronomers – and Cook had two aboard his ship – hoped to calculate the distance of the earth from the sun. Though Cook sailed across every ocean, his real mission extended far out into the solar system.'

'And what about you? If I gave you a sextant, a watch, and some charts.'

'I'm afraid the Air Force beat you to it.'

'You know what I mean.'

He lay back down on the blanket, and I could see the passing clouds reflected on the lenses of his sunglasses. 'Right now I'm only looking to get out of the war,' he said finally, 'alive, if possible.'

There was a long silence, punctuated only by the soft breaking of the waves. 'Did you set out to become a navigator as soon as you enlisted?' I asked.

'Uh-huh. I went into an officer training program especially for navigation. That was in 1957. There was no war then, except the Cold War. I cut my teeth flying redundant reconnaissance missions around Japan and Scandinavia, watching Russian submarines come and go. After that, I volunteered for polar and desert overflights for purposes of charting remote territory. I liked that. There are places like the Arctic and the Sahara where the topography is fluid and maps and charts need to be updated regularly. Then the war started and every navigator was told he'd do a tour here. It was a question of numbers.'

He shook his head. 'I never expected to end up in this kind of war. A few years ago I had a chance to work in the space program, which I passed up because I would have been forced to resign my commission. I was not prepared to do that then. Anyway, it was a desk job.' He reached out for me. 'Now, come lie beside me again – I'm getting lonely down here listening to the sound of my own voice.'

My boyfriends in Boston had been nothing like Cassiel. Though I'd always gotten a lot of attention from men, I only had a couple of serious boyfriends – and even they were short-lived – before I embraced my studies with a vengeance. One was a bass guitarist with a band that had a following around Boston; the other was a field biologist with whom I drove around New England in a VW van, preparing him macrobiotic meals and rolling myself joints. Each time I told myself that I was in love, but looking back I realized I had only the vaguest notion of what that was supposed to mean. And I say that taking my youth into account. My history, after all, didn't help me much in matters of the heart. I had never seen my mother – a martyr unwavering in her widowhood – in any kind of intimate relationship with a man. And then there was Luna, who had been drawn to Milo as surely – and hopelessly – as a leaf is drawn to a whirlpool. And of course my grandmother, whose great love was the bottle. My old girlfriends in Brooklyn, the crowd I hung out with, didn't help much either. Their motto might have been that it was better to be screwing, and screwing up, than to be idle. Anything was better than idleness. And recklessness was best of all. So when I became something of a loner with my books, it was a step up for me. Beneath the surface I had become that much hungrier for love – not the kind of love I'd known, but the kind that would nourish me – even as I stopped looking for it in the usual ways.

Now that I thought I'd found it, I saw it wasn't just the external circumstances which made things so different with Cassiel. At thirty-one – seven years older than me – he was older than my previous lovers, and there was no escaping the fact we had come together in the overwhelming context of the war; but, far more significantly, I had never before encountered a man like him. Unique yet unassuming, intelligent, physically powerful but reserved – someone, in short, who was attractive to me in every way. Drawn to him with a pull I could neither explain nor control, I realized this was the real thing, which I had never known before. There was one other quality about him, crucial to me, to which I became particularly sensitive because of the war. Cassiel was a warrior and a man of action, and though I had known hundreds of such men in Vietnam, I sensed something in him that few of the others possessed. Cassiel had been seasoned and scarred by experience long before he arrived in Southeast Asia, but somewhere along the way he had learned the rare and difficult skill of allowing himself to be gentle – with himself and with others – when caught up in the brutal machinery of this world. Even at twenty-four, I knew that this can only happen with those who suffer much and do not absent themselves when witnessing the suffering of others. But I certainly had never expected to find such gentleness in a member of that elite group who guided the B-52s and their fearsome cargo of destruction to their targets.

On the *Repose* a pilot I had to X-ray several times, who was stationed with Cassiel on Guam, gave me the only facts about him that I would have from an outside source. He told me that Cassiel was well-liked by the other fliers, but was a loner. Given to poring over celestial charts in his free time and listening to the keyboard music of Orlando Gibbons and William Byrd. An expert parachutist, to the astonishment of his comrades Cassiel liked to unwind by going up on training runs to jump with the paratroopers. He preferred free-falling until the last possible second before pulling the cord.

My cabinmate Sharline noticed at once that there was no telltale band of pale skin on Cassiel's ring finger. And she let me know that she very much admired his rugged good looks. 'But since he's the first guy over here you've shown any interest in,' she had added with a sigh, 'he's all yours, honey.' Indeed, just entering his prime and in top physical condition, Cassiel was a very handsome man. When I asked him during one of our bedside chats if he'd ever been married, he replied no. A girl back home? Again, no. 'Anyway,' he had added as I adjusted the pillows propping him up, 'there is no "back home" for me anymore in the States. And I don't just mean Nevada. Except for brief stays in Washington and Honolulu, I was posted abroad for six straight years. When I went on leave from Iceland or Germany, I traveled around the rest of Europe. I've been to Tokyo,

Bangkok, and Djakarta. Guam is the first piece of U.S. territory I've lived on for so long.'

So there was no sweetheart. But I would also come to know firsthand that he was highly sexed, and while he might be a loner in the barracks, he didn't seem to be the celibate type. Nor did I think, after living on a ship with three hundred men myself that Cassiel was the sort that came on to every woman who crossed his path. In Tokyo and Bangkok – and certainly in Guam – I imagined him seeing to his sexual needs in the countless brothels he could choose from. As for love, I was sure there were plenty of women who were attracted to him to whom he didn't give a second look. Maybe I was just flattering myself. But when, the first time we slept together, he pulled me close to say that he loved me, I believed him and was deeply moved. I could tell he had been in love before, seriously so, but my instincts told me it had been a long time ago. Cassiel told me he loved me again at the end of that long lazy afternoon at the beach near Orion as we embraced in the water. Then he picked a leaf from a bush he called a 'playing-card tree'. He said sailors used to illustrate the leaves and play cards with them in lieu of a conventional deck. With a ballpoint pen we each drew on the leaf: he a pair of stars, and as the #1 song of 1968, 'Jumpin' Jack Flash,' blared from our transistor radio for the third time, I inscribed our names, GEZA & MALA. Cassiel rolled the leaf up carefully, promising me that he would save it. As we left the beach, he lifted a starfish wriggling from the surf and held it up to me, flashing in the sun.

Needing so little sleep myself, I had found out on our first night at the Hôtel Alnilam that Cassiel was an insomniac. At first I thought his wounds might still be causing him pain, but it wasn't that. Earlier, running my fingertips over the line of shrapnel scars, I felt as if I were gazing beneath them, studying one of my own X-rays, and I could see that he had healed well. It was four o'clock when he turned to me, his eyes gleaming, wide open in the darkness.

'What is it?' I whispered.

'You've been awake too,' Cassiel said. 'What were you thinking about?'

'You,' I said, laying my hand on his chest.

He put his hand over mine. 'But what else?'

I had been thinking about Loren. That night he had been on my mind even more than usual. It was the first night in three years, after all, that *I* had felt so safe. And it had been even longer than that since I had last made love. When I went to bed alone, in a motel or furnished room or my cramped bunk at sea, and closed my eyes, I couldn't get it out of my head that Loren was still *out there*. In the most treacherous seas. Maybe, miraculously, he had landed safely, on some islet; more than likely, he was anything but safe. I wondered whether he was still alive. And, if so, whether he was more lonely and afraid than I could ever imagine. I tormented myself spinning out scenarios of what might have happened to him and, worse, what could still be happening. That first night in Cassiel's arms, warmed and softened by pleasure, feeling his hands and lips at last touch every part of my body, and touching every part of him, and feeling him push inside me and release all of himself, it was less my fears about Loren, but their constant companion, my guilt, that filled my head. Alongside the rush of happiness, the exhilarating release, I experienced in that hotel room, I would remember that my stay there also marked the first occasion on which the most poisonous torment of all took root in me: that I had deliberately – not carelessly, or innocently – lost Loren. This was the twisted punishment I dished out to myself for having finally taken respite from my grief: guilt with a vengeance.

To Cassiel I finally said, 'I've lost things too. But, as you know, in another way those become the very things that never leave you.'

'Tell me about it,' he said.

'No, I'm sticking to our agreement.' I knew that if I began telling him about Loren, it would never end, it would overwhelm me and take over our time together. After two years of solitary wandering, I only had those few days with Cassiel and I wasn't about to share them with my ghosts – not even with Loren, I thought with a shudder. So I pressed my body against Cassiel's and put my lips to his ear. 'There's just this moment – remember?'

Our second night together, tanned and hot still from being in the sun all day, we ordered dinner in our room. Just cold lemon soup and prawns and fruit salad. We bathed, taking turns in the deep claw-foot tub, soaping one another down. And then, right after we made love, we fell asleep on top of the sheets, holding hands. The night birds were singing outside the shuttered window and the piano music was faintly audible in the next room and Cassiel's breathing, from his lips to deep in his lungs, resonated softly in my ears.

On our third night, we went out on the town in Manila and enjoyed a seven-course meal of poached bass, crab, eel, and other seafood I had never heard of, on a floating restaurant in the middle of a lake to which we had to row ourselves. Through a skylight we saw the half-moon glowing gold. And all around the lake parrots chattered in the trees and bats swooped through the steamy air. Later, in the cluttered downtown streets that were bright as day with neon arcades and flashing marquees, we found ourselves in a nightclub called The Galaxy. There were a number of naval aviators at the bar, drinking alone, and a large group at a table, each with a prostitute, throwing back shots of vodka. Unlike us, these officers were in uniform. Two of them were dropping coins and pineapple wedges down the girls' dresses; the pineapple they fished out with their fingers, the coins the girls kept.

We had had champagne with dinner, followed by brandy, and now Cassiel ordered us another bottle of champagne. He was watching the table of officers absently. On a small stage, a band was accompanying a young woman in a silver dress who sang Filipino love songs. She had a thin soprano voice. A girl in a miniskirt and boots was circling the room, selling cigarettes from a basket. Having grown increasingly subdued, Cassiel bought a pack of Camels from her and lit up, the only time I ever saw him smoke. 'Hashish, too,' the girl murmured, pointing to the bottom of her basket, but he waved her off. Then, though we had made love most of the afternoon and spent our meal discussing the sights of the city, he suddenly picked up our conversation of the previous day, at the beach near Orion, as if we had just left off.

'You know that because I was wounded I can end my tour a few months early. I've already put the paperwork in motion.'

'When did you do that?'

'Before we left Subic.'

I froze. Ending his tour meant leaving combat, which couldn't have made me happier; but it also meant being shipped out of Southeast Asia, and where would that leave the two of us, at least in the near future?

The waiter brought our champagne and uncorked it and Cassiel tipped him with a twenty-dollar bill. 'Think this stuff is really French?' he muttered, studying the label.

'Where will they send you?' I asked, keeping my voice even.

He shrugged. 'First I'll have to return to Guam. Then I'll get my orders.'

'Can you go back to the mapmaking flights?'

'I didn't make any requests.'

I sipped some champagne, which was barely chilled. Or maybe it was just me. My lips and hands were particularly dry and hot that night. 'Will you resign your commission?' I said.

'That's a separate issue.' He glanced at the officers' table, where the din was increasing, and put down his glass. 'Definitely *not* French,' he said.

'Do you want to go to another club?'

He seemed surprised. 'No, why?'

'Geza, look at me.'

His hair combed back, shining, he was wearing a sky-blue sports shirt and white slacks. His arms and chest were darkly tanned. I had on an ankle-length, flowered green dress which I had gone out and bought that morning while he was asleep. When I modeled it for him, he took it off me slowly, kissing my shoulders, my breasts, and then down my sides, before pulling me onto the bed. Later at a stall near the hotel he picked out and bartered for a pair of triangular jade earrings to go with the dress.

'You're telling me things', I said, 'without telling me anything at all.'

His eyes locked on mine. Refilling our glasses, he said, 'All right,' and then drained his glass.

It wasn't the drunken officers that was bothering him. Or even that he had put in for a transfer. After one more glass of champagne, he brought up the subject which, even on the ship, he had been holding in. 'When we were hit on Christmas Eve,' he began, tapping out another cigarette and tearing off a match which he didn't light, 'the missile exploded right up through the belly of the ship. The pilot and three airmen were killed immediately. In the back, the bombardier was screaming that his legs were gone. In the cockpit, Corelli the copilot and I were covered with blood, but I couldn't find my wounds. Then I saw that the pilot's midsection had been blown open. We were going down fast. We couldn't make Saigon, and crash-landing a B-52 in the jungle is suicide, pure and simple. Suddenly we were being strafed by antiaircraft guns. Corelli was hit and the cockpit filled with smoke, but he still managed to bring us in level, skimming the treetops. Then we hit the ground, there was an explosion, and we skidded in flames through the trees. The wings were sheared off. And somewhere in there I caught that shrapnel, which knocked me facedown. The noise was deafening. I could barely breathe. I didn't feel anything. I was waiting for another explosion. Then we stopped. Corelli was dead and I thought I must be dead too. But I could still move, so I crawled to the back and rolled out with that one remaining airman. When search and rescue found me in the bush, I had blacked out. If the NVA had found me first, I'd be a statistic now too.'

Cassiel lit the cigarette, took a drag, and stubbed it out. Crushing the rest of the pack, he signalled the waiter for the check.

'That was my twenty-eighth run out of Guam, Mala,' he went on, 'and my last. This much I knew already: carpet-bombing, killing by the acre, from eight miles up is obscene. But watching my whole crew get it like that, up close and dirty – gagging on it – that's something else. Tasting shrapnel yourself is a lot different than watching six tons of bombs spin down on the radar screen like confetti.'

I drained my own glass, though, as usual, the alcohol was having no effect on me.

He leaned forward. 'That X-ray you took, where the shrapnel looked like the stars the X-ray telescope had photographed: that was a message to me.'

'A message?'

He tossed another twenty onto the table and pushed his chair back. 'If all my stars are lined up that straight, I should go with it. I joined the Air Force just before I turned twenty. I had a whole other life I had to escape. And I needed to fly – I mean really fly – which only they could teach me. But that was in peacetime. Now it's time to move on.'

Back at the hotel, we undressed completely and he fell asleep as soon as he stretched out on the bed, his head in my arms. The room was stifling, and I had to remind myself that the heat was much harder on him than on me. The ribbon was fluttering on the fan's cage, but again I could barely feel the effects of the blades. In the courtyard, one of the macaws was complaining. Motor scooters were whining by on the street. A truck back-fired. And from the hotel bar I heard glasses and bottles clicking onto shelves as the bartender closed up for the night. After a swift downpour, it was drizzling, and a fine green mist was seeping through the venetian blinds.

Stirring in my arms, Cassiel might as well have been in another world. Of the four nights we spent together, this was the only one on which he slept through until dawn. So I was able to gaze upon his face, and his body, uninterrupted and unselfconsciously. Lightly I stroked his shoulder and arm. His skin, over firm muscles, rippled like water under my fingertips. I ran the back of my index finger over the stubble on his cheek. His natural scent – like salt and honey – was unlike any I had experienced, on a man or a woman. The dark hair on his chest and legs was so soft I could barely feel it. I had never known a man with stronger hands, more sensitive in their movements even than those of the surgeons on my ship.

We had come together so naturally, and seamlessly – under the most unnatural and fragmented of circumstances – that it spooked me, first on the *Repose*, and now, even more so, in Manila.

If Cassiel was spooked, he didn't let on; my feeling was that, for whatever reason, very few things in life held the power to surprise him anymore.

Suddenly my thoughts were broken by a small red spider that scurried across the sheets and up the wall to the ceiling. I recognized it from my days in Zaren Eboli's basement, a female *Uloborus*, a master weaver of orb webs, huge concentric constructions which she completes in a matter of minutes.

Immediately the spider began spinning out such a web, and watching her at work, going round and round, had a hypnotic, dizzying effect on me. My palms had grown hotter and my lips felt numb and parched. Bits of color, bright shavings, began breaking away from objects and swirling into my field of vision – like a kaleidoscope. When I closed my eyes the colors disappeared, so I kept them closed. And from cradling it in my arms, I gently shifted Cassiel's head into my hands. At once my own head filled with images, flickering by as they did when I scanned the remoter byways of my memory. But

112

these images were alien to me. There were no half-familiar guideposts – a name, a face, a piece of clothing – to let me in on what part of my past life I was reviewing.

I saw a whirling sheet of sand sweep across the base of a mountain range that glowed red. From one of the peaks a red hawk with a tremendous wingspan and fiery talons sped toward me, streaming a shower of sparks.

Then a woman running through a dry riverbed. She wore a yellow bandanna and a red dress. Coming to a pillar of boulders, she raced into its long purple shadow and never reemerged.

And then a red car with a sand-coated windshield rolling toward the edge of a ravine in the last rays of the setting sun. One of the car's headlights was burning, the other was smashed. Suddenly the car burst into flames. Through the windshield I could make out a shadow slumped behind the wheel just before the car, a fireball, plunged into the ravine.

Finally I saw an impenetrable ceiling of slate-colored clouds through which I was ascending in a plane. I was in the rear of the cockpit. The green and blue lights of a radar screen danced before me. Finally the plane leveled off. The pilots' seats were topped by two white helmets which I saw from behind. All at once the windshield lit up with fire and the plane lurched hard before plummeting, down and down, and smoke poured in, filling my mouth. Then those two seats spun around and under the helmets were slumped what was left of two men in blue uniforms, one of them cut in half floating in his own blood and the other with a gaping hole in his chest.

I opened my eyes and cried out, and there above me on the ceiling the spiderweb turned blood-red for a moment before it disappeared altogether.

Cassiel jumped up. 'Mala, what is it?'

I closed my eyes again, and he grasped my shoulders. 'Mala!'

'I'm all right.'

He was looking into my face, his eyes bloodshot, and

I realized with a start that those were memories of his I had been looking at. Among the powerful aftereffects of the *Ummidia Stellarum*'s bite, I could now add this: the ability to scan not just my own memories in excruciating detail, but also, under the right conditions, those of another person. And what were those conditions? Holding Cassiel's head, making love . . . I had not done these things with anyone else after leaving New Orleans. And maybe there were other conditions I couldn't identify so easily: the Hôtel Alnilam, the presence of the spiderweb, the alignment of the stars over Manila. Or maybe it was just Cassiel and me. Something chemical, as Sharline would say. But these were chemicals with which Sharline had no experience.

'You were dreaming,' Cassiel said.

I didn't want to tell him that I hadn't even been asleep.

It was dawn. The birds were singing in the colvillea trees. The early traffic was starting up.

'Lie down,' he said, and then curled his body around mine. I couldn't get that scene in the cockpit out of my head. Turning my face into the pillow, I kept my eyes open, listening to Cassiel's breathing deepen, feeling him fall away from me, back into sleep – as if it were a place distinct and remote to both of us, which we seemed destined never to share.

Later that morning, our fourth day in Manila, I still felt shaky and told Cassiel I wanted to go for a walk. Wearing straw hats against the sun, we walked for a couple of hours on the periphery of the city, through overgrown deserted parks, over cement expanses and bridges that seemed to lead nowhere, down streets where the shops were closing for the midday siesta. It must have been 100° in the open spaces. As usual I seemed to soak up the heat, and Cassiel, conditioned and trained for tropical warfare, appeared unfazed by it. Eventually, though, we wandered into a coffee bar, out of the blistering sun. It was a bright tiled place with Formica tables and metal stools under long fluorescent lights.

'I feel like you're not afraid of anything,' I said

suddenly as Cassiel stirred sugar into his thick reddish coffee, for despite the walk I had remain fixated all day on what I had seen – or imagined – in that cockpit. He was surprised. 'What makes you think that?'

I shrugged.

'Is that what you want to think?' he said, looking at me closely. 'Is it true?'

'There are things I'm afraid of.'

'Not dying.'

'That's one you can't know until the moment arrives.'

'Were you afraid when your B-52 went down?'

'There wasn't enough time to feel afraid.'

'So, then, what are you afraid of?'

He ran his fingertips down my arm, then laid his hand over mine. 'That when you find what you really want, you know that losing it would be worse than losing your life. That makes me afraid.'

'It makes me afraid, too,' I said. I hesitated, then went on, 'Is that what you lost before – someone important to you?'

He nodded.

'And now—' I began, but he put his fingers over my lips and drew me close.

'Now that we've said it, we don't have to be so afraid,' he said softly. 'The worst thing about fear is what it does to you when you try to hide it.'

On that last night in Manila neither of us had much appetite. We showered and dressed and went down to the hotel restaurant, where we picked at our food. After the waiter cleared the table, we drank tea and Cassiel talked about Guam, where he would be landing in less than twenty-four hours. After telling me about his routine there, he described the place itself as 'snake- and mosquito-infested, with more weapons and explosives per square mile than any other island in the world. It's more aircraft carrier than island. A nexus of bad karma I'll be glad to leave.' When he went on to mention the terrible battle that had been fought there in the Second World War, my heart quickened.

'In July, they're going to have a ceremony,' he said. 'It's the twenty-fifth anniversary.'

'Yes, I know. My father was killed in that battle. Before I was born.'

It was the first and only time I saw Cassiel look astonished.

'He was a marine, and he's buried on Guam,' I added.

'We pass over that cemetery every time we fly in or out,' he said. 'I'm sorry.' He shook his head, still digesting this information. 'But you've never been there.'

'No.'

'If you give me his name, I'll put some flowers on the grave.'

'I appreciate that, but no,' I said, touching his arm. I didn't want to think of Cassiel in one of those overly green, manicured fields with the endless rows of identical crosses. Also, my father's last name was different from mine now, and I didn't want to have to tell Cassiel why I had changed it, along with my first name.

'I'm glad you'll be leaving there,' I said.

'The next time you see me, we'll be on a different sort of island altogether.'

My tour was to end in August, and we had agreed earlier that no matter where he was transferred to, I would meet him there. Before that, if he was still in the Pacific in June when I was next scheduled for R&R, I'd hop a transport plane and we'd rendezvous in Hawaii. We had been willing to plan this far ahead, and no more, though I couldn't imagine living my life without him anymore.

Because we had to leave early the next morning, we had already packed our bags. I was to drive the jeep back to Subic Bay, and a car was coming to pick up Cassiel and take him to the Air Force base at Luzon. So before going upstairs, we stopped at the desk to settle our bill. The owner himself came out of his office, where he had just finished his own dinner, sipping Pernod and puffing an aromatic Thai cigarette. His napkin still

116

tucked inside his striped vest, he was clutching a wad of papers, one of which he handed to Cassiel.

'Your receipt,' he said, stubbing out his cigarette. 'May I buy you both a drink?'

'No, thanks,' Cassiel said.

'Thank you for the flowers,' I said. We hadn't spoken to the owner since the day we checked in, but every morning with our coffee, guava, and brioche, he had sent us up a different flower, each more beautiful than the last. That last morning, the thin vase on our coffee tray contained a bright flower with alternating red and yellow petals around an orange center.

'My compliments,' the Frenchman replied, and the lenses of his heavy glasses flashed.

'That one this morning,' Cassiel said, 'I saw once before in my life. But I'd swear it's a desert flower.'

The Frenchman turned back to his office. 'And you would be correct. I used to have a garden full of them in Las Vegas.' Closing his office door, he glanced back at us with a small smile and said, 'Until we meet again.'

In the cage lift ascending to our floor, Cassiel glanced at the receipt and turned pale.

'Did he toss in some surprises?' I smiled.

He looked up at me, but his eyes were far away.

'What is it, Geza?'

'Nothing,' he shook his head, stuffing the paper into his pants pocket. 'You go in,' he said, unlocking the door to our room. 'I think I'll bring up a brandy from the bar. Would you like one?'

'Why don't you ring down for it?'

'This will be quicker.' He kissed me on both eyelids. 'I want to be alone with you as much as possible.'

'Then ring down,' I whispered.

He kissed me again. 'I'll be right back.'

He did return quickly, but even paler and more pre-occupied. And he had brought back two double Rémys. He took a long sip from one of them, and without a word removed his shirt and pants, washed his hands and face, and wrapped a towel around his neck.

'Everything okay?'

He finished the brandy. 'Everything is fine.'

He came over to the bed, where I was sitting half undressed, and forked his fingers into my hair. As much as I wanted to ask him why he had needed to go see the old Frenchman, I knew that if he wanted to tell me he already would have. Without my asking.

We often went for long stretches without saying a word. And that was what happened for the next few hours. Cassiel held my head to his chest, stroking my hair. I could hear his strong heartbeat. Then he kissed me, and, unhooking my bra and peeling off my underpants, eased me back on the bed and ran his lips and tongue over my body from my toes to my mouth, and then back between my legs. He was very slow, and thorough, before he moved up and slid inside me, and as I closed my eyes, it was not the spiderweb I saw overhead, but the constellation Scorpio, with Antares, the red star, glowing at its center.

An hour later we made love again, for the last time in that room, after which Cassiel fell asleep, spread-eagled on the sheets. The deep silence of the hotel at two a.m. was broken only by the phonograph in the next room where the same music that had been on all day was still playing: the jazz pianist improvising around a theme. Whoever was in there – and all I had heard was someone with a cough, pacing – was wearing out that record. Cassiel was in exactly the same position, and feeling his breath brush my cheek, I finally fell asleep.

Two hours later I awoke with a terrific thirst. I made my way to the bathroom and in the darkness drank half a liter of bottled water and splashed cold water on my face and throat. Then I tiptoed to the chair over which Cassiel had draped his pants. With two fingers I fished the piece of paper from his pocket and took it into the bathroom. I flicked on the lamps shaped like seashells that flanked the mirror, and in their dull, rose glow unfolded and examined the paper. Of course it was not a receipt at all. Hotel stationery – not the Alnilam, but one whose name had been torn off the top, leaving only some digits of a telephone number – the paper was yellowed with age and centered with a block of cramped script:

> *And the fifth angel sounded and I saw a star*
> *fall from heaven to earth: and to him*
> *was given the key of the bottomless pit.*

I didn't know what this quotation was, but it made my head spin as I memorized it and returned it to his pants. And those words kept going round in my mind when I stood by the bed gazing down at Cassiel. In the gray shadows his strong features were immobile as a statue's and his thick hair shone black against the pillow. I had never seen him look so peaceful, and I had a premonition at that moment that I would not see him in June or August – that I would not in fact see him for a long time. He had pulled the sheet over him, and slipping under it, I drifted uneasily into sleep.

It seemed only seconds elapsed before I heard my name repeated softly and opened my eyes to Cassiel standing over me in his crisp tan uniform. Sunlight was slanting into the room through chinks in the blinds.

'My car is downstairs,' he said. 'No, don't get up. We said goodbye last night. I want to think of you like this, until next time.'

He leaned over and I put my arm around his neck and kissed him.

'Geza . . .'

'I know,' he whispered.

And he was gone. I put on my bathrobe and rolled up the blinds. The sunlight dazed me, and feeling cold suddenly, I hugged myself close. Then I spotted an envelope propped against the mirror on the bureau. On the outside, he had written, *I wanted you to have this*, beside which he had drawn this symbol: ⌂

The envelope contained a gold bracelet with seven stars affixed to it. Black iron, highly polished, the stars

119

were forged in the exact shape of my volcanic pendant from the pieces of shrapnel that had been removed from Cassiel's shoulder. The bracelet fit my wrist perfectly.

I was running my fingers over those stars three days later, in the communications room of the *Repose*, as we sailed northward, seventy miles off the coast of Vietnam. Cassiel had promised he would wire me that night. But no wire came. The next night I returned and sent one myself to his base on Guam. While waiting for a reply, I asked our communications officer about the triangle with the C inside it.

'It's the navigational symbol for a celestial fix,' he told me. 'It's when you get a proper lock on the star you're navigating by.'

An hour later he read me the reply I received from the command headquarters at Andersen Air Force Base that Captain Geza Cassiel was not on Guam. I sent a follow-up, and then another, but that's all they would tell me. Finally, two days later, I asked our second officer to inquire officially on my behalf, and he received word that Cassiel, aboard a small plane, had been missing in action since January 18, four days after I had last seen him. When we queried again, the Air Force would not confirm that Cassiel had been en route to Guam, or anywhere else, much less tell us why he was aboard a small plane or what kind of action he could have been involved in. Claiming it was classified information, they weren't exactly intimidated by inquiries coming from a hospital ship. In the meantime, the war was escalating on all fronts, our influx of casualties was three times what it had been when I had first come on-line, and everyone on the *Repose* was working even more over-time than usual. Personal inquiries like mine were decidedly low-priority material. As the weeks crawled by, I grew frantic and fired off a dozen letters, to both Air Force and Navy brass, in Manila, Guam, Honolulu, even Washington, and every response was the same: MIA.

In the meantime, I learned the origin of those words

on the scrap of paper at the Hôtel Alnilam. I was poring over her Bible when my fundamentalist cabinmate, Evelyn, came in exhausted from her shift one morning. Surprised and pleased to find the Bible in my hands, she asked what I was looking for.

'Why, it's from Revelation, Chapter Nine,' she said, before I had even finished reciting the lines. 'In those verses, when the fifth angel sounds his trumpet, a star falls from heaven to earth, and the angel is given the key to the bottomless pit from which locusts emerge in a cloud of smoke. They take the form of scorpions in order to torment evil men. You see,' she went on, 'St John claimed that each star in the sky is an angel,' and I recalled the similar assertion by the pagan Cicero – which I did not share with her – that each star is a god. One that might fall to earth at any moment. Unbuttoning her uniform and leaning against her bunk, Evelyn darkly declaimed the sixth verse of Revelation, Chapter Nine, to me in her best Alabama drawl, with more passion than I had ever heard her invest in anything: '"And in those days shall men seek death, and shall not find it; and shall desire to die, and death shall flee from them." Not exactly what's happening around here, is it,' she added bitterly, for even she had sickened of the war by then.

Unable to eat, unable to sleep, I wandered the ship – the decks, the corridors below – every night for hours when I came off duty. I was more restless than ever. And so it was late one night, passing the seamen's lounge, in a part of the ship I rarely visited, that I encountered again the incessant phonograph music I had heard through the wall of Room 9 at the Hôtel Alnilam. Since leaving Manila I had heard that music so often in my head that it took me a moment to realize it was also playing outside of me now. I stopped short and returned to the open door of the lounge. Inside it was dark. I saw the orange glow of a burning cigarette between the fingers of a sailor whose face I couldn't make out. He was hunched over a portable phonograph against the wall.

The record he was playing hissed with static: but it was the same jazz pianist, all right, improvising variations on that same theme.

'Excuse me,' I said. 'Would you tell me what that music is?'

The sailor's voice was low, and scratchy too, but even over the music I didn't have to strain to hear it. 'It's called "Dead Man Blues",' he replied.

'Jelly Roll Morton?' I whispered, and to my surprise he heard me. 'That's right. Come in, if you like.'

But I was already running down the narrow corridor, my sandals slapping on the tiles as I swallowed the scream that was rising in my throat.

In their final communication with me on February 20, which happened to be my twenty-fourth birthday, the Air Force would no longer confirm that there had even been such a flight as I was inquiring after, in any kind of plane, on January 18, out of Luzon or anywhere else. Information-wise, I was going backward, finally being told that there was no information at all, for, incredibly, they refused to confirm that Captain Geza Cassiel had been a crew member on a B-52, or even that he was stationed on Guam before December 24, though I knew full well that he had been shot down while on a mission out of there. I thought I was going out of my mind. His medical charts and the X-rays I had taken were now on file at Subic Bay, and the only tangible proof I had that Cassiel existed was my gold bracelet with the stars forged from the shrapnel that had been removed from his back. Or maybe I had bought the bracelet, too, in Manila, all by myself, along with the red transistor radio and the pearldiver's goggles, which I had kept. Rubbing the patch of concentric circles on my palm, I thought maybe he had never been in Manila with me. Maybe there was no Cassiel, and those four wonderful days at the Hôtel Alnilam had been a product of my delirium, courtesy of the *Ummidia Stellarum*'s venom. Or so I told myself, over and over again, to deflect my fears that he was really dead. But it was no consolation.

As in New Orleans I had begun to cry myself to sleep again. Often I took refuge on deck, under the stars, so as not to disturb the other nurses. It was on one such night, gripping the railing in rough seas until my fingers were white, with my father's Silver Star in my pocket, that I finally began screaming, right into the teeth of the wind. A petty officer found me out there and took me down to the infirmary. One of the doctors gave me a sedative which had no effect. I didn't understand what he was saying to me, or why he was saying it. All I knew was that, like Loren, Cassiel had disappeared off the face of the earth, and once again there was nothing I could do about it.

9

The Education of Enzo

In the first three years that I lived at the Hotel Canopus
I grew accustomed to the large floating population. I
hardly bothered keeping track of the overnight and
weekend transients, but I came to know the permanent
residents, for better or worse, as well as one comes to
know the members of a family. Even those who were
most reclusive often indulged me, at least by their
standards, because of my closeness to Samax. More
permanent, even, than the permanent guests was the
constellation of women around Samax, whose dynam-
ics and tensions, I soon realized, were as complex as
their individual relationships with him.

Dolores was the hotel manager. She was ninety years
old at that time and never left the hotel grounds. She saw
to it that every operational detail met Samax's specifications and that the place in all respects ran according
to his expectations. I seldom saw Dolores, who remained in her office most of the time, in the upper
basement. On Wednesdays from noon to six she sat
alone in the maze of the garden, in a nook where no one
was to disturb her, ever, in a stiff rocking chair beside a
glass table. This was her time off. And she drank gallons
of chamomile tea, iced, from a tall glass, which
she claimed to be an elixir for longevity – but only if
consumed in vast quantities, without sugar. A thin,
craggy woman, Dolores kept her white hair drawn back

124

severely in a bun. Her eyes were still sharp, but she used a monocle, which hung from her neck on a red cord, to read by. Even with glasses, she said, her left eye could not focus close up on things.

In my first and only private meeting with her after my arrival, in her office, I fixed on the monocle's flashing lens which spun slowly when she leaned forward in her wooden swivel chair. Later, I would look back on this meeting as closer to a job interview than a cordial intro-duction. For one thing, I stood the entire time: no other chair graced the room, just a long hard sofa on the wall behind Dolores. Across the front of her desk – a for-midable line of defense – there was a row of potted fishhook cactuses, long-needled and crowned with startling profusions of purple flowers.

Peering at me closely with her right eye, dark as blue ink, Dolores remarked enigmatically, 'I see family resemblances.' Her thick, oily voice sharply contrasted with her desiccated features.

Since, so far as I could tell, I barely resembled Samax, I wondered what or who exactly she saw in my face. Did she mean my mother, Bel, I wanted to ask her; but more intimidated by her than I was by my uncle, I refrained.

'They tell me you picked up another name along the way,' she went on bluntly, her sole reference, wildly understated, to my entire history.

I nodded.

'So now we'll be taking care of you,' she said. She sat back and the monocle rested flat on her thin black cardigan. 'Even if I was blind, which I'm not, I'd know you were related to Junius. Like him, you don't talk a lot, huh?'

I cleared my throat. 'Only when I have something to say.'

She smiled thinly. 'Proving my point, 'cause that's exactly what he would say.' Cracking her knuckles, she turned over some papers on her desk by way of dis-missal and said under her breath, 'You'll do. Keep your eyes and ears open and you could learn a few things around here.'

When I stepped outside her office, my face was hot and I felt as if all the breath had been sucked from my lungs.

Dolores's daughters, Della and Denise, were the two women I had seen at the desk in the lobby my first night at the hotel. But I had spoken only with Della, the tanned one with the slate hair. Denise was the bleached blonde with the aquiline face. The sisters were responsible for the hotel's day-to-day operations, under the firm – sometimes iron – hand of their mother.

Della and Denise seldom spoke to each other and made no secret of their mutual disdain. Denise was cool to me and indifferent, and Della – as she had been that first night – friendly, solicitous, and as time passed, and we came to know each other, affectionate and loving. Certainly it was to her that I went when I had a cut or scrape to be tended; Denise, who nominally shared responsibility for taking care of me on a daily basis, would see to my needs, but not with Della's genuine tenderness. This applied both to routine matters and emergencies. For example, when a pot of coffee spilled onto my arm in the kitchen one morning, it was Della who rushed to my side and took charge, icing the burn and applying a salve which prevented my incurring the faintest scar.

During my first year at the hotel, until my eleventh birthday, one of the sisters always spent the night across the hall from me in Room D. Because of the nature of my previous lives, loneliness in the wee hours was not one of my problems. And my grandmother had not been a touchy-feely person. Still, in that first year, in an environment as exotic and complex as the hotel, I had enough questions every week to fill a small notebook. Samax was often busy, his trusted aide and right arm Calzas traveled, and Desirée was otherwise absorbed, so Della was my primary source of information, especially for stuff with which I did not want to clutter my time with Samax. Not to mention those questions about him which I did not, or could not, ask Samax himself. For example, the specifics of his relationships with certain residents, highly intricate by definition since nearly all activities at the hotel radiated from him on some level. More to the point, when I first arrived, it was Della who expressed the most down-to-earth curiosity about those previous lives of mine. Whether at my bedside or in the upstairs kitchen over sandwiches and milk, she often asked me about my itinerant life with Luna and Milo, about Brooklyn and how I had adapted to a correspondingly sedentary life with my grandmother. Sometimes we spoke of Alma, and once in a while of my mother, Bel, whom Della had known when Bel was my age. I was intensely curious about Bel, for obvious reasons; and for her own reasons, Della was not as forthcoming as she was about other things.

'She loved animals, as you do,' Della remarked to me. 'She loved music. And she read a lot. That's how I remember her, propped up against a tree with a book in her lap and a transistor radio.'

'Did she like rock-and-roll?'

'I guess,' she said. 'She always wore an earplug.'

'What did she read, then?' I asked.

Della furrowed her brow. 'I don't know,' she said, a pained expression crossing her face. 'I can't remember now. It was such a difficult time,' she added awkwardly.

Only later would I come to realize that the difficulty she referred to was a kind of retroactive one. That is, the apparent anguish Della and Samax suffered around Bel's untimely death radiated backward and tinged their memories of her short life. Because of the way she had died, they could seldom speak of her life – which anyway didn't seem to be a happy one – without anguish. And when I was young, especially, and new to the household, they were reluctant to transmit that anguish to me, even if at times this meant avoiding the subject of Bel altogether. The simple fact, which I absorbed with stark clarity from the first, was that my birth and her death were inextricably bound: Bel ran away from home, gave birth to me, and soon afterward died.

In age, Della and Denise were spaced two years apart. There had been a third sister, Doris, the eldest, but she had died some time ago. In bits and pieces, during my first year at the hotel, I had put together a few essential facts about Dolores and her daughters. Their history at a certain point – which I had yet to determine – had become inextricably tied to Samax's. What I had managed to learn more than anything reinforced the fact that I knew very little. And much of that, on the surface, appeared contradictory. The three sisters each had a different father, and Dolores was a widow three times over: everyone agreed on that. And also on the fact, which I learned quite early on, that Samax had been married briefly to the late Doris – the only hiatus in his lifelong bachelorhood. No one – not the sisters, or Dolores, or Desirée, or other people at the hotel who must have known – would ever say much about this marriage. Nor would they discuss the circumstances of Doris's death, and I was told in no uncertain terms (by Calzas) that these were two subjects which were not to be broached with Samax. Even Calzas himself wouldn't touch these subjects if I brought them up – which told me a lot. So, inspired by a shortage of information, I wondered frequently about this late Mrs Samax. I wondered why Samax had not married Della, about whom I felt so warmly. Desirée, who was twenty-three, was Della's daughter; even if it wasn't Della who had been married to Samax, I still suspected, and wished, that Samax might be Desirée's father. I had seen soon enough that he had an eye, undimmed by his age, for a pretty woman, yet I had never seen him look at Desirée – whom every man in the hotel looked at – with the slightest flicker of lust.

Though Desirée was Della's daughter, I seldom saw them speak to each other. In fact, Desirée spent little time with either her mother or her aunt Denise. Sometimes she could be found at Samax's elbow, doing

128

intensive research on the antiquities he was interested in acquiring. But mostly she was a loner, sitting by the pool under an umbrella with her portable Olivetti perched on a footstool, wearing wraparound sunglasses and one of the bikinis from her inexhaustible collection. I never saw her wear the same one twice, and with her perfect figure, it wouldn't have mattered to me if she had. Even before my formal adolescence began – my thirteenth birthday, on December 16, 1968 – Desirée had become the object of my fantasies. Many times a day I undressed her, to the point where I was certain I knew how she would look, to the last detail, if ever I did see her naked. I knew she had lovers in town, but none of them ever came out to the hotel. And, while envying them – I had calculated that when I was twenty, she would still be only thirty, hopefully within reach – I was more curious about the contents of those pale yellow pages she piled neatly beside her as she typed effortlessly yet with great concentration for hours, days, at a time. To me, she was always kind, and could be warmly intimate – or so I fancied – while remaining spacily detached, gazing far beyond whomever she was looking at, even as she had the night I met her, on our flight from New York.

It was also in that first year at the hotel, on Samax's orders, that Della or Denise always came to my room at bedtime to read to me from the *Arabian Nights* (thus we covered 365 of the 1,001 nights before I completed the entire work by myself, one night at a time, over the next two years). Denise was perfunctory, and cut me short when I asked her too many questions about the stories, until finally I stopped asking her any; the moment she shut the book, I turned on my side and she walked to the door and switched off the lamp, mumbling ' good night' without looking back. Della, in addition to being the superior reader, stayed for as long as I wanted and often asked me questions about what we had just read. When I was particularly lucky, Desirée would sit in for one of them – my very own Scheherazade, I thought – and, perched on the side of my bed, would read aloud in her low, velvety voice while I inhaled the perfume of her long hair, and studied the movements of her beautiful hands, and took enormous sensual delight in the fact that whenever she shifted her weight on the mattress, or moved at all, the subtlest ripples and tremors were wonderfully transmitted to me. In short, I was entranced by the illusion that, for even the briefest time, and by the loosest definition, Desirée was sharing my bed with me. And so it was that the 'nights' which she happened to read to me would always be among my especial favorites, forever associated with her voice, her scents, and her body.

Among their primary duties, either Della or Denise always oversaw dinner at the Hotel Canopus. When Samax was home, he insisted I dine with him, either alone in his quarters or more elaborately with other residents in the large tenth-floor dining room at the long oak table with its high-backed chairs. Above the table was a skylight and through the floor-to-ceiling windows we had a panoramic view of the desert. Those dinners were an important element in the complex structure of my formal education. Calzas and Desirée were nearly always there, as were the hotel's more long-term residents. As an overseer, Della was usually talkative, joining in the conversations, but Denise hardly ever spoke. Samax never betrayed impatience with her, though he usually disliked it when people were silent at dinner. All the same, Denise was more skilled than Della at keeping the meal flowing – no mean feat with a kitchen ten stories removed.

When I first arrived at the hotel, my mother's sister, my aunt Ivy, always occupied the seat opposite Samax, at the foot of the dinner table. Following the discussion around the table, while rarely contributing to it, she usually ignored me completely. When her dark brown eyes did leave the radius of the plate before her, they seldom betrayed her feelings. Except when they alighted on me. Then she would cast me a withering look. If

Denise was cold to me, Ivy was positively sub-Arctic.

My mere presence there, sitting literally at Samax's right elbow, was an affront to Ivy. It was not that I had displaced her – for the simple reason that he had never held her dear. Close to her father, Nilus, and knowing of his hatred for his brother, Ivy had from the first been hostile to Samax. He had tried to bring her around, but her hostility was hopelessly intertwined with her sense of loyalty to her dead father; Samax's kindnesses inflamed her all the more. Bel, on the other hand, had been close to Samax – at least until she was eighteen and had run away and given birth to me. And Samax had loved Bel, which made Ivy all the more bitter and jealous. It was not surprising, then, that Ivy should have such hard feelings toward me.

The feelings were mutual. Though I had come to enjoy my life at the hotel, which I would not easily have exchanged for another, and to love Samax as a devoted and doting uncle, I never forgave Ivy for abducting me on that chaotic winter day. My fate may have been altered for the better, but I resented that Ivy had been an agent of that alteration. It wasn't difficult to hate her, because she so hated me. In New York, she had been acting on (while not strictly following) Samax's orders, so it did occur to me more than once that I had rather neatly channeled whatever rage I felt toward Samax onto her. But maybe that was too neat, because Samax and I had many times discussed my feelings about my abduction – it was never a taboo subject. They ranged from gratitude that I had been rescued from the strong possibility of a hand-to-mouth existence with Alma (whose life would be wrecked in the process, thanks to me) to resentment that someone, anyone, should play god with my fate, however sterling his intentions. Many times, I confessed to my uncle, I had plotted my escape from the hotel, from the life he had set before me like a sumptuous and overly organized meal, but in the end I had balked. I had no one, and nowhere, to flee to, after all. I had gotten a taste of the open road, of drifting aimlessly, friendless and penniless, with Luna and Milo all those years, and had found it to be, not a pathway to adventure, but a dead end. No, even if I couldn't define it as such until I was an adult, I, too, preferred living by Samax's unspoken assumption that if you didn't try to give shape to your life, life would shape you – usually for the worse. If, at the same time, life at the hotel was isolated, cut off from the hubbub of so-called reality, then it was a splendid isolation. On the worst days, I would not have traded it for what Milo had thought of as freedom. True, there were other ways than Milo's to negotiate the open road, but I wasn't familiar with them at that time, at thirteen, when, anyway, I tended to think in absolutes.

Ivy's hostile feelings for me were further complicated by the fact that she had a son of her own, named Auro, and she was terrified Samax would disinherit both her and her son for me – now his only other living blood relative. In a very short time this fear became an obsession with her. To make matters worse, a year before my arrival, Auro had been sent away from the hotel. Then ten years old, Auro began attending a school in Chicago for students with speech disabilities. He suffered from echolalia – the pathological repetition of what other people say. He was a walking echo who could literally throw a room into chaos by parroting everything that was said around him. The local private schools couldn't handle him, and the tutors Ivy brought to the hotel quit, despite their lavish salaries. They all said he was unteachable. Finally Samax insisted he get specialized help, and making inquiries, discovered the school in Chicago; Ivy grumbled, but with little choice in the end, acquiesced.

Ivy's husband, Nestor, who hated living at the hotel, accompanied Auro, leasing an apartment a few blocks from the school. And Ivy remained at the hotel, regularly flying to Chicago. Nestor was the man in the brown hat and coat who drove the blue sedan – and started weeping – when Ivy spirited me from the planetarium.

As it turned out, that day would be the one and only time I would ever meet him. And it would be ten years before I even saw, in a photograph, what he looked like. I had not seen his face that day in the car, and the only photographs of him at the hotel were in Ivy's quarters, which I never entered. High-strung, frail of constitution, riddled with anxieties, Nestor was constantly fighting off illnesses. At the same time, he drank heavily and chain-smoked. He was twenty years Ivy's senior, a piano player on the Strip and something of a dandy when she met him. No sooner had he abandoned his bachelor life in a green bungalow off Paradise Road than his health began to go. A few years under the same roof, and in the same bed, with Ivy took a major toll on him. Though she was barely twenty when they married and had Auro, she dominated Nestor utterly, and as the years passed, he had few reserves to fall back on.

So when he left Las Vegas, what was left of his health the Chicago winter finished off. With his fragile lungs, Nestor was a natural desert dweller; in Chicago he contracted double pneumonia, pleurisy, and then St Vitus' dance, losing control of his facial muscles and hands. So quickly did he deteriorate that his doctors insisted he go to a clinic in Zurich to undertake a severe cure; anything less, they said, and he was a goner. It turned out the Swiss had an even better school for someone with Auro's condition, and so, two months after I moved into the Hotel Canopus, Ivy moved out, accompanying her husband and son to Switzerland, where they had remained ever since.

In those two months, nevertheless, I came to a realization that was unfortunately to prove all too true: whenever she could, and by whatever means, Ivy would try to make my life a living hell. She was a master manipulator. And whether by innuendo or distortion, subterfuge or outright sabotage, she would do her best to undermine me in Samax's affections – as she had never been able to undermine my mother Bel – hoping, scheming, working overtime to get me out of the picture

133

as abruptly as I had entered it. And as cut-down-to-size as possible. Her relationship with me aside, from what I had seen in those two months, Ivy was generally unpopular around the hotel. The fact that her favorite reproach, freely tossed at the staff – from the doorman to the gardener – was 'shit-for-brains' didn't endear her to anyone. Her relationships with Dolores and her daughters were more complex and problematic, as I was to discover later. But for three years running I had been free of her, and in that time it was always one of the sisters who sat across from Samax at dinner.

What I was to learn over the years was that the crux of Ivy's hatred for me was a carryover of her feelings for my mother, Bel, her half-sister. At first I thought Ivy wished Samax had never found me; then I realized she wished I'd never been born.

My longest discussion about my mother with Samax was a very formalized one, initiated by him. Taking me up to his study one day a few months after my arrival at the hotel, he unlocked a wall cabinet and took out a small leather-covered chest which he unlocked with a tiny key. 'You asked me how I came to find you in Brooklyn,' he began, 'and I promised I would show you. The answer is in here, where I've kept a few of Bel's possessions – things she had with her when she died.' He paused and studied my face, as if to assure himself I wasn't going to get upset. 'Though I had sifted through these things many times before,' he went on, 'one morning last October I suddenly spotted something I had never seen before – that is, I had not seen it clearly. It was thus I discovered the fact of your existence, unknown to me until then.'

Peering at the chest's contents, I tried to imagine which object contained the momentous clue. There was a red felt cap. A brown handbag with a brass snap. A gold hairbrush, monogrammed with a *B*, in which a single strand of blond hair was still wound. A hand mirror with an ivory handle. A slim red fountain pen. A set of car keys. A silver pendant on a chain. A blue bankbook. And

134

several unused – but stamped, with 2¢ stamps – post-cards depicting a low skyline and captioned RENO – THE BIGGEST LITTLE CITY IN THE WORLD.

I held the brush up to the light and the blond hair appeared red-tinged; I looked at my face in the mirror; I jangled the car keys, which I noted were for a Buick; I examined the pendant, on which a small bird was embossed, and then unscrewed the top off the fountain pen.

But it was the bankbook that Samax lifted from the chest and opened flat on the table.

'The clue was in here,' he said, slowly turning the pale blue pages.

The numerals, punched in by machine in black ink, dated in red, showed that the bankbook's owner, *Bel Samax, Hotel Canopus, Las Vegas*, made only six deposits and one withdrawal in all of 1953 and 1954, but in the last two months of 1955 and the first month of 1956 made dozens of withdrawals for small sums – fifteen, twenty-five, a couple of times fifty dollars. These transactions abruptly ended in February, 1956, at which time her balance had dwindled from $2,982 to $366.40.

'I opened this account with her on her sixteenth birthday,' Samax said. 'Every three months, I added five hundred dollars. As you see, only at the end of her life did she begin using the money. But what I want to show you is here at the end.'

He flipped to the very last two pages in the bankbook, well beyond the tellers' entries. There, scrawled in pencil in a small hand, was a maze of figures. Numerals scattered in all directions – being subtracted, added, multiplied and divided, erased and crossed out.

'Obviously Bel used these pages to make her calculations,' Samax continued. 'I glanced at them years ago, and never paid attention to them again. But if you closely examine these particular numbers in the lower right-hand corner,' he said, putting his index finger on the page, 'concealed among many other numbers – it's clear they're not calculations.' I bent low over the book and saw the numerals: *33-879*, and below that, *6244511*.

'After toying with them,' Samax said, 'it hit me that the second set is simply a phone number. I called the number, and it was an adoption agency in Reno. The first set of numbers, I then realized, referred to one of their case files. Right away, I thought, oh my god, Bel must have had a child and put it up for adoption. Why else would she have that number? At first, the agency wouldn't give me any information about the file. Quite properly. But I have a few connections in this state, and eventually I got to see that file. You can judge if that was the right or wrong thing to do. But the file led me to the County Clerk's office you yourself visited, where I found your birth certificate.' He put his hand on my shoulder. 'And here you are, Enzo. Probably with as many questions as I had when I first saw all this, but I don't know much more than I've told you. The other circumstances around Bel's putting you up for adoption are still in the dark for me. I know now when and where it happened, and then who adopted you, but not much more.'

I took all this in wide-eyed, hanging on his every word, my lungs seemingly frozen. When I drew my breath again, I said, 'So the adoption records didn't say who my real father was.'

He shook his head, not surprised at the question. 'They read *unknown*, just like your birth certificate.'

I looked hard again at those numbers, camouflaged and circumscribed by other numbers, as if I might find some further meaning in them.

Samax seemed to anticipate my thoughts. 'We'll never know whether or not Bel left those numbers there as a deliberate clue,' he said. 'I tend to doubt it — maybe because it took me ten years to decipher them. But certainly, subconsciously, she must have known she was leaving them there . . .'

'You mean, she wanted you to find me.'

He smiled faintly. 'I think we can say now that she would have been pleased I did find you.' He locked the chest after returning all the contents, including the bankbook, except for the red pen and pendant. 'You can have these other things someday, if you want them. But the pendant and the pen I'd like you to have now. That bird on the pendant is the desert hummingbird, sacred to the Zunis. The pendant was made by a craftsman at the Zuni pueblo, and Bel cherished it, wore it all the time. The pen is one I gave her many years ago.'

When I returned to my room, I examined the hummingbird for a long time, running my finger over it, imagining the smooth side of the pendant pressed to my mother's chest. The pen I filled from the inkwell on my desk, and after holding the tip poised above a sheet of paper for a long moment, I signed *Enzo Samax*. Then, just below it, I signed *Bel Samax*, as I imagined my mother would have signed her name. It would be several years before I saw what her handwriting actually looked like.

Samax was a man of fixed habits. He woke at five o'clock punctually, swam a dozen laps in the pool, did his Qigong regimen (the eighteen ancient 'stork' movements that direct vital energy), spent twenty minutes in the sauna, and then was served his customary breakfast: strong maté tea with a sliver of lime, a pint of mixed fruit juices, fresh figs with yogurt, and amaranth toast with jam. (My suspicion that Desirée was Samax's daughter truly began when I realized that, just as I dined with him every day, she shared his breakfast, usually out in the garden.) Befitting his boundless appetite for fruit, but unusual for a man who chose to live in the desert, Samax's great passion after antiquities was pomology. He had a full-time gardener named Sofiel – a dark diminutive man, half-Tunisian, half-Korean – who looked after the trees and bushes. Wearing a broad straw hat and loose white smock, chamois gloves, and his darkest glasses, Samax often joined Sofiel in the impeccably tended orchard, digging, hoeing, and watering.

The garden was as much a wonder as the hotel itself: it was a quincunx. That is, a series of rhombuses with a tree planted at each corner and one in the middle. Like so: ◊ Samax told me that the ancient gardens around the Tigris and Euphrates and the fantastical plantations of India that filled entire river valleys were all quincuncial. As were the hanging gardens of Babylon, the orchard of fig trees Laërtes planted for his son Odysseus on Ithaka, and even the Garden of Eden itself. At the Hotel Canopus there was a self-contained quincunx within the larger one that consisted of forty-nine female date palms and, at its center, one male, which was sufficient balance for them to propagate. The quincunx was carried over to architecture, Samax explained, where it was evident in the walls of both Roman and Gothic buildings, and even in the Egyptian pyramids. Once, in his library, Samax took down a small volume bound in red morocco from the set containing much of Roman literature that filled four shelves.

'This is Quintilian, first century A.D.,' he said, and after reading me the Latin, he translated: 'What is more beautiful than the well-known quincunx which, in whatever direction you view it, presents straight lines?'

In the large greenhouse at the foot of the orchard Samax usually worked alone. The greenhouse was state-of-the-art for its day, its daily upkeep overseen by Samax himself, who approached pomology philosophically. He liked to say that the fruit cycle was emblematic of man's cycle, in accelerated form: from seed to blossom to a fruit that ripened, withered, and fell to the earth, decaying, as the flesh decayed, leaving behind only the pit; one in a hundred of these regenerated and the rest dried up, like bone, and turned to dust.

Samax grew many varieties of fruit trees indoors and out: date palm, pomegranate, Japanese persimmons, loquat, fig, prickly pear, azarole, passion fruit, and blood orange. They spanned extremes, like the rambutan and the durian, from the same province in Malaysia, that grew side by side in the tropical section of the greenhouse. The rambutan's pendulous fruit was covered with soft red or yellow spines, exuded an intoxicating scent, and was centered with succulent flesh; the durian

138

tree had slimy bark and was notorious for the mushy pulp of its hard, spiked fruit, which smelled and tasted like sewage. Samax spent countless solitary hours in the greenhouse, before long mossy tables in the aquamarine light, grafting shoots, planting seedlings, perfecting some species and attempting to create unique hybrids with others. (Early on I sometimes wondered if I was like one of his tree graftings, nurtured carefully in the hothouse of the hotel, provided – like Calzas and Desirée before me? – with the conditions that ensured I would produce a certain kind and quality of fruit, as yet unknown.) With hybridization, he'd had his share of failures, but as Desirée informed me, he had also successfully produced a hybrid that had officially been given his name. Grafting cuttings from quince and Egyptian pear trees, he had cultivated a light green, oval-shaped fruit with tart flesh and a triangular pit. In the pomology register, it was listed as *Cydonia Samacis*. There were now three of these trees in the garden, and on my birthday – a high honor – the cook had baked me a pie with their fruit.

'The one he's working on now,' Desirée told me one morning, as we awaited Samax at the table beneath a Saharan pear tree, 'is a combination star apple and starfruit, or carambola. It's never been done, and he says it will be his masterpiece. He's even got a name picked out: the *Samax Astrofructus*.' She leaned forward, spooning sugar into her coffee. 'It will be like biting into a fleshy spice.'

At breakfast, Samax was at his most voluble. And so over the course of many mornings, often far apart, when I was able to get myself out of bed at six a.m. to join him in the garden, I heard much of his personal history in the cool mauve air as the sun appeared over the rim of the desert. Desirée, after finishing her fruit and black coffee, would casually lapse back into her typing, her eyes bright but distant; if there was a connection, as I sometimes suspected, between the words Samax was speaking and the ones she was tapping onto the sheets of yellow bond, I was unable to discern it. In his terry-cloth robe and sandals, occasionally stroking his white moustache with his fingertip, he told me the stories, in no particular order, it seemed, which to this day comprise the foundation of his biography as I know it and played an important part in shaping my own life.

To begin with, living in Las Vegas, I lost count of the number of times I heard that there was no such thing as a successful gambler, even as I was told how my Uncle Junius had methodically become a rich man at the casinos. His seed money, as a young man, had come from a more conventional source – real estate – but in a highly unconventional way. He had had a falling out with his younger brother Nilus – my grandfather – over their inheritance from their father, a well-to-do manufacturer of ladies' hats, amateur astrologer (he was devoted to Ptolemy's *Tetrabiblos*, which Samax said catalyzed his own interest in the classics), and kinky raconteur in San Francisco. After a protracted legal battle that ate up nearly the entire inheritance, Nilus got the hat business – which he promptly sold for cash – and Samax ended up with nothing. The brothers never spoke again, but after Nilus's unexpected death at thirty-four, Samax undertook the upbringing of his two daughters, my mother Bel and my aunt Ivy, with surprising devotion, but mixed results.

Though throughout his life Samax negotiated the criminal underworld as comfortably as the mazes of finance and scholarship, his great fortune was based, not Balzac-style on a great crime, but a plate of bad oysters. Some years before his brother's death, in the late 1920s, Samax, age twenty-eight, dead broke, scraped together some loans for a suburban housing tract outside New York – a novel idea at the time. With a real estate agent and two of his backers, he drove out of the city one July afternoon to look over the piece of land he hoped to acquire as a construction site. In the Bronx, they stopped for lunch at a roadhouse, and while the other men ordered the blue plate special, pot roast and mashed potatoes, Samax polished off two dozen oysters on the half shell. A half hour later, midway to their destination, he was gripped by fierce intestinal pain.

'It was like someone was going to work on my guts with a paint scraper,' he told me while paring a nectarine. 'For about thirty seconds I thought I was going to die. The real estate guy pulled over to the shoulder. His car was a big Cord sedan, heavy as a truck, and the backers were sitting in the rear smoking cigars. I stumbled out and ran through the high grass undoing my belt, and when I hit the woods I got my pants down a split second before I would've shitted in them. I was green, rocking on my heels there in the dirt, and even after I got it all out of me I still felt woozy. Gripping a branch, I pulled myself up and stood there with my pants around my ankles, taking deep breaths. The foliage was thick around me. I remember the pollen filling my nose. And some crows making a racket in the treetops. Then suddenly I got the feeling there was open space beyond those trees. I lifted that branch high, then pushed another one aside, and the sunlight flooded in on me, with a strong breeze.

'There before me was this panorama, a flat green valley dotted with shade trees, that stretched to a line of low hills. It was the most beautiful thing I'd ever seen. Exactly what I'd been looking for – the perfect place to build. I pulled up my pants and ran back to the car, and showed that land to my backers. But they were against it! Said it was in the middle of nowhere. Well, I've always been attracted to the middle of nowhere. Though my heart was no longer in it, we drove on to the other piece of land, and they were dead set on building there. So I let them have it all for themselves. After that, it took me several months, but I got new backers and I built forty houses in that other valley without cutting down a single tree. In fact, we planted two hundred more trees. I made my first million there – actually $860,000 before taxes.' He chuckled. 'Happy to dispense with my cut, those original backers built too, on the other land, which turned out to lie over an ancient swamp. Poor guys lost their shirts. What shirt I had left I would've lost too, if I hadn't eaten those bad oysters.'

This was the beginning of Samax's fabulous run of luck. Following the formula he would stick to over the next twenty-one years, he sank half his profits into further real estate and used the other half to bankroll his life as a gambler, first in Havana, Miami, and Monte Carlo, and then in Las Vegas. Amassing a fortune large enough to perpetuate itself indefinitely, he quit gambling on his fiftieth birthday, and never again placed a single bet.

'Gambling professionally, how did you beat the odds?' I asked him one day.

'Memory,' he replied simply. 'No tricks, no scams, no system. Nothing a single casino ever could, or did, reproach me for. Mind you, lots of gamblers have good memories: how fast you assimilate and distil what you're memorizing, how you read the results of that assimilation, and how you then apply it – all in the shortest possible time, under pressure – is something else altogether. And that's just the beginning.'

'Where did you learn to do that?'

Here, for the first and only time in the years I had lived under his roof, he looked away evasively. 'That's another story.'

'Was it Mr Labusi?' I asked.

'No,' he shook his head. 'Though it was the reason I first met him.' He looked me in the eye again. 'Someday I'll tell you.'

Doméniko Labusi was one of the hotel's three most prominent and permanent guests. He was a man of interesting contradictions: a memory expert, capable of amazing mnemonic exertions, who routinely forgot people's names and missed appointments; a chess grand master, winner of international competitions in his youth, who otherwise had an aversion to games; a scrupulous Pythagorean who was a caffeine addict. And he was also my tutor. In this, his only contradiction was

142

of a Socratic nature: prodigiously knowledgeable himself, he never failed to remind me that the more I learned, the more I was to realize I knew nothing at all. Understood properly, *The Apology* and *Critias* were the pinnacles of wisdom, he insisted – unusually bitter texts for a Pythagorean to be so enamored of.

I liked Labusi from the moment I met him, despite the fact he could be irascible, cranky, and incredibly aloof. He was also generous to a fault, not with money or affection or even with his time, but with that most valuable of rare materials: his knowledge. As far as knowledge went, he was one of the wealthiest men I ever encountered.

The day Samax took me into the library on the third floor of the hotel to introduce us, Labusi was bent over a semicircle of opened books, making notes on an index card. A thickset, swarthy man with close-cropped gray hair, he was in his mid-fifties at that time, a month after my arrival at the hotel. You had to watch his brown eyes for a long time – and I often did – to see him blink. He had identical moles beside each eye, which could be disconcerting, as he once told me they had been to his chess opponents; by falling in a perfectly straight line with his pupils, they gave the illusion at times that there were, not two, but four pupils fixed on you.

I felt that way when he looked me over quickly, shook my hand, and in a deep, measured voice, said, 'Diogenes of Sinope wrote, "If, as they say, I am only an ignorant man trying to be a philosopher, then that may be what a philosopher is." Do you understand that, Master Enzo?'

I thought about it, screwing up my eyes. Then I nodded.

'Good,' Labusi said, more to Samax than to me.

Thus, in our very first conversation he was laying the cornerstone for his ultimate lesson to me.

'Now,' he went on, ' do you know who Diogenes was?'

I shook my head.

'His home in Athens was a tub. People called him The Dog. He was the son of a forger. Famous for wandering the streets with a lantern, searching for an honest man, he claimed he never found one. He died a slave. Would you like to know more about him?'

'Yes, I would.' I noticed that Labusi had a triangular chip in his two top front teeth which made certain words – all those beginning with *s*, *z*, or a soft *c* – slip off his tongue trailed by the faintest whistle.

'Diogenes advises,' he continued, 'that a boy should first be taught poetry, history, and philosophy. Then geometry and music. Your uncle says you're ready for that and more.'

'I am ready.' Slipping my hands in my pockets, I shifted my weight from one leg to the other. 'Excuse me, Mr Labusi, but I have a question.'

'Oh?'

'Why did they call him The Dog?' I asked.

Labusi smiled.

'Yes, why,' Samax said.

'Because he lived with a pack of stray dogs,' Labusi replied. 'In Greek, the word for "stray dog" is *cynic*. At the same time, Diogenes also invented the word *cosmopolitan*, insisting that he was a citizen, not of any state, but of the world.' Turning back to his semicircle of books, he said, 'Enzo, I'll see you tomorrow morning at eight.'

So in lieu of the Las Vegas public school system, of which Samax held a low opinion, and the nearby private schools, which he considered stiflers of the imagination and spirit, for ten months of the year I spent six hours a day five days a week – as required by county law – in a reading room off the library being tutored by Labusi. In all the years he tutored me, we missed maybe a dozen days, and then only because I had the flu or chicken pox or because he had an acute gout attack. And gradually, through his anecdotes and object lessons, I came to learn his personal history, too.

Born in Cyprus, educated in London, twice married and divorced as a young man, Labusi was one of those guests who had come to the hotel for a visit years before and never left. Samax had first met him in Cairo where Labusi was part of a research project at the mnemonics institute attached to the university. Just as he had been comfortable in a desert climate in Cairo, Labusi had found Las Vegas – a city in all other ways so different! – very much to his liking. He played the cello for his own pleasure, usually alone, in his two-room suite, and he would only listen to music if it was performed live, never on a stereo or tape recorder. So he subscribed religiously to what few concert opportunities presented themselves in Las Vegas and at least twice a month took the train into Los Angeles – he didn't like airplanes – to hear visiting symphony orchestras. He no longer competed in chess professionally, but with his memory skills he could still play twelve simultaneous games while blindfolded. With Samax he often played three such games at a time, and on occasion Samax would win one of the three. Labusi always kept a small bowl of rosemary beside him when he played, and stuffed porous bags of it in his jacket pockets; renowned for its memory-nourishing properties, rosemary was his other great addiction. He even put a few drops of rosemary oil in his hair every morning.

A typical six hours under Labusi's tutelage consisted of the following, which more than satisfied, and often astonished, the inspectors who came around annually from the Las Vegas Board of Education, and certainly would have impressed Diogenes himself: in varying doses, mathematics, geography, geology, world history (with an emphasis on the ancients), mythology (Greek, Chinese, Scandinavian), zoology, and musicology. In addition, Labusi presented me with an outline of the Pythagorean doctrines, but under clear strictures laid down by Samax, who wanted me to examine philosophy and religion in good time like everything else, without prejudice. Nevertheless, knowing of the subject's personal importance to Labusi, I listened with particular attentiveness when he spoke of Pythagoras, a Greek born twenty-six centuries ago on the island of Samos.

In order to 'tend and purify' the soul, Labusi instructed me, Pythagoras's followers practiced silence for long stretches, studied mathematics and astronomy, and trancelike drew musical harmonies into the depths of their inner selves. They were strict vegetarians, also avoiding beans (Labusi took his caffeine, not from cocoa or coffee, but black Russian tea), who believed in the mystical significance of numbers, the eternal recurrence of events, and in metempsychosis, which he succinctly explained to me one afternoon.

'Have you ever felt suddenly,' he began, 'as if you were seeing or hearing something with which you were familiar, though you were sure you had never seen or heard it before? "Déjà vu," some people call it, as if it were a parlor game. But serious people, including Buddhists, who also believe in the transmigration of souls, insist the phenomenon represents a memory from a former life. Pythagoras once ordered a man in the street who was beating a dog to desist at once, saying he heard in the dog's yelps the voice of a deceased friend. Our bodies die, but he believed our souls at death enter another human being or an animal. That is why he abhorred eating an animal's flesh. It is also why he said that when we encounter a person or creature who reminds us of someone we once knew, it *is* that person, in another earthly form.'

Because I had noted certain human characteristics, and high intelligence, in my dog Sirius – who had been given to me by Calzas – this notion did not strike me as particularly bizarre. Far stranger to me was the idea that when our bodies die, our souls, still somehow in human form, travel straight to either heaven or hell. When everyone, without exception, as Samax liked to point out, was an uneasy, ever-shifting amalgam of saint and sinner, how – by what determination – could it be such an either/or proposition in the end? At any rate, at one point, for a week, I attempted heavy purification of my soul, to better the quality of my subsequent lives. (For someone like me, who even at thirteen felt he had already moved in and out of several lives, this notion that there were more to come also did not seem far-fetched.) I enjoyed silent meditation, having in all my lives been an only child, listened to plenty of music from Bach to hard rock (electronically, alas), and was good at mathematics, but my vegetarianism soon lapsed and I liked Mexican cooking, to which Calzas had introduced me, far too much to give up beans for very long.

But Labusi planted some important seeds, which would come to fruition later in my life.

'Pythagoras's school peaked and then disappeared from view in the fourth century BC,' he concluded his instruction, 'but he has always had his followers. In the first century AD, they revived his doctrines, enriched in Egypt by the wisdom of Hermes Trismegistus, the father of astrology and alchemy, who some say could travel to the stars at will. Out of this fusion of Greek and Egyptian mystical beliefs grew Gnosticism, which is, at heart, salvation through self-knowledge. Something the Zunis understand well.' He put his finger to my chest. 'In short, Enzo, look in here for your gods.'

But even with all the time I spent under Labusi's tutelage, Samax covered some areas of my education himself, tutoring me in the subjects dearest to his own heart: Latin and art history, and more informally but no less seriously, botany and pomology, about which we had long, ongoing conversations while working in the greenhouse or the orchard.

Self-taught himself, Samax was an eccentric but surprisingly effective teacher of Latin. Every evening except Friday, which was his personal day of rest, we met for an hour of intensive instruction. At first, he put me through the usual exercises, with the same focus and rigor he might have brought to instructing me in the catechism, had that been one of his passions. I memorized declensions and conjugations, explored the nuances of moods and tenses, the thickets of irregular verbs, and the tricky byways of the subjunctive. I learned to distinguish between gerunds and gerundives and I mastered the ablative absolute. And there were other fine points to which Samax taught me to be attentive. For example, the fact the English word *desert* comes from the Latin *desertare*, as in 'to desert,' and means, not an empty, but an abandoned place. A distinction which caused me to look at the desert in an entirely different way.

This was the way it went for the first two years, until I had the fundamentals of Latin down; after that, we read the schoolboy staples – Julius Caesar, Cicero, and Catullus – and by the time I turned thirteen, my assignments reflected Samax's idiosyncratic tastes: Sallust and Lucretius and selections from the thirty-eight books of Pliny's *Natural History*.

As with all the important activities in his life, Samax was ritualistic about these tutoring sessions. We always sat across from each other at one end of the long marble reading table in his private library, which was off-limits to everyone except by invitation. The other end of the table was usually piled high with books newly arrived in the mail as well as Samax's correspondence with various art dealers, museums, and university libraries. I was perched on the edge of a leather-cushioned, high-back chair beneath which I often slipped off my shoes. The base of the lamp before me was a jade carving of a sea nymph standing atop a wave. Her body was green jade and her eyes and hair were white jade. In her hand she clutched a fishing net filled with books. Her face was serene, and on some days her lips seemed to curve up into a smile. The lamp shade itself was hand-painted, depicting a vivid seascape for 360°. It cast a wide circle of amber light in which Samax arrayed the books we would use. There were the two well-thumbed grammar books, now bound in green leather, from which he himself had learned the language, the red Loeb Library editions of the texts, and a dictionary the size of a telephone directory. We each had a lined yellow pad, and I wrote out my vocabulary lists, exercises, and translations in red ink with the red fountain pen that had belonged to my mother. I would always associate writing in Latin with that ink and the nymph's smile and the seascape on the lamp shade, a turquoise expanse flashing with whitecaps, which I stared at whenever I paused to work out a phrase in my head. If the problem took me long enough, I felt as if I could hear the muffled breaking of those waves and smell the salt spray in the air. During our early sessions, Samax, in a cashmere cardigan and glove-leather slippers, would quiz me at a steady clip, insisting I write out my answers.

'Give me the third-person plural, pluperfect subjunctive of *moneo*,' he'd intone, and in my large, overly neat hand I would write *monuissent*. 'The accusative plural of *lux*,' and I would write *luces*. When translating, he operated methodically, unraveling sentences as if they were threads he had pulled from a particularly dense fabric. He found satisfaction in translating, I think, as some people do in crossword puzzles or riddles, unlocking meanings, making connections, discovering how an initially indecipherable jumble of words worked in simple harmony. Running his thumbnail over his moustache, pulling at his chin, he once said to me, 'A good translator is a detective, solving a mystery that has already been solved many times before and making it feel like a revelation.'

At the end of each session, Samax would have me read him a passage from some text – Virgil or Livy – that was still too difficult for me to take on, so the sounds and rhythms of the language would become familiar to me. He was especially pleased when I began to translate bits and pieces of these passages, and then to commit them to memory.

When it came to art history, Samax's instruction, like his tastes, was even more eclectic. He was constantly acquiring new works, and in the passion of the moment, it was they, and not paintings or sculptures he had possessed for many years, that he wanted to discuss with me. For example, when I was twelve he went through a phase of amassing all the Cycladic and pre-Minoan stone figures he could lay his hands on. For months they dominated his monologues to me about sculpture more than any Rodin or Brancusi, including the ones he owned. When he discovered a cache of Vermeer miniatures, the discussion of Rembrandt and Titian which had been absorbing us went by the wayside. And it was always monologues he delivered – more like a museum guide than a teacher – hands thrust in his pockets, chin grazing his chest, as we strolled around the rooms in the hotel, where the cream of his treasures was on display, or the warehouse downtown where he kept the rest. It was amazing to me, when I thought back on it later, that I got my art history, not from slides or photographs in coffee-table books, but from viewing the objects firsthand, close enough to touch.

The pockets of mini-collections within Samax's larger collection ran the gamut: delicate Japanese scroll paintings from the Edo period, early Russian ikons from monasteries in eastern Siberia, West African wood carvings, mosaics from Syria, Matisse's pen-and-ink notebooks from Morocco, and Frederic Church's Jamaican landscapes. There were also Samax's Fauvist paintings – Derain, Dufy, Ernst, Vlaminck – which adorned the walls of a gallery on the tenth floor. He was very proud of the fact that of the sixty-five featured canvases in a landmark Fauvist show organized by one of the museums in New York twenty-one were borrowed from him.

My favorites were his collection of botanical water-colors by John White, William Bartram, and William Young. He kept their work in a little-used sitting room on the tenth floor, along three walls in illuminated glass cases. I remember the first time he took me in there, late one afternoon, soon after he had purchased what would be the final addition to the set, a pale yellow lotus.

'You see,' he said, pacing the shiny marble floor, 'Bartram and White were photographically accurate. Their watercolors, often executed in the field, were indispensable to European botanists who were cataloguing the flora of the New World in the eighteenth century. Look at the detail in the roots and buds, the fine veins in the leaves.' He tapped the glass with his pen. 'Bartram was the first American flower painter. Many botanists thought of him as a colleague because he discovered several plants. But, unlike them, he wrote that plants had senses, like animals, and were to be approached as organic creatures, not inanimate objects. Now, look down here: White was a far more scientific draftsman, extremely conscious of painting to scale. His mantra was "exact proportions." He also made discoveries, like the horn plantain and the rose gentian, which – see here – he labeled *Sabatia stellaris*. Young was the most fanciful of all – a real artist. He worked so much from his imagination when he was cataloguing that to this day, many of the plants and trees he painted defy identification. But, wouldn't you agree, his watercolors are really the most beautiful of all.'

I did agree, for it wasn't just the realistic detail and delicate coloration, but the strange beauty of these watercolors that drew me in.

Not all of my schooling was so esoteric, by any means. Della gave me piano lessons every week (and, Pythagoras notwithstanding, I had no talent for it) and also taught me a bit about cooking. Much of the rest of my education, beginning with basic draftsmanship and exploration of the outdoors, fell to Calzas. He was one of the most important of the hotel's small circle of permanent residents, and by far the closest to Samax. But he was also the one who traveled the most, and I missed him when he was gone. It wasn't just the role he assumed as teacher and guide that endeared him to me, but his genuine affection for me, which I sensed from the first; knowing how cautious he could be with other people, it was all the more precious to me.

Among other things, Calzas came to serve as my guide and overseer in the urban world of Las Vegas that existed beyond the Hotel Canopus. By this I do not mean

151

the famous casinos and nightclubs, though to satisfy my curiosity about them, Samax himself had taken me on a tour when I turned thirteen. Years before my time, he had multiplied his fortune repeatedly in those casinos, but he never visited them anymore. As he put it, he still gambled, but with ideas, not money. It was clear that he frowned on the notion of my spending any time in casinos, but he knew the best antidote to my curiosity was simple exposure. With his connections, I was permitted entry to the gaming rooms, despite my age. So I saw close-up the blackjack and crap tables, touched the gleaming levers of slot machines and the chips at the roulette wheels, all the while studying the faces of the gamblers and gazing hard at the scantily costumed hostesses, miniskirted prostitutes, barroom cowboys, and hangers-on who populated the Strip. Samax gave me a total immersion course and got the results he wanted: within a week, my fascination turned to boredom, and as we were leaving the Tropicana I told him I had seen enough for the time being, could we do something else. The next night he had me assist him in the greenhouse, cleaning the leaves of the persimmons and azarole trees with sponges dipped in watered-down goat's milk, and I couldn't have been happier.

The part of Las Vegas Calzas showed me was not one that the planeloads of tourists came in to see. Though I had spent most of my childhood with Luna and Milo in the world of cheap motels, furnished flats, and fast-food drive-ins, I had always had a roof over my head – even if it was just a car roof on the occasions when, pulling into a new city late at night, we had to sleep in a parking lot. In Brooklyn, living in a poor, blue-collar neighborhood that abutted even poorer ones, I had seen my share of down-at-heels and brokenhearted people. But in Las Vegas Calzas took me to two places utterly outside the range of my experience: a homeless shelter run by a group of Navajo Indians, where a nurse he dated on occasion served as a volunteer; and a halfway house for ex-convicts that on Sundays also operated a soup kitchen for the poor. Though I could see that he had given a good deal of the little free time he had at these places, Calzas did not moralize to me about it. Just as when we set out on one of our camping expeditions, he told me nothing of what to expect, preferring to let the experience speak for itself. 'Action is the thing,' he once said to me – about as close to a philosophical credo as I ever heard from him. But even as a boy I knew well that charity was an area in which not everybody cared to act. Because of his hardscrabble roots, growing up on a reservation, Calzas's motivations were not difficult to intuit; Samax's, on the other hand, were still unclear to me at that time. Though I knew that he too had seen his share of hard times, and been tremendously generous to a lot of people, I was still surprised to learn that he had founded the halfway house just after the Second World War and remained its sole benefactor.

He had named it Asterion House, and I came to know it well, visiting with Calzas at least two Sundays each month to help out in the kitchen, spooning out vegetable stew and mashed potatoes to the men and women who lined up at the door at first light and helping to clean up afterward. I grew close to several of the residents, including a one-time car thief named Claude Tsing, a Taiwanese refugee who had learned his trade while living in Macao. Tsing was a thin man about forty years old with a shaved head and a goatee. He wore thick eye-glasses, V-necked sweaters, and high-top sneakers. According to the police, he had stolen more than two hundred automobiles in a single year in California and Nevada alone, constantly crossing the border to elude capture. After serving an eight-year stretch at the Marbella State Prison near Carson City, he moved into Asterion House and started training to be an electrician.

'It's a natural,' he told me, stirring lemonade mix into a six-gallon tub of water. 'With my eyes shut, in the dark, in less than twenty seconds, I can cross a car's transmission wires – any make of car, any year. Within a minute I'm driving away. Wiring somebody's house is a piece of cake in comparison.'

When I first visited Asterion House, it was managed by an elderly man named Acamar. But a year later he died of internal hemorrhaging after falling from a ladder, and Claude Tsing, despite his expectations of becoming an electrician, was given the manager's job by Samax. He turned out to be very good at it, and with May Ting, his mail-order bride from Taipei, he ran the halfway house for many years. Though I was Samax's nephew, they took my visits in stride, treating me like all the other volunteers who regularly showed up. Whenever I did visit, I kept my mouth shut and my eyes open.

If the Hotel Canopus was a house of dreamers, I thought, Asterion House was a scrapyard for those whose dreams had been busted. While the hotel provided a gateway to the strange and the wondrous, the shelter was the place you might hope to land after plunging through some trapdoor of failure or bad luck and finding that your worldly goods could be contained by a satchel, shopping bag, or the thin pockets of a hockshop overcoat. Standing behind the long table with its steaming vats in the shelter's basement, I would study the faces of those who silently filed in from the street, their straight-ahead eyes and cracked lips, their often swollen hands and wine-colored skin. I returned their smiles when they smiled, but more often lowered my own eyes when I saw they weren't going to look at me, heaping their plates as high as I could and looking to Calzas beside me when someone in a particularly dire state shuffled by. During my earliest visits, I saw the shelter as the hotel's dark mirror image, a kind of cautionary alternative reality.

Sensing this, perhaps, Calzas remarked to me one day as we drove home, 'From here to the hotel isn't all that far, Enzo. On this earth, no one place, and no condition of life, is very far from any other. There is a Zuni saying, that the distance between the living and the dead is thinner than a strand of hair.'

Around this time Calzas told me that Azu, Yal, and much of the hotel's kitchen staff were also ex-cons. Samax had a soft spot in this area, and if Dolores had not insisted otherwise, every worker at the hotel might have been a parolee or other graduate of the penal system.

It was Calzas who, when he wasn't busy reinforcing my social conscience, also saw to my athletic pursuits. Our trips into the vast wilds of desert and mountain around Las Vegas are among my most cherished memories. In a household humming with intellectual activity, and crowded with some exclusively mental personalities, Calzas was the sole natural athlete with a powerful connection to his physical self. No slouch in other areas – from his esoteric sensibility as an architect to his fine eye for antiquities as Samax's trusted agent – he seemed constitutionally unable to remain sedentary very long. And so it naturally fell to him, a man nearly forty years Samax's junior, to teach me the fine art of archery, the essentials of rock climbing, and a half dozen swimming strokes. For hours at a time we would also play catch with a baseball and hit one another high flies or kick a soccer ball around on the hotel's enormous lawn. Milo had been woefully unathletic, and considered sports a waste of time – though he was a consummate time-waster and procrastinator himself – so Calzas's athleticism was that much more significant for me. Undergoing a steady bombardment of intellectual stimuli, I needed plenty of physical activity to keep myself in balance. Not to mention the fact that I was an athletic kid myself, with energy to burn, exhilarated by competition and sheer exertion. Early on, I came to seek Calzas's approval as much as I sought Samax's. And though a man of few words, Calzas was unstinting in his encouragement of me.

I realized just how much he cared about me when, on my eleventh birthday, he made me a present of Sirius. The bond we formed at that time is one that was never broken. Sirius was a mixed breed, part German shepherd, part Labrador, and a small part wolf, according to Calzas. Jet black, with small white markings on his muzzle and underbelly, Sirius had pale gray irises with white striations, unusual for a dog with his coloring. He was a stray whom Calzas had found in New Mexico on the tortuous foot trail that wound up the steep mesa to the ancient sky-city of Acoma. Acoma was one of the seven desert cities of the Zuni Indians, not far from Mesita, where Calzas himself had been born. Calzas told me that though Sirius was nearly starved and dehydrated, he was also alert, and had barked at him from atop the pyramid of rocks where he was lying on his side.

'No way he could have climbed up there, even if he wasn't so weak,' Calzas had said to me, shaking his head. 'It was as if he had dropped from the sky.'

When I asked him how he knew Sirius was part wolf, he said, 'That's easy. He never comes to us in a straight line when he's called. That's the wolf in him. It's nothing to be scared of. There's a poem that says, "A wolf is a dog without a master."'

And, it was true, as a puppy and then a grown dog Sirius had never followed a straight line to me when I summoned him. In my room at night he slept on a black mat by the southwest window, and often when I awoke I found him sitting very still beneath the telescope gazing out at the sky over the desert. We often walked into the desert together, and from the very first, no matter what he was doing at the time, Sirius always ran back to sit beside me and watch the sun set. With his calm, intelligent eyes, he sought out the moon and the stars at nightfall. Rather than bay at the moon, he seemed to study it, though he barked at meteor showers, eclipses, and the occasional comet we witnessed.

Calzas had surprised me with Sirius the first time we went camping together. It was the first of many such trips into the desert or the mountains in which Calzas instructed me on how to live in the wilderness. First I learned to identify plants and animals, to read weather conditions, and to travel with or without a compass.

Then he taught me how to extract water, not only from cacti, but also, with a blunt knife, from the fissures in cave walls where moss was visible; how to sleep in the rain with only a poncho and remain absolutely dry; and how to start a fire, not with two sticks (as in cowboy movies), but with a piece of string or a shoelace. This was a whole new world for me, infinitely fascinating, though I wasn't sure when in my later life I might be called on to walk ten miles in the Mojave carrying a thirty-pound backpack without taking a sip of water, or to sleep perched on a rock ledge as I did with Calzas in a canyon of the Painted Desert. But, then, I learned a great many things from various people at the Hotel Canopus which at the time seemed unrelated to what I imagined – however vaguely – my life might become.

On that first camping trip, we were heading for the Eldorado Mountains, southeast of Las Vegas. We had put on thick-soled hiking boots and canvas jackets and wide-brimmed hats that would shield us from blinding sunlight in the stark white canyons. It was dawn, still cool, and the eastern sky was shot through with pink and orange flames. I came out to Calzas's jeep, and there among the provisions packed neatly in the back was a flat, handwoven basket in which a puppy was curled up on a red blanket. Over breakfast, Calzas had been quiet as usual, even poker-faced, but now he was smiling broadly as I vaulted into the jeep and took the puppy up in my arms. He put both paws on my left shoulder and rested his head against my own, breathing warmly onto my neck.

'His name is Sirius,' Calzas said. 'And he's all yours now.'

That night in the mountains, after the three of us had eaten by the fire under a half-moon, Sirius curled up inside the crook of my arm in my small tent, his fur sweet-smelling and soft, just as he would curl up in my bed at the hotel for the next few months, until he got too big and started sleeping on his mat.

Because I was not only privately tutored, but was the

only child at the Hotel Canopus, Samax had the good sense to ensure that I had the opportunity, if I wanted it, to play with other boys. I played second base for a Little League team – but only for a single season. And I had the chance to play games and roughhouse with various boys whom Samax brought out to the hotel as my guests, to sleep over or spend the day. Invariably these playmates were the sons and grandsons of people with whom Samax had business or civic connections. I didn't become close friends with any of them, but then, even in Brooklyn I had lots of acquaintances but no best friend. And I confirmed what I had intuited there: I wasn't the Little League type. My teammates thought me a good fielder and base stealer, a player who, while not unfriendly, very much kept to himself. In fact, among other children I was as shy as I was outgoing in the company of adults. That's just the way I was after my years with Luna and Milo.

Needless to say, after school-hopping for a couple of years with them, and attending a public elementary school in Brooklyn, this flood of learning could have been overwhelming had it not been informed by Samax's eclectic curiosity and the general passion for knowledge around the hotel. In a place where nine in ten residents were engaged in idiosyncratic, often mystical, research projects, the intensity of my own education soon felt perfectly natural. And I never for a moment missed attending a conventional school. In Brooklyn I had chafed at the necessity of sitting rigidly in a classroom with forty other children under the thumb of an overtaxed and uninspiring teacher. True, with my grandmother I had come to enjoy the security of living in one place, but now I relished the more electric environment of the hotel, with its exciting through-traffic; while remaining happily stationary, I could enjoy a variation on the pleasures of the road – as in silent movies where scenery revolves rapidly behind firmly rooted pedestrians who appear to be in motion. In this respect, I realized, I was a lot like Samax, who joked that when the time came for him to settle down, he could only do it in a hotel, among transients. And so it was – perhaps genetically – that I seemed naturally inclined to the way of life he had constructed at the Hotel Canopus.

I also still had a lot of free time in this new life, and in addition to roaming the desert, cycling, and generally idling in the many nooks and crannies available to me, I did a lot of reading on my own from the books of exploration and fable with which Samax had stocked my bookshelves. While the various libraries boasted forty thousand volumes, there was only a single television set in the hotel, in the downstairs lounge. Except for the game-of-the-week during baseball season, television barely interested me, and few of the adults around me ever watched it. There was a small projection theater where Samax had the latest movies played on Friday nights, and I usually took a front-row seat for these. But by my thirteenth birthday, I had become a devoted bookworm, and the sum effect of all this intellectual activity was that years later, when I arrived at college and discovered what was expected of me, I was so well prepared that I felt at times as if I had been through it all before – and then some.

The cornerstone of my unusual education – while not reported to the Las Vegas Board of Education – was in fact Labusi's memory technique, the world of memory palaces. The concept of the memory palace was developed in Greece long before Aristotle, who wrote of it with enthusiasm, as did Cicero and that same Quintilian who so admired the quincunx. All agreed that the classical model of the memory palace originated with the story of Simonides of Ceos, known as the inventor of the art of memory.

'Simonides was a poet,' Labusi told me one day, pacing behind my chair with an unlit pipe between his teeth, as was his custom. He never smoked, but each day he put fresh tobacco in the pipe, and to emphasize certain points of instruction he tapped its stem against one of the three silver rings he wore on his left hand. 'A wealthy nobleman named Scopas hired him to entertain at a banquet. Plucking the lyre – like the one in your uncle's collection – Simonides chanted a poem in honor of his host, but included a passage of praise for the twin warriors, Castor and Pollux, whose images Zeus later set among the stars as the constellation Gemini. When Simonides finished performing, Scopas paid him only half his commission, suggesting sarcastically that he try to obtain the other half from Castor and Pollux. Soon afterward, Simonides was summoned from the banquet by two young men who were waiting outside to see him. He went out, but found no one, and at that moment the roof of the banquet hall collapsed, killing Scopas and all his guests. The corpses were crushed so badly they could not be differentiated, but Simonides remembered exactly where each guest had been sitting and so was able to identify them all. The twins Castor and Pollux had repaid the poet for the respect he had shown them, and in the process enabled him to discover the twin pivots – *loci*, which is the word for "places," and *imagines*, the word for "images" – for the memory systems that would preserve the bulk of ancient thought.'

I took notes with my fountain pen as fast as my hand could fly, filling up one of the dozens of blue notebooks I accumulated in those years.

'There are digital and alphabetical memory systems,' Labusi went on. 'The alphabetical system dates back to the great library at Alexandria that burned down, whose layout mirrored the alphabetical memory system its scholars developed. There is another system based on the chessboard and its pieces. But the greatest memory system is the architectural one. Quintilian's description of it is the best and simplest.

'Take a building you know well, the more spacious and varied the better, including all its corridors, stairwells, and rooms, throughout which, in and around their furnishings and ornaments, you arrange your *loci*, by the dozens or the thousands. The *loci* must form a series and be remembered in a precise sequence along which you can move backward and forward, from room to room, furnishing to furnishing. On the *loci* place evocative images of the concepts or things you wish to remember. Let's say you wanted to memorize the names of the fruits growing in the greenhouse. Having placed the image of each fruit on a successive *locus*, as you strolled through the memory palace you might see a lemon on an end table, a plantain under a lamp, a papaya on the windowsill, grapes on a shelf. The *loci* remain in your memory indefinitely – the same windowsill, shelf, and so on – while the specific images fade or are replaced. Cicero compared the *loci* to wax tablets on which images may be traced and erased repeatedly.'

Of course I chose the Hotel Canopus as the site of my memory palace, superimposing throughout the building the series of *loci* I chose for my images. On the third floor, for example, I used the reading room off the library, with *loci* on a succession of chairs, several dozen shelves, and various potted plants – over a hundred *loci* altogether. And that was just one medium-sized room! Thus, as I expanded into many other rooms, the hotel became as palpable to me in my mind as it was in reality. Gradually the hotel and my memory palace conflated, and I sometimes felt when I wandered the hotel at night as if I were roaming corridors in my head. Conversely, there were times I was sure I had made a circuit of the hotel's rooms when, never leaving my own room, I had merely closed my eyes and entered my memory palace, approaching the very first of my *loci*, the desk in the lobby where Della or Denise always sat. Except that in my memory palace, there was no Azu at the front door and the desk was never manned; in fact, in this realm, I had the entire hotel to myself.

Because at the same time I was developing my memory palace I was also accumulating intense personal memories in the hotel, this duality between the 'real' building and the 'imagined' one would always be with me: alongside my own memories were the facts and figures – the underpinnings of my learning – for which the imagined hotel had become my repository within the memory system. The conjugations and declensions of countless Latin verbs, Spanish vocabulary lists, the periodic table, and a vast menu of historical subjects. With my memory palace I could quickly retain a list of the American presidents, the kings of England and doges of Venice, and every world capital along with its population.

Such stuff seemed routine, however, beside the feats of the memory exemplars listed by Quintilian: Mithradates who spoke twenty-two languages fluently, and the Persian king Cyrus who could name all the soldiers in his army, which was mind-boggling until you encountered Lucius Scipio, who could list the entire population of Rome, and Charmadas, an Alexandrian Greek who could repeat the contents of any and all volumes in the great library from memory just as if he were reading them. In the same section of his treatise, right after this daunting list, I was delighted to find that, without apparent irony, Quintilian offers up the simple bit of advice which people the world over with a minimum of memory needs have followed ever since: when you want to remember something, tie a piece of string around your finger.

I had been strolling through my memory palace – around that very same third-floor reading room – reviewing a list of famous volcanic eruptions in the Pacific, as I sat down to dinner the evening of New Year's Day, 1969. Desirée and Calzas were at the table, as well as two Tibetan monks who had been staying at the hotel since early December. In that time, they meditated in the orchard nearly twelve hours a day, and though they dined with us each night, never said a word, even to each other. (They did, however, teach Samax a set of supplemental Qigong movements.) Dinner with Samax was a far less private affair than breakfast. He discussed ideas, juggling them like oranges, but seldom

162

talked about himself and often reverted to one of the things he did best – better than anyone else I'd ever known: he listened. That night, he was quite talkative.

Sirius was curled up as always behind my chair, and Labusi and Samax continued a discussion they had begun that afternoon, concerning the destruction of the Temple of the Moon and the imperial library that adjoined it in the great fire of Rome in AD 64 when Nero was emperor.

'A great number of Greek statues were lost in the temple,' Samax was saying, 'including one by Praxiteles. But the library was a secret one and the only clue we possess regarding its contents is a passing reference in Tacitus to "astronomical and navigational" tracts.'

'Books of discovery, in other words,' Labusi said, crushing some fresh rosemary between his thumb and index finger and inhaling its scent, 'of the heavens, and of remote places on earth.'

As always when I visited my memory palace while inside the hotel, I felt – sometimes with a rush of adrenaline – as if I were in two places at once: in this case, in the reading room following my *loci*, and in the tenth-floor dining room where we were sitting. And, listening to Samax and Labusi, gazing up at the stars through the skylight, it struck me powerfully that for as long as I lived, I would be one person who always carried the hotel in his head, down to the last detail, regardless of its earthly fate. When the library at Alexandria burned to the ground, it nevertheless continued to exist for a time, volume by volume, word by word, in Charmadas's memory. Who was to say this was not also true of this secret library in Rome. Undoubtedly many of its texts had been memorized, and some would have been transcribed after the fire, perhaps with no mention of their origins.

I was about to join the conversation, inquiring after this point, when Denise rang down to the kitchen for the meal to be sent up. For our New Year's feast, Samax himself had prepared the menu – cactus salad, tomatillo soup, a casserole of octopus and beans, quinoa bread, and of course a platter of assorted fruit – which all of us except Labusi would enjoy. While using Pythagoras's doctrines as a base, Labusi modeled his diet on a regimen concocted by a sixteenth-century Swiss physician, Gugliemo Grataroli, to strengthen the memory. That night he was dining on one of its staples, bulgar wheat boiled with dandelions and beets. Grataroli also recommended calves' brains and pickled tongue for breakfast – both of course out of the question for Labusi.

Finally Dr Deneb and Hadar came into the dining room and took their seats. With Labusi, they were the hotel's longest-running permanent guests – men who had come to the hotel for short stints and never left. Hadar was the man with the oversized gloves and the metal detector whom I had glimpsed outside the abandoned factory where Ivy took me to Samax; Deneb was the equally elusive character in the white suit and dark glasses, reading the book about Atlantis, whom I had encountered in the lobby on my first night at the hotel. It turned out that Deneb always wore a white suit and those glasses, and he was always reading about Atlantis.

Unfolding his napkin, he immediately picked up on the topic of discussion. 'The records of the northern voyages of the Carthaginian general Himlico,' he said in his high-pitched nasal voice, 'off the Iberian peninsula in 500 BC, were lost in that library, and they certainly contained his speculations on the possibility of Atlantis being situated at the mouth of the Mediterranean. It's a shame because Himlico's observations when he circumnavigated Africa proved to be remarkably accurate.'

A self-described Atlantologist, Deneb had spent five years visiting nearly every conjectural site of the lost continent. Now he planned to read all the serious literature he could find on the subject of Atlantis, absorb it without taking a single note, and then, as he put it, 'write a distilled monograph that will be the quintessential word on the subject.' He told Samax and me one night that he was perhaps two years from completing his reading and picking up his pen. Always fascinated, I had heard him expound dozens of Atlantis theories that variously placed the island's ruins in places as far-flung as Brazil, Antarctica, and the Sahara Desert. I had several favorites. One was that Atlantis had indeed been an island-continent opposite the Strait of Gibraltar which sank around ten thousand years ago after its mountain ranges erupted volcanically. Another was that the earth once boasted a second moon which burst out of its orbit and crashed into the ocean, destroying Atlantis. Variations of this story, Deneb asserted, are found in the many ancient mythologies, notably the Bushmen's, whose primary myth concerns a continent west of Africa that disappeared in an epoch they identify as 'when two moons revolved around the earth.'

Though Samax was often bemused by Deneb's fantastical digressions, my uncle's interest in Atlantis itself was genuine. It did not spring, as I first thought, from his passion for the ancient world, but from something at once simpler and stranger. Samax was of Basque descent (which meant that I was, too, at least partially) and many Basques were convinced that their ancestors hailed, not from the Pyrenees, but the island of Atlantis. More Basques lived in Nevada than in any of the other fifty states, and I had heard a number of them speak matter-of-factly of their Atlantean roots. It's true that anthropologists have never ascertained the Basques' origins. Definitely not a native Iberian race, the Basques reject any ancient connection to the Spanish or French. Their language is untraceable. Samax didn't let on to what degree he accepted the Basques' claims to be Atlanteans. But he grew animated when Deneb explained to us that the southern Spanish city of Cadiz, with its large, anomalous Basque population, was in ancient times known as 'Gades.'

'It is Plato, Junius, who tells us that this city was named after Gadeirus, a king of Atlantis, suggesting that Iberia was an Atlantean colony. If so, the Atlantans probably colonized even farther eastward, for alone among

Europeans, the Phoenicians and Etruscans shared with the Basques the unusual fact that ninety-five percent of their people shared the Double-O-negative blood type' – and here Samax cast me a knowing glance – 'with hardly any strains of the A type. That is still true of Basques today, while the opposite ratio is found among Frenchmen and Spaniards.'

At this particular dinner, Hadar took over the conversation, a rare occurrence. Rare because he often traveled abroad, and when he was around was naturally laconic. In fact, he spent more time away from the hotel than he did under its roof. Unlike Deneb or Labusi, Hadar had been specifically hired by Samax during his first visit. But when he listed his occupation, on travel visas and the like, I couldn't imagine what he put down. He was a meteorite hunter, scouring the earth for them under Samax's sponsorship. He was on Samax's payroll because in the course of his travels he scouted and acquired antiquities for him. Calzas went on special missions for Samax, but Hadar simply roved, always on the lookout for rare objects.

I never got along with Hadar, as I did with most of the other guests. He was gruff and impatient, and there was something about him, a remoteness, that made it seem as if in spirit he truly inhabited the cold realms in which his meteors traveled. Usually he wore a blank expression, only his sharp black eyes, screwed deep in their sockets, betraying the fierce mental activity going on behind the mask. A loner who stood out among other loners, Hadar treated me just as he did everyone else. He didn't dislike me; in fact, I doubt he had much feeling for me at all.

Only once did I think I had glimpsed another side of him. It was a simple incident, which might have had terrible consequences for me. I was eleven, and had slipped out of the hotel by the back entrance to go for a late-night swim. I was forbidden to swim alone in the pool, and rarely did so. But as luck would have it, that particular night, after swimming for a half hour, exhausting myself, I took one last lap underwater and bumped my head against the side while surfacing too fast. Groggy, afraid I'd pass out, I began flailing and swallowing water while the hedges and trees surrounding the pool spun around on me like a carousel. Then out of nowhere a hand with fingers like steel closed around my arm, lifted me out of the water, and deposited me on the grass. I spat up some water and gulped for air. My eyes were closed, burning with chlorine, and when I opened them finally, there was no one near me – all I saw was the bleary image of a man's back, fifty yards off, rounding the hedges. I was sure it was Hadar. Shy and taciturn, he was the only person at the hotel who would have left my side at such a moment. But when I sought him out the next day to thank him, he gazed at me as blankly as ever. Finally he shook his head, and in his watery voice, as if delivering a biblical command, growled, 'Obey Samax.' Then he walked away. And for a while afterward I felt he was watching out for me at times when I wasn't watching out for myself.

Hadar, characteristically, worked out of the remotest corner of the hotel: a windowless office at the end of the very last corridor in the second subbasement. The adjoining laboratory was filled with meteorites, labeled and set out on metal tables. He also had a spectrograph, an X-ray machine, and an assortment of microscopes. With these he analyzed specimens for the eight minerals – most of them combinations of iron and nickel – that, in varying mixtures, make up the content of all meteorites. The latter, he once explained to me, are simply the roughly two thousand meteors out of a billion each year that survive the earth's atmosphere and reach the surface.

Hadar subscribed to the theory, put forth in 1800, that meteors share their origin with asteroids: they are the fragments of a planet which once revolved around the sun between Mars and Jupiter. The planet exploded – for reasons unknown – leaving behind in the same orbit nine concentric asteroid belts, consisting of billions of asteroids. About 3,500 of these are large enough to have been given names. By collecting and examining meteorites from all over the world, and analyzing their shared properties, Hadar hoped to prove the hypothesis of the planetary explosion. So, while the two men seemed so different, at heart Hadar was very much like Deneb; but instead of a lost continent, Hadar's Atlantis was a lost planet.

In fact, I thought, pouring myself some iced tea, the Hotel Canopus was filled with people looking for lost things, Samax most prominent among them, and with people who had once been lost – like me.

Hadar informed us that he had just returned from Mexico. Before that, he had been in Australia, criss-crossing the Tamani Desert in a Land Rover.

'A different kind of desert,' he said in his clipped voice. 'Red stone juts from the ground. Slashes your tires. Pretzel-shaped cacti. Lizards the size of dogs. Mountains with names like "Destruction". 116° at noon. Found two glass meteors. Type 3 chondrites. Olivine and pyroxene crystals surrounding pure glass cores. But in Mexico there was real booty.'

Reaching into a scuffed briefcase beneath his chair, he took out three shiny arrowheads and pushed them to the center of the table.

I saw that Labusi's mind was elsewhere, for meteorites were not one of his passions, but Samax listened intently while serving each of us from the platter of fruit.

'Tell us about it,' Samax said.

'I found the arrowheads in a mountain valley south of Matahuala. They're also chondrites. Valuable, but not surprising. As you know, Eskimos fashioned arrowheads from meteorites. Indians in Patagonia, too. But *this*,' he said, again dipping into his briefcase, 'this is a surprise.' With a self-satisfied twitch of his nose, he produced a shiny black dagger with a bone handle and passed it down the table to Samax. I held it for a long moment – it was heavier than I had expected, and the curved blade was razor-sharp, with a six-pronged silver star near its base.

'Obviously Aztec,' Hadar continued, 'used in sacrificial ceremonies. Animal and human. The star on the blade is a royal marking. Like the Egyptians with their pharaoh, the Aztecs had a god-king. Quetzalcoatl. Also had pyramids, of course. Aztecs and Egyptians believed their king was reborn as a star.'

Samax admired the dagger, holding the blade up to the light.

'For your collection, Junius,' Hadar said, sipping his tea.

Samax nodded his thanks. 'So the king himself would have used this?' he asked.

'He would have attended the ceremonies. And kept the dagger in his temple.'

'I have seen a similar dagger,' Deneb put in, 'but of clear quartz, in Morocco.'

Samax smiled. 'I'll tell you about a clear dagger,' he said, sitting back slowly. 'In Florence. For their most important and dangerous murders, the Borgias used one which left no trace.'

'How so?' Calzas said.

'They had a dagger-shaped mold which they filled with water and froze. Then, with a dagger of ice, timing became everything, for their victim had to be stabbed while the ice was still hard. Once it had penetrated the victim, the dagger melted, leaving no trace in the body except a tiny puncture and a bit of extra water. There might be a small amount of water beside the body, too, if the victim fell a certain way. Even today's medical examiners and police laboratories would be hard-pressed to determine the cause of death. There would be no incriminating weapon. And water doesn't hold fingerprints. I'm only surprised it's a method that's not caught on,' he added, smiling faintly.

I knew my uncle had made some serious enemies, and that in business dealings he was reputed to be as tough and ruthless as the occasion – and the antagonist

– demanded. If he had been the sort of man to have one of those plaques with a motto facing outward on his desk, it might have read: *Bend, but only when you're sure it's a way to make the other guy break.*

Later that night, after he and I retired to his library for my Latin lesson, Samax finally told me where he had discovered the memory techniques that had served him as a gambler; at the same time, I also learned a piece of his private history to which only a few people were privy. We were sitting facing each another in leather easy chairs while Sirius sat attentively between us. I was eating fig ice cream with whipped cream while Samax carefully sectioned a white apple on a crystal plate.

'Uncle Junius, what were the other tricks the Borgias used?'

'Oh, so you liked that story. Well, they were big on poison. Hollow rings, for example, filled with poison that they could squirt into your glass when you weren't looking. Hat pins dipped in arsenic, that kind of thing.' He slipped a wedge of apple into his mouth. 'But one of their favorites they could do with what I'm holding right now.'

'You mean, you stab someone with a knife dipped in poison?'

'Nothing so crude. Observe, Enzo, that I am holding a knife *and* an apple.' He laid the knife flat in his palm. 'Cesare Borgia would smear poison along only one side of a knife blade. While dining with his victim, he would halve an apple with the knife and casually eat his half. The victim would follow suit, but eat the half where the poison had come off the blade. Even to the most suspicious person, even to an enemy, it might not occur that one could so easily poison *half* a piece of fruit.'

Desserts were finished, Sirius was snoring softly on his side, and Samax had related a few more anecdotes about the Borgias before he came to what was really on his mind. It was unusual for him to let me stay up with him there so late, just past ten-thirty. Usually at that hour he played a game of chess with Labusi or retired to read or spend time alone with his sculptures and ceramics. Sometimes he got on the phone with dealers, agents, and curators in Europe and the Middle East – where it was morning – in order to set in motion or complete the acquisition of some new piece.

Samax lighted a *petit-corona*, a Havana, and studied me for a moment through the smoke.

'Last year, Enzo, you asked where I had picked up the memory technique I used to gamble, and I said I would tell you sometime.'

I nodded.

'The technique itself is nothing to me now. It was a simple placement method which, because you have studied with Labusi, you would be able to learn yourself quite rapidly. Originally developed by astronomers, it is deceptively simple. Instead of a palace, a small circular garden should be the site of the *loci*. Like the flowers and plants on a gaming table, the garden repeatedly "sprouts" new cards as they are dealt and turned over. Remembering a sequence at poker, blackjack, or chemin de fer became child's play for me.' He smiled grimly. 'It was at that time I discovered my love of gardens. Which was not surprising, considering where I was.' As he laid his cigar in the groove of a marble ashtray, I noticed that his other hand was tightly balled into a fist. 'You see, I was in the Ironwater Federal Prison in Colorado. Now that you're getting older, I thought you should know about this – and hear it from me, not some-one else.'

If his eyes had evaded me when we skirted this subject the previous year, now, pained as they were, they re-mained fixed on mine. It was I who had trouble not looking away; whatever dark and soiled image I had at that age of a prison cell, one thing it could not accom-modate in my mind was Samax as its inmate. With his dignified bearing, it was impossible for me to see him in the cartoonish striped shirt and baggy pants of a convict's garb.

'I served time for exactly one year,' he went on, visibly

less tense now that he'd gotten out the bare fact, 'for something I did not do. This was in 1926, two years before I made my first fortune on that land in New York I told you about. My cellmate was the one who taught me the memory technique – and a good many other things as well. Had I not gone to prison and met him, I would not be sitting here today. As often happens, the worst thing that ever happened to me was at the same time the luckiest thing. Fortunately, I realized this soon enough to make the most of it.' He picked up his cigar and tapped off a neat cylindrical ash. 'My cellmate's name was Rochel, and he was the most extraordinary man I ever knew.' He paused again. 'Would you like some juice, Enzo, or soda?'

Listening raptly, I shook my head.

'I was twenty-five years old,' Samax went on, 'and he was only five years older, but it seemed like twenty. He had been sentenced to six years, of which he had served three when I arrived. His crime was desertion from the army during the First World War. As you know, I served in that war, and in the Argonne forest witnessed such carnage as I hope never to see again. Rochel was half Zuni, half mixed blood – mostly French and Mexican. And he was a crack shot with a rifle. In 1916, even before America entered the war he was a sniper with a small expeditionary force, attached to the British command, behind the German lines in Arabia. Having grown up in Arizona, near the Four Corners, he was well adapted to the desert. He was the only non-British soldier in his platoon, a dark-skinned man, and the other soldiers treated him as they would an Indian – the other sort of Indian – in their own army. He kept to himself, slept alone, and was often sent far afield on solo missions. He was good at his work, and by the time America did enter the war, he'd had a bellyful of it. By 1918, the Germans were on the run, but Rochel was informed that he was too "valuable" to be sent home and would be transferred to the American forces in Salonica. Instead, he buried his uniform and rifle and went AWOL, across the desert, into Egypt. "For one man, I had killed more than my share of other men," he told me. "Others fought for twelve months. I was a sniper for two and a half years. I was sick of killing." This was his defense when he returned to the US two years later and, to his surprise, was arrested at customs in New York Harbor. But it didn't wash. Despite his war record – even the British had decorated him – the judge threw the book at him. Guys who had deserted without firing a shot were routinely given two years, but Rochel wasn't a white man so he got the maximum.

'Certainly after two years in southern Egypt he looked and felt more Zuni than when he had left the States. In the mountains beside the Red Sea he fell in with a group of Sufis, the mystical Islamic sect, and was amazed at the similarities between some Sufi and Zuni practices. Fasting, for example, to sharpen inner vision. Desert meditation which may evolve into active hallucination. Moral precepts delivered through fables and parables. But, according to Rochel, among the Sufis all this was accompanied by ferocious discipline, of which the Zunis had been sapped by the Spanish conquistadors and missionaries. Centuries of occupation had relegated the intricate, cyclical Zuni religious myths to the shadows. So Rochel sailed across the sea, infused with Sufism, ready to return to his people with a vengeance, and instead he went straight to jail.

'And that's where I come in. Rochel had had other cellmates – bank robbers, a swindler, and a child murderer, but they had all been guilty, he told me. "You are an innocent man," he asserted, moments after I was locked in with him and before I had said a word. Thus I became his first and only student in prison, the recipient of some of the fervor he had been holding in all that time. And I *was* an innocent man. My supposed crime was tax evasion, for which I had been framed by none other than my brother Nilus, whom you've heard about before. For all his ruthlessness, Nilus was a weak man, easily swayed. And he was swayed on this

173

occasion – the absolute nadir of our relationship – by his partner, who was also his lawyer, a man named Vitale Cassiel.'

Here Samax paused to relight his cigar and pour himself some pomegranate juice. It was nearly midnight. Through the large windows, the stars were glittering over the desert. Sirius was still sleeping. But I was wide awake, and felt as if I had scarcely drawn a breath for the last hour.

'That is another story, whose particulars I will leave for another time,' Samax continued. 'Suffice to say, Nilus needed to get me out of the way, and he left it to his partner to incriminate me, with an airtight set of false documents, in a scam – a complete fabrication – of which I had no knowledge. I had little money for a decent lawyer myself, and when they maneuvered me before an unsympathetic – in fact, bribed – judge, I was lucky I only got one year. But that year changed my life. Here is the first Sufi proverb that Rochel passed on to me. "If a gem falls into mud, it is still valuable. If dust ascends to heaven, it remains valueless." That helped when I thought about my brother.'

I repeated the proverb in my head, and seeing my lips move, Samax smiled.

'Rochel taught me various spiritual exercises,' he went on. 'How to breathe. How to hone my five senses and clear my mind of debris. How to sleep properly, in what he called "the lion posture," lying on my right side with my head resting on the palm of my right hand. All of this enabled me to travel deeper into my dreams, exploring portions of my past life that had been confined to darkness. Rochel said that he himself had found doors in his dreams through which he could leave that prison in all but body and roam the earth. Less important to him – in fact, almost as an amusement – he shared with me several of the Sufis' memory techniques, for they were expected to know by heart vast sets of verses and meditation prayers. The placement method I used at cards was a rudimentary version of the one the Sufi astronomers used to memorize, from night to night, the positions of the stars and planets in order to record their movements. An astronomer would concentrate on one portion of the sky at a time, but even that is an incredibly tedious task, performed today by a multitude of cameras. The Sufis invented chess, and Rochel taught me how to play a game between us in our two minds, without a board or pieces. I tried it once with Labusi, but he still won handily.

'Needless to say, Enzo, all of this was like a bolt of lightning to me, from where I came from. It turned my entire life inside out. I was someone who really would leave prison a changed man. For, on top of all this, one day Rochel told me that he was close to understanding how to take his body along the next time his mind wandered beyond the prison walls. I had only a month left on my sentence, but he had two years, and he was no longer willing to let them slip away in that cell. "Until now," he said, "I have been here and not been here at the same time. Now I am too much here. I have given them enough, and will give no more." That night I fell asleep watching him across the cell, his long black hair tied back with a piece of rawhide, his eye catching the moon's rays over the mountains as he gazed through our small barred window. Just before my eyes closed for the last time, he turned to me – which he never did – and nodded with a small smile. The next morning I re-alized he had been saying goodbye. His bunk had not been slept in and there was no trace of him anywhere. The guards searched the prison from top to bottom. His few possessions – toothbrush, comb, meditation beads, a photograph of Acoma, the sky-city – were all gone.'

'But where did he go?' I asked, breaking my long silence.

Samax shook his head. 'I didn't know then, and I can only guess now.' He glanced at his watch. 'But it's late, and you've heard enough for one night. Before you go to bed, let me show you something.' He slid open the drawer of a lacquered blue end table and took out a small box. 'The warden was angry. No one had ever escaped from Ironwater. Search parties fanned out for many miles, and all day they questioned me. But they found nothing, and I knew nothing. I only had to lie once.'

'About what?'

He opened the box and handed me a piece of polished blue stone – a beautiful blue, deep but luminous. 'I said Rochel had left nothing behind,' Samax said. 'And while it was true that he left none of his known effects, he did leave this. Now, with all I own, it is by far my most cherished possession.'

It was an amulet, flat, three inches in diameter, with a simple but accurate depiction of the earth etched on its surface, all the continents and oceans rendered exactly to scale. The other side was inlaid with three lines of tiny emeralds, a crisscross with a vertical line through it.

'As you see,' Samax said, 'the continents appear as they would in a modern atlas, drawn from satellite photographs. They were etched on that amulet as they would look from space.'

I looked up at him.

'Except that amulet predates even the earliest navigational maps made by marine explorers,' he went on. 'I've had it tested and studied – Hadar's analyzed it spectroscopically – and there's no doubt about that. Whoever etched on that stone, around the time the Egyptians erected the pyramids, had a near perfect picture of the earth's geography, which would be unavailable for centuries.'

'You mean, they flew?'

'I didn't say that. Dr Deneb can offer you an enticing theory about ancient astronauts, but I have no answers. The map aside, the symbol formed by the emeralds on the other side is a navigational sign, for a fixed star, thought to be unknown before 1700.' He sighed. 'Whatever enabled Rochel to disappear from Ironwater remains beyond my comprehension. The same is true of this amulet.'

'How did he get it?'

'I don't know. I found it under my pillow that morning before they searched the cell. But clearly it came into his hands in the Middle East. In the course of my travels there, I have heard from different sources that there is a similar amulet, of Egyptian origin, which depicts the far side of the moon as only someone orbiting the moon could have viewed it. Calzas and I have searched hard for this other amulet, so far without success. Separately, each amulet is worth a fortune; together they are price-less. But that's not the reason I want to have them both.' He sat back slowly. 'Part of it is that they comprise a great mystery – maybe one of the greatest of all. But it is also that the amulet Rochel left me marks the point at which my true life began.'

'Did you ever see him again?'

Samax shook his head. 'No. At least, not that I know of. He was a master of disguise – altering his features through sheer muscle control – and sometimes I half expect him to walk into the hotel and reveal himself to me.' He grinned. 'Or else I'll learn that he has been living here, under my very nose, as a guest. I do believe he sends me a sign or message every so often.' He stood up. 'Finally you look sleepy. We can continue this some other time. Few people know this part of the story. The rest – that your Uncle Junius was a jailbird – I didn't want you to find out without knowing the facts.'

I knew now why Samax had founded Asterion House and hired so many ex-convicts around the hotel: he was one himself. And the halfway house, I also realized, was a natural outgrowth of my uncle's preoccupation with lost people and lost things, for both the transient residents and the soup kitchen regulars were, more often than not, lost souls, or at the very least, souls who had literally – not intellectually – lost their way.

'Did your brother or his lawyer ever get caught for what they did to you?' I asked Samax as we walked down the hall to my room, preceded by Sirius.

'My brother died unremorseful. And Vitale Cassiel is

still kicking, still a dangerous man. He lives up in Reno, though he has a place here in Las Vegas, too. He and I have tangled again over the years, from a distance, but, no, he never answered for what he did. Not yet.'

Six months later, I was sitting in the desert on a flat stone beside a saguaro cactus gazing at the full moon in the night sky. The stars around the moon were washed out by its aureole – an electric orange – and the silver rays beyond it. From the mountains, a cool wind was blowing. I was wearing my Astros cap and had the collar of my denim jacket turned up. Sirius was digging in the sand at the tip of the cactus's long shadow. In a cluster of boulders behind me I heard a rock rattler stalking a lizard. But I never took my eyes off the moon.

It was 8:47 p.m. on July 20. Six and a half hours earlier the first men had landed on the moon. I had left Samax, Labusi, Deneb, and nearly everyone else at the hotel in the lounge, clustered before the television – the one and only time I recalled seeing such a gathering. But after watching the lunar module touch down, I was restless and wanted to be alone. I felt a powerful urge to go into the desert. I told Samax I preferred to be out there when the astronauts took their first steps onto the lunar surface.

He searched my face, and nodded. 'Go, then. You have your watch? Armstrong will be leaving the module at 8:56.'

The luminous green numerals and the hands of my watch glowed on my wrist in the darkness. It was 8:50. Suddenly Sirius ran back to me, barking. I tried to get him to sit, but he circled me twice, nudging my shoulder with his muzzle and tugging at my cuff.

I got up and he led me to a small patch of bur sage and silver pebbles to its right. He placed his ear to the sand beside this patch, looked me in the eye, then flopped down into a sphinx position and planted his nose a few inches from the bur sage. I glanced at my watch – 8:53 – then at the moon.

'This had better be good,' I said to Sirius, knowing that

a jackrabbit or ground squirrel would not arouse him to this extent.

Then I saw two of the silver pebbles roll away from the sage. Sirius's tail twitched and his ears stiffened. Dropping to my knees, I discovered a circular lid of hardened earth, maybe two inches across, camouflaged by sage leaves. I pried it with a stone, and had just lifted the lid when Sirius, with a yelp, shoved his paw into the narrow burrow beneath it. With a single scoop, he tossed up a writhing creature – a large black spider with a speckled abdomen – I noted with astonishment as it landed and stuck on my chest. Grabbing it, I felt a fluttering and then a sharp jab in my palm. I threw the spider to the sand, and he scurried off into the boulders with Sirius barking in pursuit. Rubbing my palm against my side, I inspected the spider's burrow. Digging his hole beside it, Sirius had obviously heard the insect moving within. The camouflaged lid I had lifted was like a miniature trapdoor, hinged with gray webbing, which also lined the entire burrow like a silk sock.

Soon the stinging I felt in my palm had grown into a hot pulsing that moved into my wrist and up my arm. Breaking into a sweat, I inspected my palm more closely, but saw only the tiniest nick – the skin barely broken – below my thumb. I sucked hard at it, as Calzas had taught me to do, hoping I could draw out the venom, and indeed I tasted the faintest metallic trace on the tip of my tongue. At my elbow, the pulsing enlarged and accelerated, until hot and cold rushes flew up into my head. My tongue was dry, and for an instant my fingers and toes went numb, as did my lips. Then, just as quickly, all these sensations receded. When Sirius lost interest in the spider and returned to me, licking my hand, I felt unsteady on my feet, but strangely calm.

I looked at my watch. It was 8:55. I sat down in the sand again with Sirius beside me. Throwing my arm around him, I gazed upward, and he followed suit, tilting his head back, his ears twitching. The moon was an enormous radiant circle – as if a hole had been cut in

179

the black fabric of the sky. At the exact moment Neil Armstrong planted his boot in the silvery lunar dust, that circle brightened to the point of incandescence, until I squeezed my eyes shut and Sirius let out a sustained howl. And then my head swam with stars, flowing in at me from above.

I will never forget what happened next as long as I live. All around us the velvety stillness deepened. The wind stopped blowing. My own thoughts swirled to a standstill, and I experienced a sense of clarity so acute it was as if I was seeing, not with my eyes, but something in me far more powerful. From the vast white sea of the desert, I observed the equally vast dust seas of the moon. The moon suddenly looked so large that I was stunned to discover I could make out its features even more clearly than if I had been studying them through the telescope in my room. I scanned the craters, whose positions I had memorized in my star atlas. I knew all their names, *Vasco da Gama* and *Balboa*, *Pliny*, *Hipparchus*, and *Strabo*. I scanned their outlines, studying whether they were steep or shallow, filled with dust or scattered with rubble. Finally, I focused on the Sea of Tranquility, at whose southern shore, beside their landing module, I knew the two astronauts must be walking around, crisscrossing their own tracks in the lunar dust, making gravity-defying leaps, and planting the wired American flag – just as I would see them do on television the next day. But at that moment sitting with Sirius in the Mojave Desert, closing my eyes, I felt I could almost see the tinted visors of the astronauts' helmets reflecting the blue sphere of the earth suspended in space, lucent in the sun's rays.

Two hours passed – seemingly like a few seconds – before Sirius and I returned to the hotel. The television had been turned off, but Samax was holding court in the lounge, where champagne and fruit drinks had been served with hors d'oeuvres. A lively discussion was under way about the ramifications of the moon landing. Dr Deneb was certain that the geological samples the astronauts were bringing back would answer once and for all the two-moons-in-the-sky theory of Atlantis's destruction, while Hadar (who scoffed at the theory) was about as excited as I ever saw him, declaring the moon a gigantic treasure trove for meteorite studies, with thousands of perfectly preserved samples strewn everywhere.

I bypassed the discussion and went off in search of Calzas, who had left the lounge. He knew all about the desert's flora and fauna, and I wanted to ask him about the spider bite. After searching for him upstairs, I learned from Azu that he was in the greenhouse. There were two ways to get to the greenhouse: across the lawn or through a tunnel, once secret, that in the hotel's former incarnation led to a cottage which had been torn down. Why the tunnel was 'secret' back then was still murky to me (and to Samax), though it was apparently connected to illicit activities on the part of the former owner, Canopus. What he could have been doing in that cottage to warrant such an elaborate egress – in Las Vegas, of all places, where anything goes – made for interesting speculation. The greenhouse now stood on the site of the cottage, and immediately behind it was the hotel's oldest flower bed, containing dozens of the red and yellow flowers that Samax wore in his lapel.

I always used the tunnel to get to the greenhouse – I liked the mystery of it. To enter the tunnel, you descended a stairwell off the elevator bank and went through a green steel door one flight down. Semi-cylindrical, its floor and ceiling completely brick, the tunnel was illuminated by green overhead bulbs. The moment you entered it, you were flooded with the sweet, tropical scents of the greenhouse. The sudden downdraft of humidity always felt, at first, as if it were lifting me several inches off the ground.

Two hundred feet long, the tunnel was a straight line broken by a single wide loop at its halfway point, where it circumvented one end of the swimming pool. When you traversed the loop, you could not see the half of the tunnel behind you. That night, emerging from the loop and making my way to the spiral stairway that led to the greenhouse, I thought I heard someone behind me. Just a rustle, and an intake of breath. Tired from our outing, Sirius had stretched out on the cool marble in the lobby, so I knew it wasn't him. I strained my ears for several seconds, and hearing nothing more, continued on.

The greenhouse was deserted. In the ultraviolet light, I saw that someone had been working at one of the tables, where the lamp was still hot, but if it was Calzas, he had left by the door to the garden, which had been locked from the outside. The greenhouse was half the size of a football field, with a forty-foot-high ceiling to accommodate the taller trees. Great humidifiers lined one wall, streaming out clouds of mist. Vents that cooled or heated the air, depending on the sharp fluctuations of the desert climate, purred on all sides. There were large, slow-bladed fans in the corners. The density of foliage – greens and blues that swayed and flickered subtly in the artificial breezes – was always a shock to me visually, especially if I had just come in from the shimmering flats of the desert. Seedlings sprouted in glassed-in cases. Grafts were planted in boxed beds that were themselves miniature quincunxes. All the trees were labeled as to their ages, origins, and special needs. Recent arrivals from around the world awaited repotting in an even more closely monitored chamber – a glass room within the greenhouse.

I picked a handful of white cherries from a gnarled Japanese hybrid and returned to the tunnel. My palm was still tingling, and my eyes burned from staring at the moon, but the other, immediate effects of the spider bite seemed to have receded. Munching the cherries, circling the loop, I was even growing sleepy finally after all that stimulation. Then I heard someone behind me again: this time I was sure of it. Another rustle, and a shoe scraping on the brick on the other side of the loop.

'Calzas?' I called out.

Calzas, my voice came back to me.

I stopped short and spat a cherry pit into my hand. I had never heard an echo in that tunnel before; maybe, I thought, the effects of the bite were even trickier than I suspected

'Calzas! ' I called again, and again the name came back to me. On an impulse, I shouted the first words of Marco Polo's *Travels*: '"Emperors and kings, dukes and marquises . . ."' Again the words seemed to echo.

But I realized with a chill that it wasn't my voice I was hearing. 'Marquises' had been inflected differently – too much so to be an echo.

'Calzas, this isn't funny.'

Calzas, this isn't funny, the voice repeated.

'Who are you?'

Who are you?

That was it. I ran back into the loop, circled it, and was astounded to find on the other side, about fifty feet down the tunnel, a boy about my own age. He was standing alone, his head cocked sharply. Shorter and slighter than me, he held his arms stiffly down his sides, his wrists locked awkwardly and his fingers splayed outward. His thin white hands reminded me of a frog's. He had a small triangular face and black hair, slicked down with hair tonic, beneath a slanted black beret. The style of his clothes was completely alien to me: a long-sleeved white shirt with a plaid bow tie, black vest, plaid shorts, and buckle shoes with black knee socks.

He betrayed no surprise at seeing me, which at first was more frightening to me than reassuring. I took several tentative steps toward him, and he followed suit. His face became clearer. Brown eyes, a small hooked nose, and a straight unhappy mouth that seemed to have been penciled onto his pale skin. Over his left eye half the eyebrow was gone, replaced by a welt of scar tissue.

And it struck me all at once who he was.

'Auro?' I said.

'Auro,' he echoed me, nodding assent.

It was Ivy's son. I had never met him, and had only seen a single picture of him, taken five years earlier when he was nine, but even in that time he had changed. His eyes were more hollowed, his mouth even thinner, his chest more concave. One thing that obviously had not changed: the doctors in Geneva had had only slightly more success than their Chicago counterparts in curing Auro of his echolalia. He could still only echo what was said to him, though now, as I discovered, he was able to bite off the ends of sentences – single words, phrases – rather than repeat everything he heard verbatim. This was progress, but the Swiss specialists also felt it might be as far as Auro would ever go.

I extended my hand to him. 'I'm Enzo.'

'Enzo,' he said.

'Glad to meet you,' I said.

'Glad to meet you,' he replied.

Already, I realized, I was arranging the words I spoke to him, however simple, with the knowledge that they would be echoed. I was instinctively attempting to shape the coherence of that echo, and as we grew older, and the words became more complicated, this reflex was to become a strange facet of my life. For despite Ivy's hatred of me, from the first I felt sympathetic toward Auro.

'You must have just arrived,' I said.

'Just arrived,' he nodded.

By then I had also recovered enough to know that if Auro was there, then Ivy was back, too. Just the thought of her put a cold knot into my stomach. I had learned a few things in the previous three years, and I reminded myself that physically I was bigger and stronger, but I still dreaded her. The fact she had once been able, literally, to carry me off against my will was not something I could wipe out so easily. Nor was the paradoxical fact that of all those concerned, she was the one who had least wanted me to be carried off into my new life at the hotel.

'We'd better go in,' I said, indicating the direction of the hotel.

'Go in,' Auro agreed, and we started walking side by side.

He had been studying my face. Though his speech disability made it sound as if he had a constricted thought process, that was anything but the case; in fact, as often happens, his limitations in this one area had made him precocious in others. His sensitivities were unusual, as was the intelligence that was as evident in his face as his considerable pain. In taking my measure in those few minutes – I felt he was looking right into me – he obviously decided he trusted me enough to unburden himself. For no sooner had we emerged from the loop than he turned to me suddenly, his lips trembling and tears welling up in his eyes.

'What is it?' I said.

He shook his head violently, and raising his hand to his face, clamped it over his mouth.

'Tell me.'

With enormous effort, he pulled his hand away finger by finger and in a high-pitched voice – completely unlike his echoing voice – blurted, 'My father's dead.'

'Oh no.' I reached for his shoulder, but he backed away. I felt awful, though my own contact with his father had been so bizarre; what I remembered most clearly about Nestor that day was his bursting into tears, to Ivy's chagrin, behind the wheel of the car. I knew now that his death was the reason Auro and Ivy were back in Las Vegas.

'I'm so sorry,' I said to Auro, just as he himself burst into tears.

He cried openly, his thin chest heaving and his nose running. 'So sorry,' he echoed through his sobs.

Seeing how forcefully he rubbed his knuckles into his eyes, I was afraid he would hurt himself, but I let him have his cry. Then I said, 'Auro, let me help you. We're cousins, you know.'

This time he hesitated. 'Cousins, you know,' he said finally.

And I had learned something else: that in moments of

185

severe crisis, Auro could and did speak words that were not echoes, but only with the greatest anguish – first sealing his lips, so he wouldn't echo, and then drawing the words out slowly, as if from his guts – in that voice which seemed to be purely his own.

He dried his eyes with a plaid handkerchief, blew his nose, and together we went through the green door at the end of the tunnel and climbed the stairs to the hotel lobby. There in the elevator bank, hands on hips, was Ivy, whose Easter lily perfume wafted over me even before we were off the stairs.

She was imposing as ever, in a long black dress, her brown hair drawn back severely in a bun, her eyes locking on mine. Her taut face was more sharply angled; what edgy beauty it had possessed seemed gone. Only thirty-two at that time, she had come to look much older. Any hopes I might have harbored that Nestor's death would chasten her were quickly dashed.

'I've been looking everywhere,' she said, still glaring at me. 'I should have known he was with you.'

'I should have known . . .' Auro said, casting his eyes to the polished floor.

'I'm sorry about Nestor,' I said to her.

'. . . Nestor,' Auro shook his head, stifling another sob.

'Honey, have you been crying?' Ivy said, ignoring my words and leading Auro away from me. She dabbed his eyes with a tissue. 'It was such a long trip, now you need to sleep.'

'Sleep,' he nodded, walking off.

Then she stepped up to me, her high heels clicking. Up close, she did not seem so tall; in fact, at around five seven, she was only a couple of inches taller than me now – far different from when I was ten years old. 'Don't ever take him off somewhere like that again,' she said.

'I didn't. He found *me*.'

'Just leave him alone and keep out of my way. We're back now, to stay. Do you understand?' Her breath, with each word, was like a dry blast on my face.

Almost as dry as my throat. 'I live here, too,' I said.

'And, you know what, I'm not afraid of you anymore.'

With no change of expression, so fast I didn't see it coming, she slapped me across the cheek. Then turned away abruptly.

I was stunned. Face stinging, fists clenched, I froze. Maybe because she was in mourning Ivy thought she could get away with this. But a moment later, it hit me, harder than her slap, that I had to deal with this myself then and there – had to put an end to it.

Hurrying after her, I tapped her shoulder, and she wheeled around.

'Don't ever touch me again,' I said, biting off each word. 'I don't have to go running to Uncle Junius anymore. Do *you* understand?'

My voice was quavering, but so were Ivy's lips and right hand, which she had begun to raise again. For an interminable moment, we stood like that, eye to eye. I didn't flinch, and she didn't strike me.

Finally she hissed through her teeth, 'Shit-for-brains. You'll be sorry.' Then spun around on her heel.

Auro, who had witnessed this scene with horror, picked up her last three words. 'You'll be sorry,' he echoed plaintively, as the elevator door slid open and they disappeared, the scent of Easter lilies lingering in my nostrils.

Later, lying in bed with Sirius stretched out by my feet, my palm throbbing where the spider had bitten me, I stared out the window at the vast array of stars in the sky. I had a lot to think about that night. But I began and ended with the two astronauts in their module still sleeping on the moon, a pocket of oxygen in the enormous vacuum of space, the green and blue lights on their control console twinkling and through the small thick window the earth sinking below the horizon – the first men ever to sleep and dream on another heavenly body. I recalled the amulet Samax's cellmate Rochel left him in Ironwater Prison. Whoever etched the earth on that blue stone had seen it from the same perspective as the Apollo astronauts. Even with all I heard, and often believed, from the dreamers and explorers at the Hotel Canopus – the theories, fantastical yarns, and grand obsessions that came at me on a daily basis – I could scarcely believe what this amulet, passed on to my uncle by a Sufi-trained Zuni Indian, must mean if its dating was accurate. And I wondered if in the years to come I would feel different about it, as with so many other things I had learned since arriving in Las Vegas.

Whenever I blinked, I saw green and blue lights flashing on my eyelids. Like the ones on the astronauts' console. Or the bright pinpoints in ocean water. Or finally, when I closed my eyes for good, like millions of stars swarming at me. As if in drifting slowly, inwardly, into sleep I were at the same time hurtling at great velocity away from the earth, the moon, the other planets, with only interstellar space before me, and Sirius, stirring slightly, still at my feet.

10

Islands

On the twenty-fifth anniversary of my father's death I watched the moon-landing on a television set in a bar in Tamuning, the largest town on Guam. He had fallen in fierce fighting on the morning of July 21, 1944, near a beach in Tumon Bay less than a mile from where I sat.

At dawn I had visited that beach. A small granite obelisk marked the point where the first wave of marines landed. Wading in from their landing craft, half were cut down by machine-gun fire from Japanese pill-boxes on the cliff and another quarter were shot or mortared on the beach. My father was among the remaining hundred men in that group to reach the cliffs and plunge into the jungle in hand-to-hand combat. As near as I could ascertain, consulting the rolls in the memorial chapel, that was where he was killed a few hours after hitting the beach. Alongside his name was the citation for the Silver Star which I carried in my handbag, informing me that before his death he had pulled a wounded comrade out of heavy gunfire and helped to destroy a pillbox.

The military cemetery, at the northern tip of the island, was just as Cassiel had described it. A series of rolling, treeless lawns, it could as easily have been in Ohio or Georgia as in a tropic zone 13° north of the equator. Fighter jets, cargo transports, and Vietnam-bound B-52s taking off from Andersen Air Force Base passed directly overhead, so close I could make out the numerals on their tails and even the treads in their tires as their landing gear retracted. How many times, I wondered, had Cassiel flown over my father's grave, in planes whose gliding shadows like ghosts momentarily, coolly, darkened the grass in the blinding sunlight?

It took me a half hour to find my father's grave, one of hundreds of white crosses in an emerald expanse along the flank of a high plateau. At the foot of his cross, FRANCIS VERELL was chiseled onto a limestone slab. My old name jumped out at me as I knelt down on one knee. I had switched around two letters when I left New York, so just as Alma had become Mala, Verell had become Revell – Mala Revell – the name by which Zaren Eboli, the US Navy, my shipmates on the *Repose*, and of course Cassiel all knew me. Perhaps because I had not seen or heard my former name for three years, it was all the more startling to have it stare up at me suddenly. This was the one and only time I was ever near my father's physical self – whatever was left of it. My mother told me she had written him a letter in early July 1944 to inform him that he was going to be a father again, but he never received it. Two days after he was killed, the letter arrived on the troop transport that had brought him to Guam, and then was returned to her around the time she was presented with the Silver Star by a marine colonel in the Federal Building in lower Manhattan.

I had bought a cluster of yellow allamanda flowers at a roadside stall outside the cemetery and, sinking to my knees, placed it on his grave. Then, feeling as if my heart were going to burst, I cried and cried, first for my mother and father, and then for myself, a fatherless child even before my life began, but most of all for Geza Cassiel, who I was sure was lost to me forever. My parents had been lost to me long ago, but it didn't seem possible that Cassiel, so new to my life – as Loren had been – could have joined them so quickly.

After my arrival in Guam the previous day, I had spent four futile hours at Andersen trying to get information about him. Everywhere I turned, I hit a brick wall. No one would tell me anything more than what I had last heard five months earlier aboard the *Repose*: they could not confirm that a Captain Cassiel had ever been based there, flown as a navigator in a B-52 squadron, been shot down, or disappeared flying solo from Manila to Guam. They would not deny outright that he ever existed, but they refused to state that he was missing in action, as I had first been told, or even that such a person had ever been a member of the US Air Force, which anyway was classified information for someone without a security clearance. That I had been a nurse on a hospital ship where I claimed an officer by the name of Geza Cassiel was treated was interesting, but without his medical record, beside the point. And so on, round and round, from the file clerk in a sweaty trailer right up to the commandant's adjutant in a sleek office beneath a photograph of the president, until I left the base exhausted, past the statue of Ferdinand Magellan – bearded, frowning, whitened by bird droppings – which Cassiel had described to me.

For the fact was that *I* was beside the point, as was brought home to me politely but firmly. No longer even an active-duty nurse, with what negligible clout that position carried, I was now a civilian with a medical discharge – and even less clout in the civilian sector: which is to say, none. And perhaps all the clout in the world wouldn't have helped me. Though I knew Cassiel existed, what the military bureaucracy knew, or didn't know, or didn't want anyone else to know, was something else. In Manila, disgusted with the war, Cassiel had already requested reassignment: that much I was sure of. I could only guess how that request had gone over. Had he been treated punitively because of it? The fact that, in the course of my inquiries, his status had devolved from an airman missing in action to a frankly non-existent person could mean any number of things. He could be a prisoner of war, a spy, a deserter, a casualty in a secret operation, or any combination of those four. And they were just the obvious possibilities.

Obvious to me now, but not so clear when I fell apart completely on the *Repose* and was shipped out to the Navy hospital in Honolulu. Aboard the *Repose*, where bed space was precious and the wounded were being ferried in by choppers around the clock, there was no room – and rightly so – for nurses who broke down. Instead I found myself on the fourth floor of the Admiral Perry Hospital, where my room overlooked one of the brown mountains that ringed the city. There were three other beds in my room, but my sole roommate was another nurse who never spoke to me or anyone else in the sixteen days I was there. Stationed in a small field hospice near Da Nang that had been overrun by the NVA, she was one of only two survivors out of a staff of five and nineteen patients.

My first week, I didn't speak either, and our mutual silences, night and day, became almost palpable, as if we were suspended underwater. After many months as a nurse, it was strange to find myself a patient suddenly, tended to – even X-rayed – by other nurses. The doctors had diagnosed me as suffering acute battlefront stress and depression bordering on psychosis. Had I been a soldier, they would have just said I was shell-shocked. When they inquired about the red dot and concentric circles on my palm, I told them the truth, even to detailing the aftereffects of the spider bite on my appetite and sleep patterns, and describing my ongoing hallucinations and acute sensory abilities. They didn't believe a word of my explanation, and wrote it off to my disturbed mental state. Nor did they believe that the seven stars on my gold bracelet had been forged from pieces of shrapnel removed from an airman's shoulder. They promptly suggested drug counseling, figuring that, like so many burnt-out cases in the war, I had been heavily into dope. They also prescribed powerful antidepressants, which I didn't take. Whatever chemical and emotional crosscurrents were running riot in my bloodstream, I was terrified of these drugs, which my instincts told me would only exacerbate my condition. I had learned a few tricks as a nurse, and so was able to palm the pills, or slide them up beside my molars, and then flush them when my nurse had left the room. I rarely got out of bed that first week, yet my chronic insomnia had not lifted: hour after hour, day and night, I lay awake, my mind racing, my body listless, feeling alternately heavy as iron and weightless as silk. Finally, desperate for sleep, I did allow myself the two Nembutal tablets they brought in the evening, but like alcohol and ganja, they had no effect on me.

And all the while – like steel shavings dancing, drawn inward, around a magnetic pole – my thoughts revolved around Cassiel. Still able to scan portions of my memory closely, I went over and over the intense days and nights I had shared with him in Manila – our meals, our love-making, our fitful sleep – and before that the more fragmented moments aboard the *Repose*.

One of our bedside conversations in particular kept spinning around in my head. Two days after Christmas, the third time I visited him, he was feverish and in pain; fearing infection, the doctors had upped his dosage of antibiotics and administered morphine. He was very drowsy, and after a minute or so too exhausted to talk. When his eyes closed and stayed closed, I waited quietly, then stood up to leave. But before I could turn around, his hand shot out from the sheets and gripped my wrist. This was the first time he touched me. Though his hand was burning, his grip was strong.

'Hear bells there,' he murmured, barely parting his lips. 'Must go. Must go back to her.'

Then his eyes flipped opened, and I don't know which of us was more startled. 'I'm sorry,' he said, letting go of my wrist and turning his head on the pillow. The next day, it was as if it hadn't happened, and I never brought it up.

What bells he heard, and with whom he associated them, I couldn't guess. But later, at the Hôtel Alnilam, this brief moment only reinforced my feeling that he had been deeply in love at some point in his not-so-recent past. Lying now in my hospital bed in Honolulu, I couldn't get this phantom he had referred to out of my head. Who was she, and where, and was that what his disappearance was really about: had Cassiel been one of Sharline's territorial bachelors, after all, who had gone back to another woman, in a place where bells were ringing?

Before leaving my hospital bed, I tried to come to grips with the fact I might not find him. I knew I couldn't pursue a yearlong search as I had with Loren, even if I wanted to; the logistics, in Southeast Asia, were simply impossible. And, in fact, I didn't want to. I knew I couldn't take the emotional roller coaster – not with the one person I had allowed myself to fall in love with. Part of me just wanted to die in that hospital, and I flirted with the idea of swiping a vial of strychnine from medical stores and injecting it. But I wasn't going to do that – not when there was a chance that Cassiel was still alive.

No longer allowed to abuse my body as I had while at sea, strung out on adrenaline amid the daily insanity of blood and guts, I recovered my physical strength quickly. A month of enforced bed rest and silence, with all my needs met, had restored me remarkably. But with only six weeks remaining on my tour of duty, the military shrinks were not about to send me back to the *Repose*. They offered me a choice: a mindless job in a stateside facility, or an honorable medical discharge and one-way transportation home (and where was that?) or to my destination of choice, worldwide. I took the latter, with passage, not to common favorites like Paris, Amsterdam, or Río de Janeiro, but to the island of Guam, which Cassiel had referred to as a gigantic aircraft carrier. The shrinks were stunned that I would choose a place still within the war zone to exit the war, cementing their judgment that I was crazily, perhaps dangerously, unfit for active duty.

The moment I was released, I allowed myself a short

time to take a last stab at learning Cassiel's fate. At Pacific Command Headquarters in Honolulu I made the rounds exactly as I would in Guam – obviously with the same lack of success. It was amazing how many different functionaries in two branches of the armed forces told me exactly nothing in exactly the same way. I boarded my flight out of Hawaii angry and discouraged, and heartbroken as well when I considered that I had been planning to spend my leave there, not in a hospital, but in Cassiel's arms. Yet even before arriving in Guam eight hours later, I realized deep down that I had already given up my search for Cassiel, that I was in fact traveling to that island as much – or more – to visit my father's grave as to touch down in the place where Cassiel was stationed when he entered my life. Maybe it was less painful just then to think of the father I had never known than of the lover to whom I had given myself so deeply, only to lose him.

I wasn't going to torture myself with the miraculous hope I would discover Cassiel alive and well on Guam. No, I knew only that I would conclude my formal search for him there and would then find myself feeling more emptied out than ever. But maybe, too, I would find some freedom in that emptiness; though it was not the sort I would have sought, I sensed it was a freedom I had better embrace all the same, for my sanity.

And so, sitting in the Pyramid Bar in Tamuning in mid-afternoon, beneath a bamboo ceiling fan, I nursed a ginger ale and waited for the astronauts to open the hatch of their lunar module. My head ached and the humidity beaded on my brow like perspiration, but still I wasn't sweating. The crowded bar had fallen silent, and the seconds were ticking off loudly on an old glass clock among the shelved bottles. When the first astronaut emerged on the television screen, and planted the flag, his convex visor reflecting stars, I was intrigued by his spindly movements, the delicate ballet he executed on the lunar surface in his bulky, puffed-up suit.

The patrons of the bar broke into applause, and the

bartender announced drinks on the house. This time I ordered a double Scotch, but as usual the alcohol had no effect on me. It tasted bitter in that heat. Everything tasted bitter. The food, the air, the tears with which I had cried myself to sleep the previous night. I was sick of tears and of bitterness. I was eager to move on the next morning. I had decided I would do what I first tried to do when Loren disappeared, which was to disappear myself. To lose myself. Except this time I would finish the job. Without falling in love or ending up on a psychiatric ward.

Instead of wandering from city to city on the American mainland, I would island-hop in the South Pacific – two days, a few weeks, finally months – on islands and atolls, hundreds, sometimes thousands, of miles apart. I would disappear into those myriad island chains with one clear criterion for each successive destination: it had to be an island I had never heard of, literally, each name a complete mystery to me. And that covered just about every island for seven thousand miles, from Micronesia to the Marquesas. I traveled by air and sea, flying standby on small commercial airlines, bumming occasional rides on private planes, or paying my way on schooners and small freighters. In addition to my severance pay, I had saved nearly all of my paychecks during my eighteen months in the Navy, and it was this money I would live on now, until it ran out.

I began by flying south seven hundred miles from Guam to Truk Island. Truk was really a single exploded volcanic island that had become forty islets and atolls within an enormous lagoon. While there overnight, I dreamed of the original island reforming itself beneath me, all those fragments rising from the lagoon's still depths and fusing into the huge circle that Truk once was. It was also American territory, one of the Caroline Islands, and little did I know when I set out the next morning for the Gilbert Islands, which were British, that I would not officially set foot in the United States again for a year.

I landed in Naura, spent two nights in a seaside pension, then went on to Ocean Island. Only three miles wide and divided in two by the equator, by day it was 100° and by night close to 80°, and the trade winds never stopped blowing. The rains were torrential, coming off the sea in black sheets, and in a ramshackle hotel in a town called Ooma I slept straight through for the better part of two weeks, waking on occasion only to eat a plate of sliced breadfruit and papaya, drink voluminous quantities of water, and stagger down the hall to the WC. It felt in those weeks as if I was catching up on some small fraction of my years of lost sleep. As if the after-effects of the spider bite were finally beginning to ebb. When the rains stopped, I woke up refreshed. I had lost ten pounds, which I never did gain back. For the first time since New Orleans, I had begun to sweat finally; the first few nights it had just been a dampness that rose up across my shoulder blades, between my breasts, and in the crook of my elbows. Then it poured off me, soaking the sheets, salt coating on my lips and crusting in the corners of my eyes. Buckets of sweat like salt-water. But I was also in pain. My breasts were swollen and the cramps in my uterus made me wince. My kidneys were burning, too. And then, for the first time in over a year, I got my period, all at once, and it was heavy, thick black clots the size of quarters mixed in with the blood. For a day and a night I lay still with two pillows propped under my back, gazing at the same two palms swaying out my window. When the cramps subsided, I drank a pot of hibiscus tea and bathed myself slowly. First I scrubbed my body with coconut soap, then rubbed it with palm oil, which I also poured into my hair, dry and brittle after weeks of equatorial sun, letting it soak in for hours before I washed it out. I didn't have to pack because I had never unpacked. I ate a meal of broiled bonito and green rice, drank more tea, then walked through the jagged, up-and-down streets of the town and booked passage for the next day to Tarawa, the Gilberts' capital, where I connected by jet and seaplane for Rarotonga, the largest of the Cook Islands, three thousand miles to the southeast.

Rarotonga was another perfectly circular island – this time intact. A road, constructed of pink coral, followed the entire shoreline – a circle within a circle at the center of which a forest ringed four mountain peaks, including the volcano that had created the island. This was the Circle Road, and a sign said it was one thousand years old. In certain spots, the coral was so polished by use I could see my reflection in it. I explored Rarotonga for a week, and liked it very much. There was a stillness to the island, at its lush center, that drew me in powerfully. I decided that after I saw the other major islands in the Cook chain, I would stay put on Rarotonga for a while.

So over the next six months I traveled by frigates and seaplanes to Manihiki and Penrhyn, to Danger Island, Mangaia, and Aitutaki. I spent a week on Aitutaki's tiny satellite island, Tekopua, which according to legend left its moorings once a year and revolved around Aitutaki, as the moon revolves around the earth. That didn't happen while I was there, but for the first time since leaving Honolulu I had begun to feel free of my own moorings. It was a tonic to be surrounded by – and one with – the vast Pacific. Each time a new island came up on the horizon my heart leapt. I lived in a small hotel on Penrhyn, rented a leaky room over a store on Manihiki, and by the time I arrived on Danger Island I had learned the ways of the islands enough to take the cheapest and most practical accommodation: a cabin or shack on the beach, with running water but usually only a kerosene lamp and stove rather than electricity. When I returned to Rarotonga, settling near Matavera in the northeast corner, I found the nicest cabin of all: peeling blue clapboard with a slanted roof and a small iron stove, it was my home for seven months.

Over the various tiny airports and post offices I encountered in the Cook Islands the flag of New Zealand fluttered; a small Union Jack in the upper left, it was a dark blue flag centered by the four stars that make up the

Southern Cross. That same Southern Cross – the constellation Crux – I could see from my beach. The ocean moisture made it look like a flaming cross rising out of the waves. Only the tip of the Cross appears in Hawaii, but in the Cook Islands, well below the equator, it is fully visible. Sixteenth-century sailors dropped to their knees crossing themselves when they spotted it. From Manilius's *Astronomica*, which along with my other books of ancient astronomy I had begun reading again while traveling these islands, I knew that the only star in the southern sky brighter than the ones in the Cross is Canopus.

When I stargazed, as I did again every night, it was in a sky 44° due south of Hawaii, entirely new to my eyes. And filled with new stars! Gazing at constellations I had never seen before, sometimes never even heard of, was very exciting, and during my first week back on Rarotonga I rarely got to sleep until dawn. Even the animals those constellations represented, none of them in the Zodiac because they were not visible to the Babylonians, were unusual: the Peacock, the Toucan, the Flying Fish, the Chameleon. There was also Scorpio, which for the first time I saw in its entirety. In the vast curvature of those skies, with Antares pulsing at its heart, it looked enormous. On clear nights I could also see the Clouds of Magellan, the twin galaxies discovered by Magellan just weeks after he discovered his strait, on that final voyage which Cassiel had told me about.

In fact, whether exploring the night sky, the sea, or the island itself, I could never get far from the influence of those two navigators whom Cassiel deemed the greatest of all time. Magellan had been the first European to map those skies and Captain Cook, in 1777 on his third voyage, the first to chart those waters and discover the islands that would eventually be named after him. And those he named himself, purely on the basis of his personal experience: Christmas Island because he spent Christmas Day there; and, for obvious reasons, Danger Island, the Friendly Islands, and Savage Island. One of the few books available in the musty, ramshackle general store in Matavera was a secondhand edition of Cook's *Journals*, which I began reading by kerosene lamp once I could tear myself away from the sky at night. I learned that the island natives thought that Cook and his crew, because of their white skin, colorful clothing, and incomprehensible weapons, were gods, the sons of Tetumu, the creator of the universe.

Reading one night about Cook's third voyage, I made an amazing discovery of my own. By process of elimination, I realized with a thrill that the volcanic eruption in 1753 which produced my star-shaped pendant had occurred on Rarotonga. Because Cook never actually landed on Rarotonga twenty-four years later, it must have been on Mangaia, to the southeast – where he did anchor – that the member of his crew who later sold the pendant in England originally bartered for it with bits of iron. So I had brought my pendant back to its place of origin. And still, whenever I swam in the sea, the pendant trailed bubbles of steam, as if it were red-hot as the day it sprayed off a jet of lava.

At the general store I also bought a pocket phrase book of Rarotongan and a glossary of local reef fish. In the latter I studied the pictures of countless species – some familiar to me from Manila Bay – including twenty different varieties of angelfish alone. The phrase book, meanwhile, gathered a lot of dust: though the islanders, from the Anglos to the indigenous people, were friendly, and alternated between English, pidgin English, and Rarotongan – a Polynesian dialect – I hardly spoke to anyone in any language. In fact, I had few conversations except around the acquisition of my daily necessities. At the open-air market and the store I exchanged niceties about the weather, the quality of a piece of fish, the ripeness of a mango; when asked about myself, I replied only with the obvious: that I was an American, traveling from Honolulu, formerly a nurse. On one such occasion, the minister of the Church of the Angel Gabriel, an emerald-green building on the road to

Avarua, introduced himself and invited me to his Sunday service. Built in Queen Victoria's time, the church was small, seating maybe forty people, but with a steeple tall as the tallest palm. The bell rung there had been salvaged from a grounded schooner and could be heard clearly in both towns. I put on the only dress I had kept – the green one Cassiel had bought me in Manila – but only got near enough to the church to hear the congregation of high voices singing 'Parting the Waters' before I turned back down the Circle Road to Matavera. I just wasn't ready to put myself in the midst of any gathering, however small.

Six thousand miles from North America, on an island six miles wide which felt like a bit of confetti in that dazzling, dizzying expanse of open sea, I might as well have been a million miles away from everything I had ever known. Never in my life had I been so starkly, elementally alone – to such a degree that, paradoxically, I seldom felt lonely. In my isolation, the lack of contact with other people limited my capacity for loneliness. It was as if the basis from which loneliness must spring, the raw social interaction – already drastically diminished in my case – had nearly disappeared. Breaking off my dead-end search for Cassiel, I had implicitly broken off with other people. Letting go of Cassiel in turn jarred loose some of the guilt over Loren that had so long weighed on me. Much of that guilt I never would – and maybe never wanted to – shake off. But to be free of even a fraction of it was a relief. In rushing to that particular edge of the world, a volcanic island which on the map approached invisibility, I had also reached an internal vanishing point, from which I hoped to reconstitute myself.

I swam. I dove for shellfish in the lagoons, wearing my pearldiver goggles from Manila. I bought fish and squid and jellyfish from the fishermen, and learned to fish with a net myself in the shallows when the tide came in. The women on Rarotonga fished with twin nets, one in each hand, which they brought together like cymbals, trapping their prey. The black and red angelfish were edible, but I could not bring myself to catch them. Where I did not find fruit growing wild, blood oranges, guavas, and papayas, I bought it in Matavera along with fresh speckled eggs and taro. I learned to make taro cakes and yam pudding. I fried fish in coconut oil on the small stove, or steamed it in banana leaves, or ate it raw cut into thin strips and dipped in vinegar. There was little meat on the islands, except wild pigs and chicken and the ubiquitous tins of corned beef from Auckland. But that was all right with me because I had stopped eating meat in Vietnam.

The days poured into one another and the weeks slid by. At that latitude, the hours of sunrise and sunset vary little from season to season – seven a.m. and seven p.m. And the two seasons are summer and winter, dry and rainy. Gradually, by necessity and desire, I had stripped away layers of clothes and possessions, even before I reached Rarotonga. I wore either a two-piece bathing suit or shorts and a T-shirt, invariably with a straw hat or a baseball cap. When I wasn't barefoot, I put on sandals or thongs. In Tarawa, I had discarded my Navy duffel bag for a single medium-sized knapsack. I bought the darkest sunglasses I could find and a Swiss Army pocketknife, and I traded my watch for a Zippo lighter and a tin of lighter fluid. On Rarotonga my body went from tan to brown to bronze. The sun lightened my hair – it was nearly auburn – and I let it grow very long, halfway down my back. After all those months on the ship, I was getting stronger, leaner, and more muscular from swimming daily and hiking everywhere. With my steady diet of fish and fruit, my eyes were clear and my nails harder. The soles of my feet were toughened, and smooth as teak, from walking barefoot in sand.

In the mountains the rains were intense. The sea winds, full of moisture, hit the steep cliffs and billowed up into black clouds which condensed, drenching the lowlands, before drifting out to sea. Every morning it rained hard before first light. And often at that time, when the foliage was slate-colored through the window of my cabin, I felt the room fill up with silent visitors. Pale and weightless, with downcast eyes, they were the shades of all the dead I had known. My grandmother, my mother, Luna and Milo. Never my father, whom I knew only from photographs. But the legions of dead I had seen, smelled, and tended aboard the *Repose* came in force, overflowing the small room. I had X-rayed every one of them. Looked inside their bodies, occasionally glimpsing in the smoky swirls and deep shadows flickers which I took to be pinpoint windows onto their souls.

To my horror, Cassiel was sometimes among them, emanating dark light. Never for long – I would catch only a fleeting glimpse of him – but I knew it was his handsome features and powerful body. And I despaired when I thought he must be dead. His skin that just ten months before had rippled like water under my finger-tips, his lips, the soft hairs on his arms and legs, his powerful fingers – all gone. To ashes or dust, I wondered with a shudder, buried in scorched earth or in the silt of the seafloor. Or perhaps he wasn't dead at all, just skirting death somewhere in this world in those few seconds while his spirit flashed before me. This was what I told myself with little consolation. My only real consolation was that among all the shades I saw, from the newly dead whom I remembered blood-smeared and torn apart on surgical tables to the distant dead who must now truly be bones and dust, Loren was not among them. In my cabin on that tiny island I dreamed of him still, as he was at ten and as I imagined he might be now at fourteen, but he never came to me in the predawn. Perhaps because he was alive.

One evening near the end of my stay on the island I was reading beneath the banyan tree near my cabin. The moths were ticking around my lantern, hung from a branch, and at the periphery of its light, toads were snapping mosquitoes out of the air. From behind the mountains, a full moon – the last I would see on the island – was rising through a swirl of clouds. After completing Captain Cook's *Journals*, I had found a slim, yellowed *History of the Cook Islands* among a bunch of maps in the tackle shop. Written in dry Victorian prose by a vicar named Ormas, who retired to Penrhyn Island, I didn't get past the first page because of the tears streaming down my cheeks. Ormas begins with a myth of the Cook Islanders about a girl and her nephew at the dawn of time. On his way across the great ocean to Hawaii, the god Maui drew the islands we call by Captain Cook's name up from the depths with his fish-hook, carved from an ancestor's bone. Then he hurled his fishhook into the sky, where it became a constellation on the underbelly of Scorpio, called 'the Spider' by the Polynesians. Of the four stars in the Fishhook, two are side by side, wedded at the hip. One is the girl Piriereua, which means 'the Inseparable'; the other is her nephew. They have fled from home, into the sky, after being ill-treated by their relatives against whom they must struggle, always.

The inseparable, I thought bitterly, drying my eyes and remembering the moment at the planetarium when someone tapped my shoulder and I let go of Loren's hand. He and I had been brought together in that place at that moment by the actions of relatives who had failed us, and against whose spirits, apparently, we had lost our struggle. I was sure of that; but I didn't think I would ever know who had snatched Loren away from me and sent my life spinning like a top.

During that last month on the island, I became restless – not to wander more, but to settle down, however tenuously, and work out my next move. To do this, I still wanted to be alone, but not quite as alone I was on the Cook Islands. Also, my money was running out, and I needed to act before it was gone completely. So I decided to go back to the States. But though I had grown up in New York, and Massachusetts remained my legal state of residence, there was only one state I even considered going back to: Hawaii, the one state in the union comprised completely of islands, 122 of them in all.

On the last morning I was to awake on Rarotonga, after sipping my tea and spooning the flesh out of a papaya, I took a long swim and closed up my cabin. Then at noon, my knapsack on my back and a straw hat pulled low against sun, I set out for the airport at Avarua. I spotted a pair of Cook's petrels, two black V's, circling high overhead. At the beginning of the summer, I thought, I would have been able to examine their gray and white plumage in detail; but those moments of visual hyperacuity were gone.

In my seven months on Rarotonga, one by one nearly all symptoms of the spider bite had disappeared. Most obviously, I began getting my period regularly, more punctually in fact than ever before. Mornings I coughed out lots of phlegm, and as had begun to happen during my stay on Ocean Island, I sweated freely. It felt like my body was ridding itself of deeply embedded toxins from the spider's venom. As the symptoms disappeared, so did the red dot on my palm and the twelve concentric circles that surrounded it. On Rarotonga, a circle disappeared roughly every seventeen days, and each time one did, the red dot faded a little more. Until finally all that remained was a kind of palimpsest on my palm that shone faintly when my hand was tilted at a certain angle to the light.

At the same time, there were other changes. I couldn't hold my breath underwater nearly so long anymore, or soak up the hot sun all afternoon. Gradually I began sleeping uninterrupted for seven hours most nights and eating two complete meals a day. And I was no longer able to roam the corridors of my memory at will, though my powers of memory did remain stronger than they had been before the spider bit me. In spurts I could remember long-ago conversations verbatim, or entire landscapes as I had glimpsed them from a train or car, or the faces of people I had met in passing years before. And yet now there were things that seemed to have been erased completely. Everyone's memory is selective, but mine became relentlessly, and peculiarly, so. For example, while I could not now remember my last telephone conversation with my mother, I recalled in its entirety a college lecture I had attended on the illusion of time in Ovid's *Metamorphoses* including the professor's quips and asides. And when it came to Loren and Cassiel, and the brief intersections of their lives with mine – I had spent a matter of days with each of them – I had total recall. Every scent and gesture, every word and hesitation. Many times I relived that final hour with Loren at the planetarium and my last night with Cassiel at the Hôtel Alnilam, attempting to excavate clues about the riddles of their disappearances. But I never found answers there – just more pain.

Altogether the venom of the *Ummidia Stellarum* had affected me in full force for over two and a half years, from December 14, 1967, when I was bitten in New Orleans, to August 2, 1970, when I left the Cook Islands. I was twenty-five years old, and I would remain forever altered by that bite. Not only in the way my memory worked, but also in the magnetic attraction I continued to feel toward the stars – less obsessive, perhaps, but no less powerful – which did not abate. Zaren Eboli had told me that the effects of the venom could last up to three years, during which time much that was false and illusory in me would be stripped away; back in New Orleans I didn't understand the full implications of this, and on that torrid August day, walking along the coral road to Avarua, I was just beginning to grasp them. I little knew that the bite had affected me in ways of which I was not yet aware.

There was one runway at the airport – a squat shingled building with a corrugated roof – and one scheduled turboprop flight a day in and out of Auckland, where I would connect with a jumbo jet for Honolulu. Only two other passengers were aboard that day, Australians in cowboy hats, as we took off into a blindingly blue sky.

On my wrist I wore Cassiel's bracelet and around my neck my pendant.

The previous morning, I had climbed the rough mountain to the summit of the island's dormant volcano, intending to hurl my pendant into its brush-filled crater. In traveling with me all the way from Savannah, Georgia, the pendant had, over the course of two hundred years, by way of sloop, schooner, prop plane, and jet transport, circumnavigated the globe, and it seemed fitting I should now return it permanently to its source. But at the last moment I balked. There was an appealing symmetry in returning it (which I thought Cassiel, a student of circumnavigation, would have appreciated), but it had occurred to me suddenly that while one part of my own journey with that pendant might be completed, the pendant still had places to go, with or without me, outside the circle that began and ended with the volcano. Where exactly, and with whom, I didn't know, but I was sure it would be wrong to leave it in that crater. Had that volcano still been active, had I been tossing the pendant into the molten lava it once was, I might have felt different. But who was to say, after all, that it was preferable for things, or people, to return to their origins rather than to get as far away from them as circumstances and luck – good and bad – allowed? Maybe that was easy for me to say because, even if I wanted to, I had nothing and no one to go back to. But as the plane hummed out over the open sea, I tucked my pendant into my shirt and was glad it was there.

Of one thing I was certain. Over the previous year, first instinctively, unconsciously, and then by design, I had begun a pattern, choosing to live on islands, and only islands, as I knew now I would do, not just for the next few months, but for the rest of my life.

11

The Sky-City

Columbus Day 1971 has always occupied a bright niche in my memory on account of an event unrelated to Christopher Columbus. Columbus had taught all Americans, including me – who as a boy kept his *Journals* alongside those of Cook and Drake – that the most spectacular discoveries are often stumbled on, rather than planned: in seeking the East Indies, you might well end up inventing the West Indies. I was to learn this lesson again on that particular October 12, in Room 512 at the Hotel Canopus, when making a different sort of discovery, no less exciting for me: sometime around midnight, on a silk-sheeted bed in the blood-warm glow of lamps with red bulbs, I had lost my virginity. It was an event I had avidly awaited, but despite the numerous, increasingly complex erotic scenarios I had spun out in my imagination over the previous two years, I was deeply surprised at the way things actually turned out – not only by the timing, but the identity of my partner, with whom, even an hour earlier, I would never have suspected I would find myself naked, head whirling, being pulled on top of her.

The evening had begun with two other unexpected events. At dinner, to most everyone's astonishment, Dr Deneb announced that at long last he was prepared to begin writing his monograph on Atlantis. All research was completed, all sources exhausted, and he had drawn his conclusion, which he claimed – and his immodesty was so devoid of arrogance, so natural, that it seemed almost charming – would be the definitive one.

'Will my monograph be long?' he said, echoing Labusi's question. 'Absolutely not. I need no more than one hundred fifty pages to make my case.'

'And will you tell us on which theory you finally settled?' Samax asked calmly, serving himself pimento salad.

'For that you will all have to wait. Even you, Junius. Just as I will not open another book on the subject while I am composing my monograph, I must not talk out my ideas, deflating them before they come alive on the page.'

'Fair enough,' Samax nodded.

'So when will we be able to read your conclusions?' Labusi asked, tucking his napkin into his collar and smoothing it down the front of his shirt.

'In four years. No more or less.' Deneb inhaled deeply and tapped the frame of his dark glasses. 'Which brings me to one sad offshoot of this good news. For the complete solitude this task requires, I must leave the hotel during that time.'

Now even Samax was surprised. 'Surely you've enjoyed plenty of solitude here.'

'Completely. These ten years could never have been so productive anywhere else. For that I will always be grateful. But now I must carve out a harsher solitude for myself. No convivial meals, no stimulating companions – just a room with a table and simple fare.'

'A monastery?' Labusi said.

'Or a prison,' Samax murmured.

'A little of both,' Deneb chuckled. 'I shall secure lodgings on a tiny island off Amorgós in the Aegean Sea. It was a garrison for the Greek Navy after the First World War. Then it became a prison island. Now they rent rooms under conditions so spartan it scares off any misguided tourists. In three years I'll be back,' he concluded.

'And you'll be welcome,' Samax said, raising his glass of hibiscus tea.

'Here, here,' drawled the man beside me, one of the hotel's newest 'permanent' guests, raising his own glass with his four-fingered, pinkieless hand.

Zaren Eboli, whose specialty was spiders, had been summoned by Samax two years earlier when the after-effects of my spider bite began manifesting themselves. For three weeks he treated me, and then, at Samax's invitation, transported his laboratory from New Orleans to a space adjacent to Hadar's in the subbasement of the hotel. Samax told him he could pursue his research under the roof of the hotel for as long as he needed; Eboli had never spent any time out west, and he was very excited by this open-ended invitation. 'In three years,' he declared, 'I should be able to collect specimens representing eighty percent of the species in this region.' And so to the eclectic roster of studies at the Hotel Canopus – Atlantology, meteoritics, pomology, and mnemonics – was added arachnology.

At fifteen, I was already a good six inches taller than Eboli. Stooped, with thick tinted spectacles, he wore a goatee which had gone nearly all white, like his long hair. His crow's-feet were deep and his brow jaggedly furrowed. He always wore Turkish slippers and a black velvet smoking jacket to dinner, and aside from his daily field trips into the desert, his most frequent excursions from the hotel were to hear jazz bands and quartets on the Strip. Often Auro and I listened to him play the piano in the lounge, which he invariably did after dinner.

I was fascinated by Eboli's proficiency with only eight fingers, but Auro, increasingly obsessed with music – possessing near perfect pitch, he could imitate any instrument – was enchanted by Eboli on every level. Though excruciatingly shy with the other guests, from whom he fled on sight, Auro took to following Eboli around and assisting him in his lab. The two developed a strong affinity – Eboli, born missing his pinkies, empa-

210

thetic toward a boy with echolalia as others could never be. And in addition to filling the void left in Auro's life by the death of Nestor, Eboli's influence was a tonic to Ivy's increasingly malignant attitudes. Before Eboli's arrival, Auro had been a virtual recluse, furtive in the hotel corridors, merging with the shadows of potted palms, or hiding in the greenhouse and echoing the cries of the birds in the darkness. There is no doubt in my mind that, without Eboli, Auro would never have ventured into the desert, where he came to relish their spider expeditions. More importantly, I doubt Auro would have found his calling quite so early as the musician he was to become – a jazz drummer, to Ivy's consternation, of ferocious dedication. So among the surprising consequences of my spider bite was the fact that, as much as it affected my life, it surely changed the course of Auro's.

It was six weeks after the moon landing that a red dot and a circle had appeared on my right palm one morning. At first, they frightened me; I wondered if I had contracted a strange virus, or a case of ringworm, or if, having entered a state of perpetual adolescent arousal, I had brought on this shameful mark (as the old wives' tale warns) by playing with myself with increasing frequency. Only after several hours did I connect the dot and circle with the spider bite. Three concentric circles in all would appear, and just as quickly disappear a year later, leaving a faint shiny trace that I could only see from odd angles. The day after the moon landing, Calzas had set out for Morocco on business, so I hadn't gotten the chance to ask him about the bite; and by the time he came back weeks later, I felt no ill effects and frankly was so preoccupied with the return of Ivy and Auro that all my other concerns had receded. Samax, too, had his hands full with Ivy at that time, as was to be expected, and I wasn't going to bother him about an insect bite.

But all that changed when the dot and the first circle appeared. Both Samax and Calzas – the two people least prone to alarm I had ever known – were distinctly alarmed. Calzas recognized the circle as the aftermath of a spider bite.

'For six weeks you said nothing?' he demanded.

'For six weeks, nothing happened,' I replied.

'Find me the best – the most creative – arachnologist in the country,' Samax had instructed Desirée, and within forty-eight hours I was sitting in Samax's library with him, Calzas, and Zaren Eboli.

Calmly Eboli interrogated me, and before I had finished describing its burrow, he knew the type of spider it was. He asked me the spider's size, how quickly I had sucked out its venom, and what symptoms I felt. He noted the date of the bite and the date the dot and circle had appeared. He asked me what I had eaten that night before I was bitten (Samax remembered) and what I ate the next morning (nothing). He asked me my weight, medical history, and date of birth. Concerning the latter, we had an unusual exchange.

'December 16, 1955.' I said.

'Really.' He peered hard at me through his spectacles. 'You know, December 16 is a special day in some circles.'

I shook my head.

'It is the day, in 1941, on which Ferdinand La Menthe died.'

Calzas and Samax exchanged glances, and Samax shifted uncomfortably in his chair.

'He was the greatest jazz pianist who ever lived,' Eboli added, then got back down to business.

He asked me some more questions, and then, after taking my pulse and temperature, looking down my throat with a flashlight, and examining my eyes through a magnifying glass, turned to Samax and said, 'He'll be all right. We'll do a blood test to check the exact amount of venom in his system, but I'm certain it will be minimal. Had the circle appeared within a week of the bite, it would be a different matter. The spider is a trap-door variety called the *Ummidia Stellarum*. Because its fang is long, and twice-jointed, one has to work at it to receive a full dose of its venom. That is, it has to be almost a self-induced bite after the spider is trapped in one's hand.' He paused. 'I know of only one person, in my own experience, who has suffered such an intentional, prolonged bite, and she brought it on herself.' He stared out the big plate-glass windows into the desert. 'I have often wondered what happened to her,' he added softly.

'What could have happened?' Samax asked.

'Oh, with a full dose of the venom, many things, good and bad. Your people have used it for centuries in purification rituals, Mr Calzas.'

Calzas nodded. 'When I saw the circle, I knew. The shamans call it the Star Spider. They say some who use its venom often become obsessed with the heavens, stargazing endlessly, and others become master architects – like the spider. That is because the Zuni believe the universe was created by a spider god, and that the stars are her eggs. From each of them springs a warrior who will eventually drop to earth. If you are receptive, the Star Spider's venom can fortify and accelerate your true proclivities, helping them to bear fruit.'

Trying to read his face, I wondered if Calzas, a gifted architect, had ever been bitten.

'It's true, whatever his interests, Enzo may find them spurred on,' Eboli agreed. 'And what are your interests Enzo?'

'Architecture,' Samax smiled, 'and astronomy. Both long-standing.'

Screwing up his right eye, Eboli looked at me with new interest. 'Is that a fact.'

I nodded.

'And you're sure the boy's in no medical danger?' Samax said.

'None. He obviously had a fever the night he was bitten, which then broke: the greatest danger comes when that fever keeps climbing. And, later, chronic insomnia sets in. I would hazard that two more circles will appear – with a full dose you can get twelve – but that should be it. His appetite and other functions have remained normal. He's sleeping regularly. At first, he felt the full power of the venom in a rush, but for him the true aftereffects of the bite will not be symptoms, but influences – often too subtle to distinguish for years – manifesting themselves in his personality, habits, choices. In short, they will become woven into the fabric of his life.' He pulled at his beard. 'And he will always look to the stars more than the rest of us.'

'Of course, if there were an antidote, you would have mentioned it,' Samax said.

'Of course. But even if there were, it would be ineffective after this much time.' Eboli turned to me. 'Did you notice anything else unusual that first night?'

'Time passed very quickly,' I replied 'while I felt completely still.'

He nodded.

'And I could see the craters on the moon where the Apollo astronauts would walk.'

'You mean, on television?'

'No, I was out in the desert. The sky was so clear, and I could make out the moon up close, in detail – even closer than with my telescope.'

'I see,' Eboli murmured.

'Later, from my bed, I could even see lights blinking like the ones inside their module.'

'Enzo has always had a powerful imagination,' Samax said, relighting his cigar. 'When he told me all this the next day, I attributed it to the excitement of the moment.'

'Assisted mightily by that rush I mentioned.' Eboli sat back slowly. 'Enzo will bear careful observation, so that I can confirm my suppositions.'

And that was what Eboli's treatment consisted of: observing me, twice daily repeating his initial examination in addition to taking my blood pressure and listening to my heart and lungs. My system remained entirely stable. The only change that I myself noted, of which Eboli could have known nothing, I hadn't mentioned to any of them – even Calzas.

The very first time I had met Calzas, at the abandoned factory, he was clutching a blueprint, and for as long as I had lived at the hotel I had been fascinated by his architectural drawings. When I was thirteen, he gave me some large drawing pads and taught me draftsmanship, as well as elementary architectural principles. These included the books of Vitruvius, whose three essential components of architecture were: *venustas* (beauty), *firmitas* (stability), and *utilitas* (utility). This became a basic part of my in-house education. Following Calzas's instructions, I had designed small houses, a Roman bath, and a gas station, all in primitive form.

What I was drawing now, after the spider bite, were fantastical buildings, with a skillfulness that startled me at first. My drawings were of enormously complex structures, filled with tortuous networks of stairwells, corridors, mezzanines, balconies, and rooms that dominoed endlessly into other rooms. Fountains cascaded on terraces jutting out from the upper tiers of skyscrapers; titanium caryatids supported a natatorium atop the tallest of these; an opera house boasted a dozen revolving stages; open walkways lined with telescopes crisscrossed thousands of feet above the multiple playing fields of a gigantic stadium. On a mile-high lighthouse a searchlight scanned the horizon. Automated warehouses shaped like beehives moved cargo on and off monorail freight cars with elaborate pulleys and derricks.

All of these structures were part of a concentric city that occupied thousands of square miles; a city that soared far into the sky and spread vast labyrinths underground. Many of its buildings, I soon realized, could only have been erected by aerial workers of phenomenal nimbleness and dexterity, unhindered by the laws of gravity; for example, a construction crew of spiders.

Over the following months, I did dozens of these sketches – all details from the same gargantuan city. For a long time I didn't show them to Calzas, Eboli, or anyone else, but kept them hidden in a panel behind my rolltop desk. All the effects of the spider bite were closely monitored, except these sketches, which remained my secret; the longer I kept them hidden, the more pleasure they gave me.

I had another, quite different, secret, which gave me a corresponding amount of pain. I shared it with Auro, and soon enough it came out, blowing up in my face when Samax became aware of it.

Auro and I got on surprisingly well in light of his mother's unconcealed hostility toward me. That first night we met in the tunnel had begun better than either of us might have expected until Auro witnessed my confrontation with Ivy. After that, she carried through with a vengeance on her pledge to keep Auro and me apart. Though she sometimes dined with the rest of us at Samax's table, Auro never did: not only was he shy, but it would have been torture for him (and everyone else) if he were placed in a position where, despite himself, he would constantly have been disrupting the incessant conversation. Ivy knew that this would have been as upsetting to Auro as to anyone else, but she resented his absence nearly as much as she resented my presence.

Because of Samax's strong attachment to me and his own rocky relationship with Ivy, bad-mouthing me to him was not one of Ivy's options in the psychological warfare she conducted against me. She had to resort to subtler – and, for me, in the end, more distressing – ruses. Soon after she returned to the hotel, for example, she began spreading invidious stories about me to others – like Denise, who had less and less use for me as time went by – and hoping that they got back to Samax third- or fourth-hand in garbled, but still damaging, form. Or she would slander me outright to the chef, telling him how much I complained about his cooking, and in a fit of pique he would refuse Sirius the scraps he enjoyed. Ivy's malevolence ran so deep that I feared she would attempt to do the dog harm, poisoning his food or water, as a way to get at me. And so gradually I trained Sirius, despite all temptations, to refuse any meal or treat unless it came directly from my hand.

But most of her cruelty came at me more obliquely. One typical example occurred about a year after the moon landing. Zaren Eboli was playing the piano in the lounge late one afternoon while Auro and I listened. He was telling us that the hummingbird, rarely more than four inches long, had no song, but produced its high-pitched music with the rapid beating of its narrow wings.

'But what is most interesting to me about the hummingbird, fellas,' he said, pausing at the keyboard, the light flashing off his spectacles, 'is that she constructs her nest with spider's silk pilfered from the orb webs strung in foliage. No other bird does that. The short-billed hummingbird does it here in the desert and her cousin the red-striped starthroat does it down in the Amazon jungle. Different spiders, same kind of nests.'

'I have a pendant with a desert hummingbird on it,' I piped in. 'It was my mother's. Would you like to see it?'

'Yes, I would,' Eboli replied, knitting his fingers together in his lap.

'I would,' Auro repeated, though I had shown him the pendant before, along with my mother's pen, and he knew how precious they were to me.

For a long time I had kept the pendant hanging by its chain from a small hook on the wall across from my desk, but lately I had taken to wearing it during the day and hanging it up at night. Unbuttoning my shirt, I pulled it out to show Eboli.

'Oh, it's beautiful,' he said. 'Sterling silver. Delicate workmanship.'

'Uncle Junius told me it was made at the Zuni pueblo.'

Ivy, who had come to fetch Auro, overheard this conversation – and must have been lingering to hear the whole of it – before she entered the room. She was annoyed, as always, to see Auro and me sharing any kind of intimacy, and with only a perfunctory nod to

Eboli and a hard glare at me, she took Auro by the hand and led him away.

'We have to go to the city,' she said preemptorily.

Auro protested as best he could, the first time I had ever heard him speak back to her. '*Go* to the city!' he repeated, converting the infinitive to the imperative. Then, as they left the room, he yanked his hand from hers – another first – and rushed off, leaving her to stare after him, slack-jawed.

The next morning, as I came in from a swim in the pool, I found Sirius waiting outside my room. The moment he saw me, he put his paws up on the door and started barking. The only time he did that was when we were inside the room and Ivy walked by on the outside, which wasn't very often since I was the only resident at that end of the corridor. I couldn't imagine Ivy was in my room, and indeed when I opened the door, there was no one there. Still, Sirius kept barking when I was in the shower. And afterward he seemed even more agitated, whining and circling me while I dressed. I had grown my hair long at that time and took great care in combing it. When I was through I reached for my pendant suspended on its hook and made a terrible discovery. Someone had pounded the silver disk out of shape, flattening it until the hummingbird was obliterated. At first I couldn't believe it was really my pendant on the chain; squeezing my eyes shut, I turned the pendant over and over in my hand, praying it would be restored to its proper state when I looked at it again. But it wasn't. Someone had hammered it beyond recognition. And I had no doubt as to who would have done such a thing. This was what Sirius had been trying to tell me.

My head spinning, I flattened myself against the wall and for a long time tried to catch my breath and figure out what I would do next.

Samax was away that week, as was Calzas, and I could never have taken a problem involving Ivy to Desirée. Ivy answered to no one but Samax. As had been the case when Ivy slapped me, I decided right away that this was a matter I had to take care of myself. Still, what could I do? Ivy made herself scarce that day, and the angrier I got, the more helpless I felt. When I crossed paths with her, was I going to pull out the pendant and confront her with it? Maybe the wisest course would have been to show the pendant to Samax when he returned, but I was too angry to wait a whole week. After what had been done to it, looking at it now – just having it in my possession – was unbearable. As was the notion of remaining inside the hotel when Ivy was there, knowing I wanted to break her neck.

I had to get out, I told myself, had to get some air. After putting Sirius in my room and pulling on my sneakers, I ran across the garden – swearing aloud and feeling the eyes of Azu the doorman on my back – threw open the garage door, and rolled out the dirt bike Samax had bought me the previous year.

It was a 50cc minibike, with extra-wide tires, heavy-duty springs, and chrome fenders, and I loved taking it out into the desert. Samax had imposed three rules when he gave me the bike: no passengers on the back, no riding on public roads, and no outings after dark. That day, I broke all three rules. Just for starters.

In low gear I had lolled the bike through the garden, and out of the fruit trees, to the lip of the desert when suddenly Auro dashed out of the oleander bushes that bordered the quincunx. Waving his arms violently, he blocked my way, then threw his leg over the rear seat and climbed up behind me. He had never done anything like this before.

He looked even grimmer than usual, his eyes narrowed to slits, and it struck me that he was still furious with Ivy for hauling him out of the lounge the previous day when Eboli was playing for us. Auro, as I came to realize, would put up with plenty from his mother, but not when it came to music. His talking back to her and pulling free of her grip had been no flash in the pan: it had been the true beginning of his overt rebellion toward her.

'Auro, you know this isn't allowed,' I said.

'*Allowed!*' he bellowed in my ear over the idling engine.

And that was that.

I gave him my goggles to wear, put on some sunglasses, and an hour later we reached the edge of the area on which a recreational vehicle was allowed. There was an old gravel road at that point, in the shadow of the mountains, which was almost never used. To the left, it led eventually to the network of roads that wound into Las Vegas; to the right, it came to a dead end in the remains of a ghost town. Not one of those colorful reconstructions for tourists, this ghost town was the real thing, a broken-down mining outpost in which the only structure still standing was an old ramshackle hotel and its water tower. Sometimes the high school kids drove out there to drink or make out or shoot their guns. But there were better places to do all of those things. I had hiked out there once with Sirius, and turned around nearly at once, hot, bored, and coated with bauxite dust. And I had never had any desire to return.

Not until that day, with Auro. The ride over scorching sand with him panting in my ear had not assuaged my anger; if anything, the heat had only fanned it further. And an idea, a means of venting that anger, had entered my head like a spark off the friction between two of those planes of light, paper-thin and metallically bright, that are forever shifting and sliding in the desert air.

Revving the bike, I pulled out onto the gravel road and turned right, breaking the second rule Samax had laid down: rough and deserted as that road was, it belonged to the county, and at age fourteen, without a license, I was riding on it illegally.

The name of the ghost town was Hydra – though there wasn't a drop of water to be found in the place – and the name of the hotel was The Vega. Calzas had filled me in on its history: in its time, The Hotel Vega belonged to the man who discovered silver in the Spring Mountains; to a famous opera singer who came there to die of cancer;

and, much later, to a former ship's captain who shot himself and his bride in the bridal suite the night of their wedding. The rusted, bullet-riddled NO TRESPASSING sign posted above the boarded-up entrance seemed comical to me in a place so obviously abandoned; but later, to my dismay, I would learn that the hotel indeed had a current owner.

When I ventured into the desert, I always kept two quarts of water and a gallon of gasoline in plastic containers in the minibike's saddlebags. After parking the bike in the shade of the water tower, Auro and I gulped down half the water. I soaked my bandanna and we wiped the grit from our faces. The goggles had left wide white circles around Auro's eyes, making him appear even more owlish than usual. He came close to smiling for once, his small dark eyes blinking fast: unless he was accompanied by an adult, Ivy never let him stray far from the hotel, so this was a real adventure for him.

Next, we climbed the winding rickety stairway to the top of the water tower. Since there was no moisture to speak of in the Mojave, none of the steps had rotted away, though many were cracked and splintered. Round and round we went until we reached the platform – two narrow planks with a flimsy railing – from which a ladder too broken to climb led to a triangular opening in the tower's roof. For several minutes, we gazed around the wide vista, the thermals undulating on the horizon and the mountain peaks shimmering as the sun arced downward in the west. The gravel road, a long diminishing line, ran for as far as we could see without intersecting another road. Directly below, we could look into the top floor of the hotel through a huge hole in the roof. Remnants of shattered furniture, shards of a wall mirror, and a steel bed frame were spattered with droppings from long-dead birds that had once nested in the rafters. Two hundred feet from the ground, I could feel a slow wind from the mountains, so hot it prickled my skin. I hadn't gone up there to admire the view, but when I saw how avidly Auro was doing just that, I

221

paused for a moment. 'It's beautiful,' I said, indicating the mountains.

'Beautiful,' he echoed, nodding eagerly.

'Auro, since you decided to join me, you're entitled to know why I came out here.'

Hearing my tone, he gazed into my face intently. I sounded calm and logical, even to myself.

I took the battered pendant from my pocket and showed it to him.

'I came to burn this,' I said solemnly. My first impulse had been to bury it in the sand, in an unmarked place, but that didn't seem enough now – I wanted to destroy it, to know it would not survive, buried or otherwise, in its mutilated state.

Examining the pendant, rubbing the side the hummingbird had been on with his thumb, Auro looked at me questioningly.

'Your mother,' I said in a low voice, and his eyes widened even further. 'She obviously overheard me yesterday, with Eboli. You know how she feels about me, and she hated my mother,' I added, beginning to choke up. 'She sneaked into my room and this is what she did.'

He recoiled, opening his mouth to speak, though no words emerged.

I touched his shoulder. 'I'm sorry. I wouldn't have told you if you hadn't come with me.'

He shook his head, not in disbelief but disgust.

'I can't bear to have it like this,' I said, clenching my fists. 'So I'm going to burn it.'

He was trying to take all this in. Suddenly he nodded vigorously and shouted, '*Burn it!*' and it was the loudest I had ever heard his voice.

Aiming carefully, I tossed the pendant and its chain up through the hole in the roof of the tower. We were both startled when it clattered to the floor just a few feet from us, on the other side of the tower's shingled wall.

'Come on,' I said, and we rushed down the stairs as fast as we could. I jumped down the last four steps in one bound and took the plastic container of gasoline from the saddlebag.

Auro's eyes lit up as he watched me.

'You understand?' I said, uncapping the gasoline.

'Understand,' he nodded, and grabbing the container he darted around the foot of the tower pouring gasoline on the stairs, the supporting posts, and the lower cross-beams. He poured out every last drop, and flung the container onto the stairs as I took out a book of matches.

'Step back,' I said.

'Back,' he said, prancing backward in his strangely hip-hop fashion, stork-like, with such light steps it was as if he were weightless.

I only needed to strike a single match: the flames shot up with a hard flapping sound, nearly knocking me off my feet. When I reached him, Auro yanked me even farther back. In thin sheets the fire climbed the tower's skeleton framework and its winding stairway, biting into the parched wood, crackling like gunfire. I was surprised how quickly it climbed. The rising hot desert air sucked the flames upward, vortex-like. It was a beautiful fire, gold and red in the blazing sunlight as it solidified into an evenly burning column which, to Auro and me, a hundred feet away, emanated the heat of an open furnace. Our cheeks and arms reddened, tears and dust smudged our eyes, and only later did I discover how badly my eyebrows and eyelashes had been singed in that initial burst of flames.

Shoulder to shoulder we watched the fire dance the last few feet to the tower's summit, its plume of smoke now nearly the same height as the tower itself. Within minutes the fire engulfed the big wooden tank that had once held the precious piped-in mountain water, jagged flames whipping around on the conical roof. Suddenly, without my saying a word, Auro cried out, 'Look!' In fact, I had also seen what he was pointing at, and just as it had impelled him to speak, the sight turned my knees to jelly. Darting from the opening into which I had thrown the pendant a bird had flown free of the tower.

A hummingbird. Silver, leaving a thin silver trail in its wake. At first, the hummingbird was lost to view in the smoke, then it shot out into the open air and climbed its own spiral, whirring high into the sky until, finally, no more than a speck, it blurred away.

My head whirling, I grabbed Auro's shoulders. 'Can you believe it?' I shouted over the roar of the flames.

For an instant his jaw quavered and his shoulders shook within my grip, as if he were struggling to speak again unprompted. But once again all he could do was echo me. 'Believe it,' he said emphatically.

Just then the tower swayed hard to the right, and collapsing as it fell, crashed onto the roof of the hotel. Something I hadn't counted on – or had I? Because of their close proximity, and the certainty that desert fires spread wildly, there was little chance things could have happened any other way. When the tower hit The Hotel Vega, it was as if a two-hundred-foot torch had landed on a hill of tinder: the hotel seemed not so much to burn down as to combust all at once. Rising several hundred feet into the air, spewing a cloud of black smoke even higher, the fire would have been visible for many miles – maybe as far as the nearest real town, I thought, as the realization of what I had done began to sink in. To citizens in that area a fire – *any* fire – was a serious matter. Auro, his eyes wider than ever, had been thinking along the same lines, and moments later he nearly outran me to the minibike.

I opened up the throttle and we bounced hard on that rough gravel road and didn't look back until we reached the point where we turned into the desert. Pausing there, I raised my sunglasses and Auro wiped the goggles and we watched the fire in the distance. All that remained of The Hotel Vega was a pyramid of livid scarlet, streaming embers into the sky and glowing like a bonfire against the purple mountains, almost as brightly intense as the setting sun to our left. Quite an enormous and dramatic bonfire, I would think many times afterward with a pit in my stomach, just to destroy a single silver pendant. But as Auro and I, reeking of gasoline and covered with ashes and sand, crossed the desert in the darkness beneath the first twinkling stars – breaking Samax's third rule – I knew the fire had not been nearly large enough to consume the real object of my rage: the cold, implacable image of Ivy I couldn't get out of my mind.

For a while, nothing happened. I heard passing mention of the fire in the kitchen the next day, but not a word at the dinner table, even when Samax returned at the end of the week. This wasn't particularly surprising. In a household where current events – including the Vietnam War, then at its height, and the race riots on both coasts – cropped up less in conversation than the wars, riots, and arcana of ancient Greece and Rome, a local fire would not arouse much interest. Only scientific breakthroughs and spectacular feats like the moon-landing seemed to penetrate the filters, invisible and otherwise, with which Samax had insulated the Hotel Canopus.

As for Ivy, I barely encountered her in the ensuing days, and when I did, she looked right past me, deadpan, as always, and I returned the favor. I could not prove she had disfigured the pendant; if I confronted her, she would just deny it. Somehow, some way, her day of reckoning would come, I told myself.

After two weeks I was both breathing easier and tormented by the notion that I had to confess to Samax what I had done. He had always trusted me completely – something which I understood better, and valued for its rarity, as I got older – and I never lied to him. At first I was afraid to tell him about the fire; then I had to admit to myself that, more than anything, I was ashamed. And so I vacillated, until one morning a pair of state troopers in taut khaki uniforms and white Stetsons drove up the cul-de-sac to the Hotel Canopus in a black and white patrol car and asked for Samax. Denise showed them up to the tenth floor and ten minutes later came down to the lounge where I sat disconsolately picking at the piano keys.

'He wants to see you,' she said, expressionless as always. 'Now.' Then, uncharacteristically breaking her studied detachment toward me, she added, 'You're going to catch it this time.'

Samax was sitting behind the plain mahogany desk in his business office (in his study he worked at a quarter-moon-shaped desk of dazzling blue glass), a small stark room adorned with a long-needled red cactus and a rough Etruscan urn – singular adornments of pain and death. There were no fruit trees, none of his many works of art, and no personal effects. It was exactly the room he would choose to receive the police. From his prison stint he equated them with correction officers, and bore them no love. The only other times I knew him to entertain in that room were when his accountant or lawyers came by, or, on a personal level, when he had to impart unpleasant news to a guest or relative. When he asked Ivy and Nestor to leave the hotel, for example, he did it in that office. So my associations with the room were decidedly gloomy, and until that moment I had never met with Samax there.

He nodded toward a straight-back chair directly opposite his desk, identical to the ones the state troopers occupied. They both looked me over, then turned their attention back to Samax. Whatever his long-standing feelings toward the police, it was at me that he was staring hard, his pale blue eyes unflinching.

'These officers have come here with some questions for you, Enzo. Answer them as honestly as I've always known you to answer me.'

Two hunters tracking desert bighorns in the mountains had seen the fire and through their binoculars and rifle scopes watched me flee from it on the minibike. Making inquiries, the police had ascertained finally that my destination must have been the Hotel Canopus. They had no physical proof whatsoever that I had been in

Hydra: just a sighting from miles away. And of course the hunters had reported seeing two boys.

I listened to the troopers, but rather than wait for them to pose their questions, I turned back to Samax. 'It was me, Uncle Junius. I went to Hydra that day.'

Samax's shoulders tensed up and he exhaled slowly. 'You were there. And the fire: were you in any way responsible?'

I nodded, and though my guts were churning, my voice remained calm. 'I started it.'

'Accidentally, you mean – were you smoking out there?'

'No. I purposely set fire to the water tower. Then the fire got out of control and spread to the hotel.'

Never in all my years with Samax – before or after that day – did I ever see him so shocked by anything I said. The troopers didn't seem surprised: my frankness told them only that I was someone who had been waiting to confess.

Samax's hand had balled up into a fist, which he brought down onto the desk with exaggerated slowness – worse, I thought, than if he had pounded it. 'But why would you do such a thing?' he said in a low voice, his most serious voice, for he seldom spoke loudly and never shouted.

I sucked in my breath and tried to fix on a wavering circle, a watery reflection of sunlight off the desktop, on the wall beside him. 'I had to burn something.'

'You what? Enzo, I've never known you to be smart with me.'

'I'm not being smart. Please don't misunderstand me. I was really angry, and I had to burn something.'

'You mean, just anything? What are you telling me – that suddenly you're a pyromaniac?'

That churning was spreading from my gut: my arms began trembling and I had to separate my knees so they wouldn't knock. The troopers' silence only reinforced that fact that I had just confessed to a crime, and suddenly I had visions of myself in reform school, behind

227

fences, barred windows, locked doors, far from the friendly confines of the Hotel Canopus, far from Desirée, Calzas, and Sirius, institutionalized at last, the fate (in its more benign forms) I had precariously avoided so often before as an orphan – the fate that my aunt Alma had so feared for me before Samax snatched me away. 'No,' I replied at last, 'what I mean is that I had a thing in my possession which I had to burn. I threw it into the water tower and set the tower on fire.'

'Something illegal?'

'No, nothing like that.'

'And to burn this thing, small enough presumably so that you were able to carry it into the desert, you set a whole tower on fire?'

'I know that doesn't make sense, but that's what happened.'

'Enzo, you're trying my patience. If you were smoking pot and the fire started, just say so.'

'But I wasn't. Uncle Junius, I'm telling you the truth. I'm sorry.'

Samax tilted back in his chair and peered through the parted white curtains at the desert, then leaned forward again. 'All right. You say you were angry. At what or whom?'

'I can't tell you that.'

'Enzo . . .'

'I can't.'

Samax shook his head. It was as if suddenly it weighed a hundred pounds on his neck. I knew he was in pain, not only because of what I'd done but because I'd kept it secret – I was still keeping it secret. Still, I couldn't bring myself to tell him about Ivy and my mother's pendant: I had made my choice not to go to him in the first place and I was going to stick to it. And, sitting there with the troopers, I thought the truth – already a muddle – would sound even more preposterous.

'Who was the other boy?' one of the troopers asked suddenly.

'There was no one with me, Officer.'

'The hunters were certain there were two of you.'

'They were wrong.'

From his eyes I saw that Samax knew I was lying now. But I saw, too, that he didn't want this point to be pursued. Gently he deflected the focus. 'Why didn't you tell me about the fire?' he asked. 'Is it for the same reason you can't tell me why you were angry?'

'No,' I said, biting my lip, holding back tears, 'it was because I felt so ashamed.'

Looking him in the eye at that moment, seeing how he took in my grief without losing his temper, was my most difficult moment in that room.

The troopers piped in again with more specific questions: what had I used to start the fire; why had I chosen the ghost town; had I set any other fires in the area, and if so, when. At that point Samax cut them off, politely but firmly.

'He's fully admitted to starting the fire, gentlemen. He's fourteen years old. He has lived with me for four years. His adoptive parents were killed seven years ago in an automobile accident. He's never done anything wrong before – certainly nothing involving the law. That ghost town has been food for termites for over forty years. I'll pay whoever owns the property whatever they ask. If they like, I'll erect a new hotel on the site. Now, are you going to charge this boy with a crime? If so, I want to get my lawyers out here before any of us says another word. I can have them in this room within thirty minutes.'

The troopers exchanged glances. Samax kept to himself more than most of the truly powerful people – on both sides of the law – in Las Vegas County, but he was no hermit, and many of those people were his friends and acquaintances on various levels. After conferring briefly, the troopers said they would have to take the matter up downtown with their superior after contacting the owner of the property.

'And who might that be?' Samax inquired, and I could see in his face that he was sure they would never file charges against me.

'Hydra is part of a large parcel owned by Xaphan Landshares. They've been buying up desert property.'

'Never heard of them,' Samax said.

'They're a subsidiary of VC Enterprises up in Reno.'

At this, Samax blanched. 'Have you had contact with them?'

'With VC? No. Just with the general manager down at Xaphan.'

Samax recovered his composure quickly, and his voice was smoother than ever. 'Why don't I just have my people offer him compensation for the damages?'

'Sir, we still have to take it downtown. It won't take long.'

'Fine,' Samax said, and he showed them to the door. I sat frozen until he returned to his desk. 'Now will you tell me why you did this?' he asked in his lowest voice.

Finally the tears came to my eyes. But I didn't cry. 'I can't. I'm sorry this ever happened. I'm sorry for all the trouble—'

'Never mind that. I just want to know why, damn it. You know they could take you away from me because of this. If you really have no explanation to offer – if you risked so much for nothing – the thing becomes ten times worse.'

I shook my head slowly.

He threw up his hands. 'Have it your way. The other boy – was it Auro?'

I nodded. 'I didn't want to drag him into this, Uncle Junius. He'd freak out. Anyway, it was all my fault.'

'You were right to shield Auro, but that's the only thing you were right about.' He turned away and fixed his gaze on the desert again. His cheek twitched and he was pressing his fingertips into his temple. 'I've never been so angry with you, Enzo. And so disappointed. I'm sorry you see fit not to level with me. Maybe you'll change your tune later, but right now just go to your room and stay there. I have to deal with this man at Xaphan so the matter stays here in Vegas.'

'Why would they care about a ghost town?' I said, pausing at the door. 'Nobody ever paid attention to it.'

He spun his chair around again. 'And you think that gave you the right to commit arson?'

'No.'

'It's not the town they would care about in Reno, it would be hearing my name connected to the fire.'

'You mean, VC Enterprises? Do you know them?'

'Know them?' he said sharply, picking up the phone. 'Remember I told you about the man who sent me to prison?'

'Vitale Cassiel.'

'Vitale Cassiel is VC Enterprises. He'd like nothing better than to get at me – especially through someone close to me, and at this time there is only one person in my life who fits that description who actually shares my name.'

'I'm sorry, Uncle Junius.'

'I hope you're sorry about more than the fact that you were caught.'

For the next six hours I lay in my bed ruminating hard on the fact that if this Vitale Cassiel had been able to maneuver someone as wily as Samax into jail – not to mention the fact that he could still make him blanch – he certainly would have little trouble getting me sent to reform school. When Della brought me a cheese sandwich and a glass of milk and told me that Samax had called off the customary sit-down dinner that night, I really started to sweat. Even with all the strings he could pull, maybe it wasn't going to be enough.

Meanwhile, Auro couldn't talk, but he could write, and when he got wind of what had happened to me in the meeting with Samax and the state troopers, he sneaked out of his room late that same night, went up to Samax's library, and handed him a short letter in his cramped script. Samax was horrified.

'This is terrible,' he said.

231

'Terrible,' Auro echoed, the tears streaming down his cheeks.

Samax wrapped his arms around Auro, and later told me it was the first time he had ever seen Auro cry. It was also the first time in a long while that Samax had held Auro so close – another unintentional but beneficial offshoot of our burning down the ghost town. Actually, the best development of all was to come about an hour later when Samax was sitting at the end of my bed while I read Auro's letter myself.

'How long has this sort of thing been going on?' Samax asked when I was finished.

'Since the day she brought me to you in New York.'

'I'm not going to ask you why you wouldn't tell me, because I already know. You were thinking you had to handle this yourself, to fight your own fight, because otherwise it would never end – not *really* end.' He stood up and went over to the window, where Sirius was sleeping, and toyed absently with the telescope. 'I know that kind of thinking,' he went on, 'because I've done it myself, and there's a lot of me in you. Sometimes you have to fight alone. But thinking you have to do it all the time, on principle, is stubbornness to no purpose. If you're going to be stubborn, have a good reason for it. The situation with Ivy is my fault. I've looked the other way with her once too often, and what was always bad in her has festered into something much worse. For her to destroy that pendant of Bel's is not just mean, it's crazy. She's crazy. Now, I can't banish her outright from the hotel, because she'll take it out on Auro for betraying her. And I promised him I wouldn't betray his confidence. Since she seems to have declared war on you, and your mother's memory, and who knows what else, I will deal with her as Sun Tzu advises us to with difficult adversaries – that is, by their own methods – so that this sort of thing never happens to you again. If it should happen, you must promise that you'll come to me.'

I knew Sun Tzu's book about warfare – along with von Clausewitz, it was one of Samax's favorites – but I never

232

knew exactly what Samax did with regard to Ivy, and I never asked. It had the desired effect, however: for a long time, she avoided me like the plague. As for Auro's letter, he succinctly told Samax about everything except the phoenix flight of the hummingbird we witnessed. That was something we would always keep between us. For, if anything, we became closer after our misadventure in Hydra. On occasion we would meet up in the quincunx orchard at midday – something we had never done before – and Auro would bring out two spaghetti sandwiches, on pumpernickel with ketchup, his favorite meal. Also, without Ivy hovering so close, he was able to join me for the first time in the swimming pool, where I taught him some basic strokes.

Auro went through other changes as well. He was less reclusive, less fearful when he encountered unfamiliar guests at the hotel one on one. One day such a guest, a gypsy friend of Labusi's who came to visit for a week, gave Auro a parrot. The parrot, with fiery orange plumage and pinwheel eyes, was from Madagascar. Auro named him Echo, though it was *he* who parroted the parrot, the latter chattering fluently from his wicker cage or while perched on Auro's shoulder. But the biggest change in Auro after the fire was the fact that he took up the drums, with a vengeance. A positive outgrowth of his echolalia, and its unique effect on his hearing faculty, was that he turned out to be a natural percussionist and rhythm man. A room was cork-lined for him on the third floor, where he practiced with a full set of black-pearl Ludwig drums and Avedas Zildjian cymbals which Samax bought him. He went at them night and day, working out his fury at his father's death and his mother's tyranny and his increasing frustration with his own muteness. In the process, he became a jazz drummer of phenomenal eloquence, articulate with drum skins and sticks, tempered brass and steel brushes, the high hat and the floor tom-tom, bell, maracas, castanets, tambourines, and the triangle, as he could never be with his voice.

Around the same time, to escape some of this domestic turmoil myself, I plunged into a colossal memory project: to memorize the names of all 3,445 numbered asteroids in the asteroid belt. When I mentioned it to Labusi, he dismissed it out of hand. 'Why undertake such a useless endeavor when there are so many important things you can memorize?'

Now, Labusi himself had memorized subjects as esoteric as the catalogues of defunct museums, the names of every member of the Hohenzollern dynasty, and entire games of chess from obscure tournaments, so, aside from his lack of interest in the subject, I knew his true resistance stemmed from the fact that asteroids were Hadar's domain, and between the two of them there was an intellectual rivalry – based more on vanity than anything else. At any rate, had I confided to Labusi my true reason for memorizing the asteroids' names, he would have objected even more vehemently, for I knew that deep down he was more pragmatist than Pythagorean. Which was a shame, because in terms of harmony – musical and metaphysical – my notion was surely Pythagorean to the highest degree.

I was convinced that if I could memorize the names of all those asteroids I would in effect be reconstituting mentally the bulk of the exploded planet between Mars and Jupiter of which Hadar claimed the asteroids were the fragments. In short, the planet would become whole again in my head. So from a green astronomical manual I began memorizing the forty pages of asteroid listings, placing the names in sequential slots around my memory palace. However, from the first, the listings obsessed me in a completely unanticipated way: the simple fact, of which I had been ignorant, that most of the asteroids were named after women. The list began with three thousand women's names! Memorizing them – *Iris, Flora, Victoria, Irene* – filling my memory palace with them – I began deriving an increasingly erotic pleasure. By the time I reached #s 208 to 211, *Lacrimosa, Dido, Isabella, Isolda*, I was arranging the names on a long set of shelves on the ninth-floor corridor of my memory palace, outside Desirée's room – a *locus* where I wanted to linger. Desirée's rooms themselves were not a part of my memory palace because, even after five years, I had never entered them in reality.

In fact, the very first time I did enter Desirée's rooms was a year later, on Columbus Day, 1971 – the night of the valedictory dinner at which Deneb announced his departure, to write his monograph on Atlantis. After that dinner, everyone retired to the ballroom for an impromptu farewell party. And that was where the second – and for me, far more important – auspicious event of the evening occurred, for I danced with Desirée, not once but twice.

The party was the kind Samax liked, because he was the impressario, improvising as he went. First he ordered up a case of Dom Pérignon '57 from the wine cellar. Then he had the cook lay out a spread of black, white, and red caviar, lobster medallions, roasted prawns, shellfish salad, fresh and pickled fruits from the garden, and a cart of cheeses. Aromatic flowers were brought from the greenhouse and arranged around the room in slender Japanese vases. The lights were dimmed and the curtains opened on the enormous windows overlooking the desert night, a half-moon in the sky over the jagged silhouettes of the mountains.

Eboli was in heaven at the piano, running through his jazz repertoire, from the Jelly Roll Morton rags that were his passion to some Ellington and Monk. His eight fingers flew over the keyboard with amazing fluency and precision, and though Ivy had made only a perfunctory appearance, Auro sat on a stool beside Eboli, watching him raptly. At first, Eboli played solo, but then after Samax, tapping his glass with an oyster fork, had offered Deneb a farewell toast, an extraordinary ensemble took shape around the piano, a trio that played, not jazz or classical pieces, but an eerie, other-worldly music which sounded as if it were emanating from some remote source across a vast, timeless expanse. Rising and falling, sometimes clear, sometimes vaporous, this music carried everyone in the room along with it.

The trio consisted of Deneb himself, playing his Atlantean flute, flanked by Labusi, who had fetched his cello, and of course Eboli, tinkling his keyboard on the highest octaves, eyes closed behind his glinting spectacles. It sounded as if the three of them must have rehearsed many times for just such an occasion as this. Yet Labusi told me later that, while he and Deneb had once in a while played together in the privacy of his rooms, neither had ever collaborated with Eboli. Their synthesis on such disparate instruments, its sinuous harmonies and rippling fugues, eventually configured itself into a waltz, and instinctively people wanted to dance to it.

Through the shifting silken shadows, I glimpsed Calzas dancing with the wife of a visiting archaeologist from Kenya, and Sofiel the gardener moving stiffly with his wife, Kim-Yung, whom he towered over, though he was only five two, and Samax following a neat ellipse with a pretty French lawyer who had come for the weekend to negotiate the sale of some Corsican urns he wanted. I had never seen Samax dance before, and while not surprised by his nimbleness, I noted his pleasure and wondered why he didn't dance more often.

Making a beeline for Desirée the moment her partner – the archaeologist – dropped her hand, I soon found myself holding her close while she instructed me in her throaty whisper in the fundamentals of the waltz. The lights had been dimmed even further, and as Deneb and Labusi traded off solos, and then Eboli offered up a great waterfall of sound, we wheeled around the ballroom and I hoped they would never stop playing. It was the closest I had been to her, feeling her body up against mine, her breasts, hips, and shoulders, her arms wrapped around my back and her long fingers resting lightly on my spine. We were the same height at that time, so I looked directly, frankly, into her dark faraway eyes while inhaling the fragrance of her jet hair. The most exquisite moment for me, though, came just before she laid her cheek against my shoulder, when I felt her breath, warm against my own cheek as I turned her slowly on the black marble dance floor. The piece of music Zaren Eboli was playing on the piano was one I would never forget, and when I inquired afterward he told me it was called 'Stella by Starlight'.

For several weeks I had been dreaming of Alma, and her image in my dreams often conflated with the image of Desirée. Near the end of each dream, in a room with a domed ceiling, Alma glided up alongside me before a full-length mirror, but it was Desirée's reflection that stared back at me. Alma still looked as she did the last time I saw her, wearing a long black coat, and it wasn't difficult to figure out that the domed ceiling in my dreams was the planetarium of my memory; Desirée meanwhile appeared in my dream exactly as she did at that moment, in a long black dress with her hair swept back. But as we glided along the marble dance floor, my dream and my memory seemed to merge: the woman in my arms was as much Alma as she was Desirée. It had struck me long before that Desirée and Alma were the same age. On that night in October 1971, Desirée was twenty-six years old, and wherever she was, Alma was the same. I knew, too, that it was not just mirror images, or planetariums and ballroom ceilings, that were merging, but that my sexual longing for Desirée was mingled with my yearning, which had intensified over the years, to see Alma again, to hold her close as she had held me on that last night we spent together at my grandmother's house; if not to initiate intimacy, I wanted at least to effect closure where instead there had always been something like a severed wire crackling in the background of my life.

My arms around Desirée in the near darkness, the desert stars twinkling in the distance, she put her lips to my ear and whispered, 'Enzo, I need you to do me a favor. Will you come to my rooms?'

237

My heart was beating fast against my rib cage.

'It concerns my cousin Dalia,' she went on, 'who's visiting for the next two weeks.'

I was surprised. 'Your cousin? I didn't know that you had a cousin visiting.'

'A very distant cousin. She just arrived this morning.'

'Is she here?' I said, looking around.

'No, she doesn't care for parties. But I think you'll like her.'

The waltz was fading away and one by one the musicians fell silent, Labusi first, then Deneb. Only Eboli played on, slower and slower, for about a minute, as the lights came up and Desirée took my hand and led me to the door. We stepped into the cool silence of the lobby, the thick glass door closing behind us with a hush.

Smiling faintly, she squeezed my hand. 'You've never been to my rooms, have you?'

We both knew I hadn't. Stepping off the elevator on the ninth floor, Desirée led me to her door, and as she unlocked it, said, 'I want you to take something to Dalia for me. It's a map and she'll need you to identify some points on it for her. I know you're good with maps.'

'A map of what?'

'Oh, a piece of the desert.'

I followed her across a bare white foyer, through another, leather-padded door, into her living room. It was pitch-black, silent except for our breathing. Desirée switched on a pair of lamps and any other questions I had for her – and there were a few – evaporated at that instant.

The large room was sparsely furnished, but the furniture itself was plush: a long white sofa flanked by black lamps and a pink marble coffee table inlaid with topazes cut in the shape of suns. The thick, soft rug was also white. The room was centered by a gleaming baby grand, which surprised me because I had never heard Desirée play the piano downstairs. But what surprised me even more was the room's truly central, and overpowering,

238

element: not the piano or the furniture, but the dozens of photographs that adorned the place.

The photographs had two things in common: they were all 8×10, black-and-white, glassed within identical black lacquer frames, and they were all of men. Most were posed head shots, some were full-length portraits, and a few were blowups of snapshots: a young man in a train station with a suitcase, another sitting on a wooden terrace gazing at the sea, another smiling with a towel around his neck. The photographs were hung on three of the walls, covering about half the available space. The fourth wall was covered with taut silk with an oval mirror at the center.

My mouth must have been open, because Desirée didn't wait to hear my obvious question.

'These are friends of mine,' she said simply, brushing the hair back off her cheek.

'Oh.'

'Excuse me a moment, I'll get the map,' she said, and disappeared into the bedroom.

I studied as many of the photographs as I could. Could these all be her lovers? The youngest looked about twenty, the oldest no more than forty. They were all good-looking, but were not of any one type. Some looked athletic and outdoorsy, others looked bookish and brooding. It was clear to me from their style and perspective that all of the photographs had been taken by the same photographer, and that was Desirée. And they had been shot in many different locales: in some, there were bits of furniture and wall hangings in the background; in others, beaches, forests, and mountain lakes were visible through windows or doorways. In the lower right-hand corner of each photograph a date was inscribed in white ink. Just the year, in tiny numerals. I ascertained that the earliest year was 1962, when Desirée would have been seventeen.

As she returned from the bedroom, I saw a desk in there on which her typewriter was perched. Beside it was a stack of those yellow pages, maybe two feet high. More than ever now, I wondered what it was she was writing.

'Sorry I took so long,' she said.

She had changed into black pants, lizard boots, and a leather jacket. She had changed her earrings, too, from teardrop pearls to silver rings. In her left hand she carried a handbag and a set of keys, in her right a rolled-up sheet of thick paper.

'Going out?' I said, disappointed that my visit was to be so short.

'After one last turn at the party,' she replied. 'Here's the map. Dalia is in Room 512 and she's expecting you.'

'Desirée, I didn't know you played the piano.'

'I only play when I'm alone.'

'You've never played for Uncle Junius?'

She shook her head.

'Or for your friends?' I said, indicating the photographs.

'Not even for them.'

When I got off the elevator on the fifth floor, she held the door and said, 'See you at breakfast.'

'I won't be having breakfast with Uncle Junius. I'm flying to Acoma with Calzas at dawn.'

'Ah. Then I'll catch you after dinner.' She waved. 'And by the way, you're a wonderful dancer.'

Room 512 was at the end of the corridor. I heard flute music from within, and I had to knock twice before the door was thrown open onto a room bathed in red light. It was like looking into a photographic dark room, or a furnace, and it took my eyes a moment to adjust.

'You must be Enzo,' the girl before me said. 'Come in.' She had a strong Spanish accent.

She was tall and fair and very pale, as I could see even in that light. And very pretty. She had wide slanting eyes, a small nose with flaring nostrils, and thinly curving lips. Her platinum-blond hair, pulled back off her broad forehead, was long and curly, and she had thick eyelashes and pencil-thin eyebrows. Her long

240

fingernails were painted bloodred. She wore a sleeve-less shift of white silk and a pair of red silk slippers. On her left shoulder she sported a tattoo of an iceberg among whitecaps radiating fire.

She saw my eyes were drawn to the tattoo. 'Where I come from, the icebergs look like that, at sunrise and sunset.'

So I knew she didn't come from Spain or Mexico – but where, then?

'I'm Dalia,' she said, rolling the *l* hard, just as she lisped her *s*'s. 'I heard so many nice things about you.'

'Here's the map Desirée said you wanted.'

'Oh yes. Thank you.' Without opening it, she tossed the map onto an end table stacked with old and battered books. 'Like some tea?' she asked, arching one eyebrow. 'It's maté with hibiscus buds. Very stimulating.'

I didn't need much more stimulation, I thought, watching her cross the room to a hot plate on the dresser. She snapped her small hips rhythmically from side to side, the white silk gently riding her buttocks with every step; from the back, at least, she seemed to be wearing nothing under the shift.

I had met all kinds of people in my nearly six years at the hotel, but never anyone like Dalia. Eighteen going on thirty, she seemed light-years older than me, though I considered myself someone who had been around a bit in my short life.

'Honey?' she called over her shoulder, drawing out the word on her tongue, so that for a moment I thought she was addressing me. Well aware of this, she laughed. 'In your tea.'

'Sure.'

I had never been in that particular room before. Aside from the lighting – red bulbs in all the lamps, red candles burning on the desk and dresser – it was no different from the typical room Samax kept for the shorter term guests: a bed, divan, the dresser, some chairs, and an alcove with a well-stocked writing desk and shelves. For someone who had just arrived, Dalia seemed to have settled in rapidly: two of the shelves filled with more old books; a reel-to-reel tape recorder on the bedside table; discarded clothes draped over the chairs; a red attaché case filled with makeup spilled out on the dresser; and several pairs of shoes strewn over the divan. Bringing me my tea, she knocked the shoes to the floor with a deft sweep of her foot.

'Please, sit.'

The tea was also bloodred. 'It's delicious,' I said, sipping while the steam ran up my nose.

Dalia sat beside me, crossing her legs so that the shift hiked up well above her knee. Like everything else about her, her legs were long and streamlined. Her stomach was flat, and she had full, prominent breasts. She cradled her teacup delicately within her palms.

'So,' she said, 'did Desirée tell you what I was doing?'

'No.' I was still trying to discern the color of her eyes. In that light, it was difficult to say if they were brown or blue.

'I am translating a lost book,' she went on, and the way she said 'book,' it rhymed with *spook*. 'That is, it was lost until very recently. Originally, it was written in Catalan, with some Latin thrown in, though the author was a Spanish speaker. Later he translated it into pure Spanish.'

'And you're translating it into English.'

'Yes. What's tricky is that he left a number of, how would you say it, *Catalanismos* – Catalanisms – in the text that I'm constantly untangling.' She paused. 'I know it must sound confusing.'

'Not at all.' It sounded, I thought, like a perfectly appropriate project to undertake at the Hotel Canopus.

'The author was a Spanish missionary named Varcas, lapsed in his Catholicism. He stayed or traveled with other Spaniards, and he wrote in this mix of Catalan and Latin so they wouldn't know his subject. If they did, he could have suffered terrible punishment.'

'He was a revolutionary?'

'Nothing like that.' She leaned closer to me, wetting her lips. 'He was writing about *vampiria* – vampires – here in your Old West in the 1840s.'

My eyebrows must have gone up.

'Oh, there certainly were such creatures,' she went on. 'Of that there can be no doubt. Let me read you something.' She hurried over to the desk and returned with a wad of pages. 'I just finished this section. I've been working on it since I left Santiago.'

'Oh, is that where you're from?' I interrupted her.

'I am a student at the University of Chile. With this project, I will receive my degree, and maybe even publication. Who knows?'

'And the icebergs?' I *was* good with maps, and I knew that Santiago was a landlocked city.

'What about them?'

'You said you have them in the place you come from.'

'That's right,' she said. 'I come from Tierra del Fuego. I was born on *Los Estrechos de Magellanes* – the Strait of Magellan. Do you know where that is?'

Of course. I had read about the Land of Fire, and the Strait, in Captain Cook's *Journals*.

'I see you do. We have tremendous icebergs in the Strait,' she said, raising her arms over her head and joining her fingertips, 'as tall as the mountains that overlook them. I grew up traveling with my father among the islands of the Strait: Gilbert, Dawson, Lennox, Nuñez, Navarino – they got their names from Spanish and English navigators. This music you hear I recorded on the Isla Cook. It's a shaman who played on the winter solstice.' She took a deep breath. 'Any more questions?'

I shook my head.

'*Bien*. At the time Varcas wrote his book, after wandering all over this country, he was forty-two years old and all his hair had turned white because of what he had seen. I'll read you a passage from the second chapter, where he is traveling north to Albuquerque, which was then called San Felipe de Albuquerque.'

In a solemn, measured voice she began to read:

243

On the night of July 21, 1843, I had traveled northeast for four days from the Gallo Mountains where I encountered all variety of wild beasts. Following the Río Puerco, I hoped to reach Los Lunas the next day and was searching for a place to pitch camp. The night was hot and windy. I led my burro over a dry riverbed, and moonlight illuminated a plain dotted with small trees. Suddenly I heard a woman's screams, and the burro stopped and would go no farther. So I proceeded alone with a heavy heart. When I reached the first of those trees, I came on a terrible sight: a young woman crucified with glowing spikes. Her dress was torn and her chin rested lifelessly on her chest. I lifted it with a trembling hand. She was cold as stone, yet suddenly her eyes flipped open, completely white, and blood poured from her mouth. Taking to my heels, I saw among the trees a wolf standing on his hind legs, laughing, then spinning into the air. Surely this was the Evil One, I thought, running as I never had before. Thus began my odyssey, and I have witnessed such horrors as the Church Fathers ascribed to the place they called Hell, which I know now is on this earth, nowhere else . . .

'More tea?' Dalia murmured, dropping the pages onto the divan.

I had grown up in that hotel having women read me fantastical stories, but I hadn't been quite prepared for this.

'That's amazing,' I said, as she took my cup. 'And you're treating it as history?'

'It is history. Real history which, large or small, must always be – what – *un viaje por el inferno:* a journey through hell. Varcas then visited mission towns and settlements and you begin to see that this incident is nothing compared to what he found later. And he documents everything: dates, descriptions of victims, witnesses who give sworn statements. The Indians encountered these creatures, as did the Spanish conquistadors. The Spanish suppressed this information

– obviously. They were colonizers – why would they want to frighten away immigrants from the old country? To the Indians, the vampires, like ghosts and other potent spirits, had always been a natural part of the nocturnal landscape.'

'So what did Varcas find later?'

She smiled. 'I'll read you some more tomorrow, if you like. But you know what's really exciting – and terrible to contemplate?' she said, narrowing her eyes. 'These creatures never die. To them, the decades since Friar Varcas perished are like this' – she snapped her fingers – 'which means they are still roaming this country. That is why I came here: to see the places Varcas wrote about, and also to breathe the air these creatures inhabit.'

'You're going to retrace his steps?'

'Of course. As much as I can by automobile – Arizona, Colorado, New Mexico, all over.' She raised her hands. 'This is what I am working on, but there is more to me than that. And there are other things to discuss.' She fixed her eyes on mine. They were pale blue, I saw now. 'I understand you've had a wanderer's life – *un vagabundo* – like me,' she said, lowering her voice to just above a whisper. 'Tell me about yourself, Enzo.'

I have little recollection of what I related to her, outside a superficial outline of my recent history. Maybe it was the maté tea. Or the fact that it took me a while to put the tale of Friar Varcas and the vampire out of my mind. Or, more likely, that I simply found it difficult to concentrate on the particulars of my own life when my eye kept gravitating to Dalia's dangling leg or her lovely breasts, the dark disks of her nipples pressing against her silken shift, when she locked her fingers behind her head and leaned back on the divan. Soon enough the shaman playing his flute on the Isla Cook gave way to some reggae, and Dalia took a plastic bag and a blunt pipe out of a velvet pouch. I had smoked marijuana a number of times and lost interest: alongside the effects of the spider bite – however subtle their evolution – it didn't do much for me. But this wasn't ganja Dalia was tamping down into the pipe.

'It is the ground-up buds from a tree we have in the mountains of Chile,' she said.

'Coca?'

'No, nothing so strong, but much rarer. These buds when they blossom are called *flores de luna* – flowers of the moon. They are silvery white circles with black dots, like the moon's craters. A couple of puffs, it just makes you feel kind of dreamy,' she said, passing me the pipe and putting a match to the bowl.

The smoke was bittersweet, tinged with a lilac scent. Expanding in my lungs, it constricted my throat, but I held it in for a long time.

'The fruit of this tree', Dalia went on, 'is white, the size of an olive, and if you rub it in your palm, and say some magic words, it glows in the dark.'

'What are the words?' I said, taking a second puff off the pipe.

Dalia ran her fingertip along my eyebrow and then down my cheek. 'Enzo, you've got very nice eyes.' Her fingertip traced my mouth. 'And lips.'

My mouth went dry as she slid closer to me. 'Those are the words?' I laughed nervously, exhaling the smoke.

'No', she said softly, her eyelids at half mast.

I felt a lightness to my body, but my mind remained clear. At least, I thought it did.

'The words', Dalia whispered, 'are, "Let's dance".' And, taking my one hand, she placed the other lightly on her breast, which felt hard, and the nipple even harder, through the silk.

The next thing I knew we were dancing cheek to cheek, our bodies pressed together tightly and the throb of the reggae pulsing the air so that gradually I felt like I was underwater in a bright red sea, feeling every ripple of her body against mine. I closed my eyes and we moved in slow circles around the room, much slower than the tempo of the music, and didn't exchange another word. But we did kiss, on the eyes, cheeks, and lips, and then for the first time I had a girl's tongue in my mouth when she licked my upper lip and slid her tongue in, revolving it slowly. The more we danced, the longer and harder we kissed until finally one of our slow lazy circles ended abruptly at the bed, onto which we tumbled as if it had been awaiting us all along. As of course it had.

'Enzo, I feel famished,' Dalia whispered, running her hand up my thigh and unzipping my pants.

I had a hard-on like a rock as she sat astride it and threw off her shift. Then she got on all fours, her breasts inches from my face, and I slid out of my pants and kicked them away. I took her breasts in my hands while she unbuttoned my shirt and then put her mouth over mine. She didn't have on underwear, just an inverted triangle of silk beneath which was a nearly identical triangle of soft light hair that emerged when she unsnapped the elastic band that circled her waist. I put my mouth greedily over one breast, then the other, and rolled over on top of her.

My instincts took over – with some help from Dalia. The platinum spirals of her hair fanned out over the pillow as she wrapped her arms around my shoulders, her fingernails poised sharply on my skin. Then she spread her legs into a wide V, opening up to my fingers even as she caressed me, gently pulling me into her. My whole body felt on fire, from my skull to my toes. Behind the roaring blood in my ears I heard a clear, high-pitched ringing, as if a small silver bell were being struck at regular intervals. Intervals that shortened with every passing moment as I buried myself deep inside her, thrusting, too hard and fast at first in my ardor, even as she thrust back more deliberately, drawing me into a slower surer rhythm. I closed my eyes and felt her lips slide across mine and flutter down to my throat. And then quickly, almost too quickly, every force in my body seemed to be coming apart at incredible velocity and merging into one at my burning center. We moved faster and faster, and then slower and more conclusively, our bodies pounding together, the sweat pouring off my back and the air tight in my lungs, as in one long burst all that fire at my center streamed into Dalia.

As I lay beside her, catching my breath, everything in the room falling away from me, the names of those asteroids began lighting up in my mind suddenly, in sequence as always – such was the staying power of Labusi's method! – but a fractured sequence now, like my breathing – *Pia, Renata, Palma* – and I thought of all the girls I might meet in my life, and all the women in the world – *Chloë, Olivia, Jena* – and I realized how much pleasure it had given me holding all those names in my head, until finally, at the end of that sequence – *Esther, Violetta, Philippina* – bringing a smile to my lips, I arrived at #643, *Scheherazade*, the weaver of tales, of desire.

At that instant I saw on my closed eyelids a perfect sphere, pale green with red streaks, rotating slowly, backdropped by stars. It was a planet. A year after memorizing the names of the asteroids, I had succeeded in reconstructing mentally Hadar's lost planet between Mars and Jupiter. It had come whole suddenly – all those names cohering and transmuting in my head – just as the rest of me had burst apart. After several seconds, the image disappeared, spinning away through space until it was just another tiny light among so many others.

Like the stars in the sky over Acoma the following night when I concluded my second visit there with Calzas and Sirius. Sirius had not been back since Calzas found him as a pup. We had flown into Albuquerque and rented a jeep. Four hundred miles east of Las Vegas, Acoma was fifty miles southwest of Albuquerque. About 150 miles to the north on Route 666 was Four Corners, which I had visited with Calzas on my first trip to Acoma three years earlier. I had wanted to see Four Corners ever since Samax pointed it out to me from the air on that first plane ride from New York to Las Vegas. And just as he told me he had done, I walked around the

248

monument with the four state seals, following a small tight circle from New Mexico to Colorado to Utah to Arizona. The dirt was orange there, a slow wind blew hard, and it was 110°.

On this trip we drove straight to Acoma. We arrived at noon and left just after nightfall, and as eagerly as I had anticipated my return to the sky-city, my mind was elsewhere that day. From the moment we left the Hotel Canopus at dawn until our return at midnight, Dalia – her scent, her touch, the coolness of her white skin – was never far from my thoughts. In everything I did that day, from climbing the mesa and hiking over a field of boulders to feeling the sun pounding my bare back, my body felt different. Though still fifteen, legally, officially, a minor, it was as if overnight much more than a night had passed; though no stranger to the company and ministrations of women, from Luna and my grandmother to the two sisters and Desirée at the hotel, it seemed to me now that I had truly entered their world, which was also the world of the heart.

At Acoma, it was Calzas's world I entered. No sooner had we started driving west out of Albuquerque than I felt he was completely in his element. He didn't change much around other people, whether at the hotel or in Las Vegas itself when I accompanied him on business errands. But in New Mexico something dropped away from him – he seemed more alert to his own needs rather than the needs of others. In his wraparound Polaroids and long-brimmed baseball cap, he always enjoyed driving in the open air, the top down, no matter what the temperature. And he was naturally taciturn: if I didn't speak, he wouldn't; but if I brought something up, he was always open – though never voluble – regardless of the subject. That particular day, though, barreling down the shimmering desert highway with sand stinging our cheeks and the backdraft fiercely hot, he was far more preoccupied than usual.

Over time I had discovered the exact nature of Calzas's employment with Samax. In addition to his far-flung troubleshooting with antiquities, Calzas had a ten-year contract with Samax for his exclusive services as an architect. His projects were Samax's various real estate acquisitions: hotels, office buildings, several theaters, and an opera house, which Calzas gutted, re-designed, and renovated. His contract expired in 1973, at which time, with Samax's blessing (and regret), he planned to go into business for himself. So when I turned eighteen, his role in my life – part surrogate brother, part godfather – would come to an end. On account of his youth alone – when I was otherwise living exclusively with men in their fifties and sixties – I never underestimated the importance of that role, despite the fact that Calzas was on the road more than he was at home at the hotel. As with Desirée, the age difference between Calzas and me was such that the older I got, the more I became his peer. For a while, though, I had often imagined him and Desirée as my ideal parents – talented, beautiful, and happy reincarnations of Luna and Milo, or better yet, of my ever-mysterious real-life parents – even though I knew Calzas had a fiancée in Santa Fe, a Zuni girl named Cela whom he visited every other weekend and planned to marry as soon as he set up his own business. Calzas looked hard at Desirée on occasion, but, the son of a philanderer, he was faithful to a fault.

Aside from his fiancée, Calzas rarely brought up his personal life or his family in New Mexico. So I was sur-prised when he broke into my thoughts about twenty minutes into our drive.

'We're going to see my father's grave,' he said.

In the years I had known him, Calzas hadn't said much about his father, but I had assembled a thumbnail sketch from others. Like me, Calzas had never known his true father, who left him, his mother, and his two brothers when Calzas was two. His father ran around with other women and worked as a sheet metal cutter in an airplane factory in Phoenix. Later he went east and became a construction worker, on skyscrapers and suspension bridges. Like many Indians, because of his extraordinary sense of balance he was made a riveter assigned to the greatest heights. Eventually he died in a fall on a job in New York City and was buried there. That was all I knew.

'You mean, we're going to New York?' I said, sitting up.

'Of course not,' he replied. 'I don't know where he's buried there.'

'I don't understand.'

'When the Zunis don't know where one of their own has been laid to rest, they bury some of his possessions on their land and erect a marker on the site. When the dead man's spirit returns here, as they believe it must, it will have a resting place. Outside of Acoma, near Mesita where I grew up, there is a small burial ground called the Hill of the Lost. Most of the 'graves' there are from the last century, warriors who never returned from the wars with other tribes and with the army. A couple are GIs who were lost in the war in the Pacific. My father is one of the few civilians represented there. I thought this trip you're old enough to come with me. Okay?'

I nodded. 'You must have searched for his grave in New York,' I said.

'Many times. I wanted to find it, just to put him to rest in my own head. Even using your uncle's connections, I had no luck,' he said ruefully. He turned to me, and I saw myself twice, reflected in his sunglasses. 'You must have traveled over the George Washington Bridge when you lived in New York.'

'Sure.' With Luna and Milo, I thought, and once with Alma in her white Impala.

'That's where my father fell.'

'Oh.' I had a feeling in my stomach as if I were falling.

'The police fished him out of the Hudson River and took him to the morgue. But there's no record of him in any cemetery in New York, including the potter's field. Most of the riveters were Mohawk Indians and Cayugas. My father was one of three Zunis who went east for these

251

jobs because they paid top dollar. I tracked down the two other Zunis, living in Brooklyn, by the way, but they were working in Philadelphia when he died. They thought his body had been sent back here, but that never happened. He always mailed my mother half his salary – no letters ever, just a money order – and she got the last one the day she found out he died. A year later, she erected the grave here.'

The Hill of the Lost was just that. Sun-baked and dusty, it rose on the edge of a hazy salt flat. The graves were circles of smooth stones, about two feet across. Calzas went up to one of them, doffed his hat, and looked down with no visible show of emotion. I wondered what his feelings were for his father, whom he knew only from a handful of photographs, and whether he came to this place strictly out of a sense of tribal respect. A few minutes later, we were back on the road and Calzas's somberness lifted at once.

I found myself wondering where my own father – if he was dead, that is – was buried. Maybe one day I would feel compelled to raise a surrogate grave, as the Zunis did. But I had no information on which to base such a gesture: no name, no image, no place or time of birth and death, and certainly no possessions of his. My father may as well have been a spirit pure and simple, unattached to any corporeal life. Discovering who Bel was the day I met Samax hadn't gotten me any closer to discovering my father's identity six years later. The person most in a position to offer me clues was not Samax – who flat out told me that, despite strenuous efforts, he had never been able to find out – but Ivy, who was more privy than anyone else to her sister's activities at the end of her life. And of course whatever Ivy knew – it might be a lot or nothing at all – she wasn't going to pass on to me.

That phantasmal figure shadowed in the photograph of Bel afforded only a cursory description that could fit millions of men – tall broad-shouldered, with long legs. It could fit the cowboy climbing into his pickup beside the tire pump, I thought, as we pulled off the highway into a gas station, or the soldier going into the men's room, limping slightly.

While Calzas filled the jeep with gas, I went into the office to buy some soda. The man behind the desk, his thatch of red hair plastered down flat, rolled a pencil in his fingers and peered at me through his cigarette smoke. I pulled two bottles of Crush from the machine, popped off the caps, and gave the man five cents for the deposit before stepping outside. A white convertible, a rental car, was parked in front of the office. Draped over the back of the front passenger seat was the soldier's jacket. It was part of an Air Force uniform, a major's, with several rows of ribbons and medals. But it wasn't to them that my eye was drawn; as I lowered the soda bottle from my lips, what nearly sent a stream of Crush down my windpipe was the name tag on the jacket pocket, which read CASSIEL.

'Enzo,' Calzas hollered. He was already behind the wheel of the jeep, pulling away from the gas pumps.

I stood there, frozen in place.

'Come on, what are you waiting for?' he called again, and Sirius in the rear seat barked at me for good measure.

Slowly I walked over to them, looking back several times at the convertible. What was I waiting for? It was true I didn't think *Cassiel* was a common name, and of course I immediately associated it with Samax's long-time enemy, Vitale Cassiel; but common or not, surely other people possessed the name, some of whom might be Vitale Cassiel's relatives. Still, I couldn't take my eyes off the convertible, even as I handed Calzas his soda.

'What's the matter with you?' he said, for he was eager to get on to Acoma.

It was then, as I circled around to my side of the jeep, that the soldier reemerged from the men's room and got into the car. From behind his sunglasses he stared at us for several seconds across the steaming asphalt. Then we swung onto the highway and he spun the wheel and left the gas station by its other exit, heading toward Albuquerque. Over my shoulder I watched the convertible disappear into the heat haze and then rubbed the moisture from my soda bottle onto my forehead.

I hadn't realized how close we were to Acoma, which emerged suddenly as we rounded a series of ridges: a steep, enormous sandstone mesa that rose four hundred feet in the air, from sheer cliffs to precipitous terraces and finally the broad, tabletop summit. Beyond it was a twin mesa nearly as tall and even more box-like, called the Enchanted Mesa. Within a few miles, we turned off the highway onto a winding road of two-lane blacktop. I had been distracted since we left the gas station, but the sight of the mesa, as exhilarating as the first time I had visited, brought me out of myself. Calzas had been watching me sidelong while he negotiated the sharp curves.

'What was it back there?' he asked.

'Nothing.'

'There was something.'

I told him about the name tag on the soldier's jacket, but this information didn't elicit much of a reaction.

'Anything else?' Calzas said.

I shook my head and looked out over the scrub brush and boulders that bordered the road.

'So of course you thought of Vitale Cassiel. Still spooked by the notion that he's going to have you locked up for arson?'

'Not so much that. Uncle Junius told me about their feud. How much does this Cassiel really hate him?'

'Your uncle told you about his going to jail. But there's a lot more history, some of which I know. I can tell you that, given the opportunity, Vitale Cassiel would destroy your uncle – and vice versa. Financially, physically, I don't know where they'd stop. For a long time there's been a stalemate between them, which is not the same as a truce.' Downshifting into the last bend on the road, Calzas looked at me. 'So, should you take notice when you encounter that name? I suppose so. But

254

will it always tie in somehow to Vitale Cassiel? I doubt that.'

The moment Calzas parked the jeep, Sirius leapt out the back and ran to the foot of the rocky trail that spiraled up the mesa. At Acoma, Sirius behaved as he did nowhere else. At first, he was very much himself, and as we began our ascent to the sky-city, he preceded us energetically, never more than twenty feet ahead. Every so often he sniffed at the thick weeds off the trail or froze, nose twitching, at the scent of another animal. Or he paused to track the flight of a bird; he had a phenomenal eye and was often mesmerized by the receding speck of a hawk circling skyward far out in the desert.

After a short time, we reached a small plateau before the last stretch of trail to the summit. Calzas took off his knapsack and I passed him the canteen I had slung over my shoulder. The sweat shone on his bronze arms. The air was noticeably thinner now, and the wind stronger. Rock dust fine as pollen gusted off the overhangs. I could taste it on my lips, and gradually it coated my face and arms a dull red.

It was on this plateau that the change came over Sirius. As soon as we reached it, rounding a thicket of brambles, he froze, then slid down onto his belly. Growling softly, he stealthily approached a pyramid of rocks surrounded by tall lavender grass.

'That's where I found him as a puppy,' Calzas said.

I was about to follow Sirius, but Calzas laid a hand on my shoulder.

'Let him go,' he whispered.

The pyramid was as Calzas had described it: flat black rocks piled about twelve feet high, where there was just enough room for a dog to lie down. But he was certainly correct in saying no dog could have climbed there. His pale eyes fixed on the pyramid's peak, Sirius crawled within a few feet of its base, then leapt up suddenly, ran around the pyramid barking, and bolted up the remainder of the trail to the top of the mesa. He still never came to me in a straight line when summoned, but he always stopped when I ordered him to. Not this time, though. Disappearing in a cloud of dust, he did not so much as glance back when I called out to him – the first time ever that he had been openly disobedient.

'He'll be all right,' Calzas reassured me, but I could see that even he was puzzled.

When we reached the unpopulated southwest corner of the mesa, the site of the Zunis' ancient city, we heard cicadas whirring in the gray ruins, sparrows fluttering in the brush, and toads croaking, but there was no sign of Sirius. He had hidden somewhere, and though when I was younger we had often played hide-and-seek around the hotel, this wasn't the way the game went. I called to him repeatedly, walking up and down the narrow packed-dirt streets that wound among the roofless adobes, but he simply would not come out. Finally I gave up and joined Calzas on a ledge overlooking the desert to share the bag of avocado and tomato sandwiches and the thermos of iced tea we had brought with us.

'Those are the Gallo Mountains,' Calzas said, pointing to a distant line of mountains, white behind a curtain of haze. 'That tall peak to the right is Madre Mountain. And there across the plain, that winding silver thread is the Río San José where it branches from the Río Puerco. In the other direction, there's no river for a hundred miles. The only water is artesian.'

I took a long draught of the tea, which was sweetened with thyme honey. 'So that town beyond the river', I said, pointing east, at a low cluster of houses, 'would be Los Lunas.'

'That's right. Have you been studying the map?'

'Sort of.'

The Río Puerco was the river Friar Varcas had been following en route to Albuquerque. Late the previous night, while we were still naked in her bed, Dalia had unfurled the map I had brought her. It was a map Desirée had borrowed for her from a friend of Samax's at the

256

historical society in Las Vegas. Roughly drawn in pen and ink, with the place names in Spanish, it was a copy of one of Friar Varcas's maps, dated 1886, twenty–five years after his death. To my surprise, I saw that the map was centered around the same area for which Calzas and I would be heading in a few hours, including Albuquerque, Acoma, Santa Fe, and the San Juan Mountains to the north, in present-day Colorado, where the source of the Río Grande was marked with an X. Aside from villages, indicated by circles, the markings on the map were all single crosses, †. There seemed to be no pattern to them: some were in settlements, others in the mountains, and many more on rivers or out in the desert. Altogether there were twenty–seven crosses.

'You know what those crosses are?' Dalia asked, loading her little pipe with more of the moon flower blossoms.

'There couldn't have been that many churches, especially in the wilds.'

'They're not churches.' She flicked her lighter and the flame sprang up gold in her irises. 'Those are where he recorded his sightings.'

'Of vampires.'

She nodded and lit the pipe. 'Desirée told me that you would be able to help me determine the locations on a current road map. I plan to visit each site, so I need to know how close they are to roads and to motels where I can spend the night.'

For the next two hours we sat up in the tangled sheets surrounded by maps: Varcas's map, a US Geological Survey map, and a Shell Oil road map, on which Dalia penned in her itinerary. We drank more of the red tea, and listened to more flute music from the Isla Cook, and soon we were making love again. Having never been so intimate with a woman, I was stimulated to the point of exhaustion, and when Dalia woke me three hours later, running her lips along my cheek and forehead, I found myself still sprawled out on top of the Geological Survey map, clutching the sheet across my chest.

257

'You said you had to be up an hour before dawn,' she whispered, pushing a lock of hair from her eye.

As I threw on my clothes, she remained naked in bed, curled around the pillows, one foot dangling over the carpet. 'I thank you from the heart', she smiled, 'for all your help, Enzo. Now, Varcas drew two other maps: one detailing this part of Nevada, and one covering northern Arizona. This Albuquerque map has the most sightings by far, but I hope you'll return to help me with the others.'

'I'll be back,' I said from the door, and within the hour, showered and changed, I was boarding the plane with Calzas, pulling Sirius along in his traveling case.

'I hear there used to be vampires around here,' I said to Calzas.

Unwrapping his second sandwich, Calzas turned to me. 'Who told you that?'

'That girl visiting from South America. Desirée's cousin.'

He didn't know who I was talking about.

'She's translating a book about it,' I went on.

'Is she,' he grunted. 'And what exactly is in this book?'

I told him what I had learned from Dalia. Calzas's expression never changed. For a long time, his eye locked on an orange butterfly flashing in the light, dancing off the cliff face below us.

'I never heard of this Varcas,' he said finally, 'but I can tell you, there are stranger stories than that out here. See that smaller mesa toward the mountains?'

I could barely detect a dark, boxy smudge on the horizon where he was pointing.

'That's close to the caves where the Zunis believe our ancestors first emerged into this world. It's called the "Forbidden Mesa," and even today no one ever goes there. No one could, even if they wanted to.'

'Why not?'

'Because no matter how far you travel toward it, it always stays that distance from you. You can't get any closer. And that's just as well, because if you did, you wouldn't come back alive.' He poured himself some more tea. 'See, it's said that there are four underworlds through which our people journeyed to arrive in this world. Each is illuminated by a different light: blue, white, red, and yellow.'

'Like the stars,' I interrupted him, my eyes widening, 'from dwarves to novas.'

He nodded. 'And the light is like starlight. In each world, its intensity grows. This world was darkness and gloom until the sun was placed in the sky, and then the world became all colors. But not at the Forbidden Mesa, where some of the first Zunis settled. Because they were half-blind and misshapen from their long climb through the bowels of the earth, which no one had marked before them, in this surface world they became monsters and strange beings – including werewolves and vampires. When there are earthquakes, more of them emerge, two, three at a time, and they go right to the Forbidden Mesa. There they can come and go, raising hell in this world, preying on the unsuspecting, nourishing themselves on blood, but no one can disturb them. Yes, your friar got it right, they never die because they are walking dead, and by now there must be thousands of them, so the fact he saw a few dozen a hundred years ago doesn't surprise me a bit.'

'So you believe this?' I said.

'That he saw vampires? Sure. But they didn't come here with the Spanish: you can't "discover" something that's already there. You know, it's the same old story, like "discovering" America, or Mexico, or wherever. But I'll tell you the most interesting thing about that mesa. The shamans say that these phantoms have built a city on the mesa the same size as the ancient sky-city whose ruins we're sitting in. Houses, meeting halls, even cisterns that contain, not water, but blood. But it's a ghost city, literally. The building materials are not stones and clay, but blocks of vapor and sheets of mist that are continually shifting and rearranging them-selves. So from day to day the city's contours are never the same, except one night every year. On the night of the winter solstice, the residents of Acoma stay indoors with their lights burning. They're warned that if they venture outdoors and even once close their eyes in the night, when they open them they may find themselves transported to the ghost city, at the mercy of its inhabitants and with no hope of seeing the sun rise again.'

Shielding my eyes, I peered at the Forbidden Mesa. 'And no one's lived to tell of this place?'

'Only the earliest shamans, who possessed great powers. And they died soon after recounting what they'd seen. You know, if you take an aerial photo of Acoma at night, it appears as a gray grid lit up silver. Well, no aerial photos ever pick up the Forbidden Mesa, much less its ghost city. That's a fact. Some Zunis claimed that in trance states they saw the ghost city, and that ancient Acoma was modeled on such a vision, recorded by an old soothsayer called the Spider Woman.'

I thought about this. 'You mean, like Newgate Prison?'

'Something like that.'

On the plane that morning he had told me that when the English rebuilt Newgate Prison in 1780, they used as a blueprint the terrifying etchings of imaginary prisons and torture chambers the Italian artist Giovanni Battista Piranesi concocted thirty years earlier. 'Or, as usual, life imitating art,' Calzas had observed drily. He had lectured me before that fantastical architecture was nothing less than the architecture of the future. Of cities and buildings, as yet unimagined, which in the present seem impossible, but must evolve eventually as a matter of course.

'Nothing is fantastical,' he said now, 'it's just unimagined. Think of the structures and contraptions visionaries put on paper long before they were ever built: skyscrapers, undersea tunnels, helicopters, submarines. Even interplanetary spacecraft, which were imagined by ancient astronomers centuries before the development of the science *behind* the science that could produce them. Space flight was like any new invention or piece of architecture: it first took form in the vapor of the human mind, then leapt into reality after a while, at some crucial juncture, and assumed earthly form.' He squinted into the hazy light at the Forbidden Mesa. 'Ancient Acoma is one of those rare cities, like Alexandria and St Petersburg, which was conceived in a single stroke and sprang up whole. Who knows how that happened.'

For a while we sat in silence. Then, with all the talk of vampires, and people transported to ghost cities against their will, I began to worry about Sirius again. 'You're sure Sirius is all right?' I said, scanning the ruins behind us.

Calzas nodded. 'He can take care of himself.'

'I hope so,' I said, stretching back into the sun and mopping my brow. 'You know, you mentioned ancient astronomers who only imagined space travel. What about Uncle Junius's blue amulet, and the other amulet you've been searching for – the Egyptian one that shows the far side of the moon?'

'What about them?'

'Well, they may prove that there was space travel back then.'

'If that's so, you can be sure someone imagined it even earlier,' Calzas said, slipping his sunglasses on. 'Don't you see, that's the way everything comes about, including people. Maybe the people, the objects, even the places that we glimpse in dreams, but have never seen on earth, are the ones which haven't made the jump from our collective minds into reality. When they do, and we encounter them in solid form, we sometimes can't understand why such a person, place, or thing seems so familiar.'

'Is that also something the shamans teach?'

'No,' he smiled, 'that's a theory of mine. Private stock.' He stood up. 'Come on, let's get going.'

I knew more about architecture on this trip and Calzas spent the next several hours leading me through the ancient city, showing me the sorts of foundations the early Zunis laid, the ingenious use of stairways and ladders to connect ascending warrens of apartments, the underground caves they expanded into granaries and storerooms, the hydraulics of the irrigation system in a place with little natural water. What most intrigued me, though, was the shamans' healing chamber, which we visited at dusk.

The chamber was a spherical room carved out of the stone interior of the mesa, accessible only on all fours through a winding tunnel. The wind that hummed past us in the tunnel sounded like a chorus of low voices, maybe of all the men who had practiced their craft in that chamber. Whether they were welcoming us or warning us off I couldn't tell as I crawled behind Calzas and the beam of his powerful flashlight. In the chamber itself, remarkably well preserved because of its isolation from the elements, the shamans' essential furnishings remained in place: in the center a low stone platform on which a man could lie down, a shelf carved into the wall, a deep basin, and a stone stool. Nothing made of wood, Calzas told me, or straw, or any other impermanent substance was allowed in the chamber. Only the naked human body on which the shaman, also naked, concentrated his healing powers. He could also make use of the narrow aperture – maybe three inches wide – bored into the smooth rock directly above the platform, revealed when Calzas slid a flat stone along runners grooved into the ceiling eight centuries before. This aperture turned out to be one end of a long cylindrical shaftway that rose on a diagonal into the open air, where a perfect circle of sky was visible. Watching the first stars appear in the darkening sky, I lay on the platform and imagined the thin beam of sunlight or moonlight that at precise times would shoot down like a laser onto my chest.

Before Calzas and I reached the head of the foot trail and, flashlights in hand, began our descent from the sky-city, I called to Sirius so many times that his name echoed through the ruins. I was really worried now, thinking he might never emerge. Calzas was worried, too, though he didn't say so openly. He didn't have to, for he had broken his silence and in his sternest voice begun calling to Sirius himself. Still, there was no sign of him, not a bark, nothing.

'I'm not leaving here till we find him,' I told Calzas. 'Even if we have to search every adobe.'

'That would take more than one night,' Calzas said.

'I don't care. What if he's hurt somewhere?'

Furrowing his brow, he looked hard at me. 'Let's try something else first. We'll descend as far as the plateau where he left us and summon him. If he doesn't come, we'll return here.'

'What good will that do?'

'Just a hunch. Trust me.'

I was certain we were wasting precious time and energy as we edged our way down the steep sandy incline to the plateau. The weeds clotting the trail smelled like ashes. In the dancing beams of our flashlights the rough terrain came alive. Not just the darting moths, clouds of mosquitoes, and wind-whipped grass, but suddenly things that shouldn't have moved at all: the bushes and trees, the loose stones, and even the mammoth boulders, shifting this way and that as the light caught them. The boulders shot off sparks when they bumped together, and beneath my feet the ground tilted. Only the pyramid of rocks surrounded by tall lavender grass appeared immobile.

'What's going on?' I whispered to Calzas.

'Just stand still and everything will be still with you.' For once his voice betrayed his excitement. 'It's this place. This happens when the spirits are active.'

'You mean, from that other mesa?'

'No. The spirits of Acoma, which are benign. I've only seen it happen once.'

'When was that?' I said, stepping onto more level ground, to steady myself, even as I watched everything move with me.

'Shhh. Be still.'

By now night had fallen completely. Still low over the mountains, the moon bathed the desert in a pearly glow. Bats swooped from their perches in the cliff face, flashed into view, and then were swallowed up again by the darkness. The wind was picking up, too, howling through the rocks. But it was the stars over Acoma, blazing as if they were embers being fanned, that overwhelmed everything else. In that sky, the constellations glittered into place so distinctly that I could pick them out as easily as if I had unfolded a celestial map on which they were illustrated. Scorpio directly above, Libra, Centaurus, Hydra, Virgo, Pyxis the Compass, and, far to my right, Canis Major just above the mountains. Except that, oddly, I could not find its largest star, just off center, the Dog Star for which Sirius was named.

'Enzo,' Calzas said, taking my arm. 'Call to him now. Just once, as loud as you can. And shine your light on the trail where we came down.'

When both our flashlights were trained there, I shouted, 'Sirius!' drawing the syllables out even as they began to echo off the cliffs.

Both of us held our breath and strained our ears, for ten, fifteen, thirty seconds, when suddenly we heard a faint bark from high above. Then another.

I was about to shout again, but Calzas squeezed my shoulder and put his finger over his lips.

The barking grew fainter, then loud again, clearly in the ruins now, as it approached us. The closer the barking got, the more the terrain grew still. Only the wind kept howling. But now when I moved, the bushes and boulders barely moved with me.

Finally, at the instant Sirius appeared in the beams of our flashlights, skidding down the trail, kicking up a cloud of sand, the earth fell still.

As I ran to greet him, he kept barking all the way into my arms. Then, throwing his head back so his eyes shimmered with moonlight, he growled deep in his chest – his entire body trembled – at that pyramid of rocks.

'Sirius, where were you?' I said, pulling him close.

Even Calzas was puzzled. Sirius's head and chest were dry, the black fur coated with gray dust, but his hindquarters and tail were dripping wet. Neither Calzas nor I could think of a place in Acoma where Sirius might have been drenched like that. The only water was in cisterns, inaccessible to him down sheer drops.

Now he seemed eager to get off the mesa, and he barked at us to follow him down the trail.

'Why do you think he hid like that today?' I asked, turning to Calzas as we walked single file over the jagged rocks.

He shook his head. 'He'll always act strangely when he comes here,' he said finally. 'You asked me when it was I saw the spirits move the stones here. It was the day I found Sirius, five years ago.'

All the way down the mesa, I thought about this and peppered Calzas with questions. But to what he had said he would only add that the Zuni spirits became active on very specific occasions: before a natural disaster, the birth or death of a powerful person or creature, or a visitation from what the Zunis called the outer world.

When we were able to walk side by side near the bottom, he pointed skyward into the great swirl of stars. 'You see the Milky Way. The Zunis believe it is the spine of an enormous beast, seen from within its bowels. That's where the earth is. Where human history is confined. Beyond the body of the beast is the outer world, populated by spirits more powerful than those here below. The Zunis say the Milky Way holds up the night, keeping fragments of darkness from falling on us. And just as Christians believe an angel in the form of a falling star may visit this world, so the Zunis receive rare visitations from beyond the Milky Way, the shell of the night. What little we know of the outer world – which otherwise is like peering into blackness through the chink in a wall – comes to us in this way. Usually, we're not even aware of such visitors.'

If Sirius was weary when he joined us on the plateau, by the time we reached the jeep he was utterly exhausted, eyes half-lidded, tongue hanging out. I brushed the dust from him and dried his hindquarters with a blanket before he jumped up into the rear seat and immediately fell asleep. It would be close to midnight before we were back at the Hotel Canopus, and at that moment, as Calzas raced the jeep along the snaking road to the main highway, I could not know that my life at the hotel, and the entire charmed world of Samax and his circle, were about to reach a turning point and would never again be the same. No, at that moment, I was still pondering Sirius's disappearance in the sky-city and wondering if Dalia would be awake when we got home. And glancing up at the Milky Way, I was so taken with the notion that it prevented the darkness from raining down on us that I didn't think to look beside it at Canis Major, where earlier I had seen no sign of Sirius, the Dog Star. Had I looked, I thought later, it must have been there – the brightest star in the sky.

12

Kauai

I was dancing with a man named Philippe and he had just put his hand on my breast. We were on the terrace of a long white house jammed with revellers on New Year's Eve. It was a hot, humid night. Down a flight of smooth wooden steps bordered with sea grapes the Pacific breakers rolled in high under a new moon. Flickering blue lights were strung through the arbor, dense with the flowering branches of hau trees, that overhung the terrace. A pair of toucans were perched on a rod overhead. Out in the garden the flames of tall torches leapt in the wind. The music on the stereo, 'Crossroads' by Cream, was deafening. And though the song was fast, we were dancing slowly cheek to cheek. I had met Philippe less than five minutes before when he passed me a joint laced with THC.

I took his hand from my breast and placed it on my hip as we danced around knots of people sitting cross-legged on the tile floor smoking hash from hookahs and sipping champagne from goblets. Each hookah held a different colored liqueur – crème de menthe, cognac, grappa, Pernod – that bubbled softly whenever someone inhaled and sent ghostly curls of smoke swirling up toward the mouthpiece. Some guests were decked out in their best tropical finery – silk shirts and pantaloons, Nehru jackets, batik dresses – while others wore bathing suits and tank tops. A darkly tanned man with hair halfway down his back and a long beard, naked but for a net loincloth, had just come up to the terrace dripping from the sea and assumed the lotus position on a prayer mat below an enormous Japanese fan. The fan depicted two storks mating in a rainstorm. Hanging from his neck on a gold chain was a medallion of a lion's face with a sun for one eye and a moon for the other. He dipped his finger into a goblet and coated his lips with wine. Then he introduced himself to all of us as Olan and announced that he had just hiked and swum up the coast to Kilauea from Anahola. To do so, I calculated, he would have had to set out late that afternoon, which I doubted was the case. Not least of all because that stretch of sea was particularly rough, with fierce riptides.

Olan raised his right arm and untaped a waterproof packet from his armpit. 'Five hundred milligrams of pure mescaline,' he said in a high clear voice, smiling and brandishing the packet, 'no speed, no impurities, spiritually sound.'

Philippe immediately made me a little bow and joined Olan on the floor, indicating that I ought to follow.

I declined and drifted into the house, crazy with the shadows cast by Chinese lanterns, where someone handed me a goblet, kissed the back of my neck, and disappeared into the darkness. I drank deeply and wiped the champagne bubbles from my lips. My eyes were burning and my mouth was dry. Both downstairs bathrooms were occupied, so I picked my way around people sprawled on the stairway in order to use the one upstairs. A small Christmas wreath blinking with stars was hung on the banister. I was halfway up the stairs when all the lights came up below, the music stopped suddenly, and a woman's voice from the throng in the living room began counting down from ten.

' . . .7, 6, 5, 4,' she cried, '3, 2, 1 – Happy New Year!'

Cries of Happy New Year resounded inside and outside the house. A couple rose from the steps before me, kissed each other, and then kissed me simultaneously, one on each cheek. Like me, and a lot of other people at the party – including my lover at that time, a hematologist who was somewhere in the living room with his wife, and the host, an orthopedic surgeon whose wife had just done the countdown – this couple also worked at the hospital in Lihue. She was a physical therapist named Jeannie and he was the cafeteria manager. Like my old friend in the Navy, Sharline, Jeannie seemed to have a different boyfriend every month. 'Do you ever dream of Jeannie?' was her favorite come-on line. I'd had a few boyfriends myself in the last year and a half, but I let them provide the come-on lines. My own come-on after a while was nonverbal and obvious: I was wide open, for companionship, a good time, sex. I had had enormous gaps in me waiting to be filled ever since I arrived on the island. Those near the surface were evident even to a man with the weakest antennae; the deeper ones, I thought, could never be filled, and so were off-limits to everyone until I felt otherwise. In short, I was available for anything but love, and instinctively gravitated to men who didn't have it to give.

'Happy 1972, Mala,' Jeannie said. 'Lots of luck.'

I nodded, clinked her goblet, and continued on to the upstairs bathroom.

Sitting on the toilet, I began to feel dizzy. When I stood at the sink and poured the rest of my champagne down the drain, I didn't have to glance into the mirror to see that I looked as bad as I felt. It had been seventeen months since I had arrived on the island of Kauai and it wasn't long before I discovered I was no longer immune to the effects of alcohol and drugs. Not only was it impossible for me to imbibe freely anymore, but I was more susceptible to getting very high very fast than I had ever been before the spider bit me. But that didn't stop me from drinking or smoking ganja. My hope of continuing the clean and stripped-down lifestyle I'd enjoyed on Rarotonga had fallen by the wayside. Unfortunately, I was not even deterred by the fact that, of all the places I had ever been, Kauai was by far the most intensely beautiful. The fact is, being around people again turned out to be much more difficult than I had imagined.

I first heard of Kauai, one of the eight major Hawaiian islands, during the week I spent in Honolulu after leaving the Cook Islands. A woman I met at breakfast in my hotel had just spent a year on Kauai. She was selling her house north of Honolulu before leaving Hawaii for good. 'It's time,' she said. 'I've been here since 1944. Maybe I'll end up in Australia, maybe in South America, but I'll never go back to the mainland.' She was a striking woman, a tall blonde about fifty years old, who said she was the widow of a wealthy hotelier, and added acerbically, 'He helped to build up Waikiki as you see it – a crime for which he ought never to be forgiven. At any rate, he was my first – and last – husband.' Then she started talking rapturously of Kauai, describing its rainforests, and the inherent healing powers of its climate, and the mystical properties visitors since the ancient Polynesians attributed to its natural features. (Later I would hear of the devotees of a certain yogi who believed the core of the island to be an enormous quartz crystal.) This woman – her name was Stella – whom I never saw again, had gone to Kauai after being diagnosed with terminal liver cancer. Within six months of bathing daily in the sea and subsisting on a diet of taro and fresh fruit, her cancer had gone into remission. If the island worked miracles for cancers of the vital organs, I told myself, think how it might heal parts of the innermost self equally damaged.

With these expectations, I once again rented a bungalow a short walk from the ocean, in Haena on the northern tip of the island. The bungalow was at one end of the single main road that ran along the periphery of three-quarters of the island, a horseshoe that began at the green volcanic peaks of Na Pali coast and ended in desert terrain. Driving the length of this road was like traveling from the Philippines to New Mexico in just ninety minutes, passing through dairy country, sugarcane fields, and even a miniature version of the Grand

Canyon, in Waimea. About ten miles apart on the island were the desert-like village of Mana, where the annual rainfall was eleven inches, and Mount Waialeale, which a rusted sign proclaimed to be the wettest spot on earth with 462 inches per year.

To reach my house, you drove through the Hanalei Valley, a quilt-work of taro fields, and then over a dozen one-way wooden bridges that forded the many streams and lagoons carrying that tremendous rainfall into the sea. There were three bungalows widely spaced on my crooked dirt lane, one belonging to an old fisherman named Lon and the other to a widow on Maui who came for two months every year. I was hemmed in by the sea in front and a lush valley in the rear that ran to the foot of the jagged green mountains. My bungalow, painted pale green, had four rooms and a shaded lanai. There was also a small shed where the original owner, a potter, had set up his wheel and which I eventually used as a developing room when I began taking undersea photographs. But that was much later.

From the lanai I saw nothing but open sea. Or as my neighbor Lon put it, in his singsong fashion, 'If you was to continue north by north-west, the next piece of land you hits is *Ja*pan.' Yes, I thought, and if you go due west, the next piece of land is Vietnam. Hanoi, in fact, lies on the same latitude as Kauai. Except for February, March, and April, the trade winds never stopped blowing; having crossed the entire Pacific Ocean from Alaska, they cooled my house on the hottest days, ruffling the palm trees that circled my tiny lawn. There was bougainvillea, like a blanket of fire, up one wall of the bungalow, lush ferns along the north side, and a pair of papaya trees beside the shed that produced fruit with sweet, delicate flesh. Flanking the front door in wide, deep beds there were plants with white flowers that bloomed constantly. I had never smelled flowers more fragrant. Year-round they filled the bungalow with their perfume. After a few weeks, when I asked Lon about it, he told me the plant was called a spider plant.

But idyllic and solitary as this place was, I could not long have tried to replicate my life on Rarotonga, for the simple reason that what money remained after my year of island-hopping had been exhausted – even sooner than I'd anticipated – by my move to Hawaii. I needed to get a job, pronto. Not a waitressing job that would keep me scraping along in a furnished room, but something that would provide a steady paycheck to support my bungalow and the secondhand VW on which I had put a down payment. At first I thought of applying to teach Latin and Greek at the high school in Hanalei, despite being a few credits short of my B.A. But the secretary there informed me that they didn't have classes in those languages. Probably a good thing, since on second thought I doubted I was prepared to enter a classroom and work with kids sixteen years old – Loren's age, if indeed there still was a Loren drawing breath somewhere. Since there probably wasn't much call on the island for an arachnologist's assistant, that left the only profession in which I truly had formal training: X-ray technician.

The notion of spending half my waking hours in hospital was not very appealing to me. But X-raying people on Kauai, I told myself, would be something altogether different than it had been aboard the *Repose*. No matter how sick they were, or how terrible the injury they might suffer, it was doubtful they would have stepped on a landmine or been strafed with shrapnel. In fact, I was informed there hadn't been a homicide on the island in ten years.

'And that', said Dr Samuel Prion, the elderly radiologist whom I saw in my second interview at Wilcox Memorial Hospital in Lihue, 'was a hunting accident.'

'I didn't know there was any hunting on the island,' I said.

He was a slightly stooped, soft-spoken man with sharp blue eyes and white hair ringing his bald head. 'Aside from pheasants,' he replied, 'the only game are the wild goats. Once a year it's legal for them to be hunted in

Waimea Canyon. They're the descendants of a few domestic goats, brought here by Captain Cook, that ran off into the mountains.'

'Captain Cook?'

'The first European to discover Kauai, in 1778. Came just that once and left the goats, among other things.'

No wonder I had felt so at home there from the first. 'I should have known,' I said, and at the end of the interview Dr Prion hired me, subject to the approval of his oversight board.

I was nervous when I came before the board at Wilcox Memorial the following week. I had had my hair cut and set at a beauty parlor in Lihue – there were none in my part of the island – got a manicure and pedicure, and had my legs waxed. I bought an overpriced white linen dress and even pricier Italian sandals. I wore my pendant, of course, and for good luck Cassiel's bracelet and the jade earrings he had given me. And I put on makeup for the first time since being discharged from the Navy. Peering into the rearview mirror as I sped down the coast road, I hardly recognized myself. I look like Luna, I thought, who always wore makeup and kept her hair carefully coiffed, even when she was broke. And I had done my makeup very much like hers – mascara just so, a narrow cloud of blue shadow on my eyelids, and lipstick a soft rose – which was not that strange seeing as it was Luna who had taught me how to do my face one long-ago summer day in our house in Brooklyn.

But none of this, or the little I was called on to say, seemed to matter one way or the other to the tribunal of three doctors, two administrators, and the head nurse whom I faced for the next twenty minutes in a conference room. The Vietnam War was still peaking, and whatever their political views (they never did ask what I thought about the war), the fact I was a medical corps veteran, one of the nurses who had volunteered to be in a combat zone – and the first to be sighted on Kauai, apparently – went a long way toward assuring me the job. I was actually well qualified, but through all the frantic running around over the previous days, that fact hadn't really registered on me. I had been alone so long that I hadn't realized how much my self-esteem had fallen.

As for the war, I seemed to think about it incessantly now. Part of this was due to the fact that I was back on American soil, seeing newspapers and hearing radios and televisions regularly for the first time in over two years (though I had only a radio in my own house). I also had daily conversations with people, many of whom were angry and anxious about the war, which at that time was spreading deep into Cambodia.

Many mornings I walked down to the green sea and thought of the B-52s three thousand miles across those same waters streaking inland after their overnight flights from Guam, veering up the Ho Chi Minh Trail to carpet-bomb Hanoi or to soar over the Northern Highlands into Cambodia to drop their massive payloads into the jungle. I didn't know where Cassiel was at that time, in early 1971, but if he was alive, I couldn't imagine him participating in either of those missions. In Manila, he had requested a transfer and then disappeared. Now more than ever I asked myself how those two things could possibly be unrelated. I was resigned to the fact I would never find the answer and would never see him again, but I didn't know how or why I should stop loving him, a man I had only known for three weeks, a period of time that now seemed like the compressed vital center within the broader, gloomier expanse of my life.

If that advisory board at Wilcox Memorial had asked me what I thought about the war, what would I have replied? Maybe that I never regretted serving as a nurse and helping the men I had encountered in that capacity. Whether those men were oppressors or victims or both was a question I had put aside when I arrived in Vietnam. I had wanted to be a nurse, and to me that meant I wasn't going to be a judge. Certainly after leaving the service I had no desire to judge those men. But for their superiors, the politicians and military brass who began and mismanaged that war, manipulating its effects for their own ends, I had only contempt. Whatever repulsion I had felt for the war as a student had been intensified a thousand times by the suffering I had witnessed as a nurse. I realized too that the deeper I tucked away my love for Cassiel, trying to keep it whole against the erosion of time, the more my loathing for the war grew.

Meanwhile, I started working for Dr Prion in the small but up-to-date radiology department on the second floor of the hospital: two X-ray rooms, a developing room, and his office. The patients were what I had expected: standard preoperative types, fractures and cancers, and a surprising number of children who swallowed all sorts of objects like marbles or tacks. But no keys. Once again I experienced the simultaneous detachment and intimacy of taking and reading an X-ray, the wave of cool solitariness that washed over me when I was gazing into a person's inner workings. Once again hearts, lungs, kidneys, spleens were like familiar islands in a dark vaporous sea, places in which I could discern any irregularities and intrusions. Once again I became acquainted with the geography and physics of the bones, the names of all 206 of which I had now memorized.

Yet the daily reality of a hospital was quite different from that of a hospital ship. I had never held a straight job of this sort before. A ship was hermetic; soldiers were the patients, and sailors, doctors, and nurses were the crew, everyone governed by strict military codes, even, especially, in the chaos of combat. What occurred outside the codes – dope-smoking, casual sex – was seldom a surprise and was always overwhelmed by the inexorable universe of the war. In that universe, Cassiel and I had been the exception, not the rule. In the hospital, I suddenly found myself in a microcosm of a society that as a whole still felt alien to me. Working solo – odd hours, odd tasks – for Zaren Eboli or toiling with moth-eaten books in the morgue of an obscure branch of the New Orleans library had been more my speed. It was no accident that in college my refuge had been the ancient world, which I studied in classes of ten students or less.

All of which is to say that, despite my wartime experiences and unusual travels, I was still on unsure footing when it came to dealing with other people. Maybe it was those very things that had left me ill-prepared for the emotional transactions others found much simpler. I was not comfortable with large populations; on the *Repose*, it had been easy to carve out a niche as a loner. In one way or another, even the most gregarious of my shipmates – like Sharline – became loners. In Wilcox Memorial, being a loner only drew more attention to me, and increased my allure for those who already found me attractive, mysterious, and even exotic on account of my history.

I couldn't keep the men at the hospital away from me. I knew I was pretty, and I knew that on an island, especially one of moderate size, the men were on the lookout for new pretty women. Maybe a part of me was flattered and didn't mind it so much. There was one man, especially, who had his eye on me from day one. He was privy to more of my history than other people at the hospital because he had sat on that advisory board which approved my hiring. But he bided his time while I routinely turned down requests for dates from other doctors. Comparing them to Cassiel, as I did every time, I found – predictably – that none of them measured up. After a couple of months, completely alone, I thought I couldn't keep it up much longer. I felt the need for private companionship as well as solitary privacy, and most of all I needed to have sex. But I decided not to look for it at the hospital.

On Rarotonga I had learned to handle a sea kayak. During those first months on Kauai, I often rented a kayak in Hanalei on a Sunday morning. I slid down the river into the bay and then up the coast to Ke'e Beach, passing my own beach on the way, where two beach dogs who had taken to sleeping on my porch followed me along the shore barking. So when I received my paycheck the first day of my third month at my job, I decided to blow it all on my own kayak.

It was a real beauty, all Plexiglas, purple with an orange cockpit and storage holds fore and aft for food and supplies. It was built not just for hugging the coast but crossing the open sea. If you had the stamina, and the stomach for the waves, it could carry you the ninety miles to Oahu, and beyond. I bought it at the place where I had been renting, from the manager, Val, a tall, tow-headed young waterskier and rower with a terrific build who had given me the eye, but in a nicer way than any doctor I'd yet encountered. He offered to deliver the kayak personally in his pickup, following me in my VW to Haena.

Afterward I made sandwiches and we drank beer on the beach. Val was wearing his typical business attire: a red swimsuit and a T-shirt. It was late afternoon, but he was in no rush to get back to town. Business was slow, he said. So we drank more beer and went for a swim. Val had grown up on the island and he swam effortlessly, powerfully, like a dolphin. I brought a portable radio down from the house. The dogs, whom I had named Castor and Pollux, fell asleep on either side of the new kayak. The sun set. We took another swim and this time he glided up and rose before me silently, through the clear, shallow water. He put his arms around me and kissed me. He unsnapped my top. And I shuddered as he kissed me again, running his hands over my breasts, cupping them, and then peeling off my bathing suit and running his hand between my legs. No one had touched me there since Cassiel, but I didn't hold back from him. After he slipped out of his own suit, we lay on a blanket on the sand. He spread my legs and was very gentle, first with his tongue, and then pushing into me. I came almost at once, and tightening my embrace, waited for him to follow.

Afterward, I rested my head on his chest and for the first time noticed a small tattoo on his left shoulder, a pair of crossed swords over a numeral 7. I had seen it many times on members of the 7th Air Cavalry in Vietnam. So he was a vet. But I said nothing about this, or the fact I had been in the war.

Val came out to see me a few more times, but we both knew it wasn't going to turn into anything serious. He had told me that first time together that he had a girl-friend, and after I found out who she was – a young redhead who worked at the bakery whom I liked very much – we agreed to stop. But we stayed friends, too, and later, after I'd surprised him with the fact I had been a Navy nurse, we would talk about the war, but not too much. Mostly we went kayaking along Na Pali coast, alone or with other friends of his, and he taught me everything I knew about the North Shore's peculiar currents and reefs. One day, after I had built up my stamina, he took me on my most ambitious excursion, to the island of Niihau, seventeen miles across the Kaulakahi Channel from Kauai.

Niihau was known as the 'Forbidden Island'. It was privately owned by a single family who bought it in the nineteenth century from a Hawaiian monarch in need of funds. No visitors were allowed. Its population was under three hundred, all pure-blooded Hawaiians who raised cattle and sold rare shells gathered on its beaches. It had been known as the Forbidden Island long before it became private property. The ancient Hawaiians had shunned it as a haven of ghosts and demons, elusive lizard-men reputed to be capable of sucking the blood from a man in less than minute. On nights when the west wind blew, it sometimes carried the howls of the demons – and the moans of their victims. It was said that on such nights, if you were trying to escape the currents around the Forbidden Island, the harder you rowed the more you were drawn back to shore, and certain death. After Val and I had paddled most of the way across the channel, we turned around, the wind whipping up whitecaps, and rowed back to Kauai without meeting any resistance. But that was because we had not actu-ally reached Niihau, Val told me, where the demons could pick up our scent. That would have been a different story.

In May, after nine months on the island, I attended a surprise birthday party for one of my few friends at the hospital, a young urologist from San Diego named Seth Vinson. His lover Marvin threw the party at their house in Hanalei, and I was the decoy who had taken Seth for a drink to get him out of the house. Seth was a slight, bearded man with an easy wit and a passion for sailing. We had dinner together every week, and I always felt I could let my hair down with him. From the start, he was generous, sharing his other friends with me.

Among the most interesting of these was Estes Shaula, whom Seth introduced me to that night. Estes didn't go to many parties. He was an astronomer at the NASA Observatory, high in the mountains of Kokee Park near Waimea Canyon. Twice I had driven up through the canyon to the Kalalau Lookout, from which I had seen the stark white dome of the NASA Observatory down a gated road with a sentry box; like Niihau, it was a forbidden place.

Built in 1960, the observatory had a small permanent staff with frequent visitors from the main US observatory, at Mauna Kea on the Big Island, which housed the largest telescope in the world. In my time on Kauai, stargazing every night, I had found a density of stars in the sky to match the Cook Islands'. I had promised myself a telescope when I could afford one, but even with field binoculars I had seen dizzying concentrations of secondary and tertiary stars that were invisible to the naked eye. I had glimpsed Europa, the brightest of Jupiter's moons, one night, and Triton, a moon of Saturn. Until I crossed paths with Estes Shaula, however, I had heard only vague rumors of what the NASA scientists on the island were undertaking. He confirmed that, in addition to tracking conventional satellites, manned space shots, and planetary probes, they were part of a secret project picking up signals from interstellar space with a radio telescope.

'And, more importantly,' Estes confided to me in his soft drawl, twirling the ice cubes in his Eclipse rum as we stepped onto Seth's lanai, 'we're searching for galaxies beyond this one where stars are born. To me, that dwarfs all the other stuff we do. You yourself work with X-rays. You know that, unlike visible light waves or radio waves, they can't penetrate the atmosphere. That's why X-ray telescopes don't work on earth. I'm helping to lay the groundwork for setting them up in space within the next twenty years.'

Gazing out over the bright crescent of Hanalei Bay, I thought it strange that, despite my obsession with the stars over the previous four years, I had never met an astronomer. And now that I had, it turned out he was one who happened to be more than happy to talk astronomy to me all the time, the way other men might talk baseball or politics or sex.

Estes Shaula was a native Texan, a very handsome man just under forty who looked far older. Part of this was the premature graying of his long hair, and the compressed seriousness of his face – his brow was deeply furrowed over his wire-rimmed glasses, crow's-feet, blue eyes, and nervous smile – but much was due to the quantities of speed and ganja he consumed daily. In thumbnail fashion, Seth had told me that Dr Shaula was both a scientist with a brilliant future and a dope smoker with a prodigious habit. Even before I met Estes, I knew it was the downward of those two trajectories he was following that would prevail. Initially he had used marijuana to come down off the methedrine with which he fueled his fourteen-hour workdays. I had learned in the Navy, where so many of the doctors and nurses operated on the speed-and-smoke monorail, that it was only a matter of time before its riders were derailed – or worse – denying all the while that they had a problem.

In his own denial about Estes, Seth, a very sober person, had surprised me. 'He works hard and he parties hard,' he said as blithely as any of the medicos aboard the *Repose*.

But after spending time with Estes, I understood how Seth could rationalize that way: speeding or stoned, Estes was a charming and interesting companion. While his appetite for stimulants seemed boundless, his control rarely faltered. He was well-spoken when he chose to converse and politely silent at all other times. His silences could be monumental, but never felt hostile. Whether at their center he was reeling and inchoate, utterly serene, or icily walled-off, I couldn't tell. But I never heard him say an unkind thing. And to me, at that first dinner, he said a number of kind ones. 'Most people who come here', Estes said, as I munched on Seth's birthday cake and he rolled a joint, 'don't appreciate the place with any depth because they haven't really suffered. So it's always nice', he nodded, 'to meet exceptions to the rule.' Not surprisingly, he wasn't a good listener, but then, he was the kind of person I preferred listening to. At first, I wished I could have stolen some time with him when he was sober – there must have been such hiatuses - but as time passed I was soon smoking more ganja myself and drinking more steadily.

At that time, good grass was cheap and easy to find all over the island. Since the mid-Sixties, there had been a hippie influx from California. Small communes had cropped up in the northern half of the island. The public campsite in Haena had become a tent city, overflowing into the forest. A couple of babies had been born there. A Hindu cult was meeting in one of the caves near Ke'e Beach, chanting by torchlight. There were squatters in the state forest; a trio of self-proclaimed dryads who lived on berries and roots in the Valley of the Lost Tribe; and nomads, barefoot, with backpacks, who hitchhiked, picked fruit for two dollars an hour, and slept out in the open. Many of these people were growing and smoking amazingly powerful dope all around Hanalei. I found that a few puffs off the local Thai stick had as strong an effect as some synthetic hallucinogens.

Estes grew his own stash in the forest near his house,

a half mile from the observatory. Unlike the local foot soldiers of the counterculture, however, he wasn't smoking it after a day of surfing, practicing tai chi, or tending an organic garden; by the time he lit up, he was totally wired in a small silent office where he once told me he could hear with clarity the silver numbers spinning off his calculations and tinkling in the air. On top of this, he had begun to moisten his throat when smoking, not with peppermint tea, but rum and bitters.

When, a few weeks after I met him, he invited me up to his house for a 'candlelight dinner' and a look at the night sky through the observatory telescope, I jumped at the opportunity. Whether I was excited about the candlelight dinner or the fact I would see the stars as never before, I wasn't sure. The two things spilled into one another. But I dressed with more care and expectation than usual, slipping on a pair of white jeans and a new black jersey embroidered with white flowers.

Estes's home, in a bamboo forest above Waimea Canyon, was not at all what I had imagined. A simple, lemon-colored ranch house on the outside, the five rooms inside were neat and austere. Instead of the gaudy carpets and wall hangings and overflowing ashtrays I had expected, the teak floor was highly polished, the white curtains were neatly pressed, and a silent ceiling fan revolved in the living room. There was a meditation cell with a black mat and an incense burner beside the bedroom, which was centered by a large futon behind a silk curtain. There were three framed portraits in the kitchen, of Albert Einstein, Edwin Hubble, and Clyde W. Tombaugh, the discoverer of Pluto. And in the living room a photograph that looked like star clusters etched on a slab of sandstone; in fact, it was a fossil, a billion years old, that preserved the movements of the oldest known organisms on earth. There was not a single book or paper in that room. All his books were in the study, shelved from floor to ceiling around a solitary rocking chair with its reading lamp. If Estes was walking a razor's edge with his mental stability, the diligent housekeeper, a young woman from Niihau named Wind, certainly kept the daily machinery of his life in order.

Wind had left a vegetable casserole in the oven. Spooning eggplant and zucchini over brown rice, Estes passed me a predinner joint and a tray of cheese and grapes. We drank rum. Our plates were set out on a low table, lit by candles, where we sat on large cushions and ate with chopsticks. Estes never let the stereo cool: first one Bill Evans record after another, then a set of Coltrane duets called 'Interstellar Space'.

'These are just to get you in the mood. . .' Estes said, pouring me some more rum.

I smiled and crossed my legs in front of me, fully extending them off my cushion.

'. . . for the telescope,' he added, slipping yet another new record onto the turntable.

Long before we took his car to the observatory, I had stopped keeping up with him joint for joint. I was afraid that everything would blur on me if I got any higher. Just before we arrived at the sentry box, Estes spritzed some Binaca into his mouth. An armed Air Force guard shined a flashlight into the car, wrote down my name, and waved us through with a crisp salute.

It was eleven o'clock. One of Estes's assistants was on night shift, monitoring the radio telescope behind a semicircular control panel. He was accustomed to seeing Estes come in at all hours, but he was surprised to see me. It was obvious that when Estes made the time to go on a date, this was not one of his usual stops. Estes didn't have regular girlfriends and he didn't conduct love affairs. Without a word spoken on the subject, I realized this even before we had finished dinner. But I chose to persist in the illusion that he and I might enjoy something more than a one-night stand. After all, he had made an exception in taking me to the observatory.

The dome that housed the telescope was dark and empty. Its tile floor gleamed. The air was chilled round the clock, its unvarying temperature calibrated to prevent distortion in the delicate lenses. On all of the island, even the hospital's pathology lab, I had never been in such a cold place. I climbed the spiral stairway to the telescope's cage and settled in, adjusting the reclining seat according to Estes's instructions. Putting my eye to the telescope's shuttered eyepiece as Estes went to switch on the power, I waited with the expectation of a child for the heavens to unfold before me. Even so, I was completely unprepared when suddenly I found myself zooming among the stars at high speed, encountering them up close – in a rush – on their own terms. I had never looked through a telescope of this magnitude, and it made me feel as if I myself were out in space.

There were white stars phosphorescent as exploding flashbulbs, and icy blue stars like diamonds, and stars embedded in swirls and clusters like particles of mica. Other, remoter stars, even at that magnification, were no more than faint pinpoints. I kept thinking about something Estes had said at dinner: if the sun were the size of the dot in the letter *i*, the next nearest star would be ten miles away; and the nearest to that, several hundred miles, and so on.

'Space', he had concluded, pushing his long hair back, 'is just that. It's basically empty. What we employ in creating a constellation – a two-dimensional figure – is anywhere from four to four hundred stars at vastly different distances from us and from one another. In three-dimensional space, they're completely unrelated. Their connections by straight lines on a single plane make them constellations, which exist only in the human imagination, an invention of the navigators. In ancient times, they used animals and religious symbols on their charts. But in the eighteenth century the European navigators who came to these waters placed their own tools in the sky: a sextant, an octant, a triangle, a compass. Even a telescope. Navigators have always been the poets of the constellations.'

Estes had come up beside me, and was manipulating

the controls so that I was slowly scanning the sky, from west to east. 'The constellations are as transitory as we are,' he said, picking up his earlier line of conversation. 'Both physically and imaginatively. There are constellations, recorded long ago, that have disappeared from the charts. Solitaire was named after a bird peculiar to an island in the Indian Ocean: the bird became extinct and the constellation soon followed. Another is the Fox, which used to lie beside Scorpio. That's all we know about it. Its stars are still there, but there's no telling which ones they are or how they were connected. Even among modern constellations, the Electric Machine came and went while the Air Pump is still with us. Physically, the stars are always moving – even the sun, at twelve miles per second. One day, billions of years from now, the Big Dipper will look like a semicircle. In the time of the ancient Egyptians, the North Star wasn't Polaris, but Thuban.'

'I've never heard of it.'

He touched my shoulder. 'You're looking at it, Mala. In the tail of Draco, the third star. The Egyptians oriented the pyramids toward it. In 14,000 A.D. – if there's anyone to see it – the North Star will be Vega. But what else would you like to see?'

'How about Scorpio?'

He adjusted the telescope, the focus swung, and I was gazing into a cluster of stars.

'There's Antares,' I said. What looked like a drop of blood through my binoculars was now an enormous red disk wreathed with smaller white disks. While the white stars twinkled, Antares seemed to pulse. Next to it was a faint green star. 'It's so large,' I said.

'Four hundred times the size of the sun. Larger than Mars's orbit around the sun.'

'Do you know what *Antares* means in Latin?' I put in. '*Similar to Mars.*'

'I didn't know that,' he murmured.

'Because it's so red.'

'It's the greatest of the Supergiant Reds. The first star

285

observed through a telescope in daylight. The old Chinese astronomers called it the 'Fire Star', *Who Sing*, and invoked it for protection against fire.'

I wasn't sure Estes intended all his talk of stars and constellations as a form of seduction, but it had that effect on me. Still, the mention of navigators made me think of Cassiel, and he was still on my mind as we drove away from the observatory, the headlights cutting a tunnel into the darkness.

Back at his house, Estes mixed me a rum and tonic and rolled himself another joint. 'I have a surprise for you,' he said, blowing out all but one candle. He put a tape on his reel-to-reel and a soft sweeping hiss, punctuated by a delicate crackling, filled the living room like an electric wind.

'This is our greatest-hits tape here at the Kokee Observatory,' he said, exhaling a stream of smoke. 'The music of the stars.'

'From the radio telescopes?'

'Two years of our best receptions, edited down and stripped of all interference. Pure interstellar sound.' He laughed. 'Even purer than Coltrane.'

We lay side by side on our backs on the rug in his living room listening to the stars. The circle of light from the candle expanded and contracted on the ceiling and slowly fell into the same rhythm as my breathing. Or maybe it was the other way around. I was pretty high myself at that point. Slowly we stopped talking and started kissing, and then Estes rolled on top of me. And soon enough we had left a trail of our clothes to his futon and quickly made love. For the first and last time. Not badly, not even unsatisfactorily, but much too quickly, with the single burst of energy necessary to slice through the haze of all that rum and ganja. I don't know what I had expected from a man as cut off from his body – and abusive of it – as Estes. He had been skilled in a mechanical way, and gentle certainly, but with so little feeling for himself that I didn't imagine he could have had much left for me. After he made me come, and then came

286

himself, he plunged immediately into a deep sleep, his breathing still raspy, one arm thrown over his eyes.

I switched off the tape recorder, blew out the candle and drove home across the island at two a.m., fortifying myself with black coffee at a gas station in Lihue. I took Cassiel's bracelet out of the drawer in my night table. I hadn't wanted to be wearing it if I went to bed with someone else. I had taken it off when I made love with Val, too. Now I sat on the edge of my bed running my fingers over the stars and crying. And I didn't put it back on for a long time.

The next afternoon, a messenger in a NASA van brought me a package at the hospital. It was a tape of the radio telescope recordings, with a note attached that was notably devoid of sentiment; it said only that we should get together again soon. We didn't; he never called me, and I was certain he was avoiding places, and gatherings, where I might have crossed paths with him.

At the time I was more upset than I let myself admit, maybe because I had finally, painfully, had to face the fact that I was on the rebound from Cassiel. Postponed, to be sure, for two years had elapsed since I was with him. Nevertheless, first with Val, and now with Estes, I had made a break. With Val the break had felt clean. With Estes, I didn't like how I felt. I had allowed myself to be far more vulnerable with Estes, in my heart – no matter what my mind told me – seeking romance with someone who so clearly wanted to avoid it. Punishing myself, in effect, for seeking it at all. That Estes had rejected me after a one-night stand revived in me the feeling that Cassiel had rejected me, too, by the mere fact of his disappearance – no matter whether he had been captured, or killed, or had simply found another woman. No sooner had I come to this realization than I suppressed it – and then I felt something snap in me. I began to plummet.

Doing more dope and drinking more heavily than I ever had in my life, I did exactly what I had promised myself I would not do, taking up, in quick succession, with two doctors at the hospital. And what a pair I chose. First, I had a fling – his word for it – with a pathologist. For a week, we slept together every night. Each time my body lay beside his I thought about the fact that he had spent the day cutting up the bodies of the dead on a steel table, probing lifeless organs which he weighed on a hanging scale, extracting fluids from veins and glands, and dissecting tissue to be examined under a microscope. I couldn't get this out of my head, though he was a mild-mannered middle-aged man, divorced after a long marriage, energetic – even ecstatic – about my more youthful body. I had been around plenty of surgeons and a few pathologists in the war, shared meals with them and worked at close quarters, and had had no feeling about them one way or the other, but then, none of them had ever laid a hand on me, much less touched me in bed. So all that week I tortured myself with these thoughts of what he did in his lab, and with logic equally tortured began to blame Estes for the fact I was with this other man. Estes could have caught me on the rebound, I told myself, but instead had let me tumble past him, spinning. I began to hate Estes, and that rapidly turned into hatred for myself.

The pathologist and I never once went out that week. From the hospital I drove straight to his house in Lihue. He brought home take-out food. I smoked dope. He drank white wine from an iced glass. We stripped and got into bed in his cluttered bedroom. His skin was very pale, except for his face and forearms, because he rarely went out in the sun. From the constant scrubbing with antiseptic soaps, his fingers were especially soft and white. His dull brown eyes seemed to be floating in his face. I felt utterly removed from my body even while absorbing myself in its rawest sensations: my spasms of pleasure were short-lived, insulated, numbed by pain. He felt and fingered, sucked and licked me, and he fucked me, standing up, lying down, on the floor, on the bed. We exchanged only small talk, and even that in small doses. I felt he could have gone on with this arrangement indefinitely. And me? I didn't know. Then, on our seventh night together, we woke a couple of hours before dawn, fucked, and sat up in bed talking – a first. This time I drank with him, and as always with wine, two glasses went right to my head.

He ended up telling me, with sudden fervor, that after cutting all through the human body, exploring the remotest nooks and crannies of bones and organs and magnifying single cells a thousandfold, he had never found any evidence of 'what people call the soul. If it's there,' he added acidly, 'its primary trait must be that it evades detection.'

I was surprised and offended in a way that I hadn't been by his blunt, nonstop appetite for sex. Despite my general torpor, my detachment from myself, a line had been crossed. His words made me feel, more than ever, that in his embrace my body was no more than its physical components. I didn't bother to share with this man all those definitions of the soul I had read in Cicero. (What would a pathologist say to Empedocles's notion that the soul is the blood in our hearts?) I believed I had seen human souls, in all their complexity and elusiveness in the recesses of my X-ray plates. But I was not about to tell him that. So why, I asked myself dully, was I allowing him to enter my body.

To his bewilderment, I jumped out of bed, gathered up my clothes, and hurriedly dressed. Had he proposed more sex two minutes earlier, I would have acquiesced without a second thought, but the one time he actually revealed something of himself it sent me flying from his door. With tears running down my cheeks, I made my second late-night drive up the coast in as many weeks. I never spoke to him again, and at the hospital he avoided me (no doubt wondering why the raw sensualist he had thought me to be would get so riled up over metaphysics) and looked away when our paths did cross.

The second doctor, whom I took up with a week later, was the one who had his eye on me from the first, serving on the advisory board when I was hired. That was his first impression of me – all dolled up – and evidently it had stuck. Cat-like, he had been waiting for the moment when I was dazed and disorientated enough so that he could pounce. Unlike his predecessor, he certainly believed in the human soul, and was very interested in mine – but only as something he might devour or destroy.

His name was Francis Beliar and he was a hematologist. My relationship with him lasted six months – the last six months of his life, as it turned out. In some ways, it was the pathologist redux, but with far more trimmings, more camouflage, and a great deal more surface charm concealing far deadlier manipulative powers. From cheap motels to the luxury resorts in Poipu, his accountant's office in Kapaa to his cabin cruiser docked at the marina, using elaborate aliases and sometimes even disguises, we shacked up all over the island. Several weekends we hopped interisland flights, and posing as honeymooners, or a doomed couple – one of us dying of a fatal disease – or whatever other deception Francis found stimulating at the moment, checked into a resort. On Oahu, for example, we took a suite at the gaudiest hotel on Waikiki and Francis told people we were a married couple making a last-ditch attempt at staving off divorce, and then for two days we screwed on an oval water bed. It was under such circumstances that I first visited, and promptly forgot, some of the other islands – Maui, Molokai, Lanai.

I didn't see Francis daily. Sometimes a week would go by. But when we did meet, the elaborate lies and feints he employed with me, his wife, his longtime on-and-off mistress, and his more occasional and even more secret girlfriends, were sometimes breathtaking in their audacity. Gliding between ever-shifting circles of secrecy was his true pleasure; sex was merely the compass with which he drew those circles. To him, the game was everything, and he liked it best when he could include a cast of supporting players. But in the end it was always a tawdry game. At times, he might have wanted no more than to fuck you in a deserted parking lot in the dark, but he'd get you both there with enough plotting and deception to fill a detective story. By comparison, my 'fling' with the pathologist seemed tame. If I hated myself when I first got involved with Francis, by the time we were done with each other, I was pushing the envelope of my self-respect. Hard.

Francis approached me on King Kamehameha Day in June, the island's biggest holiday, at the hospital's annual barbecue. He was holding a sprig of yellow ginger and smiling. I was standing by the entrance to the tent that had been set up on the lawn. The tent was crowded and noisy, and quite openly he held the sprig over my head, told me it was Melanesian mistletoe, and kissed me on the lips. At the time, I thought it was cool. During my first year at the hospital, when he had business in the X-ray Department he would stick his head in my office to offer a pleasant greeting. But that was all. In the corridors, he nodded hello, at most. I knew little about him except that he had an attractive wife with money of her own and two daughters in college. Also, that Dr Prion didn't like him, but never told me why. Distinguished looking, slim and tall, a tennis player – doubles always – with a thatch of fair hair going white at the temples, Francis was fifty–two years old, twice my age.

We slept together the day after the barbecue. And it took less than a month for me to realize just how uncool Francis was when I caught him out in a flagrant lie involving another woman – another man's wife. Of course I knew he lied to his wife reflexively, and to hotel clerks and friends alike, but it was the first time he had lied to me. Still, it didn't deter me from seeing him again. What did I care if he saw other women? Or committed adultery. That's what I was doing, after all. I pretended to discover what I surely knew from the first: it wasn't that he should not be trusted, but that I ought to *distrust* him actively. And for whom, for what part of myself, was I pretending?

Two months into our liaison, he proposed that we take another woman to bed with us. I played his occasional blindfold and handcuff games, but this I declined, and he dropped the subject at once. Soon afterward, when we were registered in a suite at the Hyatt in Poipu as father and daughter – another favorite masquerade – he said he was calling down for a masseuse. I should have known at once that the woman who came up to the suite was not a hotel employee, but I swear that whenever I was with Francis, I didn't see things clearly. It was as if I always had those ophthalmologist's orange drops in my eyes that dilate your pupils. But it was worse than that. Francis was a special kind of hematologist, I realized – one who literally got into your blood, like a vampire.

We had been drinking champagne – he knew it got me drunk right away – and after leaving the masseuse and him in the bedroom, I smoked a joint laced with black hash in the bathroom and took a shower. He had said he'd be waiting for me – loosened up – when I got out. To take my time. When I returned to the bedroom, it was pitch dark. I was very high. Francis called me to the bed. I slipped in beside him, under the cool sheet. He put my hand on his cock, which was already hard, and then another hand – not his – stroked my leg. I cried out.

'It's all right,' Francis purred. 'Nina is a friend. And she'll do only what we ask her. Isn't that right, Nina?'

And I felt a woman's breasts press up against my back.

I'd like to say that was my nadir with Francis. But now I was smoking even more ganja – the strongest I could find – and I had taken up Estes's drink, Eclipse rum with a dash of bitters, in a serious way. My other favorite, which I stumbled on in a Honolulu nightclub, I reserved for my solitary drinking: a variation on the White Angels I drank in the navy with Sharline, it was called a White Goddess – gin, Cointreau, lemon juice, and sugar shaken with ice. So I don't remember a lot of the things I did with Francis. My time with him is a blur, a continuum dotted with unconnected and unpleasant

292

images. After five months, I had grown isolated from my friends. I had given up my kayaking expeditions, and when I did not return a succession of his calls, Val stopped phoning. Seth came to Haena one night and told me flat out that I should not see Francis again. Just put an end to it, he kept telling me. But that wasn't what I had to put an end to. I thought my year in Cook Islands had cleaned me out, body and soul, of my grief over Cassiel. What it had done was open me up wide. And now that I was so susceptible to booze and dope, it didn't take much for me to set my internal wrecking balls in motion. That bottle of bourbon I had poured down the sink in New Orleans – my fear of becoming like my grandmother – had caught up with me after four years. By then the bottle was filled not just with booze but plenty of demons. Francis Beliar in the end was its primary genie, risen in a cloud of smoke to torment me.

By the time of the New Year's Eve party in Kilauea when I was swaying before the bathroom sink while the other guests were proclaiming a happy 1972, I was desperate to put the cap back on that bottle and hurl it into the sea. To stop seeing Francis and pull my life together again. That was my New Year's wish, and it came true – though not in the way I would have liked.

I tried to clean up the makeup that had smeared under my eyes, but my vision felt off, as it always did when Francis was around – that night, even more than usual. And I had drunk even more than usual. About all I could manage was to reapply my lipstick and rinse out my mouth with cold water before making my way back to the stairway. The music came on suddenly – Hendrix wailing 'Hey, Joe' – and under my feet the floorboards were throbbing. Downstairs the lights were dimmed again, and I could barely discern people milling and dancing. I just wanted to make my way through all of them and find the door. I wanted to get out of there. Jeannie was still on the same step, necking with her boyfriend. She didn't see me until I was past them.

'Mala!' she cried, pushing him away and rising

unsteadily. Coming down five steps, she nearly fell. 'I been looking all over for you.'

It was obvious she hadn't moved since I went up.

Her eyes were red and she was slurring. 'I got something for you,' she said.

'First tell me, is Seth still here?'

She tried to concentrate. 'He left.'

'Damn.'

'Come on, he doesn't have any fun, anyway.'

What she meant was that he didn't get high.

'We'll give you a ride. Your car broke?'

Just then, three people brushed past us, toward the front of the house. Two tall men and a pretty woman with long braids. One of the men had long brown hair and a moustache. I recognized him at once, even as he stopped and looked at me.

'Do you need a lift?' he smiled. He had a soft British accent. His voice was kindly, and his eyes, blue as crystal, were equally clear.

I shook my head. He was wearing a denim shirt, white slacks, and sandals, but his face, deeply tanned, with a long nose and pointed chin framed by the wavy hair, looked to me at that moment like the face of Jesus.

'You're sure?' he said, studying my own eyes closely.

There was all that THC in the joint, I thought, blinking hard, but he really did look like Jesus.

I nodded. The last thing I needed, I thought, was to get involved with another man.

He put out his hand. 'Alvin,' he said.

'Mala,' I replied, taking his hand. I didn't feel he was coming on to me.

'Mala,' he repeated softly. 'Another time, then. That's an open invitation. I live at Four Crosses in Haena. Come up anytime.' And he was gone.

I knew where he lived. Most everyone on the North Shore did.

'Do you know who that was?' Jeannie sputtered.

Alvin was Alvin Dixon, *the* Alvin Dixon, a rock star, formerly of a band called T-Zero that had been at the top

294

of the charts all through the late Sixties before he quit abruptly two years earlier and settled on Kauai. Now he was a retired millionaire who lived in a huge house on Tunnels Beach. I had glimpsed him in town a few times, like everyone else, but I'd never spoken to him.

'I can't believe you didn't take a ride from him, Mala,' Jeannie moaned. 'You must be really out of it.'

'Yeah, and I've got to go.'

She grabbed my arm. 'Wait, I want you to have this.' She took a ring off her finger, a large oval of amber on a gold band.

'Thanks, but I don't wear rings. You keep it.' I was beginning to feel dizzy again, and my mouth was so dry it hurt to swallow.

'See, he's trapped in there,' she said, holding the ring up into the feeble light. There appeared to be a drop of blood in the amber.

'Who?'

'Trapped back when there were dinosaurs.'

Someone slid between us, going upstairs.

'Jeannie, I'll see you tomorrow,' I said, turning away.

'But it's good luck,' she insisted, pressing the ring into my palm. 'Spiders are good luck, you know.'

'What did you say?' Raising the ring to my face, squinting hard, I finally saw that it was a small red spider suspended in the amber. A female *Uloborus* frozen at the moment of her death.

I wanted to scream as I pushed the ring back into Jeannie's hand, but my jaw wouldn't open. My look of panic, though, was enough to make her recoil, and this time she didn't call after me when I twisted through the circle of people around us and plunged headlong across the living room, bumping into couples dancing, knocking a glass out of someone's hand, tripping on a woman sprawled out smoking. Finally I was out on the terrace, stepping over Olan and Philippe, who were sitting beneath the Japanese fan holding hands in a circle with two girls wearing sunglasses, all of them waiting for the first rushes of the mescaline they had dropped. As I slipped by, Philippe looked up, heavy-lidded, as if he had never seen me before.

Out on the grass, I was even less steady on my feet. Heavy mist was streaming through the garden. Inhaling the jacaranda scent, I was circling around to where the cars were parked when a man stepped out of the bushes, black against the darkness, and blocked my way.

'You're in no condition to drive, Mala,' a familiar voice intoned.

Seeing me lurch across the living room, Francis had slipped out the front door to intercept me.

I shoved him as hard as I could. 'Fuck you Francis.'

Though I considered myself strong, he didn't budge. 'You still shouldn't drive,' he said.

'We're through. As of now. *Finito.* Kaput. Understand?'

'Still upset about that girl at the marina?' he said calmly.

'You must be kidding.'

'Who else could it be?'

'Oh. I get it. There's just one girl. Right. The one at the marina also doubles as the hostess with the mostest at the Green Dolphin – that is, when she's not your best friend's daughter who you spoon-feed coke before she blows you.'

'You're hysterical,' he said with a harder edge. He didn't appreciate that last reference.

'You're right. Here I thought there were lots of girls. And it's just one! Now, get out of my way,' I shouted.

He stepped toward me, and I thought he was going to hit me.

'Get another playmate to mind-fuck,' I continued to shout, shoving him again.

But he didn't hit me. He had no intention of hitting me. In fact, I never knew him to strike any woman. He dealt in violence, all right, he got off big-time on inflicting pain, but he didn't do it with his fists.

'Stop shouting, Mala.' There was a trace of mockery in his voice.

I swung my hand up as fast as I could, to slap him, but

he caught my wrist. Immediately he let go of it, and smiled, as if he wanted me to do it again. In my rage and drunkenness I had forgotten that this sort of torment was what he really thrived on: he liked to provoke anger and then soak it back up, as fuel.

When I took another swipe at him, I missed and fell down hard, and he tried to help me up.

'Let go of me, you bastard,' I said through my teeth.

Gripping me firmly around the waist, in his best doctor's voice he said, 'I'm taking you home.'

'Gonna fuck me when I pass out?'

He was half-dragging me to a sports car convertible parked under the banyan trees. I really was too drunk to drive, and needed to go home, but not with him. As we reached the car, I tried to pull free one last time. 'This isn't your car.'

'It's my wife's,' he said in his flattest voice.

'Even better! Bet you *love* to screw in it – anyone but her.'

'Come on.'

The car was Campari-red like the shirt he was wearing. As he leaned over, pushing me into the passenger seat, I smelled for the first time how much booze there was on *his* breath. His speech didn't change when he drank, so you couldn't tell from that.

'Hey,' I said, groping for the door handle, realizing just how bad an idea this was. But it was too late. He had already turned the key in the ignition, and, throwing the stick shift into reverse, he made a hard U-turn out of the yard, past a long line of parked cars.

Suddenly we were hurtling down the winding, muddy road through the forest where the fog itself was thick as mud. It was a mile to the main road and Francis was driving very fast. Trees and bushes flew by, and the rays of the headlights splintered wildly in the fog. Crushed mosquitoes streaked the windshield. Stones kicked up sharply under the rear fenders, clattering in my ears. Already dazed, I felt as if the entire world had been turned upside down.

'Slow down!' I shouted.

Francis opened the throttle another notch. As we skidded around every curve now, I was sure we would spin out in that mud. I slumped down and closed my eyes until, with a thud of the chassis and a grinding of gears, we veered onto the two-lane blacktop of the main road and Francis gunned the engine and accelerated even harder. Like a long runway the road was dotted blue and orange down the double line as plastic reflectors picked up our lights. Francis had always been a show-off, in both his car and his speedboat, skirting the coral reefs at full throttle, but this was different.

'What the fuck are you doing, Francis?' I shouted as the needle inched up to 95, then 100.

He turned to me, and though his expression never changed, in the green glow of the dashboard lights his eyes flashed, wide and blank in a way I had never seen them before, even during sex when he was at his most strung out and frenzied.

'I'm taking you home,' he said, gripping the wheel so hard his knuckles whitened. He passed a car on the right, on the narrow shoulder, then several others on a steep hill, barely edging back into our lane against oncoming traffic.

'You're trying to kill us!' I screamed over the wail of car horns.

He began to pass a bus, and suddenly we were staring into the high-beam lights of a truck bearing down on us.

'Francis!' I shrieked. The bus's tires hissed a few feet from my head and gasoline fumes burned my eyes.

The truck was closing fast on us. Teeth bared, his face gleaming with sweat, Francis jammed his foot to the floor. The wind whipped his sandy hair flat against his skull. The truck's Klaxon horn was deafening, and its blinding lights flooded us.

We swerved hard to the right and I felt an enormous, sickening rush of steel – tons of it, like a freight train – as the truck flew past us and the bellow of the bus's horn, close on our tail, blasted my ears before we pulled away.

Francis never really regained control of the car, and several seconds later we had sped off the straightaway and were descending into the Hanalei Valley. All the way down the long snaking road, the car zigzagged back and forth across the double line, inches from the wooden railing. Everything was spinning on me, and as I tried to brace myself, my hand closed on my seat belt buckle. Fumbling frantically, I managed to fasten it.

Moments later we skidded around the last curve, onto the one-lane bridge over the Hanalei River where Francis lost control of the car once and for all. The brakes screeched, the tires squealed, and there was a crash of lights and a ripping sound as if the air itself had been torn like a curtain, to swallow me up. After that, I remember nothing.

My next memory is of another sound: the wind blowing through a window, ruffling curtains. A wind redolent with the scent of plumeria, the graveyard flower. Then I heard those words from Revelation I had read in the hotel in Manila, not in my voice but in Cassiel's:

> *And the fifth angel sounded and I saw a star*
> *fall from heaven to earth: and to him*
> *was given the key of the bottomless pit.*

I was lying between cool smooth sheets. The top sheet was taut over my toes and my hands were flat at my sides. I opened my eyes and could see nothing but blackness.

Maybe I'm dead, I thought.

Then, off to my right, I heard a glass clink onto a tabletop and a rustling, as of clothing. But so light as to be nearly inaudible.

'Who's there?' I said as the rustling approached me. My voice was rough and small, as if I hadn't spoken for some time. But I did still have a voice.

The rustling stopped and I could feel someone leaning toward me.

'Who are you?' I said.

'I am Wind,' a woman replied in a soft faraway voice.

For several seconds I was certain I had indeed died and somehow ended up in a kind of heaven, a chamber beyond the clouds where the wind was distilled into musical notes. A heaven where, however, I was blind.

'What's your name?' I asked.

'Wind,' the voice repeated, a kind voice.

'And where am I?'

'In your bed in your house,' she said.

'My house . . .'

'In Haena.' She softened the *n* as only native Hawaiian speakers did.

'I can't see.'

A warm hand with long thin fingers touched my shoulder. 'You will see again,' the voice said, then paused. 'You were in a terrible accident.'

I remembered: Francis, the red convertible, the bridge.

'Oh,' I said, feeling as if a heavy weight had shifted in my chest. 'When was that?'

'Two weeks ago. They sent you home from the hospital the day before last when you regained consciousness. You don't remember that?'

'No.'

'I have been looking after you. I fed you last night, and this morning.'

'I don't remember that. How do you know I will see?'

'They did tests,' she said simply.

I thought about this. 'Are you a nurse?'

'No. I work for your friend Estes Shaula.'

And then it struck me who she was.

'Yes, I am his housekeeper,' she said. 'He sent me down from Waimea to take care of you. I will stay until you can see again.'

I cleared my throat. 'And what happened to Francis?'

'Dr Beliar? I'm sorry.'

'He was killed, then.'

'They found his body last week.'

'What do you mean?'

300

'It disappeared, then washed up on Niihau. That is where I am from.'

That evening, when he came with Seth to visit me, Estes related to me the details of the accident and I listened almost as if I had not been in it myself. Sober for once – he drank three cups of black tea during his visit – he sat at the foot of my bed and told me that the car had hit one of the bridge posts. I had been knocked unconscious. The right side of my head was still tender to the touch. I also had severe abrasions and contusions up my right leg, a gash on my right arm, still stitched, a broken finger, and two cracked ribs, which I had felt when I tried to turn on my side. And I had lost my power of sight, of course.

'It's a miracle you weren't killed,' Estes concluded softly, laying his hand on my ankle.

'From the X-rays,' Seth put in, 'we know there was no neural or retinal damage to your eyes. Everything points to temporary blindness – from shock.'

'When will I see again?'

'Maybe next week, maybe in a couple of months. We had Dr Takasa come in from Honolulu General. He's their top ophthalmologist. He has no doubts you'll regain your sight as the constricted blood vessels reopen.'

'And I'll see as before?'

'Yes. He said you may need reading glasses at first.'

'Oh, I'm sure I'll be doing a lot of reading,' I said drily, after which there was a long silence. 'And Francis?'

Seth coughed nervously.

'All of it, please,' I said. 'Estes, you tell me.'

They had found me covered with blood and vomit. I was alone, buckled into the passenger seat. The right front fender and wheel of the car protruded through the bridge's supports and dangled over the river. At first, the police thought the driver had fled the accident, or staggered away for help, or maybe crawled from the car and collapsed in the tall river grass. But seeing how I was so banged up, they couldn't understand why there was no sign of blood in the driver's seat or anywhere on his side

301

of the car, which had borne the brunt of the crash. My head had cracked the windshield, but over the steering wheel the glass was intact. And there was no blood outside the car, not on the bridge and not in the muddy ground on either side of it, where there were also no footprints. After I was rushed to Wilcox Memorial by ambulance, they searched for several hours around the bridge and in the taro fields at that end of the valley. Then, near sunrise, about the time I was being X-rayed on my own X-ray table, the police chief directing the search suddenly arrived at the solution, which at the time seemed improbable even to him: at impact, Francis was thrown clear of the car, over the railing, into the swift currents of the Hanalei River. My forward velocity had been severe, but because of the seat belt, I had at least remained in the car.

Two police boats dredged the river, joined by several fishing vessels. All day they dragged nets along the bottom, from the bridge to the mouth of the river a mile away at Hanalei Bay. The next day, they brought the Coast Guard cutters up from Lihue and began searching the bay. Just in case he was wrong, and Francis was either a delirious missing person or a fugitive from the scene of an accident, the chief issued an all-points bulletin. But after three days, the police were even more convinced he had drowned and been carried out to sea after floating down the river. When they found his body on the ninth day, this proved to be what had happened, but not exactly the way they first thought. For one thing, the autopsy revealed that Francis broke his neck the moment he hit the river, and that's what killed him. Also, he was carried out to sea, but only as far as another island; the strong currents in the Kaulakahi Channel had deposited him on a beach of shattered coral on the eastern shore of Niihau, the Forbidden Island. Bloated, with writhing barnacles attached to his scalp and back, he was found by a teenage couple, out for a midnight swim, who ran home claiming they had seen one of the lizard-men, a demon whose hair had a life of its own and

302

who stared at them without eyes and smiled without lips.

I didn't shed any tears, and I had a lot of bitter feelings just then. 'I'm sorry for his wife and daughters,' I said, 'though I'm sure they're not too sorry for me.' Then I turned to where I had last heard Seth's voice. 'And what happened at the hospital?' I asked.

'You mean—'

'You know what I mean.'

He sighed. 'It's caused quite a scandal. A lot of people were at that party. And the search for his body was in the newspaper every day. It even made the *Advertiser* in Honolulu.'

'Go on.'

'The day they released you from the hospital as a patient, you were also put on suspension. Dr Prion is fighting it.'

'But I'm still going to lose my job.'

He hesitated. 'I'm afraid so. When they brought you in, Mala, there was a lot of alcohol in your blood.'

'No kidding. It's good that's all they tested for.'

'You can fight the suspension.'

'We'll help you,' Estes said.

I shook my head. 'I don't have the energy for that. Anyway, I have a lot of thinking to do.'

And I had plenty of time to do it now. I went for twenty-two more days – thirty-six in all – before regaining my sight. It was Pliny who called the eyes windows to our soul. But – less well known – he also observed that the eyes, to him the most invaluable part of the body, distinguish life from death by the use they make of daylight. Without our vision, he says, in the sightless universe that borders the realm of the dead, we become as dead men, despite our other senses. And does that mean when the eyes no longer function, when blindness blackens them, the windows of the soul are closed suddenly? If so, that was all right with me, because the injuries I had inflicted on my soul would take far longer to heal than the ones I had suffered in the car accident. In the previous six months, with the likes of Francis, I had truly been among the dead, trying to kill myself off a piece at a time, despite the fact it hadn't displaced my pain or my loneliness – and it certainly hadn't gotten me any closer to Cassiel.

After reviewing the weeks leading up to the accident for the hundredth time, I resolved that I would keep my legs closed, my mouth shut, and my eyes open – when they were returned to the use of daylight, that is. And for the first time since I had recovered consciousness, I felt something give in me – something sharp, like a sliver of ice, that melted in my chest, until finally I began to cry – tears so frigid they stung my cheeks. After that, each day I was sure I moved a little further from the realm of the dead. One morning, for the first time in seven months, I put on Cassiel's bracelet and then the tears, hot and copious now, flowed for hours.

Through her diligence and care, Wind helped to draw me out of myself while I regained my strength. Every night she put the radio telescope tape on my tape recorder, looped so it would play throughout the night. I found it soothing. She herself slept on a fold-up bed in the living room. She prepared my meals, walked me to the bathroom, helped me dress, and attended to my bandages and medication. Twice a day she applied a balm of nectar and herbs to my eyelids that she assured me would hasten the return of my sight.

As my other injuries healed, I sat on my lanai during the day listening to the surf slide in beyond the trees. I came to know my garden, and the surrounding land, in an entirely different way. I heard the birds, insects, and foliage so clearly that, imposing the grid of their sounds on my visual memories – which were more precise than ever – I was able soon enough to imagine the living scene before me: a fruit fly on the railing, bees hovering over the hibiscus blossoms, the shadows of fluttering palm fronds on the lawn, a flock of myna birds swooping as one from the ohi'a tree to pick at the fallen papayas by the shed. It was even easier for me to identify the cars of my visitors, or to hear Lon the fisherman in his thongs pad by on the dirt road, or to follow the buzz of small airplanes over the beach.

To my astonishment, I discovered one day that I could visualize other – completely intangible – things as well. Like Wind's mental activities, incredible as that seemed. To be exact, every so often I seemed able to glimpse one of her memories from the inside out. That particular day, a week before I regained my sight, she was sweeping the lanai and I was sitting cross-legged on the lawn, performing one of the few chores of which I was capable: picking the ticks off Castor and Pollux. My legs were healed by this time, and my shoulder, where the stitches had been removed, ached only when I tried to raise my arm too high. The dogs sat patiently while I probed their fur, removing the ticks with a single turn counterclockwise. Suddenly my concentration was broken when a sharply etched image leapt into my mind's eye – and came to life.

My vision unsteady, as if I were running, I was staring down a steep, rough mountain trail that led to a circle of turquoise sea. I had hiked several times on Na Pali coast with Val, but I didn't remember descending a trail like this – and certainly not so fast, the foliage around me blurring, that circle drawing me toward it like a vortex . . .

Then, just as suddenly, the scene disappeared. Pollux licked my cheek, Castor barked, and I was catching my breath, my heart pounding – as if I had just stopped running.

When this happened again the next afternoon as I sat on the lanai drinking tea – the same sequence but even longer – it frightened me much more. Wind was in the kitchen, and I called to her.

'Wind?' I said, as soon as I heard her come out.

'What is it, Mala?' she said, coming through the screen door.

'Please do me a favor. Would you tell me what you were just thinking?'

305

She paused. 'I was fixing dinner.'

'But thinking about something else?'

'Yes. I was remembering a place near Pueo Point where I used to swim.'

'On Niihau?'

'That's right.'

'A cove at the foot of a mountain trail?'

'How did you know?' It was the only time I ever heard her sound surprised.

I had known because, while I couldn't run down a trail like that, I sensed that as a runner she would live up to her name.

Val drove out to visit later that day, and the moment I heard his pickup pull into the driveway, my mind filled first with an ocean vista – from a swaying vantage point, like a kayak – and in the foreground, just before me, a well-tanned topless, long-haired woman was paddling vigorously in her own kayak; and then – far more startling – an image of my own face appeared, gazing up, laughing, my hair spread out on white sand. I knew at once that I was observing a memory (of me!) from our first days together which was running through Val's head at that moment. I didn't have to ask him about it.

This happened again, with Seth once, and with Wind many times. It recalled to me the one other time I had experienced this ability in myself: in Manila, in bed with Cassiel, when I had witnessed the woman in the red dress running through the desert, and the burning car on the edge of the ravine, and then the horrific interior of the B-52 as it was shot down. I was sure those had been Cassiel's memories, and that, with the spider venom in my blood, I had been privy to them because he and I were lovers. So all I could deduce was that the concussion I had incurred, in tandem with the acute memory powers I retained – the one vestige of the venom remaining in my bloodstream – had heightened my psychic capabilities to the point where I could now glimpse other people's memories even as they experienced them, and without making love.

Even after regaining my sight, I retained this ability, but only one week of each month. It took me some time to figure out what characterized that particular week, thinking it might be related to my menstrual cycle or sleep patterns or some subtle form of synchronicity until I realized it was always the week of the waning moon. After a couple of months, no longer fearful, I learned how to employ this ability at will, and from then on it never occurred involuntarily. Soon it would change the course of my life.

When I regained my sight, it happened as abruptly as the doctors had predicted. I had been asleep, and thought I was dreaming when I found myself looking out my bedroom window into the dawn light, where snow was falling into the bougainvillea vines. They were large snowflakes spinning down against the backdrop of the jagged green mountains. I had to be dreaming, I thought, for while there were many natural wonders on the North Shore of Kauai, no snowfall had ever been recorded. Only after I saw the bruises on my arm atop the rumpled sheet did I realize that I was indeed awake. Slipping out of bed, I put my nose to the window screen and saw that the snow was actually a cascade of white petals the wind was blowing out of the rain forest.

'I can see!' I called out to Wind in the other room. 'I can see again.'

She did not reply. I thought I heard the screen door shut softly, but I could not be sure. When I went into the living room, the fold-up cot had already been neatly stowed in the closet, the table was set for my breakfast, and the dogs were eating theirs on the lanai. But there was no sign of Wind, except in the simple fact, now visible to me for the first time, that she had kept my house immaculate during my convalescence, and had even weeded my vegetable garden and flower beds. I gazed into the mirror at my face, which was taut and wan despite all the rest I'd gotten; it was the first time I had looked at it since standing, swaying, before the bath-room mirror at the party. I began examining my various injuries, but seeing the spider plants drip with overnight rain and then watching Castor and Pollux, white petals stuck to their fur, run in to me excitedly, I fell to my knees and, hugging the dogs, with a flush of joy burst into tears.

That afternoon I called Estes. Wind had still not returned to my house, and I inquired after her. He surprised me, saying she had already informed him of the good news before asking for the day off.

'I'm so glad you're better,' Estes said. 'Better than ever, it sounds like.'

'How can I thank you, Estes, for everything?'

'You don't have to thank me, Mala. Just watch out for yourself.'

The following morning, Wind phoned me from Waimea to say how happy she was, too, but she seemed uncomfortable with my expressions of gratitude. When the doctors gave me the green light to drive again later that week, I called Estes's house to tell Wind I was coming by, but again she seemed uncomfortable, and rather vaguely replied, 'There has been so much for me to do here after being away so long. But of course you should come by . . .'

I had hoped to see Estes, too, at the observatory, but he had flown to the Big Island that morning for a meeting with his colleagues there. I had brought gifts of thanks: for him, a basket of papayas from my trees, and for Wind a well-worn figurine of the Melanesian moon goddess that I had bought on the docks in Rarotonga, which she had once admired in my bedroom.

Around noon, as I came up the path to his house under the tall, sun-dappled trees, I heard the faucet running in the kitchen and a kettle whistling on the stove. But when I knocked on the door and called out, 'It's me, Mala,' the house fell silent.

I knocked again, then let myself in. 'Wind,' I called out, again and again, looking into all the rooms. But she was nowhere to be found, not in the house or on the lanai or in the garden beyond. I had only visited there that one night when I dined and went to bed with Estes, but everything was just as I remembered it. The teak floors highly polished, a whiff of strong incense in the meditation cell, and the glass sparkling clean over the photographs of Einstein, Hubble, and Clyde Tombaugh in the kitchen, where the kettle was still hot. Pausing in the bedroom, I thought back to that night in May as the beginning of my seven months of lurching around in one kind of darkness before being flung into another. I had often tortured myself with the notion that I might have avoided a lot of grief had I headed straight home after visiting the observatory with Estes, at the same time knowing it would have made no difference at all. As I had intuited then, it was not my fleeting disappointment with Estes, but my deep-seated grief over Cassiel that had propelled me into the arms of Francis. And I had no doubt it would have propelled me, inevitably, from some other angle, even if I had not stripped off my clothes and lay down on Estes's futon that night, stoned out of my mind.

I never did see Wind on that visit, and I realized that I never would. This had been a long outing for me after being bedridden so many weeks; before making the drive home, I sat on Estes's lanai for nearly an hour gazing into the trees. When I returned to the living room, the basket of papayas was sitting where I had left it on the table, but the figurine of the moon goddess, which I had set down beside it, was gone. And suddenly, in a great rush, the wind, powerful there in the mountains, blew right through the house – entering by the windows and screen doors on the lanai side and leaving by the windows and door in front. Along with the curtains and tablecloth, my hair billowed up, my dress fluttered, and cool air poured into my lungs, making me light-headed until, seconds later, as everything settled back into place, I walked out of the house and down the path, through the thick dark ferns, without looking back.

For the next few weeks, I slept fitfully, plagued by chaotic dreams that began with Francis embracing me and ended with my finding Cassiel's body washed up on some beach fitting the description of Francis's corpse on Niihau: bloated, his eyes gone, and barnacles writhing on his skin. This was one of my oldest nightmares about Cassiel, and circumstances had played right into it. Invariably I woke in a sweat and stumbled out of bed, terrified that I was still blind until I realized it was the middle of the night.

In my waking life, things were not going much better. Despite the strenuous efforts of Dr Prion and Seth, I did lose my job at the hospital. And though there was plenty of blame to lay at my own feet, I was much more angry and ashamed about my dismissal when it actually occurred. Too much so even to attend the advisory board hearing at which I might have defended myself. Francis had been a longtime member of that board, and it was his colleagues and friends who drew up my dismissal report, which boiled down (by omission) to a whitewash of him and an indictment of me as *ethically unfit for duty* – making me feel like I was back in the Navy. That I had several times, at Francis's side, smoked ganja and chewed peyote with two of the signatories on the report – and well knew of their own extracurricular sexual activities – made it especially bitter for me to swallow. Even so, in my heart I knew I couldn't have gone back to the hospital anyway: there were just too many bad memories and foul associations. But my friends kept petitioning in my behalf, the end result of which was that I was given a bigger severance package than anyone expected, just so they could be rid of me: five months' full pay. Since it was already mid-April by that time, I figured this money, if I stretched it out, would last me to the end of the year. And then I'd be back to square one, hoping I wouldn't have to wait tables to survive.

Gradually, though, other parts of my life fell into place. I began swimming again, and kayaking, and tending my garden. I cooked for myself every night and spent as much time as I could alone, flanked by my dogs, sipping hibiscus tea on my lanai from twilight until the stars appeared. One thing I did not do was pick up another drink. No more White Goddesses or Eclipse rum, and no more Thai stick laced with THC. Instead I went to the weekly AA meeting on Friday nights in the rec room of the Methodist church, never talking much, just listening to other people's stories, which made me feel like I hadn't been the only person on the island to undertake my own destruction so systematically.

Still, though I didn't drink, I eventually drifted away from the meeting. The last time I attended, I met a man in the parking lot who seemed vaguely familiar to me. Very tall and thin, he was clean-shaven, with long fly-away hair and friendly brown eyes. He smiled when he saw me, but with no flicker of recognition. He was dressed simply, in jeans, a white shirt, and sandals, and it was only when I spotted a medallion hanging from a gold chain on his chest that I was able to place him. The medallion depicted a lion's face with the sun for one eye and the moon for the other. I was about to turn away when he walked up and extended his hand.

'Hi,' he said. 'I'm Olan.'

He looked so little like the bearded man in the net loincloth I had met at the New Year's Eve party in Kilauea that I doubt I would have believed him had he not been wearing the medallion. The medallion, it turned out, was about the only thing from that time – just six months earlier – which remained in his life.

He didn't remember meeting me at the party – in fact, he didn't remember the party at all, nor much of any-thing else that happened to him in the months between November and March when he was dropping large doses of acid or mescaline every other day. He had started out living in a farming commune outside Lawai and ended up in a tent on the beach near Anahola. His sole source of income became the drugs he sold. To get around, he hitchhiked, and that was still his primary means of transportation.

That evening he had a dinner invitation in Haena, so

311

I offered him a ride. On the way, he told me some of the story which he had shared at another meeting, earlier in the day, in Lihue, where he had been the speaker.

'I'm from Phoenix originally,' he said, in his quiet, hoarse voice. 'I studied mathematics at the university there. Later I lived in Santa Fe. That's where I got into acid. I heard that weed, Grade-A stuff, grew so wild here on Kauai that you could just pick it up by the roadside. And that some cats from Berkeley had set up a little LSD factory: "pure Sunshine from the rain forest," that's what I heard. So I came out on the next plane.' He shook his head. 'The rest – I don't know if I can get through it twice in one day, so I'll just skip to my bottom, seventeen months later. I was down to one hundred ten pounds. I had uncontrollable trots. Nothing stayed in me longer than ten minutes – and all I was putting in were the rolls I fished from the trash at the burger stand. And green bananas that I stole. The park rangers found me shivering like a skeleton in my tent one afternoon when it was eighty-five degrees. Tripping. Shitting in the sand. I was in detox for a month. Now I'm on food stamps. Working at beach cleanup for the state – two-fifty an hour. But I'm clean. I have a room in Kapaa. A bicycle. In a coupla months I'll be able to buy a used motor scooter. Day at a time.'

We had crossed the last of the twelve wooden bridges into Haena. It was a misty night. Long gray clouds streamed out of the mountains like plumes and poured down torrents of rain when they slid to sea. Just above the horizon the sliver of a moon was barely visible.

'So we're here,' I said. 'Where can I drop you?'

'A place called Four Crosses. Just up a ways.'

'I know where it is.' I looked at him. 'Alvin Dixon's house.'

'Yeah, the rock-and-roll guy. A sweet cat.'

'You've been there before?'

'Once.'

'Since you were sober?'

He was offended. 'Why yeah. I don't go to the places

312

where I wasn't sober. When I can remember, that is.'

'Sorry.'

But now he was looking at me. 'Ever met Alvin?'

'Briefly. At the same party where I met you.'

'Oh.' He brushed his hair from his eyes. 'Well, he's not like you think. Not like that party. Alvin's cool. Nobody does dope at his place. Hardly anyone drinks.'

'He's straight?'

'As a ruler. Listen, the cat who invited me out the first time is one of his best friends. Used to be his bass player. I met him at the meeting in Kapaa, okay? Alvin's cool.'

The big houses on Tunnels Beach all had long dirt driveways off the main road. At one of these, with a chain across it and an unmarked mailbox, Olan said, 'This is it.'

After he got out, I said, 'You know, that night in Kilauea he invited me out here. He said to come anytime.'

Olan shrugged, opening his palms. 'You should do it,' he said, slipping under the chain. 'Thanks for the ride.'

A week went by, and another, and then I did go up to Four Crosses. I was restless for a change, and I thought, why not. It was only about a mile and half from my place, so instead of driving, I simply walked west along the shore, around the deep horseshoe of Tunnels Beach, where wind-gliders were riding the swells, and through a cypress grove. A sandy path led to a weather-beaten gate with a NO TRESPASSING sign. Beyond the gate, nearly concealed by a line of palms, was the rear of a sprawling white house. It was a modern two-story design, with harmonious Mediterranean lines. There were several canopied balconies, a widow's walk, and wide picture windows. Looming behind the blue roof were the greenest and most imposing mountain peaks of all, at Ke'e Beach.

A black Labrador burst from the tall grass when I opened the gate and, sniffing the thongs I carried, escorted me up to the terrace that wrapped around the house. At the far end, two men were playing cards at a glass table. Near the steps I ascended, a woman in a yellow bikini was looking out to sea through binoculars from a beach chair. She was about my height, with long, bright blond hair and an athletic figure. I was wearing a two-piece black bathing suit – not quite as skimpy as hers – under an open white shirt, a baseball cap, and the black wrap-around sunglasses I had to wear constantly since recovering my sight. This was what I would typically wear for a walk on the beach. The light makeup I had applied, and the coral nail and toe polish, were not so typical.

When she lowered the binoculars, I saw that the woman was a few years older than me, pretty, with widely spaced eyes. I recognized her as one of Alvin Dixon's companions at the party.

She came up to me, and after I introduced myself, extended her hand. 'My name is Claudia. Come, sit.'

Claudia was Alvin's girlfriend. She was Italian, but she had met Alvin in Kyoto just after his retirement from music. A ceramicist, she had studied in Japan, and now she also imported ceramic pieces from there and sold them in Italy, where they were much in demand. She and Alvin spent two months of every year in Tokyo and Kyoto, and she made regular trips to Milan. The rest of the time they lived at Four Crosses. I learned all this in our first half hour together, sitting beside her on another beach chair. I also learned that Claudia had a pretty good memory herself: not only did she recall running into me at the foot of the stairs at the party, but she informed me gently that I looked a lot healthier now.

'Your eyes are clear as the sky,' she smiled.

I flushed, wondering if like so many other people I ran into she had followed the lurid newspaper accounts of the car accident. Somehow I didn't think so.

'Thank you,' I replied. 'That was not a happy time for me.'

The two men, who I thought were playing cards, had just stood up to go for a swim. In fact, the one – a houseguest – had been giving a tarot reading to the other, who was a neighbor.

'He's very good with the tarot,' Claudia said to me of the houseguest, a short, bald, powerfully built man about fifty, 'though he doesn't use it professionally.'

'And what is his profession?'

'Jorge is a mind reader. He's performed all over the world, in nightclubs and theaters. Once, even at the Royal Albert Hall, for the Queen.'

'Really.'

'Yes. And he *can* read your mind. You'll see. In the meantime, here,' she handed me the binoculars, 'you can have a look at Alvin while I get you – what? – juice, soda . . .'

'Juice is fine. But where is he?'

She pointed to the sea, fully extending her arm. 'Far out. With those you can make out the sail, just to the left of the point.'

The deep water was indigo and the waves were high. At first I couldn't see a sail among so many white-caps. Then I spotted it: like a white saw going up and down through blue wood, the spray flying like shavings. The hull flashed into view for an instant, then disappeared.

'It's very rough today,' Claudia said simply, returning with a pitcher of grapefruit juice and two glasses.

An hour later, the man who had been at the wheel of that ketch was sitting with us at the glass table, pouring himself the last of the juice. His eyes were still intense, his face a strong V framed by wavy brown hair, and his thin wiry frame was as dark as a desert wanderer's, but Alvin Dixon no longer looked to me like Jesus. For which I was grateful. However, my instincts about him had been correct during the brief encounter at the party – and I was pleased that something good might come of that ill-fated night. He was an exceptionally kind and private man. A good listener. I hadn't met anyone quite like Alvin, in disposition, since Cassiel.

Like Claudia, Alvin too remembered where we had

first met. 'I'm so glad you accepted my invitation,' he smiled.

'Yes,' I said, 'I'm only sorry it took me seven months.'

'You're here now. You'll stay for dinner?'

I stayed that night, then returned the following night, and one night that weekend. Other guests also came and went: some were people I knew in passing, others were islanders I had never met before, and a good many were visitors touching down briefly before returning to Honolulu, en route to Asia, Oceania, or the mainland. Some were people like me, others were individuals of great notoriety. Artists, musicians, explorers, global wheeler-dealers, aesthetes, even a taciturn man en route to Australia who was a meteorite hunter – Alvin and Claudia knew all kinds of people, the sort of people with whom I had little contact previously. But, then, I had never been around anyone as wealthy and famous as Alvin Dixon. And Olan had been right: I saw none of these guests, including the most sophisticated, break the unspoken house rule prohibiting drug use – which was saying a lot in 1972, on Kauai, when things were so free and easy.

Yet despite all this activity, Four Crosses mirrored its two principal residents in that it seemed a calm and un-hurried household. This was what impressed me most about the place. Alvin and Claudia were Buddhists: they had met in Kyoto at a retreat. Not the sort of Buddhist-one-month, Hindu-the-next faddists who were so common in those days, Alvin and Claudia were serious adherents, and many of their guests, for all their glitzy trappings, were fellow adherents they had met at temples, shrines, and secluded inns during their travels in Asia.

There was a beautiful Steinway concert grand in the living room which Alvin evidently played on occasion, but seldom when anyone was around, and an elaborate, rarely used, stereo system, but otherwise very little around the house that had to do with music. And nothing at all – no framed gold records, photographs, or mementoes – related to his musical career. It seemed to be an off-limits topic in his home – banned as strictly as drugs. But I couldn't help bringing it up one day later that summer after I had been a frequent visitor. We had all just come in from a long sail and Alvin and I were sitting alone on the terrace, relaxed and tired. Having heard one of his songs that morning on the car radio, I remarked to him that I had been a great fan of his band, T-Zero. In fact, I went on, warming to the subject, their take-no-prisoners LPs had been favored even over the Stones and the Dead in our rec room on the *Repose*.

His face darkened, and I was afraid I had not only crossed a line, but offended him. 'Because of its violence,' he said finally.

'No. Because of its sexual energy, and its anger.' I sat up in my chair. 'It was a release for people trapped in a war.'

He just looked at me, and I was surprised he wouldn't have known this.

'I'm sorry for bringing it up,' I said.

'Don't be,' he said, leaning closer. 'You know, I've worked at making my former life feel like it belonged to somebody else. When people went into how they listened to my music while having sex, or tripping, or seeing God, or whatever, I just shut down. Everything about that life shut me down. That's why I had to start over.' He smiled. 'Forgive me, Mala. I haven't run into many people who were in the war. I'm glad you told me what you did.'

After that, he sometimes played jazz for me on the piano – especially early stuff like Fats Waller and Jelly Roll Morton – just as Zaren Eboli once had. We became much closer friends. So much so that when Claudia had to fly to Rome late in September, I spent a good deal of time with Alvin. At Four Crosses, on his boat, and one day at my house for lunch, just the two of us. But in all that time, when I felt as if with the slightest nudge – and a ton of guilt – I could have fallen for Alvin, he never once came on to me. I was his friend, he wanted to keep our friendship, and he was faithful to Claudia. It was that simple.

'Can you believe it?' I said to Seth one night over dinner in town. 'At Wilcox Memorial I got mixed up with a bunch of respected physicians who – present company excluded – were among the most depraved people I've ever encountered, and here I'm hanging out with a world-famous rock star and we drink green tea and do yoga and he never cheats on his girl.'

Just before Claudia's return, Alvin and I visited the Blue Room one afternoon. The Blue Room was a cave within a cavern at the northern tip of the island, where the road ended. To reach it, you had to climb halfway up a mountain, then descend into its bowels through a chasm, down a rocky slope, to a pool of fresh water, cobalt-colored and very cold. You then had to swim across the pool to a tunnel in the rock face that led deeper into the mountain. The tunnel allowed you just enough room to breathe above the waterline, and after about sixty feet it ended in a small cave. The sides of the cave were smooth stone that formed a perfect dome – like the upper half of an eggshell. In fact, the cave was the topmost portion of a vertical shaftway filled with cold water that ran to depths no plumb had ever reached. It was called the Blue Room because its water was a stunning, luminous blue – like the color of a swimming pool lit up at night – as if from that great depth light were shining upward. No one could explain the source of this light.

'Olan told me the ancient Hawaiians believed sunlight enters the mountain through a hidden shaftway and reflects off seawater far below us,' Alvin said, as we trod water, his voice echoing sharply. 'But no one has ever been able to find the shaftway.'

Afterward, we sat on the bank of the cobalt pool in the outer cavern. The rock walls there were smeared with bat droppings and the air was damp and cool. As we sat wrapped in our towels, I found myself discussing my passion for, and grief over, Cassiel; Alvin would be one of only two people to whom I ever related that part of my story completely. The Blue Room's waters, rich in minerals, were reputed to possess healing properties, restoratives of the spirit, and perhaps they had gone to work on me, for it surprised me that the story should spill out more easily with Alvin than it ever had with my women friends. A wordly man who was detached from the world, nonjudgmental, he listened quietly while for nearly two hours I related the entire tale. Though his eyes lit up, as they did when I showed him the palimpsest of rings where the spider had bitten my palm, he didn't once interrupt me.

When I was through, he took my hand. 'You say you and he only had so little time together as lovers. Whenever I come here, I'm reminded of a story I heard when I visited India. Long before there were telescopes, Hindu cosmographers concluded that the universe was composed of billions of galaxies. They defined the life cycle of a galaxy as an eon. Asked the length of an eon, they replied: "Imagine a mountain of solid rock, bigger than the Himalayas, which a man brushes with a piece of silk once every century; the time it would take him to wear away the entire mountain is an eon." When you consider time in that light, days, years, centuries begin to blur, don't you think? How you fill any one day – while emptying it of distractions – is all that matters. It sounds as if you filled your few days to the brim. Also, Mala,' he smiled, 'I do believe that there *are* stars which fall to earth. Sometimes we're lucky enough to be around when they do.'

I kissed his cheek. 'It's no mystery why you were a star yourself, Alvin,' I said. 'For me you always will be.'

High above us, at a forty-five-degree angle, the oblong chasm leading to the open air was golden with light. The foliage rippled brightly in the mountain breeze. It was as if we were truly in the underworld, gazing up at the world of the living. And though I was not his Eurydice – nor anyone else's, despite Francis's efforts – that day Alvin Dixon felt to me as if he were Orpheus himself

319

who with his music could charm the animals and even the rocks. When I followed him up that rough slope, grasping his extended hand over the last, steepest portion, Alvin seemed to be leading me back into the sunlight once and for all after my extended sojourn in the darkness.

Jorge Gaspard, the mind reader, was nothing like Alvin. And he was decidedly *not* one of the many Buddhist visitors to Four Crosses. I had barely spoken to him during his visit in the summer, but when he returned just after Christmas, after touring in Canada, Claudia invited me over for dinner. Gaspard was their only houseguest, so along with Olan, who had also been invited, there were just five of us at the big table. Olan and I had arrived at the same time, and he proudly showed me his motor scooter, which he had finally saved up enough money to buy. I was seated between Olan and Gaspard, and it was clear to me that Olan didn't much care for Gaspard. Superficially, I could see why: Gaspard was not unfriendly, but he was humorless, even smug.

Over coffee, Claudia, just back from Tokyo and in an expansive mood, told Gaspard about the telepathic powers that manifested themselves in me during the week of the waning moon.

'She can become privy to, and visualize, fragments of memories passing through your thoughts,' Claudia said. 'I have seen it many times.' And indeed she had, but only when I had been alone with her and Alvin. Then she turned to me suddenly. 'You don't mind my talking about this, Mala, do you?' she asked, for my expression must have betrayed some of my discomfort.

I shook my head. Out of the corner of my eye, I saw that Alvin, too, was uncomfortable, and obviously not pleased that Claudia had brought this up. He didn't take an invasion of privacy lightly.

Gaspard turned his dark, direct eyes upon me and compressed his thin lips. His round face and bald head were glazed with moisture, for it was a stifling night and the trade winds had stopped blowing. 'This only occurs during that one week?' he asked in a deliberate bass voice.

'Yes.'

'You have never tried to induce it at other times?'

'I've never wanted to.'

He grunted. 'You need to be in the person's physical presence, correct?'

I nodded.

'And if there is more than one person present, you can choose among them?'

'Yes.'

At that point, Alvin ended the interrogation by changing the subject, but later, when I went out to the terrace to look at the stars, Gaspard came up to me out of the darkness.

'I'd like to make you a proposition,' he said bluntly, lighting a thick, short cigar with a gold lighter. My defenses went up, but he surprised me. 'My current stage assistant is experiencing burnout,' he went on. 'She's talking about marrying some fellow she met in London. We've both agreed that she should move on in March. Thus I need a new assistant. I think you would fit the bill perfectly, Miss Revell.'

I shook my head in astonishment. 'Are you serious?'

He waved away my question. 'I perform thirty-eight weeks of each year. Four ninety-minute performances a week. The pay is one thousand dollars per week, plus all expenses. For two weeks I rehearse and you receive full pay. The weeks you don't work at all you receive half-pay and do as you please. What do you think?'

I was thinking I still couldn't believe my ears: 'But what exactly would I have to do?'

'In a nutshell, the assistant is my conduit to the audience. Her duties are threefold: she goes out into the audience, soliciting questions and collecting cards on which people have written their queries; she deals me cards and handles other props; and she sits blindfolded onstage and passes on people's thoughts to me. I'll be frank with you: I'm offering you more money than any previous assistant because with them the blindfold portion of the act was accomplished through technical manipulation – word codes, inflection patterns, and the like. With you, at least one week per month – one-quarter of all performances – we'll evidently be able to employ genuine telepathy. There is a new moon now, or I would ask you for a demonstration, but I have no doubt your ability is just as Claudia describes it. If you utilize it onstage, I predict that I'll almost certainly be giving you a raise very soon. My wife, who was my partner before I went solo, had similar powers, and they were what launched me. But she lost them.'

'You have a wife?'

He was put off. 'What of it?'

'Does she travel with you?'

'Ah, I see,' he snorted. 'No, she lives at our house in the Bahamas.' He grinned, his lips compressed. 'She is the guardian of my tax shelter. The three months I don't tour I am there with her. Anyway, I have no romantic involvements ever with my assistants. Neither serious nor casual. Never. And I have had many assistants.'

'Why so many?'

Because it is a demanding job. My sense is you'll be good at it. And, I'll be honest, you'll be good for me. In this business, no one is completely authentic, but without some authenticity you cannot flourish. In the end, never forget, it is show business. You are poised, attractive, intelligent, and possess an unusual skill. With me, you will get the finest international bookings and make invaluable contacts.' He shrugged. 'It is likely that at some point you'll be able to go off solo yourself, if that interests you.'

The job was unusual, but despite our surroundings the job interview had come to sound much like any other, complete with the promise of a raise dangled before me as well as the prospect that I could someday parlay the work experience into a business of my own.

'Since it obviously concerns you,' he concluded, 'you

will have total privacy in the time that is your own. For one thing, I prefer sitting alone or with strangers on airplanes – never with my assistant. And I always dine alone. You will have first-class accommodations, and eat where you like, but you will not have to reckon with my disturbing your privacy. In return, I ask that you respect mine. For professional concerns, or illness, knock on my door, but do not come to me with personal problems. So, you see, if you have anything to be concerned about, it is loneliness, not invasion of privacy.' He cocked his head, drawing deeply on the cigar. 'But you strike me as a solitary person, accustomed to being on her own.'

'I am.'

He continued to look hard at me. 'At the same time, you're worried about leaving your first real home and being on the road so much – as your sister was.'

I started. 'How—'

'Please,' he cut me off. 'You see, I do have some skill at what I do,' he added drily, as if he had just handed me his calling card. 'Well, then, enough for now,' he said. 'Sleep on it, and give me your answer in a day or two.' And blowing a chain of smoke rings, he turned on his heel and set out for a walk on the beach.

I lay awake for a long time that night with those figures he had tossed out dancing in my head. Forty-six thousand dollars a year was a lot of money for me. And with all my expenses covered, I'd be able to bank most of it. There was almost nothing left of my severance pay from the hospital and I had been anxious for weeks about what I would do next. This seemed like an amazing stroke of luck, but with a big catch: I would have to leave Kauai and bounce around in the world in the company – however detached – of a dour, self-absorbed employer. At the same time, my job prospects on the island were not good, and though I now had some real friends, and felt healthy again, I had been itching to get away ever since the accident. This would be a way to do so while traveling to cities I had never seen, working in a strange and intriguing profession, and piling up money for the day I returned to Kauai, which, in the long run, I knew would be my home. It sounded almost too good.

Which was what I said to Alvin the next day when I sought his advice. He was uncharacteristically edgy, even evasive, about the whole subject.

'You want a character reference about Jorge?' he said.

'No, I want to know what you think it would be like working for him and traveling with him.'

'I met him in Paris four years ago. He was the friend of a very close friend. I've always known him to be an honorable person. He's gruff, he doesn't suffer fools, but he's very smart. You can never really tell about people's private lives, but from what I've seen, he dotes on his wife.'

'You've met her, then?'

'Oh yeah. Heléne was a very famous clairvoyant. She's older than him. Originally it was her act, and Jorge assisted her. Didn't he tell you that?'

'In a way.'

We were in his kitchen, and Alvin paced back and forth, fidgeting with a knife sharpener.

'Alvin, what's bothering you?'

He shook his head.

'Are you holding out on me?'

'It's nothing like that. I think you'll be fine working with Jorge. And I understand why you might need a break from the island. But if it's really just the money, Mala – you know, I have so much money . . .'

'I can't take money from you, Alvin. And if I borrow, how would I pay you back?'

'Look, I know you've been fretting about getting a job. Claudia and I were talking, and we thought you might be able to help her. You could go to Japan as her buyer.'

'She doesn't need anyone to do that. Anyway, that would be very part-time. It's sweet of you both to think of it, but don't you see, this is a chance for me to earn some real cash. I'm sick of worrying about it. And I'd like to buy my house. If I do this, I can.'

'What about the house – do you want us to look after it while you're gone?'

'Olan's going to stay there, with the dogs.'

When I said this, I realized I had already made up my mind. I had spoken to Olan that morning, and despite his dislike of Gaspard ('a burrow-dweller in his previous life' was his description of him), he encouraged me to take the job.

'I'll miss you, but you need to get away,' he added.

When I saw how much Alvin would miss me, too, I was deeply touched, for I had never left any place before – not home, school, or the Navy – where I felt I was leaving anyone behind who really cared. And when I left other places and was churning with deep feelings – New York after Loren's disappearance and Manila the day of Cassiel's departure – the two of them were already gone.

Late in March, I flew to Honolulu to meet up with Gaspard and proceed on to Australia, where he would break me in to his act. The night before, Alvin and Claudia threw me a farewell party and invited all my friends. Seth and Val came, and Estes, who obeyed house rules and smoked only cigarettes, and Olan, who offered me his medallion.

'You've heard of Janus,' he said, 'who looks forward and backward at the same time. This is his Ethiopian counterpart. He'll protect you night and day.'

'Olan,' I said, brandishing my star bracelet and my pendant, 'I already have more protection than I need. You keep the lion to watch over you, and my house, okay?'

Seth gave me a watch that kept time in different time zones, so I'd always know what time it was on Kauai, and Estes gave me a pocket atlas, so I'd always know where I was. 'With a twist,' as he put it, showing me the table in the back that listed the world's major cities and their respective distances from Hawaii.

'See, when you arrive in Sydney, you'll be 5,070 miles away.'

Alvin waited until the end of the party, and then, without a word, put a record on the stereo and asked me to dance. The record was his last T-Zero LP, and its first cut was a slow number that we danced to in the middle of the living room. I was stunned, but when I recovered a little, my heart full to bursting, I whispered in his ear, 'Thank you.'

When the song was over, Claudia and everyone else clapped, and I looked up at Alvin, still holding his hands.

'There's one thing I've never asked you,' I said. 'Why did you invite me out here that night we first met?'

He tilted his head quizzically.

'I mean, I was so stoned and drunk, Alvin, and you can't stand being around people like that.'

'Yeah, you were pretty wasted,' he said. 'I don't know, just an instinct – a flicker in the back of your eyes.'

'A pretty faint one.'

He shook his head. 'It wasn't so hard to see.'

At dawn tears streaked my cheeks as my plane lifted off from Lihue Airport and I watched the green mountains fall away beneath the clouds. Just before boarding, I was sure that one last person, absent from the party, had come to say good-bye when a strong cool wind swept over me suddenly on the tarmac, lifting my hair and fluttering my skirt.

Two weeks later, on April 13, 1973, after two rehearsals a day for twelve days, I made my debut as Jorge Gaspard's assistant at The Bellatrix Theatre in Sydney. That night I wore a long black dress that shimmered with rhinestone chips, like stars. My hair fanned over my shoulders, dusted with sparkles. I had applied my makeup severely – eyeliner, shadow, mascara, lipstick – so it would stand out even at the back of the theater. I had to get used to walking rapidly in high heels, and also to dealing cards while wearing long velvet gloves. At different times onstage I wore a silver headband, a black domino studded with moonstones, and during the one part of the act in which I took center stage, a black silk blindfold that Gaspard applied nimbly from behind my chair.

The last time I had walked onto a stage wearing a costume and makeup was in a college production of *The Bacchae*, in Greek, in a cast of classics majors. And once, when I was asked to read a paper I wrote on Seneca's *Letters* to the members of a lecture course, I discovered that, while my voice never quavered, addressing one hundred people made my hands shake terribly. When Gaspard and I were rehearsing in the cavernous theater with just a few stagehands present, these memories kept going through my head, making what I was about to do seem overwhelming in comparison. Gaspard, however, was blissfully unconcerned about my lack of stage experience.

'One, when you get onstage, your mind will be on other things and you'll be too busy to be afraid; two, though you will obviously be more appealing to look at, after you receive the once-over, the audience will be focused on me; three, like the rest of us, you're probably more vain than you would like to think and you will relish the spotlight.'

Opening night I was still dubious. I knew I had my part of the act down, and I was comfortable in my costume, but as the minutes ticked away in my tiny dressing room, my stomach coiled into knots, my mouth dry, I had the powerful urge to bolt the theater, lose myself in the night, and wait tables after all, safely, anonymously, somewhere in the immensity of Australia.

Once onstage, however, though I hated to admit it, I found that Gaspard was right: after following him out of the wings ('Jorge Gaspard – Mentalist Supreme' was his introduction; 'assisted by the lovely Mala' was mine), I had to concentrate on the opening routine. And the audience *did* focus on him exclusively. And, yes, by the time we reached intermission, I felt a tug for the stage even as I left it. Not once had I faltered. When the following week we performed in a fancy nightclub in

Melbourne, with a far smaller stage and the audience nearly upon us, my stomach knotted up again. But soon enough, whatever the venue, instead of feeling trepidation, I began looking forward to our performances.

The act was straightforward, and Gaspard played it with few variations. He didn't like surprises, which was no small paradox in a performance that required so much audience participation – by its very nature a series of improvisational unknowns. But, as he told me, you must only *seem* to be improvising while actually controlling everything: when you were truly forced to improvise, the performance was in trouble. These tenets of his seemed hopelessly abstract until I saw them in action – for he was a consummate performer – and that helped make my job simpler.

He began with a short tour-de-force routine. Opening and shuffling a sealed deck, I distributed two playing cards each to ten different members of the audience. Gaspard asked these people to exchange their pairs of cards, randomly, not once, but twice. He then stared hard at each audience member in turn, and closing his eyes, correctly identified the cards they were holding.

For the centerpiece of the performance, I descended into the audience again and picked out a succession of people. While Gaspard sat with his back to us, I stood beside these people and announced their names and places of origin through a portable microphone. Then I would read aloud the questions they wrote down for him to answer. These were the only things the audience could hear me saying. What they didn't hear were the subtler messages encoded in my matter-of-fact recitations. It was these messages that provided Gaspard with the raw material which he would expand and refine in 'reading' these people's minds.

The code had been passed along to him by his wife, Heléne. She in turn had learned it as a young woman from a mind reader in Lisbon during the Second World War. This mind reader, a Venetian who had fled the fascists, told Heléne that the code could be traced back to the clairvoyants who came out of Alexandria in medieval times, hid from the Crusaders on Cyprus, and then roamed the Mediterranean as carnival performers.

Gaspard taught me the code in a single week of intensive sessions at the outdoor café of our hotel in Sydney. Because of my facility with languages, and the memory skills that sustained it, I picked up the code easily, impressing Gaspard, who said it had taken him over a month to instruct his previous assistant. After first playing detective, examining a given audience member, I read his or her question aloud to Gaspard, employing certain key words and numbers, each with its own set of variables, and stressing or syncopating others in order to communicate my observations: the style of the person's clothing; whether he wore a wedding ring, cheap or expensive jewelry and cologne; his visible scars, tics, and mannerisms; whether he bit his fingernails down, had a smoker's wheeze, or alcohol on his breath; and, most importantly, who his companion was, along with all the same details about the latter. I always sought out people who obviously had a companion. For, while the rest of the audience focused on the person I had chosen, I could glean much crucial information about the companion that would help Gaspard to make his revealing – hopefully startling – pronouncements from the stage. Sometimes he answered their questions directly; other times, he used them as stepping stones to what he had extrapolated from my observations – especially when he couldn't answer the questions with confidence.

For example, if a woman asked whether or not her husband really loved her, and I had already reported to Gaspard that she wore no wedding ring – the first thing I always looked for – and was twenty years old, in the company of an amused-looking young man, it was easy for Gaspard to reply, 'He would – if you were married.' Equally easy were the questions meant to catch Gaspard out: a man asking if he would ever go bald when, as I detected, he was already wearing a toupee, or a woman inquiring how many children she was planning to have

329

– when she was well past sixty. More difficult were the oblique questions: *I'm thinking of the city in which my favorite composer was born,* a woman wrote on her card. *Can you identify it?* Gaspard worked at deducing the questioner's musical tastes from my description of her, insisting – while rubbing his forehead – that he required more information, until, snatching a couple of facts out of the air by way of my queries to the woman, he could nail down the city. As he told me that first night in Sydney, it worked out that for every twenty questioners, he successfully satisfied nineteen of them. 'The twentieth,' he added drily, 'is a good thing, anyway. It reassures the audience that you're not tricking them.'

As for my own routine, it went like this. One week of every month, just before intermission, I took the spotlight for fifteen minutes. Soon enough, this became thirty minutes. Finally, the routine caught on so strongly that we doubled the number of our performances the week of the waning moon. Gaspard knew a good thing when he saw it. He first announced to the audience that I possessed a rare psychic skill, unlike any he had ever encountered. He offered no explanation beyond the vague – and darkly intoned – suggestion that my 'telepathic powers were aligned to the movements of certain celestial bodies.' In fact, Gaspard knew nothing of my spider bite, nor did he have any idea that my 'telepathic powers' had been amplified after a traumatic automobile accident. Once, when he probed rather insistently as to how and when I had become aware of my ability, I replied – improbably, and sharply – that I didn't remember. He waited some time before asking again. To the audience he described in the simplest terms how I would demonstrate my skill.

'Mala will respond to six members of the audience – more than that would prove exhausting, considering the amount of psychic energy she must expend.'

This was of course untrue, but Gaspard had told me it would add 'spice' – one of his favorite expressions – to the routine.

330

'The six', he continued after a pregnant pause, 'will be drawn by lot, and one at a time will approach the stage, so as to be within twenty feet of Mala physically. Then she will relate the contents of a specific memory that is passing through that person's mind at that instant. You may ask no questions of her.' He lowered his voice, and with a significant look scanned the audience from left to right. 'Should you possess a memory that you do not wish to share, or that ought not to be shared publicly, do not allow it into your thoughts when you come before Mala. That said, understand that she will use her discretion before disclosing the contents of any memory.'

This provision was my idea, in case, as indeed would occasionally happen, someone purposely or otherwise called forth the memory of a graphic sex act or of some particularly gratuitous violence. Gaspard heartily approved of it, not because he wanted to spare my sensibilities, but because it added more spice. Still, some people summoned less sensational but incredibly painful personal memories, and I had more difficulty, in the time allotted me, in separating these out.

Once I concentrated on a person, his memories always came to me the same way: a helter-skelter rush of fragments that quickly ordered themselves, proceeding as a single set of moving images – as if a jumpy film projector were alternately run forward and backward at the highest speeds until it slowed down, fully focused. At first, on Kauai, memories like Wind's and Val's had just invaded my thoughts and remained as long as I fixed on them. Once I could control my intake of memories by entering other people's minds, I felt responsible for what I was doing. Now that people were volunteering to open themselves up to me, and I was making money off my ability, I felt even more responsible – to myself, as well as to them. Being blindfolded helped in this respect, not only by enabling me to concentrate and creating the illusion of privacy onstage, but by ensuring that I never saw the people to whose memories I became privy. Young or old, ugly or pretty, they were all the same to me. Aside from their voices when they identified themselves, I had only the contents of their memories, for a few seconds, to differentiate them.

In Sydney, on the night of my debut performance, after Gaspard had drawn the silken blindfold over my eyes and knotted it, the six people who approached the stage proved to be typical of the groups I would face in subsequent performances.

First, a woman remembering a family picnic by a stream on which a blue rowboat was moored, tethered to a tree; it was the detail of the rowboat's color that made her cry out.

Second, an old man remembering himself with his brother in sailor caps mugging before a store window near the turn of the century.

Next, a man's recollection of someone (I saw only a pair of hands) quartering a melon on a flight of steps drenched in sunlight.

Then a teenage girl who remembered seeing a warehouse on fire from a passing train. ('How did you do that?' she shouted incredulously – to Gaspard's delight – when I concluded my description.)

Fifth, a young man who remembered a pair of tigers pacing their cage at the zoo during a rainstorm.

And finally, an older woman with a murmuring voice who summoned the most chaotic memory: a door swinging open in a dark corridor, a lightbulb flickering on a cord from the ceiling and a bed in the corner over which a man was leaning—

At that point, I broke off, not sharing with the audience that there was a dead child laid out on the bed, and that the man was digging his nails into his palms, drawing blood.

Instead, I concluded by saying, 'And he's in great pain.'

Later, when word came backstage that this woman had asked to see me, Gaspard refused her request categorically, as he told me I must routinely do, without exceptions. 'Because of crazies,' he explained, 'and

332

because we're not psychologists. Not to mention that the sense of mystery you're building onstage would be constantly undermined.'

Two hundred twenty-nine performances and twenty months later, on the night of December 15, 1974, in The Stardust Casino in Las Vegas, Nevada, twelve people approached me before a full house. (This was the limit I myself had set over time, for it turned out that the psychic energy I had to expend was exhausting.) I was restless and distracted that night. Not because of the performance, the mechanics of which had long since become second nature to me. Or even because, as I was well aware, the next day, just a few hours off, would have been Loren's nineteenth birthday. No, my anxieties stemmed from the fact that I had never before been in Las Vegas or any other part of Nevada, and Nevada was Cassiel's home state.

In the previous year I had been up and down the east and west coasts of the United States, along the Pacific rim, and through half a dozen South American capitals with Gaspard, but I had not been in the desert since I drove west after Loren's disappearance – and on that trip I had never strayed farther north than Tucson. All day at the hotel my thoughts had been full of Cassiel. Accustomed now to diving easily into others' memories, I found it was my own that had been weighing on me from the moment our plane touched down that morning.

Memories from the *Repose*: that first time Cassiel kissed me, his arm still in a sling, as we stood on deck crossing the South China Sea.

And memories from Manila: the first time we had made love, with the small fan blowing onto our bed; and the envelope containing my bracelet on which Cassiel had drawn the navigational symbol for a celestial fix.

And then there were the disturbing memories of Cassiel's which I had visited at the Hôtel Alnilam. As I took a taxi to The Stardust, gazing at the stark mountains beyond the lights of Las Vegas, I felt sure those memories had occurred near this city. Closing my eyes, I could see the woman in the red dress running – could smell gasoline fumes before the red car burst into flames. An hour later, as I applied my makeup before the humming, incandescent bulbs of my dressing-room mirror, those fumes were still with me, leaving me light-headed when I took the stage a half hour later.

Gaspard was playing as a headliner, so he was in a good mood that night. But just before we went on, he grew alarmed to see that I was – uncharacteristically – pacing and wringing my hands. When I rebuffed his inquiries, he grew even more alarmed. I had put on a new black dress, with twice as many rhinestone chips as its predecessors, and new heels to match, and I had dusted more sparkles than ever into my hair, which I was wearing very long again. On this particular engagement, a warm-up for a European tour that summer, I wore a black domino onstage until I was blindfolded just before the intermission; only in the second part of the act would my face be fully visible.

Walking into the lights, I realized suddenly just how tired I was. Sleepless the previous night, I had tried all afternoon to nap, without success. The Stardust, like every other casino in town, was air-conditioned well below 70°. But I was boiling. The new dress, custom-made for me in Hong Kong of the lightest silk, seemed heavy as canvas. Beneath my domino I felt sweat beading around my eyes. Only by working rotely did I make it through Gaspard's first routine without throwing him off.

During my own routine, I needed all my energy to concentrate. The layout of the main lounge at The Stardust didn't help: huge, with a domed ceiling, it was called the Star Room, and its low, curved stage, flanked by enormous palms, was backdropped by a gold curtain with silver stars. Two bright spotlights, one on Gaspard, one on me, crisscrossed the stage, following our movements, and a machine in the wings wafted clouds of mist past us, to produce an atmosphere in keeping with our psychic activities. The stage had two runways into the audience, where semicircular tables ran to the back of the room. The closest tables were twenty feet from center stage. The star motif of the room was repeated everywhere: lamps, ashtrays, the waitresses' star-speckled leotards, not to mention the constellations reproduced on the ceiling and the enormous white marble star embedded in the black floor.

The place was packed. Men in black or white dinner jackets, women in pastel gowns. Diamonds and sapphires flashed in the blackness when the houselights dimmed – dazzling as a night sky.

After his introduction, while he was affixing my blindfold, Gaspard whispered urgently in my ear. 'Is everything all right?'

I nodded slowly, but my head was whirling.

The twelve audience volunteers lined up on the right-hand runway. The first two proceeded routinely. The third was a man who identified himself, in a low brooding voice, as 'Lieutenant Gregory Castro.' I had heard that sort of voice dozens of times and knew right away that he was not a cop, or an active-duty military man, but a Vietnam vet. Braced for his combat memories, I was about to fix on Lieutenant Castro when a sequence of images far more explosive to me burst into my thoughts. Someone in the first two rows stood up and pushed his chair back so abruptly – at a moment when the rest of the audience was absolutely still – giving off such powerful emanations, that my concentration immediately shifted to him. To my astonishment and exhilaration this was the memory I saw passing through his head:

He was descending a flight of stairs, into a cramped foyer with a frayed Persian carpet. There was a coatrack on which a green woolen coat hung beside a smaller blue one. Two suitcases sat by the open front door. Down a short slate walk, on a quiet street, a car was idling at the curb with its headlights burning. His cigarette ember glowing, the man behind the wheel was blowing smoke out the window. Overhead the tree branches were lined with snow. The person who descended the stairs took the blue coat off the rack and paused before entering a room off the foyer.

My heart was racing wildly, for I knew that stairway and the carpet and the green coat – they all could have been lifted from my own memory. Which was what I thought for an instant: *your own memory has intruded and this has nothing to do with the person who left his seat.*

But then I became certain it was not my memory, that it was someone else who remembered entering that room off the foyer, a small living room with heavily curtained windows and old overstuffed furniture before a familiar fireplace, and that the scene he witnessed was one I could have witnessed: two women, old and young, arguing toe-to-toe. The older woman's gray hair was tightly bunned, and her hands were on her hips; the young woman, with dark hair flowing onto the shoulders of her motorcycle jacket, was jabbing the air with her finger, making points.

Neither woman took notice of the person with the blue coat who had just joined them. Then suddenly the older woman slapped the younger one across the cheek, and the person remembering all this backed out of the room with the young woman, flushed and furious, following him, picking up the suitcases, and kicking the front door shut behind them. Only when she was out in the cold air, illuminated by the silver ray from a street-light, did the tears become visible, glittering like stars on the cheeks of her pale, pretty face.

The face of my sister Luna!

The memory broke off there, and an instant later – to Gaspard's horror and the surprise of Lieutenant Castro, still waiting on the runway – I tore off my blindfold. Half-blinded by the spotlight, I glimpsed bewildered faces in the audience before focusing on an empty table for two, with drinks, in the second row. There were three red EXIT signs in the rear, and my eyes darted from one to the other. The middle door was shut; two men were entering the right-hand door; and the door on the left was just closing on a red dress and a man's white-jacketed shoulder and sleeve. I tried in vain to remember who had been sitting at that second-row table.

Debating which exit I ought to rush for, I instead found myself, on rubbery legs, being assisted offstage by Gaspard, who gripped my arm and, over the buzz of the audience, kept saying, 'What is it? What's gotten into you?'

'Let me go!' I cried the moment we were offstage, and bolting from him, I rushed out into the house.

'Mala!' he shouted after me.

The audience gawked at me as I hurried up through the tables, still clutching my blindfold. I pushed through the right-hand door into the lobby and stopped cold. It was peak hour in the casino proper, and gamblers were milling everywhere. I saw literally dozens of men in white jackets and a good number of women in red. I zigzagged through the crowd desperately, then gave up, fighting back my tears. I got the maître d' for the Star Room to find the waitress who had served that second-row table, but she remembered only that it had been occupied by a young couple; they had arrived just as my routine began, ordered a mescal Bloody Mary (for her) and a glass of champagne (for him), barely touched them, and walked out minutes later, leaving a big tip. They seemed agitated, the waitress said, as if they'd been arguing, but she couldn't remember much about them physically except the fact the man was 'good-looking' and the woman was a blonde wearing sunglasses. From the rear of the Star Room I saw Gaspard alone onstage, improvising. But I couldn't concentrate on what he was saying and I didn't care.

I made directly for my dressing room, locked the door, and sat trembling before the mirror as I went over every-thing that had happened. Perhaps the fact I had gone on so frazzled and exhausted, pained by my memories of Cassiel, was the reason I had picked up on the wrong person's memory during the performance. That had never happened before. But it was the identity of the person that staggered me: I felt sure it was Loren who had ordered a glass of champagne, argued with his date, and while leaving the Star Room revisited a boyhood memory of my mother and Luna arguing in my mother's house. And moments later he and Luna joined Milo, smoking outside in the car, perhaps to begin that final, fatal cross-country trip.

Had the memory broken off, and my blindfold come off, a few seconds earlier, I might have seen him. But as it was, I was sure he was alive – Loren was alive! – and burying my face in my arms on the makeup counter I began to cry, wrenching hard sobs from my gut, and only stopped, much later, when Gaspard's banging on the door finally reached my ears.

Afterward, I was not so sure what I had experienced that night. But at the time, wanting so badly to believe it so, I told myself that I had crossed paths, however fleetingly, with Loren. This in itself, regardless of his circumstances – and what could they be that he should turn up at a Las Vegas casino? – felt like a miracle. If I was right, then for several precious seconds I had been inside his memory. A particularly accurate memory, I thought, drying my eyes with the blindfold, for even my father's Silver Star had been present in its green frame over the mantelpiece, exactly as I remembered it, in the lamplight glinting as sharply as Luna's tears out on the street.

13

The Stardust

In Las Vegas, 'the crossroads of limbo', my tutor Labusi used to call it, it sometimes felt as if everyone was lost, or in the process of losing something or someone, or of losing themselves in the end. Perhaps that was the real reason – as much pragmatic as esoteric – Samax had settled there and filled up his hotel with people looking for lost things. At that moment, crossing the parking lot of The Stardust Casino behind Dalia, I felt I was about to lose something with her – and it wasn't going to be as pleasurable as losing my virginity. Suddenly she wheeled around, her eyes flashing in the moonlight, and raised her hand to slap me across the face. When she had tried to slap me in the casino not thirty minutes earlier, I had caught her wrist in midair, infuriating her even more. This time she stopped herself at the last instant, and curling her fingers into a fist, waved it at the sky.

'Don't tell me what I can and cannot do,' she said spitting out the words as if they were hot on her tongue. 'Not *tonight*. Not when I've found out that back home I've lost *everything*.'

'Dalia, I wasn't telling you what to do.'

'Bull*shit*!' she shouted.

When we reached my car, she opened and slammed shut the passenger-side door, then, hands on hips, began pacing rapidly up and down and kicking at the loose gravel with her red pumps.

I slid behind the wheel and turned the key in the ignition. The car was a black 1959 Ford Galaxie convertible that Samax had given me on my eighteenth birthday – exactly a year ago, I thought, watching the luminous minute hand on the dashboard clock inch past midnight. Her red dress flaring in front of the headlights, Dalia circled the car a half dozen times, broke a heel, flung her shoes across the parking lot, and stopped abruptly to light a cigarette which she smoked with her back to me, red neon from the casino's sign setting her mane of hair on fire. The top was down on the car and I gazed away from the moon, away from Dalia, toward the mountains, where the stars were brightest and the night was still.

On the Strip, between the human and mechanical traffic, things were anything but peaceful. Even at this hour – especially at this hour – the Seventh Day Adventists in their street-corner booths were bringing their message to the sinners. They warned that Las Vegas, like Nineveh in seventh-century BC Babylon – teeming with erotic dancers and courtesans, gamesters and conjurers – would soon be swallowed up by the desert sands. In addition to the city's round-the-clock frenzy, the nearby (almost suburban) testing of atomic bombs only encouraged such speculation. Nevertheless, in my nine years there, Las Vegas had nearly doubled in both size and population.

The act in the lounge that Dalia and I had begun to watch would have fit in at one of Nineveh's nocturnal bazaars. I was sorry to be torn away just as I began observing the mind reader's svelte assistant enter the labyrinth of someone's memory on cat's feet and calmly report its contents. With her dress like the night sky, her glittering blindfold and star-speckled hair, this woman especially was right out of my old *Arabian Nights*, which I still dipped into on nights when I couldn't sleep. Which of late, because of recent developments at the Hotel Canopus, meant almost every night.

My evening with Dalia had been eventful, even for us.

And not a little frenetic. I hadn't seen her in a year, after all, and she had only arrived at the hotel that afternoon, from Santa Fe, in a rented car. After being expelled from Chile in January for political 'crimes', Dalia had flown to Albuquerque and begun driving eastward, covering another line of those crosses on Friar Varcas's old map. We had dinner at a gaudy Moroccan restaurant in Paradise City, drove out into the desert at 100 mph, smoked some of her moon flower buds, drank mescal from a bottle with a green worm tumbling at its base, and made love on a blanket spread out on the sand.

'The first time we made love,' she murmured, opening the bodice of her red dress like the petals of a flower, 'you were a boy, and now you are a man.' She slid the dress up to her waist, and pushing me onto my back, climbed on top of me. 'Let me show you something. I learned it once from a sailor in Punta Arenas. It's called *Lo Sacacorchos* – The Corkscrew.'

I had dated and slept with a good number of girls since that first time, some who lived near the hotel and others whom I met at the university. But there was no one quite like Dalia. Two years before, when she had returned to the Hotel Canopus for a week, we had taken every opportunity to tear off our clothes, in my room, her room, the billiard room, the greenhouse – where Samax nearly stumbled on us beneath his prized loquat tree – or to drive into the Mojave, and with the car radio blaring, to make love as we were now. Then seventeen, I was beginning to realize just how attractive I was to women. About six one, strong and well-proportioned, I had benefited from all those years of Samax's rigid dietary standards – an unceasing flow of fresh fruit juices and organic vegetables – as well as from the varied physical activity around the hotel, from swimming and archery to rock climbing in Kyle Canyon and jujitsu lessons. I had briefly grown, and shaved off, a beard, then a moustache, and I still wore my hair long at that time, combed straight back. But I also discovered that when it came to women, it was my upbringing – not

341

just my good looks – that made me feel at ease around them and they around me. Not just girls my age, but young women several years my senior. The pattern I established with Dalia – I fifteen and she eighteen that first time together – I repeated several times afterward. Many of these young women, I would one day see, resembled the image of Alma that I had reconstructed and fixed in my memory from the days we had shared nine years before: tall, slender, blue-eyed brunettes around twenty years old. As for Desirée, who for me had conflated with Alma in even more powerful ways, I was moving closer chronologically – but in no other way I could discern – to my boyhood fantasy of making love to her when I was twenty and she thirty. I didn't know how my carryings-on with her cousin Dalia, of which Desirée herself was well aware, having instigated them in the first place, might affect my slim possibilities with Desirée one way or the other.

When Dalia and I finally zoomed back to the Strip, we took in an early show at the Sahara, and went on to The Stardust. Her dinner conversation had swung back and forth between two poles: from discovering that morning that the military dictatorship now running Chile had stripped her of her citizenship to the harrowing details of her latest foray into northern New Mexico in search of vampires. She broke off in midstream with both subjects, announcing suddenly that we must make love, not back at the hotel, but right away, in the desert, under the stars. And until we did so, indulging in 'The Corkscrew,' among other things, she was lost in a revery. Once we arrived at The Stardust, it was a different story: the lilac smoke of the 'flowers of the moon' and the ninety-proof mescal seemed to catch up with her, so that when she returned to her earlier conversation it was with a much fiercer slant. At first, ranting about Chile's dictator.

'That sonofabitch *maricon* Pinochet has banned Marx and Hegel and Thomas Paine, none of whom he has read, but not *Mein Kampf*, which he has. He murdered

342

Allende, he executed José Gonzago, and Hugo Rozzel and María Filomárte and Niño Vallar, and now he will try to murder my father, and if I went back again he would murder me along with all the others at the university – though he can still do it here, can have me shot or blown up anytime, because your fascist government are the ones who put his fascists in last year – but the sonofabitch has taken away my passport, so now I am a refugee, a persona non grata, a piece of driftwood they would like to see rot.'

She raved on like this, veering between Spanish and English, while downing mescal Bloody Marys and betting wildly at the roulette table. When I tried to stop her on all counts, she became furious, and there among the gamblers, in a swirl of lights and faces, we began arguing. Not only did I lose the argument, but she lost her money.

'This is my dirty Chilean money,' she said through her teeth, signing a check with a flourish at the cashier's window.

Drawn on a bank in Albuquerque, the check was for ten thousand dollars.

'That's American money, Dalia. You'll need it here to travel.'

'I'll make new money. This is dirty money that I smuggled out with me. Six hundred thousand pesos. Pinochet's face is on every bill,' she added darkly, though I doubted this was the case. 'I'm going to turn it into clean money at the roulette wheel. *La Rueda de Fortuna*.' Pressing her face to mine, she whispered, 'You know how? I'm going to bet *red* every time. *Rojo, rojo, rojo . . .* Did you know the color red is outlawed in Chile now? They've made the color a crime. For wearing this dress, I would be arrested. I'll bet red, and this filthy money, after I double it – maybe quadruple it! – will come out clean.'

There was no point in arguing with her, but after she had dropped five thousand dollars in five minutes, I tried once more.

'Dalia, you're not getting back at anyone, you're just screwing yourself.'

Her eyes narrowed. 'Excuse me,' she said to the croupier, and led me around a marble pillar behind a potted palm. 'You're trying to humiliate me, Enzo?'

'If that's what you want to think,' I said, 'fine.' The casino din, on top of the mescal and the moon flower buds, was making my head pound.

'Are you?' she demanded.

'The hell with it,' I said. 'Go lose all your money.'

It was then she spun around and tried to slap me. Squeezing her wrist tightly, I lowered her hand back to her side.

Within minutes, Dalia doubled her remaining five thousand and then lost it all on a single spin of the wheel. At that point, we attempted to patch things up by attending the mentalist's act – a mistake – and twenty minutes after leaving the Star Lounge we were still in the parking lot, the car idling and Dalia lighting another cigarette off the butt of the first one.

Three hours later, just after three a.m., we were sitting at the butcher-block table in the tenth-floor kitchen of the Hotel Canopus. Dalia sipped maté tea with lemon juice and a dash of Tabasco and told me she had no regrets about losing the money.

'I know you don't understand,' she said, peering across the table at me with bloodshot eyes, 'but it made me feel better. I apologize for losing my head. Getting violent like that,' she shook her head, 'I don't like it.'

'Forget it.'

Sweating and hungover already, I was wearing only pajama bottoms, and Dalia had slipped into a red silk bathrobe. She had also removed her makeup and her face looked even whiter than usual, and much gaunter than I remembered. Though we were both exhausted, she still had one last surprise for me – by far the most bizarre of the evening – beside which her losing the ten thousand dollars paled.

'I've been having a lot of trouble with my temper

lately,' she murmured after a long silence. And then she picked up the other strand of her dinner conversation, exactly where she had left off back at the Moroccan restaurant. 'Remember I told you I came to a road stop east of a town called Puerto de Luna, near the Gallo Mountains?'

I nodded. 'Where the waitress was strange.'

'She was not just a waitress,' she said, shaking her head violently. Then she lowered her voice until it was barely audible, though we couldn't have been more alone. 'This road stop was at the site of one of Varcas's crosses. A place he passed through on September 10, 1849. Back then, it was a horse-relay station beside a salt flat. The air there was stifling, yet the woman began kindling a fire in a giant hearth as soon as I entered. She was a dark woman, but not Apache or Kiowa, and not Spanish – though she spoke our language. Her feet were bare. She wore a coarse brown dress and her hair was the color of smoke, billowing around her head. However, it was the fumes from the fire that truly alerted me to the danger I was in,' Dalia whispered.

'And what was that?'

'Varcas said when he smelled those fumes, the woman turned white eyes upon him and he brandished his cross. Immediately she disappeared, but for three days afterward he resisted sleep while a single wild dog and then a buzzard kept to his trail. Like Varcas, I have no doubt what she was. Before leaving the road stop, I examined the fire and confirmed that it was fueled not by common wood, but by the four elements with which a *bruja* enchants before she feasts on the blood – capulin branches, copal, century plant roots, and dry zoapatl leaves sweeter than honey . . .'

My head throbbing, I spiked my tea with another shot of Tabasco.

'Enzo, it was the same *bruja* Varcas describes,' Dalia added emphatically, 'now, 125 years later, and she is not a day older. Who can say how many travelers she has entrapped over the years.'

'She was dressed the same?'

'Not just that,' she said impatiently. 'Did you listen to what I said? *Everything* about her was the same: the bare feet, the smoky hair, the eyes. And that fire is the only one a vampire can stand. She was feeding it the four elements of enchantment. As for the dog and buzzard, it is those forms – not a bat's – that a vampire assumes when pursuing someone for a prolonged period.' Suddenly Dalia covered her face and her matter-of-fact tone fell away. 'But, Enzo, I was not so lucky as Friar Varcas,' she sobbed, and I saw how badly her hands were shaking.

'What happened?'

She shook her head, biting her lip. 'I breathed too much of the fire's fumes and could not escape so quickly.'

I waited in vain for her to stop sobbing. 'And?'

'And this!' She pulled the robe off her left shoulder and, just below the tattoo of the iceberg on fire, there was a swollen red and blue welt.

'What's that?'

'What do you think?' She was crying hysterically now. 'She bit me.'

'The woman bit you?'

'She's not a woman!'

'Dalia, why didn't you tell me about this earlier?' I said, grabbing her arm. I was trying to believe her, but at the same time I didn't want to.

'Don't touch it!' she cried.

'Dinner, the casino – all that time you said nothing.' And now I knew why in the desert on the blanket she – who always preferred making love stark naked – had kept her dress on.

'I wasn't ready to tell you,' she said defiantly, wiping her tears, her eyes more bloodshot than ever.

'Look, you have to see a doctor.' Whether it was a bite or not, she needed help.

'Doctors cannot help me.'

'Don't talk crazy – when did this happen?'

346

'Two nights ago.'

'And you didn't even dress the wound?'

'It would make it worse.'

Slowly I put my palm against her cheek fighting the wave of nausea that was passing through me. 'Dalia, listen to me. We can get help.'

'No.'

'There's someone here who can help. Remember Zaren Eboli?'

She knitted her brow. 'The man with the spiders? He cannot help me.'

'He knows about these things, about bites and poisons.'

She shook her head. 'He doesn't know about this. It's not the same – this is not spiders. I wish it were.'

'But he'll know what to do.'

She leaned across the table and her breath was hot on my face, and sickly sweet now, like the fumes she had described. 'I know what to do,' she said urgently. 'Enzo, I didn't show you this for nothing. There is someone I can see. You can take me to him tonight.'

'It's three-thirty.'

'Enzo, this is how you can help me.'

'And he's not a doctor?'

'He is a kind of doctor,' she said slowly. 'Can you do that for me? Now. Without any more talk.'

Fifteen minutes later, I was pushing the Galaxie hard, northward into the desert, on the two-lane secondary road that Dalia insisted on. I followed her directions despite the fact she seemed to be wasting away beside me with each passing minute. I thought eventually she'd exhaust herself and I'd take her to the hospital. She wore my gray trench coat over her red bathrobe; the trench coat was large on her to begin with, but by the end of our journey that night she was not so much wearing it as floating within it, animating its form more as vapor than bone and sinew. The journey was strange and alarming in itself, through places I had never seen at night, and then places I had heard of but never seen, and finally places I had never heard of – though they were only two hours from Las Vegas – and would never see again. Even when I later tried to find them.

Gradually we veered northwest, encountering fewer and fewer cars in either direction. We passed the federal maximum-security prison at Indian Springs. Samax once told me he often thought about the prison, since it was just ten miles from the hotel, and about the innocent men he knew must be in it; he added with only a trace of irony that while he had met some evil men in prison, he had also known several innocent men at Ironwater besides himself and Rochel, and they too were no better or worse than other men just because they were terribly wronged. Wronged, however, in a way no man on the outside could understand. 'No more than we can understand, but can only imagine, what it's like to be murdered,' he had concluded, 'because what they say is true, when you're put away, a part of you is killed off.'

Dalia's conversation, meanwhile, was lapsing into delirium. By the time we reached Mercury, the off-limits Air Force town at the lip of the Nevada Test Site, she was speaking strictly in staccato fragments. We were in the strange, charged corridor in southern Nevada where the Mojave and Great Basin Deserts overlap. On our right there was a stretch of radioactive sand flats – scene of both above- and under-ground atomic tests – and on our left the eastern border of Death Valley. Still, it wasn't the local geography, but that of New Mexico, that so obsessed Dalia suddenly. Specifically, a peculiar fact which she claimed was evident on any map of that state.

'Can you picture it?' she said, wringing the sleeves of the trench coat as the wind whipped her hair. 'A triangle . . . three points . . . each of them a town: *Luna . . . Los Lunas . . . Puerto de Luna . . .* You think those names are a coincidence? . . . a triangle of lunar towns . . . at its center the mouth of the Río Puerco . . . Do you remember the Río Puerco?'

In fact, I did, for I had seen it from Acoma when I was

348

there with Calzas four years earlier: a faint brown ribbon in the east that fed into the Río San José.

'It is the river Friar Varcas was following', Dalia went on, 'when he encountered the crucified woman and that first vampire. Near Los Lunas,' she added emphatically. 'Just as the road stop was in Puerto de Luna.'

The high clouds over the test site were stationary, and faded, as if they had been painted onto the sky long ago. And in the wind blowing from that direction there was a faint hiss of irregular static, an edgy whine – the residue, I thought, of all those atomic blasts, the afterbuzz and debris of split atoms. A wind of free-floating electrons which lent an incandescence to Dalia's tightening features. Her voice, though, was drifting, increasingly free-floating itself. And I was increasingly alarmed. Over the course of the drive, and from the moment she had shown me the welt on her shoulder, I had been running on adrenaline. At first I had been skeptical of much she was telling me, but that changed. And the more apprehensive I grew, the more I fell back on old instincts, withdrawing into silence and holding my feelings in check.

'But Puerto de Luna made those places look tame,' she started up again. 'That's where I was two days ago . . . where Varcas disappeared in the end . . . where his book breaks off . . . February 29, 1852. The last entry is just seven words: *Found the lost Mansion of the Moon*. Do you know what that means? The cabalists said there are 301,655,722 angels abroad . . . and that they live in the twenty-eight mansions of the moon. But there is a twenty-ninth, a lost mansion, here on earth where the fallen angels live . . . *los angelos infiernos* . . . the ones from hell. Under the full moon, one night each month, it opens its door . . . *Puerto de Luna* . . . Varcas found it . . . he entered and never came out again – never as Varcas, that is. A mansion with many occupants and many outposts. That way,' she concluded, pointing through the windshield, 'the left-hand fork to the next town.'

We had just passed Beatty, where the wind's static jumped from a hiss to a sizzle and those high clouds darkened from indigo to black, barely visible against the sky. Dalia was back to wringing her sleeves, clawing at them with her long fingers, and I was trying to keep my eyes on the road.

'I went to Puerto de Luna', she continued, 'on a clear night, but without a single star shining . . . as if all the stars had burnt up and fallen into the mountains. I came to a crooked road . . . all the trees dead, the earth scorched, the wind foul . . . I left my car and walked . . . it was as if I was walking the length of my entire life, and at the end of the road there was a huge lodge . . . black stone . . . a single door . . . a window glowing with moon-light . . . and in the surrounding darkness, cries and howls . . . the ground moving . . . a carpet of snakes . . . some dogs with human eyes. Despite all I had seen following Varcas's path, I was overcome with fear, yet I didn't want to leave . . . not when I had found my way to the center of his labyrinth. A woman in a gown came out the door and took my hand . . . there was blood under her fingernails but I could see right through her hands . . . she led me to the door . . . behind her there was a press of bodies . . . dancers, gliding in pairs, their features part human, part animal . . . I glimpsed an owl's stiffened ears, a wolf's snout, an ant's many-lensed eyes. Suddenly the dancers parted and a man with a beard stepped out to greet me . . . he wore a black coat and high black boots . . . he had long white hair, a beard, and a hooked nose . . . his wide-set eyes stared through me as if I were glass . . . it was – turn right here,' she interrupted herself. 'Go up the hill.'

She didn't say another word as I drove up to a sign with phosphorescent letters that read ENTERING RHYOLITE, past abandoned mining shacks in a cratered hollow, a crumbling depot, and the skeleton of a burnt-out church. Then, just over the crest, she pointed at a boxy black building sitting solitary to my left, in utter darkness.

350

'Stop here,' Dalia said, her eyes widening.

Gazing down the long street illuminated by my high-beam lights, I realized that Rhyolite was a ghost town. We were at one end of the main street, which was lined with broken-down buildings and rubble. I knew that rhyolite was a volcanic rock, the lava form of granite; along with the vast gold deposits, the rhyolite must have long ago been mined out of that windless bluff over-looking Death Valley. On mild days, it would reach 110° up there; even at five a.m. in December the air was stifling, rank with sulphurous fumes.

I pulled up outside the building. It was all stone, windowless in front, with a metal door and a narrow walk covered with dust white as snow. The few trees near the building were dead, and up the walls there were thick vines that looked just as lifeless.

At Rhyolite, the feelings I had been holding in all that time, listening to Dalia rant, flooded over me. By the time I sat in front of that building, the nausea in my gut had coalesced into a rush of fear. My lips were so numb it felt as if I would have to pry them open. Gripping the steering wheel hard, squinting into the inky darkness, I read the plaque beside the building's door: THE LOST MUSEUM.

'After traveling this country, I can tell you they are everywhere,' Dalia said, startling me, for her voice was suddenly cold and precise. 'Just as Varcas said. Only their occupations have changed: now they're croupiers, rodeo riders, store clerks, cocktail waitresses – oh yes, and priests. The ones who avert their eyes from the crosses in their own churches. Some of them go back to Varcas's time, others just fifty years, and some,' she whispered, 'just a few days . . . But all of them will live forever.'

'You mean, Varcas—'

'I mean, it's all true – everything he reported.'

'And this museum – what is it?'

'Just what it says,' she replied evenly. 'For those who are lost, never to be found. You once told me your uncle's hotel is filled with people who are lost, or who are looking for lost things. You are one of those people, just as I was. But in finding what I was looking for, I have lost everything else. Perhaps that is always the way it is.' She wet her lips and they gleamed sharply. 'Now you see why that money was nothing to me. At this museum you pay a different kind of admission.'

'Dalia, let's get out of here.'

'That's exactly what you're going to do,' she said, slipping out of my trench coat. She was no longer shivering and her hands were finally at rest.

'Without you?'

'Leave here as soon as I enter that door,' she said. 'And don't look back.'

'And the man who was going to help you?'

'He's here.' Her eyes were wide again, and the color seemed to be draining from her irises. 'You are a deep soul, and I enjoyed our times together,' she said in a distant voice. 'I wanted to see you once more. And I had some business to finish. I was given two days and they're over now, at sunrise.'

I had been afraid, but for the first time I was afraid of her.

'Let's not pretend I have to explain, Enzo.' Her mouth curled into a tight smile as she leaned close and whispered, 'Make no mistake, I would love to take you with me.' Then she pulled away and opened her door. 'So just go . . .'

When she stepped from the car, I made no attempt to stop her. She came around to my side and said, 'The manuscript of my translation is in an envelope in the desk in my room. Mail it for me.'

My lips parted, but I could not speak.

'Will you do that?' she said, squeezing my wrist. My hand was cold, but hers was like ice. Then she brushed my cheek with her fingernails – not hard enough to scratch, but nearly so. 'You will,' she nodded.

Turning toward the Lost Museum, she whispered, 'Can you see him?' But I saw nothing.

Dropping the red bathrobe from her shoulders, Dalia was naked when she walked up to the door of the museum. Her white skin shone against that black door, which swung open the moment she reached it. She stepped through it and never looked back.

I hesitated, then got the flashlight from the glove compartment and rushed up the stone path. My hand was shaking as I entered the single rectangular room that was the Lost Museum. It was hot as a furnace and absolutely bare. There were cold ashes in the fireplace. The cement floor was thick with dust, but did not bear a single print from Dalia's feet. Where could she have gone? The only other exit from the room was a window in the rear wall, barely large enough to accommodate a child. Through that window I saw a small red light streaking across the desert, growing fainter by the second. It was going too fast to be a motorcycle, I thought, and then I watched it rise suddenly from the floor of Death Valley and disappear altogether.

I jumped into the Galaxie and spun it around, keeping my eyes glued to the rearview mirror. Straining to suck down some air, flooring the accelerator, I rode the double line the four miles back past Beatty, then got onto the interstate just as the sun was peeping over the mountains.

During the drive home, I resisted rushing into State Police headquarters near Indian Springs, even after pulling off the highway to do so. How could I have told the police what had just happened to me without provoking them to administer a Breathalyzer test – which I would have failed – and locking me up? Could I have explained that after a night of dinner, lovemaking, gambling, and other diversions, my date had stripped naked and vanished into a phantom museum? And if I just reported Dalia as a missing person, what would I become – the only person she had been with all night, and the last one she was seen with – but a murder suspect who was deranged. No, the police were out of the question. And when I arrived back at the hotel, still frightened, I also resisted the impulse to rush into the garden to Samax, who was eating breakfast. He was having enough trouble at that time without my adding this particular madness to the mix.

Instead, I went directly to Dalia's room. At first glance, it appeared she had not left a trace: no clutter, no personal effects, the dresser bare, the bedcovers taut. Maybe she just hadn't unpacked the previous afternoon, I thought, but then I found her suitcase in the closet, containing only the red dress and shoes she had worn when we went out. Since the red bathrobe was standard issue to guests, when she arrived at the hotel her suitcase's sole contents must have been the fat red envelope in the desk drawer which she had asked me to mail. A gray address label had already been affixed to the envelope, with the following typed in red ink:

> REVENANT PRESS
> 3000 DAEDALUS CIRCLE
> ALBUQUERQUE, NEW MEXICO

The envelope was sealed, and I did not open it. But behind it, far back in the drawer, I did find the old Spanish edition of Friar Varcas's memoir, titled *Vampiri en Española Califorñia y en Gran Mexico*, from which Dalia had made her translation. Brown, with a heavy battered binding and yellowed pages, it was a book I had seen in her hands many times, but had never opened myself. When I did, I didn't get beyond the frontispiece, where there was a faded photograph – the only one known to exist, according to the caption – of the author. With wide-set eyes, a hooked nose, and long hair – but without the beard – it was obviously the man Dalia claimed to have seen at Puerta de Luna, and again, just hours before, at Rhyolite.

Putting the book back into the drawer, I hurried to my own room. With Sirius at my feet, I stared out the window onto the brightening desert sands until I dozed off fitfully around noon. I was up all night, and the follow-

354

ing morning I returned to Dalia's room. I found the envelope where I had left it, and I promptly mailed it, but there was no trace of Varcas's book in the desk drawer. And I never saw Dalia again – at least not as I had known her, though I felt in subsequent years that I might have glimpsed her on occasion in other incarnations. Always benign – to me, at least. And not always in my dreams, which she sometimes frequented, standing out more vividly than anyone else, as if it were her true element.

If I hadn't been sleeping well before, Dalia had ensured that I wouldn't be for some time to come. But even the incredible circumstances of her disappearance soon receded in my consciousness, so intense did the swirl of events at the Hotel Canopus become later that winter. Many gears on the complex apparatus that was daily life at the hotel began spinning out of control at the same time. At first this seemed coincidental, a matter of bad luck, but it soon became clear that these simultaneous events were of course connected in subtle ways.

In fact, much had transpired at the hotel, with people of great significance and long standing in my life, well before Dalia's sudden arrival and departure. Labusi, for one, had been paralyzed in an automobile accident two years earlier – a horrible blow, and a shock to all of us at the hotel. There was a railroad strike at the time, and, terrified of air travel, rather than miss a performance of *Turandot* he had been looking forward to, Labusi hired a car and driver to take him to the opera house in San Francisco. On the return trip, he told me later, as he dozed in the rear seat, dreaming of the moment when Turandot first sings, a van of tourists who had lost their way ran the car off the highway. His driver escaped with a couple of fractures, but Labusi would spend the rest of his life in a wheelchair. His intellectual processes were unaffected, but for nearly a year he tumbled into a seemingly bottomless depression. Even the elaborate chess problems and mnemonic challenges that all of us brought to him failed to arrest his descent. He made a pathetic figure, propelling himself through the lobby in his chromium wheelchair, his large head cocked stiffly to one side, or sitting in mutual silence and sipping iced chamomile tea all afternoon with Dolores in her little niche of the garden, encircled by hedges. What an unlikely, and unhappy looking, pair they made. I hated to see him like that, stripped of his vitality and wit. Silence, however, was the only element of his Pythagorean beliefs to which Labusi continued to adhere. His dietary strictures – he began eating beans, then fish – had fallen by the wayside. And by the end of that year, when he even stopped listening to his extensive music collection – including the late string quartets of Beethoven, without which, he had once told me, life would literally be meaningless – I truly feared that he might have become suicidal. Evidently this was a red flag for Samax as well. For what finally snapped Labusi back to some measure of his former self was an inspired notion of Samax's.

'It's not delicious puzzles from Capablanca's secret journals,' Samax said one night in the solarium to Hadar and me, 'or ever more intricate memory palaces that will get through to him – those are the things he's always gone after. He needs to take up something completely different.'

'Like what?' Hadar said.

'Just leave it to me,' Samax replied confidently, which made me squirm, for in my heart I was as skeptical as Hadar.

'But we can't even get him to leave his rooms most of the time,' Hadar grumbled.

'Exactly my point,' Samax said. 'Because what he needs is utterly unavailable to him now. I can't believe I didn't think of it before. What's the one thing Labusi ever left the hotel for, gentlemen? Not women and wine, but . . .'

'Song!' I said.

Samax nodded. 'We'll give him something new,' he murmured, 'and something old.'

Samax began bringing in chamber groups from the

area to perform in the ballroom every Friday night. The first such Friday, when a string quintet arrived, he simply went up to Labusi's quarters himself, and without a word conveyed him to the ballroom. Every Friday after that, at eight o'clock sharp, Labusi would be in the ballroom waiting for the musicians to arrive. The night they played Boccherini's 2nd String Quintet, one of his very favorites, the tears ran down my old tutor's cheeks – the first time I ever saw him weep.

The 'something new' that Samax provided Labusi was even more ingenious, and I marveled that it had occurred to Samax at all. He had commissioned a company in Carson City to construct a customized billiard table, fully convertible to pocket billiards, of regulation size and specifications, but resting on electronically adjustable legs that could rise at the touch of a button from thirty-two inches – exactly the right height for someone in a wheelchair – to the customary forty-five inches. The legs operated with such precision, and the table's internal honeycomb, springs, and balances were so perfectly calibrated, that when the legs went up and down not a single ball on the table stirred a millimeter. So Labusi could play pool or shoot billiards with anyone. And play he did, sometimes for ten hours a day. With his still-steady cellist's hands and steely chess player's nerves, his Pythagorean passion for geometry, and of course his memory skills – filing away countless variations of bank and combination shots – Labusi was a natural at all billiard games. He could best any of us at the hotel in the game of our choice – mine was always 8-ball – and when he craved stiffer competition, he found that, living in Las Vegas, there was no shortage of first-rate players with whom he could compete seriously. First in pickup games, for which various pool sharks came to the hotel, and then in formal competitions in town to which Labusi traveled with his custom-made table in a small truck. 'Like a pianist,' he said to me drily, the *s* whistling faintly through the triangular chip in his front teeth, 'with his Steinway.'

For thus, through his own and Samax's perseverance – a quality my uncle perhaps prized above all others – Labusi began his third career, following a painful yet surprisingly symmetrical route in his life's journey: from chess champion, to scholar and tutor, to the billiards champion he would soon become.

Would that the other catastrophes occurring in and around the hotel at that time had lent themselves to such constructive, even happy, resolutions. In fact, happiness was fast becoming a scarce commodity at the Hotel Canopus; Labusi aside, Samax's Midas touch and vaunted ingenuity, rather than overcoming that trend, seemed to aggravate it. In ancient days, heroes single-handedly diverted the courses of rivers to alleviate drought or prevent flood; in our own times, deciding on your own to divert the course of someone's life in order to secure his happiness might be a comparably dramatic achievement. And a tremendous gamble, too, as Samax had acknowledged on the day he undertook just such an action with regard to my life, informing me right away that he had once been a gambler. But, whatever the magnitude of their feats, those ancient heroes I had read about in Homer and Virgil were convinced that no man could change his or anyone else's fate, which was written in the stars. When a man thought otherwise (signalling, in effect, that he had gone mad), he was struck down. I doubt that Samax shared this conviction.

Since that first day, and all through my boyhood, he had always seemed a kind of magician to me: passionately whisking people around the globe in the service of their own passions; delving into history's murky by-ways and bringing the rarest objects back into the light; even cultivating the most delicate fruit in one of the world's hottest deserts; and all the while presiding over an enormous extended household and successfully maintaining a set of private – if not secret – lives within the confines of his public one. But when it came to the elemental issues that underlie all others – the fragility of life and inescapability of death – Samax was, of course, as powerless as any other man and well aware of it. With lesser issues, he was not so philosophical. Philosophy, magic, and even his gambler's instincts were not the things to which he automatically turned when confronted with crises in the real – the fallen – world, where he had had to make his way against fierce adversaries. Deep down I think he fell back on the ethos of the streets he had been forced to incorporate, as a young man, among his other beliefs. One of Samax's great paradoxes was that, for someone who had thrived as a gambler, in most matters he was terribly unwilling to leave things to chance. He was not an accepting man. Blind acceptance of his condition, or of the hand dealt him, was never a part of his emotional vocabulary; instead, he concentrated his tremendous energy on making sure that *he* would be the one – quite literally – who always dealt the cards.

Even so, the deck, like all decks, always contained a joker, a wild card over which even the likes of Samax had limited control, as became clear later that year when Dolores, still firmly rooted in her shadowy cul-de-sac in the garden, became the passive hub at the center of an amazing turn of events after Labusi's accident. At least, they amazed me at a time when I didn't think I could still be amazed by anything that happened at the hotel. Those events would be the catalyst to all that unfolded soon afterward.

It started with Denise suffering a fatal heart attack one night at two a.m. in the red elevator. She had been on her way to the lobby after bringing Samax a pint of freshly squeezed blackberry juice – his choice of soporific – in the penthouse. But Samax was not the last person she spoke with (in fact, they barely exchanged a word) before her death. While switching elevators on the ninth floor, she ran into Della, and the two sisters quarreled loudly, awakening Desirée, who ran into the corridor to intervene. Before Desirée could say a word, however, Denise stormed into the elevator and Della returned to her room, locking the door behind her.

Shortly afterward, up late playing his drums, Auro found Denise sprawled facedown in the elevator. She was already dead when the door opened before him in the lobby, and it became the rare occasion for one of his spontaneous cries that did not echo someone else.

'De-*nise!*' he shouted, kneeling beside her. And then: 'Help me! *Help!*' which, even more torturously, he was able to cry out over and over again until Yal the doorman ran to his aid.

The next day, with the household in turmoil and Samax bereaved, Desirée emerged from her rooms sleepless, distraught, her long hair wild, and embraced me outside the library, blurting out, 'Oh, Enzo, my mother is gone. I'll never see her again.'

For a moment, I thought she had really come unhinged, referring to Denise in this way. But Desirée knew exactly what she was saying: her mother, Della, was indeed gone, fleeing the Hotel Canopus in her car just hours after Denise's death without a word to anyone but Desirée.

Why she left without any goodbyes I would learn two days later, shortly before Denise's funeral. Desirée and I were sitting on a wooden bench in the garden waiting for Samax and Dolores to emerge from the hotel. I was wearing a shiny black suit, she a long black dress, gloves, and wraparound sunglasses. Long legs crossed, one foot tapping in the grass and the sunlight rippling over her, Desirée had never looked more beautiful to me. In the circular driveway, around the fountain with its beatific female figure, three black limousines awaited us. Desirée spoke to me in barely above a whisper. Still shaky, her guard down, she alternately choked on her words and spat them out.

'So my mother split without looking back. I always knew it would happen like this.'

'But how do you know she won't come back soon – did she tell you that?'

'She didn't have to. Trust me, she'll never be back. It's

360

been building for a long time, Enzo. A long time. Maybe I ought to fill you in on a little history.'

And she did, crossing and uncrossing her legs, but growing more composed as she went along – as if recounting the history took her out of herself.

'Samax and my other aunt, Doris, were married for ten years,' Desirée began. 'Doris died when I was ten years old. My mother and I had just come to live at the hotel. My grandmother had been living here from the first, all those years. Dolores's connection to Samax is not as simple as you might imagine.'

'Simple? I've never been able to figure out what it is.'

'You know the story of how Samax bought that land in New York after eating the bad oysters. The deal that was the cornerstone of his fortune. What you probably don't know is that Dolores lent him the down payment after all the banks turned him down. He was desperate, on the verge of borrowing from loan sharks when she stepped in.' Desirée tilted her head into the shadows. 'In those days Dolores owned a small residence hotel in lower Manhattan, not far from the Brooklyn Bridge, and Samax was one of her tenants – one whom she'd become friendly with. He never forgot her generosity, and when he had money he bought her two other hotels in New York. There isn't anything he wouldn't have done for her. And that was still the case even after she made some money in her own right, and retired, and wanted to come out here to run this place. Samax agreed at once, so Dolores brought her three daughters and they did what they knew best.'

All of this *was* news to me, but I was still trying to figure things out. 'And Uncle Junius fell in love with Doris?'

'I don't know about that.' She hesitated. 'If he felt deeply about any of them back then, it was Dolores. He never knew his own mother, you know.'

Like me, I thought. 'I did know that,' I said.

Grief, which can silence a talkative person, had made Desirée, who kept to herself more than anyone else I knew, talkative. At least with me she had a lot to say that afternoon – more than in any other conversation over the previous nine years.

'After they were married,' she went on, 'Samax developed other feelings for Doris. But in the beginning, it was just a business arrangement – between him and my grandmother. This was really his way of paying Dolores back: Doris was the eldest daughter, and the arrangement ensured that the Hotel Canopus went to her. Samax said wills could always be contested, but in Nevada it was practically impossible to prevail in such a case against a spouse.' She exhaled softly. 'He didn't want there to be any legal loopholes. We all know how cautious – even paranoid – he is on the subject, having been disinherited himself. Before your arrival on the scene, no one could say who would get the bulk of his fortune. And don't think for a minute that Ivy will step aside easily, for you or anyone else.'

I knew that Samax had provided for me – he never had to say so outright – but no one had ever spoken openly about it to me. Not even Ivy, who wasn't shy about such things and whose obsession with the topic I didn't have to be reminded of. Desirée was the last person at the hotel I would have expected to break that precedent.

'Well, there's no doubt Dolores now wants the hotel to go to Della, the only remaining sister, and no reason to believe Samax would not go along with her, as he always has. If it were just up to them, everything would be hunky-dory. But my mother's not going to play along.' She shook her head. 'I'm sure glad I wasn't in Samax's shoes two days ago. Breaking the news of Denise's death to Dolores couldn't have been an enviable task.'

That was an understatement, for what Samax had had to explain to her was that she had lost not one daughter, but two. Years before, when Dolores had learned of Doris's death, it had nearly killed her – and the old lady had only been eighty at that time! So we were more than apprehensive, now that she was almost 100, at the effect the death of her second daughter and the disappearance of the third would have on her.

'You see, it's not just that Della's gone,' Desirée said, 'it's that she made it clear all along that she never wanted sole responsibility for the hotel. She's the youngest, so as long as her sisters and mother were around, that seemed a remote possibility. Denise always felt quite the opposite: once Doris died, she looked forward to inheriting the hotel, and Samax changed his will accordingly. But she always expected Della would help her run it. Dolores, who was always closer to Denise, had the same expectations. Della told both of them that she had other plans. You know she's always dreamed of living alone somewhere. She often told me that in her entire life she'd never been completely on her own – with just a few rooms someplace, or a cottage or something.'

I nodded. 'Reading to me one night when I was small, she told me she wished she could live on a houseboat.'

'Did she. That sounds about right.' She brushed aside a yellow jacket that hovered between us. 'Well, back in reality, with Dolores closing in on her one-hundredth birthday, a lot of this stuff obviously came to a head. I mean, when someone hits one hundred, you realize they're not going to be around much longer. Recently, to get Della to come around, Denise offered her a fifty-fifty split of the hotel after Dolores dies. Denise said she would ask Samax to make it official and change his will. And Della told her to forget it, that she had no intention of sticking around once Dolores is gone. Between them they've been quarreling about this ever since, with Dolores weighing in behind the scenes, pressuring Della. The other night was just the explosion of that quarrel into the open. Denise thought that because Della was always cowed by Dolores, she too could cow Della. But that wasn't the case. And the moment Denise died, Della knew she had to take off, rather than deal with Dolores, who would have made her life hellish. She didn't see any point in waiting around to find out just how hellish.'

'Is that what she told you before she left?'

Desirée smiled. 'What she told me was that she'd send me a letter. And that she hoped I understood.'

'And what did you say?'

'That I don't want the hotel, either, and that I didn't appreciate her making me the heir apparent by flying the coop.'

'But why can't Dolores accept that Della doesn't want the hotel?'

'The same reason she can't accept that she's going to die. In rejecting the hotel, my mother's rejecting her – that's how they both feel about it. At least, it's always been obvious to me, looking at it from that angle.'

I shook my head. 'And they were all so afraid of Dolores?'

'You don't know the half of it, Enzo. Hey, Doris was always Dolores's favorite. Dolores adored her, doted on her, as she never did on her other daughters. When Doris died, it was Della and Denise who found out about it first. And it took them a week to get up the nerve to break the news to Dolores. They were that afraid of her reaction. Samax was in Cambodia at the time, so it was three days before he came home. When he got back, he was so shell-shocked that he went along with Della and Denise for a while before telling Dolores himself. Think about it. That's how much power Dolores had over all of them.'

'But how *did* Doris die?' I asked, as finally the front doors of the hotel opened and we watched Zaren Eboli emerge, followed by Labusi being pushed in his wheelchair by Azu. 'Was there an accident?'

Desirée shook her head. 'Suicide,' she said abruptly. 'Carefully executed.'

This wasn't what I had expected. 'Here at the hotel?'

'No. She went down to the motel on Route 15, across from the Shell station. The Twin Stars. I've spent one or two nights there myself,' she said with a crooked smile. 'The rooms have little efficiency kitchens. She sealed the door and windows with electrical tape, turned on the gas in the oven, and lay down on the floor. That's where they found her.'

'But why did she do it?'

Desirée skipped a breath. 'Because of me.'

'You?'

'It was coming for a while, but I was the last straw.'

'I don't understand.'

'When I arrived here with Della, Doris was convinced I was Samax's child. His "love child," she called me.'

I felt a flutter in my stomach. 'And are you?'

Now it was she who was surprised. 'No, I'm not. Before he married Doris, Samax and Della had a brief affair. I mean, a single night. Doris knew about it, and from that concocted her entire fantasy. In fact, it happened over a year before I was born.'

Desirée was toying nervously with the fingertips of her black gloves. 'My father was someone Della got involved with here at the hotel several months after her affair with Samax. She became pregnant, and in those days, abortion wasn't always an option. Anyway, she didn't want one. Samax didn't know she was pregnant, but Dolores did, as did her sisters. Dolores sent Della away and told Samax she had run off with a man. Actually, she went to Miami alone. That's where I was born. Then we lived in New Orleans before settling down in the Florida Keys until I was six years old. All that time Samax knew nothing of my existence. Della went out with other men, never for very long. She worked at a small hotel. We lived in an apartment that overlooked the ocean. Dolores sent us money every month. Then one day Della wrote Samax a letter telling him what had really happened ten years earlier: that she hadn't run off with a man, but a baby. He was dumbfounded to learn she had a child. First he requested, then demanded, that Della and I come back to Las Vegas. Denise warned him that this could be catastrophic for Doris. Doris was still certain I was Samax's daughter, on top of which, though they had tried for several years, she and Samax were unable to have children. But Samax wanted us here. And Della was sick of her life in Florida, tired of having to take care of me by herself. I was lonely there, too.'

'What about the man she got involved with?' I asked.

'My father? Oh, he was long gone. Gone even before Della left for Miami in the first place. She never saw him again, so far as I know.'

'But who was it?'

Desirée pulled one of the gloves halfway off, then pulled it back on even more tightly. 'Until we left Florida, Della had told me my father was a French pilot who had died in the war. But that wasn't true. Anyway, we returned, and it was catastrophic, all right. Not for me – Samax gave me a lot of love right from the start – though for a long time I blamed myself for what happened next. Doris hadn't been well for some time. Her marriage had reverted to its original state – a legal stratagem, a piece of paper – and when she laid eyes on me, it completed the rupture and put her over the top. It was as if all her worst delusions were realized, seeing me there in flesh and blood. Furious with Della, and with Samax, who in turn was furious at all of them – especially Doris, for her insistence that I was his daughter – Doris felt utterly humiliated.'

'And she killed herself.'

'A week later. In the note she left, she mentioned none of this. Without explanation, she requested that her ashes be scattered from a plane over the Atlas Mountains, a place she had never visited. And Samax had it done.'

'And your father . . . ?'

She pursed her lips and nodded toward the driveway.

Just then Samax and Hadar came through the glass doors of the hotel and descended the steps, supporting Dolores between them.

'But you said—'

'No, not him. The fountain, that sculpture – for that matter, the hotel itself,' she added with a sigh.

Still uncomprehending, I gazed at the sculpture of the woman behind her curtain of spray.

'My father was a man named Spica,' Desirée said softly, 'the architect of the hotel and the designer of that sculpture.'

'What!'

'So you know who he is.'

'Sure. Uncle Junius told me about him.'

'Ah.'

'How Spica finished installing the sculpture after Uncle Junius bought the hotel.'

Desirée stood up and smoothed down her dress. 'That wasn't all he did,' she said drily.

Crossing the cul-de-sac, Dolores and Samax and Hadar looked ashen in the blinding sunlight. Samax was particularly unsteady, as if he were being supported by the other two even more than he was supporting them. Dolores wore a long pearl necklace that dangled on her plain black dress. A veil fluttered from the boat-shaped hat perched on her head. Through the veil's black gauze her large, off-center eyes stared straight ahead, frozen wide, as they had been staring from the moment she was informed of Denise's death and Della's disappearance. I was certain just then that Dolores would remain fixed in that moment for the rest of her life, and that the next, the only, moment to which she could progress would be that of her death. Indeed, from that day forth, Dolores, five months short of her one-hundredth birthday, stopped drinking the quarts of iced chamomile tea that she claimed promoted longevity. And the next time she shared her tucked-away spot in the quincuncial garden with Labusi, less than twenty yards from the vault that now held the urn with Denise's ashes, she rejected his expression of condolences with a snap of her head and a terse reply, her eyes still wide and unblinking: 'I never had any daughters,' she muttered.

I missed Della, who had been so kind to me. But I did not miss Denise, whom I had never liked for the simple reason that she didn't like me. After I heard Desirée's story, it seemed obvious why she wouldn't. Maybe perceiving from the very beginning that I would be Samax's heir, she feared that all her and her mother's well-laid plans with regard to the Hotel Canopus would be disrupted. To Della, who had always been warm to me, this would have been a blessing in disguise.

Though on the surface it did not seem connected to these events, two months after Della left the hotel, Auro lit out as well. That is, he ran away from home. And stayed away. The move took nearly everyone by surprise, especially Ivy, who became darker and more inturned than ever, a recluse among recluses, retreating so far into the shadows that, like Auro before her, she became a shadow herself for a long time, removed from the daily life of the hotel, to be glimpsed only at night, solitary and furtive.

I for one was not particularly surprised to hear of Auro's flight. I knew that he had been badly shaken when he found Denise's body in the elevator, but I had seen his departure coming, for other reasons, well before that. For one thing, he had begun practicing his drums round the clock, stopping only to eat twice daily and to catch maybe five hours of sleep. And unknown to Ivy, he had also begun sneaking down to the Strip to hear jazz bands at the casinos. He knew, and could emulate, the playing of every major jazz drummer in his encyclopedic collection of EPs and LPs, from Art Blakey and Max Roach to Buddy Rich and Tiny Kahn, who died a master at twenty-four. Big band, bebop, jive, jump, and swing – Auro could play them all. Not to mention the other percussive music he absorbed, from Morocco and India, Turkey and Trinidad. To my ear, he had become a phenomenal drummer, not just proficient but unique in his style. He was either going to do something with all this talent, I decided, or he was going to bust.

There was also the fact that he had asked me late one night, writing it down on the pad he now carried at all times – in itself, for him, a leap toward communicativeness – if I would care for his parrot Echo if he ever had to take a trip one day. Of course I told him I would take good care of the bird. We were sitting in the garden in the darkness stargazing, as we often did during that time, our bond as we grew older lying not in exchanges of information – both of us, after all, were for our own reasons close-to-the-vest types – but in mutual silence. This was how we confided most intimately. And I felt that while I knew little about my cousin in the usual way – his thoughts, his ideas, even his aspirations – I had learned a great deal about the content of his heart during those long evenings when we sat facing each other while the desert winds ruffled the leaves of our uncle's rare trees.

I knew, for example, that Auro's restlessness had grown dramatically in the previous year. Then eighteen, he was eager to break away from his mother. Stifled sexually and emotionally, Auro found his only release in drumming. But he was tired of doing it in a super-insulated room in the hermetic atmosphere of the hotel. He wanted to play for other people, wanted his drumming to be heard. Such was his agitation on the subject that I was stunned others hadn't picked up on it. But because Auro was a nervous type to begin with, Samax and even Ivy hadn't seen beyond his general edginess to the deeper turmoil. At the same time, he hadn't been nearly as direct with them as he was with me. 'I need to find work as a jazz drummer *now*,' he had told me one evening, by way of his scratch pad. 'I'll start out as a sideman, first in the recording studio, then in clubs where they have live gigs, until I can put my own group together.'

So, though I would miss his silent companionship, a part of me was relieved to hear one August morning that Auro had taken off. I was glad for him. I hoped he was already playing his heart out as a sideman. Two weeks after he had walked out of the hotel and got into a waiting cab with a suitcase, his drum set, and Echo in a traveling cage, I received a postcard from New York City. The photograph on the card was of Times Square lit up at night. In the card, a second-floor window in a sooty building over a nightclub called The Adhara

369

Lounge was circled in ink. The message, in Auro's tiny left-handed print, was short:

DEAR ENZO,
AUDITIONED HERE LAST NIGHT.
IN THIS CITY PEOPLE DON'T NOTICE IF YOU REPEAT WHAT
THEY SAY — THEY ALL DO IT.
LAST NIGHT I GOT A FORTUNE COOKIE THAT SAID
THANKS FOR THE MEMORIES.
IN THE END, COULDN'T LEAVE ECHO BEHIND.
YOUR COUSIN,
AURO

To Ivy he sent a Postal Service postcard with no picture on it, just two words besides his name: I'M OKAY. And that was the last we heard from him for some time.

Still, all the traumas and crises, the deaths and disappearances at the hotel at that time were overshadowed by the escalation of Samax's bitter, ongoing feud with his severest and most formidable antagonist, Vitale Cassiel, a menacing shadowy figure to me — for I still had never laid eyes on him — but real enough to Samax, who now traveled with a pair of bodyguards whenever he left the grounds.

The bodyguards were Tunisians, recruited in Tunis through connections of Sofiel — of all people — the gentle, introverted, half-Tunisian gardener. Former paratroopers, mutes who had lost their voices in a freak war-games accident (diving through a cloud of nerve gas released by an exploded truck), they were named Alif and Aym, which, as I soon learned, are the two letters in the Arabic alphabet that have no sounds attached to them. Alif was an Olympic marksman and Aym a kendo champion; both were expert boxers with short, compact builds that might have been lifted off a gymnasium frieze. They looked so much alike they could have been brothers: short-haired, thin-lipped, with square chins and sharp cheekbones. They lived in adjoining suites on the third floor of the hotel, ate together always, communicated in sign language with one another, and took orders from Samax in French. Intense physical culturists, they added a welcome nonintellectual dimension to our extended household. First to rise and first to bed, every day at four a.m. they ran three miles, pressed weights for a half hour, and swam two miles of laps in the pool. At first I enjoyed watching them fence with sabers or spar with kendo sticks on the lawn, race one another in wind sprints, and practice their marksmanship in the garden. In the case of Alif, this meant watching an artist at work, for he was capable with a single round from a .38 automatic of forming an *A* in the bull's eye – with either hand. My enjoyment dissipated, however, the first time I accompanied my uncle on what would once have been a routine trip to Phoenix and saw Alif and Aym, grimly alert, in trim cotton suits with pistols holstered under their arms and daggers strapped to their calves, precede him like pilot fish through two airports, a bank, a penthouse restaurant, and several art galleries. I realized that afternoon just how much danger Samax – as fearless a man as I ever knew – thought he must be in.

Yet while it was true that Samax had good reason to feel threatened by Vitale Cassiel in a variety of ways, it was never clear that he was in imminent danger of the sort of mob-style execution which Alif and Aym had been hired to prevent. When gently questioned about this, Samax declared that their mere presence had served as a deterrent. 'That's the whole idea,' he said stiffly. And with the sort of logic I had never before heard him employ, he went on, 'The very fact they haven't been put to the test in a life-or-death situation is what tells me they're indispensable at this time.'

Still, in the many years he had been at odds with Vitale Cassiel, Samax had never felt the need for bodyguards, and I wasn't the only one at the hotel who thought the larger source of his fears for his life was the unexpected blow he had been dealt in recent years with regard to his health and mortality. In private, it was more than his logic that had changed. He now would speak with intensity and a newfound intimacy of the Angel of Death, whom he was certain he had glimpsed, not once but several times of late. 'I'm talking about an entity more real than I had ever imagined,' he solemnly observed. As was his custom, he did a prodigious amount of research and discovered that the Angel of Death manifested himself under many names, in many guises, over time: he was Michael for Christians, Azrael for Arabs, Mot for the Babylonians, Mairya for the Zoroastrians. The Jews, Samax learned, believed there were six Angels of Death, including Af, who held sway over men's lives, Mashhit over children's, and Meshabber over animals'. But it was the description of the Angel of Death by a tenth-century Talmudic scholar named Saadiah Gaon that truly seized Samax. 'This is what I've seen,' he intoned, as we sat in his library one night and he handed me a large leather-bound book with silver-edged pages in which the following passage was bracketed: *The angel sent by God to separate body from soul appears to man in the form of a yellow flame, full of eyes shining with a blue fire, holding in his hand a drawn sword pointed at the person to whom death is coming.* 'I saw it that night,' Samax said, 'and every time since then it's been the same. A walking fire . . .'

The night he was referring to occurred in the summer of 1973, when, after a lifetime of robust health, exercise, and a near fanaticism about his diet, out of nowhere he had suffered a stroke. I was just about to go off to college at the time, and there were a great many other matters weighing upon him. Even so, it was quite out of character for him to disrupt all his other long-standing routines by seeking relief, then escape, working in the greenhouse straight through the night, every night, for several weeks. In the process, he achieved a small break-through in his quest to graft the star apple and the starfruit into the *Samax Astrofructus* that he hoped to have catalogued in the pomology register. And on that fateful night, bathed in the glow of the blue-green lamps while I sat listening on a stone bench running my toes over the velvety moss that grew between the floor tiles, he rinsed some seeds in the zinc sink and explained the botanical hurdles he had cleared and those that remained.

'You know that grafting and hybridization are like night and day,' he said.

'Or apples and oranges,' I quipped.

If he got my joke, he didn't acknowledge it – as if he were only half there with me. 'You can easily graft an apple on a pear tree,' he went on, 'but you can't hybridize them – they won't reproduce after that one tree. Grafting between genera can be done: there's peach on plum, pear on quince – which, as you know, I've done myself – medlar on hawthorn. But try apricot on quince or quince on plum a thousand times and a thousand times it will fail,' he concluded, placing the seeds on a glass tray which he slid into a small incubator.

Seeing Samax at work in his greenhouse was not like seeing him anywhere else. A man who had grown more formal with age, in the hotel he rarely wandered around in anything less casual than a jacket or silk robe. In fact, he rarely wandered around at all anymore. Even in his private quarters he favored the red smoking jacket monogrammed in yellow that he had specially made for him in Milan every couple of years. But in the greenhouse, off-limits to everyone when he was at work, Samax had worn the same long white lab coat and scuffed rubber shoes – the outfit of scientists in old movies, I used to think – for years. The coat was thin from repeated washings, with countless plant stains and snags from thorns and twigs. In the lapel pocket he kept his reading glasses and a couple of cigars; in the side pockets, a pair of well-worn chamois gloves. He liked to handle soil, humus, peat moss, fertilizer. He liked the mud under his fingernails, the water drenching his sleeves, the fetid air clinging to his nostrils. Sensations alien to his everyday life in the hotel. He lost himself at that zinc sink, at the long wooden tables, on the ladders and platforms enveloped in mist in the upper reaches of the greenhouse. His movements were as precise and unhurried as ever – the legacy of his years as a professional gambler – but his face was far more relaxed and his eyes seemed fixed on what was before them. They seldom strayed into the middle distance, where he might have entered the more difficult byways of his memory, or, worse, the urgent, treacherous terrain of worry and calculation which so preoccupied him at that time.

'When I started out with this graft,' he went on, 'everything indicated that it belonged to that category of failure. Not only had no one attempted to graft the *Averrhoa carambola*, or starfruit, of the wood sorrel family, on the *Chrysophyllum cainito*, or star apple, of the sapodilla family, but no one had ever successfully grafted other members of their respective families across genera. All problems of scion and rootstock aside – and they are big problems – as far as I know no one has attempted this graft because it would be considered problematic fruitwise. The star apple is purple and apple-shaped, with a rough skin. It grows in Central America. The starfruit is bright yellow and five-angled, with a waxy skin. It grows in Indonesia. The one has many tiny black seeds, the other a few amber ones.'

'So what will your fruit look like?' I asked.

A smile played over his lips. 'I appreciate your confidence, Enzo,' he said. 'If I'm successful, I foresee a star-shaped fruit when it's cross-sectioned, with a hard, waxy skin. Its flesh will be indigo, speckled with yellow seeds. The fruit will appear in profusion, many to a branch, as it does on both these trees. This guy is my best candidate,' he added, pointing to a large grafting planted in black humus and bathed in ultraviolet light. 'If the graft takes, I'll know in a year whether or not it will produce fruit. The scion will become the aerial portion and the rootstock will form the roots. On my previous attempts, the scion got killed off because buds and suckers sprouted on the rootstock. I also have to keep an eye on the nutritive balance, to prevent leaf scorch and chlorosis, which is like botanical jaundice.'

He held up the grafting for which he had high hopes and examined it carefully. 'Right now the balance appears to be just right . . . so the only question is whether it can sustain fruit,' he said, his voice trailing off.

At the sink he drank two glasses of water before joining me on the bench. 'I got so thirsty all of a sudden,' he said, unbuttoning his lab coat and loosening the collar of his shirt.

To me, he looked uncharacteristically pale. And his irises, usually the clearest blue, seemed smoky. 'Uncle Junius, it's late, maybe we should go in.'

He glanced at his watch. 'Two-twenty. You go in. I'll be finished here soon.'

'No, I'll wait. I'm not tired.'

'When you are tired, go,' he said, mopping the back of his neck with his handkerchief. 'I haven't been able to sleep lately.'

'How come?'

He shrugged, averting his eyes. 'The years are catching up with me, Enzo. When you get older, you sleep less.'

'You're in better shape than men half your age,' I said. 'You can still swim a mile without stopping.'

'You know I haven't been swimming in weeks.' He shook his head. 'I'm going to be seventy-three years old soon.'

I had never heard him bring up his age in this way. 'You're worried about something. What is it?'

He waved this away. 'Why should I be worried? I want this tree to succeed, yes. And there's that other amulet . . . we have some new leads . . . we're getting closer.'

'I know all that.'

'Well?'

'Come on, Uncle Junius, you've always told me to level with you.'

He opened his hands slowly and examined his palms. 'It's Vitale Cassiel,' he said simply, evenly, but the mere mention of this man's name sent a chill through me. 'He's been occupied elsewhere,' Samax went on, 'but he always comes back, always from a different angle. Always with the same objective.'

'What's that?' I asked quietly.

'My destruction,' Samax replied. 'He may make it look like something else, he may be blunt or subtle, but that's what he wants to accomplish.' He looked up at me. 'And he never will, I promise you that.'

'But why?' I said. 'It was *he* who wronged *you*.'

'It's not that simple.' He hesitated. 'You'll know the whole story one day. To hear it now would be of no help to you. In fact, it would be a hindrance.'

Later I would be astonished to learn that one small part of that story which had taken on great importance was the fire I started in the ghost town of Hydra. An embarrassment in my own life, what should have remained an obscure incident had become the trip wire of the most recent flare-up in Samax's private war with Vitale Cassiel. Through his own sources in the Las Vegas Police Department, Vitale Cassiel had discovered that the two boys who had burned down The Hotel Vega were none other than Junius Samax's great-nephews. Because I was a minor at the time, he sued Samax for damages and tried to have Auro and me charged with arson and malicious mischief – charges that Samax used all his influence, and considerable energy, to block legally and also to keep from ever reaching our ears, which was no small feat. This sequence of events could have been just another drop in what was already an ocean of bad blood, but because Auro and I were involved, it enraged Samax that much more. And, in retrospect, it became apparent that it marked the first moves in the endgame of Samax's tortuous relationship with Vitale Cassiel.

'Did you know,' Samax said, veering to another subject, 'that all imposed grafts go back to a single fruit tree in Florence?'

I shook my head, not happy to be put off in this way.

'The year was 1644,' he said in a leisurely voice,

leaning back and changing his tone as abruptly as he had changed the subject. 'The tree came to be called the "Bizzarria Orange" – for obvious reasons if you were a Florentine gardener at that time. Root grafts occur naturally on tropical plantations where all sorts of trees mingle in the soil. But in Italy, where species are more segregated, they're unheard of. So when a certain Guido Angelli one spring day in a forgotten corner of the garden of his employer, the Barone Zelo, found a single tree with oranges on some branches, lemons on others, and combinations of the two fruits on still others, he dropped to his knees. Not in ecstasy or devotion, but because he was terrified that Satan himself had touched down in that garden. In fact, somehow, a scion of sour orange had been naturally grafted onto a stock of lemon. The tree turned out to be a true hybrid, eventually producing only lemon-oranges – the first known chimera in pomology. Years ago, I acquired one of its descendents, but I donated it to the Botanical Gardens in Albuquerque. It's still there today . . .'

His speech became increasingly slow, as if his voice were a phonograph slipping into the wrong speed. 'We are all of us accidents of nature,' he concluded, 'refined by thousands of graftings . . . some that take, some that don't.' He ran his handkerchief over the back of his neck. 'My history, yours – we can control our destinies up to a point. What shapes us is the extent to which we can adapt beyond that point . . .'

His eyes were closed now. Samax was not a man given to rambling, and it frightened me to hear him go on like this. I sat stiffly for nearly a minute, waiting to see if he would continue. The giant humidifiers whirred overhead and the palm fronds rustled in the artificial breezes stirred up by the floor fans. Through the vapor on the ceiling panes the desert stars twinkled faintly. Samax was rocking his shoulders, gripping his knees. I had never seen him look so tired and frail. His spine was bent. The creases in his brow seemed to have deepened, merging at his temples. His usually crisp white hair was damp. Suddenly his eyelids snapped open and he surprised me by standing up in one clean motion and walking to the sink, sure and steady on his feet.

What happened next I would watch again many times over the next two years on the nights I found it difficult to fall asleep myself.

Samax turned on the tap and began washing the leaves of a small quince tree with a piece of cheesecloth. For several minutes he neither spoke nor looked at me. In fact, he acted as if I weren't still sitting there behind him on the stone bench. At first this was a relief: I told myself I had read him all wrong, that he was feeling fine after unburdening himself. That the rambling had been cathartic. He picked up a pair of scissors and snipped away several torn or wilting quince leaves. He loosened the soil at the tree's base with a miniature pitchfork. Then, rising up on his toes, he reached toward one of the overhead shelves for an aluminum sprayer. His fingers closed around the sprayer's handle, but he never lifted it from the shelf. For an eternity he remained frozen on the balls of his feet, his right arm fully extended. Then without warning he wheeled around, wearing a quizzical expression. He opened his mouth to speak, I heard my name die on his breath, and then he started shaking violently and the sprayer crashed into the sink. In a matter of seconds, he lurched forward, tried to right himself, and, knees buckling, toppled sideways against the worktable before I could leap up and break his fall.

'Uncle Junius!' I cried.

His left arm and leg continued to twitch. His eyes stared up at me helplessly. I heard only a single word, just a whisper, escape his lips before his jaw locked: 'Fire . . .'

He's going to die and there's nothing I can do, I thought, my heart hammering.

'Just hold on,' I whispered, stripping off my shirt and sliding it under his head. His skin was clammy and cold. All the blood seemed to have drained from his face: it looked white as a piece of paper. I didn't want to leave him even for a moment, but I raced across the greenhouse and called Azu on the house phone. Within fifteen minutes an ambulance had backed up to the greenhouse door and a pair of attendants were lifting Samax onto a stretcher.

Desirée and I followed the ambulance in her silver Corvette. Aroused from sleep, she had slipped into jeans and a denim jacket. Her hair was uncombed, her eyes heavy. She was chewing gum nervously. And all the while, I thought I was checking the tears welling up in me, until I felt the wind turn them cold on my cheeks. And though I had never cried in front of Desirée, I made no effort to conceal it.

Samax's left hand remained numb for months, and his eyelid fluttered, but aside from a faint limp which he had from then on, he seemed to suffer no long-term damage to his faculties. 'What does "long-term" mean when you're seventy-three?' he said drily when I visited him at the hospital one day. 'Until I hit a hundred, like Dolores? No, that's not in the cards for me.'

In fact, because of his strong constitution and rock-steady habits, his physical rehabilitation was hugely successful – a marvel, the doctors insisted, for a man his age. The emotional aftereffects were something else, especially for those of us who knew him well. His fixation on the Angel of Death was by far the most dramatic of these. 'I saw him, Enzo, as surely as I see you now. He swooped down through the glass ceiling, through the trees, and bent over me, yellow with hundreds of eyes, and then pointed his long sword at me, the blade tilted so I could see my own eyes reflected in it.' Subsequent sightings, always when he was alone, took place in the quincuncial orchard, at the edge of the desert, and again in the greenhouse. Generally, however, after the stroke he kept to himself even more than usual – which meant he practically became solitary. He traveled little and entertained less. And of course he hired the bodyguards, which I was now certain had less to do with Vitale Cassiel than with the increased frequency with which

Samax said he glimpsed that yellow fire with the blue eyes – as if two martial arts specialists and crack shots could protect him from his visions, much less from death itself.

During this period, it was not unusual for Samax to cancel dinner in the tenth-floor dining room four, even five, times a week; and when we did all dine together, he seemed distant, preoccupied not with archaeological digs or auctions in Hong Kong and Venice, but other matters, much closer to home. It was also around this time that Calzas finally married his fiancée Cela and moved permanently to Santa Fe. He went with Samax's blessing, even his encouragement, and a good deal of financial support to set up his own architectural firm. Samax missed Calzas, and said as much, but I don't think even he knew how much of a loss it was to him; certainly none of us realized at first how great a toll the younger man's departure would take on my uncle. Calzas had not only been a business confidant and trusted friend, but also the closest thing to a son Samax ever had. That is, until I had arrived on the scene. Now that I was becoming a man, as Della had once pointed out to me, I was stepping more and more into Calzas's shoes. Or, to be more exact, a moment came when I realized that I was *expected* to step into them. While affectionate to me as a child, Samax on many levels had always treated me as an adult, but even before he fell ill I saw that he had truly begun to rely on me, both in business and personal matters – and that was something quite different.

For all of these reasons – but especially Samax's stroke and Calzas's departure – I changed my plans at the last moment with regard to college. Thanks to Labusi, I had passed my entrance and equivalency exams at sixteen and been accepted at Stanford; this would have been my first extended time away from the hotel, and though I had mixed feelings about it at first, I was excited about attending. Samax, who had never gone to college, had always spoken of my attending Stanford, a dream of his own as a young man, shattered first by his being drafted and then by his legal battles with his brother. But in the end, over his objections (though I sensed that deep down, with the pressures he had come under, he was relieved) I stayed in Las Vegas and in an accelerated program attended the University of Nevada, to which I could commute. So it was that in the spring of 1975, six months before my twentieth birthday, I would take my degree in architecture.

What exactly was going on again between Samax and Vitale Cassiel at the time of all these other crises, and what had transpired in the past, was first told to me in snatches by other people, especially Calzas before he got married, and Desirée. As I got older, Samax himself filled me in more on what he would not tell me in the greenhouse the night of his stroke. The stroke hastened this; he had said that I would learn the whole story one day, but I don't think he imagined it would be so soon.

Nearly fifty years had passed since Vitale Cassiel had engineered Samax's imprisonment at the Ironwater Federal Penitentiary. At seventy-seven, Vitale Cassiel was two years older than Samax. But it was as if the wound left after all those years had never healed – never been allowed to heal. The source of Samax's resentment was obvious to me from the start: disinherited, betrayed, framed, and jailed for a year in the prime of his youth, he had plenty to be angry about. But the ongoing virulence of Vitale Cassiel was more difficult to fathom. Especially since he had so clearly come out ahead all those years back, effectively funneling all of Samax and Nilus's assets into his own pocket. What was Vitale Cassiel's gripe? I asked myself.

Finally, one evening when we were sitting in the dining room drinking maté tea from black bowls, Calzas clued me in on some of the events *after* prison that Samax had never gotten around to in our breakfast or after-dinner conversations. For starters, Calzas told me that as soon as Samax had made his fortune on that land he stumbled on, he set out to exact revenge on Nilus and Vitale Cassiel. By then, Nilus was very much the junior partner in all their ventures. While Vitale Cassiel wheeled and dealed, Nilus was relegated to paper shuffling at their home office in San Francisco; for this, he was paid a fat salary that enabled him to carry on a full-time social life in the high-blown style of his father. So long as the money rolled in, this arrangement suited Nilus fine. As the years went by, Vitale Cassiel primed him with just enough cash to keep him happy, always but a fraction of the overall profits. Following in the family tradition, Nilus was a collector – not of rare antiques, like his brother, but of beautiful women, like his father. He never married, but instead lived with a succession of mistresses, among whom were the mothers of his daughters Bel and Ivy. For, outdoing himself, Nilus Samax in a single year, 1937, fathered his daughters on two different women.

Bel's mother, Astrid – my grandmother – was the orphaned daughter of a doctor and his wife who perished in a Colorado mining camp during a typhoid epidemic. Astrid died within a month of Bel's birth. Ivy's mother, the other object of Nilus's affections, gave birth to Ivy three months later. Her name was Stella, and she lived with Nilus less than a year before running off with another man, leaving Nilus with both his daughters.

The other man was Vitale Cassiel. Nilus apparently never knew this, but Samax, who had kept tabs on both men through private detectives was fully aware of their activities, including Nilus's amazingly chaotic domestic circumstances – the lifelong bachelor suddenly bequeathed, through death and desertion, two infants – and the fact that Stella and Vitale Cassiel lived briefly in San Francisco before moving to Reno. It was there that Stella gave birth to a boy, Vitale Cassiel's son, twelve months after Ivy was born. Thus within a two-year span, like a mirror image of Nilus, Stella had two children by two different men. And so Ivy had a half-brother, whom I had never heard mentioned before. When I asked Calzas who and where this half-brother was, he couldn't answer on either count; he knew nothing about him, and he had never heard Samax or Ivy speak of him.

It was also in Reno, Calzas told me, that Vitale Cassiel had begun setting up VC Enterprises, the sprawling company that would eventually control a large chunk of Nevada real estate, from office buildings and shopping centers in Carson City and Reno to the insignificant ghost town of Hydra where Auro and I burned down The Hotel Vega. How could we have known that it belonged to Auro's grandmother's onetime lover, much less that the seed money for VC Enterprises had come from the cash proceeds of our great-grandfather's hat business? For while keeping Nilus busy, Vitale Cassiel not only snatched away his mistress, but transferred all the remaining assets of their partnership into the accounts of the company he was forming. This final transfer was accomplished gradually, secretly, and above all – on paper – legally, for Vitale Cassiel was nothing if not a crack attorney, skilled at perverting the law in order to commit a crime, whether it was framing an innocent man or embezzling his fortune. The upshot of all this was that when Nilus Samax died of cardiac arrest one rainy spring morning, slumping over in a taxi en route to an assignation after a breakfast of oysters Rockefeller and champagne, he had no idea that for all intents and purposes he was bankrupt. Leaving an estate so bare – for a man who lived so extravagantly – that it stunned everyone but his personal attorney, Vitale Cassiel. This was when Samax intervened, after his brother's funeral (which he did not attend) taking charge of his daughters and putting them under his own roof.

And what was the revenge Samax inflicted upon Vitale Cassiel and Nilus? With Nilus, it was simple: once he got wind of how Vitale Cassiel was fleecing his brother, Samax simply sat back and watched it play out. Knowing Nilus the double-crosser was being double-crossed by his accomplice was far sweeter to Samax than anything else he could have concocted. Added to this was Samax's knowledge of where Stella was and the fact that he was keeping it to himself. It was true Samax could have informed his brother of Stella's whereabouts, thus poisoning the well between Nilus and Vitale Cassiel; but this might also have ended the possibility of a financial debacle for Nilus, which was what Samax most desired. Anyway, he wasn't sure that his dissolute brother, involved with countless women after Stella left him, would have cared much at that point.

With Vitale Cassiel, revenge was more complicated – and more personal – because Samax knew that Vitale Cassiel, not his brother Nilus, was the brains behind the plot that had sent him to prison. To avenge himself on Vitale Cassiel, Samax bided his time, waiting for the opening that he hoped would allow for a blow akin to the one he had sustained: a year in prison and the loss of all his money. He knew Vitale Cassiel was too clever and vigilant to be set up for jail time, and bankrupting him would be nearly impossible with the tools at Samax's disposal. So he got very personal.

This part of the story I heard in Samax's own words one afternoon during his convalescence when I followed him on his rounds of the orchard, up and down the grassy corridors of the quincunx. He wore his red silk robe, rope sandals, and a big straw hat against the strong sunlight. He had to walk slowly, favoring his right leg and taking deep breaths at regular intervals, often as he poked his cane through a tree's foliage to examine a cluster of fruit.

'You're eighteen now,' he said, glancing at me sidelong. 'You ought to hear the whole story.'

I understood from this that he was about to tell me something highly personal which did not cast him in the best light.

'You'll meet women in your life like Stella,' he said ruefully, for he was well aware of my pursuit of girls at that time, 'or maybe you already have.' Then he shook his head. 'No, if you had met a girl like Stella, you wouldn't be here now with me.' He shook his head. 'How beautiful was she? An old man's memory embellishes, it's not to be trusted. But I'll tell you what I remember. Blond hair that shined like gold. A sly turn to her lips when she smiled. Eyes blue as this sky that stayed lit even at night. And a laugh you could hear, like a piece of a tune, long after she'd left you.' He folded his hands over the top of his cane. 'She was something, Enzo.'

'When did you first meet her?'

'October, 1938. On Belmont Street in San Francisco. I can't tell you the exact day,' he smiled, 'but I remember it like it was yesterday. She was someone you never forgot. On my brother's arm, crossing the street to enter a restaurant, she wore a midnight blue dress with a diamond choker. Every man they passed turned to look at her. I froze in my tracks. I was thirty-eight years old, and in the twelve years since my release from prison, this was one of only two occasions that I crossed paths with Nilus – the other was in a lawyer's office. It caught him flat-footed as well. He never knew what to say to me anyway – what *do* you say when you've betrayed your own brother and seen him get locked up? – so kind of to deflect things, he mumbled an introduction between Stella and me. She was surprised – probably to find out that Nilus even had a brother – and looked me in the eye, and then he hustled her into the restaurant. I felt a shudder go through me, I wanted her so bad. I'd never felt that way with any woman right off the bat. But there wasn't much I could do about it – not just then. When Vitale Cassiel encountered her for the first time a few months later, he had a similar reaction, but he came at it entirely differently. Whatever his lust for money and power, it was nothing like what he felt when he gazed upon Stella. She became the great and abiding passion of his life.

'And so Vitale Cassiel stole her away from my brother, and Nilus was left alone in a big house with two babies, Bel and Ivy. When Nilus died five years later, Stella was still living with Vitale Cassiel. In 1944, their son was six years old, but they had never married. Stella didn't believe in marriage. She was the runaway daughter of a ship's captain – at sixteen she ran away and never stopped running. Her six years with Vitale Cassiel in Reno had been her longest interlude with anyone, anywhere. *Wild* was the word that had attached itself to her, as if it was a part of her name. In 1944, she was still only twenty-six years old, twenty years younger than Vitale Cassiel, eighteen years younger than me. And she was restless. Chafing at the bit. Vitale Cassiel may have been one of the richest guys in Reno, but during the war, on the heels of the Depression, Reno was a dusty backwater – unbearable for a girl who had grown used to the high life in San Francisco. He took her all around Europe, and there were Caribbean cruises, and he piled on the jewels and furs, but she took those things as her due. If anything, they made her even more restless. At the end of those six years, she was more than primed to jump ship: she was overdue. That's where I come in. My revenge on Vitale Cassiel, I decided, would be to seduce Stella away from him myself.' He paused for a deep breath, and winked at me. 'How unpleasant a task could that be? And how much faith I obviously had in my own powers of attraction,' he added drily.

Then he looked closely at me. 'What, you can't imagine me playing such a role?'

'I can imagine it.'

'It was messy. Like something out of an Italian comedy,' he muttered, 'where you never get love served up without vengeance, and vice versa, and often it all comes out as tragedy in the end. One thing was for sure: Vitale Cassiel wasn't laughing.'

We sat down on one of the wooden benches, in the shade of an apricot tree. A blackbird was singing in the higher branches. Samax fell silent, probing the tufts of onion grass at our feet with his cane.

'I can tell you', he said suddenly, 'that I did possess considerable charm with the ladies in those days. I had made some money. I dressed sharply. I knew how to have a good time. In the spring of 1944 the world was preoccupied with the war; Europe was in flames and all across the Pacific there were vicious battles over remote islands. But I was engaged in a different kind of warfare – obsessed with Stella and only Stella – utterly focused.'

'What did you do?'

He leaned back, his eyes faraway. 'First I should tell you that I ran into her one more time after San Francisco. It was here in Vegas, at some charity function at the old Avior Hotel. Very stodgy. I doubt it was something Stella did very often. I was just leaving with a bunch of business guys I knew when I crossed paths with her. It was just for a few seconds on the front steps, but I know she recognized me from that time with Nilus six years before. She looked into my eyes, she smiled at me, I smiled back.' He paused for a long moment. 'I felt like I was drinking her in. And then she was gone.' He chuckled softly. 'That's what gave me the idea that I could seduce her, and make her mine. I told myself I was taking revenge on Vitale Cassiel, but really I was just hooked, like him and my brother before him. So the comedy began. A few weeks later, I moved into a fancy hotel suite in Reno and started pursuing her. I found where she spent her time, and that's where I began spending my time. Finally, I was following her outright. Well, it didn't take me long to accomplish my mission, and instead of making me wary, this merely reaffirmed to me that I was pretty hot stuff. Then I found out that for Stella I was no more than a means to an end: getting away from Vitale Cassiel. Stella used me even as I was using her – except she did it better. We ran off together just two weeks after I first approached her, outside the auditorium of the Fleischmann Planetarium one afternoon. She was there with her son, but that didn't stop me.' He sighed. 'Vitale Cassiel and her son never saw her again. I took her to Acapulco, where we lived together for two weeks in a rented villa. I couldn't get enough of her. I gave her anything she asked for, including plenty of money. So it hit me like a ton of bricks when she ditched me. She boarded a Hong Kong-bound ocean liner late one night in July, 1944. In addition to the money I had given her, she had cleaned out two of her joint bank accounts with Vitale Cassiel and sold a bunch of jewelry he had given her. Thus she could do whatever she liked, which evidently included sailing into a war zone at a time of fierce naval engagements from Midway to Guam, where the marines were landing even as her ship passed a hundred miles to the north.

'I went after her, flying by clipper to Hong Kong, but when I met her ship, Stella was no longer aboard. It had put in at only one port, in Honolulu, and evidently she had disembarked there. I flew back to Honolulu and searched for her in vain, knowing full well that from there she could have sailed or flown anywhere – the mainland, Australia, Mexico again. Before coming home, I hired several private detectives, and even a psychic, but none of them could pick up her trail.' He shook his head. 'I was in the same boat as Vitale Cassiel: I never saw her again.'

'So what did you do?'

'I tried to come to my senses. But, in trying to get over her, I realized that, despite her treachery – maybe because of it – I was still in love with her. I tried other women, solitude, intense traveling – nothing worked. Loving Stella was a form of insanity for which there was only one cure – unattainable – which was Stella herself. At the same time, when I finally began thinking of something besides my own interests, I was left to ponder the hard fact that, thanks to my scheming, both Stella's young son in Reno and Ivy in San Francisco would never see their mother again. I told myself that Ivy never saw Stella anyway, and that Stella would certainly have taken off soon enough – if not with me, then with someone else. In fact, by the time she reached Honolulu there was a good chance she was with someone else. But, no matter how I sliced it, I had instigated her flight and now she was gone for good. I had been so busy trying to wreck Vitale Cassiel's life that it never occurred to me I might have been wrecking the lives of these children. And so, in my own way, I tried to make amends, and it helped me regain my sanity.'

What he did, back in San Francisco, was to begin looking after Nilus's daughters as if they were his own. Because of their closeness in age, six and seven at that time, the girls were often taken for twins, and in their earliest years had been treated as such by the servants in Nilus's household who cared for them, dressing them alike, cutting their hair identically, and so on. But as soon as the girls became aware, for example, that their birthdays were celebrated three months apart, they began asking Nilus questions. Not much of a father otherwise, he was honest with them on this count – up to a point. That is, he told them that they had different mothers, both of whom were dead. In Bel's case, this was true, of course; and, only two months old when Stella ran off with Vitale Cassiel, Ivy obviously had no memory of her. Because Stella had severed all contact with Nilus – he had no idea where she was in those last years of his life – this lie must have seemed to him more than an expedient. Nilus could tell himself that he was sparing Ivy undue pain: an unresolved disappearance was likely to torment someone more than a confirmed death. On top of which, it was not too far-fetched to think that Stella might really *be* dead. He knew she had run off with someone – with her history and their own stormy relationship that hadn't altogether surprised him – and that anything could have happened to her afterward.

But the fact is that Stella was alive, and when Ivy, just turned sixteen, learned this nine years after Nilus's death, she was heartsick and furious. She did not blame Nilus, of course, whom she revered and recalled only as a doting father. In fact, with his daughters Nilus had been anything but doting; paying only sporadic attention to Ivy, he had compensated in timeworn fashion, spoiling her with lavish gifts and elaborate outings. And this was the part of their relationship Ivy fixed in her memory. All the rest she blocked out: the topsy-turvy household, the caretakers who were changed with alarming frequency and no explanation, the lonely nights, Nilus's erratic comings and goings and the detritus of his intrigues. She chose sheer denial to prop up the shaky edifice of her illusions, and eventually, inevitably, it led her to become the custodian and defender of the memory of a man whom she hardly remembered.

Ivy diverted the anger and resentment provoked by Nilus's neglect onto Samax, who was anything but neglectful. It only made matters worse that from the age of seven on, Ivy had no other adult in her life who took even a fraction of the interest in her that Samax did. In short, Samax's care and generosity worked against him: he provided Ivy with a target for her rage that happened to be the only target, outside of Bel. That rage – and the size of that target – increased exponentially after Ivy discovered that during Nilus's lifetime Samax had known not only that her mother was still alive, but where she could be found – and that he had withheld the information. Forget that Stella had run away, and that it was doubtful Nilus would have acted on this information had he possessed it. Forget, too, that in over six years Stella had made no effort whatsoever to see her. When Ivy made the additional discovery, about a year later, that Samax had caused the rupture in her mother's relationship with Vitale Cassiel, running off with Stella before she disappeared once and for all, she declared to Samax that she could never forgive him. And she never did.

Samax in turn never forgave himself – for letting Stella get away. But he also couldn't understand from whom Ivy had learned these secrets, which he had so carefully guarded. At the Hotel Canopus, where Ivy and Bel lived in their teens, not even Dolores and her daughters knew any of this. And that included Doris, Samax told me, whom he had married, very much on the rebound, in 1945. For a wild moment, he thought Stella might have returned and was in contact with Ivy. But it wasn't that. And not until later did he suspect that Ivy had met Vitale Cassiel around the time she came into all this information; but knowing Vitale Cassiel to be notoriously close-mouthed, Samax couldn't imagine him opening up so freely with a teenager. At any rate, Samax never denied Ivy's accusations, but when he demanded to know how she had learned these things, she took some delight in refusing to tell him. And, to his credit, considering the guilt he felt, Samax didn't use that occasion to inform Ivy what had motivated him; it would be some years before she learned – and promptly denied it could be so – that Nilus had conspired to put Samax into prison. For Samax Ivy had about as much compassion as Stella and Nilus had had for her.

Samax also knew that Vitale Cassiel had long suspected his role in Stella's disappearance (that he *wanted* him to suspect it was a prime underpinning of his revenge), but hadn't been able to prove it – at least not for a long time. Oh, but he had tried. Samax had been told how Vitale Cassiel hired one private investigator after another (how the tables had turned in that regard!) to find Stella, but they each reported that her trail went cold in Honolulu. Infuriated, Vitale Cassiel advertised for, and got, a soldier of fortune – a recently discharged Foreign Legionnaire – who combed the Hawaiian Islands and half of Indochina for her, to no avail. But he was able to pick up the brief trail that she and Samax had left in Acapulco. And that was how Vitale Cassiel confirmed Samax's role in Stella's flight, which, while deepening the animosity between them, was not the end of that particular chapter in their rivalry.

It did come to an end of sorts ten years later, in September, 1955, in a rocky stretch of desert midway between Las Vegas and Reno, where a different cast of characters was playing out a notably similar game, underscored by love and vengeance, flight and pursuit. One participant was Stella and Vitale Cassiel's son, who was carrying a valuable item of his father's which the latter had sent an emissary to retrieve. Vitale Cassiel's son would disappear, and the emissary would later be found, charred beyond recognition, with a bullet in his skull, in a burnt-out car at the bottom of a ravine.

What exactly happened at that ravine would never be completely unraveled, but there was no doubt it crucially changed the course of several lives, including my own: my mother, Bel Samax, then four months pregnant with me, was also there, and barely avoided death herself. Nevertheless, the terrific shock she received in that stretch of wasteland would mark the beginning of the end of her own life and would cause her to give birth to me prematurely, and with great difficulty, three months later. Soon after she had put me up for adoption, the medical complications springing from childbirth resulted in her death.

I was intensely curious about Bel, for obvious reasons. When I turned eighteen, Samax had given me that small chest of her possessions which he showed me when I first arrived at the hotel. Sometimes I took out the gold hairbrush or the ivory-handled mirror, or flipped through the blue bankbook that held, among so many numbers, the ones that had enabled Samax to find me in the world. And though the hummingbird pendant was gone, I still used the slim red fountain pen that had once belonged to my mother. In my years at the Hotel Canopus I had discovered a few additional objects which I added to that chest; at the same time, I had tried to gather all the information I could about her, which in the end did not amount to much.

Bel simply had left very little of herself behind outside of the contents of that chest. Even in the way of photographs. Her pretty, pale face with the blue eyes, shapely lips, and straight bright teeth with the slight overbite (I saw now that they matched my own) smiled out of the slim 'family' album of Samax's, which I must have leafed through a thousand times. Not one for impromptu snapshots (he disliked photographs of himself almost as much as my grandmother in Brooklyn did), my uncle had stocked the album with generally unrevealing portraits and stiff group shots by professional photographers. His household had never formally celebrated holidays and the like, so they would hardly have been memorialized; even in my time, and in ironic contrast to the large-scale dinners each night, Christmas and birthdays were observed in small, intimate gatherings, casual yet with a decorum that would not have encouraged any of us to pull out a camera and pop a flashbulb.

Somewhat more revealing was a photograph album that had belonged to Bel which I stumbled across one day in a box of old magazines in the library stacks. Bound in green leather, even slimmer than Samax's, Bel's album was also impersonal in its way. The single shot of Desirée, at age six, sunning herself by the pool exactly as she would at age twenty-six, and one of a youthful Della kneeling on the patio feeding some bluebirds were the exception. Nearly all the other photographs, maybe twenty altogether, were of landscapes – sandstone pillars in the Painted Desert, gypsum dunes at White Sands, salt flats – that reflected excursions she had made outside of the Mojave. Always to other deserts. But how and with whom? Samax didn't know; as Bel got older, he said sadly, she came and went as she pleased, sometimes disappearing for a week or more and never discussing her destinations or her companions.

There were a couple of grainy photographs of Bel herself tucked into the album, solo shots taken in front of desert gas stations and diners, from so far off that her features were barely visible. In both, she was waving at the camera – and the person behind it, who may or may not have been my father, though this time his shadow was nowhere to be seen. These otherwise unsatisfying shots – as distant and nebulous as the verbal descriptions of her I had been given – interested me because they seemed to have been taken around the same time, and by the same hand, as the photograph of Bel that Samax had shown me at the abandoned factory, smiling in a red dress against a yellow background. And I realized that the clear, living impression of her I so desired was always going to elude me. At night, when I lay in bed and tried to fix her image in the darkness above, it was as if I were gazing at a heavenly body, remote from me in time and space – like those stars whose light takes billions of years to reach earth – that had mysteriously, all my life, held sway over my impulses, choices, and fears to a degree I didn't fathom properly until I was older.

Finally, there were two 8 × 10 photographs in the back of the album. The first was of a field of sagebrush beside a road in sunlight. The field was unremarkable. The road could have been anywhere. Neither Samax nor Della nor anyone else who had lived at the hotel in Bel's time could identify it. 'It looks like she snapped the picture from a car,' Samax remarked. I wondered, as he had, what significance, if any, that place could have had for her.

The most interesting photograph was the other 8 × 10. It was a shot of Bel and Samax. They were both in white coveralls, holding shovels, in what would become the quincuncial orchard but was still a bare lawn, with a single sapling before them, its roots encased in a ball of peat moss. According to Samax, the photograph was taken around Bel's sixteenth birthday when they planted the orchard's very first tree – a carambola tree, in fact, to which I would often retire when I wanted to be alone with my thoughts. After Bel's death, her ashes were scattered beneath it. Located at the exact center of the orchard – which had grown outwardly from it, quincunx after quincunx, like a quilt – it was a good place to be alone. The grass beneath the tree was soft, and the tree, about thirty feet tall, produced an exceptionally cool circle of shade in which I could lie on my back and gaze at the starfruit, bright and golden, clustered in the thick foliage. Samax called it 'Bel's Tree', and because it was planted by my mother as a girl, two years before my birth, I cherished it, watering and fertilizing it according to Samax's instructions and eating its fruit, which was deliciously tart, with special pleasure.

I also found a sample of Bel's handwriting – not numerals this time, but a faded list of desert wildflowers tucked into the photograph album. The list was written in violet ink on a piece of cardboard, and I was stunned to see that the handwriting was identical to my own, right down to the way Bel wrote her *e* like a backward *3* and crossed her *t*'s so high they looked like tiny seesaws. Some of the names were checked, and I thought this might indicate that she had encountered the flowers in the wild.

√*Angel Trumpet*
 Desert Bell
√*Skyrocket*
 Ghost Flower
√*Desert Candle*
√*Indian Blanket*
 Sunray
√*Whispering Bells*
 Mariposa Lily
√*Mojave Desert Star*

I easily memorized the list, the one thing of my mother's composed of words that I could hold inside me and preserve. Running through this list in my mind enabled me to feel closer to her – as if I could hear her speaking the names herself. As if they were the only words I would have known in her voice.

The handful of Bel's other possessions that I found over time, and usually by accident, were a pair of onyx earrings – ovals ringed with diamond chips – a wooden ruler in which she had etched her initials, and a small working compass with a snap-on cover and a silver chain. The compass, in effect, replaced the humming-bird pendant, for I began carrying it on me from the day I discovered it in that same box beneath the photograph album. There were also two LP records that I found tucked away behind Samax's old opera collection: Christmas carols sung by a girls' choir and Elvis Presley's *Heartbreak Hotel*. The carols I played often on the portable phonograph in my room, especially the very last cut on the record, 'The Star Carol', which began, *Long years ago on a deep winter night / High in the heavens a star shone bright . . .* and ended, *And when the stars in the heavens I see / Ever and always I think of thee.* That one I played over and over again.

There must have been other physical traces of Bel in a place as big and complex as the hotel, but I never found them. All in all, with few material touchstones, and people's memories of Bel seemingly sealed off by the grief that had overflowed and solidified around her death, the hazy picture I put together of her over the years remained remarkably unaltered. It began with a reclusive child who barely spoke while Nilus was alive, and then under Samax's wing rapidly flowered while remaining intensely private. And, to be sure, it was a conflicted picture at first: a wallflower who could also be the life of the party, a bookworm who hung out with a fast crowd, a dreamy sort of girl with a violent temper.

In a rare burst of expansiveness on the subject of Bel, Samax told me outright that I reminded him of her. It was several months after my nineteenth birthday, one of those nights in his library when he had been going on to me about the Angel of Death; by then Samax was convinced that this entity could manifest itself not just as a walking fire or other spectacular natural phenomenon like lightning, but even in the form of a plant – one whose aura, to the naked eye, would be spectral, like moonlight.

'Bel kept to herself the way you do,' Samax said, abruptly changing the subject. 'She could go for days with barely a word to anyone. And like you, she often walked far out into the desert. She loved the desert, as Ivy never did. She was a natural dancer – show her a step once and she never forgot it. As a kid, she read incessantly. Then, at sixteen, she got restless. Wandering at first, then staying out for nights at a time. When I clamped down, she sneaked out even more. She got wilder. We had been close, but I lost touch with her – even more deeply than I knew. She was so young – I remembered how I had been when I was young, and I kept telling myself the pendulum would swing. But it never did: it just stopped.' His left hand was trembling, as it sometimes did after his stroke, and he kept locking and unlocking his fingers. 'I'll never forgive myself, Enzo, for what happened to her. I've tried to make it up through you. Bel got pregnant, ran away, had a difficult childbirth. In less than three months, you came into her life and went out of it. She was in all kinds of other trouble. And I knew nothing. I who could read the most inscrutable faces around a high-stakes poker table, who had spent a lifetime playing the angles other people didn't see. Yet I didn't even know you existed, much less who your father was.'

I was astonished to hear him express such feelings – most of all, his shame – so openly. 'That's not your fault,' I said from a parched throat. 'None of it is.'

'It was my responsibility.' He shook his head in disgust. 'I was responsible for her.'

'She was already eighteen when those things happened,' I put in, trying to help him let himself off the hook.

But that wasn't what he wanted. 'Eighteen?' he snorted. 'Enzo, she never reached the age that you are tonight. The last time I saw her, she was crossing the courtyard in a yellow dress and I was rushing off to the airport. She waved to me. I waved back. She started up the front steps and I lost her in the fountain's spray. The next day, she ran away. Months later, I got a call from some little hospital. She was already gone.' He was fighting back tears. 'That night I slept in her room – your room – and I swore I could still smell her scent in the air, even in the blankets.'

From then on, some nights I thought I could smell it, too. It was only in the previous year I had learned that

Room E, my room since I was ten years old, had been my mother Bel's room from the time she was nine and a half until shortly before her death. I had not been informed of this particular bit of my history because Samax had thought it could have disturbed me when I was younger.

'Then why', I asked, 'give me that room at all?'

He looked surprised. 'But what other room could you have been given? That was always your room – even before you knew it.'

What a strange answer, I thought, and only then understood that Bel's time in that room had included a good portion of her pregnancy, which meant I had also resided there long before Samax had first brought me to Las Vegas.

Some months later, midway through the summer of 1975, Deneb returned from the Aegean exactly as he had said he would: four years after his departure. He was not as somber as I remembered him; perhaps because his work was done, or because now he didn't have his face buried in a book or treatise every waking moment. He had a leathery tan and was wearing his hair – a full shade grayer now – much longer. His dark glasses were the darkest pair yet, and his customary white suit was of a baggier cut, bought off the rack in Iráklion, Crete, and complemented by a madras tie. Copies of his Atlantis monograph in red binders were neatly arrayed on the sideboard and it was almost like the old days when, at dinner on Deneb's second night back, Samax and the rest of us sat down to hear what conclusions he had reached after his long years of research and contemplation.

Despite the buzz of anticipation in the air, it was painfully clear to me that night how much our ranks had been thinned. Calzas was gone, and Auro, and Ivy always dined alone now in her rooms. Zaren Eboli was on an extended field trip, fulfilling his quest of cataloguing all the spiders of the Southwest. And of course Della and Denise no longer choreographed the meal itself. For this, Samax had hired a laconic middle-aged woman with long red hair held in place by turquoise barrettes whom all of us knew only as Mrs Resh, the former manager of a four-star restaurant in San Francisco. Unlike the two sisters, she never sat at the table, but always hovered behind Samax or by the door. Desirée sat across from Samax now, at the foot of the table, and Labusi in his wheelchair was on his left.

The ranks of the more transient guests had also dwindled. That particular night only two of them were at dinner: Professor Zianor from Pakistan, a short, immensely fat man in a black turban, who was writing a book about paintings that depict Adam with a navel; and a lady from Malaysia named So Li who was studying the history of bells. Also present was a man named Forcas whom Samax introduced to me as an old friend. I had never heard of him before, but he would become a frequent guest at the hotel over the next few years. Often he played chess into the night with Samax, who had much less opportunity to play with Labusi now that the latter was so absorbed in his billiard career. Forcas was a trim man about seventy, of average height and weight, with brown eyes and steely gray hair. But, as with no one else I had ever met, while I could spell out the particulars of his features, I always found it impossible to retain a clear picture of him in my memory after he was gone. He possessed an air not so much of mystery as abstraction. As if he didn't really exist except when he was physically standing before you.

'That's right,' Desirée replied when I mentioned this to her. 'Even professionally he doesn't really exist. He's a gangster without a gang, famous and at the same time anonymous. Solitary, but with connections everywhere – none of which you could document. He's filthy rich, with no known bank accounts, property or investments. He's fathered a dozen children, but has no women in his life. He lives comfortably but has no home, and while he can go anywhere, and does so openly, his whereabouts are always unknown. He's one of Samax's most valued friends, though they haven't seen one another in ten years.'

My first thought, which I shared with Desirée, was that Forcas was Rochel, Samax's old Zuni cellmate at the Ironwater Penitentiary.

'I don't think so,' she said, without elaborating.

What he was, it turned out, was probably the only mutual friend Samax and Vitale Cassiel had in common, someone who had done favors for both men over the years, and had the favors returned. In fact, as tensions grew between Samax and Vitale Cassiel, Forcas would come to serve, briefly, but crucially, as an intermediary. Once, finding myself alone with Forcas in the billiard room, I asked him about the feud – why it never ended.

'Oh, I don't know how something like this ends,' he said in his low voice, puffing a cigar and crossing his legs in one of the big leather armchairs. 'It's not about ending – it's like a circle neither man will step out of.' He shook his head. 'Recently, your uncle decided to sell off a big spread up in Elko County, next to the Paiute reservation, on the Idaho border. He bought the land in 1950 and its value has sky-rocketed. The buyers were a consortium of ranchers – Junius didn't want the land to go to developers. Suddenly, as they're closing the deal, a Bureau of Indian Affairs inspector shows up with a writ, saying a third party has complained of irregularities.' Forcas chuckled. 'Then a couple of mob lawyers from Tahoe go to district court and stop the deal, claiming their clients had an option on the land. At that point, the ranchers get cold feet and pull out. After sending up a team of lawyers himself, and pouring a lot of money down the drain, your uncle discovers what he already knew: that it's Vitale Cassiel's agents, after getting the tribe a casino license, who've been empowered by the Paiute lodge to block the deal. Suddenly the Paiute say they want the land for themselves. At the same time, none other than VC Enterprises has bought and sold an adjoining stretch of land in Idaho to the mob, who now want to consolidate. Still following me?'

I nodded my head in disbelief.

'In other words,' Forcas concluded, 'Vitale Cassiel played both sides against the middle, just to screw Junius, and in the end it worked: Junius sold half the land to the mob guys and half to the Indians, at a loss. Not to mention the loss of time and energy.' He paused. 'And, in his mind, the loss of face.'

'Vitale Cassiel did all that out of pure hatred?'

'Oh, VC Enterprises made a pile of dough in the process, but you have to believe the real motivation was the ongoing revenge. Your uncle has taken his shots in the same way: undermining deals, financial sabotage, court actions. But, never forget, loss of face drives them more than loss of money. The feud only ends if that's resolved – or when one of them dies.'

Nonetheless, I thought, I had been right about the bodyguards: in his dealings with Vitale Cassiel, Samax had more to fear from cutthroat lawyers than actual cutthroats.

As always, the night Deneb made his presentation I was sitting on Samax's right, with Hadar beside me. Hadar was voluble, despite his usual hard edge, from the moment he settled his great body onto his chair. His mitts for hands were as rough as sandpaper from handling rocks. His hair looked ignitable as straw from all his hours in the sun. In fact, except for his corkscrew eyes seeming to have recessed even farther into his skull, he had barely changed in the nine years I had known him. As we waited for Deneb to speak, Hadar was telling me about a man in Zurich who had recently contacted him.

'A collector. Claimed to have the Ensishein meteorite.' He stirred his tomato juice with a stalk of celery. 'Do you know what that is?'

I shook my head.

'A famous meteorite that fell to earth in 1492. In the Black Forest. Local constable locked it in a dungeon to keep it from flying back into space. Kept it there for 105 years.' He chuckled. 'Then it disappeared.'

'Maybe it did fly back into space,' I said.

'Well, it hasn't come back now,' he grunted, then leaned his big head close to my ear. 'This afternoon Deneb told me his whole theory is built around an asteroid.'

'Really.'

Hadar sat back slowly. 'We'll see.'

Samax clinked his glass for quiet, and Deneb stood up, clearing his throat.

'Let me state categorically,' he began in his high voice, 'that the coordinates for Atlantis were 26°6'N and 42°55'W, 600 miles off the European continent, east of the Sargasso Sea in the North Atlantic. It was a land mass of 220,000 square miles – roughly the area of the Iberian peninsula. From Plato on, every ancient source agrees that Atlantis suffered a swift, explosive cataclysm and sank into the sea. That includes tribes as diverse as the Berbers, who called Atlantis Attala, the Celts, who named it Avalon, and the Vikings, on whose maps it appears as the continent of Atland. The Phoenicians referred to it as Antilla, and the Basques,' Deneb paused, glancing at Samax, 'gave it the name Atlantida, and even today in the Pyrenees call themselves Atlantika. On this side of the Atlantic, too, the Aztecs claimed their ancestors fled the eastern island of Aztlan before it disappeared.' He leaned forward, planting his palms on the table. 'Here is my solution to the mystery: Atlantis was destroyed by an enormous asteroid.'

He sipped ice water and scanned the table eagerly for our reactions. Then he spelled out his theory:

The asteroid that struck near Atlantis did so with the combined force of a hundred nuclear warheads. One of the Adonis group that are drawn to the major planets, the asteroid approached Atlantis at twelve miles per second, and before impact blazed with a fiery light, exceeding the brightness of a hundred suns. Everyone who saw it was blinded. When it hit the ocean near Atlantis, the asteroid's temperature had reached 40,000°F, vaporizing tons of seawater and hurling up a succession of 3,000-foot tidal waves – taller than Atlantis's mountain ranges – that devastated the island and drowned the entire population.

Deneb backed all this up with a dizzying assortment of geological and oceanographic facts and figures, compiled by scientists whose names sounded as fantastic as their theories – Alan H Kelso De Montigny, Count Carli de Lalande, Otto Muck. Saving his biggest surprise for last, he disclosed that he had discovered an obscure Greek codex of the Hellenistic period in the archives of the Crusaders' library in Rhodes which linked Atlantis to the lost city of Tartessos in southern Spain.

'Tartessos is the unshakable link between Atlantis and the Basque people,' Deneb concluded excitedly. 'It was a colony of Atlantis, the outpost from which the Atlantans traded in the Mediterranean. Since no one escaped the tidal waves on Atlantis, the bulk of Atlantans who survived their civilization were the colonists in Tartessos. After the Carthaginians razed their city, these colonists fled to the Pyrenees.' Deneb turned to Samax, who was listening with his head cocked, puffing a cigar. 'And those full-blooded Atlantans, Junius, who evolved into a fierce and resourceful alpine tribe, are the people we now know as the Basques. Or the Atlantika, which literally means, "those who were once of Atlantis".'

Deneb closed his red binder and bowed stiffly as everyone applauded, after which Samax offered up a toast.

But, much as he appreciated Deneb's well-wrought theory, Samax was really thinking about something else altogether throughout that dinner. Afterward he would tell me that earlier in the day Deneb had mentioned a possible reference in the Greek codex to a rare amulet: sacred to moon worshippers, this amulet was said to hold secrets about the moon never before revealed. Deneb had microfilmed the codex and sent the film out to be developed the day he returned to Las Vegas. The moment it came back from the lab, Samex was poring

403

over it – projected onto a screen in his library – with Labusi as his translator. Though it took them a while, they did find definitive mention of that amulet – aerially depicting the far side of the moon – which had for so long obsessed Samax.

As for Deneb, after his monograph was published, the section on the origins of the Basques was excerpted in the Nevada newspapers, and to his surprise he was fêted by the state's Basque-American Society and the Basque-dominated Chamber of Commerce. Called on to address civic groups, Rotarians, Masons, and schoolchildren, he became for a while, to Samax's amusement – for we all knew Deneb as one of the hotel's most reclusive residents – a local celebrity. The 'Atlantis Connection,' as the *Reno Gazette* dubbed him.

Later that night, as Samax and the others retired to the library after Deneb's speech, Desirée intercepted me in the corridor and took me aside. 'I need to see you,' she said in her velvety voice which still had the power to make my heart skip. 'Let's go outside.'

Desirée had passed up dinner. Atlantis was not one of the lost things that captured her fancy. She led me out past the fountain, into the garden. We stood only inches apart there under the stars with the desert wind ruffling our hair. Without a word, her long lashes concealing her eyes, she unfastened the buttons of her jacket. Was this, I thought, the night I had been waiting for all those years under the same roof with her? Then from her jacket she produced an envelope, which contained a letter to her from Della.

'You asked me to let you know as soon as I heard from her. I found this when I came in tonight.'

I tilted the envelope into the moonlight. 'Postmarked Santa Fe,' I said.

'That's temporary. She says when she settles down, she'll send me her address.' Desirée shrugged. 'About what I expected. She doesn't trust me or anybody else. And she's still afraid of Dolores.' She shook her head. 'All these years they all feared Dolores. And all their

404

lives they served her – and served her purposes.' She fell silent for a moment. 'There were only three bumps on that road: Doris's marriage to Samax, which of course Dolores sanctioned, my mother's fling with Samax, which of course she didn't, and her affair with Spica, of which I am the living reminder. Dolores never forgave Della for those two indiscretions, and afterward Della tried so hard to make it up to her. On some level it must have been excruciating for Della to take off like that – putting herself first – after Denise's funeral. When I was small, and we were exiled in Florida, that was Dolores's doing. She always needed to control the levers. This time Della went on her own, and that could make Dolores do something really crazy.'

'At her age?'

'Why not? Seems to me all that chamomile tea has worked: she's never been sick and she's strong as a horse. She doesn't even use a cane to walk. I hope I have just a few of her genes.'

'Does she talk to you at all?'

Desirée shook her head. 'She gave up on me a long time ago. Predictably, she did call me in right after Della split. She said, "Now that your mother's gone – as good as dead – I want you to know that I expect the hotel to go to you. And I don't want to hear otherwise."'

'What did you say?'

'What I've always said – that, like my mother, I'm not interested. But she doesn't hear me. It has nothing to do with me. Now it's something she has to thrash out with Samax, if she uses her last breath to do it. Let them deal with it.' She squeezed my arm. 'I'm going to bed, Enzo.' She kissed my cheek, and drinking in that wonderful fragrance of her hair and skin, I held on to it for as long as I could after she had slipped away into the darkness.

Minutes later I could still feel the warmth of Desirée's lips when I stretched out in the cool grass under Bel's Tree at the center of the orchard. And no sooner had I closed my eyes than I plunged into a dream.

I was back in the planetarium I had visited with Alma,

except instead of being abducted by Ivy I had gotten lost in the basement. The basement was a labyrinth of pitch-black rooms twinkling with pinpricks of starlight. In one of them the floor was littered with astronomical paraphernalia: orreries, telescopes, sextants. At the end of a long corridor, I came on a door marked FIRE, which opened, and a young woman stepped out. It was Bel. Smiling, she approached me slowly and embraced me. Her thin body felt cold, but her breath was warm and her blond hair smelled of jasmine, like Desirée's. She held me like that for an eternity, just the two of us. Then, as I began to feel her heart beating against my chest even while my own heartbeat was growing louder in my ears, she stepped back into the cool darkness. Groping blindly, I tried to find her, but she was gone.

Opening my eyes, I stared up through the foliage of Bel's Tree, into a patch of sky where the stars were blazing. Drowsily I stood up and moved across the garden like a sleepwalker, the trees in their quincuncial pattern turning to vapor before me. Like the ghosts of trees, they seemed to leave a sheen on my skin when the wind blew through them.

In my bed I did not return to that dream, as I had hoped, but instead lay awake tossing until dawn. When I finally drifted off, the last thing I heard was two different heartbeats: my own and Bel's, I thought, as I had heard them in the garden – and as she must have heard them in that room, on just such a night before I was born.

14

Naxos

In the deserts of Africa, Pliny wrote, ghosts suddenly confront the traveler and vanish in a flash. This happened in other sorts of deserts as well – the internal variety – which I could find with little effort whether I was crisscrossing the South Pacific, marooned in a northern city in dead of winter, or sailing the Aegean Sea. Hydra, Spetses, Tínos, Santorini . . . I had been island-hopping again, alone again, eventually settling down for a while for the simple reason that I found myself on an island I didn't want to leave.

For the first time in years I had begun reading again in Latin – not just the naturalists like Pliny, but historians from whom I had shied away as a student, like Livy, who was so dry, and Suetonius, who could be more salacious than a tabloid columnist. Suetonius also wrote a great deal about ghosts and apparitions: according to him, every Roman emperor from starchy Augustus to lewd Domitian during this last night on earth dreamt fantastical portents of his own death. I had also begun to read again in ancient Greek – especially Herodotus and Plutarch – and while my Latin came back to me quickly, with Greek I plodded. Even so, it made my efforts to pick up the vernacular that much easier. Having settled on Naxos – the largest and least visited of the Cyclades – in the off-season, I had little choice but to speak Greek. And the more I explored the island and

407

its five thousand years of history – Ionic temples, Roman aqueducts, Byzantine churches, Venetian castles – the more I felt that I had finally, at age thirty-four, made the trip to the Mediterranean basin that, before my mother's death, I had dreamt about in college. With a well-thumbed copy of Pausanias's *Guide to Greece* under my arm, I felt very much the student at times, one who had received a far different education than the classics department had planned for me.

Pliny wrote of ghosts in his book on zoology, which did not surprise me; I, too, had come to see them as fully animated, specialized members of the animal kingdom. The ghosts I encountered on Naxos were not like the ones that had visited my seaside cabin on Rarotonga eight years earlier – my deceased relatives and friends and the small legion of the dead I had X-rayed in Vietnam. Nor was Geza Cassiel ever among them. No, these were the ghosts of strangers, which made it no less frightening when I discovered them – materializing for an instant, silent and still – at my table in a noisy restaurant, or by a kiosk on the windswept harbor, or, worst of all, behind the curtain by the small balcony of my room at the Hotel Capella.

Then one rainswept April day the origin of these ghosts came clear to me: I had conjured them, I thought, out of the memories of all the people who had participated in my performances in the five years I had worked as Jorge Gaspard's assistant. Before our professional relationship ended – that is, before I fled both him and the act in Athens – I calculated that between 1973 and 1978 I had participated in 1,498 performances, during which I must have been on intimate terms with the memories of at least 10,486 members of our audiences. Taking into account the additional thousands of people fixed in the memories of those audience members, this meant that I had been privy, however fleetingly, to the lives of a population as great as any midsized European country's – say, Denmark. Or Greece. Now, it seemed, these violated ghosts were getting their revenge. Or perhaps they were a kind of ectoplasmic residue: once absorbed into my consciousness, they had remained there as a kind of foreign colony. When I glimpsed them, they resembled shadows with glowing outlines – like shining black auras. Or that special variety of X-ray called a skiagram – a figure formed by shading in the outline of a shadow – which I remembered from my technician days. At first these ghosts frightened me, but I almost got used to them after a while, as if they were natural shadows; indeed, if I squinted, they didn't look much different from the shadows cast by a streetlight on a misty night.

As the months passed, after years of public performances and constant travel I reverted to form on Naxos and began leading a fixed, near solitary existence. I moved from my hotel just below the Kastro, the hilltop castle that crowned the old town, to a two-room house on Karades Bay, thirty minutes south by motor scooter. The roads to my house devolved from winding asphalt to gravel to rocky dirt. There were two cypress trees in front and some cactus and thorny bushes along one side. The soil was baked, the horseshoe of mountains around the bay like a succession of gray stone skulls. In fields marked off by stone walls, goats grazed on weeds that might have been cut from sheets of tin. Accustomed to the lushness of Kauai, the multiplying gradations of green and blue, I found this stark white landscape made my eyes ache. But it was an aching clarity I welcomed at that point in my life. A clarity I found at night, too, when I sat on my porch gazing at the stars. Touring in cities, I had missed the night sky, and once settled into that house on the coast – on an island again finally – I resumed stargazing in earnest.

In those five years I had been back to Hawaii only once, one Christmas. Olan still lived in my bungalow with my dogs. Though Alvin and Claudia were spending more of their time in Japan, and Estes was visiting the mainland on that occasion, none of my friends had left the island permanently. But it had been painful to go back. I wasn't yet ready. My anger over the fallout around Francis Beliar's death had hit me with renewed force once I was away from Kauai. I was still ashamed over the nature of my affair with him – the dope and booze, the twisted sex, feeling cheap all the time – and neither my success onstage nor the fact that for the first time in my life I had some money in the bank helped. However, now that I was away from Gaspard those wounds were beginning to heal, and I realized how much they had been aggravated by my relationship with him. Zigzagging over the rocky, scattershot archipelago of Greece for several months freed me up; it felt like the Cook Islands all over again: the more erratic my route and remote the islands, the stronger their effect on me, and the more sustenance I drew. By the time I reached Naxos, I was experiencing deep tugs for Hawaii, the only place I'd ever really thought of as home. But I knew I needed to be alone for a while first.

I saw that, while I hadn't fled the chaos of a war or the pain of a severed love affair, my years with Gaspard had taken a toll on me. I had gone from distrusting to detesting him. When I spent two weeks on Santorini, the barrel-chested proprietress of my hotel in Monolithos informed me that the island was home to all the vampires in the region. *Vrykolakes*, she called them, and no matter how distant the other islands they visited nocturnally – Chios and Samos, for example, off Turkey – she said they always returned to Santorini before dawn. But it was her definition of a vampire that made me think of Gaspard: the truly powerful *vrykolakos* had no need to suck a victim's blood because he could, with far more devastating results, suck out the entire contents of a man's soul.

Gaspard had run through his many other assistants indiscriminately, but I knew that one with my gift, who enhanced his drawing power, he would try to keep at all costs. Put simply, I had become a cash cow for him, and in his greediness he had doubled our performance schedule whenever the moon was favorable. When I brought up quitting – even hinted at it – it clearly alarmed him, and during my last months with him, he focused his considerable energies on getting me to stay on. He did it overtly: flattering me, indulging my small extravagances – acupuncture sessions, hydrotherapy, weekends at alpine spas – and, most of all, paying me plenty. I grew accustomed to having more money than I needed, which made me think I needed it all the more. In European capitals I had acquired expensive tastes in clothes – never a vice of mine previously – and, to let off tension, visited casinos where I played the roulette wheel. Gradually, though, I came to believe that Gaspard, a sophisticated manipulator, was using more than money and perks to keep me tethered to him. I didn't know what, exactly; I knew only that no matter how intensely I wanted to break with him, I wasn't able to. Presented more than once with opportunities, at the last moment I always shied away from leaving, without understanding why.

At the end of this frustrating cycle, a well-known promoter in Rome contacted me with a proposition: if I left Gaspard and signed with him, he would send me on tour as a solo headliner – tripling my income while cutting my performing time in half. Over a sumptuous lunch he declared that I had become a major attraction whom people came to see in her own right. 'You are a star now, *signorina*,' he smiled, raising his wineglass, though I had trouble thinking of myself in that way. When I turned him down flat, I told myself it was because I wanted to get out of the mind-reading business, not because I couldn't leave Gaspard. Yet, perversely, I continued playing second fiddle to Gaspard, letting him work me silly without giving me any real autonomy. By this time, my salary was about seventy thousand dollars a year, but unlike my early days with him, I was banking less than a third of it.

Money aside, what neither the promoter nor Gaspard knew was that I had not only grown weary of entering people's memories, but also felt that my ability to do so was waning. The burst of clairvoyance I had enjoyed since the car accident was drawing to a close. Eventually, over Gaspard's objections, I had to shorten the act accordingly; the lie I told him I couched in prima donna terms, complaining that nine audience volunteers was simply too taxing. So we went to five, then four – and, even then, the strain was such that, by the time I walked offstage, I was suffering severe headaches. Knowing my performing days were numbered was yet another impetus to stash away as much money as I could, which made it even more puzzling that I would pass up the chance to earn more in so much less time.

Though I had been plagued by terrible bouts of insomnia for months, suddenly during this period I had the opposite problem: some nights I slept so deeply I could not even be roused by a pair of powerful alarm clocks and a wake-up call from the concierge. I saw a doctor in London, and he told me I must be depressed. Well, of course I was depressed – tired of the act, hostile toward Gaspard, increasingly wanting out – but I knew there was more to it than that.

Soon I became convinced that I was receiving visitors while I slept. At first I thought they must be from the spirit world, but gradually decided that they were very much of this world. That they were, in fact, Gaspard himself, coming into my room after hypnotizing or drugging me. This seemed an incredible, if not paranoid, notion, but I had come to see him as someone – like Francis Beliar – capable of doing anything to retain power over people. Unlike Francis, he was motivated by greed, not lust. And with my psychic energies ebbing and my defenses shaky, I felt susceptible. A master of subliminal hypnosis, Gaspard could easily have been hypnotizing me hours before I went to bed in such a way that I didn't know it was happening and only felt its full effects while asleep, absorbing first and foremost the notion that I should not leave him.

It was in Barcelona I was inspired to test my theory by buying a small sound-activated tape recorder and

412

placing it under the bed in my hotel room. It was an exceptionally quiet room. The first two nights the tape recorder remained off. The third night it was activated twice: once when I coughed, the second time when I cried out in my sleep.

The next night, in Madrid, I went to bed directly after our performance, leaving Gaspard at the theater. Though by the clock I had slept for nine hours, I was as usual tired in the morning. The tape recorder had again been activated, and this time when I played it back, I froze at the sequence of sounds: a rustling of clothes, the chair by the bed creaking, and then whispering so soft I could not make out a single word or distinguish whether it was a man or woman's voice. But I knew it wasn't me. The whispering went on for a full minute, then the chair creaked again, and the tape recorder clicked off.

My hands shaking, I played the tape over twice, turning up the volume, but still I couldn't identify the whisperer. All the same, this was the proof I had been seeking: someone had entered my room, I thought, and attempted to hypnotize me. Who could that be but Gaspard? I knew there was no point in confronting him with the tape: he would feign bewilderment, deny everything, cover his tracks, and I would never be able to catch him in the act, which I thought I must do.

The next night I returned to my room, drank two double espressos, and got into bed. And nothing happened. We flew to Paris, where I fell asleep exhausted after a lackluster performance, only to find that the tape recorder picked up the rustling and whispering again. In Venice the pattern was repeated: I forced myself to stay awake and heard nothing; when I slept, there was whispering. By the time we arrived in Athens, I thought I had better confront Gaspard with the tape recordings before I lost my mind altogether. But then something completely unexpected decided the entire matter for me.

Gaspard usually stayed at the Grande Bretagne in the hub of the city, but there had been a mix-up and no rooms were available. So we checked in to a small dark hotel called the Aldebaran on an obscure square in the Kolonaki district, near the National Garden. Gaspard took a taxi to the theater where we would be performing and I went up to my room. At first, in the shuttered darkness, I didn't see that there was someone else present. Catching a glint of silver across the room, then the gleam of a pair of eyes, I dropped my suitcase with a cry and jumped back to the door, groping for the handle. At that moment, a switch was thrown and a lamp came on, illuminating a woman sitting in an armchair.

'I'm sorry I startled you, Mala,' she said in a low, softly accented voice.

Blinking hard, I saw that she was about sixty, thin, with a long nose and a wide mouth turned downward at the corners. Legs crossed, she looked relaxed in a gray pants suit that matched the color of her hair, which was pulled back tightly in a bun. Her eyes shone just as brightly in the lamplight as they had in the darkness.

'Who are you,' I said, 'and how do you know my name?'

'How could I not?' Somehow her voice was familiar to me, though I was certain I had never seen or spoken with her before. 'You've been working for my husband for five years.'

'Your husband?' I said in astonishment.

She nodded. 'I'm Heléne Gaspard.'

I just stared, for I had never expected to meet her. In fact, I had begun to doubt her very existence. Gaspard never talked about her. And until that moment I had only a vague idea of what she might have looked like, for he always mysteriously claimed to have no current photographs. In the only ones he showed me, glossy old promotional shots, a woman with jet black hair was sitting onstage in a long dress; half her face was concealed by the same sort of domino mask that I wore during performances, below which her wide mouth was firmly set, unsmiling. In the years I had been with Gaspard, Heléne was a phantom to me, alive only by

414

way of her vaunted mind-reading technique, which in turn lived in me. Many times Gaspard had said, 'You *are* Heléne when you are onstage'; it was his way of complimenting me, but it always made me feel anxious.

'I am pleased to meet you,' she said.

I shook my head. 'What are you doing in my room?'

'Waiting for you,' she replied simply. 'I didn't think you'd mind since you hadn't yet checked in.'

I wondered why the concierge hadn't told me she was waiting.

'Because he didn't know,' she said, cutting into my thoughts as effortlessly as if I had spoken aloud.

Though I knew secondhand her skills as a mind reader, this still took me by surprise.

'But where did you come from?' I asked.

'Venice. I was there when you were. And Paris before that. Jorge didn't tell you?'

'No, he didn't.' And of course she would have known that he didn't, I thought. 'Were you in Madrid too?' I asked quickly.

'No, I have not been in Spain in many years,' she said with a thin smile, rising slowly from the chair and opening the shutters onto the night. It was only then, with a shiver, that I saw what had glinted in the darkness when I entered the room: she was wearing a silver pin on her lapel in the shape of a scorpion, with a ruby at its center. 'The food in that country does not agree with me,' she went on. 'But I know a fine place here, at the foot of Lykabettos, if you'll join me for dinner. I must speak with you.'

I would never find out why. With a hot breeze blowing in, sticking to my skin, I felt sick to my stomach; convinced that Heléne, not Gaspard, was the one invading my hotel rooms and my sleep, I decided at that moment to carry through on the impulse I had been suppressing for weeks: I would flee Gaspard and not look back. Finding Heléne in my room unannounced – even proprietary – had clinched it for me.

Trying to keep my mind blank, I told Heléne I would

be glad to dine with her after I showered and changed. She peered at me closely – and I used all my willpower to project something, anything, other than what I was really thinking – then went down the hall to her own room, agreeing to meet me in the lobby in a half hour. Within five minutes, grabbing my suitcase and leaving my performer's trunk, I bypassed the lift and rushed down the stairs. Making a fuss – so the clerk would remember – I called the airport from the front desk and reserved a seat on an eleven p.m. flight to London which I had no intention of taking. Then I hailed a taxi, and entering the fast-weaving traffic of the coast highway, headed straight for the docks at Piraeus.

I never saw Gaspard or Heléne again. I would be surprised if they fell for my ruse of flying to England, but I doubt they even considered the possibility that I would board a ferry for a random island in the dead of night. I don't know what I thought they could have done to me – ongoing hypnosis, brainwashing? – and within days, as I put distance between us, my fears diminished. But that night in Athens, everything in me had told me not to fight those fears, but to run.

I remained wary for a time that Gaspard might try to trace my whereabouts. But how? I didn't worry about his hiring a private detective; my own experiences with them had been so abysmal. First, in New York when Loren was abducted, and then in Las Vegas in 1974 when I was sure I had crossed paths with him at The Stardust Casino. And the further I got from that experience, the more I doubted it, fearing that what I had 'seen' was an agglomeration of my own memories of Luna and my mother, short-circuited into being while I was performing, rather than some highly specific memory of Loren's. Before leaving Las Vegas the following day, I had hired a former Pinkerton detective to track down the young man whose memories I thought I had glimpsed during the act. A number of people had seen him and his female companion in her red dress; it was the kind of assignment the detective himself had called difficult but routine. Yet he had come up with nothing – *zilch*, *zero*, *nada*, as he cabled me in Copenhagen two months later. So I wasn't quaking at this notion of a gumshoe on my trail in the Aegean.

Several months after settling into my house on the southwest coast of Naxos, one last mention of Jorge Gaspard crept into my life. I had brought home a bunch of newspapers – the international *Tribune*, *The Times*, *Le Monde* – as I did every couple of weeks, to catch up on the news. I didn't even keep a radio in that house, and I had no interest in reading the papers daily. In the theatrical listings in *Le Monde* an announcement caught my eye: Jorge Gaspard, the world-famous mentalist, was beginning a twelve-country tour with a new act and a new assistant, one Zuléifa Turais. And good luck to her, I thought, with a small sigh of relief.

I had spent that particular autumn day in typical fashion. Here was my life on Naxos in miniature: up early for a swim in the sea, walking a mile and back to the market for fruit, bread, and goat cheese, lunch, reading, siesta, a longer swim, and then riding into town for dinner. I had given up my Vespa and was leasing a jeep with which I explored every road on the island, dirt or paved, from the village of Moni, nestled like a white chess piece on a mountain precipice, to Apóllonas on the shore of a rocky cove. Occasionally I stayed in town late to listen to music at a taverna or have coffee with the one real friend I had made on the island, a woman about my age named Melitta, a silversmith with a studio in the maze of the Kastro.

Melitta was a small woman with short blond hair, finely shaped hands, and a high-pitched laugh. A native of Corfu, she had come to Naxos when her on-again, off-again engagement to a doctor in Athens remained stuck in its off-again stage. She had set up shop for a year, and five years later had no plans to leave. She like to wear long embroidered dresses and velvet berets fashioned in the old Venetian style, prominent in the oil paintings I had seen in the former governor's fortress. A sly, vivacious woman, she had managed to expand not only her business but her love life – quietly taking on a series of lovers – without compromising her privacy. In the closed and scrutinizing society of the island, this was no mean trick. She had many sides to her, and many friends to go with them, and through her I came to know people on the island I might not otherwise have met, from the abbess at the convent of St John Chrysostom in Grotta to the Czech artist in Lionas who had come to Naxos in order to paint the sea.

That night I had dined with her at an ouzeria, where a tinny bouzouki band played loudly and a fire crackled in the blue brick fireplace. It was the middle of October and, unlike Kauai, on Naxos no matter how warm the days, the nights were always chilly. I washed down small plates of grilled octopus and fried mullet with mineral water while Melitta tossed back smoky shots of barrel ouzo. In nearly eight years, since New Year's Day 1972, when I was dragged blind and half-dead from the tangled wreck of Francis's sports car, I hadn't touched a drink. Nor smoked, sniffed, or shot any drug. In the company of someone like Melitta, with whom I felt safe, I was tempted to have some wine with dinner, but the longevity of my abstinence always outweighed these desires. I didn't see any percentage in gambling with the one portion of my sanity that I could truly control.

After dinner, we met a new friend of Melitta's at a café on the harbor. He introduced himself to me as Sergius Voël, a onetime cat-tamer from a Belgian circus who the previous year, on his seventieth birthday, had retired to the island. Voël was his new name, he added, formally adopted after he had left the circus. 'Not an uncommon thing to do,' he said in his bass voice that pitched and rolled like a boat at sea, 'when beginning a second life. Did you know that El Greco, born in Crete, was in his first life known as Doménikos Theotokópoulos?' I thought of Zaren Eboli – a lifetime ago – telling me that

Jelly Roll Morton's original name was Ferdinand La Menthe.

Physically Voël didn't look seventy: he was a blunt, big-necked man, with large hands scarred from wielding whips and being nipped by razor-sharp teeth – a man of steely calm, with unblinking brown eyes, who had faced down tigers, lions, and panthers in locked cages. He lived alone outside of town in a stone tower surrounded by cornfields. Melitta told me he was popular around the island, with the reputation of a reclusive bon vivant, a cosmopolitan spirit in repose. At his tower he took in as many stray cats – Naxos had hundreds – as he could accommodate, whom he fed and nursed.

But Voël's latest passion, he confessed to Melitta and me, was the lost continent of Atlantis, ignited in him at the end of his circus career by a lady fire eater named Salome, from Santorini. A doctrinaire believer in the theory that Santorini, before its great volcanic eruption, had been the site of Atlantis, he regaled us with what he considered the most spurious Atlantis theories, including that of a man he had met several years earlier on Santorini. 'I liked him very much,' Voël said, 'despite the fact he had blinded himself to the truth. There we were on the scorched cliffs in Fira, overlooking the volcano's caldera, and he is telling me with a straight face that Atlantis, situated somewhere off Spain, disappeared underwater when an asteroid fell into the sea beside it.'

While we sipped our coffee and watched the big ferries whir up to the slip with their lights blazing to unload passengers, I showed Melitta and Voël the photographs I had taken the previous week. They were mostly compositional shots of cacti, olive trees, and rock formations on the beach. I took one photograph each day, had them blown up, and set them in an album, one to a page. As of that night, I had 147 such shots taken on Naxos, including three self-portraits composed by way of an old Venetian mirror with a sea-green copper frame. Tilting it away from the sun, I propped the mirror against my house's lone sink, an outdoor trough of white marble under an arbor sagging with grapevines. I placed the camera on the sink's edge, pointed at the mirror, and positioned my reflection carefully before activating the shutter at the end of a long cord. Publicity shots aside, I hadn't had a single photograph of myself taken in years; in these, wearing no makeup, illuminated by the pitiless Mediterranean sun, I saw myself as I never had before.

I had turned thirty-four in February and no longer retained the girlish looks I had carried well into my twenties. From my years in the tropics and my grueling nocturnal life as a performer, I had a faint web of crow's-feet beside my eyes, my forehead was creased by several thin lines, my nose was freckled, and my lips, too often sun-chapped, had grown puffier. But men still looked hard at me when I walked through the town, the local men and the visiting Europeans and Americans. I wore my hair long, combed straight back, and, as in the Pacific, it quickly lightened in the sun. Once again my body went from fish-white to tan to brown, and I was growing strong from swimming daily and returning to my old diet of fish and fruit. I knew, too, that thirty-four was still quite young, even though inside I sometimes felt as if I were well past fifty. After those first months on Naxos, falling into familiar rhythms, I had begun to be reinvigorated.

As for men, I had slept with no one since arriving on the island. On the road with Gaspard, I had had one-night stands when I thought I would go mad without some kind of release. With no close friends, and a scarcity of even casual acquaintances, I was sometimes desperate simply to have a warm body beside me. Living in hotels made it easy to find transitory partners – other performers, other lonely people, interesting travelers. Interesting enough, that is, to share maybe twelve hours with. Once I settled on Naxos, however, I became very cautious when it came to men. Melitta told me there were discreet men to whom she could introduce me –

'they would die for you,' she laughed – but I declined the offer. I wanted no trouble like the kind I'd found on Kauai. Anyway, I told myself there were other appetites to indulge in this place.

At the same time, being alone so much again, memories that I had tried to bury away began to preoccupy me. Memories of Cassiel in Manila which, after ten years, were still painful to revisit. I had been with a good number of men since then, some for much longer than I had been with him, but those four days at the Hôtel Alnilam, and the weeks preceding them on the *Repose*, remained alive in my head as no other period in my life. Why was that, I asked myself – what was it about him and the brief time we had together that truly kept me from wanting to be with anyone else? At one point, on Kauai, I had been looking for love; but, mostly, over all those years I had remained celibate for long stretches, or used brief affairs to keep love away. I wondered if the reason for this was that the time I had shared with Cassiel was so short. And that I was so young. In a war. Crazed out of my mind. On top of which he had disappeared so abruptly. Mysterious even when I knew him, he had become a mystery in the end. And that carried its own allure. But deep down I didn't believe it was my youth or the war or his disappearance. I had known I was in love with Cassiel that day on the *Repose* when, seeing his eyes fixed on me, I wended a path through all the other wounded men directly to his bed. It was as if I had known him always and always been in love with him. More deeply than I had ever loved anyone or anything. And nothing, and no one, I had encountered since then had supplanted or dislodged that feeling.

Voël finished his coffee and ordered a cîtron, the island's lemon liqueur, and began talking about Ariadne – another single woman washed ashore on Naxos.

'In the legend, after Theseus abandoned her, Dionysus found her on the beach, made her his queen, and when she died set the crown Aphrodite had fashioned for her among the constellations – the Corona Borealis. Before her death, Ariadne made a wish which Dionysus granted: that when the stars are properly aligned over Naxos, lost things can be found by those who pray to Zeus.'

'What do you mean by "properly"?' I asked, for he had piqued my interest.

'The position of the Corona Borealis. When it is directly over the island, look for your lost things and you will find them.'

'But when is that?' I asked.

'The Corona lies near Scorpio,' Voël replied. 'Scorpio appears over the island in the spring. In the village of Corona at the island's center – and named after that other Corona – they celebrate Scorpio's arrival in a nightlong festival. Next year it will be in April. While they search for lost things, the participants will wear masks to conceal their identities.'

'It's true, amazing things turn up,' Melitta said, 'some of them having been missing for many years. Articles of clothing, money, keepsakes, even goats and sheep. Last year, an old man found a pocket watch he had lost on his wedding night, still keeping perfect time.'

'Do they find people, too?' I asked quietly.

Voël looked at me with a crooked smile.

'I don't believe that has ever happened,' Melitta said. 'But you never know.'

Six months later, the night before the Festival of Scorpio, I barely slept. It was a windy night and the sea was crashing. Bands of moonlight streamed through the shutters and the cypress branches were swaying. But it was the cicadas in the scrub brush that kept me awake, their high-pitched, metallic drone that must have filled the ears of the ancient Greeks when they invented their Furies.

Finally I got up and brewed a cup of mandrake leaf tea, which the apothecary had recommended as a sleep remedy. At the kitchen table I went through my daily photographs that now filled three albums. I had been living on Naxos for a full year, and as I turned the laminated pages, the days and weeks passed before me: the slanting rains in late fall; the smoky winter light; forest anemones blooming in March; and then the first hint of blinding summer skies that had appeared that very week. It had been a peaceful fall and winter, cooking for myself for the first time in years, exploring the island on foot, and most nights reading until my eyes hurt. After exhausting my Latin library, I attempted some of the Greek historians, whose books I ordered from Athens. It was Strabo's *Geography*, the chapter on Naxos itself, I was poring over later that night – a first, for me, to be in an ancient place while reading about it – when the mandrake leaf took effect.

At four o'clock the following afternoon, I drove into Naxia to buy the mask required of all visitors to the festival before I headed out to Corona. Suggesting it was good luck to get the mask that very day, Melitta had shown me the shop where I ought to go. Several alleys away from her own workshop in the Kastro, down steep marble steps, it had a door constructed of driftwood with an oarlock for a handle and a brass hand for a knocker. The shop itself was very small and dimly lit. Scented charcoal burned in a brass bowl and flute music was playing somewhere in the back. The floor was a mosaic of colored seashells that formed a stingray. Mythological scenes were depicted on large tiles propped against the wall: Dionysus presiding over revellers in a moonlit vineyard; Theseus strangling the Minotaur in the labyrinth; Ariadne watching the Athenian ship disappear over the horizon. A glass case beneath the counter was filled with masks, also designed around the Ariadne myth: a young woman's face tragically frozen; a leering masculine face with grape clusters for hair; and various animal masks – bulls, owls, dogs, and foxes.

A beaded curtain parted in the rear of the store and a thin bearded man appeared. About my own age, he wore a multicolored vest and his long platinum hair was held fast with a scarlet bandanna. He had very dark, direct eyes.

'A mask?' he said simply.

I nodded. 'Melitta sent me.'

He smiled, and after looking at me closely, pointed to a small wall mirror.

Then he patiently showed me one mask after another from the glass case. We didn't exchange another word, but it was clear none of the masks satisfied me – or him. I was beginning to despair when he put up one finger and murmured, 'Wait, please.'

Disappearing through the beaded curtain, he brought back a flat cardboard box and removed a mask like no other I had seen: a mermaid with crescent eyes, tiny stars for eyebrows, and coral lips verging on a smile. I held the mask to my face, and at once the man nodded his approval. Looking in the mirror, I felt a rush of pleasure – almost of recognition, so perfectly did the mask suit me. I thanked the man and paid him while he put the mask back into its box. Then he made me a small bow and showed me to the door.

I descended from the Kastro in the direction of the harbor, where I had left my jeep. It was that strange limbo hour at the end of siesta, and zigzagging through the warrens of houses and shops, I encountered no one. Every so often a twisting whitewashed alley would end in an explosion of color, a dense flower garden or wall of bougainvillea. These squares of bright color seemed to have been precisely fitted, as if from above, into a sprawling geometrical puzzle. A jumble of trapezoids, triangles, and rectangles, the town of Naxia was as much a labyrinth as the one Ariadne had helped Theseus to negotiate in Crete. And it seemed that whenever I walked through it, I came on a place I had never seen before.

This time it happened near the archaeological museum, a neighborhood I thought I knew well. Turning a corner, I was standing before an unfamiliar church in a windy, deserted plaza. The church was dedicated to

St Antony, the desert hermit who lived to be 105 years old in a cave by the Red Sea. His church on Naxos could not have been in a less desert-like setting. Ringed by eucalyptus trees, hibiscus vines climbing its white walls, it was located at one end of a diamond-shaped orchard. A wrought-iron fence surrounded the orchard, and according to a plaque at its gate, the church had been rebuilt after the Nazis bombed the original building. Only the foundation and the west wall had survived the bombing. The enormous ceiling mural, executed in the sixteenth century by the Venetian painter Francesco Gozzoli on a commission from the doge, had disappeared after the war, carted off apparently in a thousand fragments. I was sorry, for I would have liked to see this ceiling, which the plaque described as a celestial landscape populated by hundreds of angels in concentric circles.

The orchard was so beautiful, the foliage silver, the wind fragrant, that I decided to walk through it before proceeding down the hill. It contained only fruit trees, fig, plum, orange, and lemon, as well as some pomegranate bushes. All but the fig trees were laden with fruit, but it was one of the orange trees that caught my eye. Or was it a lemon tree? Its branches contained both fruits, and also what looked like combinations of the two – big, gnarled, amber ovals. The tree was solitary, in one corner, and at its base, fringed with moss, was a wooden sign that read BIZZARRIA ORANGE. In Greek, the sign detailed the tree's history. *An offspring of the first true hybrid*, it read, grown in Florence by one Barone Zelo. Zelo married a Venetian lady born on Naxos and in 1660 brought a grafting from his famous tree to the island; since then, the tree had reproduced itself several times. Looking around quickly, on an impulse I went up on tiptoe, plucked one of the bizzarria oranges, and dropped it into my pocket.

An hour later, I was midway to Corona in my jeep, climbing the tall mountains of the interior. Night had fallen fast. The moon rose, its craters sharply visible, and the stars began to shine. As promised, the Corona Borealis and Scorpio beside it – Antares bright as a drop of blood – were directly overhead. The air was cold in the mountains, and I turned on the jeep's heater to warm my legs. In an isolated town like Corona, where I would be one of only a few foreigners, it would have been disrespectful to wear anything but a white or black dress, as the local women did, depending on whether or not they were widows. I wore white, though sometimes at that point in my life I felt like a widow. Certainly I did that night, driving into the darkness, increasingly preoccupied with thoughts of the people and things I had lost over the years, until I saw the lights of Corona twinkling in a deep valley.

I had been to the village once before, in daylight, to see its streets and buildings that were composed of marble. It wasn't because the inhabitants were wealthy that marble had been used so lavishly; on the contrary, with a quarry a kilometer away, marble was the cheapest available building material. Now as I entered those streets, they seemed, in the moonlight, to be illuminated from below. A crowd was milling in the main square, everyone in masks. In my travels I had seen Carnaval in Río and Mardi Gras in New Orleans, but this reminded me most of the Venetian Carnival, on a much smaller scale. Blinking colored lights were strung through the trees and around door frames. Several troubador bands – with ouds, bouzoukis, accordions, and drums – wandered the streets. Torches flared under the trees and fires salted with incense burned in steel drums, filling the air with the powerful scents of cinnamon and myrrh. The sweet, purple local wine was being served outdoors from barrels.

Purple was Ariadne's color. Young girls in purple tunics were performing the crane dance, a complicated step dating back to the Cretan labyrinth, where it was danced by the maidens to appease the Minotaur. Old men in black felt masks wore the military medals and ribbons of their youth. Goats festooned with flowers and bells were tethered to trees, braying, and all the caged birds in the town, from magpies to parrots, were hung outside their owners' windows, with purple ribbons through the cages. Previously lost objects, recovered during festivals past, were also displayed in purple baskets on people's doorsteps. And they were as varied as Melitta had indicated: from the mundane (key rings and gloves) to the esoteric (a glass tortoise, with a hinged shell, that was a jewelry box) to the unexpected (a pet ferret). On one doorstep there was even a forlorn little girl with onyx eyes, sitting on her heels with her legs tucked under, the sight of whom made my pulse quicken: perhaps you *could* find lost people, after all, I thought.

All at once everyone grew silent, and the air hummed with expectation as the priest offered a blessing from the steps of the church. There were at least two hundred people in the square, and all of us had fastened our masks in place. Everywhere there were foxes and bulls, Ariadnes and Dionysuses, but I was the only mermaid in sight, and I attracted a few stares. What was once a pagan event, I thought, had become a fixture in the local church calendar, and I watched closely as four men in white robes, wearing owl masks, strode single file from an unlit alley where dogs were barking. Swinging censers with burning coals, they split up and walked to the corners of the square. Drummers perched on roof-tops pounded bass drums in unison, and were answered by other drums at the edge of town. Then the men in robes simultaneously drank off glasses of wine while the crowd broke up into four groups, each one following a different man.

I was in the group that walked around the church, through a smaller square, up the tortuously steep alleys that climbed into the mountains. In a very short time, I saw two people find lost objects from their pasts. First, an old woman in a fox mask discovered a pair of cat's-eye earrings from her youth in the basin of a fountain. Then a heavyset, middle-aged man, wearing a bull mask, came on a fountain pen under an oleander bush. It was his father's pen, he exclaimed, lost at the time of his death. As people gathered around him, the man uncapped the pen and on a scrap of paper showed them that it could still write. In fresh blue ink he printed the date, *April 30, 1980*, and then rushed off, surrounded by companions now, for good luck in these searches was reputed to rub off.

That didn't seem to be the case with me: neither lost objects nor lost people came my way at the Festival of Scorpio. I followed my group around for several hours, then wandered alone until well past midnight, when I admitted to myself how disappointed I was to have come up empty-handed. As the festival wound down, I watched an assortment of islanders return to the main square to lay what they had found on a purple blanket on the church steps: a red fedora, a violin bow, a set of false teeth, a pair of green leather slippers, a white cat with a broken tail, and so on. By that time, the wine was flowing fast. Platters of roasted lamb, potato casseroles, pilaf with almonds, plates of figs and olives, baskets of grapes, and great circular loaves of rye bread had been set out on long tables. People were dancing to the troubador bands, who were now playing as one. Some of the drunkest revellers had removed their masks, though it was forbidden to do so before dawn.

Picking at a plate of food, I sat quietly on a low wall under a fig tree and watched the dancers from behind my mermaid's mask. The musicians played with increasing abandon, never stopping for a break, and the dancers kept up with them. I fingered my star bracelet, and as I had often done before, reviewed the Christmas morning on which I had first seen those stars when they were still jagged pieces of shrapnel embedded in Cassiel's flesh. The sounds of that time came back to me: the muffled *whomp-whomp* of chopper blades in the night, the hum and click of my X-ray machine, the clinking of surgical instruments, the moans and screams of men, and their death wails. And then the smells: iodine, alcohol, tannic acid, and plasma, and the sickly metallic scent of blood, and the hot winds heavy with phosphorus and napalm smoke that blew out to sea from the jungle. That smoke was in my nostrils now, I thought, raising my head as the four men in white, swinging their censers, crisscrossed the square and disappeared together behind the church, signalling the official end of the festival.

I pushed my mermaid's mask back on my head as I walked to my jeep. Someone had scattered gardenia petals on the hood, and as I drove out of town they gusted high into the air. At that moment, on an impulse, I decided to take a detour to the eastern shore to watch the sun rising up out of the sea. Living as I did on the western side, this was something I had never seen on Naxos. Though I had been up all night, I was not tired so much as overstimulated, and I thought driving by the sea would calm me.

Descending from the mountains, I crossed the great gypsum plain stretching from Apéiranthos to Moutsana that seemed, with each mile, to tilt downward toward the sea. On the narrow road, thick with dust, I passed only a farmer leading a white mule and a boy hunched over on a motorbike. A few houses were set back on treeless plots, chickens pecking in the baked yards and goats grazing on the jagged weeds. Nearer the coast, the wind grew brackish with the smells of the sea. And then suddenly, up and over a ridge, I was in Moutsana.

In its brief and improbable heyday the emery mining capital of Europe, Moutsana was now a ghost town. Cats darted across the streets and wild dogs lurked in the shadows. I passed a boarded-up restaurant, a former ferry office filled with nesting birds, and the foundation of a hotel that had burnt down years before. The town ended abruptly near the remains of the cable car trellis that had run from the mines to the harbor. Beyond that, after a rusted sign cautioning hazardous driving conditions, the road continued on between a rocky beach and jutting white cliffs. One of the few roads on the island with which I was unfamiliar, it was a soft mixture of sand and limestone powder, for which I had to downshift into first gear. I gripped the steering wheel high and stiffly, with both hands. To my left, the sea was dark, but the horizon had begun to glow a pearly gray.

After a few more miles, the horizon went from violet to pink and the stars grew dimmer. I parked the jeep on the shoulder and walked down to the sea. The shoreline there was all coarse white sand punctuated by coves with pebble beaches. Dunes dotted with salt grass and thistles separated the beach from the road. In that transitional, ashen light the entire expanse looked lunar, right down to the craters in the road and on the cliffside. Thirsty, my lips coated with limestone dust, I realized I still had the bizzarria orange in the pocket of my dress, and I peeled it as I walked on. The knobby rind pulled away in thick strips. The pulp was amber-colored and firm. When I bit into one of the wedges, my tongue was flooded with bittersweet juice.

The wind was whistling and sawing as it swept in from sea, trailing sheets of spray. As I crossed the dunes toward the nearest cove, shielding my eyes with one hand, I heard the buzz of an airplane overhead. I thought I saw some flashing lights high in the sky, but they could as easily have been falling stars as navigational lights. In an instant they were gone and the buzzing had ceased. Turning around, I scanned the beach and the cliffs, and when I had come full circle, facing the cove again, I blinked hard and rubbed my eyes. I thought I was seeing things, for there was a man silhouetted against the sea, just emerging from the surf, as if he had dropped out of nowhere.

I stood still with my head tucked down against the wind and watched him follow the waterline away from the cove, onto the wet sand. As he drew nearer, I saw that he was a tall, broad-shouldered man wearing a rubber body suit. He had blue goggles pushed back into his wavy black hair, and clipped onto his belt, beside a sheathed knife, was a small net filled with shellfish. In his hand he held a single creature, still wriggling, which I couldn't make out clearly. He walked with a firm gait, studying whatever it was he was holding. Finally, when he was no more than twenty yards away, he glanced up and froze at the sight of me. I was so intent on him that I had forgotten how strange I myself would appear in that remote place: a woman in a white dress, her hair flying out the sides of the mermaid mask pushed back on her head.

Several seconds ticked away, the waves rolling in, the wind gusting the sand, before he started walking toward me. The closer he came, the more he blurred for me against the sea – like a shadow. Another ghost? No, if he was a ghost, it was of a very different sort. His lungs were heaving. His powerful hands were flesh and blood. Muscles rippled beneath his rubber suit. Over his heart, I could now make out an insignia: a star-speckled blue circle intersected by red wings, with the initials NASA stitched in bold letters. An American – and an astronaut, I thought with surprise – on an island that didn't even boast an airport? Then, when he was just ten yards from me, I could identify that wriggling creature: a starfish. And an instant later, god help me, my knees went soft when I saw his face fully. His eyes. His eyes gray with the silver lights, older but the same as he came right up to me. Half-smiling, curious, his mouth the same too, though harder now, and his hair tinged with gray and his forehead creased, a thin scar crossing it on a diagonal. I raised my head and pulled my mask off, and watched his curiosity turn to astonishment and then fear. I saw my own face – just as astonished and fearful – reflected in his in those first few moments when we stood just two feet apart, in the same time and place, after all the fractured years of other times and places among the living and the dead.

When he finally recovered his senses enough to move, it was to touch my cheek, softly, tentatively. Then he touched my hair. His lips parted, but he didn't speak. He shook his head slowly. And then, before he took my hands in his, I held up my bracelet for him as the tears began running down my dusty cheeks and the stars faded in the broad sky, and, dripping seawater, a starfish in his hand, Geza Cassiel stood before me.

15

The Hotel Rigel

Even before noon it was 105° that day and when the
wind blew in from the desert you hoped it would stop.
From the roof of the Hotel Rigel, at the end of Corona
Street on the outskirts of Albuquerque, I could see the
silver ribbon of the Río Puerco. This was the river, I
remembered well, that Calzas had first shown me from
Acoma, the one Dalia had read to me about, which Friar
Varcas had followed northward from Los Lunas after he
was bitten by the vampire at the way station. Whether
or not Varcas ever reached Albuquerque, and what he
may have done there if he did, Dalia had never said. But
I felt sure he was there now – and Dalia, too.

Twice I thought I had sighted him: first, when I went
to the Revenant Press at 3000 Daedalus Circle to inquire
after Dalia's translation of Varcas's manuscript, and a
pale bearded man with a hooked nose peered at me from
behind a curtained window, shaking his head that they
were closed; and then, again, on a dark deserted street
corner near my own hotel where the same man was slipping into a black car with tinted windows behind a tall
woman in a red dress. I couldn't see her face, but I had
no doubt who the woman was. My heart sank, but at the
same time I had no desire to chase after them.

For this and other reasons – including the stifling heat
and bad air that seemed impervious to air-conditioning
– Albuquerque was a city in which I felt anxious and

off-balance from the moment I arrived. On previous visits, the city had struck me much the way Phoenix did: outside the glass towers at its center, a bland, character-less place, with baked vegetation, sun-blanked streets, and shabby peripheral neighborhoods. This time Albuquerque seemed oppressive in a sinister way as well: there was a crime wave that summer – a murder a day, the headlines screamed for forty straight days, as well as dozens of unsolved cases of arson, bank robbery, and car theft. Vandalism was out of control. Even the suicide rate had skyrocketed: two a day over those same forty days. Neither the newspapers nor the police could explain it, though they came up with ingenious theories, from the magnetic waves emanating from high-voltage wires to a recent series of underground nuclear tests near White Sands.

I had a different explanation. Even to a longtime resident of Las Vegas like me, the human landscape of Albuquerque seemed to be riddled with grotesques; the city felt more infernal with each passing day. Dalia had warned me on our last night together about all the people she had recently seen in this area who seemed to be one thing but were really vampires. Now I was seeing, or imagining, them, too – occasional flashes, visible for the blink of an eye, of fox ears, hawk eyes, or lizard scales on someone in the recesses of an elevator, or on the high landing of a stairwell, or in a restaurant kitchen through a curtain of steam. A floating population that was everywhere – and nowhere.

It didn't help my state of mind that I was in town, not to build something, but to destroy it; in fact, to oversee the demolition of the very building I was standing atop, surveying the desert. I was twenty-three, a licensed architect now, serving my apprenticeship with Calzas, and this was my first job. The Hotel Rigel, a twelve-story building erected seventy-four years earlier, in 1905, and vacant since 1971, was one of those orange-red brick buildings with marble and terra-cotta trim common to the Southwest at that time. It was as solid as the bedrock upon which it had been erected, and it saddened me to think I was helping to engineer its reduction to a mountain of rubble. After the rubble was cleared away, it would be replaced by a civic center – auditorium, theater, gym – which Calzas had helped design. A worthy project, I thought, but still wished they had chosen a different site. I had been in town a week, setting up the demolition with a specialized crew of eight men. The foreman and I were making a last circuit of the building before the men activated the complex set of explosive charges which had already been put in place and would be detonated at four o'clock.

Vitruvius's *Ten Books on Architecture* was among my primary reading when I was tutored by Labusi, who felt the building of earthly palaces and memory palaces were closely related activities and who once observed to me somberly that the wrecking ball and the construction crane were of equal importance to the architect. I don't know if Labusi had culled this idea from Vitruvius (I never found any such statement in his books), but I realized that he intended me to hear it as a large metaphorical statement on the human condition, for he went on to draw an analogy between the architect who must both raze and erect buildings and the physician who ought to possess both the skills required for bringing an infant into the world and for seeing an aged person out of it. Labusi often offered up his most valuable nuggets to me in this fashion.

I realized now just how much of my education had been geared to the notion that I would someday be an architect. Of course this was Samax's doing: it was he who had set Labusi's curriculum. And no mean cartographer when it came to charting the lives of others, he had mapped mine out even more closely than I had suspected. For starters, the emphasis he had laid on geometry and trigonometry, drawing lessons, and all the memory work. I recalled that on the very day my life coincided with Samax's, he was studying first a blueprint, in the abandoned factory, and then a map, while we flew cross-country in his jet. The map, which he had shared with me, was of the northern Sahara, but it was only years later that it occurred to me to ask Calzas what it was they were converting that factory into.

'A museum,' he said after the slightest hesitation. 'For collectors. Your uncle came up with the idea that people like him, with private collections, needed a place to exhibit on their own terms, outside the museum bureaucracies. To rotate in the stuff the public rarely has a chance to see, without pigeonholing it in some easy-to-swallow package. But his fellow collectors were gun-shy – they were more comfortable with the bureaucracies – and so the idea never got off the ground.' Calzas shook his head. 'As you know, quitting isn't one of Samax's strong points. He was pretty pissed, but it would have been a disaster if he had tried to go it alone.'

'So what happened to the factory?' I said.

'He sold it to a real estate company. What they did, I don't know.'

When I went to Samax with the same question, I received the same response. Within a year of my coming to Las Vegas, neither he nor Calzas ever again set foot in the former factory. And it would be twelve years before I returned there myself, soon after my twenty-second birthday, in the wake of an utterly unexpected series of events that left me overwhelmed by the need to find out what had happened to Alma all those years ago.

The first of these events was the unannounced return of Auro to Las Vegas. Touring with the jazz quintet he had formed the previous year, he was booked in the lounge at The Aladdin for a week. One member of the quintet, the bassist, a Tunisian emigré from Atlanta, was Auro's lover.

'Frankie Fooo,' the bassist introduced himself to me, extending his hand, 'with three *o*'s.' He was a short, thin man with a dark complexion, a ponytail, and teeth straight as piano keys. Smiling broadly, he added, 'The third *o* is the note you hold.'

Frankie Fooo talked fast and he talked a lot, proclaiming to me at once, and later to Ivy in my presence, that he and Auro 'were the greatest pair of rhythm men, ever. Bar none.' 'Bar none,' Auro added emphatically, tapping his fingernails on his ride cymbal. His black and silver drums glittered, the bass drum emblazoned with the band's name, THE ECHO QUINTET, and its logo, an orange parrot.

Auro had changed in all sorts of ways, obvious and subtle, in the five years since I had seen him. I still would have recognized him anywhere, but the part of him with which I had been most familiar – frightened and retiring – was not apparent. Or maybe it just manifested itself in other ways, internally. But I wasn't sure; it was my belief that taking up the drums had been a last-ditch survival instinct on Auro's part, and that the ceaseless hours he had put in becoming a professional – and then making a name for himself – had burnt away much of the fear that had crippled him all his life. On the surface, he had transformed himself completely. That night I was treated to the sight of him – who at one time had been forced to dress in plaid shorts and white shirts with bow ties – wearing a lime-green sharkskin suit with purple silk lapels, a shimmering tangerine shirt of Indian silk, a green-and-gold checkered tie, and pointy gold lizard boots. On his left hand Auro wore five rings – topaz, amethyst, turquoise, opal, cat's-eye – spread over three fingers. Gold bracelets jangled on his wrists, and an onyx medallion dangled from his neck on a long chain. And the wraparound shades he seldom removed.

Physically he had filled out a bit: his chest not so sunken, his shoulders slightly broader. His curly hair was long and he sported a goatee. His black eyes were steadier, and the welt of a scar where his left eyebrow should have been actually gave his face more character now. I believe someone's mouth reveals as much about him as his eyes; Auro's mouth had become warmer since I had last seen him. His lips were no longer tightly compressed, or chewed on, or chronically chapped, as they had always been. As for his hands, the drumming had transformed them outright: he had gone away with the thin, too-white hands of a boy and returned with the wrists and fingers of a man, tendons and veins bulging powerfully when he played.

Auro was affectionate to me, full of questions about my life over the previous years. He used our old method, writing on a scratch pad in his tiny script. He seemed glad to see Desirée, and was especially animated when Zaren Eboli came to hear him play. But from the moment Ivy walked into the lounge at The Aladdin, he tried to steer clear of her. For Ivy, that week must have been hellish – certainly she ended up making it so for me. Despite her pleas, and an invitation from Desirée, Auro steadfastly refused to come out to the Hotel Canopus. Samax happened to be away that month, on a rare trip abroad, undergoing hydrotherapy and acupuncture treatments in Kyoto to ease the continuing aftereffects of his stroke. But that had nothing to do with it. Having left the hotel, Auro told me, he had no intention of ever going back.

'I understand,' I said to him. 'You left for good.'

'For good,' he nodded vigorously.

Ivy didn't understand. And there was no reason I would have expected her to. She had been laying low for those five years, so elusive in the end that she became nearly invisible. She who had thrown her weight around so haughtily during my early years at the hotel was now even less of a presence than Dolores, who at 103 still maintained her daily routine, sitting in her niche in the garden every afternoon, alone or with Labusi when he wasn't competing in a billiard tournament. Ivy had aged badly. She was one of those women who retain their good looks unchanged up to a certain point and then lose them all at once, as if some corrosive chemical has been introduced that effects overnight what the natural ageing process should have produced over many years. The hollows around Ivy's eyes and mouth had so inten-sified that when I glimpsed her in dim light across the lobby or down a corridor, her face often resembled a skull mask, sharply delineated into pools of black and white. She always dined alone in her rooms, and barely spoke to anyone, and more and more frequently disappeared to Reno or Lake Tahoe for weeks at a time. She was almost totally alienated from Samax. The incident with the hummingbird pendant had seriously undermined her standing with him, and after his stroke he shut her out altogether. I knew how his mind worked: he wasn't going to allow anyone as untrustworthy as Ivy near him when he was so vulnerable. But it was Auro's absence that truly knocked the wind out of her. Ivy could deal with the enmity of someone like me – she fed off such negative energy – and Samax didn't really frighten her as much as he might have thought, but Auro's slamming the door in her face had been a serious trauma. For twenty years Auro had been all she had, as she often, gratingly, reminded him, especially after Nestor died. Now, aside from that single postcard with the two-word message, I'M OKAY, Auro had maintained a total silence toward her – unbroken even at Christmas and on birthdays – and it had been eating at her like a poison for which she had no antidote.

So, when she entered the empty red-and-gold lounge of The Aladdin in mid-afternoon and saw Auro adjusting his cymbals on the crescent-shaped stage, Ivy's knees buckled and her breath caught in her throat. I actually took a step toward her, to offer support, but she recovered in time to cast me a baleful glance from behind her dark glasses. She wore a long black dress, and black cotton gloves, despite the heat; according to Labusi, she so badly bit and picked at her fingers and cuticles as to have disfigured them.

At the sight of her, Auro pulled up abruptly but remained calm. He endured a long embrace from her, then stepped back, disengaging as smoothly as he could, when she placed her hand on the back of his neck and pulling him closer began whispering in his ear. With no qualms about how it looked to anyone else, this secretive posture had always been the one Ivy assumed when she wanted to relate to him intimately. But Auro was having none of it, and he abruptly chose that moment – with a sharp nod – to have the members of his band introduce themselves to us.

Ivy remained fixated on Auro, and the moment the band members were done, she approached him again. This time he politely waved her away. Being in Ivy's presence always disturbed me, but the sight of her in black gloves was in itself a shock, bringing back my very unhappy memories of our first encounter, at the planetarium. But that aside, to watch her clumsy attempt at reconnecting with Auro, acting as if nothing had changed in all that time when he so clearly had changed – that gloved hand clasping his neck, exerting its full variety of pressures – made me gag. Whatever feelings of the same sort were churning up inside Auro he successfully masked – at least to my eyes.

Playing countless gigs night after night for years in smoky dives up and down the East Coast and through the South, living in hotels that were not, by a long shot, Canopus-style establishments, getting bookings in New Orleans and, finally, at the bigger New York clubs, and now touring the West for the first time en route to Los Angeles to finish recording his debut LP – making himself, in other words, into a performer – had brought out in Auro a toughness that obviously was not restricted to his professional life. I had seen traces of it – for example on that day when I set fire to the ghost town – in our years growing up together. But never had I caught in Auro's eyes the centeredness under pressure, his pupils like sparks off a flint, that was so apparent that day at The Aladdin. Still, Auro's echolalia was unchanged, and I noted soon enough that Frankie Fooo had assumed the role I used to play as Auro's verbal prompter, tail-ending his sentences with phrases Auro could pick up on.

'We gotta ask everyone to leave while we rehearse,' Frankie announced, 'but please come back tonight.'

Auro nodded emphatically. 'Please come back tonight,' he repeated, shifting only the emphasis in the words.

We did, and the set they played that night was a gem. I had to believe Auro was pumped up, what with his relatives out there – for better or worse – hearing exactly what it was he had been up to during all those years away. The Echo Quintet played practically in its entirety the contents of the LP that was released four months later, a double album destined for cult status entitled *Echo Chamber* that would gain Auro, who composed eleven of its fourteen cuts, an instant following in the jazz world. It was the advance buzz for this album that was getting them gigs at high-end venues like The Aladdin.

I had watched Auro drum many times when he was taking lessons at the hotel, but to see him onstage, playing with, and off of, other musicians, was a different experience altogether. He was an extraordinary rhythm man, the echolalia an asset for once, enabling him with the subtlest antennae to anticipate and answer the sounds his partners produced. The intense symbiosis he set in motion made the band one of the tightest I had ever heard. When he launched into his solos, it was with passion and a minimum of ostentation – no twirling drumsticks or overwrought cymbal action – all his flourishes tightly in the service of the music. All of this was made sweeter by the fact I was watching Auro display his talents before a packed house on the Strip. I was sitting at a front-row table with Desirée and Zaren Eboli. Ivy chose to sit alone, farther back, nursing a martini. Though she had been working night and day at her silent typewriter in a corner of the greenhouse, Desirée looked ravishing that night in a blue leather miniskirt and studded jacket. Eboli, who had been holed up for weeks with a bevy of new spiders he had brought in from Utah, had put on a silver tuxedo jacket for the occasion and ordered a magnum of champagne for our table. He was particularly proud of Auro, to whom he'd given many pointers on performing from his own days in the piano bars of the Latin Quarter, never dreaming the boy would one day employ them as a big-time performer. Auro's way of repaying him came at the very end of the set when the quintet performed a tribute to Jelly Roll Morton – a medley of rags from 'Dead Man Blues' to 'Star Jam', which pleased Eboli mightily.

When I grabbed a few minutes alone with Auro backstage, it was awkward at first. We embraced; I congratulated him. But there was too much to say, too much had happened. I understood why his silence toward Ivy had had to encompass all the rest of us, including me: to effect such a difficult break he'd had to make it a complete one. But that hadn't made it any easier for me. Over the previous years, I was surprised just how acutely I had missed his companionship, our late-night communings in the quincunx garden. I knew that the telephone had of course always been an impossible device for Auro – he couldn't even say hello first – but I wished he had been able to send me a follow-up to that one postcard of Times Square lit up at night. At the same time I realized his continued correspondence might have tipped Ivy off to his whereabouts, for the Hotel Canopus could be a very small place when it came to such information. But there was more to it than that.

The most elementary verbal communication – taken for granted by most people – was the central issue of Auro's life. His frustrations thereof had defined his personality. Concentrating fiercely on an alternate form of communication like music had turned into a life-or-death proposition for him, his only hope of breaking through. With the members of his band, music was the common language; the verbal interchanges that accompanied the music's creation were secondary. With Frankie Fooo, apparently, Auro had also been introduced to the language of love, including sex – non-verbal communication in its purest form; like music, it must have effected radical alterations in Auro's internal

442

workings. When he had run away from the hotel, after all, Auro was not only a budding musician who had never performed publicly, but also an utterly inexperienced virgin. In short, aside from escaping Ivy and being on his own for the first time – huge factors in themselves – one reason he had remained strictly incommunicado had to be that he was simply overwhelmed by these powerful new sensations, sexual as well as musical.

Or so I concluded, even before I had entered his over-air-conditioned dressing room and found him sitting alone, pensive, before the long pink-lit horizontal mirror dusty with makeup powder. His face lit up when I told him how much I loved his music. Knowing the emotional pressure he was under just by being back in Las Vegas, I tried to hold some of my own feelings in check. I thought he'd do the same and – in true Samax family fashion – our feelings would somehow cancel themselves out.

'I'm really proud of you, Auro,' I said. 'And I missed you so much.'

Instead of holding back his feelings, Auro burst into sobs and said, 'Missed you so much.'

And that was it. We both had a good cry until Frankie Fooo and their saxophonist knocked on the door. Auro and I made a date for the next day, and I left. Of all the people who had disappeared in my life, I thought, Auro was the first ever to come back.

As I made my way to the parking lot, Ivy stepped out suddenly from between a pair of sleek tour buses. She had been waiting for me. Desirée had already returned to the hotel with Eboli. Behind me, the after-midnight crowd was entering the casino in clusters. In her shades and black dress, Ivy looked like the guest at a funeral who's had one too many drinks. Which caught me off-guard, for in even the worst of times I had never known her to be a drinker. But maybe for Ivy this *was* the worst of times.

'He'll talk to you,' she said disdainfully, 'but I wasn't even allowed backstage.'

443

'I'm sorry—'

'You're not sorry! You've never been sorry. And you never gave a damn about Auro, but now you pretend to be his friend.'

'I am his friend, and he knows it.'

'Don't tell me what Auro knows,' she snapped.

The gin fumes on her breath made me wince. I tried to step around her, but she blocked my way. 'I have to go,' I said.

'No,' she shook her head.

'Ivy, get out of my way.'

'You going to hit me this time?' Among her many grievances, she had never forgiven me for standing up to her when she slapped me as a kid, the night I first met Auro.

'Don't talk crazy,' I said.

'Crazy? You think you're so smart,' she sneered, 'but you don't know anything.'

I tried to step around her again.

'You don't even know who you really are,' she went on, blocking me again.

'What?'

'I thought that might grab you,' she said with a sharp laugh. 'You're a bastard so many times over, you must have lost track. Tell me again how many times you were orphaned, Enzo,' she said in a voice of mock concern. 'Or should I say *Loren*?'

'Fuck you.'

'That's more like it. Twice? Or three times, counting that "aunt" of yours – I forget her name.'

'You'd better stop now.'

'Going to hit me?'

'What do you want from me, Ivy?'

Her mouth twisted up in a smile. 'Surprise! I already got it, a long time ago.'

'Yeah? Then why don't you leave me alone?'

'I took something from you and you didn't even know it,' she said through her teeth. 'You still don't know it.'

Somehow, afterward, I was sure I had known at that

moment what she was about to tell me. Known, too, that it would change everything for me.

'The letter you and Samax wrote to your aunt, that he asked me to send her by messenger – guess what?' A long pause, then she dropped her voice to a whisper. 'I never sent it. That's right, so she never knew what happened to you. Never could have known.'

'That's not possible,' I said, knowing instantly it must be true.

'Oh no?'

'You're lying.' But as her words sank in, it was as if a gun had gone off beside my ear: my head was ringing, and everything around me for miles was crashing to a standstill, and all I could think was, god help me, Alma, what did we do to you.

Ivy was gloating, savoring the moment. 'So far as she knew, you were kidnapped and murdered,' she went on. 'And why not? An orphan, a castoff; if Samax hadn't butted in, that's probably how you would've ended up.'

'You must be lying,' I repeated, my voice coming from far away.

'You can tell yourself that,' she said.

My legs, my feet, then the ground beneath me turned to vapor, until it felt as if I was standing on nothing at all. I closed my eyes and saw Alma, not as she had appeared in my dreams all those years, but far more care-ridden and in a much darker place. It hit me what sort of fear and guilt she must have felt back then – she was even younger than I was now – and how it would have worn her down. As a child, I was convinced that what Samax had done, spiriting me away, had benefited both Alma and me, freeing her of a terrible burden; instead, an even worse one had been imposed – one that, it seemed to me now, could never be lifted. In a matter of seconds, the many alternate lives I had over time envisioned Alma leading were wiped away. Again I revisited that planetarium, seeing us rise from our seats, a twenty-year-old woman and a ten-year-old boy, and jostle in a press of bodies up the aisle where a gloved hand took mine. I watched Alma search frantically through the sea of faces. She was panicked to a degree I had not allowed myself to imagine before, having reassured myself that later that very day she would receive the letter from Samax which would alleviate her fears. But there had been no letter. And where was Alma now? Across seas of time and space, in that long-ago spot, I had slipped off the edge of her world when someone turned it upside down, and it was true, she would never, could never, have known how or why this happened to her.

Just a couple of feet away as she dropped all this on me, Ivy hadn't flinched. Admitting such an act of cruelty toward someone she had never even met, whose life she had so casually sabotaged, did not faze her. So long as she was lashing out at me, her actions were justified in her own mind. But why, I asked myself? What in her own past provided that justification? And what were her insides made of to contain a secret so toxic for many years? Labusi once told me that when Alexander the Great was poisoned, the toxin was so virulent the only container it wouldn't eat through was an ass's hoof. Ivy's stomach must have been like that.

Still reeling, I braced myself against the side of the bus even as Ivy backed away from me. I could barely focus on her now, but for a moment thought she actually looked frightened: perhaps something in my face made her believe I really was going to strike her finally. I wish it had been that easy, but with each passing moment she grew smaller and smaller until she faded into a mist of red and blue lights that had risen up like a veil between us. For several minutes I was sure I was going to be sick. Then I sucked in my breath and headed for my car, breaking into a run when I was halfway there.

For the next week I didn't stop running. I didn't confront Ivy, and I didn't contact Samax in Japan – she must have known I wouldn't – nor did I have a chance to see Auro again during his stay in Las Vegas, though I left a note at his hotel. No, the next morning, after an interminable sleepless night, I packed a small suitcase and boarded the seven a.m. flight for New York. By three-thirty New York time I was standing in front of my grandmother's old house in Bensonhurst, having gone there directly from the airport. The last time I had walked out that door, I thought, I had locked it behind me and handed Alma the key when I slipped into the front seat of her white Impala.

The house had changed, but not very much. It looked incredibly small – not surprising considering the size and scale of the place where I had lived ever since leaving it. But the passage of years had also blurred the dimensions of my old street. It was narrower and shorter than I remembered, with fewer houses which – to my surprise – were piled on top of each other like dominoes. The lawns were dime-sized, and many of the shade trees lining the sidewalk had been cut down or were stripped and dying. My grandmother's house had a different roof – green, and no longer new – and a heavier front door. And someone had dug up the two gloomy fir trees that used to flank the front steps and replaced them with azalea bushes. However, the smell that filled my head, a mix of damp leaves, wet concrete, and exhaust fumes from Bay Parkway, two blocks north, was exactly the one that had lingered in my memory.

I walked up the flagstone path to my grandmother's house and prepared a little speech in my head before ringing the doorbell. No one answered. I tried making inquiries of the neighbors, hoping to find someone who might remember Alma, but after twelve years that trail was ice cold. In fact, none of the people I talked to remembered me – nor I them. Only one old man, way down the street, who said he was a retired mailman, remembered my grandmother.

'Mrs Verell, sure,' he said, standing outside his screen door with his hands in his pockets. 'For a long time she was a widow.'

'Her husband was killed in the war,' I said, 'on Guam.'

This didn't seem to ring any bells for him. 'And she died when?' he asked.

'In 1965.'

He nodded, lighting a cigarette. 'Anyway, no, I don't remember you or your aunt – that's what you wanted to know, right?'

The neighborhood had changed: most of the old people had moved away or died, and while the street all year round had always been cluttered with children, I didn't see a single one. I wondered who did live there now.

I went around to the side of my grandmother's house, down the damp mossy gap between the houses where we used to keep the garbage cans, which I took out to the curb on Tuesdays and Fridays. I looked up at my old window, which now had striped curtains rather than the dark blue ones my grandmother had sewn. That window was directly opposite my bed, and I remembered lying there the very first night I had spent in that house when my grandmother brought me on the train from Pittsburgh after Luna and Milo were killed. I remembered, too, doing my homework at night at the little desk that had belonged to Luna, her initials carved with a nail file on the underside where my right knee touched the wood. Often when I lost my concentration midway through an arithmetical problem or a spelling list I ran my fingertips over those letters, LV, and thought that if you added two more letters you could spell out LOVE.

I checked into a midtown hotel, requesting a room in the back where I kept the curtains drawn. After ordering up some sandwiches and coffee, I set out to find the site of the planetarium Alma and I had visited. I remembered only that it was at the northern tip of Manhattan, on the Hudson River side. It was a Saturday, so I wouldn't have access to the city's building department records until Monday morning – and I didn't want to wait that long. Instead I went up to that neighborhood and combed it on foot, questioning shopkeepers and people who looked like long-term residents. It wasn't long before an old shoemaker near the elevated subway line told me that, sure, he remembered the old planetarium. It had been demolished, he said, in 1966 – less than a year after Alma and I visited it – and then gave me directions to its former site, seven blocks away, much nearer to the river than I remembered.

What I found there was a housing project wedged between a scrap of park land and a shopping center. The clerk at the rental office told me the project had been built in 1967, but he had never heard of the planetarium. He grew suspicious when I asked him if I could just roam around the project, but relented when I signed a form that legitimized me as a potential tenant. And what was I looking for there? I asked myself as I wandered the cement paths bordered by sparse trees. Buildings have their own ghosts, and using my architect's eye, I tried in vain to imagine the long-gone planetarium on that site. But it was impossible. I had scanned my memories of the place thousands of times, but it had been so altered by the housing project that I couldn't even recreate the point on the sidewalk where Ivy had propelled me to the waiting sedan.

If it was ghosts I wanted, I would have to look elsewhere.

Early the next morning, I visited the police precinct nearest the project. I told the desk sergeant that I was interested in tracing a missing persons report that might have been filed in December, 1965.

He looked at me askance. 'You know someone reported as missing back then?'

I nodded. 'Me.'

Something in my voice must have told him I wasn't a crackpot, or maybe he just wanted to get rid of me. Looking me in the eye, he said, 'You have to go downtown for that,' and jotted down the address of the Missing Persons Bureau in low Manhattan.

The bureau happened to be open on a Sunday, and after I'd answered a slew of questions and filled out some forms, a plainclothes detective sat me at a bare table in an empty room and placed a manila folder before me. When I saw the date on which my missing persons report had been filed, December 17, 1965, I felt the same mixture of astonishment and emptiness that had overwhelmed me that same day when, newly arrived in Las Vegas, I rode a bus to the County Clerk's office to check my birth certificate and confirm that my name was Enzo Samax. Now I was reading about the disappearance of one Loren Haris, age ten, last seen at the Herschel Planetarium on River Avenue and Water Street on December 16, 1965, at 3:10 p.m. Just seeing my old name on the tab of the folder had given me a shock. Over the next hour I experienced the impact of Loren Haris's disappearance almost as if he were another person. But chilling as that was, it could not have compared with what Alma must have felt over the course of those painful, drawn-out days twelve years earlier – and for how long afterward, I asked myself.

That she was beside herself with fear, panic-stricken, was clear from her initial statement, made to a pair of detectives named Kinor and Turel. This document – six typed, single-spaced pages on onion skin – covered everything Alma and I had done and everyone with whom she recalled our having had contact on the sixteenth, from the time we left the house in Brooklyn to the moment she last laid eyes on me at the planetarium. This was followed by a blow-by-blow account of the frantic hour she spent scouring the planetarium's theater and lobby, its anterooms of exhibits, its corridors and men's rooms, and then the surrounding streets. Interspersed throughout were short, often fragmented digressions – how I had come to live with her mother, the nature of her life in Boston – intended to provide the cops with pertinent bits of her history and mine. All of it was excruciating for me to read. Even in the clipped, dictated prose transcribed by the police, her terrible grief and helplessness were palpable, made all the more heart-wrenching to me finally by the detectives' obvious skepticism. In their notes accompanying her statement I was stunned to discover that from very early on they simply didn't believe her story. In his cramped script Detective Kinor ventured ominously that she might be a drug user. Or the victim of some trauma, weaving hysterical tales. For a brief time, the detectives even suspected her of foul play: supposedly driven to desperation by the sudden pressures foisted upon her as my guardian, she had bumped me off. Next they embraced some sort of Huck Finn theory: a wild, rootless boy with tragic family circumstances – my grandmother dead, Alma (by her own admission) a virtual stranger, unprovided for financially – I'd simply upped and run away.

When the cops finally did accept Alma's story of my abduction, still with a strong dose of skepticism, their investigation immediately hit a wall. In fact, they got nowhere at all. There were simply no leads, they insisted in their own report. No witnesses, no ransom demand, no trail to follow. The FBI was called in, to no avail, though my description was dispatched to police departments nationwide a month after my disappearance: five feet tall, 105 pounds, brown hair, gray eyes, wearing a navy pea coat, black watch cap, and plaid scarf; distinguishing features: my bent right index finger, broken in the car accident outside Pittsburgh, and a birthmark under my left arm. (And how had Alma known about the latter, I wondered.) The FBI flirted with the notion I had been the victim of a sexual predator who had murdered two other children in New York that winter and was still at large. They questioned some pedophiles recently paroled from New York prisons. For their part, the NYPD interrogated my schoolteacher, the school nurse, and several of the neighbors, still trying to determine if I had it in me to take to the road on my own. Why I would have done so from a planetarium, without even a change of clothes, they never addressed.

Three months later, both these investigations slowed to a crawl. Obviously frustrated, Alma then hired a private detective and he quickly dug up a witness the police and FBI had missed: an elderly woman who was the cashier in the gift shop near the exit Ivy had taken me through. Blind in one eye, this woman had seen a young woman, dressed exactly like Alma and fitting her physical description, leading a boy fitting my description, out onto the sidewalk. That clinched it for the police, who, with little appetite for the case from the first, zipped right back to their hunch that Alma was either a hysteric or a wily criminal with tortuous motives. And despite the fact that I was still physically gone and unaccounted for, the police at that point relegated the case to 'inactive' status, effectively ending their investigation. They did keep an eye on Alma, unknown to her, and Detective Kinor noted near the end of my file that she had left New York under rather suspicious circumstances: in the middle of the night on New Year's Eve, 1966, in zero-degree weather. That was the last they ever saw or heard of her.

And so, in the improbable position of reading my own missing persons report, I learned not only the immediate torments Alma had suffered after my abduction, but even more devastating, the fact that after a torturous year spent searching for me, she had not returned to school, which I knew had been her anchor, the place where she lodged all her hopes after much personal turmoil. Instead she had left town and dropped out of sight, the entire course of her life altered – like my own life, but not so benignly, I was sure. I returned my file to the officer on duty and inquired about the two detectives, Turel and Kinor; the former was dead, he informed me, and the latter had retired – to Arizona, he thought, but wasn't sure.

I was exhausted at that point, but so agitated by what I had just read that instead of returning to my hotel, I took a taxi up to the address I had possessed from the first but been saving for last. Everything I had been holding in that week – my ugly encounter with Ivy outside The Aladdin, my sudden return to my grandmother's house, hearing Alma's voice across the years in those police reports – rose up in me when I caught sight of the large white brick building my taxi was approaching. We had turned into the same narrow street Ivy and Nestor had sped down in the blue sedan when they took me to Samax. Now as then, my palms were sweating with trepidation, and when we pulled up at the curb moments later, my chest began shaking with suppressed sobs and tears welled up in my eyes.

The building was tucked into a forgotten corner of an industrial zone near the Harlem River. Mountains of rubble filled the vacant lots around it. A rooftop spotlight directed down the building's side flickered badly, casting a flashing ellipse. With darkness descending, the moon appeared through the clouds and I heard a pack of dogs baying nearby. The streetlights blinked on, their powdery silver rays pooling on the pavement.

Now even the smells of that long-ago December day – the dry stinging snow, Ivy's paralyzing perfume with the scent of Easter lilies, the smoke of Nestor's cigarette – had come back to me, and I started crying silently. My driver peered over his shoulder without curiosity, awaiting instructions. My emotions did not engage him; though I could not see his eyes, shaded beneath his cap, it was clear he was nervous and just wanted to get out of there. He hadn't expected the address I gave him when he picked me up near City Hall, and now that we had arrived at it, he wasn't pleased. I told him I wanted him to wait, and he thrust his upturned hand through the sliding panel in the security wall atop the front seat, wiggling his index finger. To have him wait in that neighborhood was going to cost me.

He had a point. We seemed to be at the epicenter of a wasteland. In the last decade, this entire neighborhood had deteriorated. While I remembered the buildings in the surrounding streets as rundown, they were now decimated – windowless, roofless, with heaps of rubbish pouring from their doors. Even taking the passage of time into consideration, I couldn't believe Samax had thought this would be a good location for a museum of rare collectibles. And the real estate outfit to which he had sold the building appeared to have done nothing with it. The building looked abandoned again, and even more neglected. The caged windows were still sealed and dirty, the doors at the loading zone were padlocked, and the sign over the entrance was now so corroded that even those few letters that had formerly been legible – CHINE – were reduced to a single faded E. Getting out my handkerchief, I tried to pull myself together there on the sidewalk. It had never been easy for me to cry, and here I had let myself go twice within a few days' time, first with Auro in his dressing room, and now in this place. Sitting alone for half the afternoon in that airless room at police headquarters, reading those reports, had sent me spinning far inside myself, until I felt all twisted up, vividly remembering the fear that gripped me when Ivy dragged me into that building.

The fare meter read twenty-nine dollars and was still running when I stepped from the taxi. I took out my wallet and offered the driver a crisp fifty-dollar bill. 'And another of those when I get back,' I said. 'That should cover the ride downtown, too. I'll also need to borrow a flashlight, if you've got one, and a screwdriver.'

The driver pondered this offer, his eyes still shaded beneath the brim of his cap. 'You ain't going to do anything illegal, are you?'

I shook my head. 'And I'll only be a few minutes.'

He looked me up and down suspiciously, assessing the value of my leather jacket, two-tone cowboy boots, and the onyx ring glinting on my finger. 'For the tools, the other fifty now,' he said finally.

My heart was thumping when I approached the metal door. Its lock was so old and rusted that I was able to jimmy it easily. As the door swung open, I was greeted by a rush of stale air. The interior, swirling with cold dust, was as dark as I remembered it, and I could hear the wind howling in a distant shaftway. The scuttling of rats, too, that preceded the tunnel of light my flashlight cut through the blackness. I picked my way down the only corridor unblocked by boxes and rubbish, and at the end of it found myself before another door. Pushing it open, I stepped onto a narrow balcony and felt a vast darkness yawning before me, its icy vapors flowing upward. I leaned into that darkness for a few seconds, holding my breath, closing my eyes, trying to gauge its depth before I directed the flashlight into it.

At first, in that open space, the beam exploded out so brightly that I couldn't see anything. Then the light contracted into a white circle, and when my eyes adjusted I saw just how enormous the space before me was, wide and deep with a high ceiling. The balcony overlooked a kind of amphitheater lined with steep tiers of seats. Knowing the balcony was at street level, I calculated that the floor of the amphitheater itself must be about four stories underground. Whatever work had been undertaken there long ago by Samax's successors was broken off abruptly. Tiny as toys below me, there was a cement mixer, a crane, a stack of lumber, and a pyramid of cinder blocks, all of them thick with dust and cobwebs. Ropes and wires dangled from the rafters. The floor was deeply recessed, with furrows full of dangling wires and large craters crisscrossed by rusty pipes. Thinking I had seen those craters before, I realized I was looking down at the very room, enormous as a football field, in which I had first been brought to Samax.

The moment this realization hit me, I felt as if I could see that long-ago scene come alive before me in the amphitheater, as if the flashlight were a magic lantern reanimating those ghosts from my past. Ivy in her black coat. Samax in his black suit. Calzas with his shiny cropped hair unfurling a blueprint for Samax. And a boy in a pea coat sitting at a small table writing on a piece of paper.

Standing there on the balcony all those years later, I recalled the words I had written to Alma at the base of Samax's letter:

455

Dear Alma,

This is so hard, but it's better for both of us, and I want you to know I'm okay and I'm going because I want to.

Love, Loren

Words lost in time, that no one ever saw.

Feeling very cold suddenly, I just wanted to get away from that place. Backing away from the edge of the balcony, I stepped through the door and sprinted down the corridor, the beam of the flashlight dancing crazily on the peeling walls, all the way to the street.

I leapt into the back of my taxi and the driver floored the accelerator and sped around the corner. The flashlight was still burning, and, as I switched it off, I saw how hard my hand was shaking.

The driver didn't ask me if I had found what I was looking for. I passed him the flashlight and the screwdriver, with another fifty-dollar bill, and he slid the plastic panel shut and negotiated the narrow streets toward the Harlem River Drive. I sat back, dizzy, disoriented, staring at the oncoming headlights on the highway, and within no time it seemed, we were back in midtown Manhattan, in front of my hotel.

When I arrived in Las Vegas the next afternoon, I found my uncle had just returned from Japan. As invigorated as he was from his trip, I was exhausted from mine. Samax knew right away that something was terribly wrong, and it didn't take him long to get me to tell him what Ivy had spat out at me in the parking lot of The Aladdin. On learning the fate of his letter to Alma, he first turned deathly white, then grew as angry as I had ever seen him. He stormed out of the library, banging the floor with the cane he was now forced to carry, and went directly to Ivy's rooms on the eighth floor.

White-haired for as long as I had known him, after his stroke Samax truly looked his age for the first time. He had the thinning hair of an old man now, as well as the concave chest, sunken cheeks, and braided throat muscles. Liver spots were surfacing on his hands and he had to wear glasses all the time because of retinal damage to his left eye. But taking all that into consideration, and the fact that he now almost exclusively wore his Chinese silk pajamas and velvet slippers around the hotel, the inner resources he had garnered over his long life and his still iron will nevertheless made him a formidable figure, capable of intimidating close acquaintances and strangers alike.

Within a minute of entering Ivy's suite and confirming what I had told him, he banished her from the Hotel Canopus forever, effectively banishing her from his life. Forbidden by Samax from saying another word to anyone, no goodbyes, nothing, even to Dolores and Desirée, Ivy put three white suitcases in the trunk of her Coupe de Ville and, at the age of forty, after living at the hotel for over thirty years, drove away. To Reno, as it turned out, where, enraged at Samax and at me, she would quickly cement her unholy alliance with her mother Stella's former lover, Vitale Cassiel.

Meanwhile, Samax had me join him in the greenhouse for a serious discussion. He was determined to right a wrong, as he put it. No matter that twelve years had elapsed, and that Alma, now thirty-three years old, could be anywhere at all, he wanted to find her.

'But you've got nothing to go on,' I said gently.

'What do you mean – there's always something. I found you years ago, didn't I?'

Relatively easily, I thought, by bribing and intimidating people once he discovered the adoption agency where Bel had taken me.

'I don't care what it costs,' Samax shouted toward the upper canopy his fruit trees formed beneath the greenhouse roof. 'We'll get Pinkerton's. And the Hopkins brothers in Miami – they can find anyone when no one else can. And, just in case, there are private investigators my friends at the casinos hire – sometimes to track down wise guys fifteen, twenty years after they think they got away with something. I have other people downtown I can ask, too. And I'll have Alif and Aym scout around, with their paramilitary friends. We can crack this thing, I know.'

He knew nothing of the kind, but he was so furious that he had to convince himself he could find Alma, even if he needed to conjure up a small army to do so. The fact is, he felt horribly guilty and ashamed, not just on Alma's account, but, most especially, on mine.

How could you have trusted Ivy, of all people, with that letter, I had been thinking for days, but Samax was already so agitated, I couldn't bring myself to ask him this question. Indirectly, he answered it moments later.

'The very first promise I made you, Enzo,' he declared, 'was that your aunt would get that letter. For chrissakes, everything was predicated on it, from the day you came out here with me. I was careless – inexcusably so – and Ivy broke my promise. At what cost to your aunt I shudder to think. Sabotage is too clean a word for what Ivy did. Now we just have to find your aunt.'

'And what will we do then?'

He didn't answer this question, and it turned out he would never have to, for the combined genius, muscle, and resources of Pinkerton's, the mob private eyes, the cops with connections, Alif, Aym, and their soldier of fortune pals, and the Hopkins brothers who succeeded when all others failed, turned up absolutely nothing about Alma Verell: last known address, 222 Cabot Place, Brooklyn; last known occupation, student, Boston University. It wasn't just the NYPD Missing Persons squad that never saw or heard of her again, it was everyone. Right away, Samax feared that she was dead, he was responsible, and there was no way now that he could ever make his amends. It didn't look good, I had to agree, and I was more heartsick about it than anyone, but still I couldn't believe Alma was dead. That just didn't ring true in my bones. Samax kept paying people to look, and spent countless hours on the phone himself, exploiting his many connections, but nothing came of it. Like that ancient amulet depicting the dark side of the moon, Alma seemed to be one lost thing Samax was going to have a great deal of difficulty finding.

Around this time, the hotel population felt skeletal compared to the days of my childhood. There were few short-term visitors anymore, and the three new long-term ones were anything but collegial: fat Professor Zianor, dry as his cough, who holed up in the library for days at a time unearthing paintings of Adam with a navel and drinking licorice tea; Harahel, an elderly archivist from Alexandria, Egypt, hired by Samax to put in order his personal papers as well as the hotel's voluminous files; and the polite but unsmiling So Li, who was assiduously studying her bells – for a long time the myriad harmonies of ceremonial bells – in Auro's former practice room. As with Zianor and Harahel, however great her devotion to her work, on the outside she appeared passionless to the point of indifference.

After a while, this cold-fish attitude seemed to infect the old-time residents: Labusi, who either shot billiards alone or sat with Dolores in the garden, an umbrella affixed to his wheelchair to shield him from the sun; Hadar, never sociable to begin with, who practically camped out in his subbasement laboratory when he returned from expeditions; and even the irrepressible Deneb, who when he wasn't delivering his stump speech about Atlantis at Basque social clubs, generally made himself scarce around the hotel. Meanwhile, to my great disappointment, Zaren Eboli had become an infrequent weekend visitor after moving to west Texas to complete his catalogue of spiders of the Southwest.

Mrs Resh, the replacement for Della and Denise from the world of four-star hotels, turned out to be a soulless woman who literally never spoke except when spoken to. She ran the hotel with great efficiency, following the model laid out by Dolores years before. As for the latter, at the age of 103 she finally began walking with a cane, and rarely spoke to anyone outside of Mrs Resh and

Labusi. Desirée avoided her, as did Samax, to whom she had taken to writing sharply worded requests, which he ignored; first, she demanded to see his will, then inveighed against him for refusing to verify that he had bequeathed the hotel to Desirée – who still didn't want it.

'What do you expect?' Desirée said to me one night as we sat by the pool drinking wine and I complained of the general torpor at the hotel. We had both just returned from trips: I to Santa Fe, where I had visited Calzas and his wife upon the birth of their second child; Desirée to Bali, on what she described as a 'pleasure trip', making me wonder if she had added a new photo to her gallery.

'It's not because of Zianor or So Li or Harahel,' she went on, 'that things have come to this. It's Samax. He's the one who invited them, and he handpicked Resh out of a slew of terrific applicants the agency sent over. The same with Harahel: there was a young guy from the University of Hawaii who had ten times the spunk and would have given some shape and vitality to the material Samax shoveled at him, rather than just compiling the stuff. Samax has got Harahel in there sifting through the history of his life as if he's already dead. It makes me crazy – like he has a mortician on call. Samax wants these people around him now because he was so knocked out by the stroke and Denise's death. Labusi's accident and Calzas's marriage didn't help either. Why should he want fascinating dinner companions, like the old days, when he never comes to dinner himself? He no longer craves distractions, or the kind of over-stimulation he used to thrive on. Again, why should he when he's always up there in his library with the Angel of Death? To my mind, all that motivates him now is finding that amulet and producing his hybrid tree. And of course making sure you're okay after he's gone.'

This last observation was not made with bitterness, but it was also not the first time she had said something to this effect over the previous few years. She may not have wanted the hotel, but that didn't mean Desirée was indifferent to Samax's making *some* provisions for her future. And because he had showed less and less interest in her activities – not the surest barometer, I thought, considering his state of mind – she was certain that he hadn't.

Soon afterward, Samax did fulfill his longtime pomological quest for the hybrid he had sought to create between the star apple and the starfruit. In fact, he succeeded. It was just before sunrise one morning when I received a summons from him on the house phone.

'Can you join me for breakfast in the greenhouse?' he asked.

Though of late such requests had often come in response to crises, this time I detected a lilt in my uncle's voice. Still, the hybrid was far from my mind just then, so, as I threw my clothes on, and made my way down to that tunnel where I had first encountered Auro, I didn't know what to expect.

Alif and Aym, in blue sweatsuits and running shoes, were playing backgammon under a plant light at the entrance to the greenhouse. They nodded when I passed, with Sirius trailing me. The first person I saw in the greenhouse was Harahel. Desirée was right, I thought: he looked like a mortician. Gaunt, with pale hands and sallow cheeks, Harahel was wearing a tan fez and a khaki jacket with an ink-stained handkerchief stuck in the front pocket. As usual, he was cross-referencing two bundles of folders that documented some aspect of Samax's earliest collecting days. So far, after a year of unremitting labor, he had covered only the years 1935 through 1940. At that rate, it would take him six more years to finish the job.

In a terry-cloth robe, Desirée was sitting near the zinc sink, fingers flying on her silent portable typewriter, filling up one of her yellow sheets of paper. She and Harahel were so absorbed in their own activities that I as utterly unprepared for what Samax was about to reveal to me.

He did it quite simply, walking out from behind a pair

461

of palmettos in his red smoking jacket, the customary yellow and red flower stuck in the lapel. His threadbare lab coat was hanging by the door, but he was wearing his scuffed rubber shoes. In his outstretched palm he cradled a piece of fruit, which I took from him. Samax's hand was trembling – from emotion, not the aftereffects of the stroke – and I too felt a welling up in my chest and behind my eyes as the coolness of the strangely oblong, dark blue piece of fruit permeated my palm. What Samax had predicted to me years before was exactly what his hybrid had turned out to be: a star-shaped fruit with a hard, waxy skin. It smelled acrid, the juice my thumbnail drew from the skin part citrus, part ammonia. And when Samax cut it in half with a pocketknife, I saw that the flesh was also indigo, speckled with golden seeds. Like a night sky, as he had promised.

'The rootstock and scion *were* in perfect harmony with this tree,' he murmured approvingly. 'But only after it had produced the first full-fledged and edible pieces of fruit could I be sure. Taste it, Enzo.'

It was as pungent as it smelled. Sharp as a tamarind, with traces of clove and pepper. Like biting into a fleshy spice, just as Desirée had predicted years ago.

'The *Samax Astrofructus*,' I said, swallowing the pulp and feeling its faint afterbuzz on my lips. 'Congratulations, Uncle Junius.'

'Thank you, Enzo,' he said, and for one of the few times in all my years with him, his eyes gleamed with tears. 'You understand, I know.'

I did. I understood that with the various setbacks of late, and the increasing friction in his life on several fronts, this accomplishment was all the more important to him. He had worked at this for a long time, with a singular concentration, responsible only to himself, and, patiently, diligently, he had produced a tree that had never before existed. Which in turn had put forth a piece of fruit with its own unique color, texture, and taste, that still lingered on my palate. The *Samax Astrofructus* was Samax's baby in every way, a hedge against mortality now that he could rest assured it would outlive him.

'There is something I wanted to do at this time,' he said softly. His tone was that of someone about to offer up a prayer, which in his own way was perhaps what he was doing. He pointed to the flower in his lapel. 'I'd like to give this flower a name, too,' he said simply, 'with which it can be officially registered.'

It stunned me to realize that in all those years, in an environment in which the names of things – whether asteroids, flowers, or stars – had been so important, this flower which I had seen nearly every day from the time I was ten years old had managed to remain anonymous. It was true I had never heard any name ascribed to it, nor had I ever sought one out. In my mind this flower had always been simply 'the flower with the red and yellow petals and the orange center,' a variety of the desert poppy which it most closely resembled. But it was not a poppy. Samax told me it was a kind of marigold.

'It's a hybrid that has no name,' he went on, 'a lost flower developed in mysterious circumstances by a horticulturist who never registered it and whose own name has been lost over the years. That sense of mystery always appealed to me. But now I feel this flower should have a proper name. Because I've cultivated it, and possess the greatest concentration of the flower in North America, I can do so. With your permission, Enzo, I want to name it after your aunt.'

This was an even bigger surprise. 'Alma?'

He nodded. 'I want to call it the *Alma*. You can do that with a flower – give it just a single name.' Shaking his head ruefully, he looked me in the eye. 'I wanted to make up, in a small way, for some of what we know she must have suffered. Is that all right with you?'

'Of course,' I replied, and now it was I who choked up.

'After two months, the flower will officially be known as the *Alma*.'

'It's a fine gesture, Uncle Junius.'

He embraced me. 'It's done, then.'

He clipped and lit up one of his Upmann coronas, for despite his doctor's instructions, he refused to give up cigars. Harahel had shuffled out of the greenhouse with the folders, Desirée was still typing, and after a long silence, Samax beckoned me over to a nearby table beneath ultraviolet lamps. 'I've saved the best for last,' he whispered, 'and for the moment I'm not showing it to anyone but you.'

'Not even Desirée?'

'No one.' He placed the other half of the blue fruit on a small plate. 'Look at this, Enzo. It's incredible.'

At first I thought that, with an old man's pride, he was reaffirming the mere existence of the fruit.

'Look more closely,' he urged me, taking my elbow.

I studied the golden seeds in the indigo pulp, and they did indeed look like stars. In that lamplight, particularly, they glittered. Then I saw that the seeds formed a familiar pattern, which I recognized after a few seconds.

'It's Gemini.'

'That's right.' He was very excited. 'Can you believe it?'

'But—'

'Enzo, each piece of fruit from this tree contains a different constellation. I've cut open four of them and already found Taurus, Orion, Libra, and this.' I heard a laugh deep in his throat. 'I don't know how it happened, but they're there.'

I held the fruit up and turned it this way and that, marveling at the sixteen golden seeds that comprised Gemini, exactly as it looked in the night sky. 'I'd say it's a miracle,' I murmured, and Samax nodded in agreement.

After this, Samax's spirits picked up considerably for a while. Though he had lived in the desert most of his adult life, he had rarely explored it much; during the considerable time he spent outdoors, he confined himself to the gardens and orchards of his own creation.

Now he began making forays into the Mojave, always at twilight when the air was cool, with Sirius at his side. Though Sirius's senses were keen as ever, he limped with arthritis now in his forepaws. Still, he could keep up with Samax, and together they circled out into the desert and returned to the hotel as the stars began to shine. At this time, too, Forcas, the enigmatic gangster, began staying at the hotel for weeks at a time; he and Samax often dined alone together, played a game of chess, and then talked late into the night. About what I didn't know, though a couple of times I saw Forcas jot down whatever it was Samax was saying, as if it were a message to be conveyed. As in the old days, Samax even engaged a string quartet on occasion to come out and play Haydn and Mozart in the lounge. His good mood was undimmed, apparently, even by his admission to me one night, in the rich silence of his library, that he now doubted he would ever find the amulet he had been seeking all those years.

'It's just not in the cards,' he said, with an equanimity that took me aback. 'The codex Deneb brought back from Rhodes confirmed, without a doubt, that the amulet first surfaced in Alexandria over two thousand years ago and was a companion to the one my old friend Rochel left me in our cell at the penitentiary. I know the amulet existed at least until the second half of this century. Then, in 1952, the trail goes cold, right here in Nevada. Oh yes, it was here, all right – so close, yet so far away. I know it for a fact.' His eyes narrowed. 'I even know who was last in possession of it. Whether that person hid it away or, more likely, destroyed it, it just disappeared at that time and there's nothing I can do about it. It could be anywhere in the world now, and I don't have the energy or the time to chase after it any longer. I told you when you got out of school that I wasn't going to have you chase after it for me the way Calzas did. God knows he must have traveled a million miles in search of that amulet. He was able to trace most of its strange path through history over the centuries – from Coptic monasteries to a caliph's library in Damascus to the royal vaults of the Byzantine Empire – but then we came up a little short.'

'The last owner died?'

'No, he's very much alive.'

'And you know him?'

'I used to.'

'But who would destroy such a rare object?'

'Only one person I know. Finding out how badly I wanted it would be enough for him.' He laid his palms on his knees and leaned closer to me, barely parting his lips when he uttered the name of Vitale Cassiel.

'What?'

'He may still have the amulet in his possession, but even now he would destroy it in a second rather than let me get hold of it.'

'How did he know you were interested in it?'

Samax waved the question aside. 'That's no mystery. Many people knew because of all the specific queries we had to make over the years. You couldn't keep it secret. Anyway, he got wind of my search and somehow beat me to the prize. Part of me would love to know how. Another part says it's better I don't because it would just make me sick.'

'But it's wrong,' I said angrily. 'Whenever this guy's name comes up, it's always the same story. Listen, I have my own gripes with him. Let me confront him and get the amulet for you.'

Samax's eyes widened. 'Don't talk crazy,' he said, grabbing my wrist. 'And don't ever go near him, you hear me?'

'What can he do to me?'

'Enzo, you don't know what you're talking about.'

'Tell me what he can do.'

'He's capable of *anything*, whether you cross him or he crosses you.' Samax was agitated, the little color in his cheeks draining fast. 'You're a young guy, full of stuff, and he's old, like me, but he'd come after you like no one you've ever known.'

'I never knew you to be afraid of anyone, including him.'

'There's a difference between fear and knowledge. Knowing your enemy, and what he would do, gives you power – unless you act as if you don't know anything. Then you have plenty to fear. Understand?'

I nodded, but I was thinking that I couldn't give up on the amulet so easily, not after all I'd heard about it since I was a boy.

'The lunar amulet is gone now,' he went on. 'It might as well be on the moon itself. I have the other amulet. And, more importantly, I have my *Samax Astrofructus* tree. That makes up for plenty. It will keep growing and you'll have it after me. Forget the amulet and promise me you'll stay away from him.'

'All right, I'll forget the amulet,' I said, but I didn't promise him anything. And that night, when I returned to the small apartment I now rented in west Las Vegas, I thought about the amulet some more.

Several months later, I went to Albuquerque. The day I was to oversee the demolition of the Hotel Rigel I woke in a cold sweat in my own hotel, hours before my alarm clock was to go off. I had been sleeping fitfully all week, but this was my worst night yet. I wasn't hungry, so after I had showered and dressed, I drank a pot of maté tea while watching the sun rise from behind the mountains. Then I drove across the city to the Botanical Gardens. I had never seen the Bizzarria Orange tree Samax donated to the Gardens. In fact, on previous visits to Albuquerque I had avoided going to see it. Thinking about this, I realized it was because I had first heard about the tree while conversing with my uncle just prior to his stroke. The tree and the stroke had always been painfully linked in my mind. Finally, though, Samax seemed puzzled by the fact I had never visited the tree, so I decided I must do so while he was still alive.

I found it prominently displayed in the glass-enclosed arboreum with a plaque stating that it had been donated by Junius Samax and was a fourth-generation descendent of the first known chimera, discovered in Florence, Italy, in 1644. I studied the clusters of knobby lemon-oranges on the tree's gnarled branches. I inhaled the fragrance of its thick leaves. I tried to imagine how the fruit would taste – sour or sweet? Samax had never told me if he had eaten one. His mind was elsewhere that night in the greenhouse, before he collapsed, telling me, 'We are all of us accidents of nature, refined by thousands of graftings . . . some that take, some that don't.' At the time he was rambling, but now I saw that those words could have been his credo.

For the next four hours, I was completely occupied with my preparations at the Hotel Rigel, running through checklists, issuing last-minute instructions to my crew. When I left the hotel roof with my foreman at one o'clock, completing our final circuit of the hotel, I was thinking again of Vitruvius, the father of modern architecture who nevertheless – despite his professions to the contrary – was deeply superstitious, constantly picking apart his dreams for portents. He subscribed, for example, to the Greek belief that it was beneficial to the strength and stability of a building to kill a cock and bury it under the foundation stone. Sometimes an architect instead enticed a man to the building site and maneuvered him into casting his shadow onto the foundation stone. It was believed the measured man, no longer able to cast a shadow, would die within a year – that his very soul had been fatally stripped from him. Eventually there sprang up a network of shadow-traders whose sole business it was to provide architects with men's shadows, stolen by sorcerers.

Calzas told me one day that the Zunis shared this belief, as did people in places as far-flung as Japan and Finland. In all these places, as in the Zuni pueblos, burying the shadow as a substitute for the even more ancient custom of immuring a living person in the walls, or crushing him under the foundation stone, of a new building. (When I mentioned this to Samax, he observed with amusement that maybe the mob had read Vitruvius, too.) Whenever construction was about to begin, Zuni shamans customarily traveled as close to the Forbidden Mesa as they dared to rendezvous with shadow-traders. So for every building in Acoma, the sky-city, a man had literally lost his soul.

Superstitious himself, whenever he broke ground for a new office building Calzas had a Zuni shaman pay a visit, much as an architect in Hong Kong brought in a geomancer who practiced *feng shui*. At that particular time, Calzas was erecting many such buildings across the Southwest. His practice was thriving, and he was banking as much of his profits as he could in order to underwrite the project that truly consumed him, his magnus opus in the realm of fantastic architecture: an agronomically self-sufficient city atop Acoma. What he hadn't told me with regard to the job at the Hotel Rigel was that a shaman would also be on site for the demolition. So I was startled when, on the landing to the fire stairs, the foreman and I suddenly came face to face with a reed-thin, moon-faced man wearing a multicolored vest, buckskin boots with fringes, and a blue fedora with a black feather in its ribbon. He held a tambourine in one hand and a stick in the other. Nearly his height, the stick was painted the same blue as his hat and was adorned with white stars and yellow moons. And there was a large white star dyed into the tambourine's sky-blue skin.

Unblinking, unsmiling, the man looked me in the eye.

'Calzas sent you?' I asked. 'You know, we won't be laying a foundation stone for some time.'

He shifted his weight from one foot to the other.

Studying the feather in his hat, I decided it was a raven's. 'Well?' I said.

In the shaftway off the stairwell updrafts of hot wind were swirling pieces of trash. They hovered like paper fish outside the dirty window, then disappeared. There was a humming of machinery from the street. And the sound of hammers, drills, and crowbars on the lower

469

floors as our crew stripped away the few remaining valuable fixtures that I had marked for salvage.

Finally the shaman raised his stick a few inches off the floor – he would never speak while it touched the ground – and addressed me in a thick voice, 'Sometimes when you wreck a building, the soul of the dead man under the old foundation stone is released. That's why I am here.'

The foreman, a burly, city-bred Zuni, said, 'I never heard that before.'

'The spirits in this building are agitated,' the shaman said, stone-faced. Tucking his stick under his arm, he cupped his hands over his ears. 'The moment I entered, I heard them.'

'Why this building?' the foreman asked. A seasoned demolition man – no squeamish soul – he was visibly shaken by this information.

The shaman slowly opened his palms.

'We set off the charges at three o'clock,' I said to him. 'Where will you be?'

'Beside you, of course,' he said with a faint smile.

'You must know why,' the foreman persisted.

But the shaman's stick had returned to the floor and he wouldn't say another word. He followed the foreman and me down the stairs, chanting almost inaudibly under his breath. When we reached the elevator bank, I glanced over my shoulder and the shaman was gone, though there were no other doors off that stairwell. Then, as we rode down in the elevator, I was sure I could still hear his low murmur. Maybe the foreman could, too, but if so, that was the least of what was upsetting him.

'I worked on plenty of buildings, but I never heard of that,' he said, picking at the fingers of the heavy gloves he clutched in one hand. 'It's the *new* foundation stone those guys come in for. No, I never heard of it.'

In the lobby, through the opening where there had previously been revolving doors, two of the men were wheeling a cart filled with brass wall clocks and crystal chandeliers. Others were carrying out large mirrors with gilt frames that flashed wildly in the heavy sunlight. And still others were coming up from the basement, where they had inspected the charges and the nitroglycerine cannisters one last time. There was also a lone member of the crew with a crowbar prying a brass mailbox from the marble wall near the former front desk.

It was two-thirty. In ten minutes, we were all due to rendezvous in the parking lot across the street so the foreman could take a head count before I began the countdown to detonation.

I watched the man at the mailbox for a few moments, then turned to the foreman, who was still mumbling to himself.

'Did you tell him to remove that?' I asked.

He shook his head.

'I don't remember even seeing a mailbox,' I mused.

The foreman started walking toward the man, but I took his arm.

'I'll take care of it,' I said.

Coming up behind the man, I recognized him – the loner in a group of loners, the one with whom I had barely exchanged a word, a pale, spindly man with a thin red moustache. 'Red,' I said, 'there isn't enough time for that. Just leave it.'

'I'll have it down in no time,' he said, without pausing in his work.

The mailbox, brass with an eagle embossed on the front, was hanging by a single L-brace now. Red yanked it free in a cloud of marble dust and laid it on the floor.

'Who told you to take that down?' I said, waving the dust away.

'See, it was covered with a thick spiderweb,' he replied without looking at me, pointing his crowbar at a sticky ball of silver webbing that he had tossed off to one side.

'A spiderweb?'

Red whipped a large screwdriver from his belt and went to work on the four ancient screws that secured the front panel of the mailbox.

471

'What are you doing?' I said.

'There's stuff in here,' he replied matter-of-factly.

'What?'

'Must be some mail, right?'

We had fifteen minutes to demolition, but I stood there raptly watching him open the mailbox. For a man his size, Red was exceptionally strong: those large screws had obviously never been loosened before, and in less than a minute he had whirled them out. Then, prying it loose at the corners, he lifted off the panel. Sure enough, there was a single white envelope lying in the bottom of the box, beneath several layers of webbing.

'Looky here,' he said, whistling softly.

With the tip of the screwdriver he brushed the webbing from the envelope before reaching in and lifting it out. The envelope was a piece of hotel stationery, yellowed along the edges and bulging.

'Here,' he said with a nod of satisfaction, handing me the envelope.

The envelope had a row of 10¢ stamps along the top – immediately dating it for me – and was addressed in a compact masculine hand, in black ink. Obviously posted after the final mail pickup, in the closing days of the Hotel Rigel – on the very day, in fact, that the hotel permanently shut its doors – it was addressed to:

> *Miss Mala Revell*
> *c/o Combat Nursing Corps, 2nd Division*
> *U.S. Navy Pacific Command*
> *Honolulu, Hawaii*

There was no return address, and at the bottom of the envelope was printed the odd instruction, *Please Hold/ Forward When Possible*. But there had been no occasion for holding or forwarding; I knew that the hotel had closed in the fall of 1971, which meant for eight years that mailbox had effectively become a dead-letter box. That's what that envelope contained: a dead letter.

Red was staring at me with a faint smile.

'Have that mailbox carried out,' I ordered him, slipping the envelope into my briefcase. 'And get out of here yourself now.' It took two men to load the mailbox onto the truck at curbside containing the chandeliers, clocks, and other items that would escape being buried beneath a mountain of rubble.

This was to be the fate of every other remaining object in the Hotel Rigel, for at 3:06 p.m., after the foreman took his head count and sounded a two-minute evacuation warning with a siren, I signalled the explosives man to set off the charges by remote control. The police had cordoned off the surrounding streets and a large crowd, many with cameras and binoculars, had gathered behind the barricades. There were news crews from two television stations. And in the blistering heat a hot dog vendor and an ice cream truck were doing a brisk business. I was standing beside one of our trucks with the foreman and some of the men, our eyes glued to the Hotel Rigel in its final seconds as a solid entity in this world, as the explosives man punched out the activation code on his remote control bar. I could visualize the twelve three-gallon nitro cannisters in the basement – in the corners and below the reinforced concrete piles – as I began counting under my breath *1 . . . 2 . . . 3 . . .* On *4* the charges set off the nitro with a quickening roar and twelve plumes of smoke and dust merged into one expanding gray cloud. The building shook violently and collapsed in on itself, for an instant resembling a grotesque, square white cake whose center had evaporated. Midway down, the rest of the square followed, and out of the crashing chaotic mass of rubble a swirling black cloud, twice the height of the former hotel, rose rapidly into the sky. As the roar ebbed, I heard the rattle of a tambourine and a stick pounding rhythmically on the pavement a few feet to my right. When I turned, however, the shaman was nowhere in sight.

That evening, back at my hotel, I pulled off my boots and ordered up from room service – tostadas, rice and beans, and a fifth of El Toro 5-Star mescal, a green worm

473

tumbling at its base – before switching on the television. The lead news story on the local stations was the demolition of the Hotel Rigel. It had even bumped the murders du jour – a bookie shot in his car and a beautician found on the roof of a warehouse – from the top slot, a rarity during the crime wave. At the hotel, the television crews had operated side by side, so the footage looked almost identical as I switched back and forth with the remote control: the building intact, the simultaneous explosions, and the toppling mass beneath the billowing dust cloud. Then, briefly, there was footage of my foreman and crew, and for a few seconds I even saw myself in wraparound sunglasses and the khaki pants and white shirt I was still wearing. Hard hat pushed back on my head, I was surveying the smoking remains of the hotel. I had never before seen myself on television, but what startled me out of my chair at that moment was the image of the shaman on the flickering screen, just to my right, shaking his tambourine and pounding his stick, exorcising the angry spirits that might be released by the collapsing building. I saw myself glance in his direction with a surprised look, but no one else in the news footage even registered his presence. Could we all somehow have missed him in the glare of sunlight?

At midnight I took out the dead letter that had been recovered from the hotel mailbox. For a long time I just sat with it in my lap and sipped some mescal. It was so quiet I could hear the cold whisper of the air-conditioning vent. When I finally brought myself to open the letter, I felt it had somehow been intended for me all along, through all those years it had lain beneath the spiders spinning their webs. Why else, I asked myself, sipping mescal, had it been placed in *my* hands at such a critical moment, seconds away from certain destruction? Even so, I was completely unprepared for the contents of that letter, which, to my amazement, would not only be populated with people out of my own life, including Samax and Ivy, but would fill in some of the crucial gaps in my history, revealing things I had thought lost forever in the mists of time – the fate of my grandmother Stella, the activities of my mother Bel at the end of her life – and, most amazing of all, things I had no idea were even a part of my history, such as my true relationship to Vitale Cassiel. That these revelations were made in passing, in the larger context of the writer's life, rendered them all the more heart-stopping for me. Part love letter, wound around a story of the Vietnam War, and part confessional, the letter was divided into four parts. I read and reread it that night before falling into a fitful sleep. And early the next morning I read it again. Parts of it I would reread many times over the ensuing months.

The letter was thirty-seven pages in all, also on hotel stationery, the same concise, even handwriting as the address, covering both sides of each sheet. I had to smooth it out carefully, for it had been folded over twice and tightly packed for all those years. Composed over the course of five days in the fall of 1971, the four parts of the letter were dated the 13th, 14th, 16th, and 17th of October. The writer was an Air Force major named Geza Cassiel, and, discovering at the beginning of the letter that he had injured his leg in the war, I realized with a jolt that I had actually crossed paths with him on October 13, 1971. This happened to be a moment in my own life that I remembered very clearly, for it was the day after I lost my virginity with Dalia – on Columbus Day – when Calzas and I had been en route to Acoma in a jeep. We had stopped at a gas station outside of Albuquerque where I had seen a rental car with a US Air Force jacket draped over the seat. The name tag on the jacket read CASSIEL. An officer with a limp had emerged from the washroom, and for several seconds, as I recalled with a cold thrill, he and I had stared at each other across the steaming asphalt before he drove off toward Albuquerque. Little did I know that eight years later I would be privy to his thoughts at that moment, for on that very night he began writing this long letter in

Room 1216 of the Hotel Rigel, one of the 178 rooms whose destruction I would personally oversee.

Whether that officer was still alive, or like the hotel was already a ghost, by the time I was halfway through that fateful letter, pouring myself a stiffer glass of mescal, I realized that, no matter what else happened in my life, I had to find the woman to whom the letter was addressed. Whoever and wherever she was – assuming she was still alive, too – she was my only link to Major Geza Cassiel. A link that had taken on immense importance in the previous hour when, under a wave of vertigo – so many of my assumptions about my life collapsing before my eyes with the same finality as the Hotel Rigel – I had discovered that Major Cassiel was not only the son of Vitale Cassiel, but was also my real father.

16

Dead Letter

13 October 1971

Dear Mala:

Where to begin.

How about 1,500 miles due west of Luzon Air Field, on the 15th parallel, flying up the Mekong River at 10,000 feet. Into Laos. January 18, 1969. 2 a.m. The night of the new moon. Four days after I left you at the Hôtel Alnilam in Manila.

I have never been a letter writer. Never had anyone to write to. Outside of Official Air Force correspondence, I haven't written a letter in ten years. I've started this one over four times now, and then torn it up. Now I'm not going to read it over, not even when I finish it. I don't know when it will reach you. Maybe I'll find you first.

For four months I've been looking. In Honolulu, Manila, even on Okinawa where I'd heard that many Navy nurses leaving the war zone were restationed. A nurse at the Admiral Perry Hospital in Honolulu told me she knew you. Thought you had gone to Tokyo. Or maybe Bangkok, to work for the Red Cross. I went to Tokyo. And searching for you blind, lost myself. Went to Bangkok, too, but the Red Cross had never heard of you.

Now I'm in the desert, back where I came from. But just passing through. Not looking for you here, in the place where at one time I thought I had lost everything. I never dreamed I'd be back after losing everything all over again. After losing you.

Mala, I should have started out by telling you how much I love you. Again. And again. More than ever. And how I didn't foresee that this could have happened to us. But I should have, knowing the war. Knowing the war, it seems inevitable now. It's true, I should have started this letter differently, but I'm not going to tear it up and start over. It was hard enough to get this far. Know that I love you, across time and space. How much time and how much space I don't know. When it's really important, we rarely seem to know. I'd give anything to see you now. To touch you.

I'm in a hotel called the Rigel. The place is nearly empty, going out of business, about to close down. There is no one else on the twelfth floor with me. The clerk told me I may be the last guest, depending on when I check out. The only other one I've seen is an old gangster – real Vegas type – who plays solitaire all day in the bar. My room has soundproof windows. And up this high, I can't hear any traffic. It's like a decompression chamber, or an isolation room – and maybe I could use a little of both.

I'm drinking tea by the quart. I brought my own, a green, mountain tea I discovered in Bangkok. The Thais say it clears the bloodstream, promoting clear thought. Maybe that's why I crave it.

Two blocks away, there's a small park where I go for walks. With a cane, like an old guy myself. I was wounded again, in the left leg, three inches above the knee – and no Mala to find the shrapnel! Two bullets, actually. One that fragmented. They cleaned out everything but one sliver, which lodged a couple of millimeters from the bone. I can feel it when I extend the knee. They had to cut through a lot of muscle, so I'm rehabilitating. Walking two miles daily. That's the prescription. The Air Force doctors told me that in six months I won't be limping. In a year I'll be able to run again.

Aside from these walks, I hardly leave the hotel. I take my meals here. I don't want to go out. I know this place too well. Bone-white, bone-dry, the only moisture you feel is what beads on your neck or drips off your brow. Right now, after so many months in the jungle, in the closed-in, compressed atmosphere, I don't want to be venturing into the tricky light of the open spaces. The even trickier, outsized shadows. The vastness and the roads that never end.

I know all about this place. You leave things here, when you come back they look the same, but they've changed. The opposite of the tropics, where everything looks different after you haven't seen it for a while, but nothing's changed.

My leg is only sore at night. In this climate, it should be easier, but it's been sorest here. I saved the bullet they got out whole. Maybe you'll want to add it to your bracelet. The gift of an NVA sniper in Laos. Chinese bullets from a Russian rifle – it's amazing that they fired. They operated on me at the 85th Evacuation Hospital in Phu Bai. Accommodation's not nearly as nice as the *Repose*. My last bit of surgery in Vietnam, though, no matter what.

But I'm getting ahead of myself.

On January 18, 1969, on that run up the Mekong River, my plane, a two-engine OV-10, was shot down over Laos. The pilot never made it. I parachuted and landed without a scratch. Then I was captured by a band of Pathet Lao irregulars working with the VC.

This happened east of Xepone, at 106°40', 16°50' – coordinates I'll never forget – 110 miles north of the point where Laos, Cambodia, and Thailand meet. You could call that point Three Corners, if you had a perverse sense of humor, but it doesn't have a monument, like Four Corners here in New Mexico, just border guards on all sides with shoot-to-kill orders and no questions asked. North, along the river, the jungle is dense as a wall. East, where I came down, the yellow plains end abruptly after many miles in another wall of jungle, and then a green mountain range. The plains are so dry that grass fires start up on their own and burn for days.

As you well know, I left Manila making preparations to be transferred *out of* Indochina. Instead they sent me right into the burning belly. That's what the CIA guys call that zone in southern Laos. The place that vomits fire. And fire is what I thought I was going to get.

First the Pathet Lao trussed my hands behind my back and threw a noose around my neck. Yanking me by a long rope, they doused me with gasoline and started lighting matches and tossing them by me. One of them – he was about sixteen – had a Zippo off a dead GI which he flicked inches from my face. They kept this up for an hour, leading me into the jungle. I thought the payoff would be to turn me into a human torch. But finally they just blindfolded me and every so often prodded me with their rifles or kicked me in the shins. Later I would learn that the gasoline-and-matches routine was a standard welcoming technique for prisoners. The first of their psych-out games.

How did I come to be there? What was my mission – and why did I even have one? For starters, I was practically shanghaied. When I got to Luzon after leaving you at the hotel, I was called in to the CO's office. I was pleasantly surprised, thinking my transfer had gone through at record speed.

The CO is a one-star general. Tall, with a gut. He has a crossbow hanging behind his desk. Pictures of himself fly-fishing. He sits me down. We drink coffee. He smokes a meerschaum pipe, brown with nicotine. Two other guys come into the room. A bug-eyed blank-faced lieutenant who has a skull above crossed swords tattooed on both forearms. He's been flying Spookies – AC-47 gunships – over the Ho Chi Minh Trail, knocking out truck convoys. He's my pilot, who won't make it. The other guy is wearing a Nehru jacket, rope sandals, and black shades. He looks like a blind man. He barely says a word. Clearly he's CIA.

The CO tells me what a hero I am. Shot out of the sky, pulling a crewman from the burning B-52, twenty-eight combat missions to my credit. You've done your part, Major, he says, knocking some ashes out of his pipe. Oh yes, you've been promoted, and there's a Purple Heart and a Silver Star on the way. Maybe a Distinguished Flying Cross in the cards, too. Depending. On what? Well, you've got your transfer, it's yours. But you have one more run to make. It's been in the works since before you requested transfer. One more mission. Then you get your medals and you wake up on a NATO base in southern Europe. Aviano, Malta – you name it – a year of Mediterranean sun. But first.

First I have to go into the burning belly. Just once. After which I'll be sipping wine with cheese and olives at sunset.

Someone's told the CO I'm the best navigator out of Guam. That I can read the stars without a map – *the way other men read a book*. Also that I'm experienced in surveillance and night photography, from my days flying over Russia and Japan which I told you about. And cartography, too. In short, I exactly fit the bill for the mission: a navigator who can use a camera, know what he's looking at, and map it. And here I am in Luzon, the right place at the right time.

I feel exactly the opposite: that I'm in the wrong place at the wrong time. I don't like any of it. Especially the part about fitting the bill so exactly. For what purpose?

My pilot and I are to be flown to Saigon at once. From there, in an OV-10 with extra fuel tanks, we'll take off at 1 a.m. on the 18th of January and fly north over the whole of Cambodia to the Laotian border at Khong Island. That's about 300 miles. We'll follow the river north another hundred miles, over a ridge of mountains that puts us within thirty miles of the Ho Chi Minh Trail. The Trail runs through Laos, the lifeline of the NVA in the south. I'm supposed to guide us to a very small wedge the CO has pencilled onto a map he spreads out before me. A narrow valley between the river and the mountain highlands through which the South Vietnamese border runs. I'm to photograph and chart the means of access to this valley, which they think is two winding dirt roads. High-flying surveillance had not been able to detail the area enough. We'll draw rocket fire, but the plane has a radar-blocker and under cover of the night we should be all right. As soon as I'm done, we'll veer east out of Laos and fly south to a base near Da Nang.

What's in this valley that's so important? It's top secret, the CO says, but they're going to tell us – because we're volunteering for the mission. Volunteering by this definition: if I don't do it, medals or no medals, they're going to make me finish out my tour back on Guam, navigating bombing runs on B-52s. This little trip into Laos is my ticket out of the war.

The top-secret item in the valley is an Air Force officer being held in a VC compound. They want him out badly. Why? Mr CIA in his shades clears his throat to say that this is high-security clearance information. Then the CO informs us that the officer is a former Air America pilot who has in his head the locations of every secret landing strip and rendezvous point in Laos. The VC may not have a clue who he is; and it's doubtful they could know that he knows so much. But working him over they'll find out. Maybe in a month, maybe in six. So he has to come out. Special Forces commandos are poised to do it. But only after they have a detailed map and photos of the compound.

If they can't get the officer out, I realize too, they're going to kill him.

My pilot's name was Basus. For three days in Saigon, in Division Headquarters at Kendall Air Force Base, he and I were briefed. In that time, we barely exchanged a word. At the canteen we shared a couple of cold meals together, in silence. Our quarters were far apart. And in the dark, early morning hours of January 18th when he

482

was killed, he was less than a thousand feet from me, but I could barely see him. We were high in the air, para-chuting into the jungle after ejecting from our plane. From beneath camouflage nets, the antiaircraft battery that caught us flying so low – never mind the radar-blocking and the moonless night – had then turned its 20mm gun on our parachutes. The Pathet Lao don't bother themselves with the Geneva Convention. They strafed Basus, and the last I saw of him, his helmet was tilted severely and his body limp as his parachute sailed into the black trees like a ghost.

I closed my eyes and waited for them to turn the gun on me. My whole life didn't pass before me: just a single moment, which I had often revisited, even when I wasn't awaiting a hail of gunfire.

It was on the afternoon in February 1945 (the month you were born) that I visited the Fleischmann Plan-etarium in Reno, Nevada, with my mother. I was seven years old. We were standing in a room with black walls just outside the auditorium before an enlarged X-ray photograph of the Andromeda Galaxy. The galaxy nearest our own. We were waiting to see the show that ran every two hours, called 'A Trip to the Stars'. My mother was wearing black gloves and a black dress and her long hair flowed out of a wide-brimmed hat. She was holding my hand and reading me the card on the wall next to the photograph when a man came up to us out of the darkness. He was wearing a white suit and he tipped his hat to her. The hat was white, too, with a black band. His face I never saw clearly; for someone my height, it was impossible to distinguish in the gloomy light of that anteroom.

In a low voice he began speaking to my mother. A voice I will never forget. Confident and confidential, with a tinge of urgency. A seducer's voice, I would realize only when I was older. At seven, all I knew was that it was a type of voice I had never heard before. My mother was a very beautiful woman. I was aware that men looked closely at her. On the street. Even in our house. And I knew that she and my father had many acquaintances in Reno. I was used to people coming up to them when we were out. But never like this, with this kind of voice. Or with this man's body language, as he smoothed his yellow tie leaning into and away from her at the same time.

As she talked with him, my mother let go of my hand. I waited for her to take it again, but she didn't. Maybe three minutes had passed. Yet I knew instinctively that in that brief time I had lost her. I knew it in the following weeks when she and my father argued even more than usual. Knew it when she kept slipping out of the house without a word, first in the afternoons, then at night. Knew it before the commotion one morning in March when the maid breathlessly descended the spiral staircase to tell my father, just returned from Vegas, that my mother was gone. And that she had taken her two largest suitcases and all her jewelry and a swath of clothes from her walk-in closet.

The rest of her bedroom my father tore apart. I had seen him angry many times, but coldly so. Never enraged. Never breaking things over his knee or hurling them against a wall or tearing them to shreds, as he did with the things my mother had left behind. If he was looking for something in that big corner room flooded with desert light, he didn't find it. My mother was not the type to leave a note. Or send a letter afterward. In fact, she never communicated with him again. Or with me, to whom she had not said goodbye.

All I ever heard was that she had first traveled to Honolulu and then possibly disappeared into Southeast Asia. When I was looking for you over the last few months, in Thailand and Japan and Hawaii, following hunches, chasing after third-hand information, it struck me it was the way I might once have set out to find my mother. A quest that would have proved equally futile, I'm afraid.

The only thing I knew for sure when my mother left was that she was with that man in the white suit who had approached us at the planetarium. Looking up at her profile, her smiling eyes, I felt a cold thread of fear wind its way around my heart. I would never forget the two of them in that black room, she in black, he in white, before the blazing ring of Andromeda.

I never saw my mother again.

When I opened my eyes all those years later in Laos, swinging from my parachute, waiting for the artillery flash out of the darkness that would mean my death, I gazed up quickly at the night sky, at the stars, certain I would never see them again. That they would be the last things I ever saw.

Descending fast over the jungle canopy, I braced myself, but the artillery fire never came. I hit the ground as my plane exploded into a hillside several miles to the south. Cutting loose from my parachute, I took out my pistol and plunged into the brush. I heard an animal thrashing nearby and all around me the birds were clattering. Without a machete, in the darkness, I knew I wasn't going to get far. There was a lot of bamboo, sharp as razor blades, cutting my hands and face.

Within minutes I heard men approaching me, slashing through the bamboo. First to my right and left, and then from behind. There can be few worse feelings than being surrounded, hearing a circle tighten around you. They saw me before I saw them and one of them switched on a flashlight, trained it on me, and started shouting. As I spun around, half-blinded by the light, searching for an opening, they emerged from the brush, a dozen men in motley uniforms. Rubber ponchos, NVA jackets, Chinese battle fatigues, plastic sandals, Russian boots, even an American infantryman's uniform, torn up in the back where he'd been shot. His name tag, still sewn on, read SAFKAS.

I dropped my pistol and raised my arms over my head. Immediately one of them slammed a rifle butt into my back and another clubbed me on the head with the heel of his machete handle. I fell to my knees, sharper lights flashing in my eyes and the mud seeping through my pants as I waited again for a bullet, this time just one, in the back of the head.

But they had no intention of killing me outright. They wanted to take me alive, to interrogate me. And this was even before they had ascertained my rank. Why they had mowed Basus down without hesitation – why him by chance and not me – preferring one prisoner to two, I would never know.

When they searched me and discovered that I was an Air Force major, they got very excited. But they didn't treat me any better.

Five hours later, after they had blindfolded me and tied my hands and run me through the jungle, they beat me across the shoulders when I refused to eat something still moving – an insect – that one of them pushed into my mouth. My back and head were still throbbing, on fire, from the previous blows I had taken. When my hands were finally untied, I would find a lump the size of a plum on my skull and my hair matted with blood.

We reached our destination, wherever that was, and I was made to stand against a tree under a blistering sun. I heard men barking out commands and cursing. Once a truck came and went, and a couple of motorbikes. My knees and elbows were raw, and the flies and mosquitoes were going after the blood on my face. Twice someone slapped me. Once I was spat on. For the third time that morning, I thought I was going to be executed. I strained my ears to distinguish the sounds of a firing squad: men shuffling into a line, rifles being loaded and cocked. Had they in fact wanted to kill me, it was more likely my executioner would have been another sixteen-year-old shooting from the hip with an M-1.

Standing against that tree, exhausted and hungry, I was the most scared I had been all day. And suddenly I had the time to think about it. My eyes were open beneath the blindfold and I tried to keep the rest of my face taut, to show nothing.

Finally someone led me away from the tree and pushed me into a dank place with a dirt floor. The stench was overpowering – excrement, urine, vomit. I got sick myself, and tried to roll away from the smell. I wasn't alone anymore: beyond my blindfold there were moans, whispers, coughing. I could hear breathing close up, could feel myself being studied. 'Are you Americans?' I said after a long time, my own voice sounding miles away. No one replied.

I lay there in the dirt. The hours crawled by. I had begun to realize that this was not going to be over anytime soon: I could be facing months, probably years, in a hole just like this one – maybe worse.

It was night when they removed my blindfold and untied my hands. At first, even the darkness in that place hurt my eyes. Then things came clear and I saw that I was in a long, narrow, windowless hut with about twenty other men. The others all had a wooden block secured around one ankle, to immobilize them. I hadn't gotten mine yet. Only two of the men were Americans: a helicopter gunner and a marine corporal. Then there were South Vietnamese Army soldiers and six montagnard guerillas.

The marine told me all this. He had been a prisoner for two years, the gunner for eleven months. All he ever thought about, he told me, was escape. After less than a day of captivity, I could understand that.

His name was Geal. He was from south Texas. He had been captured in a fire fight near Par Kung after the rest of his platoon was wiped out. He told me the Pathet Lao moved him and the others around all the time. He said that as an officer above the rank of lieutenant I would be taken to a special compound for interrogation. Probably, I thought, the very place I was to have photographed from the plane. I might even meet the captain who knew too much. And maybe now the Special Forces commandos would come in and kill both of us. Except they didn't have the map I was to have drawn for them. So instead the Air Force would just carpet-bomb the place.

This was the way my thoughts were running, lying there in the dirt.

Geal told me another thing: the montagnards were the last men captured before me, just two days earlier. Montagnards means mountaineers, the thirty-three tribes that inhabit the Central Highlands which straddle Vietnam and Laos. Centuries before those two countries came into existence, the montagnards' ancestors were settling the steep mountain forests. Tough and independent, they survived the French and now the NVA by uniting their fighting men under one command – FULRO, a French acronym for the 'United Fighting Front of the Oppressed Races'.

The montagnards imprisoned with me were from the Bru tribe, the toughest of all the FULRO forces. They despised the Pathet Lao and the VC, who in turn feared them. Geal said the Pathet Lao didn't like to take Bru prisoners. The Bru believe imprisonment is tantamount to death. Their comrades did everything they could to free them, regardless of the risks. If the prisoners were executed, their Bru comrades pursued the executioners to the death. So even after a battle they'd won, the Pathet Lao seldom rounded up the Bru that hadn't been killed. It was better to let them slip back into the forests.

I didn't know it at the time, but if I was going to be shot down again, I couldn't have picked a better time than that day or a better place than that district. The fact I had then been brought as a prisoner to that particular penal way station probably saved my life.

The next day at dawn, two guards pulled me outside the hut. They gave me a cup of water and a lump of dried rice, and then tied my hands again behind my back. Next they brought out the six montagnards and with mallets knocked the wooden blocks from their ankles. They gave them water but no rice, and after tying their hands behind their backs, ran a rope between them, so the six had to walk as one – like a centipede, I thought – as they preceded me into the jungle along a narrow trail. I never again saw Geal, the copter gunner, or any of the other men in that hut.

By midday, we had forded two rivers and entered a scorched valley where most of the trees had been cut down. We were heading due east, I realized with alarm, toward North Vietnam. Toward the prison compound near the border that I was to have photographed. I tried to put out of my mind the inquisition that would await me there. I only hoped my aerial cameras had been destroyed when my plane crashed. The NVA were known to be especially brutal with fliers doing surveillance work, blinding them with acid, cutting off their ears. If they found out the object of the surveillance had been their own compound, I would really be in for it.

After we had walked several more miles, a jagged green mountain range appeared suddenly on the horizon. At the sight of these mountains, the Bru became visibly animated, though they tried to conceal it from our captors.

My few previous encounters with montagnards had been in Saigon, where they were like fish out of water. Ears attuned to the sounds and silences of alpine forests, they found the clatter of the city intolerable. They always seemed rigid and uncomfortable in the regulation combat boots and khaki they had been issued. And few Vietnamese understood their guttural tribal dialects.

In their own element, in the mountains, wearing scant, loose-fitting clothes, they were a handsome, wiry people, lithe and well-proportioned, with coppery skin and choppy black hair. Just over five feet tall, the Bru men were generally bowlegged, which is an asset on steep slopes and dangerous cliffs. Their small feet were so callused they could travel over the roughest terrain barefoot, as if they were wearing sandals. Nearly all of the Bru – men and women – were tattooed. Some had barely noticeable markings: a circle or a line of dots on their ankles. Others had elaborate images – the heads of birds or fishes – painted on their backs and chests, or even their faces. The prisoner just ahead of me that morning had a tattoo of a dog with stars for eyes. As we trudged into the swelter of midday, I tried to focus on it, to distract from my pain.

I would soon discover that, among their other attributes, the Bru possessed an acute sense of smell and extremely powerful eyesight, like the mountain tigers they worshipped. The Bru claim that the only man they truly fear is the one who might come into their village carrying some part of a tiger's anatomy on his person. It doesn't matter if it's a tooth, a piece of fur, a bone. They believe such a man can turn himself into a tiger at will. Later, the prisoner with the dog tattoo, whose name was Nol, would tell me matter-of-factly that it was just such a man who came to our rescue that day.

Whoever it was struck with the swiftness of a tiger just as we were preparing to ford yet another muddy river with the rifles of the Pathet Lao on our backs. I heard successive arrows hiss by me and saw two of our guards crumple to the ground. The arrows were short, with black-and-orange feathered arrows. Panicking, the other guards opened fire point-blank at the montagnard prisoners and five of them toppled facedown on the riverbank. Instinctively I dived into a thicket of reeds, grabbing Nol's shirt and dragging him along with me. Then, as the guards fired blindly into the bush, they were picked off one by one, black-and-orange feathered arrows through their hearts. When the smoke cleared, of seven prisoners and fifteen guards only Nol and I had survived.

Bok-Klia, he cried, still tethered to his dying comrades, *Bok-Klia*. Later I would learn that this meant 'Lord Tiger', the man-tiger whose quiver contains arrows feathered with the colors of the great cat. He is also called 'Mister 30' because, when enraged, he will kill a different man every day for a month.

I would learn many things after Nol and I managed to make our way deep into those green mountains I had first glimpsed from the scorched plain. But whether we had been rescued by a band of men or one man with the power of ten, I never found out. Nol's answer to my queries was always the same: *Bok-Klia.*

It took us three days through the roughest country I had ever seen to reach his village. Torn up by mosquitoes and nettles, we ate what we could find. Plants, mushrooms, and roots handpicked by Nol. According to the Brus' law, for saving his life I was now more than a brother to him. Which was how he treated me.

On the third day of our trek, he ended up carrying me on his back, a dead weight. I don't know how he did it. The previous night, I had slashed my ankle right through my boot while crossing a swamp. At first I didn't realize I was cut and the swamp water went to work on me. Within an hour I was feverish, my leg throbbing all the way up to the hip. Nol packed my ankle with a white moss held fast by sticky blue leaves. He made me chew a bitter black root and keep the pulp in my mouth as long as I could. And he tied a stringy fern tightly just below my knee, like a tourniquet.

We took shelter from a heavy downpour in a shallow cave, and the last thing I remember is watching Nol rig up a kind of stretcher out of bamboo. When I next woke up without fever, clear in the head, I was lying on a straw mat in a dark room with a thatched ceiling. I had no idea how much time had passed. The walls of the room were thick bamboo. A black macaw with an orange bill was perched in the open window. Incense was burning in a brass bowl. A pair of ox skulls painted bloodred flanked the low doorway. And there was a crossbow hung on the opposite wall, just like the one in the CO's office back in Saigon.

14 October

I used to fall asleep in that bamboo room, Mala, trying to put myself in your place when you didn't hear from me after Manila. I tried, but it was too painful. I knew the Air Force would have told you nothing. Less than

491

nothing. As only they can do. You must have thought I was dead. Even now, as I write this, watching the desert sun rise through my window, I know you must think I'm dead. If you're thinking of me at all, that is, wherever you are.

In fact, for a long time the Air Force knew nothing about my whereabouts. I had been on a mission about which maybe six people knew the details. The wreckage of my plane had been sighted. Ditto my dead pilot, hanging from a tree in his parachute. I was listed as MIA. Later, I would begin to materialize, like a wisp of vapor, a rumor that wafted to, and barely registered with, the informers and double agents who comprised the outermost reaches of the CIA's tentacles. An American in a place where no Americans ought to be. If this rumor ever reached Saigon, it would have been too faint and insignificant to make any impression at all.

The Bru village in which I recovered my strength was technically across the DMZ, in North Vietnam, in a zone where none of our forces operated. A place so remote that the only montagnards who had ever seen an American were the FULRO fighters who passed through on occasion.

I would be there for five months.

It was the rainy season when I first arrived. The point – about twenty miles off – where the mountain footpaths were said to connect with a real trail was washed out. Where the trail connected with a safe route (or where I imagined a safe route might be) out of that country I didn't know.

For weeks I couldn't walk. My foot was badly infected. I was terrified of gangrene, of losing my leg. I lay in that room in a house on stilts in a village of twenty such houses nestled high in the rain forest and thought, this is where I'm going to die. And no one will ever know.

You would never have known.

You and I were together for such a short time. First in chaotic circumstances, among all those wounded men

492

and exhausted nurses. And both of us wounded and exhausted in our own ways. Then we were alone together even more briefly, and intensely, in a city neither of us knew, before being torn apart.

Now, two years later, the idea that you could be with someone else torments me. When I tell myself this isn't possible, it's not out of false pride, but because I believe deep down that you must feel as I do. That for both of us there will never be anyone else.

Yet, with the passage of time, I fear I've become a ghost to you. Forever inhabiting the limbo of Manila. In our heads, a ghost can assume a whole other life, so fixed in the past that we convince ourselves it can't ever return to this life. That's a subject I know something about.

I know about possessiveness, too. My fears of losing you are still more painful to me than any wounds I've suffered. What two people can love each other deeply without wanting to possess, and be possessed? Isn't love the only place we can give everything and honestly expect it may not be in vain? Even after we're dead.

This is how my thoughts were running my first weeks in that bamboo room in which incense burned day and night. On the straw mat under the thatched roof I had plenty of time to think. The room was always twilit. In the upper corner of one small window I could see the sun light up the tall trees at midday, and in the same space I might watch a few stars flicker to life before I fell asleep. For six weeks I never saw the moon or sun directly.

As my fever abated, my mind fixed on more concrete and particular things. I thought of the bracelet I gave you. Of the slenderness of your wrist, and the scent of your skin when I kissed you there, and then on your shoulders and breasts. Many times as I lay in that room I felt your lips brush my cheek. And settle on my mouth. And part slowly before we were kissing hard, embracing, in our room in Manila with the shutters and the slow fan.

Over and over I revisited our time together there.

Every moment, from different angles, but always with you at the center of the picture. The drive down the coast. The beach at Orion. Diving for shells. The bazaar where I found the jade earrings. The green dress they matched and the soft sound it made when you walked. The playing-card leaf on which you wrote our names. The hibiscus in the hotel courtyard and the cries of the cats on the high wall. But most of all our room. The ribbon on the fan and the muffled piano music in the next room. The narrow bed. Your body pressed up against mine. The red dot on your palm where the spider had bitten you in New Orleans. The spider with the stars on its belly.

In the Bru village there was a woman who nursed me, a sorceress. Like all the montagnards, the Bru are animists. To them, every rock, tree, plant, mountain, and stream has its own spirit and consciousness. The same goes for floods and fires, and even particular sections of the sky. Their word for this spirit-force is *ae*. When you're sick, they believe the illness to be spirit-induced, adversely affecting your own spirit. Thus they insist that, more than the organs of the body, it is the spirit which must be dealt with. Left unattended, malignancies of spirit can spread and wipe out an entire village. (Or even a country: it occurred to me that the war itself has been perpetuated by such runaway malignancies in Washington DC and Hanoi.) With a high fever and lingering infection, added to the fact that I was a stranger of an alien race, my case was seen as especially dangerous. This was why the chief sorceress, the caretaker of spirits, actually moved into the hut belonging to one of Nol's cousins where I had been lodged.

The first time I saw this woman she looked thin as a reed sitting in the corner of my bamboo room staring at me. Smoking a pipe. Among the montagnards, men and women alike smoke a bitter mountain tobacco laced with mint. I had seen many sorts of tattoos since arriving in the village, but this woman's was particularly elaborate and gave me a jolt: a red spider, finely drawn on her left cheek, complemented by a concentric web that covered the right side of her face. At the center of the web there was a silver star. Through the dim light of the tallow burning beside me, the spider at times looked real. And at night, as the woman sat very still, the star twinkled. I came to look for it when I awoke half delirious in the darkness.

That first night, when she came out of the shadows to mop my brow and repack my ankle, the woman told me her name was Ji-Loq. Which in the Bru language means 'spider crossing the stars,' a being with enormous powers in the world of spirits.

It was Ji-Loq who informed me (by drawing a circle of figures with upraised arms on a mountaintop under the stars) that the Bru I was among were a distinct branch of the tribe who worshipped the stars.

She brought me tea and boiled rice. And those bitter black roots which I chewed several times a day. I communicated with her by sign language. And by drawing pictures on a flat stone with a splinter of charcoal. When I grew afraid one night and drew a picture of a man with one leg, she shook her head vehemently and gripped my wrist. She was not going to let me lose my leg.

And I trusted her because of her name. Because of her name, I thought you had sent her to help me.

At first, during the long days and nights I drifted in and out of sleep and dream, I did not participate in my dreams so much as I observed them from the outside. For a while, they were strictly dreams of my childhood: roaming the peripheries of the desert with a compass; watching my mother comb out her hair on the terrace when she woke at midday; sitting on the floor of my father's study while he was at his desk without our once exchanging a word; building model airplanes out of balsa wood; and, most frequently, lying on my back on the lawn to study the clouds and the stars and the meteorites that flared brilliantly over the desert.

This part of my childhood didn't last long.

I began getting in trouble when I was still very young. I was born in Reno, and after my mother left, when I was seven, I remained there for another eleven years. My father raised me – when he was around. He still lives there.

I never got over my mother's disappearance. My troubles really began when I told myself that I had. The anger it fired up in me was going to burn for a long time. It started out with fights at school.

As I said, my parents were well known around Reno. My father is a rich, powerful man. For that reason, he has plenty of friends, but their loyalty is about as thick as a sheet of paper. With his enemies, on the other hand, the feelings run deep. They last lifetimes. His vendettas, and the vendettas against him, have been known to take on lives of their own.

One of the things my father never did well is play the fool. You could argue that his entire adult life was a tortuous exercise in erecting defenses against ever having to do so. My mother knew that. And the role of fool was exactly what she handed him the moment she very publicly ran away with another man. Having overheard their quarrels, and knowing how unhappy my mother was, and how cruel and difficult my father could be, I could almost forgive her just taking off like that. But I couldn't forgive that she hadn't given a thought to the consequences of her actions on me. For starters, the ridicule to which I would be exposed.

In some ways I resembled my father: swallowing my pride was not one of my strong suits. Not when it came to being taunted in the playground about my mother. All my pent-up anger for her I let fly against the kids who taunted me. It didn't matter if they were twice my size, or came at me in pairs, I took them on. I became very free with my fists, and the more I got beaten up, the harder I fought.

I don't know how many times I was expelled from school – lots of schools. If it hadn't been for my father's influence, I would have been in reform school. As it was,

I was lucky to have avoided juvenile prison, having moved up to petty larceny – shoplifting, picking pockets (without extracting a single dollar before throwing the wallets into trash cans) – and then to grand larceny, stealing cars off the street. I'd jump the ignitions, joyride the cars on the interstate, and ditch them in the desert.

I was a rich kid slumming, a dilettante criminal with the flimsiest of motives: that I was pissed off. Where my mother had left off setting my father up to play the fool, I was going to finish the job. Between the two of us, I thought, we could put him through the wringer. How wrong I was, and how dearly I paid for it. My father's business was putting other people through the wringer. My mother had gotten to him, all right, but that made him all the more determined that no one else should get to him. And certainly not her son.

Which, as my troubles multiplied, is what he came to see me as: *her son*, not his.

I haven't spoken with my father in sixteen years. Though our rift was many years in the making, it became completely and forever uncrossable on September 10, 1955, when I learned once and for all just what kind of man my father was.

It's a complicated story. It begins and ends with the only other woman I ever loved, Mala.

Her name was Bel. My childhood sweetheart. She was a year older than me – nineteen when she died. My father, who barely knew her, hated her because of who she was. That is, who she was related to. She was the daughter of a former partner of his, whom he had betrayed, and the niece of his most hated enemy, whom he had cheated even worse. When he got wind that I wanted to marry Bel, my father not only forbade it, but promised to make my life miserable just for contemplating such a move.

In truth, her uncle, who hated my father every bit as much as my father hated him, and who wouldn't have liked anything he might have heard about me, would never have approved our marriage, either, if he had gotten wind of it. But Bel kept our relationship a secret. She said we were a Romeo and Juliet story, born on the dividing line of an ugly feud, people on all sides thwarting us. Still, she told me, love would win out.

I wanted to believe that. To believe that love, not destruction, would win out. Yet I knew that, even in the most favorable conditions, love is fragile. And because of my history, I had a strong hunch then about what I know now: that destruction always wins out. But even people under the gun sometimes get some breathing room. Five years, six, for some people upward of ten.

Bel and I had less than two years. Time that seemed like it was ours alone – and therefore felt much longer – because we didn't share it with anyone. It wasn't that we were together all the time – far from it – but when we were, it was as if there were no one else in the world. And no one who knew anything about what we were doing or how we really felt.

We were going to elope, which meant running away together without a dollar between us. But because of a blowup with my father, my own foul temper, and a reckless chain of events he set in motion, everything backfired on Bel and me. We got badly burned and never recovered.

Events moved very fast at that time. Whenever I thought I had a grip on them, they changed. Even now, as I try to reconstruct them, they keep moving. Like a jigsaw puzzle some invisible hand scatters every time you're poised to add a pivotal piece.

When you and I were in Manila, one of those pivotal pieces that had always eluded me just fell into my lap. It seemed to arrive across many centuries, but really it had only been fourteen years. And how strange that this should happen when with you I was living each day as if it were a year, when once again events were about to speed up and fly out of control.

Remember the proprietor of the Hôtel Alnilam, the Frenchman from Las Vegas? Our last night there, when we settled the bill, he passed me a note. After we went up to our room, I said I was going down for drinks, but really I went to his office. I was sure I hadn't fooled you – it was the only time I ever lied to you – but you didn't call me on it.

His name was Canopus. While I had heard of him back in Nevada, I had never met him. He used to own the hotel where Bel lived. When Canopus went bankrupt, her uncle bought it from him. Canopus was bitter about that, and plenty of other things. He had wandered through Indochina and settled down in Manila. He recognized my name the moment you and I checked in to the Alnilam. He had a grievance against my father, too, who he claimed had swindled him in some real estate deal that led to his insolvency.

I didn't doubt it, and when he saw that, he assured me that he had nothing against me personally – but I didn't believe him. He claimed he just wanted to buy a cognac for someone from back home – that no one from Vegas or Reno had ever passed through his hotel. And that was why he left the flowers in our room. Do you remember those red and yellow ones? He had cultivated them in the garden of his hotel in Vegas and then carried the seeds all over Asia.

But it wasn't flowers he wanted to talk about. Pouring the cognac, he said he knew my story, the story of Bel and me, including some things even I might not know. Did I want to hear them?

I was stunned. A part of me didn't want to hear any of it – not with you upstairs, not when I hoped I was finally putting all that behind me. But I had to hear him out.

Canopus told me that Bel had given birth to a child before she died. And that neither my father nor Bel's uncle had known about this at the time. Neither had I, and it was as if he had struck me a second blow with a sledgehammer.

Until that moment, I was sure no one else had known that Bel had been pregnant. After we were separated, she told me she had had a miscarriage. That was in her fifth month. I never saw her again, so I had no way of being sure that was what had happened. I also had no reason to doubt her. She would have needed a good reason to lie to me about something that important.

It occurred to me even while Canopus was relating his tale that Bel did have a good reason: she had been protecting me. Not from my father or her uncle, but from myself.

I killed a man, Mala. In this lousy war I did terrible things. I'm lucky I don't know the real numbers: how many hundreds of dead for the bombing runs I navigated. Back in Nevada, before I ever thought of enlisting, I killed a single man, but I did it up close, with his own gun. Afterward I hid out in Colorado, and Bel was afraid that if I returned to Nevada I would be arrested. Knowing it was hard enough for me stay away, she wasn't going to tell me anything that might have brought me running to her.

I had killed this man in self-defence – actually, to save Bel's life – but the police might not have seen it that way. That I had fled the scene was damning in itself. But for many other reasons, I was sure my version of events would never be believed. Not least of which was the fact that the very same cops I would be dealing with had several times picked me up for car theft. I was actually on probation. The fact that Bel had been at the scene with me, and so would be treated as an accessory to murder, made it impossible for me to risk arrest. On top of all this, the man I killed was an ex-cop.

He was also my father's strong-arm man, a shady jack-of-all-trades named Dupont. He had been at various times a diamond courier and union organizer. As an undercover cop, he had been on the take, and though never convicted, he was eventually busted from the force. A large, dark man with black hair and long sideburns, he had blunt features and a square jaw. He favored flashy tropical shirts and a Stetson. For my father he performed an assortment of tasks: keeping an eye on his friends, delivering messages to his enemies, serving as bodyguard when my father traveled, and in earlier days, bringing my mother home from her nights-on-the-town. After my mother was gone, he had the run of our house, and even as a kid I had never gotten along with him, never trusted him. The feeling was mutual. He looked down on me as the boss's spoiled son, and when I started getting in trouble I was convinced that he put in a bad word about me with cops who were still his friends. Worse, whenever he got a chance, he fanned the animosity between my father and me. Not that it needed much fanning.

What happened to Bel and me that day on a rocky flat in the desert might never have happened if my father – furious that I had taken something of his – had not chosen to send Dupont after me for it. Bel and I would have moved away together. She wouldn't have died so young. I would have known my child. Maybe my father and her uncle wouldn't have spent another sixteen years at each other's throats.

One day after I'd been arguing with my father – that's about all we did that last year before I took off – I found myself alone in his study, in a rage. As was often the case, the argument had started over my mother. Grown ever more embittered, he often made disparaging remarks about her to the people around him, like Dupont. To get under my skin, Dupont would then repeat these things to me. When I complained to my father about it, he exploded, and as always took out his anger at my mother on me.

This particular time he shouted that as far as he was concerned my mother had died the moment she last walked out of that house; the fate she met in Honolulu or Hong Kong or wherever she ended up was no concern of his. When he added that he hoped she *was* dead – something I had never before heard him say outright – it really set me off. Why then, I shouted back, did he continue to sink a fortune into private eyes to try to find her? He looked at me as if he wanted to take me apart right then and there, and without blinking an eye he said that as long as I was with *that girl* I was dead to him too. That was another first, bringing Bel into the whole ugly mix about my mother, and I knew with him it wouldn't end there, it would never end, that I had been right and Bel was wrong: love wouldn't win out where we came from; while we were around my father, and people like him, we would never have any peace.

I was shaking all over, but before I could come back at him, my father stormed out and left me there, wanting to turn that room upside down and smash every single thing in it. Instead, I broke open his desk drawer and took something I knew was irreplaceable to him, something that would drive him crazy to lose; worth little in itself, without it he wouldn't have access to his most prized possession. For years, long before he had Bel and me to attack, my father had tried to obliterate what little good of my mother still lived in my heart. Now I was going to repay him for his efforts.

You see, despite her long absence, until then my mother had continued to play a dubious role in our little family: arguing about her had usually kept my father and me from clashing about our more immediate differences. She served as the kind of buffer between us that she would never have been if she were still around. When she was around, she shopped for clothes, lost money at the casinos, and had her affairs in hotels downtown. My picture of her had altered as I got older and better understood what her life in Reno had really been like. When I was a boy, I often just sat gazing at her, and she was so beautiful I couldn't imagine her doing any wrong.

In fact, even then I knew what she was capable of. I knew, for example, that she had disappeared on us far sooner than my father thought: not when she last walked out of the house, but the moment she let go of my hand at the planetarium while talking to the man in the white suit. How many times in my head had I taken revenge on that man. Usually with my hands around his throat. Sometimes with a knife under his ribs. Or a gun jammed into his stomach, wiping away the smile I imagined he had flashed at my mother that day. A man whose face I would not know if I passed him on the street.

Dupont's face, on the other hand, I will never forget. Especially as I last saw it, contorted, with glaring eyes, behind the wheel of a red sedan bearing down on Bel as she tried to run clear of him along the edge of a ravine; I had gotten down on one knee just ahead, steadying a .44 pistol with both hands, knowing I would only get the chance at one more shot as his car flew past.

How, in a few short hours, did I get from arguing with my father to shooting a man dead?

After running out of my father's office, I threw some clothes in a suitcase and telephoned Bel. I told her to take, not her car, but a taxi, to a place where we used to rendezvous, a Mexican joint called El Neón, midway between Las Vegas and Reno on Route 95. I said she should bring what she needed, that we were heading for California – to start our new life, once and for all. Brave words for someone just turned eighteen, with three hundred dollars in his pocket and no prospects. Though we had discussed running away together many times, I would never know if she agreed that this was the best time to make our move. In her brief hesitation over the phone, I could sense her uneasiness, but she said only that she would be there in an hour, at five o'clock.

We never had the chance to discuss how she felt. No sooner had I picked her up at El Neón and doubled back toward the California state line than a red car appeared out of nowhere in the late-afternoon light and began riding our tail. Suddenly the car slammed into us, crushing the rear fender and forcing me to pull onto the shoulder. As I slammed on the brakes, I saw it was Dupont behind the wheel, wearing a Stetson and a black duster. He leapt out and was at my window in a flash.

Leaning in, he gripped my shoulder like a vise. He told me I had something of my father's that he wanted back, and I realized how careless I had been: leaving the desk drawer open, running from the house. Obviously my father had discovered my theft within minutes. I could have denied it, argued with Dupont, called his bluff – instead, I bit his hand, spun the steering wheel to the right, and floored the accelerator.

For a couple of miles he ate my dust, but then suddenly the red sedan was back on my tail, closing fast. Skilled as I was at jumping car engines, I had little experience of car chases, and Dupont, the ex-cop, was very comfortable driving at breakneck speeds. Again he slammed into our rear, and I had to grip the steering wheel with all my strength.

Bel couldn't believe what was going on. Bracing herself against the dashboard, she kept asking me who Dupont was and what he wanted. But it was too late to explain. And I was panicking. We were on a stretch of road under construction, between Luning and Pilot Peak, a mountain northwest of Las Vegas. The desert there was truly a no-man's-land – bare rocky flats for miles in every direction. When I saw Dupont was going to cut us off again, I got desperate and pulled off the highway altogether, hoping that somehow Dupont would spin out of control and I'd lose him.

But as I sped across the flat, his red sedan was still bobbing in my rearview mirror. Forty, thirty, twenty yards back and gaining fast again. There were scattered boulders to our right and a steep ravine dead ahead. About a hundred yards from the ravine, Dupont cut me off a second time, jumped out, and put a pistol to my head.

He yanked me from my car and motioned with his pistol for Bel to get out too. Ordering us to put our hands on the car roof, he kicked my legs apart. He took my wallet from my back pocket and flipped through it. Then he yanked all my pockets inside out. He tore my jacket pockets away, and put the pistol back to my head, but still I wouldn't give him what he was looking for. He told me to have it my own way, and walked around the car to Bel, adding that searching her would be a real pleasure. I told him he'd better not touch her. He laughed, stepping up behind her, keeping the pistol pointed at me while he ran his fingers along her cheek, then down her shoulder slowly toward her breasts. I said, all right, enough, let her go and I'll give you what you want. This is what I want now, he said, running his hand under her breasts. Bel was biting her lip, frozen. Oh yeah, he said, she kind of reminds me of your mother. I told him I was going to kill him. He laughed again, then lowered the pistol and pushed Bel aside and invited me to try.

I realized that he was off on his own with no turning back: the reason my father had sent him after me was beside the point now. My father might not have minded my being knocked around, and he wouldn't shed tears if I didn't come home again – but I didn't think he wanted me killed.

Before Dupont changed his mind and raised that pistol again, I jumped him. He decked me with a forearm to the head. With Bel screaming, I leapt up and charged him again. And I got lucky. Looking to sidestep and club me with the pistol butt, Dupont's feet went out from under him. With a cry, he fell and the pistol flew from his grasp. He scrambled for it, but I got it first. He was quick, though, and by the time I turned it on him, he was in his car again, grinding the key in the ignition and backing up hard, trying to run me over. I rolled out of the way, but he barely missed Bel, and in her terror she started running. I cried out to her, but she wouldn't stop. Dupont fishtailed his car around and went after her. I was still screaming as he nearly overtook her, but she dove off to the side. Then he wheeled the car around again, kicking up stones, and came after her even faster as she ran back toward me. Her face was white and her red dress was flapping against the yellow sand.

Dupont swerved right, slowing down in order to be sure he hit her. He saw me with the gun, but he must have calculated that I couldn't make such a difficult shot. Or maybe he was so enraged he had stopped calculating altogether. In fact, growing up in that part of the country, growing up with guns, I was a very good shot.

Still, the first shot I got off was wild, shattering one

of the car's headlights. The pistol recoiled hard, and bracing myself, I aimed again, at Dupont's open window, sliding the gun barrel to follow the car's path. At the same time, I saw Bel trip and fall, and I knew this was going to be my last chance. Stopping the breath in my throat, when he was twenty yards away I squeezed the trigger again. There was a streak of smoke. The report echoed sharply across the ravine. And the red sedan skidded to the left, spun around, and lurched to a stop. The horn was blaring. Dupont was slumped over the wheel.

I ran over to Bel, who was sprawled out on her back. Unknown to both of us, the damage to her was already done, just as surely as if Dupont had struck her with the car. She had fallen badly the second time, cracking a rib. It was this rib that would cause complications in her pregnancy, and it was those complications that would kill her.

But at that moment our minds were fixed only on the fact that I had just shot a man. As I helped her up, she kept asking me if Dupont was dead. The scream of the car horn reverberating across the ravine was the answer to that question. I made my way to the red sedan and saw what was left of Dupont's head resting on the steering wheel.

I gagged. I had never seen a man's brains before. And there was so much blood on the seats and windows that I couldn't believe it had come from one man. I reached in for Dupont's shoulder and pulled him off the wheel. Bel was shouting to me, but I couldn't take in her words. On the rear seat there was his Stetson, also blood-spattered, and the gasoline can he carried with him on long drives. I switched off the car's ignition and threw the transmission into neutral. Then I took the gasoline can and emptied it inside the car and all over the hood. Slowly I pushed the car toward the edge of the ravine. I had to push it about forty yards, but down a slight incline, so it didn't take me long. And even though Dupont had just tried to kill me and the only person in the world I really loved, I felt sick when I tossed a lit match into that car and watched it burst into flames as it rolled over the edge of the ravine. I knew that it could have been Bel and me in the car, our brains blown out, our bodies engulfed in fire, as it fell, slamming off the wall of the ravine and flipping over. I remember seeing a hawk circling overhead. And the clouds catching fire too as the sun set. And then a fireball on the floor of the ravine as the car exploded.

Bel and I sped away from there as fast as we could. Several miles out, we passed another car, driven by a solitary man in a baseball cap. This man checked out our faces, and my license plate, as he passed. I thought I recognized him. He could easily have been another of my father's employees. Or a complete stranger about to stumble on the fact I had just committed a murder. Or he could have been nobody at all.

It hit me then that I wasn't just in over my head, I was drowning. My hope that Dupont's body might not be found for a while was fading fast. And when it was found, someone – it didn't matter who he was – could now place me at the scene. My eyes glued to the rearview mirror, I wondered what that man in the base-ball cap would do if and when he reached the ravine and saw the burning car, but I would never find out.

As soon as Bel and I drove a couple of miles down 95, she had to get out and throw up. She became hysterical, and it took me some time to calm her down, though I was half out of my mind myself. We both knew I had to get out of the state, pronto. She said she wanted to come with me, but we also knew that, with me on the run, that was out of the question. She especially knew this was impossible, because of the pain she must've been in, which she kept to herself for fear I would insist on taking her to a hospital. At that moment, I couldn't have imagined I would never see her again, but I think she knew. The way she looked at me, the things she said and didn't say. She always had a strong sixth sense. I did know that, after what I had just done, my life was never going to be the same again. That evening, the last thing she said to me – the last thing she ever said to my face – was, 'Don't come back here until I tell you it's safe.' Well, it's never felt safe and I've never gone back. Even now, sitting in the next state, I'm not tempted to do so.

I dropped her near the hotel where she lived with her uncle, the place Canopus had once owned. I drove all night, not to California, which was the direction the man in the baseball cap had seen me heading, but across Utah into Colorado, where I painted my car, and stole plates for it, and rented a cabin behind a broken-down motel, and hid out for the next few months. It was Canopus, in Manila, who told me the rest. That, in the meantime, Bel was in and out of the hospital, then stayed in a place outside Vegas, bedridden, keeping her condition to herself, keeping her uncle in the dark, until in December she went into labor suddenly and gave birth to a child. A child, Canopus said, whom she put up for adoption weeks later when her health deteriorated to the point where she knew she wasn't going to make it.

He didn't know if it was a boy or a girl.

Over those months, Bel and I had just a few phone conversations. At first, we were so terrified by what had happened that I remained incommunicado. I'd been in trouble before, but not like this. I sold my car and affixed the stolen plates to another car I bought for cash. Outside of buying food and gas, I talked to no one. I was barely across the state line in southeastern Colorado, near Four Corners, just outside the Indian reservation. About 150 miles from where I'm sitting right now. I figured at Four Corners I had four states to choose from: if they tried to extradict me in Colorado, I could jump to New Mexico, and if they came after me there, I would slip into Utah. Round and round and round – my head was spinning.

Twice in the dead of night I drove all way across Utah to the Nevada state line, but I didn't cross it. I was afraid that if I was picked up, I'd never see Bel again. They'd just lock me up and throw away the key. And my father would be happy not to use his connections. My phone conversations with Bel became impossibly frustrating. Convinced the police were on to us, we feared my calls would be traced and so we never stayed on more than a minute. We were certain we had little very time to maneuver. Day and night I plotted desperately for a way out, and what did I come up with? Mexico. I told her that when I raised some money we'd rendezvous there. And lay low. She wasn't going to have her baby in some dusty village. We'd find the most modern hospital in Mexico City, whatever that was. But for that you needed money. Money I couldn't borrow and couldn't afford to steal. If I got picked up in a hot car, I'd be finished. My head was still spinning . . .

And so I made another big mistake. To get the money, I confided in someone besides Bel. The last person on earth I should have turned to.

My half-sister, Ivy.

It's a curious – maybe more than curious – fact that Bel and I shared the same sibling, our one and only sibling. Ivy was my mother Stella's daughter by a man named Nilus Samax, who was Bel's father by another woman. Soon after giving birth to Ivy, Stella left Nilus and ran off with my father. I was born a year later. In the meantime, three months before Ivy's birth, Nilus had fathered Bel on a woman named Astrid.

Follow all that? What a strange and cursed trio we were, spun off two wild women and two betraying men.

Ivy hated Bel – a naturally affectionate girl everyone was drawn to – and when she got wind of our relationship, she hated me, too. Before that, Ivy and I had been okay. That is, for the two years I even knew she existed, after she first came into my life when I was fourteen. Showing up unannounced one day at my father's house in Reno. Each of us embraced the notion that the other might shed some light on the enigma of our mother Stella, and we shared and compared what crumbs of information we had. The runaway, we called her. That was my link with Ivy, and it was tenuous. What else could it be when our links with my mother were nonexistent.

Two significant facts, however: from those crumbs Ivy and I deduced that it was her uncle who had accosted my mother at the Fleischmann Planetarium. He was the man in the white suit whom I had repeatedly murdered in my dreams. When I discovered that my mother had promptly gone on to abandon him – just as she had abandoned all of us – I didn't feel quite so murderous anymore. For my mother, he had been an intermediary, not a great passion. The other fact, even more important perhaps: it was from me that Ivy learned our mother was still alive.

For a while Ivy came to Reno pretty regularly and we would talk, and soon she became friendly with my father. Their link? Their mutual hatred of that same uncle of hers and Bel's; he was also their guardian – Nilus's brother, Junius Samax.

It was through Ivy that, quite accidentally, I met Bel. I went to Las Vegas once to meet Ivy and, to her consternation, while waiting for her in my car on the road to the Hotel Canopus, ran into her sister. Bel and I knew of each other, but only through the filter of Ivy, so when we actually met, the shock of our mutual attraction was that much more powerful. I fell in love with her at first sight – just as I did with you, at a time when I thought I could never again love anybody like that.

Ivy knew at once what happened. Like a lot of people, she knew all about love from the outside in. What I didn't want to see then is so clear to me now: Ivy was the most jealous person I've ever known. And the most effective, when she wanted to be, at concealing the venom that fueled that jealousy. From that day onward, after seeing Bel and me laughing together beside my car, she evidently began working overtime at how she could get at us. She felt me pull away from her as I grew closer to Bel, and she obviously knew I was hearing about the side of her she had kept under wraps, her cruelties to her sister, her cold rage. For better or worse, I had seven

510

years with my mother before she disappeared; Ivy had had a few months. How much crueler that had made her, and how much colder, I could only guess.

Soon enough I found out, when she got her opening and struck out at Bel and me in one quick stroke. An opening I gave her.

Feeling particularly strung out one night when I was holed up in Colorado, unable to get hold of Bel, I opened up to Ivy, who had answered the phone in Bel's room at the Hotel Canopus. I told her everything that had happened at the ravine. That I was at my wits' end. I begged her to get hold of some cash for us.

Instead she made sure that Bel and I never saw each other again.

And months later – with how much pleasure I can only guess now – it was she who told me that Bel had died.

If Ivy knew Bel had given birth to a child, she never let on. Maybe she kept it to herself as yet another form of revenge. Early on, I knew that Bel had not told Ivy she was pregnant. In fact, she had done all she could to conceal her pregnancy. But somewhere along the way Ivy had found out. To me, she backed up Bel's story of a miscarriage. Not, of course, out of loyalty to Bel, but because it served her own purposes, to manipulate and keep us apart. One thing was for sure: in the end, Ivy knew that there was no way Bel and I were going to Mexico or anywhere else. Bel was too sick to travel, even to Colorado. So long as she was weak and bedridden, it was too dangerous, especially since I had to be prepared to light out on very short notice.

In the meantime, Ivy not only kept putting me off about the cash she had promised to scratch up, but she fed my paranoia about the police. Telling me how they had been poking around, looking for me. They didn't find Dupont's body for months. And I wasn't a suspect when they did. At the same time, colluding with Bel, Ivy didn't let me know how sick she was.

Again, it was Canopus who told me that in the end,

when Bel couldn't hide her pregnancy anymore, she hid out in a rented bungalow in Paradise, south of Vegas, until she gave birth to a child, which soon afterward she put up for adoption. He didn't know when or where, exactly. Nor did anyone else who might have cared, so far as I knew; her uncle Junius, for example, didn't even know that Bel and I had had a relationship, much less a child. The last time I talked to Bel was in a prearranged call, from one gas station pay phone to another, in February, 1956, nearly five months after we'd fled the ravine. With trucks roaring by on the interstate, and heavy static, I could barely hear her. I told her soon she would be well enough to travel to Mexico. Yes, I'll be ready, she said through an ocean of static. Then we were cut off.

Finally Ivy assured me that she had gotten five thousand dollars and a pledge of secrecy out of the old lady who ran her uncle's hotel. She sent me a check, but it was no good. I nearly got arrested trying to cash it at the bank in a town called Chiba, but I talked my way out of it. When I called Ivy about this, from another town, the sweat was pouring down my back. She heard me out, never denying anything or apologizing. She just waited, listening, and then put a knife through my heart.

Bel is dead, she said. Just like that. She died last night. In Paradise.

I didn't care about the check anymore. About the police or anything else. I've never been much of a drinker. But I started drinking that day, alone, in Vega, Colorado, and I kept drinking, and I drove around as fast and hard as I could for two days and nights, trying to get myself killed. Except when you're trying like that, you need some luck to get killed. Instead, I found myself sick and hungover in Boulder and the next thing I knew I had enlisted in the Air Force. You told me how you joined the Navy after the spider bit you, when you were at the end of your tether – it was something like that for me.

In fact, joining the Air Force probably saved my life. It certainly changed the course of it completely. And that's what I wanted, if I wanted anything. Before I knew what hit me, I was stationed at a base near Bremen, in northern Germany, in the middle of winter. Two years later, I entered officer training school, specializing in navigation.

I never saw Ivy again, or my father. I don't know any more now than I did then about where my mother Stella ended up. When I asked Canopus how he had come by his information, he just smiled and said he used to know people who knew such things – or something to that effect. Vague as he was, I believed him. For though he was motivated by vindictiveness (if he couldn't hurt my father or Bel's uncle, both of whom he despised, at least he could hurt me) and greed (promising that, for a modest amount the secret of my having killed Dupont was safe with him), my gut tells me that Canopus didn't invent the story of Bel's having given birth to a child. From afar, I hired a detective to check the adoption agencies, but with so many agencies and so much confidentiality to cut through, a blind search was nearly impossible. So if such a child is still alive, I don't see how I'll ever cross paths with him. The trouble is, I don't see how I'll ever cross paths with you, either. And that is the fear which weighs heavily on me each day now.

16 October

As soon as I was on my feet again, Ji-Loq took me to the longhouse at the center of the village to meet the Bru elders. The village which was my home for so many months consisted of several dozen bamboo houses built in concentric circles in a clearing surrounded by dense forest. The design of the village was patterned after the heavens, which the Bru saw as a gigantic circular web in which the stars had been caught, like flies.

Like all the houses, the longhouse rested on six-foot stilts, protecting it from flash floods at that time of year. Protection from spirits came in a different form: as is customary in Bru villages, all the windows and doors were on one side of the houses – in this village, the western side. The Bru believed that evil spirits were only able to approach a village from one set direction, so they put access to their houses on the opposite side.

The interior walls of the longhouse were adorned with crossbows and the painted skulls of water buffaloes. The principal constellations of their zodiac were outlined in red chalk on a wooden disk fastened to the ceiling: a rat, a hawk, a scorpion, a fox, a tiger, and of course a water buffalo. At the center of the room, around a low fire in a circle of mudbricks, a group of old men were sitting on thatch mats, smoking short clay pipes. They all had heavily tattooed faces and lizard bone earrings. In the corner, with his back to the others, a one-eyed man was squatting on his haunches mixing herbs in a wooden bowl by tallow light. He was the shaman, and he always wore only a loincloth and a blue hat. He never spoke to me or looked me directly in the eye. Beside the fire a green liquid simmered in a metal vat. This was reimu, the rice wine which as a visitor I was expected to drink before I could address the elders. The wine was sour and made my throat close up, every time.

In the amalgam of pidgin English and Vietnamese with which we communicated, I told the elders I appreciated all they had done for me, but that I needed to get to Quang Tri, and then Saigon, as soon as possible. I had waited for Nol to return and serve as my guide, but Ji-Loq told me he had rejoined his FULRO unit in Laos, near the Thai border, and would not be returning any-time soon. The fact I had saved his life was between him and me, so far as the elders were concerned. They had their own interests at heart, and their own plans for me. As I was about to find out.

The chief, a wiry man with long white hair named Ren, heard me out and then replied that, with all the foot trails washed out, no one could get out of the forest during the rainy season. Not even the Bru. Furthermore, Ren added, Ji-Loq had told the elders I could read the stars, and so I might be of some use to the tribe while I was waiting for the rains to stop. I didn't like the sound of that, and I insisted that I was trained to traverse the jungle in the worst of conditions. Go ahead, the old man exhorted me, but no Bru could accompany me. Not during the rainy season.

And so for four more months I was held captive in all but name by my rescuers. To them my astral knowledge was magical, obviously acquired during my years as an aviator, flying among the stars. None of them had ever been in an airplane. They imagined the stars to be situated at a low altitude. They peppered me with questions about their sizes and distances from one another. Who was it who said the sun is the size of a human palm? The Bru believe the stars are no bigger than a man's teeth. I explained to them the principle of a lightyear, but the notion that starlight reaches us many thousands of years after it has been emitted was inconceivable to them. When I told Ren that the night sky is a window onto the past, he corrected me, saying, no, it is a map of the future. For the Bru, too, believe that you can foretell the future in stars.

On paper I showed Ren some of the basics of celestial navigation. He enjoyed posing problems: for example, how many stars had to be visible for me to navigate properly. He had never seen the ocean, and because he imagined it must reflect all the stars in the sky, causing endless confusion, he wondered how I could sail across it.

Every two weeks I was permitted another audience in the longhouse. Each time I petitioned Ren and the others for an escort to Quang Tri, I got the same answer, politely but firmly. I was beginning to worry that when the rainy season did end, they still wouldn't let me go. Especially when Ji-Loq let slip that perhaps before the next rainy season I could direct the construction of a wooden watchtower from which the stars might be observed more clearly. So, when I was sure I was strong enough, I took matters into my own hands. I had been telling Ren how easy it would be to cross the ocean using only a pocket compass and the stars: now I'd find out if they would be enough to help me thread my way out of the mountains through forests so dense, with canopies so uniform, that they felt nocturnal at noon.

I picked a moonless night after the rains ended. Ji-Loq had long since stopped watching over me, and Nol's relatives, on Ren's orders, allowed me my privacy so that I might occupy myself – as he hoped – in astral meditations. Around 2 a.m. I slipped on my Air Force boots and vinyl poncho, neither of which I had worn since being brought to the village, packed some dried meat and yams into a pouch, stuck a machete in my belt, and set out along one of the hunters' trails that zigzagged across the mountain.

The village dogs all knew me, and none of them barked. The Bru always kept two lookouts in tall trees, but they were on the other side of the village. Everyone else was asleep. For a moment, as I left the last house behind, I thought I saw the shaman in his blue hat peer at me from behind a tree, but when I looked more closely it was a snake coiled around the trunk. Hours later, feeling as if I had been closely followed from that point on, I wondered whether I had been right the first time.

I traveled as far from the village as I could that first night and morning. I didn't stop to rest until the following afternoon – and then only for two hours. Ji-Loq's medicine, all those black roots I chewed and the white moss she kept wrapping around my slashed ankle, had done their work. The ankle had healed well. I was out of shape, but I had tried to prepare myself for my trek by doing push-ups and sit-ups and running in place barefoot in my room every night over the previous few weeks. And it turned out I was strong enough to walk at a steady clip for two hours, rest a half hour, and then continue on. In this way I crossed the mountains from north to South Vietnam in five days. If Ren sent a search party after me, I had managed with phenomenal luck (for the Bru are tenacious trackers) to elude it. More likely, knowing the deadly difficulties of the terrain, he had written me off as a goner and decided not to waste time and energy in locating a corpse.

Once I was in the South, things got a lot tougher. First, I suffered acute fatigue from hunger. After stretching out the dried meat and yams for four days, I was eating plants and roots, as I had done with Nol, and beetles from under rocks, which I had been taught to do in Air Force survival courses. Lack of food aside, the heat exhausted me, and the dampness that penetrated my bones when I was curled up on the ground at night. After a couple of sleepless nights in a row, feverish again, drenched in sweat, I was lucky I could push on. But I wondered how long my luck would hold.

I had navigated a course south-by-southeast toward Quang Tri and followed it to a T, and I had not encountered another human being the entire way. Nor even the trace of a village. I was in country so wild that no one inhabited it and no one was fighting over it – a small miracle in Vietnam. The air teemed with mosquitoes bigger than moths. In the lowland swamps, water rats proliferated, their yellow eyes shining even by day. And every night I had to pick the leeches from my legs. I saw monkeys in packs and giant lizards that walked on their hind legs. And even a tiger at one point, fording a river, about whom I felt a thrill of fear, thinking *It's Bok-Klia and because I ran away, offending the Bru, he's come for me*. If that was the case, I even managed to elude him, for no volley of orange-and-black feathered arrows materialized.

On the seventh day after I left the village, I came on the first signs of the war I had seen since escaping the Pathet Lao: a line of bomb craters along a dirt road, a riverbed red with chemical residue, and a smoldering barren expanse where an entire valley had been napalmed, maybe a week earlier. In a matter of a single mile, the wilderness turned into wasteland.

Until then I had been wary of wild beasts: now I had to be wary of men, which was far worse. Dressed as I was, in loose Bru clothing and my poncho, I could easily be shot on sight by either side. Certainly, in an active battle zone, the NVA would ask no questions. And no GI would have any reason to think me an American. Not to mention the fact that bombers might return. I knew that they rarely hit a target area just once. Those craters could have been left by payloads from Phantom F-4s, T-28s, Skyraiders. Or even B-52s out of Guam.

As twilight descended that day, I heard gunfire – the first since I had been shot down. At first, sporadic small arms, maybe a mile off. Then a real firefight that made the hair bristle on the back of my neck. I couldn't tell if I was walking toward, or away from, the firefight. All I knew was that it was growing louder by the minute. Approaching me faster than I was approaching it. I was nearing jungle again, the darkness deepening, when suddenly the gunfire tapered off. Maybe too suddenly. Just a lull.

The good news about the fighting was it meant both sides were in the area. The bad news was that when I did encounter the NVA, they'd see me before I saw them.

The moment I entered the jungle again, all hell broke loose. Flares lit up the treetops and gunfire flashed on either side of me. First I hit the ground. Then, when I heard gunfire behind me as well, I jumped up and began zigzagging as fast as I could through the trees. I fell twice in the brush. I heard shouts and a scream far to my left and veered in the other direction. Finally the fighting seemed well behind me.

After crouching behind a fallen tree to catch my breath, I sprinted off again and immediately felt a tremendous blow, and then an explosion of blood, in my left leg. I never heard the shots that caught me in quick succession just above the knee. Maybe the sniper was in a tree a thousand yards off, or a foxhole fifty feet away. I know I screamed, but I couldn't hear that either as my body crumpled and the jungle, upside-down, flew away from me and the wet grass swallowed me up.

When I opened my eyes again, I smelled the iodine

that someone was pouring onto my wounds. He was an American medic with a red cross on his helmet. I was on a stretcher. In a clearing. Beside six other stretchers with shot-up GIs in battle gear. It was night and several lanterns lit a circle around us. A tremendous racket started up just outside the circle. A Jolly Green Giant helicopter revving its blades. *The Army's going to take you home, fly-boy*, the medic said. The first words of English spoken to me in months. And they lifted me into the chopper and we rose straight up over the trees into the black sky.

I must have passed out again, because the next thing I remember is being indoors looking up at a nurse. I was on a cot in the field hospital at Quang Tri, the post-surgical ward. My leg was throbbing and my head felt on fire. A bare lightbulb burned behind her, so I couldn't see the nurse's face, just her silhouette. The electric lights hurt my eyes. Everything else ached as well when I lifted my hand toward the nurse. In her palm she was holding the bullets they had taken from my leg, which, as they put me under, I asked the surgeons to save for me.

I thought it was you, Mala, standing there beside me, and my heart leapt. Then the nurse leaned closer and her face came clear. And now, a year later, I still wake up from dreams thinking it was you there with me in Quang Tri. Feeling you take my hand. Feeling your breath on my cheek.

17 October

In Honolulu six months later I looked everywhere for you. Bribed, pleaded, pulled rank strings. I requisitioned files. Demanded interviews. Questioned people who had been on the *Repose* with you. And others who encountered you in Honolulu. Yet I learned very little. You had a hospital stay. You received an honorable discharge. After that, nothing. As far as the

519

Navy was concerned, your last known address was the Admiral Perry Hospital. They couldn't find you, they said; that wasn't their business. If you contacted them, they would notify me. If I wrote to you, they would hold the letter until they could forward it.

Here in Albuquerque it's 6 a.m. I'm checking out of the Hotel Rigel in an hour. They tell me I'm the last guest. I have two more days' leave. I lay awake last night thinking how close I was to Vegas, and to Reno. I flew into Holloman Air Force Base, near the Mexican border, before driving up here. At nine o' clock I'll be flying to Chicago for a night, and then on to North Dakota. That's where I take up my next assignment. I had my pick because of my war record. Never mind that I never completed my surveillance mission: for getting shot down and wounded again, for being captured and escaping, I was awarded that Distinguished Flying Cross the CO in Saigon had dangled. A big-ticket item, he called it.

It was my ticket back to aerial observation. Not high-altitude espionage, but cartography. First I'll have a desk job until my leg heals completely. Then I'll be charting remote places from the sky, far from North America and Southeast Asia. Most likely working out of New Zealand. After being in the war, this is the only assignment I would even consider; if I hadn't gotten it, I would have resigned my commission. And that would have been a shock. The only legitimate employer I've ever had is the Air Force. When my life blew up on me, the first time, the military gave me enough structure so that I didn't lose my mind. Now that my life's blown up on me again – especially in my losing you – I need that same structure more than ever.

One night in Manila when I was dreaming beside you, I was sure you had entered my dreams. As a kind of observer yourself. Was it the dream of Dupont in the burning car at the ravine that you saw? I dreamed it often back then. I rarely do now. Now I dream of waking up in Manila that last morning when you were still asleep.

Of needing every ounce of my strength to leave you in bed and dress and drive to Luzon. Of wanting to run away with you. To Malaysia. Or Indonesia. The thousands of islands where no one would ever have found us. Or the chaos of some provincial town. To run away as my mother did. I can still see you lying there just before I woke you. And I still go cold with the fear which filled me at that moment. That I would never see you again. That what has happened would happen.

If you ever get this letter, you'll know what happened to me after I left you that day. Why I disappeared. And I wanted you to know about my life before we met, at least the crucial events before that Christmas Eve when I was shot out of the sky.

In this room the last few days, sitting at this desk, it feels as if time has stopped. The atmosphere could not be more static: the temperature and humidity never vary by a single degree; the food is uniformly bland; the silence, set off by the hum of air conditioners, deep and unwavering. Time had to stop for me to write to you like this. Thinking of how we both disappeared on each other, I sometimes ask myself, as you perhaps do, whether we were ever in Manila at all. I have many memories, but only a single tangible object from that time remains in my possession: the leaf from the playing-card bush on which you wrote our names one afternoon. I've kept it in the only large book I own: the Air Force's *Star Catalogue*.

The Bru have a saying. One of those things that's so simple you're sure you heard it before: *Only when you stop looking for something will you find it.*

I can't imagine not looking for you. If I have to stop looking, I will. But I'll still find you. Until then, my love,

Geza

17

Honolulu

There was a ceiling fan revolving slowly over the bed. A garden outside in which the birds were chattering. Hibiscus and jacaranda scents wafting.

We were up high in a hotel called The Altair, out beyond Diamond Head. From our lanai in the early morning, when the mist lifted over the sea, we could see the island of Molokai smoky on the horizon.

For the first time since Manila we were in a room that was not just his or mine, but ours. Neither of us wanting, ever now, to be apart again.

Yet knowing that soon we were going to be as far apart as technology permitted two human beings to be in the year 1980. A separation fraught with risks, technological and human. And after that – what? – maybe we would be together always. Which, as I had learned with considerable pain, could mean a single day or many years.

And so I was holding on to each moment: a skill I thought I had been honing my entire life, not in the way of my Buddhist friends, but as a woman accustomed to losing the people and things she loved – and even those she didn't. In my twenties, when I lost first Loren, then Cassiel, I would have thought this fatalism hopelessly self-pitying. But I was thirty-five now and I knew that I'd better hold on to the present moment for dear life because it was all I might ever have. I had learned that I could either insulate myself, nursing the illusion I had nothing to lose, or push on, taking risks, with the knowledge that in the end we all lose everything, never on our own terms, and never in the way we would like. All of us come into this world crying, and some of us leave it crying. Those who don't aren't necessarily stronger or weaker. Luckier or unluckier. Maybe they're just cried out.

All the same, the very real possibility that I could lose Geza Cassiel a second time, forever, at that point in my life, was one blow I knew, in my heart, I couldn't afford to absorb.

My fears would be tested, but not because Cassiel ever wavered in his devotion. He loved me a great deal – maybe more than I had imagined. Maybe as much as I loved him, though I told him that was not possible. His love for me, more enduring and unconditional than any I had received in my life, was what I had hoped for after Manila. I had believed in him so much, after all. But, in the back of my mind, I could not be sure over all the years that he hadn't forgotten me, fallen in love with someone else, or even married. In fact, those were the easy torments: for a long time I had doubted he was even alive.

Lying in bed together at The Altair, running my fingertip along the stubble on his jaw, I asked him if he had been in love again since Manila.

'I was with other people, here and there. But it wasn't like with you, Mala. All the time there was only you.'

I had forgotten how direct he could be, though it was one of the very qualities that had attracted me to him. 'It was the same for me,' I said. 'Why do you think it's like this? We were together so briefly – how did we know? I mean, I was so young, I didn't know anything, but I always knew about us.'

'Maybe because it's not something you can learn. There's no wisdom involved. You can't explain it. That's why some people let it slip through their fingers, though they're handed all the breaks.' He pulled me closer. 'We didn't allow that to happen, even when it seemed we got no breaks at all.'

For two months we had waited for this long weekend in Hawaii – the rendezvous we never had during the war. After meeting on the beach, we spent one night together in my house on Naxos. Then he had to go back to Crete and I remained on Naxos, two islands separated, not by an unknowable, unbreachable expanse, but a hundred-mile stretch of open sea. It was a shock – finding each other, having to separate so soon, yet at the same time, after the years of separation and silence, being able to communicate and see each other. Communications were limited, for Cassiel was restricted to his base, in training for a mission which he wouldn't discuss much at first. Gradually I learned just how highly classified, top-security, his mission was.

In those two months we did have a weekend in Xanía, in eastern Crete, and a night in Iráklion, but otherwise had to rely on the telephone and the mail, either speaking or writing to each other every day. In this way, I learned a great many things about him, and he about me. Before, he had known that my father was buried on Guam, that my mother had died suddenly, and that I could speak a few ancient languages. I tried to fill him in on the rest, beginning with the aftermath of my mother's death and Loren's abduction and the twists and turns my life had taken before and after I met him on the *Repose*. It felt good to get this part of my story out to him; he comforted me, and also told me that he understood better now the fear and dread he sensed had been at work in me in Manila, which he had attributed to the war.

'You entered the war looking for refuge,' he said as we walked along the promenade in Xanía one night. 'For something that might be bigger and more oppressive than your own grief. I can understand that.'

'Then you know it didn't make my grief any smaller.'

'But it sounds like you did everything you could to find this boy.'

'He would be twenty-four now, twenty-five in December. I had to let go, Geza. Even more than I let go with you. Or I really would have gone insane. As it was, I took myself to the brink.'

And more difficult than telling him about Loren, I related the entire tale of my first years on Kauai, my job at the hospital, my affair with Francis Beliar, including the accident, and all the drinking and drugging. By the time Jorge Gaspard entered my story, he seemed – in comparison, in retrospect – a welcome figure.

Cassiel told me that, likewise, over the course of the long years, through countless lonely nights, he had spun out endless scenarios to fill the enormous gaps in his knowledge of my life.

'You were too beautiful and too unique, Mala. At times, I was certain you must be married, or with someone else, and that you had become a classics professor at some university. At one point when I was searching for you, I actually got in touch with a national association of classics professors. I envisioned you in a big colonial house on a green campus translating *The Peloponnesian Wars* or Plato's *Symposium*.'

He also said he had written me a long letter nine years earlier, while staying in a hotel in Albuquerque, and was disappointed that I had never received it. In the letter, he too had tried to fill in some gaps: his boyhood, his parents, the circumstances that led him to enlist in the Air Force before he was twenty years old. Who he had loved before me, and what had happened to him after he walked out of the Hôtel Alnilam in Manila in January, 1969.

Over time, Cassiel shared most of the contents of that long letter with me. It had been written, he said, in a furious burst when he was just out of the hospital, recovering from bad wounds, disgusted with the war and heading for his next assignment with decidedly mixed feelings about remaining in uniform at all. He had wanted me to know the events that had shaped his early life, and everything that had happened to him in the war after Manila, from being shot down again, and taken prisoner, to his long rehabilitation. I saw that my fears about him – short of my fear that he was dead – paled beside the actual events. In the eyes of the Air Force, Cassiel had been a genuine hero. But he had known that, after Vietnam, his days in the military were numbered. He gave me his various medals in Honolulu, saying only that he preferred me to have them because during the war I had saved, rather than taken, lives. And so I slipped his Silver Star into the velvet-lined box beside the one my father had been awarded.

And yet what happened to Cassiel in the war seemed no more harrowing than the story he told me of his early life: his mother abandoning him, his estrangement from his father, his short tragic relationship with Bel, the one and only girl in his life besides me he said he had loved. None of the scenarios I had concocted about Cassiel's past could match what had actually happened to him. Especially, for me, the most shocking fact of all: that he had enlisted in the Air Force at eighteen only because he had just killed a man – bravely, in self-defense, but also brutally with a gunshot to the head and a gruesome attempt at covering it up.

So, in addition to all those long-standing questions, I had an answer now, too, to the biggest question of all: how and where Cassiel had spent the previous eleven years. And that, too, was a surprise. For he had become an astronaut.

Five years earlier, he decided to take the step he had flirted with before the war, resigning his commission as an Air Force colonel and enrolling in NASA's astronaut-training program. That he was a highly decorated veteran opened doors for him. But, in truth, NASA was happy to have him for reasons of its own: namely that he had developed a reputation as the best navigator in the Air Force, specializing in exploring and charting difficult and unknown territories. A specialty that would be no small part of his NASA mission as the navigator on a three-man spaceflight in a modified Apollo spacecraft. A secret flight – all three crewmen volunteers – which the public might not know about for some time. By the time we left Greece, I knew he was going to the moon – which seemed incredible enough – but only when we were in Honolulu did he confide to me the exact nature of his mission and the reason it was being kept under wraps. I had just flown in from Athens, having closed up the house on Naxos, and he had been on the Big Island all week in his final on-site training, in the lava fields that so eerily approximated the lunar surface.

Before joining NASA, Cassiel's last Air Force assignment was in the Falkland Islands, where he had worked with cartographers and geodesists to remap the islands off the western half of Antarctica. Coordinating aerial photographs and laser measurements with high-resolution radiometer pictures from satellites, they had charted the coastlines and interiors of places previously too remote to be surveyed by plane. Over several years, Cassiel and his partners had created or updated hundreds of conventional, geodesic, and contour maps, detailing geologic folds and glacier lines and establishing alpine landmarks and coastal boundaries down to the meter. Before that, stationed in New Zealand, he helped to chart the numerous island groups in the South Pacific – Society, Gilbert, Caroline, Phoenix, Cook – which had not been looked at since the 1920s. All those islands I had hopped through, I marvelled, he had charted. The mapping of islands was Cassiel's specialty. In fact, as bit by bit we compared notes, we were astonished – and heartbroken – to discover that his tenure at an air base in Auckland, New Zealand, overlapped my stay on Rarotonga by a couple of months. And that Rarotonga was one of the islands he charted from the air.

In Manila, Cassiel and I had spent at least half our time in bed, and that didn't change in Honolulu. We made love before we fell asleep and soon after we woke up. He was as gentle and thorough in giving pleasure as he was in taking it – just as I remembered him to be. I loved, as before, to run my hands over his body and drink in his scent, still like salt and honey. The hair on his chest had begun to gray, but his skin remained smooth, and he still had the strongest hands and fingers I had ever seen. In fact, despite the passage of years, and the severe wounds he had incurred, his entire body felt even stronger to me than it had in Manila. He was far better conditioned as an astronaut than any Air Force officer could have dreamed of keeping himself during the Vietnam War.

When we did leave our room, it was to take long excursions in a rented convertible, visiting remote beaches on the north shore of Oahu and diving for shells. We browsed through the open-air flea markets, and after late-night suppers strolled through the city parks with their eucalyptus groves and carp ponds. Like our love-making, all of this was just as it had been in Manila. Yet in some ways everything had changed. We were eleven years older, and at thirty-five and forty-three felt much closer in age. We had each been around the world several times. Our years of separation, of loss, had scarred and defined us, individually and as a couple. At the same time, it was apparent that those years had also brought us closer together and burned the superfluous edges, the false connections, off our conversation. Long into the night we sat on the lanai looking at the stars set low in the sky, in the velvet darkness, and barely exchanged a word. I had expected us to have a million things to say, but most of those things didn't need to be said.

For me, the weekend went by in a flash. Our last night in Honolulu I came out on the lanai to find Cassiel lying on a chaise longue, gazing at the blinking lights of the transoceanic jets out of Melbourne and Hong Kong and Djakarta as they descended on Honolulu International. Nestling beside him, I was reminded of the moment on the deck of the *Repose* when I saw his squadron of B-52s pass overhead, and then the day I first met him, lying in the postoperative ward, a Christmas wreath strung with lights flashing on the wall behind him. The powerful forces and impulses which had first drawn us together, I thought, were still at work when I went to the Festival of Scorpio and found him – one of the two people for whom (in my heart, at least) I had long been searching without truly expecting to find them. Before Cassiel and I left that deserted beach near Moutsana, he made that same point in his own way, drawing the symbol for a celestial fix in the sand, just as he had drawn it on the envelope containing my bracelet in Manila. We both knew that in the vast expanses of time and space we had somehow homed in on each other. The disparate worldly events that brought this about seemed fated because they felt so accidental. In fleeing Gaspard, I had caught the first boat out of Piraeus one sultry night and ended up on Naxos; many months later, going on leave from an intensive survival course on Crete, Cassiel had chosen Naxos out of dozens of Aegean islands for the simple, and perverse, reason that it had no airport and, up to his neck in matters aeronautical, he had a whim to travel somewhere accessible only by boat.

Maybe it was a similar whim the following afternoon which prompted him to suggest that he fly me to Kauai in a small plane, just the two of us. I had never flown with him, after all, and I had always wanted to. We were to have left Honolulu that night separately, me on a Hawaiian Airlines flight to Kauai, he in an Air Force fighter to Houston.

'We can land at the airstrip at the Barking Sands Missile Range and someone will drive you home. I'll have just enough time to turn around, change planes here, and get to Houston by eleven o'clock Central Time, when I'm due back.'

He had caught me off guard. Anticipating the distractions that would arise on Kauai after my long absence, I had preferred to spend the few days I had with Cassiel in Honolulu, undisturbed. At the same time, I was dying to share with him the one island where I had truly made a home for myself. To share my treasures: my house by the sea, the garden, the mountains, and the only permanent set of friends I'd ever had. Kauai was the place, after all, where I now dared allow myself to dream that Cassiel and I might one day live together.

'But I want you to see the island,' I said.

'I will see it.'

'I mean, from the ground.'

'I'll see it next time,' he replied. 'And not just for one night.'

While I packed, Cassiel drove over to Hickam Air Force Base, where he requisitioned a sleek two-engine Learjet with the NASA insignia on the fuselage. It was a four-seater that NASA used to ferry astronomers, engineers, and other personnel around the islands between their various observation posts, like Mauna Kea on the Big Island, which housed the world's largest telescopes, and the Kokee Observatory in Waimea Canyon, where Estes worked.

Cassiel took the controls and I strapped myself into the copilot's seat. I had been around a lot of planes and helicopters in Vietnam, but I had never before sat in the cockpit of a jet. Doing so with Cassiel, seeing him for the first time in his element, I enjoyed it all the more. It was five o' clock, still sunny, as we taxied into position, past rows of gray military transports and silver F-16s. Cassiel checked with the tower, raised the flaps, and opening up the throttle, hurtled us down the runway. The small jet got up speed incredibly fast, and within seconds I was pressed back flat as we climbed a steep arc through the clouds while Honolulu – the pink and white skyline, the beachfront hotels, Diamond Head, our own hotel where an hour before I had stepped from the shower – fell away from us, toy-sized.

Cassiel did not take us on a direct route from Honolulu to Lihue, which was only a twenty-five-minute hop across the Kauai Channel. If he had had his way, I would have seen the entire Hawaiian chain as far as Midway, two thousand miles to the northwest: Nihoa and Kure, inhabited by birds and monk seals, and the atolls and shoals named after ships' captains who went aground on their reefs – Pearl, Hermes, Laysan, Necker, Gardner – and Disappearing Island, which I would have loved to see before it lived up to its name completely. Instead, for the next two hours, we zigzagged over the main islands: Molokai, Lanai, Maui, the Big Island (where we swooped down low over Mauna Kea, enveloped in snow), and then, after an hour of open turquoise sea punctuated by whitecaps, Niihau, the Forbidden Island.

It was seven o'clock, and as the sun set we circled Kauai and I pointed out landmarks to Cassiel. The dome of the NASA Observatory in Waimea, cloud-capped Mount Waialeale where it never stops raining, the chess-board taro fields of the Hanalei Valley, and my house in Haena, pale green and tiny, the sight of which, with Cassiel at my side, brought tears to my eyes.

After flying through the last, deepest band of sunlight, the darkness was flowing in around us. Before we landed, we were going to see the stars, from five miles up, flickering to life around a three-quarter moon.

'The mission was officially confirmed today,' Cassiel said suddenly. Just before we took off from Honolulu, he had been called to the telephone in the NASA hangar. Now I was to find out why.

'It's in two legs,' he went on, 'and we were waiting on the second one. Now they're both go. I wanted to be sure of what we'll be doing before I filled you in on it completely.'

'You're still going to the moon.'

He turned to me. 'That's only the first stop. The second is a point in space they're calling Nova 1. You know, the last Apollo mission was eight years ago. Then there was the Skylab, and next year they're sending up the Space Shuttle. We're a transition flight. Either a bridge to the future, or a holdover that was ahead of its time, depending on how you look at it.' As he banked the plane, moonlight spilled into the cockpit through my window. 'Mala, we're going to the far side of the moon,' he concluded.

He must have heard my breath catch in my throat.

'I was surprised myself when they first told us,' he said. 'Lots of unmanned satellites have landed there – Orbiters and Rangers and Russian Lunas – but none of the Apollo spacecraft. No men have ever walked on the far side.'

'That's amazing. But why all the secrecy?'

By way of an answer, he said, 'That's the first leg of the mission. Our lunar module will land near the moon's equator, like Apollo 15, on the edge of a crater called Icarus. We'll spend three days there setting up some instruments before returning to the command module. At that point, astronauts have always flown directly back to earth, but we're going to use the moon as a jump-off point and proceed farther into space. We'll take readings of light conditions, gamma rays, and solar dust beyond the moon: everything that might affect the space telescope they hope to launch into interplanetary space in ten years. A telescope that will observe the stars as we can't even imagine them now – stars nine, ten thousand light-years away. Galaxies where we'll watch stars being born thousands of years ago. Maybe by the millennium they'll be able to send the same sort of telescope into interstellar space. Imagine what we'd see from out there, beyond Pluto.'

Through the windows I could see the stars clearly now, twinkling into place, and I wondered how Scorpio, and red Antares, would look from out beyond Pluto. 'Considering how important it is, how do they expect to keep your mission secret?'

He shook his head. 'They've done it before. They can keep a very tight lid on things when they want to.'

'Still, there must be a lot of people directly involved.'

'Fewer than you'd think. And, let's face it, the press lost interest in the Apollo program after Apollo 12. By the time of 16 and 17, NASA could barely scare up TV coverage of the launchings.'

'I think it's thrilling. Especially after all you went through in the Air Force. But you still haven't told me why it's a secret. Is the military involved?'

'There are some military imperatives. And technological reasons. But that's not why.' He was choosing his words carefully. 'The fact is, the NASA engineers think this mission has a lot of risks.'

'Don't they always?'

'They think this one has more than usual.'

'I see. And what do you think?'

'That there are a lot more variables than on any previous spaceflight. That's what it comes down to.'

What it came down to was that NASA was going to keep the mission secret until the crew returned. Only a limited number of people in the government would know about it. That doesn't sound so bad, but according to Cassiel, those were very tough odds in the space program. Acceptable in the Air Force, in test flying, but unprecedented in NASA. If the crew made it back, they would be heroes. If they didn't, it would be treated like a covert military operation and a discreet report would be filed.

This brought me up short. Though I was excited for him, and happy to be a part of it with him, I was also afraid that I might lose him now, forever, just when I had found him again.

'How long will you be gone?' I said, trying to keep that fear out of my voice.

'Twenty-two days.'

'Geza, I have to say this up front: you know I'll be with you all the way, but if something does happen, I don't want to go through that MIA stuff again. No matter what.'

'I know,' he said, taking my hand. 'I've taken care of that – just in case – both officially and otherwise.'

I knew that those seventy-thirty odds would grow tougher by the day right up until I joined him in Houston three weeks before his scheduled launch date, in Florida, in mid-December. Those last weeks would be the most exciting and also the hardest of all, especially after I left him again, but they would also bring me even closer to him than I was before, closer even than that very moment in the small jet, over the western coast of Kauai, just the two of us, circling under the stars, feeling removed from everything and everyone in the world, feeling safer than I had in years.

'We're going farther into space than anyone's ever gone,' he said. 'Closer to the stars than anyone's ever been. In a way, I've been waiting my whole life for this.'

'God, I wish I could go with you,' I said, letting out my breath and gazing at the moon.

'You will be with me,' he said, as we began the descent into Barking Sands. 'Mala, it won't be like Manila. I'll be back.'

I focused on the lights of the runway, the parallel strips of blue lights glittering. And the nose of the jet bisecting them as Cassiel brought us down with barely a jolt, the tires hissing on the cement, the flaps dropping silently, and the lights flying past us now.

'Just like that,' he said.

18

Ice

The day Samax died, I woke from a dream I could not remember. Bells were ringing far down the corridor. Drowsily I thought it must be So Li, the bell expert, but then I remembered that she had left the Hotel Canopus months before. As had Professor Zianor, frustrated in his search for paintings depicting Adam with a navel. In fact, nearly every guest had left. If a couple of years earlier the hotel population had been skeletal, it now felt positively barren. In fact, at eighty, in the last year of his life, Samax perhaps realized his worst fear, for he was practically living at the hotel alone.

Deneb had settled in Reno, where the Basque-American Society had underwritten him a chair in Atlantean studies at the university. Zaren Eboli, having moved from El Paso to Houston, never returned to the hotel now, even for weekends; as he wrote me in a post-card featuring a pair of tarantulas, he had finally made it back to the Gulf of Mexico and was gradually edging his way to New Orleans. Of the longtime residents, only Hadar and Labusi remained, but it was as if they had exchanged routines: now it was Hadar, a virtual recluse in his laboratory, who seldom traveled anywhere, and Labusi, with a sheaf of invitations to billiard tourna-ments, who had uprooted himself from his niche in the garden and taken to the road with a vengeance in a super van specially modified to carry both a billiard table and

535

a wheelchair. Harahel the archivist continued his deadly compilation of every document Samax had ever handled and was only glimpsed on occasion, around four a.m., the tassels of his fez bobbing as he paced the hotel corridors in order to stimulate the circulation of blood in his legs. Lastly, the old gangster Forcas continued to visit, but with far less frequency than before. As Samax closed down or liquidated his various business interests, Forcas served as his negotiator, really his emissary to the outside world, fulfilling some of Calzas's old functions.

Desirée, too, was around the hotel much less now, coming and going as she pleased, traveling abroad much of the time, living in hotels in out-of-the-way places, often acquiring works of art on commission for collectors she had met through Samax. Long gone was the ritual of her daily breakfast with him. When I did see her at the hotel, she was doing what she had always done, filling up those yellow sheets of paper with the Elite type of her silent Olivetti. She had just turned thirty-five, and if anything she had gotten even more beautiful over the years. Ten years her junior, I was as attracted to her as I had ever been – maybe even more so now that I had had a good number of lovers myself. Of late I had pondered my relationship with Desirée – what was it exactly? Having lived under the same roof with her all those years, I thought of her as much more than just a friend. But that did not mean she was anything like a sister, or even an aunt – which had always been a problematic relationship for me one way or the other. If I tried to pin it down, we seemed like not-so-distant cousins who are nevertheless strangers to each other underneath. Because Desirée, from the very first, had carried – even cultivated – the aura of a stranger, I had never felt impelled to resist my attraction for her. Not as a boy, a teenager, or a man. She had to be aware of this. Whether she liked it or didn't, she was never coy and she didn't tease – but, then, she never had to tease anyone to get attention. With me, she maintained both a sense of intimacy and a detachment that never wavered. I knew I would always be a little in love with her, and I hoped that maybe one day she would share with me the contents of those yellow pages, maybe even read some of them aloud to me as once upon a time, when I thought she was Scheherazade herself, she had read me the *Arabian Nights*.

Like me, Desirée was visiting the hotel that weekend when Samax died. I had come up from Santa Fe, where I had taken a studio apartment while working in Calzas's office. Knowing that my uncle's health was failing, I tried to fly to Las Vegas at least every other weekend. What with his vegetarian diet, the myriad fruit juices, and his exercise regimen, I had always assumed Samax would be one of those people who literally lived to be one hundred, expiring finally of that most wonderful of euphemisms, 'natural causes', words which had for me always conjured a mechanistic image of the internal organs silently, painlessly shutting down – like a power generator, or a complex clock that can no longer be rewound. Samax's stroke years before had been a shock to me, but I had convinced myself it was an aberration in an otherwise healthy continuum. I may have been lulled into this conviction by his remarkable recovery. More likely, it was my need, because of our history together, to think of Samax as immortal. He knew better, even before the smaller deteriorations that followed the stroke – bronchitis, gallstones, bladder infections, an enlarged prostate – began to mount at an alarming rate, each malady making the next more difficult to deal with. And always hovering was the specter of another stroke – one that would finish him off, Samax declared matter-of-factly, because he was that much weaker.

'Dolores is one hundred and five,' he remarked to me in the fall of 1980, two months before his death, 'and she got there by doing everything I stopped doing: glued to her rocker, eating lots of eggs and red meat, salting her food heavily. The closest she ever came to a health food was those quarts of chamomile tea she used to put away.

She hasn't seen the inside of a hospital in seventy years – since Della was born – while at eighty I'm in and out constantly, being jabbed and prodded.'

Indeed, Dolores, who kept to her routine of sitting in the garden, with or without Labusi, continued to oversee the management of the hotel under Mrs Resh and the far-reduced staff. With so few guests, there simply was no need for an army of employees, and of the oldest of these, only Azu the doorman remained – balding now, with gout in his knees, but still wide as the door he manned. Sofiel the gardener continued to maintain the quincunx orchard, and Alif and Aym were still on the payroll. Though they too were operating at diminished strength ever since Aym had lost his vision overnight – not, according to him, in an accident, but during a dream in which he had found himself flying into the sun, unable to stop. The doctor who examined him confirmed (and could not explain) the fact that Aym's optical nerve had been singed like a piece of straw. Yet though Aym was now blind and mute, Samax kept him on, convinced that with his acute sense of hearing and still-crackling martial skills, he continued to be a formidable force. Maybe this was true. Or maybe Samax had come to realize what I had intuited long before: his bodyguards were intended to deflect not assassins dispatched by Vitale Cassiel, but the Angel of Death himself, whom my uncle continued to glimpse in visions of his own. Perhaps he was hearing him now too, closing in, and so thought Aym's sharp ears would be valuable in the end.

In November, just a week before Samax's death, a new guest did arrive at the hotel who was more unusual than any of his predecessors. Which was saying a lot. He would turn out to be the final guest to check into the Hotel Canopus, someone I knew at first only as 'the Man of Smoke'. For a simple reason. When you entered his room on the fifth floor, it was always filled with smoke – not wood or incense smoke, but a scentless variety – and the man himself was never visible. Once you were inside the room, his voice remained equidistant from you. He took all his meals – milk, fish broth, and sauerkraut juice twice daily – in his room, as well as a tumbler of ouzo mixed with water (which turned smoky in the glass) in the evening. As far as anyone knew, he never left the room. No one ever saw him. When I asked Samax about him, he was even more secretive than usual.

'He's someone I was looking for for a long time,' he said cagily, though it was not like him to be mysterious for the sake of mystery.

Immediately I thought of Rochel, his cellmate half a century earlier. 'When did you find him?' I asked.

'Just last month. You'll find out soon enough who he is. It's a surprise – for you and Calzas. In the meantime, go by his room and introduce yourself.'

I did just that. And was met with a low, somewhat singsong voice that floated from the depths of the smoke, inquiring about my recent work for Calzas. I had not expected that he should be so interested in my activities as an architect (was he just trying to please Samax, or was the surprise that he himself was an architect?), for I saw immediately that he conversed on the subject like a professional.

'I know the Hotel Rigel,' he said. 'I once stayed there.'

'You did? When was that?'

'Oh, a long time ago. Before you were born. And what is your next assignment – demolition again?'

I shook my head. 'No.'

In fact, the Hotel Rigel was my first and last demolition job. For Calzas, I had begun designing a hotel to be built on a seaside cliff in the Baja; in my free time, with my truest mental energy, I had completed work on the blueprints for a planetarium. Months earlier, I had heard that the city of Phoenix intended to build a planetarium and was announcing an open competition for a plan. I had pulled out all the stops, creating a design that owed as much to my youthful immersion in fantastic architecture and star lore as to the conventional needs of a public place. The story Calzas had once told me,

539

about the British using Piranesi's *Carceri*, the drawings of an imaginary infernal prison, to lay out the very real Newgate Prison, had always inspired me. I had found it exhilarating, despite the grimness of his subject matter, that Piranesi could create such a dynamic – of life not just imitating, but being determined by, art.

But in the weeks after I had helped to demolish the Hotel Rigel, I was so distracted by the contents of the letter I had found in the defunct mailbox that I nearly missed the deadline for the Phoenix competition. Instead, I directed my energies into trying to locate the man I now knew to be my father, Geza Cassiel. Suffice to say that reading that letter had been like poring over a very different sort of blueprint, tantalizing, dangerous, and incomplete – destined, perhaps, never to be completed. Finding the letter marked the second great fateful crossroads of my life – standing out amid many detours and byways – as significant in its way as my abduction by Samax when I was a boy.

Among the most powerful shocks were the fact that Vitale Cassiel was my grandfather, and thus a closer relative than Samax, and – even more incredible – that Ivy turned out to be my closest relative of all, the half-sister of both my father and my mother. If the letter was a blueprint, it was for a particularly tortuous labyrinth – filled with dead ends and trapdoors. When I first reviewed its revelations – Ivy my aunt twice over, Stella my grandmother, Stella's son and Bel's lover one and the same person – I felt as if I had plunged through a trapdoor and were falling through space. From the tumult created forty-three years earlier by my grandfathers, Nilus Samax and Vitale Cassiel, had come both my mother, whom I would never know, and Ivy, whom I knew only too well. And now, it turned out, my father as well, who might still be alive with as little knowledge of me as I had had of him before finding the dead letter. No, less – for he wasn't sure I even existed.

To hear his story in his own words, including some crucial chapters in the life of my mother Bel – and, out

of nowhere, the first, long-lost chapter of my own life –
was an incredibly painful and exhilarating experience
for me. I had known many wanderers in my life, both at
the hotel and during my years with Luna and Milo, but
my real father was in an entirely different class. Not
only a nomad, from his youth on the lam to his far-
flung military postings, but also a warrior. Someone
who could negotiate the jungles of Vietnam with a
pocket compass and fly over the North Pole in the dead
of night with unerring precision. Who could find his
way anywhere, yet in his letter sounded utterly lost.
Learning about his passions, fears, and sorrows, his
horrific wartime experiences and the murder he had
been forced to commit at eighteen was all the more
intense because I became certain that I would never be
able to find him. It was strange that, in reading his letter,
I, his son, should be feeling the same despair about him
that he had obviously felt toward the woman he was
addressing – whom he feared he would never find again.
A lost son searching for a lost father who in turn was
searching for his lost lover.

I concluded there were two possible avenues I could
explore in trying to find my father: Vitale Cassiel, still
alive in Reno, who might no longer be estranged from
his son (though Geza Cassiel's letter made that seem
highly unlikely), or the woman to whom the letter was
addressed. In the nine years since he had written the
letter, my father might well have found her. She might
know of his whereabouts – or he might even be with
her. At any rate, I reasoned that if I could find her I had
a good chance of finding him. Of course this was only
after I had come up against a brick wall when I tried
to learn his whereabouts through the Air Force;
they would tell me only that he had resigned his commission and they were not permitted to give me
additional information unless I was an immediate relative. I was his son, I replied. When asked for proof, all
I had was a birth certificate that read FATHER: UNKNOWN.
And a different surname, on top of it. The Navy was

equally unforthcoming about the nurse named Mala Revell. I tried to play the sleuth myself, but with such old, scant information, I wasted many months going down dead-end streets. Finally, I followed Samax's advice of last resort and hired the Hopkins brothers out of Miami, who he said could find anyone anytime anyplace – except for Alma, whom they had never found.

I paid them dual commissions, to locate my father or the nurse, whoever they tracked down first. And then I waited. With Geza Cassiel they too hit a wall, once removed from the one that had stopped me: it seemed he had indeed resigned from the Air Force, a full colonel, but was still working in some way for the government, his current activities and whereabouts tightly classified, top secret. Could he have become a spy? I thought. That covert action he was ordered to undertake in Vietnam was obviously CIA. He mentioned them outright in the letter. And before the war he was doing espionage surveillance. Joining the CIA would have been a natural transition after the war.

Reading of Geza Cassiel's adventures in Laos and his captivity with the montagnards, I had been enthralled in much the same way as when I pored over the journals of Captain Cook and Sir John Mandeville that Samax gave me as a boy. This was a man of action, and courage, and for someone like me who had grown up around men of ideas – enterprising, iconoclastic men, to be sure, but idea men all the same – action of the life-and-death sort was always impressive. At the same time, I had been heartened to read of my father's disgust with the war, and equally saddened to think that – if indeed he was with the CIA – it might have been a passing emotion. I could understand how someone like him, not a gung-ho enlistee but a career military man posted against his wishes, would have ended up in combat in Vietnam; but with all the information about the CIA's unsavory wartime activities that had surfaced, the possibility he had joined that organization was harder for me to swallow.

Samax was the most apolitical man I ever knew, and I had grown up in an environment shaped by his belief system. Later, going out into the world, and being on a college campus in the early seventies as the war dragged to a close, I found that my eccentric education at the hotel, at its core almost fanatically humanist, had left me with a very definite, if unintended, set of political beliefs. Samax, who was repelled by the killing of animals, could never have endorsed organized slaughter between human beings. At the same time, however strong his pacifist tendencies, he was a man who did not hesitate to retain armed bodyguards when he felt sufficiently threatened.

Maybe I shared some of that ambivalence. For no matter how powerful my own revulsion for the Vietnam War, I confess that I was also proud to read of my father's combat decorations, the Purple Hearts and the Flying Cross and the Silver Star – like my adoptive grandfather's – in Brooklyn. But I wondered if this weighing of my father's actions – and my notions of him based on what he had written, not to me, but to someone he was in love with – was really one way of cushioning the shock I felt in discovering his identity as I did. Even at the age of twenty-four, maybe I was just trying to protect myself in case I should actually find him, a virtual stranger with whom I might discover I couldn't get along. Living with a romantic like Samax for fifteen years had not necessarily made me a romantic – not when it came to family relationships. Quite the opposite, in fact, after what I'd witnessed around the likes of Ivy, and Dolores and her daughters, and Luna and Alma and my grandmother in Brooklyn. At any rate, it looked as if I wouldn't have to deal with these questions concerning my father anytime soon, for in the end the Hopkins brothers couldn't find a trace of Geza Cassiel, not even a photograph.

They had a hard time with the nurse as well – a civilian now – but after a protracted search, they found her. In fact, I received the Hopkins brothers' report on Mala Revell, in a special-delivery envelope, on November 30, 1980, just moments before Sofiel knocked urgently at my door – still Room E when I was visiting the hotel – with the news that Samax was dead.

Mrs Resh had found him slumped on the floor in his private library at one o'clock when she brought up his lunch – baked plantains and apples and some of his own *Samax Astrofructus*, neatly pared. When I ran into the library ahead of Sofiel minutes later, still clutching the Hopkins brothers' report, I found this meal scattered on the carpet where Mrs Resh had dropped her tray and run from the room in terror.

I knew why the moment I saw my uncle's body. I felt as if I had been struck in the chest and had all the breath knocked out of me. His posture was not that of an old man who had dozed off. He was contorted grotesquely, one leg extended and the other tucked up behind him, clutching the side of his chest, as if he had suffered a heart attack or that monster stroke he so feared. His eyes were open, rolled back in his head, his lips were blue, and his teeth clenched. His free hand was balled up tightly, the arm stiff, and his white hair, which he had begun to wear long, was spread out on the dark blue carpet. As always, he was wearing his red robe over Chinese silk pajamas. He appeared to have fallen in agony from his favorite reading chair, by the picture window that overlooked the desert. There was a book beside his body, inches from his stiffened arm.

I rushed to his side and sank to my knees. I could still smell his cologne, faintly citric, and the scent of the greenhouse's moisture on his pants cuffs. There was a cut on his lip, which he had apparently bitten through in his death throes. For an instant I went blank, I panicked, telling myself, no he's not dead, just unconscious – how can I revive him? I put my fingertips to his cheek, then his throat. Both were cool, but not yet cold. I saw that my hands were shaking. My stomach was all balled up. And suddenly my eyes were burning so badly that I had to close them. When I opened them – it felt like hours later – Samax's body was still there.

In my previous experiences with death, a kind of protective icing had come over me from within, helping to keep me intact. Even in the car crash with Luna and Milo, or when finding my grandmother facedown in her bedroom, or as a teenager seeing Denise sprawled out in the elevator. Now, when I needed that icing most, I felt it wasn't there. And I knew that all those other deaths had not prepared me for Samax's, which I had long dreaded.

I loved my uncle dearly. And I knew he loved me, maybe more than he loved anyone else, as Desirée insisted. He was a generous man, but I was well aware that he didn't share a great deal of himself, his real self, with others as he had shared it with me. I knew, too, that I could never have repaid him for the new life he had given me – a second chance on the largest possible scale – though he said I had done so, many times over. However, at that moment in his library, where I had sat alone with him so many evenings, hearing the tales of his travels or diagramming Latin sentences, my feelings were not so much sentimental as angry. I simply couldn't believe he was gone. Having for the better part of my life thought him invulnerable, and finally immortal, I still expected him to come to and pull himself out of that horrible position and stand up and tell me he'd had a close shave, but it was going to be all right, and he even had a few new things he'd seen on the other side of the river that he wanted to share with me.

But it wasn't going to be all right, and there would be no more new things for him to share with me, not ever, for he had certainly crossed that river from which no one comes back, where the ferryman, as he once told me, looks right through your eyes and reads your soul in an instant, like a map, before seeing you on your way on the other side, down one of millions of dark paths.

What tears I had, I held back. I told myself to keep my head. Mrs Resh wanted to telephone for an ambulance. I told her to wait. I wanted to move Samax, to straighten his limbs and lay him peacefully on his back and cushion his head, but something stopped me. It wasn't just the way he had collapsed: I was struck suddenly by the absence of Alif and Aym. Where were they? And where was Sirius, who, even before I moved to New Mexico, had gravitated to Samax's side; slow and plodding in his own old age, Sirius was more comfortable in the company of an equally plodding old man. An old man whom I was certain at that moment had not suffered a heart attack or stroke. Someone had helped Samax get to the river. But who?

After sending Sofiel out in search of Alif and Aym, I turned to Mrs Resh. 'Has anyone been up here since you last saw him?' I asked.

Usually cold and distant, she was weeping silently behind me, her red hair for once in disarray. 'Not so far as I know.'

I examined the book beside Samax's hand: it was Sir Thomas Browne's *The Garden of Cyrus*, a nineteenth-century private edition which I had read myself years before. An obvious favorite of my uncle's, it was all about the quincunx, especially the history of quincuncial gardens and plantations. I knew that, whatever else he was reading, this was a book Samax always kept, along with a dozen other such favorites, piled on the table beside that chair. And so when I saw that the top half of the pile had been knocked over – despite the fact Samax had fallen in the other direction – and when I also saw no sign of his eyeglasses, it struck me that he had not been reading *The Garden of Cyrus*, but had deliberately, and with obvious effort, yanked it out of the pile as he collapsed.

Why would he do that, I asked myself. Why that particular book?

Just then, Desirée rushed into the library, wearing a black robe over a black bikini, fumbling with the sash.

She had been swimming, and her skin and hair were still wet. She stopped short, and took several steps backward before approaching Samax's body, never taking her eyes from his face. 'Oh no,' she whispered, laying her hand on my shoulder.

'He hasn't been dead long,' I said. 'Have you seen Alif and Aym?'

Desirée cleared her throat. 'Sirius was missing this morning and Samax sent them to find him. He's been wandering into the desert alone lately, at night, and staying there for hours.'

Of the three of us in the library at that moment, Mrs Resh had been the last to see Samax alive, and then the last to speak with him. I was still sleeping when she said he left the greenhouse alone around nine-fifteen. And Desirée was at the pool, where she glimpsed his red robe through the foliage of the sycamore trees along the drive-way. Crossing the lobby to the elevator, he said nothing when he passed Mrs Resh seated behind the front desk. Then, at nine-thirty, he called down to her and ordered his lunch, specifying the hour he wanted it brought up. Aside from the fact he could have told her this minutes before in the lobby, he customarily made this call at noon, not early in the morning. He also told Mrs Resh that he didn't want to be disturbed by anyone – no exceptions – which I only thought unusual because Desirée and I were just in for the weekend and at dinner the previous night he had twice mentioned that he wanted to spend the day with us.

My last conversation with him, after dinner over coffee, revolved around his renovation plans for the Hotel Canopus, to be implemented by Calzas after his death. Samax was not bequeathing the hotel outright to anyone – including me, once he realized that I would never go on living in it without him. Rather, I encouraged him to convert it into that private museum for rare collectibles he had never brought to fruition in the abandoned factory in New York. He found this notion particularly attractive because it meant he could keep the hotel alive while realizing – even posthumously – his dream of the museum, complete with a visitors' park consisting of his orchards and gardens. If he was going to leave behind any one monument to himself, like the princes and emperors whose most precious possessions he had spent his life collecting, then this would be it. Calzas, Desirée, and I were to be the museum's trustees. In working with Calzas, I would have the opportunity as an architect to transform the hotel even more radically than Samax had when he first bought it. Aside from its being predicted on Samax's death, the renovation was an unsettling proposition for me on many levels. Not least of which was that the Hotel Canopus in its current incarnation was the basis for the memory palace I had constructed in my head. Would I be altering my memory palace as we altered the hotel?

As for Desirée, she was a reluctant trustee. Dolores was still vehement about Samax leaving Desirée the hotel, to run as a hotel – though Desirée had repeatedly made it clear that she had no wish to do any such thing. When Samax designated her a trustee, she was wary of even that much involvement in the property. After his death, she said, she wanted a clean break. Meanwhile, rather than being placated by Samax's gesture, Dolores was only further enraged: converting the Hotel Canopus into anything else was to her a slap in the face.

'She's getting to be impossible,' Samax muttered to me that last night. 'I don't have the energy for it anymore. But on Monday my lawyer's bringing out all the papers, and once I sign them, it's done.'

As on my previous visits since discovering the dead letter at the Hotel Rigel, I had been on the brink of telling Samax about its contents, but once again resisted the impulse. With his health so frail, I thought the emotional impact would be too tough on him, especially when he learned the identity of my father and the stark fact that by birth I was half-Cassiel. No less than the grandson of Vitale Cassiel.

Now that Samax was dead, part of me was relieved

that he would never have to absorb that particular shock. Another part of me was saddened, for perhaps it would have been some small comfort, after the decades of antagonism, for him to know that he and his archenemy had something in common besides their enmity. That it should be me was something Samax, a man with the keenest sense of irony, would surely have appreciated. As he would have appreciated the many ironical layers pertaining to him and Vitale Cassiel that were implicit in my father's revelations. Samax was an intensely curious man. At its core, his life had been constructed around his curiosity, and around the raveling and unraveling of secrets. That is why, in the end, whatever the pain and repercussions, I believe he would have regretted – as I did – that he hadn't shared in the discovery of my paternity.

At the same time, whatever his other regrets might have been, Samax was not one to talk about them. Even to do so obliquely, as he had the previous night, was unusual. He had walked me to my room just before going to bed, and standing in the corridor in these same pajamas and robe that he wore in death, he told me he had been having trouble sleeping.

'It's not the physical stuff,' he said dismissively of his various ailments, 'though the plumbing problems wear on me, getting up to piss every hour on the hour. And even if I dose myself with herbs, I don't sleep deeply enough anymore to have nightmares. It's an ongoing unease that eats at me – like the fungi that get my trees, working their way beneath the bark. I'll be tossing, drifting in and out of sleep that's indistinguishable from the darkness of my room, and suddenly I'll be looking in on myself, watching scenes from my life play themselves out – as they happened, but with the smallest, disturbing variations. I'll be with some people, having dinner, say, just as it was except that one person will be wearing another's clothes, and another will say something, verbatim, that really someone else said, and through the window I'll glimpse the streets of a city

– Chicago in a rainstorm, say – though that dinner really took place in Miami on a clear night. It brings me up in a sweat. I know it doesn't sound bad, but it's as if I've lost my dreaming function; it seems what I do now in my sleep is alter my memories in strange ways, all the time knowing what occurred in reality, so the alterations aren't even pleasurable. I mean, it's not like you get to go someplace you always wanted to go but didn't, or find a woman you had looked for everywhere but could never find.'

These were Samax's last words to me before he shuffled down the corridor in his velvet slippers. It was a curious and poignant confessional for him to have delivered out of the blue, and I wondered what place he could have had in mind, world-traveler that he was, where he had never gone. As for the woman who could never be found, I had no doubt that must be my grand-mother Stella, whose disappearance, Samax would have been interested to know, had also been one of the great obsessions of my father's life. Twelve hours before his death, Stella was still on Samax's mind.

For several endless minutes, Desirée, Mrs Resh, and I stared down at Samax's body.

'It must have been a massive stroke,' Mrs Resh remarked, wiping her eyes.

Without replying, Desirée said to her, 'Would you find out what the delay is in finding Alif and Aym.' As soon as Mrs Resh had left the room, Desirée turned to me. 'Look more closely, Enzo.' She indicated the place on his side which Samax was clutching when he died.

'And move him?'

'Why not? It's not like we're going to call the police. We both know how he felt about them. But, more to the point, there is nothing they could do about this.'

Steadying my hands, I pried Samax's hand away with difficulty, and was surprised at once by how wet it was. His robe, too, was soaked through at that spot on his side.

'Why, it's blood.'

'No, not blood,' Desirée interjected. 'Do you see a tear in the robe?'

I smoothed and tugged the fabric, but saw nothing.

'It will barely be visible,' she went on. 'More like a puncture.'

'This might be it,' I said, pressing my fingers up behind the wet patch.

'Now look beneath that spot at the pajamas.'

The pajamas' silk was thinner and I was able to find the puncture in it, barely the width of a pencil.

'But if that's not blood, what is it?' I said.

'Water,' she replied. 'Ice water, to be exact.'

All at once I saw what she was getting at. My mind flew back to a long-ago dinner when I was a boy at Samax's side, hanging on his every word as he regaled the table with a description of the Borgias' special methods of committing murder. Foremost among them stabbing the victim with a dagger of ice, frozen in a mold, that left no fingerprints or evidence of a weapon, just a puncture wound – if one was looking for it – and a bit of water.

'He was stabbed?' I said incredulously.

'By the thinnest of blades.'

Just then, there was a deep howling in the corridor before the door burst open and Alif and Aym ran in with Sirius barking at their heels. Alif brandished a drawn pistol, and Aym in his blind man's black glasses froze, cocking his head, alert for sound.

'You're a little late,' Desirée said.

Sofiel had found them finally at the edge of the property, bringing Sirius back, and informed them of Samax's death. Extremely agitated, Alif several times circled Samax's body, examined it, circled again, and finally stood beside it, his hard black eyes shot through with grief. Aym also circled the body, his ear tilted toward it, listening intently, biting his lip. Then Alif burst into tears and Aym fell to his knees, wringing his hands. After all those years at my uncle's side, watching over him wherever he went, seeing to so many of his needs as he grew infirm, his bodyguards had grown close to him. But, after all, their real mission was to protect him from death. And when the Angel of Death had finally come for him, stepping out of the spectral light of his visions, Alif and Aym were nowhere to be found.

'Who would want to murder a dying man?' I said, turning back to Desirée. This was the question I kept asking myself, like a mantra, thinking that if I answered it philosophically, I would be able to answer it practically.

Desirée took a blanket from the closet and spread it over Samax's body. 'Someone running out of time themselves, Enzo,' she said bitterly. 'It doesn't take inordinate strength to thrust a dagger. Especially when your victim isn't expecting it.'

'You're talking about the Man of Smoke?' I said, and she seemed puzzled for a moment.

Then she looked me in the eye. 'Enzo, just so you know: the person you call the Man of Smoke is my father, Spica. He came back after all these years,' she said with a rueful smile, 'not to see me, but to help redesign the hotel.'

'Spica?'

'Yes. Samax told me last night who he was.'

'Have you spoken with him?'

'Not yet. But I know this: he didn't kill Samax.'

At that moment, we caught our first whiff of smoke. Desirée and I both knew immediately that it was a kind of smoke we had never smelled before around the hotel. Only once had I smelled it elsewhere, I thought, as all the fire alarms around the hotel began going off.

'We'd better get downstairs,' Desirée said, grabbing my hand and pulling me into the corridor with Sirius at our side. 'You, too,' she called back to Alif and Aym, but they shook their heads defiantly as if to say that if they had failed Samax in life, they certainly weren't going to leave his side in death. Then Alif made a sign indicating they would bring Samax's body down.

'Shouldn't we wait for them?' I said to Desirée.

'They can take care of themselves. And nothing can hurt Samax anymore.'

At the door to the fire stairs she stopped suddenly and leaned closer to me. The clatter of the alarms was growing louder and we heard shouts from the lower floors. 'It was Dolores who killed him,' Desirée said, her breath warm on my face. 'And god only knows what she's done now.'

19

Houston

I tilted the book into the rays of a small yellow light as I read. *'All the other moons in the solar system are either captured asteroids, like Phobos and Deimos around Mars, or satellites created at the same times as their planet, like Io and Europa around Jupiter. Our moon is neither.'*

Cassiel had his head in my lap. 'There have been plenty of theories about its origin,' he said, 'all disproven. We've mapped it and broken it down geologically, but we still don't where the moon came from or how it got there. It's one of the great mysteries.'

I shut the book, a history of the solar system which I had picked up that morning. 'Did you know', I said, 'that the Babylonians thought it was a mirror reflecting a lost portion of the earth which no one would ever discover?'

'I like that.' He closed his eyes and I began massaging his temples.

'Pythagoras, on the other hand, was convinced that the gods created the moon as a dwelling place for the souls of the dead.'

'Everyone from here who ever died? It would be very crowded.'

'Not in his time.'

'Hmm. I hadn't thought of that. What else did you find out?'

'Oh no, it's your turn. What has NASA discovered about the moon's origin?'

'That would take me all night.'

'We have all night.'

We were lying in the rear seat of his speedboat, in the darkness, anchored far out on a misty lake. The sky was overcast, with low blue clouds. It had been overcast all week: we hadn't once seen the moon. On the shore, nestled among thickets of maple and elm trees, the houses twinkled with lights. In one house a blue light glowed in an upstairs window, where I had screwed a blue bulb into the bedside lamp.

This was where Cassiel lived, a small ranch house in Clear Lake City, on the outskirts of Houston, a mile from the Johnson Space Center. A lot of NASA people, including astronauts, lived around that lake. Cassiel said it was the first real house he had lived in since he was a boy. He had been renting it for two years, yet it contained very few possessions outside the basic furnishings. He had bought himself a stereo, an aquarium stocked with neon fish, and a pool table, and there was a black BMW motorcycle and a white Corvette in the garage. That was about it. For him, it was a lot. A career nomad, accustomed to carrying everything he owned in a pair of sky-blue Air Force duffel bags and a trunk, he simply wasn't one to accumulate objects of any sort.

I had been visiting him for ten days. Five months had passed since our rendezvous in Honolulu. At the end of the week he and the other astronauts would fly from Ellington Air Force Base to the Kennedy Space Center at Cape Canaveral; twelve days after that, they would be launched into space. In Florida, they would live in quarantine in the Spartan quarters of the Space Center. Cassiel would have his own bedroom, but would share a living room, mess hall, and conference room – its walls adorned with lunar and astral maps – with the others. They would be served high-calorie meals, work out in an exercise room, receive endless briefings, and continue the daily sessions in the flight simulator that had been their second home in Houston. Eight hours a day for six months they had worked the complex control panels of switches, levers, and valves, learning to read every nuance in the dense array of dials and displays before them while they simulated hundreds of planned maneuvers and countless variations that might arise in a crisis.

Seeing the pressures Cassiel was under, feeling them palpably, vicariously, as I slept beside him, I understood why a number of Apollo astronauts a decade earlier had become religious zealots or alcoholics after their missions. Gazing back on the earth while standing on the moon might make me very religious, too – as if I'd seen the light and then some – but there was also a time it might have made me want to drink a great deal. In fact, Cassiel would stand on the far side, at the dead center of the forty-one percent of the lunar surface that is never visible on earth, looking out to the stars – something no man had ever done. I thought that this image of himself, gazing into an enormous glittering expanse, must have been hovering in the back of his mind for months.

My own feelings about his mission remained the same: I was at once excited and fearful. He had explained the mechanics of the flight to me, and shared many of the briefing materials that he brought home at night. Many of the facts that related to the flight, crucial to him as a navigator, I now knew by heart.

For example, that the moon, 234,000 miles from earth, orbits it at a speed of 2,300 mph and is an elusive moving target, especially if you yourself are traveling at 5,000 mph.

That the three-stage Saturn V rocket which would propel him into space was 363 feet high, with five enormous engines to power the first stage alone. At liftoff, the combined thrust of those engines would be 160 million horsepower. 160 million horses pulling them into the sky. Burning half a million gallons of kerosene and liquid oxygen for 2½ minutes in order to travel 40 miles. And then falling away.

The flight to the moon would take 66 hours. Half the time required for a transatlantic voyage by ocean liner. Or the time it would take to drive nonstop from Miami to Anchorage.

To enter lunar orbit, they would decelerate to 3,700 mph. On the far side of the moon, whether orbiting or on the surface, they would lose all radio contact with mission control. During their third revolution, Cassiel and one of the other astronauts would board the lunar module, detach from the command module, and descend to the surface. Landing on the far side, in pitch-darkness, would be treacherous. To be sure they touched down on clear, level ground, Cassiel would override the onboard computer and navigate manually, scanning quickly with infrared viewfinders. The only natural source of illumination on the far side is starlight, and Cassiel said it would be strong enough to cast his shadow – something that had happened to him only once on earth, in the Sonora Desert on a moonless night.

On the near side of the moon, the temperature varies wildly, from 225° in full sunlight to –240° in darkness. On the far side, it remains –250°. Cassiel and his partner would set out a semicircle of high-intensity lights beside their module and work with powerful helmet lamps, like coal miners. They would assemble the twin 120-inch refracting telescopes, gather geological specimens, and take seismographic readings. For four nights, until their work was done, they would sleep in their space suits in net hammocks suspended within their module.

When they returned to the command module, the *Constellation*, they would immediately leave lunar orbit. The *Constellation's* engine had no fallible moving parts – no fuel pumps or ignition system. Pressurized helium forced the propellants into the combustion chamber. In the icy prison of lunar orbit, this engine – and its backup – were the crew's lifeline. It would launch them into space for another 60,000 miles before carrying them the 300,000 miles back home. The amount of fuel they could carry on such a long mission left little margin for error; and the same went for air, food, and water. If they should veer off course for very long at any point – and this would be Cassiel's responsibility – they wouldn't be able to return to earth.

From the moon to Nova 1, a point in space that would be roughly in line with Mars and Jupiter when they arrived, was two days' flying time. Each mile they traveled beyond the moon would put them farther into space than any astronauts had ever been. At Nova 1 they would take hundreds of telescopic photographs of the larger stars and the closest galaxies, including Andromeda.

Five days later, the three astronauts would reenter the earth's atmosphere at 25,000 mph along an angle of entry just 2° wide. Their projected landing point was at 148°20'E, 12°6'N, in the South Pacific between Guam and Saipan.

Their estimated time in space: 527 hours, 12 minutes, 56 seconds.

I reviewed the facts of his mission many times, and in the end was comforted by one thought above all others: the sky was Cassiel's element, whether it was earthly, lunar, or interplanetary. He had come to me from the sky, in Vietnam, and when he took leave of me someday – as he had once before, but this time forever – I was certain it would be the same way. I could live with that. But in my gut I didn't think that day had arrived. Not yet. Not even with this mission, filled with so many perils.

By the time of my visit to Houston, alone together for the last time before the mission, we had stopped talking about the perils. The launch date was fast approaching, it was going to happen; any abstractions attached to it were quickly evaporating. In Cassiel I sensed no fear whatsoever, despite the fact that at the Space Center, where he was now spending practically every waking hour, they were focusing on everything that could possibly go wrong, ironing out kinks. When he came home, we talked about other things. We still had plenty of the past to catch up on, and it was easier to do so now that the wounds of our long separation had begun to heal. He liked hearing stories about my own travels and, especially, my days in the mind-reading business. We cooked together – neither of us very good at it – and shot pool and made love and listened to his jazz records lying on the living room carpet. Each morning before dawn we took the speedboat out and went for a swim.

For much of my visit in Clear Lake City I stayed around the house. I tinkered in the small garden or canoed alone on the lake. I culled a chronology of Cassiel's mission from the briefing books, so that back on Kauai I could follow his progress each day. A couple of times I accompanied him to the Space Center and he led me on a tour that was off-limits to ordinary tourists: up into the gleaming rocket gantries and through the labyrinthine chambers of the flight simulation center. He took me into the simulation models of his command and lunar modules. In the command module I was most drawn to the small triple-layered convex window from which Cassiel would view the moon, the stars, and finally the earth, the size of a nickel, from deep in space.

I also went into downtown Houston several times while Cassiel was at the Space Center, to go to the movies or wander through a museum. To my surprise, on the last of these solo outings I ran into an old acquaintance.

I had just bought a green dress with a flowered print – so much like the one I had worn for Cassiel in Manila that I couldn't resist it – and then worn it out of the store. Next I picked up the Christmas present I had ordered for him at a map store, a highly detailed topographical globe of the moon, three feet in diameter, with his projected landing site marked by a gold star.

At five o'clock I went to the natural-science museum where I spent the next hour and a half before meeting Cassiel for dinner. After exploring an exhibit about ancient deep-sea creatures, I took a spin through the entomological wing, where there was a new selection of South American jungle moths and giant mountain butterflies. I was at the last display case when a slight, stoop-shouldered man with a white goatee hurried by, steering a pushcart through the narrow aisle. I don't know if it was his thick, wire-rimmed spectacles or the spider terrarium perched on the pushcart that registered with me first. But the moment he passed me, I realized the man was Zaren Eboli, my one-time employer in New Orleans. It took him a bit longer to recognize me after I called his name. When he did, he turned ashen. I thought he was going to faint as he approached me, taking his furtive, pigeon-toed steps.

'Mala? Mala from the morgue at the Saint-Eustace parish library?'

'Yes.' I hadn't thought of myself in those terms in some time, and for a moment I felt a twinge of regret for having stopped him.

'My god. I often wondered over the years what happened to you.'

I flushed, for it was a painful memory. 'You mean, after I got myself bitten by one of your spiders.' I shook my head. 'The *Ummidia Stellarum*. I hope I didn't kill it.'

He smiled ruefully, and I saw just how much older he looked, how time had deepened the creases in his brow and the crow's-feet beside his eyes. His nervous voice and polite manner, however, were just as I remembered them. 'No, the spider survived,' he replied, 'but I wasn't sure that you had.'

I extended my hand. 'Well, here I am. And I must apologize, however belatedly.' His hand, with the missing pinky, was small and dry. 'You were so kind to me back then.'

He scoffed at this. 'No apologies necessary. But what happened to you after that day?'

'Oh, the venom didn't affect me much,' I said drily. 'I just drove up to Savannah and enlisted in the Navy Nursing Corps and was shipped off to Vietnam.'

'Really. I remember you being very much against the war.'

'Oh, I remained so, more than ever. But things worked out unexpectedly for me in the end. I wouldn't be here in Houston right now if your spider hadn't bitten me.'

He cocked his head.

'I met someone in Vietnam,' I said, 'we fell in love, met again after many years, and I'm here with him now. He's with NASA.'

He seemed taken aback by my directness. 'He's a scientist?'

'An astronaut.'

'Well, I'm glad for you.'

'But tell me about yourself,' I said. 'What are you doing here?'

'Oh, I've just finished cataloguing the spiders of the southwestern states. 2,942 of them, to be exact. The head curator gave me an office here. You know, I'm doing what I've always done.' He cleared his throat. 'Do you have time for a cup of tea, perhaps in our modest cafeteria?'

'I'd love to, but I have to run.' I peered into the terrarium: there was a lone spider, silver-green, with black markings, which I tried to identify. 'A lynx spider? Female?'

'That's good!' Eboli exclaimed. 'Yes, she's a particularly beautiful example of the *Peucetia viridans*. I found her near Yuma, Arizona. The lynx flourishes all across this region, into Mexico.'

'Lays her eggs on cactus plants, right?'

'For protection, yes. On the spiny pads of the prickly pear cactus or the leaves of the jatropha plant.' He smiled. 'I must have taught you well back then. You know, I hired you for your proficiency in Latin, but you turned out to have the makings of a first-rate arachnologist.' He hesitated. 'You didn't by chance go into that line of work yourself, did you?'

'I'm afraid not.'

'Well, maybe you'll give me a raincheck on that tea.'

From his vest pocket he took a card. 'Will you call me tomorrow?'

I did, only to find him extremely agitated. Packing his suitcase. Trying to get the airline on the phone. He had to fly at once to Las Vegas, he said. A dear friend of his had died several days earlier, and he had just been informed of it. 'He was my patron for many years. Living at his hotel, I did some of the best research I've ever done. He was like family to me.' Through the phone I heard him stifle a sob. 'I'm sorry, Mala, but I won't be able to meet you just now.'

I gave him my address and phone number in Hawaii and told him I hoped we'd cross paths again. I felt so bad for him because I knew that, like me, he had no real family. That is, until Cassiel came back into my life.

After leaving Zaren Eboli at the museum, I drove in Cassiel's Corvette to a Vietnamese restaurant he frequented. It was surrounded by shade trees and had a rock garden at its center with a carp pool. Cassiel's motorcycle was parked in front and he was waiting for me at a corner table. His face lit up when he saw the green dress. He had already ordered appetizers and, unusual for him, he was drinking a champagne cocktail. Also unusual, he seemed a bit nervous. I found out why when he put a small velvet box and a large sealed envelope on the table before me.

I opened the envelope first: inside it, enfolded in tissue paper, was the pale, leathery leaf from the playing-card bush on which I had inscribed our names, alongside a pair of stars, in Manila in 1969.

'I told you I'd save it,' he said.

I nodded, biting my lip. Then I opened the box and found a diamond ring, the diamond cut into a seven-pronged star that matched my pendant. Inside the gold band was inscribed a single symbol, no words: $\triangle$. The symbol for a celestial fix.

'For when I get back,' he said, slipping the ring onto my finger. 'If you'll still have me.'

I had never in my life worn a ring. But, as always, I

was wearing my pendant and my star bracelet. Raising my left hand, with both the bracelet and the ring, up beside the necklace, I leaned over to him. 'I'm covered with stars,' I said, kissing him.

The morning I left Houston, he had one last thing to give me. After getting up early, we barely said a word around the house. I packed my bags while he made breakfast. It was a sunny day, with a damp wind blowing off the Gulf of Mexico. Though I knew he had settled into a zone of serenity with regard to the flight, Cassiel had slept badly the night before. I had barely slept at all. It was December 4. The next day he would fly to Cape Canaveral. Eleven days later, at 9:42 p.m. EST, he would be launched out of the earth's atmosphere.

As the time approached for him to drive me to the airport, the silence in that house had become deafening. Cassiel had gone for a short walk along the lake, and when he returned, it was he who broke the ice, sitting me down on the patio while he poured himself yet another cup of black coffee.

'There's something I have to ask you to hold for me, for safekeeping. I don't want to leave it here when I go to Florida.'

He handed me a small metal box; no bigger than a matchbox, it slid open like one, revealing a silver key with complex teeth and a circular black stone inlaid below the key-ring hole.

'The key with the black stone,' I exclaimed.

He smiled faintly. 'That's right, it's the one you saw in the X-ray in Vietnam.'

'I can't believe I'm holding it now,' I said. Studying the stone, I guessed it was onyx.

'Up until three months ago, nobody could hold it,' he said, patting his abdomen. 'I had it in here for twenty-five years. It's one of a kind, impossible to duplicate. It opens a box that will probably never come into my possession. But until I'm sure of that, I must know that the key is in a safe place. I didn't want to take it into space with me, either.'

'Three months ago you had your appendix removed.'

'Right. After it became inflamed last year, the doctors wanted it out before the mission. I told them to get this key while they were in there. A long time ago I swallowed it to keep the contents of the box out of somebody's hands. Please, just hold on to it for me, Mala, until I return.' He hesitated. 'I doubt it will happen, but if you ever encounter someone with that box, use your judgment as to whether you want to open it with them.'

'But how will I know? You're not telling me enough.'

'You'll know.' He sat back. 'You'll know if you trust that person. It's a long story, and right now you have a plane to catch.'

I knew him well enough to feel sure that, long or short, it must also be a painful story, one he didn't want to dredge up just then; had he wanted to go into detail, he would have brought up the key at another time, and not on the morning of my departure.

Even before we left his house, I put the key on the black chain around my neck where my pendant usually hung. At the airport, waiting awkwardly after checking my bags – neither of us good at, or experienced with, long goodbyes – I said to him, 'You've given me wonderful presents. This one is for you.' And I pressed my pendant into his palm. 'Take it with you to the stars, Geza.'

He pulled me close and kissed me, and before we parted a few minutes later it was he who said to me, without a trace of irony, 'Have a safe flight.'

20

Fire

The Hotel Canopus burned down in six hours. Despite the swift arrival of the fire department – six trucks and forty firemen – all that remained of the hotel in the end was a shell of charred steel beams along the western wall. Even the basement and subbasement were gutted by fire. Samax's library, most of his art collection, the rare furniture and the sacred objects brought to the hotel over the years from every continent, all of it was destroyed. While of necessity many of his secondary pieces were in a warehouse he owned in downtown Las Vegas, Samax was not a man who kept his valuable artworks locked away, out of sight. He liked to admire them openly in the course of his daily affairs. Or as he put it to me one day: 'Why should it be easier for me to make myself a sandwich or prune one of the trees than to gaze upon a piece of Cretan bronze work or a mosaic from Umbria it took me ten years to find?'

Why, indeed. Now no one would ever gaze on them again. And to the bewilderment and dismay of the various museums to which he had bequeathed the bulk of his collections, when his fireproof, floodproof, explosion-proof vault was opened, it was found to contain a handful of roughly drawn maps from the logs of explorers like Columbus, John Davis, and Martin Frobisher, a sheaf of rare terrestrial maps by Mercator and Cassini, one of Riccioli's first lunar maps, and a first edition of the very first world atlas, the seventy-map *Theatrum Orbis* compiled by Abraham Ortelius of Antwerp in 1570. Not a single painting, sketch, or piece of sculpture was found in the vault. While the maps and journals were in themselves worth a fortune, and had always been of interest to Samax, it was not clear that he had kept them beyond the reach of disaster because he valued them more highly than his other possessions or because he valued them less and didn't mind their being less accessible. I tended to the latter explanation, but even I was surprised at the contents of that fire-blackened vault, hauled by crane from the mountain of debris, when I was called to witness its inspection.

Unimportant to the insurance assessors and museum curators, but very painful to me, was the destruction of Samax's personal effects and many of my own things, from the small chest containing Bel's few surviving possessions and the trove of books Samax had given me to the other keepsakes of my childhood (the American Flyer trains, my telescope, the woolen cap I had been wearing the day I was brought to Las Vegas) and the looseleaf binders of architectural drawings I had been filling since adolescence. Gone, too, were Labusi's music collection and mnemonic memorabilia and the papers and artifacts of former guests like Deneb and Zaren Eboli that had been squirreled away in the hotel's myriad storerooms. Harahel had escaped the fire un-scathed, but the archives of Samax's life he had been assembling so tediously, the decades of files and records, the voluminous correspondence, were reduced to ashes. I must admit, that project had never particu-larly touched my heart; I suffered more grief at the notion of the raging flames devouring my uncle's yellow fountain pen with the red ink, the jade-handled razor with which he had taught me to shave, and the velvet slippers and red robe he had been wearing when he died.

Most grievous of all to me, Samax himself had been consumed by the fire, very much in the fashion of the old Assyrian kings, those astute stargazers he so admired, whose bodies were laid out on the top floor of a palace filled with their possessions that was then burned to the ground. Once I absorbed the initial shock, I knew he would have preferred this method of cremation, lying on the floor of his private library in the hotel's penthouse, flanked by his faithful bodyguards Alif and Aym, to the conventional one in a Las Vegas funeral parlor. For in the end Alif and Aym had had no intention of carrying Samax's body out of the hotel; like a king's retainers who had failed their master, they apparently decided to die beside Samax – the only casualties that day besides Dolores.

The instructions Samax had left with regard to his funeral, not just in his will, but in separate conversations with Desirée and me, were quite simple: he didn't want one. He was to be cremated as soon as possible and then his ashes were to be scattered in the quincunx orchard beneath the very first *Samax Astrofructus* tree he had planted. There was to be no service, no priest, no guests. And definitely no sermons or eulogies: he just wanted one of his favorite fragments of Heraclitus – a single sentence of seventeen words – recited when the ashes were scattered.

And so it was, as the fire engulfed the topmost reaches of the Hotel Canopus and I realized that Samax's body would never be recovered, that I recited Fragment 67 aloud while standing beside Hadar in the driveway. My throat was aching from the smoke and heat washing over us, and firemen were rushing past us with loud cries and clattering equipment, jets of water from their hoses vaporizing as they arced into the flames. Still, I heard at that instant why these words must have resonated so powerfully for a man like Samax, who obviously hoped that his voyaging days would not end just because this particular leg of the voyage, in this short life, had ended: *In death men will come on things they do not expect, things utterly unknown to the living.*

Hadar looked long and hard at me as I got the words

out, then surprised me with a response, another fragment of Heraclitus's, in fact. I knew all 124 of them, which Samax had had me memorize as a boy, advising me that if you were to read only one philosopher in your life, it should be Heraclitus.

Fire catches up with everything in time, Hadar intoned, in that voice of his that sounded like it was coming from underwater.

But that was to be the end of our philosophical dialogue. The hotel had become Samax's funeral pyre and this was the hour of his immolation, and as I gazed to the sky, Hadar turned his face to the ground. A moment later, what appeared to be a circular rainbow rose up from the column of fire the hotel had become. At first, it looked like a large halo, or a ring of Saturn. But the colors rapidly differentiated and solidified, and for a few seconds I saw an army of winged forms with shining human faces ascend in spinning concentric circles and disappear into the bright light.

Of course, I thought: Francesco Gozzoli's angels, from the ceiling mural, would find another home, just as they had when the Nazis bombed their church on that Greek island. And now, I was sure, my uncle's soul was among them.

If Hadar saw them, he didn't let on, and the next metamorphosis I witnessed would be his own, occurring so quickly and unexpectedly that afterward I doubted my own eyes.

Hadar had barely escaped the fire, his hair scorched, his face blackened, long after everyone else was out of the hotel. His hundreds of hard-found meteorites, which had survived incineration while plunging into the earth's atmosphere, reached temperatures in his windowless laboratory that caused them to melt and fuse with one another; later, when they hardened again, they had become as one – not like the lost planet Hadar had imagined, of course, but a formless and grotesque mass of pure iron.

'I failed him, too,' he said suddenly, but with the

deepest resignation. For the first and only time in fifteen years, I saw his corkscrew eyes wide open; reflecting the towering flames, those eyes were even blacker and fiercer than I had imagined them to be when I was a boy. He was the last of the old guests, on Samax's payroll to the very end, but still I was taken aback by his utter despair; it felt as if, given the choice, he would have preferred the route taken by Alif and Aym.

The next words he spoke – in a different voice, tinged with bitterness now – floored me, and I looked around to see if it was really him speaking.

'When I took my body from that prison, I found I could never reinhabit it again. My spirit roved – in and out of men near death, and criminals, and lost wanderers – until it settled in his body and found new purpose. I'd discover a wholeness, not in men's souls, but in reconstructing the lost planet from those wanderers of space we call meteors. And I'd do it here, under Samax's roof.' He drew a long breath. 'But no more.'

Then he edged away from me, onto the lawn between the hotel and the greenhouse. He moved slowly, yet put a great distance between us in seconds. With his back to me, and his arms folded, he did not respond when I called after him. For a moment he was backdropped by the intensity of the fire, and I lost sight of him. When he reappeared, it looked as if he were stepping out of a shadow, though he was in an open, sunlit space. But he was no longer Hadar, wearing the baggy white jumpsuit and steel-toed boots. Instead I saw before me a much younger man, lithe and wiry, with a bronze torso and long black hair knotted in back with a piece of rawhide. He wore a vest and khaki pants and moccasins and had a rifle on a leather strap slung over his back. A rifle with a walnut stock and an extra-long barrel – World War One vintage, I thought.

And suddenly I knew who I was looking at: Rochel, the Zuni sharp-shooter, the hero and deserter who became a Sufi in the Levant, Samax's cellmate who escaped the federal penitentiary. My uncle had intuited correctly that Rochel might have been residing at the hotel in a new incarnation, with a new calling, while watching over him all those years – and over me, too, on occasion. With Samax gone, Rochel had reverted to his old form in the seconds before he himself took flight.

Hadar was Rochel, I thought in amazement. And it struck me that he was the guest, of course, who most resembled Rochel as Samax had described him: taciturn, self-contained, a loner. The same Rochel who in 1926 had given Samax the ancient blue amulet with the earth rendered as it would look from outer space was also Hadar – the man consumed by celestial phenomena and phantom planets.

He disappeared now, stepping back into that shadow in the bright light. Just as he must have disappeared from the locked cell in Ironwater, Colorado, I thought, running over, looking in vain for some trace of him.

Instead, I saw Desirée racing across the lawn with long strides, still in her robe and sandals, her black hair streaming behind her and Sirius at her heels, loping as fast as he could. Several firemen, despite the ferocity of the blaze, stopped to stare at her. More frantic than I had ever seen her, she ran directly to the greenhouse. Once inside it, Sirius started barking so loudly that the echo carried above the commotion on the lawn.

The other outbuildings – pool house, toolshed, garage, even the cottage across the orchard where Sofiel the gardener lived – had all been set afire by flying embers and were burning down with the hotel. The fountain in the driveway had been badly damaged, too, the statue of the beautiful woman designed by Spica shattered when the firemen, finding inadequate water pressure in nearby hydrants, tapped into the pipes below. Though closer to the hotel than the other buildings, the greenhouse remained unscathed. Even after the fire was finally extinguished, none of its thousands of windowpanes had been broken.

Running in after Desirée, I found her on a stepladder, throwing open some old cabinets where Samax used to keep potting soil and peat moss. 'You were right,' I said breathlessly. 'Forcas isn't Rochel; it was Hadar.'

She glanced over her shoulder at me blankly, her mind elsewhere.

To my surprise, I saw that the potting soil and peat moss had been replaced with material completely unrelated to gardening: many thousands of pages of yellow typewriter paper in crisp yellow folders.

'So you moved them here?' I said.

'Only because I began writing here a couple of months ago. First for a change of pace. Then I got to like it.' She began lifting the folders from their shelves. 'A bit of luck, I suppose.'

'Can I help?'

She paused and looked hard at me, turning something over in her head. 'Maybe I'll show you some of this later,' she said finally.

'I'd like that.'

She handed me down some folders. 'I hope you won't be disappointed.'

Under the dark canopy of Samax's trees I began carrying them, an armful at a time, to the far side of the greenhouse, where Desirée thought the stone walls that set off the potting area would offer extra protection. I left the manila envelope containing the Hopkins brothers' report in that area as well, on a shelf beside the zinc sink. I had been clutching that envelope so long – since running up to the penthouse from my room – that I had forgotten it was in my hand. It was the only thing besides the clothes on my back that I took from the hotel when the fire alarms went off, and now it would have to wait.

So while the priceless artworks and rare astronomical objects were gone forever, it turned out that Desirée's mystery opus had escaped the flames. That very night, after everyone else left, the firemen and the police, Mrs Resh and Sofiel and his wife – for whom I would secure rooms at the Twin Stars motel – I thought I might finally get my wish and dip into those yellow folders, dated with neat red labels, beginning in December, 1961 and continuing right up to the present, November, 1980.

As we carried the last of the folders along the flagstone paths, Desirée said, 'There's just one other thing. I need to be sure about Dolores.'

'Sure that she killed him?'

'Sure that she's dead. Will you come with me?'

'Back into the hotel?' I said incredulously.

'Through the tunnel. I don't see her committing suicide. If she tried to get out, that would have been the only route from her office downstairs. Look, maybe it won't even be passable, but I have to see.'

'All right.'

First I made sure Sirius was secure in the greenhouse, resting beneath the potting table. Then Desirée and I wended our way through the trees to the tunnel and ran between the greenhouse and the hotel.

'How can you be so sure it was Dolores?' I asked.

'Who else?'

'I can think of a bunch of people. Vitale Cassiel, Ivy—'

'No, no. Think back to the book Samax pulled out of the pile as he fell.'

'*The Garden of Cyrus*.'

'You know he was trying to tell us something. It's a book about quincunxes – like the orchard. And who was it who always sat in the orchard? Dolores. That's what Samax was telling us in the few seconds he had left.'

'Just like that?'

'If you need it to be more complicated, think about this: the quincunx is an arrangement of five things in a diamond – one at each corner, one in the middle. Those things can be trees, they can be people. Dolores, Denise, Della, and Doris at each corner, and Samax in the middle: my mother always said Samax set up the orchard with that concept in mind. Whether he did or not, that book tells me it was Dolores who murdered him.'

We went through the door and down the steps into the tunnel. Instead of the usual tropical smell, of moss and stone and flora, the air was acrid with smoke.

'And she did this because of the museum – because he wasn't leaving the place to you?'

'It's even more insane than that,' Desirée said sharply. 'She always knew I didn't want the hotel. No, she killed him because he wasn't leaving the hotel to *her*. Even at 105, she was convinced she was going to outlive him. But when he finalized his will this week, endowing the museum, that became a moot point. It was premeditated murder, after which she set the fire. Knowing the hotel inside out, she could do that with a minimum of effort.'

'Alone?'

'Why not? A few gallons of gasoline, strategically placed . . .'

My head was reeling.

'I hope she's dead,' Desirée said. 'She deserved to die. Someone who lives so long and still wants to cheat death – who's still greedy enough at her age to commit murder – ought to die.'

Though as a boy I had used it daily, I hadn't been in the tunnel for a long time. And it had never felt so strange to me – not even the day I first encountered Auro there – as it did at that moment, walking side by side with Desirée over the steaming brick floor, around the loop beneath the swimming pool, toward the stairwell that spiraled down from the burning hotel. With each step, we felt the temperature climb a few degrees. The metal steps when we ascended them felt warm under our feet. The double door to the basement landing – a fire door – was shut. I gripped the handle and it was hot.

'Better step back,' I said, and as I pulled the door open, the rush of fiery air nearly blew us both off the small landing. The corridor's walls and ceiling were livid with flames. The floor tiles had melted. And less than ten feet from the door, someone was lying flat on those tiles, face upward, on fire. As terrible a sight as I've ever seen, it was Dolores, all right, black dress and white hair burned away from her scarecrow frame, her bones beginning to protrude through her flesh. Her left hand had become one with the handle of a leather briefcase that was burned to a crisp. Where she had intended to go and what papers she had been carrying with her we would never know. But even in the throes of burning alive, she had not let go of that briefcase.

'Let's get out of here,' Desirée muttered, and headed down the stairs.

Back in the greenhouse, gulping down the cool air, we locked the door to the tunnel behind us, as if to seal out not just the fire but the memory of what we'd seen. And for the next couple of hours, barely exchanging a word, we sat on one of the teak benches and watched the rest of the hotel burn. Sirius watched with us, his old pale eyes half-lidded and tears streaking his muzzle – for he knew well what was going on, and he loved Samax dearly – before finally dozing off. I put on Samax's white lab coat, and draping my shirt over Desirée's shoulders, touched her cheek. She surprised me yet again, pressing my hand to her face and holding it there for a long time before resting her head against my shoulder.

I took pleasure in feeling Desirée's breath rise and fall as she leaned against me, even as the enormity of what had occurred began hitting me in waves. Samax murdered, the hotel torched. By Dolores! She was the Angel of Death all along, living in the hotel basement, rocking in the deep shade in her hidden corner of the orchard. The *D* at the top of the quincunx of *D's*. Samax had kept Death close by all those years, had used her in fact (an efficiency expert without peer) to run the place, had even, carelessly, married one of her daughters, until the day arrived when she decided his time had come. And then, despite his bodyguards and street savvy and his gambler's instincts, she not only struck him down, but also leveled the empire he would have left behind.

For now, despite a vast endowment and meticulous blueprints, the hotel would never become a museum. The trusteeships, the bequeathals, the charitable bequests – all gone up in smoke. Home to me for three-fifths of my life, the repository of so many of my own dreams and memories, the Hotel Canopus had been

574

snuffed out as speedily as a barn filled with hay rather than a building brimming with the dreams of a man to whom dreams were everything. All that had survived on the property were the greenhouse and the orchard – Samax's trees, which were rustling behind me in the currents of the ventilation fans.

In the evening, a trio of fire inspectors began the work which would culminate, four days later, in their officially declaring that the fire was an act of arson. But when they first arrived, I didn't have the heart, or the armor, to deal with them. Before she left for the night, I assigned Mrs Resh the task, speaking with her outside the greenhouse. That was the only time I got off that bench beside Desirée. When I returned, I was certain I didn't want to leave her side again. Maybe because I knew what was about to happen between us. Looking back, I'm sure I did. The way she had looked at me, and touched me, and then rested her body against mine. I had wanted to be close to her in that way for so long, and I could never have guessed that it would happen on my very last day at the hotel. Although, looking back, I must have known, too, that it couldn't have happened any other way.

Night fell like a curtain and still Desirée and I didn't move. And then everyone really was gone. Not just Samax, and Alif and Aym, and Dolores, but all the living too. And Hadar, whatever and wherever he was now. They were all gone. There was just Desirée and me.

I said as much to her.

'Don't forget Spica,' she said. 'He's gone, too.'

Spica, her father, to whose room she had raced after we left the penthouse together.

'I know the hotel was also your memory palace,' she said suddenly, touching my forehead. 'So it will always live on, up here. You can imagine what it must have been like for me all these years, living in the hotel, knowing that my father had designed and built it and then disappeared. "The Man of Smoke",' she added, shaking her head and gazing at the smoke rising from the rubble.

'When I got there, his door was open and the room was filled with black smoke. The white smoke was gone. I called out over and over again, but there was no reply. I'll never have the chance to talk to him now. Samax told me Spica wanted to talk with me,' she said bitterly. 'I guess he was working up to it, hiding behind that cloud of his own making. But he was still my father.' Her eyes filled with tears. 'Today I lost both my fathers.' She put her arms around me and I turned her face up to mine.

When she closed her eyes, I kissed her, tentatively at first, and then, when her lips parted, harder, her tongue slowly circling my own. Everything we did, every movement and gesture, unfolded slowly, yet afterward it seemed to have happened in a flash. We rose from the bench, leaving the lab coat and her robe there, and still embracing, made our way through the maze of the greenhouse to a dark triangle of Japanese cherry trees hidden away in a circle of date palms. We lit a kerosene lantern and hung it from a branch. Then we spread a blanket on the moss that carpeted the ground. Drawing in my breath, I unsnapped Desirée's bikini top and peeled off the bottom, down her long legs and off her inturned feet, and then lay back while she removed my clothes, one by one. I had never seen skin like hers – her breasts with their pale nipples, the inside of her thighs, the small of her back where I found a constellation of beauty marks. She emanated a silvery, almost lunar, glow there in the sylvan twilight. I must have kissed and touched every inch of her, tasting the jasmine moisture of her body, drinking in her hair which was black and sweet as wine, lingering as long as I could before sliding on top of her. Her knees up high, her arms around my shoulders, I felt her yield as I eased into her, her mouth, too, yielding under mine.

At that moment I thought I heard piano music, a slow clear tune, very faintly, far away. And Desirée whispered in my ear, 'I would have played my piano for you tonight . . .'

I heard that music for the next hour while we made

love, and then made love again, before I drifted off into the sweetest sleep with Desirée's head resting on my chest.

When I opened my eyes again, she was gone. It was dawn. Exhausted, I had slept through the night. Pulling on my pants, I walked around to the potting sink. Where we had piled the dozens of yellow folders against the stone wall, I found only a single piece of yellow paper, held down by a stone. Typewritten, it read:

Dear Enzo,

You will never see me again.

All the pages I filled for nineteen years were about the men I became involved with. So many different men. I too was searching for a lost thing, trying to seduce it out of the darkness, but what that thing was, I couldn't say. For obvious reasons, some would suggest it was my phantom father, the French pilot my mother invented, others that it was the real phantom whom Spica became, but I would prefer to think it was something in me.

That is what my life has been, and I chronicled it. You are the first and only lover of mine whom I will not – could not – write about. Everything I felt about you I was able to express when we made love. And that means the end of something for me. Along with the end of the Hotel Canopus. Watching the hotel burn, with Samax and Spica inside it, I knew everything had changed for me.

By the time you read this, I will have burned all my pages. They should have burned with the hotel. But that would have been too easy. Now I will start fresh – at what, I don't know. I do know that you'll find the things you've been looking for. You were always loving to me – I already miss you.

Love,

> *Desirée*

She had never intended to read me her yellow pages; instead, she had given herself to me. And now she had confirmed what I had vaguely suspected: she had been writing a kind of history of her life, like Casanova's or Byron's, based on her sexual exploits and erotic explorations, from age sixteen to thirty-five. At her silent Olivetti she had in fact been her own Scheherazade. How many men there were, how many nights of lovemaking she had chronicled in how many different places, no one would ever know now. All I knew was that I still tasted jasmine on my lips, and that my hands, which had roved her body and lost themselves in her hair, smelled now of jasmine too. As they would for many days, no matter what else I touched.

Before leaving the greenhouse, I sat up on the zinc sink with Samax's lab coat draped over my shoulders and read the Hopkins brothers' report. They laid out every investigative step they had taken, all the twists and turns of the inquiry which led them to report that the woman named Mala Revell lived at #2 Kohale Road, in Haena, on the northwest shore of the Hawaiian island of Kauai. She was thirty-five years old, self-employed, and she lived alone. Later, from a pay phone on the road, I called the airline and bought an open ticket for Honolulu from Albuquerque, which I hoped to use within the next two weeks.

It took me nearly that long to close down the affairs of the hotel. I dealt with the fire inspectors and insurance underwriters, the county clerk and the medical examiner. The latter had only Dolores's remains to examine before they were redundantly cremated; no trace of Samax, Spica, or Alif and Aym was recovered from the ashes. Calzas flew up from Santa Fe to help me out. When I picked him up at the airport, he embraced me hard, and later, as he surveyed the smoldering ruins of the hotel, I saw his eyes well up. Then Forcas arrived, two days after the fire. When they got word eventually, Labusi arrived in his bus from San Diego and Zaren Eboli flew in at the same time from Houston, but I missed them, having gone on that particular – and momentous – day to Reno to see Vitale Cassiel, my grandfather.

It was Forcas who urged me to do so after I told him what I'd read in my father's letter.

'He hasn't a clue who you really are,' Forcas said to me, lighting a cigar. He was wearing his usual black sharkskin suit and a silver tie with a silver clip. His features that were so difficult to recall showed no visible signs – no darkening or contraction – of the grief I knew he felt over Samax's death. 'To him, you were just one of Junius's relatives,' he went on. 'Once, a long time ago, he may have suspected something, but it's his nature to be suspicious.'

'I wonder why,' I said drily.

We were in the tiny nightwatchman's office of Samax's warehouse on Paradise Road, which I had made my temporary headquarters.

'I was planning to go see him anyway,' I went on.

'About the amulet.'

'That's right. I promised Samax I wouldn't try to get it – but that promise ended with his death. Samax should have had that amulet.'

'Maybe so, Enzo. But it belongs to Vitale Cassiel. He got it first. That's the way it went with everything between them.'

'I'll make him a fair offer.'

'Money?' Forcas said. 'May I give you some advice? Don't offer him money.'

'I don't think he's just going to hand it over after all this time.'

Forcas blew softly on the ember of his cigar. 'Are you going to tell him he's your grandfather?'

'I don't feel obligated. After all, I never told Uncle Junius about the letter – though I'm glad now that I didn't.'

'You should tell him.'

I rose from the swivel chair behind the metal desk and looked out at the desert through the barred, dirty window. 'Can you tell me what else he and my uncle were fighting over?' I said. 'You would know.'

'In the last few years, nothing to speak of. They were both wearing down – reduced to leveraging, shadow-boxing with dummy corporations. That's how they got in their shots. Even buying a property out from under the other guy, like I once told you about, had become too much for them.' From his cigar Forcas tapped a perfect cylinder of ash into the plastic ashtray. 'You want me to call ahead to him for you?'

I had my hands in my pockets. Beyond the city limits, at the foot of the Spring Mountains, the thermals were swirling up curtains of sand. 'You mean, you'll tell him who I am.'

Forcas nodded. 'And that you're coming to see him. That's all I'll tell him.'

I thought about it for a long time. 'All right. Today's Wednesday – tell him I'm coming on Friday.' I turned back to him. 'And thanks.'

Forcas stood up, smoothing out his tie. 'He's dying, you know.'

'No,' I said. 'I didn't know.' But I appreciated that Forcas had waited until after I decided to tell me.

Vitale Cassiel's large white house shone in the glaring sunlight. Sitting on forty acres on the outskirts of Reno, the house had two long verandahs and a stucco roof. There was a single ancient elephant tree on the baked lawn and a line of mesquite trees around the property. Oleander bushes around the house itself. No flowers. It was too hot a place for flowers, even if you wanted them. That day it was 98°. Clouds like brown dust were fixed on the horizon, as if they were painted there. As soon as I stepped from the air-conditioning of my car, a blast of hot wind made my lungs ache.

It was about a hundred yards to the house from the cul-de-sac at the end of the driveway. There was a garage there that could accommodate six cars. Tar was boiling up through the asphalt. I walked gingerly to keep it from my shoes. On the first-floor verandah I could make out a solitary figure sitting under a slow ceiling fan. A bird-cage hung from a hook on a wooden pillar. As I got closer, I saw it was a woman sitting stiffly in a straight-back chair.

The woman was Ivy, and the caged bird was a parrot, who watched me climb the limestone steps. 'Goodbye,' he squawked.

Ivy didn't say hello or goodbye. And she didn't seem surprised to see me, though I hadn't seen her in three years. 'I know why you're here,' she said. 'I told you I knew more about you than you knew yourself. I've always known.'

Her voice was weak, and she was slurring. Her hair had turned gray, dry as straw, her pale skin was tinged yellow, and she had a thin blue robe sashed tightly around her thinning waist. Her mouth seemed off-kilter, as did one of her cheekbones, as if she had suffered a stroke herself.

'I'm glad he's dead,' she added. 'And I'm glad the hotel is gone.'

'What have you always known, Ivy?' I said.

'You know what. What *they* never knew.'

'Meaning Samax—'

'Yes, and him,' she said, inclining her head toward the second floor. 'I knew when your mother died that you were Geza's son. I told no one. Now it doesn't matter anymore.'

'You did it because Bel took him away from you. That day on the road near the Hotel Canopus.'

Her washed-out eyes flared. 'What do you know about that?'

'I know you were in love with him, too.'

'He was my brother,' she snapped.

'Sure,' I said thickly. 'And if you couldn't have him, you'd make sure Bel didn't either. That's why you lied to him when he was in Colorado, telling him the cops were on to him, sending him a bad check.'

If it was possible for her to turn any paler, she did. 'Geza is alive? You've talked to him?'

'I haven't talked to him.'

'Then how could you know all this?'

I leaned down to her ear. 'I know more about you than you think.' Then I rang the doorbell and a butler materialized from the gloom of the foyer.

'Goodbye,' the parrot squawked.

'Go to hell,' Ivy cried after me, and then started coughing.

The house was white on the inside too, and it looked and smelled like a hospital. A wave of ammonia and alcohol greeted me. A nurse with a tray disappeared through a swinging door. Through a window I saw a private ambulance parked by the rear entrance, on call. Immediately, no questions asked, the butler showed me up to the second floor. There I was met by another nurse, who asked if I would like a cold drink. Then she took me down two long bare corridors to a room where an orderly, a burly man with a blond crew cut, sat on a stool outside the door. He looked up at me without interest as he opened the door.

I entered a spacious bedroom where there were two more nurses. It was difficult to make them out clearly because the room seemed to be full of fog. In fact it was mist, from an enormous humidifier. The mist was nearly as thick as the smoke in Spica's room, and the little sunlight that penetrated the heavily curtained windows was deeply refracted, the beams crisscrossing sharply. Lining the walls were a mahogany desk, a chest, an armoire, and a long leather couch. In the center of the room was a white hospital bed surrounded by medical equipment – oxygen tanks, monitors, a breathing machine the size of a commercial freezer. There was a clear oxygen tent on the bed and a man beneath it, white-faced with a shaved head, peered at me as I crossed the room. His large white hands were nearly indistinguishable from the sheet drawn up to his chin.

His blue eyes studied me closely through the plastic tent. I could hear him wheezing as he breathed.

'Lift it,' he rasped to the two nurses hovering beside the bed.

They unfastened and lifted a small square of the tent

582

so that he and I could see each other clearly. His nose was long, his ears large, and he had once had a strong chin. I had seen photographs of him in middle age, but the man inside the tent looked nothing like the tall, black-haired, broad-shouldered man in those photographs. Now his face was as bleached-out as his hands. And his lips had more blue to them than his eyes, which never left mine. After about ten seconds, one of the nurses refastened the square.

'You're a Cassiel, all right,' he said. 'Imagine.'

'My name is Enzo Samax.'

'Ah. Have a seat, then, Enzo Samax.' One nurse placed a metal chair behind me, and another appeared with a glass of ice water. Then the three nurses took up positions, forming a triangle around the bed, just out of earshot. The breathing machine whirred, lights flashed on the monitors, the mist continued to pour into the room. Already my shirt was clinging to my back.

'I've got half a lung left,' Vitale Cassiel said, his voice slipping into the rough whisper where it would remain. 'And that half is no good. So we've got ten minutes to talk. It's all I can do. I don't see anybody anymore.'

For more than half my life, this man's name had been synonymous with fear, chaos, vengeance, destruction. Just as certain words can function in themselves as reproaches, his name, uttered without embellishment, was like a threat. I had often thought about what it would be like to meet him. I had concocted many scenarios – usually with me confronting him, sword in hand – but this had not been one of them.

'Forcas told me about the letter you found. I didn't know,' he said. 'And you knew me only as something else. You've never met your father?'

'No. I tried to find him, but I didn't.'

'I never tried to find him. He knows where to find me, but I'll never see him again. It's December. Before March I'll be dead, no matter how many machines they wheel in here.' He stopped to catch his breath. 'Your father blamed me for everything.'

'You mean, like the fact he was forced to commit murder?'

'Who forced him? He put himself in that position. He was stupid. I gave up on him a long time ago.'

Sick as he was, his vehemence stopped me for a moment.

'Ivy knew about me all the time,' I said.

'Should that surprise either of us? I've learned that everyone's a chameleon, but Ivy is the only one who never bothers to change her color. I used her when I needed to, but all the time she was using me, just like she was using Junius. That's what she is.' He paused. 'If I had known about you, things might have been different.'

'Between you and Samax?'

'No. Nothing could have changed that. Certainly not another illegitimate child.'

'Of course not.' He seemed to have no recognition of, or concern about, the cruelty in his words; he might as well have said 'bastard'. I was seeing firsthand, I thought, why Samax and my father had been so repelled by him.

'Why did you hate my uncle so much?' I asked him.

'You think you know everything there is to know about all this,' he wheezed. 'You think you know who all the heroes are, and all the villains. And who did what to whom – and why. But it's not that simple. It's not one color, like with Ivy. Remember that. If that's all you remember from me, remember that.' He paused. 'What I did to Junius all those years ago, and then to your other grandfather, Nilus – those things didn't happen in a vacuum. I lusted after money then, sure. And after women. But what do you think they were – saints? For Stella I would have cheated fifty men – a hundred – I'm not ashamed to say it. For the money to keep her, I would've put a thousand men like Junius in jail. That's the way it was.' He laughed – more a dry cough than a laugh. 'But the pendulum swung back. I ended up losing Stella, not in the end to Junius, or to a man with more

584

money than me, or a man more foolish and vain than either Nilus or me. Worse, I lost her to men I would never know anything about. And that drove me crazy. Junius took her away, but she was using him all the time: after she ditched him, how many others were there? I had years and years to ponder that question. So, you see, Junius got his revenge. He made me suffer right back. You know that. And he knew how to get at me, where it would hurt the most. Not in my pocketbook, but in here.' Slowly he raised one ghostly hand and rested it on his chest. 'Junius knew how to put a bullet through me without firing a gun.' He drew a long, rattling breath. 'You've got so much bad blood in you, Enzo. Like a mix of chemicals that ought to have exploded the minute they came together. Yeah, I can see a few people in your face – especially your father.' He nodded toward the desk across the room, where there were two framed photographs angled away from us. 'I used to keep them in the drawer, but last month I had them put out. Have a look.'

On the desk, in a plain black frame, was what looked like a graduation photograph of the same man – aged sixteen or so – I had seen in the Air Force uniform at the gas station outside Albuquerque. Here he was wearing a jacket and tie. Darkly handsome, with a pompadour, he wasn't smiling. The other photograph, twice as large, with an ornate gold frame, was of a young blond woman in a black dress. Even without the description Samax had once given me, I knew at once who she must be. She was strikingly beautiful, with full lips and clear, lucent skin; her mouth was smiling, but her eyes didn't go with that smile. I had never quite seen eyes like hers: not wicked, exactly, but knowing – in a way that was un-settling for someone her age. Of myself I saw one notable characteristic in her face: the slight upturn of her lip beside a dimple on the right cheek.

'Ever seen a picture of your grandmother Stella before this?' Vitale Cassiel said, as I returned to his bedside.

I shook my head.

'I didn't think so. Junius wouldn't have kept them around.'

'She was very beautiful.'

'She was still in love with me then. Christmas, 1940. We were in Havana. Maybe you can see now why I would've sold what soul I had left for her. How Nilus who couldn't find his own shoes in the morning discovered her in the first place, in the dung heap of this world, I'll never know. But he never lived to regret it as much as I did. He stumbled on to something else. Another girl, it was all the same to him. But not to me. Not to Junius, either, no matter what he told you. I know he filled that place of his with things, but he would've traded every one of them, in a heartbeat, to have her back. And he never did. That's my solace, I'm sorry to say. But enough. The ten minutes is up, and you came here for something more than conversation. I can see that.'

'I'd like that amulet Uncle Junius was looking for.'

'Ah, I should have known. And you want me to give it to you.'

I hesitated, remembering Forcas's advice. 'I do.'

'Maybe I can give you more than that.'

'That's all I want.'

'And here I thought maybe you were going to visit here for a while. Spend a little time.'

He's testing me, I thought. 'I don't believe you really thought that.'

The shadow of a smile crossed those blue lips. 'You're more Cassiel than you'll ever know. But that's all right.' He wheezed slowly, and ten, fifteen, twenty seconds ticked away. 'What Junius always wanted, it's in there,' he said finally, nodding toward a small chest directly across the room from the desk. 'Take the two silver keys from the bottom drawer in the bedside table here. Open the top drawer of that chest and you'll find another drawer inside it. It has two keyholes. Insert the keys and turn them simultaneously, the right one clockwise, the left counterclockwise. Then come back here.'

I did exactly as he said. The keys turned easily, and when the tumblers were fully engaged, they produced a single musical note together. What I found inside the inner drawer was a small box that looked like a music box. It was covered in black velvet with an onyx circle inlaid on its lid, and it too had a silver lock.

'When he left here for the last time, twenty-five years ago, in a rage, your father took the key to this box, but Geza made it so I couldn't have it, either.' His voice was so low now, I had to strain to pick it up. 'See, only that one key can open the box. There's no duplicate. If you try to use another key, or to force the lock, the contents of the box are destroyed at once. It's an old Japanese design. I had it made for me in Tokyo. And it's all yours. Take it with you.' Again, the laugh that was a dry cough. 'Of course you'll have to find your father to open it – providing he didn't throw the key away. Or lose it. But I'll never see the inside of that box again. There's another box waiting for me.'

I didn't say goodbye, for he had already closed his eyes and the nurses were moving toward the bed as one, like clockwork. A moment later I was escorted downstairs and out the door. The straight-back chair on the verandah was empty and the parrot was gone.

On the way out of Reno, lost in thought, I stopped by the Fleischmann Planetarium, ostensibly to check out the design for the planetarium in Phoenix, but really to see the place where Samax had begun his seduction of my grandmother Stella. In my head, however, I kept scanning the photograph of her, and the one of my father. The planetarium itself left me cold: it was difficult to conjure up ghosts there after being in the presence of a pair of living ghosts like Ivy and Vitale Cassiel. Though I hated to admit it, Vitale Cassiel had been right about one thing: there was plenty of blood – mostly bad – to go around, and it had ended up on just about everybody's hands, including Samax's. Ivy just had more of it than anyone else. All those years, none of them had ever escaped either one another or themselves.

Back at my apartment in Santa Fe, accompanied by Sirius, I found two packages in the pile of mail that awaited me. One contained an audiocassette of The Echo Quintet's second album sent by Auro, the other a signed copy of Dalia's translation of Friar Varcas's book on vampires, just published by the Revenant Press. Enclosed in a plain brown jacket, inscribed *To Enzo* in a shaky hand, it looked like any other book, but I noticed the next day, while flipping through it during my flight to Honolulu, that it had one amazing peculiarity which sent a shiver through me: when you tilted its pages out of the light, their ink appeared to be red, not black.

My flight to Honolulu out of Albuquerque was at two o'clock, and I had to make one stop before going to the airport. Actually, it was an extended detour to Acoma, for which I had to start out early in the morning. I put on the same clothes I would be wearing when I arrived in Honolulu that evening – a plaid shirt and jeans, black lizard boots, and a dark blue jacket – and with Sirius curled up beside me in the front seat, I lowered the top on the old Ford Galaxie. The sky was already a hot, clear blue. We passed the gas station where I had seen Geza Cassiel and the Zuni cemetery where there was a grave marker but no grave for Calzas's father; but Sirius, who had always enjoyed looking at the sights when we drove, didn't once raise his head.

He had been agitated for weeks, as Desirée had told me, slipping away into the desert for the night, uncharacteristically hiding around the hotel, and not eating for days at a time. Losing weight, he had begun to look haggard, concave around the rib cage. Fourteen years old now, for the first time since Calzas had given him to me he seemed every bit his age. Samax's murder and the cataclysmic loss of the hotel – the only home Sirius had ever known – were major shocks, which only aggravated his restlessness. Mrs Resh had attributed his behavior before the fire to my extended absences from the hotel, but Sirius and I knew better.

Those last days in Las Vegas and Reno, and the very

last night, in Santa Fe, he stuck close to me, and even slept at my feet on the bed, which he hadn't done in years. I knew, well before we had left Nevada, that before I did anything else he wanted me to take him to Acoma. That morning when I awoke, I found Sirius staring out the window, westward toward the desert sky.

With just a last few miles to go on the winding two-lane blacktop into the valley, Sirius sat up as soon as the mesa of Acoma, and the Enchanted Mesa beyond it, came into view. The last time I had been there with him was nine years earlier, when he had run off and Calzas and I couldn't find him. Now his ears were extended, his tail began ticking, and his eyes focused suddenly. Gazing through the windshield, he remained riveted on Acoma until I parked the car and switched off the engine. Only then did he turn to me, and laying his paws on my left shoulder, rested his head against my own. His breath felt warm against the nape of my neck. His body was trembling. I put my arm around him for a long moment and drew in his scent and whispered his name just once. Then with a yelp, and an energy I hadn't seen in him for some time, he bounded from the car and ran directly to the rocky trail that spiraled up the mesa.

I didn't call out to him. I got out of the car and walked to the trail myself. I could no longer see him after he rounded the second bend in the trail, still running hard, but I knew where he was heading: that pyramid of black rocks on the plateau where Calzas had found him.

When I reached the plateau, I followed his tracks from the trail, through the grass and brambles, directly to the pyramid of rocks surrounded by lavender grass, where they ended abruptly. There was no sign of Sirius atop the pyramid or anywhere else. I knew there wouldn't be.

Wiping my brow, I sat down on a flat boulder and gazed out across the brown valley, its bright dust rising into the sunlight, at the Enchanted Mesa. I saw the blue ribbon of the Río Puerco. And the Gallo Mountains far off in the haze. Above me the sky-city of Acoma shone gold in the midday sun. I knew that when night fell and

Canis Major rose in the eastern sky, the Dog Star would be back in its place, at the constellation's center. It was Calzas who told me that your life is a road along which you leave many markers – points in time and places on the map. The ones in time you can only revisit in your mind, and they never change. The places can be re-visited firsthand, but they're constantly changing. To keep a place the same, he said, you can no longer return to it – and then it becomes a point in time. For me, Acoma would be such a place now. And for the first time since Samax's death, and the destruction of the Hotel Canopus, and all the farewells of the previous days, I buried my face in my hands and started to cry. I cried for so long that when I lowered my hands, the Enchanted Mesa looked as if it were underwater, and the valley itself filled with tears.

Throughout the long flight from Albuquerque to Honolulu, I listened to Auro's tape, which was entitled *Star-Crossed*; its cover illustration was a silver X composed of small stars, with a red star at its center. If his first album had been eclectic and joyous, this one was elegiac, long dark understated riffs in minor keys around Frankie Fooo's heavy bass and the alto sax and the lower octaves of the piano. And behind it all Auro's drumming, his soft touch with the bass pedal and his delicacy with the brushes on muted cymbals. The music played into my own mood so exactly it was unsettling at first. Auro, too, it seemed, had come to the end of something.

Putting Dalia's book aside, I was drawn to the Hopkins brothers' report on Mala Revell, which previously I had only skimmed. Neatly typed, it was nineteen pages, and I read them all now. I was probably on a wild-goose chase, but this woman was the only lead I had. If the Hopkins brothers couldn't find Geza Cassiel, there was a good chance he wasn't alive. Back in 1971, when he had been searching for this woman, who could say if she in turn had been searching for him. Or was even still in love with him when he wrote that long letter from the Hotel Rigel; maybe by then she was already in love with someone else. If so, there was no indication of such a person in the report. She had never been married, so far as the Hopkins brothers could ascertain, and she had no permanent address before the one on Kauai. The one regular job she'd held after leaving the Navy was at a hospital there. And she had been in a bad car crash years before, in which a man was killed; the circumstances of the crash were described as *mysterious*, but they didn't say why. Most of the rest of the report was interviews, legwork, wrong turns the investigators had made in the previous months. There was no photograph of her, just a basic ID description: five seven, brown hair, blue eyes. She drove a white jeep. She had two dogs. And, an odd aside, it said her house, which overlooked the ocean, was painted pale green.

I had never been to Hawaii before, and after Las Vegas and Albuquerque the moist, tropical air, fragrant with flowers, was intoxicating. I was planning to island-hop until I found a place as unlike the desert as it could be and plant myself there for a few weeks. From what I had seen of this island during the hour-long drive from the airport, passing through incredibly lush valleys, over streams that gushed from mountain waterfalls, I might have already arrived at the place I wanted. Aside from clothes, my suitcase in the trunk contained the blue-prints for the Phoenix planetarium, Geza Cassiel's letter, some seeds from the *Samax Astrofructrus* tree which I'd found in the greenhouse, and the only memento of my mother Bel's that I'd taken before the fire from the Hotel Canopus to my apartment in Santa Fe: the small silver compass with a snap-on cover. I'd also brought the black velvet box which I got from Vitale Cassiel – in case I ran into my father. In case he was living in that pale green house, too.

I saw the white jeep first, in the headlights of my rental car as I parked it off the dirt driveway. Then I heard the dogs, who ran barking out of the darkness, past a wooden post fence, to greet me. The house was just a black outline in a semicircle of tall trees.

The dogs were friendly. Old dogs, with rough fur. I petted them and they kept circling me, but stopped barking. It was just after ten o'clock, and as I crossed the driveway and swung open the low gate in the fence, I saw a single light burning in the rear of the house. To my right, over a row of bushes and through a cluster of swaying palms, I could see the silver and black of breaking waves, could hear their muffled roar as they slid rhythmically in to shore. A strong breeze was blowing and night birds were singing in the trees, and the crickets were buzzing incessantly. Sound seemed magnified in that place, or maybe it was just my nervousness as I walked up the path to the door of the green house listening to my boots crunch on the loose stones.

When I was about halfway up the path, the porch light came on, and the dogs peeled off from me and ran up to the door. I held my breath as it opened onto a woman silhouetted against the lighted interior. She was slender and tall – easily five seven. Her hair broke over her shoulders. She was wearing a white dress. I heard a bracelet jangle on her wrist.

'Who is it?' she called out, remaining in the doorway.

I walked the rest of the way up the path, feeling her eyes following me from within that silhouette.

'Mala Revell?'

There was a moment's hesitation. 'Yes.'

I climbed the three steps to the porch. 'My name is Enzo Samax.'

I could tell my name meant nothing to her.

'I'm sorry to intrude. I've come from the mainland, looking for someone, and I thought you might be able to help me.'

She stepped from the shadows, not so much because of what I was saying, I realized, but in order to study my face more closely. As the yellow rays of the porch light fell across her own face, brightening her blue eyes, I saw her clearly for the first time. For a few seconds I just stood there blinking, taking her features in, not quite believing what I was seeing, not allowing myself to, even after it had registered clearly. I stepped back and leaned against the porch railing and felt the inside of my head begin to spin even as the night in that place grew still around me, the insects and birds and swaying trees and the rise and fall of the sea, all of it silent suddenly. It was *her*, I told myself, thinking I had lost my mind.

'Alma?' I said.

She was shaking her head, staring at me. Her lips parted, but no words came out.

'Is that really you?' I said.

'Yes, Loren,' she said hoarsely, 'it's me.'

21

A Trip to the Stars

He had come across an ocean broader than the Pacific, wider than the gulf Cassiel was about to cross to the moon. An ocean fifteen years in the crossing. And he had come to me.

Both of us with different names now. Different faces, older, yet the same. After he embraced me at the door, I didn't dare touch him again for nearly an hour: I was afraid he would disappear if I did. Dissolve like one of those apparitions when you first wake up. But he was still there an hour later, drinking the green tea I brewed for him, sitting across from me at the small kitchen table, a man now.

He had come looking for someone else. Up the path in the darkness, tall, broad-shouldered, with a swinging gait, his head tilted like Cassiel's when he walked. Looking like Cassiel. And looking for Cassiel, who was his father. He told me this in the course of that first hour, but I knew it would take days, weeks, maybe longer, for me fully to grasp it.

All I remember saying to him at first was 'We don't have to understand everything – or anything – all at once.'

Many things flew right by me while he talked. Some stuck. Bits and pieces of his history, of what happened that day at the planetarium, going back to that repeatedly, like a compass point to get his bearings – the point

where we were lost to each other. And then his life afterward, trying to compress, to explain, it. All of which
took him time, for he too was stunned, finding himself
alone in a house with me, just the two of us on that
remote coastline near the end of the state highway, the
last mile of state highway in the United States, in a room
that must have felt as if it were at the end of the world.

And what was it he was saying? *Las Vegas . . . the letter
you never received . . . a man named Samax who was
my real uncle . . . his hotel . . . his niece Bel who was my
mother . . .*

Bel. The same Bel who Cassiel had told me about, who
ran alongside that ravine in her red dress. Loren's
mother. No, Enzo's. Loren was the name my sister Luna
gave him. Enzo is the name Bel gave him.

I said to him at one point, trying to keep my wits about
me as the two names danced in my head, 'If you put
together your names, you know, you could be called
"Lorenzo."'

He smiled – the same smile I remembered seeing
in Brooklyn, but so much quicker and brighter now. In
Brooklyn he hadn't had much to smile about. He liked
this idea about the name. But he said to me, gently, 'I
know how you must feel about my other name. But
I want you to call me Enzo. Is that okay?'

Of course it was okay. And he was to call me Mala.
Which once meant 'bad,' but now meant many other
things to me, all the things I'd done and been for better
or worse, over the last fifteen years. That my former
name was Alma was the one element of my story I had
omitted with Cassiel, who had so often told me how
much he loved the name Mala. I would never change it
back. I was Mala now. Just as Loren was Enzo.

'It seems right,' I said, 'that we should have other
names now.'

He thought about this for a long time. 'You mean, it's
part of what happened,' he said.

This was the way he was, I realized. He took things in
and turned them over. He was cautious. Like Cassiel.

And he kept his own counsel – which was not surprising. At the same time, that smile, and the way he carried himself and spoke to me, told me that somehow he had had a good life with these people he was describing – the very people who, through malevolence or selfishness or sheer negligence, had altered the course of my own life with such breathtaking ease. Whatever pain he had felt and losses he had suffered, it was not like what I had imagined when he was abducted, or later when I was searching hopelessly for him, half out of my mind. Whatever resentment I felt toward those people – most of them, apparently, dead now or near death – I wasn't going to express it to him at that moment. In the end, he had been well taken care of, he had thrived – but at what ferocious cost to both of us. And it was obvious to me that he was sensitive to these feelings of mine, had been aware of them and thought them through, long before he found me that night.

'But tell me more of what happened to you,' he said. 'After that day.'

I tried to tell him, there at my kitchen table with the dogs sleeping at his feet as if they had known him forever. I tried so hard, late into the night, until finally I broke down – though that was the last thing I had wanted to do – sobbing on his shoulder and hugging him to me as if he had come back from the dead. Or as if I had. He had Cassiel's letter with him, the one that had been mailed to me from New Mexico; explaining how I had come to be the woman to whom that letter was written, and then the woman whose wanderings had brought her to this island, and finally the woman who would soon become not just his foster aunt, but his stepmother, took me the rest of the night.

I had kept up my reading in Latin after Naxos and just that week had been making my way through Plotinus, who wrote long passages on astronomy that were really about fate. It was he who observed that all previous philosophers saw the stars in two ways: as the words that spell out our fates perpetually being inscribed and

596

modified on the chalkboard of the heavens, or inscribed once and for all, like the zodiac. Plotinus argued that to approach fate in either of these ways you have to assume the earth is stationary – which he thought impossible. He held that if you trace the stars' movements in relation to a revolving earth, the map you get is utterly chaotic. No neatly inscribed words or frozen zodiac, but a jumble of circles, ellipses, crisscrosses, and zigzags – which is what he proposed a cartographic transcription of our lives would truly resemble if we mapped them out.

By sunrise, Enzo and I were exhausted from trying to recreate, and overlay, our own respective maps. There was, as I had always thought, one previous point of intersection after his disappearance. Also on the eve of his birthday. Taken aback that I should know of it, Enzo confirmed that he was indeed in the Star Room of The Stardust Casino in Las Vegas on December 15, 1974, accompanied by a woman in a red dress. When I told him that I was the blindfolded woman on stage in the mind-reading act, it took him a few moments to remember, but when he did, he remembered it all – the sparkles in my hair, my glittery dress, the audience volunteers approaching me. We had come so close that night, the two of us, but we had had to wait another six years before we found ourselves in the same place again.

For it was now the morning of December 16, 1980, Enzo's twenty-fifth birthday, fifteen years to the day after he had disappeared from the planetarium. It was also the day that Geza Cassiel, at 3:42 p.m. Hawaii time, would be launched to the stars. I had planned to be at the NASA Observatory at Waimea for the liftoff, with Estes as my host. Now Enzo would join me.

First we needed to catch a few hours' sleep, though for me that proved impossible. I was so excited to have Enzo under my roof at last that, on top of my intense excitement over Cassiel's mission, I found it almost unbearable to close my eyes. Enzo, on the other hand, having suffered a barrage of shocks recently even before he walked up my front path, was able simply to collapse at that moment. How gratifying it was to me that he felt safe enough to do so in my house. Within minutes of sprawling beneath a single blanket on the pullout sofa, he plunged into a deep sleep – a scene I had rarely permitted myself to imagine over the previous fifteen years. Outside of the day Cassiel and I had found one another on Naxos, I can think of few things in my life that gave me as much pleasure and comfort as the sound of Enzo's steady breathing over the next five hours.

When he woke, I was sitting on the lanai in my bathrobe watching the heavy clouds stream seaward out of the mountains. There had been a heavy shower, and now the sun's rays were breaking through again, glittering in the dripping leaves of the trees. I had put a pot of coffee on the stove and sliced up two red papayas, and after Enzo had showered and dressed, I fried some eggs and bacon. However overwhelmed I was, I kept trying to imagine how he must be feeling, first to learn that, of all the women in the world, I should be the one with whom his father had fallen in love, and, second, that his father himself, already an enigma – former delinquent, former airman, war hero – was now an astronaut who on that very day would begin a space mission.

So it made perfect sense to me that, after his deep sleep, Enzo retreated inside himself. I might have felt calmer myself that morning if I had managed some sleep. Over breakfast, he expressed his admiration for my house and for the beauty of the island itself, but said little else. Then, as I reached over for the coffee, I noticed he was staring at my necklace, which had swung free of my robe.

'That key,' he said. 'Where did you get it?'

'Geza – your father gave it to me.'

'May I see it?' he said.

I took off my necklace and he examined the key, especially the circle of onyx below the key-ring hole. Handing it back to me without a word, he went to his suitcase and brought back a black velvet box with an identical circle inlaid on the lid.

'Do you know what that circle is?' I asked.

'In astronomy it symbolizes the far side of the moon,' he replied. 'This box contains an ancient Egyptian amulet depicting the far side only as someone orbiting the moon could have viewed it. It had a twin, depicting the earth itself, which was destroyed in the fire I told you about. For years this box was in the possession of my grandfather, Vitale Cassiel. He gave it to me only last week. Last night when you told me about my father's mission, I was thinking of it. And now I find that you have the key.'

'Your father asked me to hold it for him while he's gone. He swallowed it a long time ago—'

'To keep it out of my grandfather's hands. I know. This key is what he stole when he ran away with my mother. Then he swallowed it. Without it, my grandfather could never open the box.' He passed the box to me. 'You open it.'

I thought of Cassiel's instructions – to make sure I trusted the person with whom I opened it – and without hesitation I inserted the silver key in the lock and turned it. When I lifted the lid, the box began playing music – beautiful high-pitched notes in slow succession. Like the music of the stars recorded by radio telescopes that Estes had once played me at his house. Nestled into a cavity in the black velvet I found the amulet, a highly polished black stone, three inches in diameter. Etched onto one side in white were the craters, seas, and mountains of the moon's far side, rendered in minute detail, just as Enzo had said they would be. In amazement I held it up to him and he smiled.

As we drove across the island in my jeep, Enzo held that amulet in his closed fist. Behind the wheel, I again experienced the fear that had shot through me the previous night, wondering if he would disappear on me suddenly – this time not if I touched him, but if I took my eyes off him too long while negotiating the road. During the night, he had asked me a lot of questions about myself, but now he wanted to know more about

599

Cassiel, and his mission, which I had barely sketched out for him after pointing out the projected landing site on a lunar map.

Where I left off, Estes picked up an hour later, greeting us at the door of the NASA Observatory. He ushered us out of the blinding sunlight into the twilit coolness, where Enzo's cowboy boots clicked sharply on the marble floor. Estes was wearing what for him was formal dress: a long white jacket with the NASA insignia on the pocket and matching white pants. He looked healthier than he had in years; he never got formally sober, but his days of smoking ganja had ended abruptly when he was stricken with pleurisy and a bleeding ulcer one winter, and so he now limited himself to a single glass of rice wine with dinner. He had also taken up transcendental meditation – his guru had a temple by one of the waterfalls above Wailua – with the same devotion that he once brought to getting high.

'It's very hush-hush,' he said of Cassiel's mission. 'You know, Mala, that you're only here as a spouse-to-be, not as my friend. Having another close relative of a crewman on hand', he nodded to Enzo, 'is an honor for us. Here on Kauai, I know about this misson, and my assistant Maxwell, and Estelle, the new astronomer who's joined us from Mauna Kea. Several other people at Mauna Kea have been briefed on the mission, and there's a communications man on Midway, but that's it for the Hawaiian Islands – and we're NASA's main Pacific outpost. In Australia two guys at our listening post near Perth have been briefed, and a couple of others on Guam. We've all been warned that if we talk to anyone about the mission, we'll get our walking papers.'

'How is the weather in Florida?' I asked.

'It's a cool night, with light fog. 52°, vertical visibility ten miles. Everything's go. The last dispatch I got, the astronauts had their final physicals and boarded the ship an hour ago.'

I thought of the doctors in their sterilized jumpsuits

listening to Cassiel's heart and lungs, checking his blood pressure, his pulse, taking his temperature, hooking him up for an electrocardiogram. Then attaching the nodes and sensors that would transmit all his vital signs back from space, into a computer in Houston. I thought of his silk undersuit clinging to the line of shrapnel scars across his shoulder and to the thicker welts where the sniper's bullets had come out of his leg. I thought of the soft hair on his arms, and his gray eyes wide and steady, their silver lights flickering, behind the blue visor of his helmet, and the adrenaline pumping through him at that moment, and my pendant in one of the zippered pockets of his pressurized suit.

Enzo looked up at the clock as we stepped into the glass-walled console room within the observatory dome. It was 3:02.

'T minus 40,' a voice from Cape Canaveral intoned over the speaker system. Then we heard the flight commander running through a seemingly endless checklist with mission control in Houston. Midway through it, he ticked off several navigational items, and then deferred to Cassiel, whose voice broke in suddenly, giving readings, confirming numbers, crisp, relaxed, concluding his portion of the checklist with, 'Navigation is go, Houston.'

Enzo's eyes locked on mine and I nodded, getting a chill in my stomach, knowing this was the first time he had ever heard his father's voice.

'December 16th', Estes said, sipping from a coffee mug, 'is one of the prouder days in NASA history. In 1965, it was the day the Pioneer 6 satellite was launched' – and this time Enzo and I didn't have to exchange glances – 'that went on to orbit the moon and Venus before circling some of the outer planets. Someday it will leave the solar system altogether, spinning out among the stars. Someday too there will be men out there, but right now this mission will do just fine,' he smiled. ' "A Trip to the Stars." '

'What did you say?' Enzo asked, reacting with the

same amazement I had when Cassiel told me the name of the mission in Houston.

'That's what the astronauts dubbed this mission,' Estes replied. 'Now it's official.'

At that moment a young Hawaiian woman, also wearing a white NASA jacket and a short white skirt, came through the door with a clipboard under her arm. She was very pretty, with long black hair and black eyes and a face at once serious and warm. Estes introduced us.

'This is Estelle,' he said. 'She'll be running the radio telescope here from now on.'

'Listening to the stars,' I said.

'Yes,' she smiled, and out of the corner of my eye I saw Enzo return the smile.

'Today she's going to track the *Constellation* on the reflector telescope,' Estes said. 'We'll be able to follow the ship visually for a while after it leaves the atmosphere.'

'Even at that speed?' Enzo asked her.

She nodded. 'It's no faster than a comet. And that's how we set the telescope to follow it – like a comet. We'll run the telescope's images into the monitors while we're filming them.'

She took her place in the reclining seat of the reflector telescope and began setting the instrumentation. Estes excused himself and, putting on a headset, took a seat at a brightly lit panel in the next room. The lights dimmed, and the monitor before him – and the one suspended overhead in the room where Enzo and I remained – came to life. There was the Saturn V on the launchpad in Florida, steam pouring from its vents and fumes rising from beneath the funnel rims of its giant engines. Blue and green lights twinkled around it in the fog blowing in from the ocean. The last of the ground crew had just descended the gantry in a cage elevator, and floodlights from nearby towers had been turned on the rocket.

The countdown was at T minus 22 and counting. There had been only one delay during the final sixty

602

minutes. A small miracle, I knew, in an operation where a single malfunctioning gauge, a loose wire, a burnt fuse could put everything on hold. At T minus 12 and counting, mission control announced that all systems were go for liftoff, and everyone knew we were nearing the point of no return: in another few minutes, a succession of silent hatches deep in the rocket would begin to open, releasing the fuel components into their combustion chambers.

Alone now, Enzo and I stood side by side in front of the suspended monitor in the console room. Shadows swirled around us, and the ventilated air was cold. For good luck I had worn my green dress with the flowered print, and during those final minutes of the countdown I was fingering the stars on my bracelet. I thought back to that Christmas Eve in the South China Sea when Cassiel fell from a sky blazing with stars in his B-52. If he hadn't, I thought, Enzo wouldn't be standing beside me now. At T minus 3 and counting, with all the NASA machinery whirring around me, and the nape of my neck tingling with anticipation, it occurred to me that, in addition to all else, Cassiel had specially come down to earth to bring Enzo and me back together, as no one else could have.

My eyes were fixed on the conical capsule atop the gleaming rocket, where I knew at that moment the astronauts were feeling the intense rumble of the five engines firing far below – like sitting atop a volcano – as the calm voice at Cape Canaveral intoned, 7 . . . 6 . . . 5 . . . 4 . . . 3 . . . 2 . . . 1 . . .*ignition* . . . *liftoff*, and then there was a great extended roar, impressive even to us, five thousand miles away, and the voice repeated, *We have liftoff.* A vast plume of fire streamed from the rocket as it arced slowly upward, those millions of gallons of kerosene and liquid oxygen igniting on contact and the 160 million horses pulling it into the clear black sky. *All systems are go, Constellation*, the voice concluded. *You're going to the stars.*

The earth was falling away from Cassiel, I thought, as

603

it falls away from few men in their lives before they die. It was not a city, a country, or even a continent that he was leaving behind at breakneck speed, but the entire planet, luminous and blue. I wanted to close my eyes at that moment and imagine myself inside his body, seeing what he was seeing, feeling what he was feeling, but I couldn't turn away from the monitor. And as soon as the *Constellation* roared out of the earth's atmosphere, just a blur of flame to the earthbound cameras, Estelle sent the image she had locked on to down to the monitors: a close-up of the Saturn V's third and final stage, well beyond the exosphere, still streaming fire, but back-dropped now by stars. And Cassiel, I thought, reclined inside it, looking through his convex window. What intricate mix of forces, the pushes and pulls of his own life and the lives of others – including Enzo and me – had put him in that place at that moment? If it were charted according to Plotinus's design, what would the map of Cassiel's fate have resembled? Even he, who could read maps with such ease, might find it indecipherable – unless that was his secret gift, the ability to decipher not only terrestrial and celestial maps, but also the vaporous, ever-shifting, far more unruly maps that delineate our fates. His, mine, Enzo's.

As the *Constellation* streaked toward the moon, covering hundreds of miles a minute, Enzo and I barely stirred. Eerily glowing in the sun's icy rays, framed by millions of stars, the spacecraft seemed farther away now than I could possibly conceive. In the silent, darkened room, Enzo and I might have been as far away as Cassiel from everything we knew and all we had lived through, together finally, gazing at the stars that filled the monitor – which meant we were gazing back in time – when without a word he reached out. And I took his hand.

THE END

OF LOVE AND SHADOWS
Isabel Allende

'ISABEL ALLENDE IS A BRILLIANT STORYTELLER'
Marese Murphy, *Irish Times*

Set in a country of arbitrary arrests, sudden disappearances and
summary executions, Isabel Allende's magical novel tells of the
passionate affair of two people prepared to risk everything for
the sake of justice and truth. Irene Beltrán, a reporter, comes
from a wealthy background; Francisco Leal, a young
photographer secretly engaged in undermining the military
dictatorship, is strongly attracted by her beauty. It does not
matter that Irene's fiancé is an army captain: each time
Francisco accompanies her on a magazine assignment, he
falls more deeply in love with her.

When they go to investigate the mysterious case of Evangelina
Ranquileo, a girl suffering from spectacular fits which are
rumoured to have miraculous powers, the arrival of soldiers
adds a sinister aspect to the mystery. And then Evangelina
disappears. Irene and Francisco, in trying to trace her and
indict the Junta, become engulfed in a vortex of
terror and violence.

'BREATHTAKING . . . AN IMAGINATIVE LANDSCAPE
WHERE FABULOUS THINGS HAPPEN'
Helen Birch, *City Limits*

'THIS IS PROPAGANDA ON THE SIDE OF THE ANGELS. LATIN
AMERICAN DICTATORS HAD BETTER BAN IT IMMEDIATELY'
Jill Neville, *Independent*

'HER PEN HAS A CLENCHED FIST AND CRIES OUT
AGAINST INJUSTICE.
VIVA ALLENDE!'
Kate Saunders, *Books*

0 552 99313 1

BLACK SWAN

THE SPARROW
Mary Doria Russell

Winner of the Arthur C. Clarke Award

'ONE OF THOSE RARE BOOKS THAT TAKES YOU TO ITS HEART
AND REFUSES TO LET GO'
Lorenzo Carcaterra, author of *Sleepers*

'After the first exquisite songs were intercepted by radio telescope,
UN diplomats debated long and hard whether and why human
resources should be expended in an attempt to reach the world that
would become known as Rakhat. In the Rome offices of the Society
of Jesus, the questions were not whether or why but how soon the
mission could be attempted and whom to send.

The Jesuit scientists went to Rakhat to learn, not to proselytize.
They went so that they might come to know and love God's other
children. They went for the reason Jesuits have always gone to the
farthest frontiers of human exploration. They went for the greater
glory of God.

They meant no harm.'

Taking you on an extraordinary journey to a distant planet and to
the very centre of the human soul, Mary Doria Russell's *The
Sparrow* is an astonishing literary début – a powerful, haunting and
exciting novel about the nature of faith and what it meants to be
'human'.

'A PARABLE ABOUT HUMAN LIFE ON EARTH, WITH ALL ITS
IMPERFECTIONS, FAILINGS, DOUBTS, WISDOM AND
ERUDITION . . . *THE SPARROW* IS A STARTLING, ENGROSSING
AND MORAL WORK OF FICTION'
Colleen McCullough, *New York Times*

'BRILLIANT FIRST NOVEL ABOUT THE DISCOVERY OF
EXTRATERRESTRIAL LIFE . . . SHADES OF WELLS, URSULA
LE GUIN AND ARTHUR C. CLARKE, WITH JUST A DASH OF
EDGAR RICE BURROUGHS – AND YET STRIKINGLY ORIGINAL'
Kirkus Reviews

0 552 99777 3

BLACK SWAN

A LIST OF FINE WRITING
AVAILABLE FROM BLACK SWAN

THE PRICES SHOWN BELOW WERE CORRECT AT THE TIME OF GOING TO PRESS. HOWEVER
TRANSWORLD PUBLISHERS RESERVE THE RIGHT TO SHOW NEW RETAIL PRICES ON COVERS
WHICH MAY DIFFER FROM THOSE PREVIOUSLY ADVERTISED IN THE TEXT OR ELSEWHERE.

99313	1	OF LOVE AND SHADOWS	Isabel Allende	£6.99
99820	6	FLANDERS	Patricia Anthony	£6.99
99619	X	HUMAN CROQUET	Kate Atkinson	£6.99
99824	9	THE DANDELION CLOCK	Guy Burt	£6.99
99686	6	BEACH MUSIC	Pat Conroy	£7.99
99715	3	BEACHCOMBING FOR A SHIPWRECKED GOD		
			Joe Coomer	£6.99
99767	6	SISTER OF MY HEART	Chitra Banerjee	£6.99
99836	2	A HEART OF STONE	Renate Dorrestein	£6.99
99587	8	LIKE WATER FOR CHOCOLATE	Laura Esquivel	£6.99
99851	6	REMEMBERING BLUE	Connie May Fowler	£6.99
99801	X	THE SHORT HISTORY OF A PRINCE	Jane Hamilton	£6.99
99848	6	CHOCOLAT	Joanne Harris	£6.99
99796	X	A WIDOW FOR ONE YEAR	John Irving	£7.99
99758	7	FRIEDA AND MIN	Pamela Jooste	£6.99
99859	1	EDDIE'S BASTARD	William Kowalski	£6.99
99807	9	MONTENEGRO	Starling Lawrence	£6.99
99785	4	GOODNIGHT, NEBRASKA	Tom McNeal	£6.99
99905	9	AUTOMATED ALICE	Jeff Noon	£6.99
99718	8	IN A LAND OF PLENTY	Tim Pears	£6.99
99817	6	INK	John Preston	£6.99
99810	9	THE JUKEBOX QUEEN OF MALTA	Nicholas Rinaldi	£6.99
99777	3	THE SPARROW	Mary Doria Russell	£6.99
99846	X	THE WAR ZONE	Alexander Stuart	£6.99
99819	2	WHISTLING FOR THE ELEPHANTS	Sandi Toksvig	£6.99
99780	3	KNOWLEDGE OF ANGELS	Jill Paton Walsh	£6.99
99673	4	DINA'S BOOK	Herbjørg Wassmo	£6.99

All Transworld titles are available by post from:

Bookpost, PO Box 29, Douglas, Isle of Man, IM99 1BQ

Credit cards accepted. Please telephone 01624 836000,
fax 01624 837033, Internet http://www.bookpost.co.uk
or e-mail: bookshop@enterprise.net for details

Free postage and packing in the UK. Overseas customers:
allow £1 per book (paperbacks) and £3 per book (hardbacks)